Seeds of Bravery

Cultivating Courage One heart at a time

By

Kurell Vidal

For my grandchildren, Armanie and Khayiome.

Dedication

To my beloved Philogene family,

This work is dedicated to the strength, courage, and unwavering support that you have always shown. Your bravery and resilience inspire me every day.

May these seeds nurture hope and courage in us all, just as your example has done for me.

With all my love.

Acknowledgment

I am deeply grateful to the entire Philogene clan for your unwavering support, encouragement, and love throughout this journey. Your strength, resilience, and unwavering belief in the importance of bravery have been a constant source of inspiration.

A special thank you to family elders for sharing stories of courage and guiding me with your wisdom.

To my siblings, cousins, and all family members, your encouragement kept the seeds of bravery growing within me.

This project reflects our collective spirit—bold, brave, and united. Thank you for being the roots that nourish this endeavor and for reminding me that true bravery runs deep in our family.

With heartfelt appreciation.

Bravery begins as a tiny seed, and with courage and hope, it grows into a mighty tree that can withstand any storm.

— Kurell Vidal

About the Author

Kurell Vidal is a passionate storyteller and advocate for women's empowerment, drawing inspiration from her own experiences and the rich tapestry of culture in her community. With a background in sociology and community development, Kurell has dedicated her career to uplifting voices often overlooked in society, inspiring and motivating others to embrace their strength and potential.

Born in the village of Colihaut and raised in Salisbury, Kurell proudly identifies as a West Coast lady and a descendant of the Philogene clan. She brings a unique perspective to her writing, skillfully weaving together themes of resilience, unity, and transformation. Her debut novel, "Woman of Valor," draws inspiration from the stories of her ancestors and the remarkable women who have faced adversity and emerged empowered, highlighting their journeys and the legacies they leave behind.

When she is not writing, Kurell enjoys traveling, hiking, mentoring young women, and engaging in community projects that foster growth and change. Currently residing in the USA with her family, she continues to advocate for social justice and inspire others through her words and actions, striving to create a world where every voice is heard and valued.

Table of Contents

Prologue: The Journey of Two Families

In a time when the world was defined by sweeping tides of change and the whisper of adventure beckoned to those brave enough to hear it, two families undertook journeys that would etch their legacies into the fabric of Colihaut, Dominica. This story begins in the early 19th century, in the wake of colonial aspirations and the promise of new beginnings.

Ledger Philogene, a man of steadfast spirit, set out on a journey alongside his beloved wife, Clara, their nine lively children, and extended family. Departing from the sun-drenched shores of St. Barts, they made their way to St. Thomas, where the sea breeze carried with it hopes for safety and a brighter future. At every stop along their challenging path, the Philogenes sowed the seeds of courage, nurturing resilience, and faith amidst uncertainty, trusting that each new horizon might offer the promise of a better life.

As time flowed onward, Ledger and family found themselves in Roseau, Dominica, surrounded by lush mountains and vibrant communities. Yet, it was in Colihaut, a quaint village nestled against the rhythm of the sea, that they would plant roots and nurture their dreams. There, Ledger became a proud farmer, tending to the fertile land while instilling in his children the values of hard work, unity, and the courage to chase their aspirations amidst the whispers of the past.

Across the Caribbean Sea, in the vibrant landscape of Venezuela, another family was charting their course. Henri Sebastien, a dreamer with fire in his heart, set sail with his extended family, wife, Isabelle, and their five children around the year 1810. Their journey led them through the tides of history, crossing the waters to Portsmouth, Dominica, where they felt the promise of a new start blossom like an unyielding flower. The whirling winds of change guided them to Colihaut, where they would join the thriving community and embrace the spirit of collaboration and growth.

The Sebastians and Philogenes weathered life's storms and celebrated its joys, drawing strength from their shared experiences. They stood united, bound by the common threads of bravery, commitment, and a longing for belonging. Within their families, seeds of courage began to take root, emerging in the laughter of children, the exchange of stories, and the forging of bonds that would withstand the test of time.

In Colihaut, where the land kissed the sea and communities were built on kinship, the legacies of these two families intertwined. They would navigate challenges, find solace in shared traditions, and embrace the richness of their diverse heritages. As each child grew under the sun and stars, a sense of bravery was nurtured—a quiet knowing that they were part of a larger tapestry woven from dreams both bold and humble.

Thus, the stage was set for a rich narrative of courage and connection, where the seeds of bravery would blossom into something remarkable, forever shaping the lives of those who called Colihaut home. This is the story of their journeys, of the trials they faced, and of the vibrant community that flourished as a testament to the indomitable human spirit. In the embrace of this extraordinary place, generations would rise, rooted in the bravery of their ancestors, as they continued to cultivate their own legacies amidst the beauty of the Caribbean.

ॐ

Part One: Foundations

Chapter One: Ledger Philogene

In the mid-19th century, St. Barts was firmly entrenched in the colonial plantation economy, primarily dominated by the cultivation of sugar cane, which was pivotal to the island's economy and a significant export commodity within the Caribbean. The island was a French territory, and, as such, it was governed by colonial powers who benefitted from the immense wealth generated by the sugar industry. This wealth came at a tremendous moral and social cost, borne by the enslaved population who labored on the plantations.

St. Barts during this time was a vivid tapestry of rolling green hills and thriving sugar cane fields, shimmering beneath the Caribbean sun. Its stunning natural beauty belied the harsh realities of life on the island, where a brutal socio-economic system prevailed. Plantations were scattered across the land, marked by whitewashed buildings, and regularly visited by overseers and wealthy owners who lived in luxury, far removed from the harsh conditions endured by the enslaved laborers.

The air was filled with the sweet scent of sugar cane during the harvest season, yet this pleasant aroma belied the harsh reality of life for those who cultivated it. Enslaved people worked long hours under the watchful eyes of overseers, facing grueling conditions without compensation or rights. Their toil was rendered invisible to many of the coastal elites who enjoyed the fruits of their labor in the shaded gardens and ballrooms of the plantation houses.

The social structure of St. Barts was starkly hierarchical, with a small class of wealthy European planters at the top and a large population of enslaved individuals at the bottom. This created a palpable tension between the oppressors and the oppressed. Amid the lush scenery, there lay an undercurrent of resistance, as enslaved people developed their own culture, blending African traditions with the influences of European and Caribbean life.

Rumors of slave revolts in other Caribbean islands spread through the grapevine, adding to the unease among the plantation owners. The enslaved population organized clandestine gatherings, communicating their hopes for freedom and discussing resistance tactics, fostering a sense of solidarity and resilience against their circumstances.

The sun was just beginning to rise over St. Barthélemy, casting a soft golden light that filtered through the wooden shutters of Ledger's room. Awakened by the call of the morning birds and the distant sound of waves lapping at the shore, he lay in bed, staring up at the ceiling adorned with simple wooden beams. The tranquil sounds of the island filled his ears, yet an unsettling weight rested on his chest.

Ledger turned onto his side, glancing at the small shrine his mother had created in the corner of the room. It was adorned with small tokens: a carved boat representing their father's seafaring heritage, a fragile flower picked on a family outing, and a photograph of his childhood home. Each item held significance, a piece of the narrative his mother had woven like a tapestry over the years.

But even here, in the sanctuary of his room, Ledger could not escape the pressures pressing down on him. As the eldest son in a family carrying a legacy steeped in both honor and expectation, he felt the burden of his responsibilities heavy upon his shoulders. His thoughts drifted to the day ahead—a day that might be filled with tension, as it so often was.

"What will it take to make them understand?" he whispered to himself, recalling the fragmented conversations that had consumed many evenings at the dinner table. His mother's passionate pleas for change often clashed with his father's stern adherence to tradition, creating an atmosphere thick with unresolved conflict. Ledger could not help but feel that the roots of their arguments ran deeper than their differing views—they were entwined in the very fabric of their identity, reflecting the complexities of colonialism and economic obligation.

He swung his legs over the edge of the bed and rose, stretching to shake the sleep from his limbs. The cool wooden floor met his feet, a steady reminder of the world that waited beyond the room. Another day meant another trip to the sugar plantation, where he would again confront the unyielding rhythm of labor that sustained both the island's economy and his family's wealth.

In the small mirror hanging on the wall, he met his own gaze. Ledger's features revealed a man caught between worlds: the hopeful aspirations of his mother and the unyielding traditions of his father loomed over him. As the eldest child, he was expected to carry the family name forward, but the path he was expected to follow felt increasingly disconnected from the legacy he wished to honor.

He stepped outside, the early morning sun warming his skin as he made his way toward the kitchen. The vibrant sounds of the island stirred to life around him. Neighbors greeted each other as they began their daily routines, the smell of fresh bread wafting from a nearby bakery mingling with the scent of ocean salt. Yet Ledger felt separate from it all, like a spectator in a world that moved with purpose while he wrestled with his inner turmoil.

Upon entering the kitchen, the comforting sight of Clara preparing breakfast brought a smile to his face. She was humming softly, her hands flipping pancakes on the stove. The warmth of their little home enveloped him like a hug. "Good morning, my dear!" she called cheerfully, her eyes brightening upon his arrival.

"Morning, Sweetheart. It smells wonderful in here," he replied, filling his plate as the sounds of their children playing in the yard filtered through the open window, mingling with Clara's melody.

But even as he participated in the rhythm of family life, Ledger needed a moment to gather himself. "Have the children gone to market with Petronel?" he asked, hoping to distract himself from the weight of the day.

"Yes, they rushed out just before sunrise. They were excited to help barter for our greens," Clara said, her voice brimming with warmth. "It is a beautiful day, dear. Let us make the most of it!"

For a moment, the tension lifted, like soft Caribbean waves brushing against the shore. Looking at Clara, radiant in the joy of their children and shared dreams, Ledger felt the weight of his duties return. Still, he allowed himself to linger in the peace of now. "I love this time with you and the children," he said at last, a real smile breaking through his thoughtful expression.

"This is our world, my dear," she smiled back, "and we have the power to shape it. Together."

Those words lingered in his mind as he took a bite of his meal. He knew he would have to reconcile his place in their family, between his mother's cries for justice and his father's insistence on tradition. As Ledger finished breakfast, he made a quiet vow to himself; he would seek a balance, a way to unite these conflicting ideals, not only for his family but for the future of the community he cherished.

With renewed determination, he prepared to face the day, ready to step into the complexity of his existence, where family dynamics intertwine with a world fraught with challenges.

Ledger Philogene was born in 1852 on the Caribbean island of St. Barthelemy, a period marked by profound transformation and turmoil shaped by the lingering impacts of colonialism and the plantation economy. Nestled in the heart of the Caribbean, St. Barthelemy was a microcosm of the complexities surrounding wealth, power, and morality, as the island's history was tightly woven with the exploitation of enslaved people.

Ledger grew up in a prominent family along with his siblings Florence, Pierre, Leon, and Margot whose fortunes were derived from a plantation that produced sugar, one of the most lucrative commodities of the time. This plantation, like many others across the Caribbean, was built upon the backs of enslaved individuals who toiled under harsh conditions, their labor fueling the prosperity of their captors. From a young age, Ledger was acutely aware of the societal framework that both supported and exploited the lives of countless men, women, and children, all trapped in an unjust system.

His identity was significantly formed by the contradiction that pervaded his childhood. On the one hand, he lived in a mansion furnished with the conveniences of colonial luxury, enjoying the benefits that came with his family's riches and prestige. However, the moral ramifications of his family's success, which came at an incalculable cost to others, plagued him. Contradictions abound in Ledger's early years: the island's lush beauty stood in stark contrast to the harsh realities of the enslaved workers who toiled diligently to preserve the plantation's history.

As he matured, Ledger's awareness of the injustices surrounding him deepened, leading to a growing conflict within him. He grappled with feelings of guilt and responsibility as he sought to understand the true nature of his inheritance, a legacy built on exploitation and suffering. This internal struggle ignited a passion for justice and sustainability, propelling him on a quest to reclaim the narrative of his family's past while forging a path aligned with his values.

Ledger envisioned a world where prosperity could exist without the sacrifice of dignity or the erasure of cultural identity. His journey became one of empowerment, not just for himself, but for the community that had long been marginalized. Fueled by the recognition that change must begin within, Ledger sought to challenge the status quo, embarking on a transformative journey that would redefine his legacy and inspire those around him.

In the face of a complex history woven into the very fabric of his existence, Ledger Philogene emerged not only as a figure shaped by the past but as a catalyst for a more equitable future, determined to honor the dignity of those who had labored beneath the weight of oppression.

The sun climbed high over the lush hills of St. Barthélemy, casting a shimmering light on the grand Philogene mansion, its whitewashed walls gleaming like a beacon overlooking the sprawling plantation. The estate stood majestically amid the rolling fields of sugar cane, a symbol of both prosperity and the dark realities that fueled its wealth.

Inside the mansion, the air was rich with the scent of freshly baked bread and the soft notes of a classical piece drifting from the parlor, where Ledger Philogene's mother, Clarissa, played the piano. With her elegant fingers gliding over the keys, she filled the ornate room with music that rang like delicate glass chimes, a fitting backdrop to the opulence that surrounded them. The adorned walls were lined with paintings of coastal vistas and portraits of esteemed ancestors, figures who had once carved their fortunes from the soil of this very island.

"Ledger!" his father, Elijah, called from the adjoining study, his voice urgent yet steady. "Come help me with these repairs!"

The voice jolted Ledger out of his reverie, where he frequently wandered the verdant fields with the cane harvesters, dreaming of exciting exploits far from the mansion. He had been seeing the rhythmic toil of the plantation workers, their strong bodies gliding over the towering sugar cane stalks while they skillfully handled machetes. But knowing that his family was the landowners, he pushed those thoughts away.

He rushed to the study, where his father awaited him amidst a disarray of blueprints and tools. Elijah, a tall, imposing figure with salt-and-pepper hair and a well-tailored linen shirt, was meticulously examining a faded map of the estate. His brow was furrowed in concentration, revealing the weight of responsibility that accompanied their fortune.

"Ledger, we need to ensure that our main barn is ready for the harvest season," Elijah explained, pointing at a chart that indicated the layout of the plantation. "The workers will rely on the barn to store the sugar. If we do not replace that roof soon, we will face losses when the rains come."

Ledger nodded, feeling a swell of pride at being entrusted with such important work. "I can help with that, Papa. I have seen how the carpenters fix those roofs."

"Good," Elijah replied, a smile creeping across his lips, though it did not reach his eyes. "You'll learn the value of hard work, even amid our privileges."

As they gathered tools and headed out, Ledger could not help but notice the stark contrast between the grandeur of his surroundings and the toil of the laborers who made it possible. The pathways leading to the fields were flanked by tall hedges, carefully manicured, and fertilized, creating an illusion of perfection. And yet, Ledger remembered the sweat on the brows of the people who labored under the sun, their hands calloused, and backs bent from relentless labor.

"Papa, we have so much," Ledger began cautiously, glancing up at his father's expression. "Why do we rely on them so much? They seem… weary."

Elijah halted briefly, a shadow crossing his face as he considered his son's words. "Wealth is a double-edged sword, Son. It provides comfort but at a cost. The sugar cane we harvest is the foundation of our lifestyle, but it is derived from hard work and sacrifice. Our fortune, as you know, is entangled with the lives of those who work our land."

Ledger nodded, wrestling with the weight of his father's words. Though they lived comfortably, feasting on exquisite meals and dressing in fine clothes, he could not shake the uncomfortable truth that their wealth was built on the suffering of others. As they neared the barn, he saw workers in the distance, diligently gathering and weighing the sugar cane.

Their sweat-soaked bodies were a stark reminder that their toil fueled the Philogene family's fortune. "Does it ever trouble you, Papa?" Ledger asked as they inspected the aging structure. "The way our lives are built on their backs?"

The question hung in the air, heavy with implications. Elijah's expression hardened slightly, but he maintained his composure. "It is an uncomfortable truth, son, one we must confront if we are to understand our place in this world. But our duty lies in ensuring they are treated well and paid fairly. That is how we maintain our honor as owners."

Ledger bit his lip, absorbing his father's words. Honor felt fleeting in the face of such disparity. He wondered what it would look like to disrupt convention, to challenge the status quo that dictated the relationships between rich and poor within the plantation's confines.

As the afternoon wore on, and they repaired the barn, the rhythmic sounds of the plantation became a backdrop to Ledger's thoughts. The wealth of the Philogene family, set against the backdrop of a labor-intensive economy built on the backs of the enslaved, echoed through every pound of sugar cane harvested and every note of his mother's piano. Ledger stood on the precipice of understanding, an awakening to the complexities of their existence that would shape the course of his journey.

As the sun climbed higher in the sky, casting golden rays over the bustling streets of Gustavia, the weekly market began to come alive. Vibrant stalls filled with an array of goods lined the town square, displaying colorful textiles, fresh produce, and handmade crafts. The rich tapestry of life on St. Barthélemy unfolded around Ledger, who had come to buy supplies for his growing family.

The scent of ripe tropical fruits and fragrant spices mingled in the air, drawing people from all walks of life. A sold-out stall, manned by an elderly woman with weathered hands, overflowed with bright mangoes, juicy pineapples, and fragrant herbs. She smiled warmly at Ledger, offering him a sample of ripe mango, its sweetness bursting against his palate. Ledger exchanged a few coins, feeling the weight of expectations as he considered not only the food he was purchasing but the legacy he wanted to build for his family.

Around him, the lively chatter of townsfolk resonated, creating a vivid chorus that echoed through the square. Families gathered to engage in animated conversations while children darted about, their laughter mingling with the melodies played by local musicians. A group of drummers set a lively rhythm, their beats forming an infectious pulse that urged others to sway along.

As Ledger walked through the market, his gaze landed on a familiar figure—his mother, Clarissa, holding his younger sister Margot's hand. She was during a lively conversation with a neighbor, her expressive gestures emphasizing the concerns close to her heart. While Ledger admired his mother's dedication to social justice, he often felt a disconnect between the principles she championed and the contradictions of their own life.

"Ledger!" Clarissa called, her voice breaking through the market's din. "Come here! We were just discussing the latest news from the enslaved community. There are whispers of discontent, and I fear we may see disruption soon."

Ledger felt a chill at her words, instinctively glancing around the market. He could sense the growing tension between the two worlds he inhabited: the cheerful marketplace filled with laughter and color contrasted sharply with the grim realities facing the island's enslaved population.

Looking over his mother's shoulder, he saw a group of enslaved individuals on the fringes of the market, their faces weary but resolute. They were bartering with local traders, exchanging handmade goods for food or medicines, but the shadows beneath their eyes told stories of unyielding labor and struggle. Ledger's heart ached at the sight, a reminder of the harsh conditions that sustained the very livelihoods of families like his.

"It's time for us to do something," Clarissa continued, her voice rising with conviction. "We must advocate for their rights, for their humanity. Ignoring their suffering would make us complicit in this injustice."

Ledger wanted to embrace her passion, to join her in championing a cause that resonated deeply with him. But swirling doubts clouded his thoughts; the financial stability his family enjoyed hinged on the exploitation of those very individuals his mother sought to support. "But Mother, what can we truly change against such a powerful system?" he asked, his voice low with uncertainty.

Before Clarissa could respond, a sudden commotion erupted nearby. A loud crash rang out as a vendor's cart tipped over, sending jars of local honey and spices spilling across the cobblestones. People around the scene gasped, momentarily distracted from their conversations.

Ledger could see the panic in the vendor's eyes as he scrambled to collect his wares, frustration etched on his face.

Amidst the chaos, Ledger saw his father, standing sternly at a distance, arms crossed and frowning at the unfolding scene. His presence reminded Ledger of the competing expectations that weighed heavily on him, his mother's desire for justice and his father's adherence to tradition.

Ledger was torn between two realities as the market came alive again, the thriving community honoring its traditions and the underlying indifference to the island's structural problems. With his heart heavy with the urgent need for change, he returned to the rhythm of the market, determined to strike this delicate balance while being mindful of the duties associated with his background.

The reliance on enslaved labor was a fundamental pillar of the colonial plantation economy, serving as the engine that drove profitability for plantation owners across the Caribbean. This system of forced labor enabled the cultivation of lucrative cash crops such as sugar, coffee, and cotton, generating immense wealth for a small elite while simultaneously inflicting immense suffering on the enslaved population.

Enslaved individuals endured profoundly harsh conditions as they toiled endlessly on plantations. Their daily lives were marked by backbreaking labor, with long hours spent in the fields under the scorching sun. The work was grueling and unrelenting, often starting at dawn and continuing until dusk, with little regard for the physical capabilities or well-being of the laborers. The tasks involved not only the planting and harvesting of crops but also the processing of these crops into marketable goods, requiring a range of physical and technical skills.

The brutality of the plantation system was evident in the treatment of enslaved people, who were subjected to frequent physical punishment as a means of control and coercion. Overseers enforced labor demands through vicious intimidation, using whips or other forms of violence to maintain discipline and ensure maximum productivity. Enslaved individuals lived in constant fear of punishment, which contributed to an environment of psychological and physical terror.

Denying basic human rights was a core aspect of the enslavement system. Enslaved individuals were considered property, with no legal rights or protections. They could be bought, sold, or traded at the whims of their owners. Families were often torn apart, as adults could be sold off, leaving children to grieve the loss of parents, siblings, or other loved ones. This dehumanization effectively stripped them of their identities and cultures, creating a profound sense of disconnection and loss.

The plantation system generated a stark societal division, creating an entrenched hierarchy that placed wealthy white landowners at the top, enjoying power, wealth, and privilege, while the oppressed Black enslaved population remained at the bottom, subjected to dehumanization and exploitation. This division was not merely economic; it was deeply social, cultural, and political, influencing every aspect of life in colonial society.

The wealth accrued by plantation owners facilitated the development of affluent communities, enhanced by their control over land, resources, and political power. They shaped societal norms, reinforcing racial hierarchies that justified the enslavement of Black individuals. Meanwhile, the absence of rights and freedom for enslaved people perpetuated a cycle of oppression, confining their existence to servitude and subjugation.

The social disparity continued even after slavery was outlawed. For descendants of enslaved people, the effects of the plantation system, economic hardship, racial prejudice, and structural inequality, persisted in influencing their lives. The history of poverty and marginalization among Black communities was solidified by the structural injustices created during slavery, making it challenging to attain equity in a society still enmeshed in historical injustices.

Enslaved labor was critical to the profitability of plantations in the Caribbean, rooted in a system that severely mistreated individuals while building vast wealth for a privileged few. The harsh treatment and brutal conditions faced by enslaved people exemplify the inhumanity at the heart of the plantation economy, creating a societal divide that has had lasting repercussions. Understanding this history is essential for recognizing the enduring legacy of inequality and the ongoing struggles for justice and equality faced by communities shaped by this painful past.

The sun had begun its descent, casting long shadows across the fields as Ledger made his way home from the sugar plantation. The rhythmic sound of the ocean waves crashing against the shore was a stark contrast to the heavy silence that hung over the plantation. He could still hear the distant echoes of the day, the thudding of tools against the earth, the muffled voices of the enslaved laborers, and the sharp bark of overseers giving commands. Each sound was a reminder of the exploitation that underpinned the island's prosperity, and with each step, a weight pressed down on his heart.

As he approached his home, the warm glow of the setting sun illuminated the plantation house, its whitewashed walls gleaming. But the beauty of the scene felt tainted, overshadowed by the grim realities he had witnessed. He paused at the entrance to the yard, taking a moment to collect his thoughts. The fragrant scent of flowering plants wafted around him, mingling with the salty air from the nearby sea, but it did little to ease the turmoil inside.

Inside, the sounds of his children playing filtered through the open windows, voices dancing with laughter and joy. Ledger entered to find Clara seated on a woven mat, surrounded by Wizen, Julien, Eliza, Koie and Nerisa who were engrossed in a game. Petronel was busy organizing stacks of freshly picked herbs from the market, while the twins, James, and Dfriel, chased each other around the yard, their laughter ringing like sweet music.

"Father!" Wizen exclaimed, breaking away from the game to run towards him. He embraced Ledger tightly. "You are back! We were just talking about our next adventure! Can we explore the cliffs tomorrow?"

Ledger smiled at his son, the warmth of his children momentarily distracting him from the heaviness of the day. "I would love to," he replied, ruffling Wizen's hair. "But first, let's help your mother with these herbs."

As they gathered around Clara, Ledger felt an overwhelming sense of gratitude for his family, a sanctuary of love and laughter in a world filled with strife. But that gratitude was quickly tempered by the reality he had just faced. He watched Clara closely as she sorted through the herbs, her face glowing with contentment as she engaged with the children.

"Clara," he started, hesitating before finding the words. "I…" He struggled to express the turmoil clawing at him. "I wish things were different for everyone on this island, for the families working the fields."

Clara looked up, her expression shifting from joy to concern. "Ledger, what troubles you?"

"I've seen the toll it takes on them," he said, his voice heavy. "The pain, the exhaustion… it is like they are not even viewed as people. They are just cogs in the machinery of profit."

She nodded, understanding the depths of his despair. "I know," she replied softly. "It weighs on me, too. But what can we do? We have our lives to live, our children to raise."

"That's just it," he replied urgently. "Shouldn't we be doing more? Standing up for those who have no voice? Your work in the community…" He let his voice trail off, feeling the tension rise again as he considered the risks involved.

Before Clara could respond, Louisa burst into the room, her eyes wide with excitement. "Look! I made a flower crown!" She held it up proudly, the vibrant colors contrasting delightfully with her dark hair.

The room erupted into cheers as everyone admired Louisa's handiwork, and Ledger felt a flicker of joy amidst the weight of sorrow.

"It's beautiful, Louisa!" he praised, kneeling to help her place the crown on her head. Her smile radiated warmth, reminding him of the innocence and joy that must be preserved in their children despite the world's harshness.

However, even as laughter filled the space, Ledger could not shake the thought of those who suffered beyond their walls. "Someday, we should make sure they know they aren't forgotten," he whispered to Clara as he observed their children, their futures bright and hopeful.

Clara reached for his hand, squeezing it gently. "I promise you, dear, we will find a way. Together."

As twilight descended upon St. Barthélemy, the contrasting realities of life weighed heavily on Ledger's mind. He glanced toward the horizon, where the sky met the shimmering sea, and he felt a flicker of resolve igniting within him. Together, they would aspire to bridge the divides that marked their island, nurturing hope amid despair, both for their family and for those whose stories lingered just beyond their reach.

The Caribbean plantation economy's use of enslaved labor cemented inflexible social structures, resulting in a structured society that had a significant impact on the social dynamics, interpersonal connections, and historical development of the area. The colonial power structures were firmly rooted in these hierarchies, which positioned white landowners and colonial officials at the top and the enslaved people at the bottom, where they faced systematic abuse and dehumanization.

At the heart of the social hierarchy were the white landowners, who wielded considerable economic power and political influence. They controlled vast plantations that generated immense wealth through the exploitation of enslaved labor. These landowners often formed the elite class, enjoying privileged access to education, resources, and governance. Their status allowed them to dictate the social norms and values of the time, establishing a culture rooted in racial superiority and entitlement.

Conversely, the enslaved population was stripped of autonomy and humanity and viewed as property rather than individuals with rights or dignity. This dehumanization was not merely a byproduct of economic exploitation; it was a key component of the social order that justified the systemic oppression of Black individuals. Enslaved people faced daily indignities that reinforced their status as the lowest members of society, including harsh living conditions, physical brutality, and the constant threat of violence.

This rigid social hierarchy created an atmosphere of fear among both the enslaved laborers and the free population. Enslaved individuals lived under constant surveillance and control, their every action subject to the whims of their overseers. The threat of punishment loomed large, instilling a paralyzing sense of vulnerability. This oppression stifled individual freedoms and aspirations, compelling many to accept their fates under duress.

Despite the atmosphere of fear, resistance, and rebellion inevitably arose among the enslaved population. Acts of defiance ranged from subtle forms of resistance, such as work slowdowns, sabotage, or the cultivation of personal gardens, to more overt acts of rebellion, including uprisings and escapes. These actions highlighted the deep-seated desire for freedom and justice among enslaved individuals and illustrated the human spirit's resilience in the face of overwhelming oppression.

Intermittent rebellions challenged the status quo and forced slaveholders to confront the realities of their brutal system. Some of the most notable uprisings, such as the Haitian Revolution, inspired enslaved populations across the Caribbean, proving that liberation was possible and igniting a fire of hope among those laboring under oppressive conditions.

The strict social structures that were put in place during the colonial era had a significant influence on Caribbean history. Deeply ingrained racial differences persisted in influencing social interactions, political power dynamics, and economic prospects in the area even after slavery was abolished. Challenges that lasted for centuries were brought about by the legacy of exploitation and oppression, which shaped cultural views and sustained cycles of inequity.

As Caribbean societies emerged from the shadows of colonialism, the remnants of social hierarchies have continued to affect identity, cultural relationships, and the struggle for equality. The fight against systemic racism and social injustice remains deeply entwined with the history of enslaved labor and the enduring impacts of colonial rule.

The presence of enslaved laborers solidified rigid social hierarchies in the Caribbean, manifesting a clear division between the elite white landowners and the oppressed enslaved population. This division fostered an atmosphere of fear, resistance, and rebellion, shaping the collective history of the islands. Understanding these social hierarchies is crucial for recognizing their lasting repercussions and the ongoing struggles for justice and equality in the Caribbean today.

The sun dipped below the horizon, painting the sky in hues of pink and orange as Ledger stepped into the gathering space of their home, the scents of roasted meat and fragrant herbs wafting through the air. The cozy atmosphere thrummed with the chatter and laughter of family and close friends, creating a warm cocoon of connection against the backdrop of societal tensions that permeated the island.

"Ledger! There you are!" Clara called out cheerfully from the kitchen, where she was busy preparing a large pot of stew. Even with the day's weight still hovering around him, her vibrant energy filled the room and spread warmth among the guests.

"I'm here, love," he replied, trying to shake off the lingering worries from earlier that day. The plantation had felt particularly oppressive, the hierarchy evident in the way workers were treated, much differently from the camaraderie he felt around this dinner table.

As he moved through the crowd, Ledger felt the familiar tug of family ties. Wizen and Julien were showing off their latest drawing on a piece of scrap paper, while Louisa and Eliza chased each other around the table, giggling uncontrollably.

"Settle down, you two!" Ledger chuckled, keenly aware of the energy thrumming through the room. He ruffled their hair, his heart warming at the sight of their unbridled joy.

The evening proceeded along the same pattern of storytelling and laughter, with each story serving as a reminder to Ledger of the ties that bound them together. Ledger's mother, Clarissa, stood among the grownups and spoke enthusiastically about the latest happenings in the local social movements. Some listened carefully, while others exchanged doubtful looks, the inescapable rift in viewpoints boiling under the surface.

"If we do not stand up for those enslaved, how can we call ourselves a community?" Clarissa insisted, her voice rising above the chatter. "We must advocate for their right to dignity and freedom!"

A whisper of discomfort rippled through the group. Ledger's father exchanged tense looks with some of the older men in the room, their brows furrowed in disapproval. "Your sentiments are admirable, Clarissa," he finally interjected, his voice steady but laced with a hint of warning. "But we must be cautious. The world is changing faster than we can comprehend and change without foresight can lead to chaos."

Ledger felt a familiar knot tighten in his stomach. This was not the first time he had seen his mother's ideals clash with his father's pragmatism. He could sense the tension rising, the push and pull of their beliefs creating an undercurrent of discomfort that echoed the broader societal divides on the island.

"But silence is complicity, Father," Ledger found himself saying, unable to hold back. "We have a responsibility to use our voice to bring about change, no matter how uncomfortable it may be."

The room fell silent, all eyes turning towards him, a mix of surprise and tension tracing their expressions. Clara paused, her gaze shifting between Ledger and his father, sensing the growing friction.

"What Ledger means," she stepped in diplomatically, "is that we cannot sit idly by when there are lives at stake. We must consider the humanity of every individual, regardless of their status."

"You idealists are brave but naive," one of the older men said from across the table. "You think you can change systems that have been in place for generations with mere words and arguments?" His voice dripped with skepticism.

"Perhaps not with words alone," Ledger replied, his heart racing, "but with the force of our unity, together, we might foster understanding and bring about hope."

The atmosphere shifted slightly as Ledger's impassioned plea resonated with some while discord swirled in the minds of others. Clara caught his eye, a mixture of pride and concern reflected in her expression. The children continued their games, blissfully unaware of the storm brewing among the adults.

"We must tread carefully, Ledger," his father warned, his tone serious. "Consider the risks we face. This is not just about us, but the ones we care for. It is easy to speak of change when you are not the one bearing its burden."

The tension in the room thickened, and Ledger could feel the weight of familial loyalty sliding into conflict. "And yet," he countered, lowering his voice, "if we do not stake a claim in the future we want, who will? Are we willing to let fear dictate our actions?"

As the conversation went on, each family member became a mirror of the larger social conflicts at work, with some advocating for the status quo to be maintained and others starting to feel the pressure of change. While the visitors engaged in a lively discussion on the market prices and the impending crop, Ledger saw a delicate balance between confidence and uneasiness that spoke a lot about the world beyond their golden gates.

His father, Elijah, led the conversation with gusto, his voice booming as he espoused the virtues of hard work, enterprise, and the booming sugar market. "With our yields increasing this season, our prosperity will only grow," he declared, raising his glass for a toast. "To our continued success!"

While the gathered men cheered, Ledger noticed his mother, Clarissa, exchange a fleeting glance with him, her expression revealing a momentary flicker of concern. She had always been the empathetic heart of their family, and Ledger felt her unease resonate with his own. She remained quiet, her delicate fingers tracing the rim of her glass as she took a moment to collect her thoughts. Clarissa had long been aware of the discomfort that brewed beneath the surface of their lives, even as she tried to maintain an air of genteel whimsy.

"Do we think about the laborers?" she finally asked, her voice steady but firm, drawing the attention of her husband and their guests. "Are we ensuring their well-being? They work tirelessly for us, yet I fear we may overlook their suffering."

The room fell silent for a heartbeat, tension coiling in the air. Elijah's expression tightened slightly, a flicker of disapproval crossing his features. "It is the way of business, Clarissa. They do what is required of them, and they are compensated accordingly."

Ledger watched as one of the guests, Mr. Fontaine cleared his throat, eager to interject. "Indeed, it's a necessity of the trade," he affirmed, shrugging off her concerns as if they were mere trifles. "As long as they are healthy enough to keep working, we are doing our part."

Clarissa's brow furrowed, and she pressed on, undeterred. "But at what cost? They are not mere commodities or tools. They are people."

"People who contribute to our wealth," Elijah interjected, his voice firm, an unyielding reminder of their societal roles. "This is how our society is structured, and it is crucial for our way of life."

Ledger felt a pang in his chest as the conversation unfolded. He watched his parents navigate the line between the comforts of their privilege and the looming sense of morality that unsettled the evening. The discussions at the table reflected the broader societal tensions that divided white landowners from the enslaved population, theirs was a world built on a foundation of inequality masked by wealth and opulence.

Among the guests, Ledger spotted Mr. Fontaine's son, Hamid, a boy close to his age. While their fathers basked in the privileges of their status, Hamid's eyes held a flicker of something unexpected, an awareness that echoed Ledger's unease. As their fathers laughed, Hamid turned his gaze away, fixating instead on the ground or the fruit scattered across the table, as though distancing himself from the mingling laughter and the unspoken resentment in their words.

"What if we could do more?" Ledger found himself blurting out, his voice rising above the din of conversation. Though just a boy, something inside him reacted to the conversations swirling around him. "What if we treated them better? Gave them a voice?"

All heads turned toward him, surprised at the sudden shift. The laughter halted, replaced by an uncomfortable hush. Elijah studied his son with a mix of confusion and concern, while Clarissa looked at him with a mixture of pride and anxiety.

"Those matters are far beyond your understanding, Ledger," Elijah said, his tone chastising yet cautionary. "You will learn your place in the world soon enough."

"Why should I have to accept that?" Ledger asked, passion igniting within him. The words felt raw and defiant. "It is not fair. They work so hard, and they deserve more than this."

Clarissa reached for Ledger's hand, squeezing it gently as if to anchor him amidst the storm brewing at the table. "It is important to care for others, even when society tells us not to. Remember, our actions have consequences," she said quietly, reflecting a depth of understanding. Her gaze darted between her husband and son, seeking balance in an increasingly fractious discussion.

"It's easy to think of this as just business," she added at length, her voice tinged with sorrow. "But we must not forget that lives are intertwined with our choices." With those words, a palpable tension enveloped the room, the laughter fading into nervous glances.

Ledger could sense the weight of history bearing down on them, an unseen pressure that echoed in the stillness of the room. The air grew thick with unspoken thoughts—each family member reflecting the societal divisions that had long shaped their lives. The legacy of wealth built on the suffering of others loomed large, casting shadows that seemed to stretch beyond the walls of their opulent mansion.

His father's jaw tightened, and Ledger could see the flicker of anger mixed with exasperation in his eyes. "This is no place for childlike idealism, Ledger. The world is complex, and the roles we play are essential to our survival. You will understand when you are older," Elijah said, his voice firm yet edged with concern for what he might be igniting in his son.

Ledger's heart pounded as he struggled with the contradiction of his father's remarks and the raging sense of unfairness that had begun to consume him. "However, there are alternative paths to success that don't require the suffering of others!" The cries of the slaves that reverberated in their head gave him the fortitude to speak.

The guests exchanged wary glances, uncertainty rippling through the room like an impending storm. Mr. Fontaine could no longer hide a smirk, but it quickly turned into a frown as he leaned back, crossing his arms as if to dismiss Ledger's plea. "The boy just needs to play in the fields with the laborers a bit more. He will learn the value of hard work in the sweat of the cane," he sneered.

Clarissa shot a disapproving glance at Mr. Fontaine, standing tall against the tide of condescension. "Or perhaps he needs to learn compassion and recognize the human dignity of all people," she countered, her voice steadier now, emboldened by her son's fervor. "Our wealth does not grant us the right to dehumanize others."

Ledger felt a surge of pride in his mother's words, yet the gravity of the situation weighed heavily on him. He had long admired his father's ambition and strength, but now he yearned for the moral courage that his mother embodied. "What if we could change things?" he ventured, feeling light-headed but determined. "What if we could treat them better? Give them hope?"

The room fell silent, the flickering candlelight casting shadows that danced eerily against the walls, mirroring Ledger's own uncertainty. His mother looked at him with eyes full of encouragement, while Elijah remained steadfast, the lines on his face deepening with concern.

"Hope doesn't change the realities of life, son," Elijah finally said, his gaze steady but tinged with sadness. "A plantation requires order and adherence to society's structure. What you see is the power that we must wield carefully. You are not called to question the foundations built over generations."

"Yet those foundations are built on broken lives," Ledger shot back, his voice steady despite the confrontation. "We should be better than this. Our wealth should not blind us to their struggles."

The tension in the room thickened, transforming what had begun as a festive gathering into a battleground of ideals. Ledger's breath quickened as he realized the enormity of what he was suggesting—not just for his family, but for the very structure of their existence. It was as if he had directly challenged the legacy of plantation owners, and a part of him trembled at the thought.

He felt the need to pull away and disregard the tension that was growing in the talk as he saw his parents' upset looks. But his will was strengthened as he looked back to the fields, where he could picture Margo's hardworking hands and the joy of the kids he had seen playing with the laborers. He could no longer ignore the irrefutable contradiction of their lives.

"Please," he whispered, desperation creeping into his voice. "They are people. We cannot just sit in our mansion while they suffer. We must acknowledge them, every single one of them."

Clarissa's eyes sparkled with tears, born of pride and heartache, as she witnessed her son's bravery. But Elijah's expression remained stern, caught between the desires of the heart and the harsh realities of the world he had known all his life.

After a long pause, Elijah took a deep breath, his voice low and measured. "Understand, Ledger, we are part of a system that rewards exploitation. With change comes uncertainty and risk, not just for us but for everyone. You want to fight an uphill battle, but you must be aware of the consequences."

"Why are we afraid of change?" Ledger pressed, his voice firm now. "Isn't that what people do when they see wrong? They fight for what is right?"

As he spoke, Ledger felt the weight of something greater than himself, an awareness of a world on the cusp of transformation, buzzing with the energy of untold stories and struggles yet to be fought. The stakes were higher than he had previously imagined, and he stood at the precipice of reckoning, ready to leap into a future fraught with challenge but filled with possibility.

That night, as laughter resumed around the table and glasses were raised in celebratory toasts, Ledger felt like a ghost hovering on the periphery of their revelry. The laughter echoed off the ornate walls, the joy felt hollow against the weight of his burgeoning awareness. While the adults resumed their discussions of business and profits, Ledger remained adrift in his thoughts, grappling with the tensions that had surfaced.

He watched as his father shared stories with Mr. Fontaine, both men relishing tales of their exploits in the sugar trade. Their voices mingled with the sound of clinking glass and the soft laughter of the guests, who seemed to revel in a reality insulated from the harsher truths of their lives. Ledger felt both distant from them and increasingly burdened by the silence that surrounded the enslaved individuals they relied upon.

"Would you like to join us, Ledger?" Hamid's tentative voice broke through Ledger's reverie. The boy leaned slightly forward, concern etched across his face amid the merriment. "It seems you have something to say."

Ledger blinked, surprised that Hamid had noticed his unease. "It doesn't matter," he murmured, shrugging, but the flicker in Hamid's eyes urged him on.

"Of course, it matters," Hamid insisted, his tone cautious yet earnest. "I could see that everyone quickly moved on. But you should not shy away from how you feel. If something is wrong, it needs to be voiced."

The words resonated with Ledger, igniting the courage that had flickered within him throughout the evening. "I don't want to shy away," he admitted, lowering his voice so as not to draw the ire of the adults. "I just... I do not know how to make them understand."

Hamid nodded sympathetically. "It is hard, especially when no one else seems to care. But they do need to hear about Margo and the others. They deserve to be more than just laborers in our eyes."

In that moment, Ledger felt a surge of kinship with Hamid, a sense of shared discomfort that lit a path forward. "Maybe we can make them understand together," he suggested. "Maybe we can change things starting right here in this house."

Hamid's eyes widened as if Ledger had just suggested an adventure more thrilling than the wildest tales of pirates or explorers. "You really think so?" he asked, a glimmer of hope lighting his expression. "What can we do?"

Before Ledger could respond, a sharp voice cut through their conversation. "What are the two of you whispering about?" Samuel, the overseer, stood nearby, his arms crossed over his chest. The tone in his voice was accusatory, and Ledger could feel the encroaching threat of his authority. "Do you need a reminder of your place?"

Ledger bristled at the challenge, heart racing. "We were just talking," he replied defiantly.

Samuel chuckled darkly, his eyes narrowing. "Talking, or conspiring? Be careful, boys. Ideas have a way of brewing trouble." With that, he turned on his heel, rejoining the adults who continued to fill the air with laughter and clinks of fine China.

Once Samuel was gone, Ledger felt a mix of anger and frustration boiling within him. "Why does he have to be that way?" he asked, the heat of emotion spilling over. "He acts as if we don't have a say in how this place is run."

Hamid shrugged, his youthful confidence waning. "He must keep the workers in line. That is how he thinks he will maintain order. He fears anything that threatens the way things are."

"Maybe that means we should work harder to change the way things are," Ledger declared, voice low but fueled with determination. "We could start by speaking to Margo and the others. They have ideas too."

Hamid hesitated, looking between Ledger and the banquet table. "But they might not want to hear us," he cautioned. "We are" the ones who own the plantation. I know," Ledger interrupted, frustrated but determined. "But if we're truly to honor their humanity, we must at least try."

As the evening went on, Ledger sensed a resolve building within him, a renewed feeling of purpose reinforced by the growing camaraderie between him and Hamid. Ledger's determination remained unwavering despite the continuous laughing outside. He would endeavor to remove the obstacles—erected by centuries of oppression, that separated his life from the lives of people who farmed the land.

Eventually, after the guests had departed and the mansion settled into a hush, Ledger slipped away from the after-dinner festivities. He ventured out onto the balcony, the cool night air refreshing against his skin, the distant stars twinkling down like distant watchers.

From his elevated view, he scanned the fields that stretched out before him. Shadows moved among the cane, silhouettes of those who toiled in the dim light of the approaching dusk. Ledger's heart ached as he watched. Each movement represented not just the physical labor of harvesting sugar but a testament to their struggle, each bend of a back, each swing of a machete a reminder that their lives were bound to the plantation's wealth yet completely excluded from its comforts.

He took a deep breath, inhaling the faint scent of earth and vegetation mingled with the sweet aroma of sugar cane. It was a bittersweet reminder of the dualities of his existence—the wealth and privilege of his home contrasted starkly with the hardships faced by those laboring in the fields below.

Suddenly, the silhouette of a figure stepped into a clearing illuminated by the soft light of the moon, a familiar shape that stirred something deep within him. It was Margo. Even from this distance, he could see her graceful movements as she worked alongside others, her determination evident in the way she carried herself. Somehow, despite the fatigue etched onto her face, she exuded a spirit of resilience that he admired.

"Ledger?"

Startled, he turned to see Hamid approaching, stepping out from the shadows behind him. "What are you doing out here?" he asked, his voice low to avoid drawing attention.

"Just… thinking," Ledger replied, gesturing out toward the fields. "About them. About Margo and the others."

Hamid followed his gaze, watching the workers with a frown. "It is heartbreaking, isn't it? All of this could change. But how do we even start?"

"I don't have all the answers," Ledger admitted, frustration weighing heavily on him. "But I know we cannot just keep living our lives while they suffer. There must be a way to make them feel recognized—like their hard work matters."

Hamid nodded thoughtfully, processing Ledger's words. "But what if they do not trust us? What if they see us as just two more entitled boys who do not know their pain?"

"Then we show them we care," Ledger urged, his voice steady. "We can approach them, listen to their stories, and understand their needs. We can be allies instead of oppressors."

"Do you really think they would want to talk to us?" Hamid asked, skepticism edging his tone.

"They might," Ledger replied, determination rising within him. "If we approach them with respect and honesty. We can start building bridges instead of walls, even if it is just between us and them.

The resolve in Ledger's words struck a chord, anchoring Hamid's gaze. "I suppose it's worth a try," he said, his voice gaining strength. "But we need to be careful. Samuel will not let us just wander into the fields, he will want to keep control."

"Then we will need to be discreet. We will find a way, together," Ledger declared, fear pushing him forward. "If we wait any longer, nothing will ever change."

Ledger's heart flickered with hope as a plan started to take shape. The injustices all around him were too much for him to overlook. The weight of history seemed to lessen at that very instant, as though the force of transformation was coursing through him and kindling a flame that may one day result in something bigger.

"Let's meet tomorrow at dawn," Ledger said decisively. "We will head out early before the heat sets in. We can talk to Margo and the others, show them they are seen and heard."

Hamid's expression brightened. "Alright, I am in. Let us do this."

With a newfound sense of purpose, Ledger returned inside the mansion, the air thick with the scent of roasted meats and the lingering laughter of guests who had departed. Yet he felt detached from it all now; the grand structure that had once seemed so comfortable felt strangely suffocating, filled with illusions that he could no longer abide.

As he lay in bed that night, sleep eluded him. Instead, he pictured Margo's face, her strength, her laughter. He envisioned a future where gratitude could replace entitlement, and where empathy could build connections instead of barriers.

The darkness of his room felt both cold and promising, a whisper of rebellion hanging in the air. He knew they were entering uncharted territory, uncharted not just for him, but for the plantation itself. Together, they would confront a legacy built on exploitation and forge a path toward dignity and respect for everyone.

17

And as night surrendered to dawn, Ledger felt a stirring within him, a quiet resolve to help shape the future, not just for himself, but for all those who had been silenced for far too long. Tomorrow would mark the beginning of their story, and he would write it alongside those whose lives mirrored the struggle within his heart.

The experience of enslaved individuals in the Caribbean plantation economy had a profound and devastating impact on family structures and cultural continuity. Enslaved people were frequently torn from their families and communities, disrupting the essential bonds of kinship that are vital for personal identity and cultural transmission. This fragmentation had lasting emotional and social consequences, not only for those directly affected but also for subsequent generations.

Families in the enslaved population often faced the constant threat of separation. Enslaved individuals could be sold at any time, resulting in heartbreaking separations from spouses, children, and extended family members. Such fracturing of family units was designed to dehumanize and control; it fractured the networks of support essential for resilience and survival. Children were especially vulnerable, as parents could be sold away, leaving them to grow up without the guidance of their mothers or fathers.

This disruption significantly hindered the ability of enslaved individuals to pass down cultural traditions, values, and practices that are typically sustained through familial connections. Languages, belief systems, and customs that formed the cultural bedrock of their communities faced erosion. In many cases, the efforts of enslaved individuals to preserve their heritage were met with resistance, as plantation owners sought to strip them of their identities to maintain control over their labor.

Despite the harsh conditions, enslaved people demonstrated extraordinary resilience by preserving cultural traditions and familial connections. They forged new forms of expression and community, using these as tools of survival and resistance. One key adaptation was the formation of extended kinship networks among those with no biological ties, a vital support system that helped them endure adversity.

Through oral traditions, music, and communal gatherings, enslaved individuals found ways to celebrate their identities. Rituals and stories served to reinforce a sense of belonging and shared history, bridging the gaps left by physical separation. These customs not only provided comfort but also became acts of defiance against an oppressive system that sought to erase their heritage.

Being born into a system that thrived on the exploitation of enslaved labor, Ledger Philogene had been acutely aware of the complexities and struggles faced by the people who worked on his family's land. As a member of the plantation-owning class, he observed firsthand the lives of the enslaved individuals who toiled in the fields and the profound emotional impact their treatment had on families.

Ledger's awareness of the suffering endured by the enslaved population influenced his understanding of justice and responsibility. The contradiction of growing up in an environment of privilege while acknowledging the immense cost of that privilege laid the foundation for his later aspirations toward reform and social impact. Witnessing the hardships of those enslaved left an indelible mark on Ledger's conscience, prompting him to contemplate issues of power, identity, and humanity.

The fracturing of familial structures and cultural ties among enslaved individuals reverberated through generations, shaping identity and experience long after the abolition of slavery. The loss of familial bonds and cultural continuity created lasting challenges for descendants, as they navigated a world that remains influenced by the legacies of this painful history.

Enslaved populations laid the groundwork for new cultural identities, weaving together remnants of their African heritage with the realities of life in the Caribbean. This fusion created vibrant, dynamic communities that spawned rich cultural expressions, from music and dance to storytelling and spiritual practices. However, the scars of dislocation and loss would persist, reminding future generations of the resilience required to reclaim and reconstruct their identities in the face of historical trauma.

The impact of enslavement on families was profound, resulting in the disruption of cultural transmission, kinship ties, and personal identities. Ledger Philogene's existence within this context heightened his awareness of the struggles faced by enslaved individuals who worked on his family's land. The complexities of familial and cultural ties are crucial for recognizing the enduring effects of slavery on contemporary Caribbean society and the ongoing journey toward healing, reconciliation, and cultural reclamation.

As nightfall descended in St. Barthélemy, the sun dipped below a cloud cover that promised rain, and the air was heavy with humidity. Appreciative of the momentary break from the tension of supper, Ledger strolled out onto the veranda. He was surrounded by the serene hum of nature, but a persistent strain persisted in his mind.

From the kitchen, the sounds of Clara and their children filled the house, laughter mingling with the clatter of utensils. He could hear Wizen arguing playfully with Eliza over who would get the last piece of pie, their innocent bickering a stark contrast to the heavier conversations that had dominated the table moments earlier.

Ledger leaned against the wooden railing, gazing out at the horizon where dark clouds rolled in like shadows of the unspoken challenges facing their community. The vibrant hues of the sunset had faded into a muted gray, mirroring the growing anxiety in the hearts of the islanders. He recalled the simmering discontent that had increasingly gripped both the enslaved population and the settlers, a tension that felt like the calm before a storm.

"Ledger?" A voice pulled him from his thoughts. It was Clarissa, stepping out to join him, her expression a mix of concern and resolve. "Would you mind helping me bring in some of the herbs from the garden before it rains?"

"Of course, Mother," he replied, straightening up. As they moved toward the garden behind their home, Ledger sensed her unease. "You're worried about this brewing tension, aren't you?"

"I am," Clarissa admitted, kneeling to gather bunches of fragrant thyme and rosemary. "Everywhere I turn, I hear murmurs of dissatisfaction. People are restless, Son. I fear that if we neglect their suffering, the consequences will be dire."

"It feels inevitable," Ledger said, swallowing hard. "Sooner or later, something is going to give." He helped her tuck the herbs into a woven basket, trying to focus on the task and not the anxiety gnawing at him.

"You must understand how dangerous it is to challenge the status quo," Clarissa continued, glancing over her shoulder, her voice barely above a whisper. "If we speak up, we risk losing everything. Your father... well, he believes we are better off staying in line with the old ways."

"But change is necessary. People cannot continue to suffer in silence," Ledger replied, his heart pounding. He set the basket down and turned to face her. "I feel it in my bones that we cannot afford to be complacent. Not when so many are crying out for justice."

Clarissa sighed, brushing a strand of hair behind her ear. "I agree, son. It is just that the reality we face is complex. Not everyone can see the truth beneath the surface."

She stood and wiped her hands on her apron, her gaze drifting toward the darkening sky. "But you must be cautious. While you have youth on your side, the risks are significant. We must find ways to support those in need without throwing ourselves into the storm."

Ledger felt a surge of frustration mixed with determination. "How do we do that, Mother? Remain safe and risk nothing while they endure such pain? They deserve so much more!"

Before she could respond, a rumble of thunder echoed through the valley, startling a flock of birds into flight. Ledger's gaze turned skyward, watching the first drops of rain begin to fall, heavy and deliberate, like the weight of the worries crowding his mind.

"You're right, Son," Clarissa said softly, her expression shifting as she regarded the storm clouds. "But change requires more than just shouting louder; it must be deliberate. We need allies, and that takes time."

He nodded, reluctantly conceding that change could not merely spring from passionate declarations. "Allies…and planning. We must find a way to connect with those who feel the same urgency."

Just then, a loud clap of thunder broke through the air, causing both to jump. The rain intensified, pouring down in sheets, drumming against the ground, and sending a cool breeze swirling around them. "Let's head inside," Ledger suggested, starting to retreat toward the house, but a thought struck him. "What if we organized the families? We could meet and talk openly about what we all face. Build a network of support."

"That might be the spark we need," Clarissa said, her eyes lighting up with a mix of fear and hope. "But it is important to tread carefully. Gather only those who understand the risks involved." She hesitated, her brow furrowing with concern. "Not everyone will be willing to confront the uncomfortable truths or the consequences that come with speaking out. We need to ensure that those we invite to join us share a common vision and are prepared to endure the fallout that may follow.

The weight of her words hung heavy in the air, and Ledger felt the gravity of the situation settle within him. "I want to help, Mother. I can reach out to some of the families I trust, those who have shown empathy toward the suffering of others. We can create a safe space for honest dialogue." Clarissa placed a hand on his arm, her touch grounding him. "Just remember, my son, that hope must be balanced with caution. Each step we take could ripple through our community, and we must be prepared for whatever may come. The urgency in her voice resonated with him as they stood together, rain pouring around them, each drop a reminder of the storm that loomed not only in the sky but in the hearts of those yearning for change.

Enslaved people in the Caribbean frequently rebelled against their enslavement, finding different methods to express their agency and oppose the dehumanizing institution of slavery, despite the harsh conditions they endured. From small-scale acts of disobedience in day-to-day activities to coordinated uprisings that sought to topple the plantation system, this opposition took many forms. Their hardships and tenacity were essential in forming Caribbean history, impacting later debates about freedom and human rights that surfaced in succeeding decades.

Day-to-day acts of resistance were a common and powerful form of asserting agency among enslaved individuals. These behaviors often took the form of small, inconsequential actions that collectively undermined the plantation system. For instance, enslaved people would engage in work slowdowns, feigning illness, or perform tasks poorly to protest their treatment and to push back against the demands imposed on them.

Additionally, some enslaved individuals would steal food or supplies, cultivating their gardens to supplement their rations, thereby reclaiming some degree of autonomy over their lives. Others engaged in cultural practices, such as storytelling, music, and dance, which served not only as forms of expression but also as communal gatherings that reaffirmed their identities in the face of oppression.

These everyday acts of defiance were critical for maintaining a sense of self and dignity, allowing enslaved individuals to resist the erasure of their identities and foster a spirit of solidarity among their peers. They also served to create an undercurrent of rebellion that would later erupt into more organized and overt forms of resistance.

While everyday defiance was integral, there were also significantly organized rebellions that marked pivotal moments in Caribbean history. Enslaved individuals banded together to challenge the status quo, seeking not better conditions but total liberation from the oppressive systems they endured.

One of the most notable events was the Haitian Revolution (1791–1804), where enslaved individuals successfully overthrew their colonial rulers, leading to the establishment of Haiti as the first independent Black republic. This revolution was both a powerful statement of resistance and a beacon of hope for enslaved people across the region. Inspired by the ideals of freedom and equality, enslaved populations in other Caribbean islands followed suit, staging rebellions of their own.

Rebellions such as the 1831 Baptist War in Jamaica and the 1795–1796 Slave Rebellion in Trinidad exemplified the courage and determination of enslaved individuals who fought against oppression. While these uprisings faced various degrees of success and were often met with severe reprisals, they highlighted the growing discontent among enslaved populations and the unyielding desire for freedom.

Enslaved people's acts of defiance and tenacity had a big impact on more general conversations about freedom and human rights. Their battles brought attention to the cruel conditions millions of people faced and questioned the morality of slavery. Enslaved people were freed in several locations throughout the 19th century because of these groups' gradual contributions to the escalating abolitionist sentiments in the Caribbean and Europe.

This legacy of resistance fostered a deep understanding of human rights, influencing future generations and shaping post-emancipation societies. Discussions around equality, justice, and social rights continued to evolve, driven in part by the foundational resistance laid by enslaved individuals. These themes remained central to social movements throughout history, particularly during the civil rights movements of the 20th century, where the fight against systemic oppression was framed through the lens of justice and human dignity.

The resistance of enslaved individuals in the Caribbean took many forms, ranging from everyday acts of defiance to organized rebellions. Their struggles and resilience were crucial in shaping the region's history, challenging oppressive systems, and influencing the ongoing discourse around freedom and human rights. The enduring legacy of their resistance serves as a testament to the human spirit's capacity for agency and the relentless quest for dignity and justice. Understanding these acts of defiance is vital for recognizing the profound impact of enslaved individuals on the Caribbean's path toward freedom and equality, laying the groundwork for future struggles against oppression.

The morning sun rose over the Philogene plantation, casting long shadows across the fields filled with lush sugar cane. The air was thick with humidity, but it was the murmurs of discontent that truly filled the atmosphere—whispers of resistance woven into the daily toil of the enslaved individuals who worked the land.

In the early light, Ledger made his way to the fields with Hamid, both boys moving quietly so as not to attract the attention of the overseers. They had decided to meet Margo and some of her fellow workers at the edge of the cane, where they could speak freely away from prying eyes. Ledger's heart raced with anticipation; they were stepping into a world that was both foreign and compelling, a world beyond the constraints imposed by their families.

As they approached a cluster of workers, Ledger caught sight of Margo, her strong hands deftly slicing through the cane, each cut precise and practiced. Her brow glistened with sweat, but there was a fierce determination in her expression. She was a leader among her peers, embodying the resilience that echoed through the stories of resistance he had begun to learn.

"Good morning, Margo!" Ledger called, breathless with excitement. The workers paused, casting curious glances at the two boys. Margo turned, a guarded smile breaking across her tired face.

"Good morning, Ledger, Hamid," she replied, her voice steady. "What brings you out here so early?"

"We wanted to talk," Ledger said, glancing around to ensure no overseers lurked nearby. "We want to help."

Margo raised an eyebrow, skepticism etched into her features. "Help? You mean help us by taking us back to the mansion for dinner, or something else?"

Hamid stepped forward, sensing the tension. "No, we mean it. We want to understand what you need. Samuel treats you like…,"

"Like livestock?" a voice interrupted. It was Kofi, a tall man with broad shoulders and a fierce glint in his eye, who had just joined the group. He stepped forward, arms crossed. His presence radiated strength, commanding attention. "We do not need charity. We need change."

"Right," Ledger said quickly, feeling the weight of their scrutiny. "Change is what we are hoping to discuss. If we work together…"

"You think collaborating with us will change anything?" Kofi challenged, his voice low and filled with skepticism, yet tinged with curiosity. "You stand in your father's shadow. What can you do that would matter?"

Ledger squared his shoulders, drawing upon the conviction that had ignited during their dinner the previous night. "I can stand with you and fight for change. You are right; I have lived in comfort while you bear the burden of toil. But I see the strength you have, and I want to help amplify that strength."

A tense silence hung in the air, the workers exchanging glances that reflected a mix of uncertainty and guarded hope. Margo stepped in beside Kofi, her gaze penetrating. "What do you propose, Ledger? Speaking out in your father's house will not change our reality."

"There are ways to resist," Ledger replied, his voice steady. "We could organize. We could share stories and tell others what truly is happening here. If we gather support and awareness, it might create a ripple effect."

Kofi shook his head, frustration evident. "And what if Samuel finds out? We could be punished, or worse. They do not just whip us, they take lives too."

"I know the risks," Ledger admitted, heart pounding. "But every act of defiance, no matter how small, is a step toward asserting our agency. I have read about what others have done, small rebellions, and uprisings. Every whisper of resistance matters."

Margo stepped closer, her voice low. "Let us say we entertain your idea. What can we do in practice? Talking will not change the world."

"Maybe we start small," Hamid suggested, catching the interest of some of the workers. "We could gather at night and share stories and experiences without fear of reprisal. Reclaim our narratives."

"What good are stories?" Kofi asked, though his brow furrowed, revealing curiosity.

"They give us strength," Ledger replied, fired up. "Knowing our history, honoring our ancestors. That, along with practical ways to disrupt our work or slow production. Together, we could make a statement, show them we are not just laborers—we are individuals with thoughts, lives, and hopes."

Margo's expression deepened, weighing the gravity of his words. "It takes courage to speak like this, Ledger. But let us not forget what we risk. Our lives depend on the will of the overseers. If they catch wind of any dissent…"

Her voice trailed off, the implications hanging heavy between them. The reality of their situation settled in like a thick fog—any act of defiance could lead to severe punishment, a fate all too familiar among the workforce.

"I understand the risks," Ledger replied earnestly, feeling a swell of determination within him. "But isn't it worth considering? Each day, we suffer together; each day we endure a system built on our backs. If we do nothing, what does that mean for us?"

Kofi was silent for a moment, the tension evident as he searched Ledger's face for sincerity. "You've no idea what it is like out there at the hands of the overseers. The whip is a constant threat, and we have lost friends and family to their cruelty. You speak of change as if it is a game, while we play with our lives."

"None of us wants to risk our safety," Margo said softly, placing a hand on Kofi's arm. "But if we take measured steps… if we create a community where we can support each other, then maybe we can begin to craft our own agency." She turned to Ledger, her eyes thoughtful. "What would you suggest?"

Ledger felt the weight of their gazes on him. "We start with gatherings, sharing our stories, our histories. We can plan ways to slow production without overt defiance, using the very system they have imposed on us against them. We might also forge connections with sympathetic whites, those who might help amplify our voices."

Hamid nodded eagerly. "We can communicate through subtle signs, ways of taking longer during our work or rearranging schedules so they seem less efficient. Let them see we are capable of more than just bending to their will."

Kofi's posture relaxed slightly. "Awareness is one thing, but if we dare to act, we need to ensure we can defend ourselves. A gathering can put us in danger if it creates too much attention."

"It won't be easy," Margo agreed, her voice steady, filled with purpose. "But a seed of resistance must be planted. If we stand together, we can make them listen."

A murmur of agreement rippled through the group. It was a fragile alliance forged in the weight of oppression, but it radiated potential—a light flickering boldly against the encroaching darkness of their reality.

"Let's meet again when the sun sets," Margo continued, her voice resolute. "We will speak freely then, share our stories, and strategize how we can assert our presence. We define our narrative."

"Agreed," Ledger said, feeling a rush of approval and camaraderie among his peers.

Kofi shot him a penetrating glance. "If this is to work, you both must understand that trust is fragile among us. Trust is often shattered by fear. You especially must prove you are truly on our side."

"I will," Ledger vowed, feeling a fire ignite within him. "I'll do everything I can to show my commitment to this cause."

There was a sense of urgency among the group as they started to disperse. With resolve engraved on their features, each laborer returned to the fields with a fresh sense of purpose. The subdued murmurs of opposition had transformed into unwavering determination, a shared understanding that spoke to their innermost selves.

As Ledger and Hamid walked back toward the mansion, Ledger's chest swelled with hope and apprehension. He knew now that their journey together would not be without challenges; the path to change was fraught with danger and uncertainty. Yet amidst that fear, they had forged something vital—a spark of agency, defiance flickering against the dark shadows of oppression.

"Do you think they'll trust us?" Hamid asked as they approached the thresholds of their sheltered lives, glancing back toward the fields now hidden by the early morning light.

"I think we have to earn their trust," Ledger replied, determination clear in his voice. "And that means not just talking about change but truly standing with them when it matters most."

With the echoes of their shared conversation hanging heavily in the air, Ledger felt an unbreakable bond forming—one that he hoped would be fierce enough to weather the storms ahead. Bound by the recognition of their shared humanity, they would strive to create a tapestry of resistance deeply woven with the stories of those who labored, creating a new path stitched through resilience, hope, and fierce determination.

Ledger Philogene's birth in 1852 places him at a transformative juncture in Caribbean history, a time when the legacies of colonialism and slavery were deeply ingrained in social structures and cultural identities. Growing up on his family's plantation in St. Barthelemy, Ledger was surrounded by the remnants of a system that had profoundly shaped the lives of countless individuals. As he navigated this complex landscape, the societal dynamics surrounding him undoubtedly influenced his worldview and laid the groundwork for his eventual destiny.

Born shortly after the emancipation of enslaved individuals throughout the Caribbean, Ledger's early years were marked by the remnants of colonial power structures. Although formal slavery had ended, the societal hierarchies and racial divisions that had characterized plantation life persisted, creating an environment in which the struggles for true equality and justice were ongoing.

Ledger's experience was profoundly shaped by these dynamics. As a member of the plantation-owning class, he had access to privileges that contrasted sharply with the experiences of the formerly enslaved population. The inequalities and injustices that played out in front of him would have been impossible to ignore, prompting him to grapple with his family's legacy within the broader context of colonial oppression. This awareness fueled a sense of responsibility and a desire for change, a response to the complexities of his heritage.

The legacies of colonialism—economic exploitation, cultural dislocation, and social inequality—were critical aspects of Ledger's upbringing, shaping his beliefs about justice, power, and identity. The environment in which he grew up also allowed him to witness the resilience of formerly enslaved individuals as they fought against the tides of inequality and sought to forge new identities in the aftermath of systemic oppression.

Ledger gained an understanding of his family's challenges, goals, and cultural diversity via interactions with the work market and the larger society. Ledger's viewpoint and commitment for social justice were impacted by his understanding of the resilience and adaptability of individuals who faced hardship. This early encounter fostered empathy, and an understanding of the difficulties associated with the continuous struggle for equality and dignity, a struggle that struck a deep chord throughout the Caribbean.

Ledger Philogene's legacy also reflects the broader historical currents at play in St. Barthelemy and the Caribbean during the 19th century. The abolition of slavery across the Caribbean was accompanied by significant social and political change, leading to a re-examination of colonial power structures and a growing discourse on human rights and dignity.

As Caribbean societies sought to redefine themselves in the wake of colonial rule, figures like Ledger Philogene found themselves at a crossroads, where personal heritage and societal change intertwined. The movement toward greater autonomy, cultural reclamation, and justice became paramount during this period, and Ledger's trajectory can be viewed as part of this collective struggle for identity and agency.

Ledger Philogene's life underscores the complexities and contradictions inherent in navigating a legacy influenced by both privilege and the enduring scars of oppression. His awareness of the historical injustices faced by the formerly enslaved population may have propelled him toward advocacy or leadership that sought to challenge the lingering inequities within his society.

His legacy lies in contributing to the ongoing narrative of resilience and resistance in the Caribbean, a narrative where individuals from diverse backgrounds strive to create a more just and equitable world. In recognizing the interconnectedness of his heritage with the broader societal movements toward justice, Ledger Philogene embodies the enduring struggle for recognition, equality, and dignity in a post-colonial landscape.

Ledger Philogene's birth and life in the context of St. Barthelemy during a pivotal historical moment provide insight into the legacies of colonialism and slavery. His upbringing on a plantation, amid the complexities of societal dynamics, profoundly influenced his worldview and shaped his destiny. Understanding his legacy is crucial for grasping the interplay of history, culture, and identity in the Caribbean, contributing to the ongoing pursuit of justice and the recognition of the enduring impacts of colonial rule.

08

Chapter Two: Philogene Family Migration

The air in the Philogene mansion was thick with anxiety as Ledger's family gathered in the parlor, the weight of colonial unrest pressing down on them like the heat of the Caribbean sun. The news from St. Barthélemy had grown increasingly dire, strikes by enslaved workers, disturbances caused by freedom seekers, and whispered threats of rebellion echoed through the plantation. Tensions swirled like a storm cloud, casting a shadow over their comfortable lives.

Elijah Philogene stood by the window, his posture rigid, arms crossed tightly over his chest as he gazed at the far-off horizon. "The situation is becoming untenable here," he said, his voice grave. "With unrest brewing among the laborers, it may only be a matter of time before our estate is caught in the flames of rebellion."

Ledger shifted uneasily in his chair, his father's words sinking like a heavyweight in his gut. He had heard the murmurs of unrest from the fields and sensed the anger bubbling just beneath the surface. But the thought of leaving home the only place he had ever known stirred a mix of fear and yearning within him.

"Where do we go, then?" Clarissa, his mother, asked, her voice soft yet laden with urgency. "What options do we have?"

"St. Thomas." Elijah's tone was resolute. "We have relatives there, and the rumblings of unrest are quieter. We may find opportunity in the growing commerce of the island. The situation there is still unstable, but the financial prospects outweigh the dangers here."

Ledger felt an unfamiliar mixture of hope and apprehension. St. Thomas was known for its bustling ports and trade networks, a place where life could be different, a glimmer of possibility amid the uncertainty. Yet he could not ignore the weight of leaving behind everything he had ever known.

"But what about our plantation?" he interjected, his voice shaky. "What about the people working for us? They should be able to live free, not live under the boot of oppression.

"Ledger," his father replied, his voice tempered with a mixture of exasperation and paternal concern. "We cannot help anyone if we are consumed by our predicament. The world is unforgiving; self-preservation is paramount. We must look to our future."

Clarissa nodded, though Ledger saw the hesitance in her eyes. "Change is never easy, but this move can bring us closer to a better life. And if we can extend help to those in need once we are established, then it will be worth it."

The mid-19th century was a turbulent period for the Caribbean, a crucible of transformation where dreams of freedom simmered beneath the surface of colonial authority. In St. Barthélemy, the air carried a different weight, thick with rising discontent among the enslaved population. Ledger Philogene could feel the pulse of change throbbing in the very soil beneath him, a reminder that the world was shifting in ways that would soon be impossible to ignore.

Each day, Ledger witnessed the gatherings grow more numerous, the conversations more heated. It became common to hear murmurs of discontent as the enslaved workers exchanged hushed words during their brief moments of respite. They spoke of their dreams of freedom, and whispers of revolts danced through the air like smoke from a distant fire. Ledger noticed the change in their expressions, fear mingled with determination, as they stood on the precipice of something greater than themselves.

The tension in the streets was unmistakable. Angry shouts filled the evening air as local meetings bubbled over with calls for abolition and rights. Prospective leaders emerged from the shadows, rallying those who dared to hope for a better life. It was a volatile mix, and Ledger knew that the plantation owners and their families felt it acutely. He could see it in their restless eyes, hear it in their wavering voices during conversations that had once been so firmly rooted in comfortable predictability.

"We live on the edge of a knife," Ledger confided to Clara one evening as they sat in their dimly lit kitchen. The flickering oil lamp cast shadows on the walls as the sounds of unrest echoed faintly from the town square. "It wouldn't take much for everything to change, for the anger of the people to boil over."

Clara nodded solemnly, her hands tightening around the edge of the table. "What if they rise? What will we do?"

He leaned back and took a deep breath, a swirl of hopes and fears battling within him. "I cannot help but admire their courage. They have every right to fight for their freedom. But the consequences for us could be dire."

The reality of their situation became more pressing as news of violent uprisings in neighboring islands reached their ears. Reports of plantations set ablaze, overseers attacked, and families torn apart fueled the anxiety that hung in the air like a storm cloud.

"The power shift isn't just affecting them; it's changing our lives too," Clara mused, her eyes reflecting a mix of resolve and doubt. "We cannot continue to live as if nothing is happening. We need to think carefully about our future here."

"I agree," Ledger said, his tone sober. "We are in a precarious position. We need to adapt to this new reality, for the sake of our children. If the tides of change come crashing, I want us to be ready."

Their conversation turned inward as they contemplated their life on the island. It was challenging to envision a path forward, with every option fraught with uncertainty. Would they stand by the status quo, risking any semblance of safety for themselves and their children? Or should they seek a way to navigate the storms brewing on the horizon?

St. Thomas, a neighboring island of St. Barthélemy, lay shimmering on the horizon like a promise, a vibrant hub of trade and commerce that beckoned to Ledger's family. In stark contrast to the instability and turmoil of their current home, St. Thomas offered a vision of hope and prosperity that seemed tantalizingly within reach. Its bustling markets, thriving businesses, and multicultural communities painted a picture of a future where hard work could yield tangible rewards.

In the evenings, Ledger listened intently as his father spoke of St. Thomas, his words brimming with possibility. "It is a place where the tides of fortune flow differently," Elijah would often say, drawing on his experience from years spent in the sugar trade. "With the influx of vessels from Europe and America, the trade opportunities are immense. If we migrate, we could find work, develop skills, and even establish our own business one day.

Over family meals, Clarissa added her thoughts, her eyes alight with optimism. "Market days in Charlotte Amalie are renowned for their vibrancy," she said, recalling tales of traders from various islands converging to exchange goods—fruits, spices, textiles, and more. "If we can tap into that energy, we may carve a niche for ourselves. We must leverage what we know about trade and our connections to create a new life."

Ledger felt a mixture of excitement and apprehension at the prospect of relocating to St. Thomas. He was aware that abandoning everything would be a huge leap into the future. But there was no denying the appeal of economic freedom. His mind conjured up images of market booths brimming with fresh goods, the cadence of commerce, and laughter resonating among the thronging crowd.

The decision to migrate began to crystallize for one evening when the family gathered for their usual discussions. Ledger could sense the urgency in the air as the shadows of unrest grew longer around them. His mother had prepared a simple meal of rice and beans, but the atmosphere was charged with a hunger for something more, hope.

"Every day I hear more whispers of unrest among the laborers," Elijah said, his brow furrowed with concern. "Reports of strikes, of people bolting for freedom—these winds are shifting. We cannot afford to stay complacent. We must seek a safer haven for ourselves."

"What if we don't find acceptance in St. Thomas?" Ledger asked, his voice tinged with apprehension. "What if they look upon us as remnants of the past, as those who once owned plantations?"

"Everyone here in St. Barthélemy knows the hardships of survival," Clarissa reassured him, her voice steady. "Many people migrate for the same reasons we would. If we approach them with respect and humility, we can build relationships. It is about showing them we are eager to contribute, not just survive."

Ledger nodded thoughtfully, pondering the idea of not just leaving behind the physical space of the plantation but also the weight of its legacy. They did not have to become defined by the past; they could forge new identities in a new land.

Days passed, and their discussions solidified into a collective resolve. The family spent their evenings mapping out a plan for their migration. They would save what little funds they had, seek out connections in St. Thomas, and gather supplies needed for the journey. The more they talked about it, the more their doubts began to fade, replaced by a shared determination to seek a better future.

As days rolled into weeks, the unrest escalated. Ledger noticed changes among the plantation owners, their confidence wavering. Once in control, they now hold meetings cloaked in secrecy, their discussions punctuated by alarmed whispers. Fear seeped into their conversations like the rising tide, transforming once casual laughter into strained smiles.

Ledger often stood among them, grappling with a growing sense of unease. He felt torn between his empathy for those who labored in the fields and the instinct to protect his own family from the fallout of any societal upheaval. Each passing day weighed heavier on his conscience, as he could no longer reconcile the comfort of their lives with the suffering of others.

One stormy night, Ledger ventured out to meet a few fellow plantation owners at a hastily convened gathering. The tension was palpable as they exchanged grave glances and hushed tones, discussing the shifting tides of power and the contentment that had begun to crack under the strain of unrest.

"We cannot ignore the signs," said a robust man named Jacques, his voice deep but tinged with fear. "The people are restless. They will not be subdued forever."

"Perhaps we should reconsider our positions," Ledger said cautiously, surprising himself with the weight of his own words. "These uprisings may call for a reevaluation of how we govern our plantations, a shift in how we treat our workers."

The air thickened with tension, and Ledger could feel the unease ripple through the group. A murmur of dissent followed his comment, a mix of disagreement and concern about surrendering any advantage they had.

"We're not here to discuss compassion," Jacques retorted, his frustration evident. "We must maintain control at all costs. This is not a matter of sentiment, but survival."

Ledger's heart sank as he watched their faces harden. He knew he was speaking from a place of humanity, a desire for change, but in that moment, it felt hopelessly naïve against the backdrop of their fears. The shift in power dynamics sparked uncertainty for everyone in the room, yet solutions and discussions of empathy were drowned out by a primal urge to protect their interests.

Normally so lively with children's laughter and the bustle of market days, Gustavia's streets have turned into a furnace of conflict. Ledger observed the sight outside from the window of his little house, his pulse pounding. The gathered mob rushed forward, their voices rising in a cacophony of defiance and rage as the sun sank below the hills, creating deep shadows that felt more sinister than normal.

"Look at them," Clara murmured, joining him at the window, her expression a mix of concern and determination. "They're gathering again."

Ledger nodded, feeling the weight of every shout and chant as if they were pressing against the glass separating them from the unrest. He could see people standing shoulder to shoulder, their faces illuminated with passion as they voiced their demands for freedom and justice. Wooden signs, crudely painted with desperate calls for emancipation and rights, bobbed above the throngs—a visual testament to the urgency of their cause.

The air was thick with tension, the thick scent of sweat and smoke mingling and pervasive. Ledger could hear the rhythmic clapping, the sound echoing against the cobblestones, punctuated by the shouts of a few bold leaders who stood atop makeshift platforms, rallying the crowd. "Freedom! Equality! We will not be silent!" they cried, their words rippling through the masses like a wave of energy.

As the group grew, so did the noise. Ledger caught snippets of their chants, weaving in and out of the shouts, rising to a fever pitch that made his heart race. "No more chains! No more silence!" echoed around him, and he felt a deep resonance with the struggle, even as fear tugged at his insides. Each shout was a reminder of the oppression that had long defined their lives, and as he looked out, he saw the faces of neighbors, people he had known for years, their eyes alight with hope mixed with the uncertainty of rebellion.

But as the night deepened, so too did the atmosphere of dread. He spotted a group of colonial officers moving down the main street, their presence like a dark cloud rolling in. Dressed in crisp uniforms, their faces betraying no emotion, they advanced on the crowd with a menacing air, a stark reminder of the power they wielded and the consequences that might follow any dissent.

"They're coming," Ledger breathed, feeling Clara tense beside him. The officers drew closer, their gazes scanning the crowd as if searching for a spark to ignite an explosion. Ledger's heart hammered in his chest; these men had the power to escalate the situation beyond control, he knew it, and so did the crowd.

The atmosphere shifted; the hopeful chants began to falter, replaced by an undercurrent of fear. Ledger watched as the tension between the crowd and the authorities thickened, like the air before a storm. "We need to go," he urged Clara, unable to suppress the urge to shield his family from the unfolding chaos.

"What if they lash out?" Clara replied, her voice trembling slightly. "What if…"

Before she could finish, a shout erupted from the crowd, a man at the front raising his arms defiantly. "We are not afraid!" he yelled, but the sentiment was swiftly swallowed by the clash of authority. A colonial officer stepped forward, drawing his weapon, his voice booming with authority. "Disperse! Return to your homes immediately!"

The command sent shockwaves through the crowd, a ripple of hesitation flickering across faces once bold in their solidarity. "Stay strong!" another voice cried, but the power of the officer's presence was unmistakable, casting a pall over their hopes. Ledger's heart sank as chaos erupted; some turned to flee while others stood rooted in place, torn between fear and conviction.

Ledger turned to Clara, their eyes locking in an understanding of the urgency pressing down upon them. "We cannot stay here. Not now. Not like this," he urged, pulling her towards the door. "We need to protect the children."

Shouting and dissatisfaction filled the air as they went outdoors, a tumultuous reminder of the world outside their door. The decision had become obvious: remaining would have meant surviving in the increasingly perilous environment of instability while leaving would have meant facing the future for the sake of their family. Ledger bore the burden of the choice ahead as they made their way through the mayhem that was erupting all around them, every cry for freedom resonating in his ears and pushing them in the direction of an as-yet-undetermined direction.

Ledger returned home that night, the storm mirrored the turmoil in his heart. He looked around at the familiar sights of his home, the laughter of his children playing in the fading light, the faint scent of Clara's cooking wafting through the open window, and the laughter that echoed from the nearby homes of friends and neighbors. It all felt both comforting and haunting. The storm rumbled again, and he felt a chill that had nothing to do with the weather.

"What kind of future can I offer them here?" he wondered, his heart heavy with doubt. The unrest swirled in his mind like the tempest outside, threatening to upend their lives. Would they continue to ignore the calls for justice and freedom, clinging to the delicate fabric of their lives? Or would they risk everything for a chance to align themselves with the dreams of change echoing through the community?

Ledger paused at the threshold, torn between the safety of the familiar and the uncertainty of venturing into the unknown. His children deserved a life marked by hope and possibility, not one overshadowed by fear and oppression. He knew the choice would not be easy, to stay amid the chaos or to seek a new beginning in St. Thomas where opportunities awaited, but so too would challenges.

"Tomorrow," he resolved silently, "I will talk to Clara. We must decide together. The time for action has come, and our family deserves a future free from the shadow of this unrest." Conflicted yet determined, Ledger stepped inside, bolstered by the love surrounding him and the hope he carried for a brighter tomorrow.

That evening, as the shadows lengthened, Ledger gathered his family around the table. The flickering light from the oil lamp cast a warm glow, but the urgency of their discussion suffocated the warmth, leaving an air of tension hanging over them. Clara, his parents, and his siblings all felt the oppressive weight of uncertainty pressing down upon them. The events of the day had ignited a spark of concern that needed addressing, and Ledger sensed that the path before them was fraught with difficult choices.

"We can't ignore what's happening anymore," he began, his voice steady yet firm as he looked around the table. "This unrest will not dissipate on its own. We need to prepare to leave St. Barthélemy."

A heavy silence followed his statement, each family member processing the implications of his words. Clara exchanged glances with Ledger's parents, her brow furrowed with worry. "Leaving?" she echoed, concern lacing her tone. "What about our home? Our community? Everything we have built here?"

Ledger leaned forward, his hands clasped tightly on the table. "I know how much this place means to all of us, but staying could mean putting our lives in danger. I have seen things, Clara, things I cannot unsee." The bitterness in his tone grew as he recalled the recent confrontation at the market, where a friend had been struck down during a protest. "The colonial authorities are cracking down, and those who stand up to them face severe consequences."

His mother, seated beside Clara, looked visibly shaken. "But what will we find if we leave? St. Thomas is a foreign land. What if it is worse? What if we struggle to survive there?" The fear in her voice was palpable, a reflection of the uncertainty that haunted them all. "This is our home. We have family and friends—we cannot just abandon them."

"We wouldn't be abandoning them," Ledger argued, a desperate edge creeping into his voice. "We would be seeking safety, a chance for our children to grow up without the constant threat of violence. I cannot bear the thought of our children facing a life filled with fear.

Wizen, hearing the escalating conversation, spoke up with wide eyes. "But, Dad, what if we end up lonely in St. Thomas? What if we do not make any friends?" The innocence of his question pierced through the tension, making Ledger's heartache. He wanted to protect his son from the harsh realities of the world, but there were no easy answers.

"We would have each other, Wizen," Ledger soothed, reaching over to ruffle his son's hair. "Families migrate for a fresh start. There are people there who share our experiences—we would find new friends and create new memories.

Clara shifted in her chair, her expression torn. "But what if leaving means losing everything? Our patterns, our traditions… we could end up losing ourselves." The worry etched on her face mirrored Ledger's fears, and it felt like a tug-of-war of emotions between the heart and the head.

"You know it's not just about us," his father interjected calmly, his voice heavy with years of experience. "It is about the world we are living in. We have seen the signs of change; it is not safe for anyone right now. You have witnessed it!" He leaned forward, placing his hand on Ledger's. "You've been on the front lines of the unrest—we can't ignore the danger that lurks around us."

"But what if we find it's a mistake?" Clara pressed, her hands clenched in her lap as she searched Ledger's eyes for assurance. "What if it is worse? We would be uprooting our children, putting them in harm's way in the name of hopes that might not come true.

"What is worse than living in fear?" Ledger countered, the urgency in his voice rising. "What is the alternative? Watching them grow up in a place where their rights and futures could be snatched away at any moment? We are at a crossroads, and we must decide whether we are going to face the waves of change or be swallowed by them.

31

The gravity of the moment pressed down on them all. Ledger's heart pounded as the full weight of the decision took hold. He glanced at his siblings, each one lost in thought, their faces marked by the fear of the unknown and the pull of the familiar. The risk of losing what they had clung to them visibly, yet beneath it, Ledger could feel something else stirring: a quiet hope, a shared yearning for safety that bound them together.

"We should come together and weigh our options," Ledger said, leaning back to regard each of them. "This decision is not just mine or Clara's; it affects all of us. We need to understand what we are willing to risk and what we can gain. Staying means living under the constant threat of violence, while leaving could open doors to a future where our children can thrive, unburdened by fear."

He paused, gauging their reactions. The room was charged with tension, the weight of the moment settled heavily on their shoulders. "Let us talk about what we might find in St. Thomas, the opportunities, the community there that awaits us. Yes, it is daunting, but it is an opportunity for a fresh start. We will not abandon the love we have for this place; rather, we will carry it with us and seek new roots to grow."

His words hung in the air, a fragile hope amidst the swirling uncertainty. Ledger could see a flicker of understanding begin to resonate in Clara's eyes, and the acknowledgment of shared fear shifted subtly to a dawning realization: sometimes the choice between fear and hope could lead them to new possibilities. "Together, we can support each other through this transition, we will face whatever comes, hand in hand."

The sun had barely risen over Gustavia when Ledger stepped out of his home, the morning light painting the village in hues of gold and amber. The unrest from the previous day still lingered in the air like an unshakeable fog, but the necessity of life continued. He felt an urgency in his bones as he prepared to speak with his neighbors about the possibility of migrating to St. Thomas, a potential path away from the encroaching chaos.

As he walked down the narrow-cobbled streets, familiar faces greeted him. He approached a group of men gathered outside the bakery, their conversations mixing with the scent of fresh bread. The camaraderie felt like an anchor amidst the uncertainty swirling around them.

"Morning, Ledger! What is on your mind?" called out Samuel, a man with a hearty laugh and a welcoming demeanor.

"I wanted to talk to you all about the possibility of moving to St. Thomas," Ledger said, taking a deep breath. He knew that such discussions would evoke mixed reactions. "With everything that's happening here, Clara and I are considering it for the safety of our family."

Immediately, the atmosphere shifted. Some faces lit up with excitement, while others clouded with skepticism.

"St. Thomas? That is a bold leap, my friend!" Samuel said, a spark of enthusiasm in his voice. "I've heard tales of opportunity there, jobs aplenty, and people making lives for themselves." He leaned forward, his eyes twinkling with hope. "It sounds like a chance for a fresh start, away from all this unrest."

However, not everyone shared his optimism. Marisol, a woman known for her practical outlook, crossed her arms tight against her chest, her brow knitted with concern. "But it's still uncertain, isn't it?" she replied, shaking her head. "What if it is not what you are expecting? The stories we hear are often colored by dreams, not reality. You could find yourselves struggling more there than you do here."

Ledger felt a pang of apprehension at her words, but he pressed on. "It is true, but staying could mean continuing to live on a powder keg, waiting for something to explode. Our children deserve more than that."

Marisol's husband, Reggie, chimed in, his voice low and serious. "And what about family? What about the roots you are leaving behind? You risk losing everything familiar to chase a dream that might crumble the moment you arrive."

A murmur of agreement rippled through a few others in the group. Ledger recognized the fear behind their words: leaving behind loved ones and a community woven tightly through shared history was no small sacrifice.

"It is a difficult decision," Ledger acknowledged, sensing the weight of their emotions. "But change is coming regardless of whether we are ready for it or not. I would rather choose the direction of that change than be swept away by it. We must consider what our family's safety means."

Samuel, however, remained steadfast in his encouragement. "We all want what is best for our families, Ledger. St. Thomas is the solution. Look, my cousin moved there last year and has already opened a shop! He says the opportunities are real."

"But at what cost?" Marisol pressed back, her voice rising slightly as a sense of urgency tinged her frustration. "We have not seen the full picture! There are, after all, uncertainties that might threaten your very existence. Those who sought new lands often faced hardships we cannot even imagine. What if you are not welcome there? Or what if you find out you have nothing in common with the others there?"

The group drifted into a heavy silence, thick with unspoken tension. Ledger understood the complexity of their thoughts, their hopes intertwined with fears, their yearning for a better future in conflict with the pull of familiar comforts. It mirrored the broader societal divide surrounding them, splitting people into camps of cautious skeptics, and daring optimists.

"I appreciate your honesty," Ledger said finally, sensing the need to bridge the growing divide. "These conversations matter. We need to discuss our fears together rather than shying away from them. Whether we decide to leave or stay, we should support each other through it.

As he looked at his neighbors, Ledger realized that no matter how the community divided over the issue of migration, the bond they shared remained constant. The pressure of uncertainty and the approaching storm outside was undeniable, but this very conversation created an opportunity for understanding and mutual support in the face of a collective struggle.

The morning passed in conversation after conversation, fluctuating between stirring hope and deep-rooted fears, encapsulating the struggle taking place not only in their hearts and families, but in the very fabric of St. Barthélemy itself. As Ledger left the gathering, he felt a rising urgency to decide—one that would define not only his family's future, but the ripple effects it could create through their community.

***

The air in Ledger's home buzzed with a palpable mixture of excitement and anxiety as the family prepared for their journey to St. Thomas. Sunlight streamed through the open windows, casting warm patches on the polished wooden floorboards, yet the atmosphere felt heavy, suffused with the weight of their impending departure. Boxes piled high in the corners of the small living room, each one a testament to the life they were leaving behind.

Ledger moved methodically through the room, folding clothes and placing them into a woven trunk. Clara sat nearby, sorting through their children's toys. She held up a small wooden horse, a gift from Ledger's father, and smiled wistfully.

"Do you think the new place will have enough space for all of this?" she asked, her brow slightly furrowed.

"It has to," Ledger replied, glancing up with a reassuring grin. "We will have a chance to start fresh, Clara. Besides, we can always leave a few things behind."

Just then, Wizen and his sister, Louisa, burst into the room, their faces alight with a mix of curiosity and amusement. "What are we taking? Can I bring my whole collection of seashells?" Louisa asked, her black eyes wide with enthusiasm, clutching a small bag already half-filled with her treasures.

"I think we should leave the entire shore behind, sister," Wizen teased, grinning as he squatted beside her. "How many shells do you need for one journey?"

Louisa pouted her hands on her hips. "But these are special! And some are big! I cannot leave my big ones behind!"

Ledger could not help but chuckle at their playful banter. "We'll find a way to make sure you bring the most special ones," he said, glancing at Clara to gauge her reaction.

"That's fair," Clara agreed, her smile returning at the sight of the children's excitement. "But you will have to help pack other things, too. We need to make sure we have enough clothes for the journey."

As they packed, the children scampered around the room, giggling and slipping away to play with their toys. Their laughter cut through the tension that clung to Ledger and Clara, a fragile reminder of the innocence they longed to protect amid the weight of an uncertain future.

"Louisa!" Wizen exclaimed suddenly, lifting a small ball. "What about this? Do you really want to take the ball? We can get a new one on the other side, can't we?"

Louisa frowned, crestfallen. "But this is a part of all our games! We cannot just leave it! What if we do not find a new one?"

Wizen, feeling the weight of her disappointment, knelt beside her. "Okay, how about this, let's take it, but you have to pick which shell you'll leave behind to make room for it!"

Louisa's brows lifted, contemplating the offer. "Okay, but can we make a game out of it? You help me choose which shell to leave behind, and I will help you decide what to take!" A pact was formed, excitement replacing their earlier worries as they found common ground.

As the children busily debated which toys to choose, Ledger and Clara exchanged a glance, sharing silent understanding. The fear of the unknown had not vanished, but it receded just a bit, replaced by bubbling hope and the thrill of adventure, the very building blocks of a new life on the horizon.

"Let's make sure to pack that horse, Clara," Ledger said, gesturing toward the wooden toy. "It could remind them of home, and stories of our journey can make it feel like a grand adventure."

"You're right," Clara agreed, her spirit lifting just a little more. "New adventures await us. And who knows what St. Thomas has in store?"

As the morning unfolded, laughter and decisions filled the air, wrapping around them like a warm blanket, enveloping them in the comfort of family. The prospect of leaving everything they knew morphed into excitement as they embraced the journey ahead, packing not just belongings, but hope, dreams, and the love that would guide them through the changes to come.

***

The sun rose slowly over St. Barthélemy, casting golden rays that filtered through the fluttering curtains of Ledger's home. Today marked the last day they would awaken in this familiar space, bathed in the scents, and sounds of a life well lived. Ledger stood at the kitchen window, watching as the world outside stirred to life, the familiar sights bringing both comfort and sorrow.

He took a deep breath, inhaling the crisp morning air mixed with the rich aroma of coffee brewing behind him. "Morning, love," Clara said softly as she entered the kitchen, her eyes still heavy with sleep but a warm smile gracing her lips. She walked over, wrapping her arms around Ledger from behind and resting her chin on his shoulder.

"Good morning. Can you believe it is finally here?" he replied, leaning against her for a moment, savoring their connection. They had spoken at length about this moment, the complexities of leaving their home behind, but the reality of it was beginning to settle in.

"There's a bittersweetness about it, isn't there?" she mused, looking out at the horizon. "All those memories... and now we're packing them up to take with us."

"That's the thing," Ledger said thoughtfully, turning to face her. "We carry those memories, but we can also create new ones. Today is a goodbye, yes, but it is also a beginning."

Clara nodded, though her eyes glistened with unshed tears. "I just wish the children understood it better. They are so excited to explore a new place, but they do not fully grasp what we are leaving behind.

"Neither do we," Ledger admitted, allowing the truth of those words to linger. They had cultivated a life rich in love and community, each corner of their home filled with laughter and the warmth of shared meals and celebrations. "But we must trust that this is the right choice for them, for all of us."

As they spoke, the children began to stir, their laughter echoing from the backyard as they chased each other with boundless energy, blissfully unaware of the gravity of the day. "Let's make this last day memorable for them," Clara suggested, her eyes brightening with determination.

"Yes, I want them to remember today," Ledger agreed. "We'll take them to the beach, show them their favorite spots, and share stories until the sun sinks into the sea."

"And let's have a farewell gathering tonight," she added, excitement simmering in her voice. "Invite our friends and the people we have grown close to over the years. They deserve a proper goodbye."

Ledger smiled, feeling a surge of warmth at her enthusiasm. "That sounds perfect. Let us celebrate our time here and honor the bonds we have built."

They moved in quiet tandem, making simple breakfasts and finishing the last of the packing. Warm aromas of baked goods and spice filled the kitchen as Clara prepared one final batch of her beloved cinnamon rolls, a recipe perfected over time. Meanwhile, Ledger gently gathered their children's favorite toys and books, each item stirring memories as he held them close.

As the sunlight streamed through the windows, illuminating the kitchen, Ledger called out to the children. "Hey, little ones! Who is ready for a beach adventure?"

Wizen and Eliza, Louisa and the other children came running in, their faces lit up. "We are!" they shouted in unison, their excitement infectious.

"Let's go!" Clara said, wiping her hands on her apron before sprinting to the door, leading the charge as the children followed, squealing with joy. Ledger grabbed a small basket of snacks and hurried after them, a smile spread across his face.

As they reached the beach, the scene unfolded before them like a painting. The golden sand glistened under the bright sun, waves crashed rhythmically against the shore, and the salty breeze tousled their hair. Ledger felt a rush of gratitude for this place that had given them so many gifts.

"Look at the waves!" Eliza squealed, her hands clenching the air as she darted toward the water. Wizen and Petronel joined her, both giggling as they splashed through the shallows, carefree near the frothy edges.

Ledger and Clara watched, their hearts swelling with pride and love. "This is good," Ledger whispered, turning to Clara. "This is what we want for them."

They spent the day swimming, building sandcastles, and reminiscing about the moments that defined their family, gatherings with friends, picnics under the trees, and stories shared in the glow of firelight. Each smile captured a story, a memory woven into the fabric of their lives.

As the sun began to dip below the horizon, turning the sky into a canvas of orange and purple, Ledger felt the bittersweetness of the moment wash over him. "Let's gather them for one last sunset view," he suggested.

They all settled on the sand, the golden light painting their faces as they sat shoulder to shoulder. "Remember this moment," Ledger said gently, watching his children's eyes widen at the vastness of the ocean. "Always carry it with you."

The sun hung low in the sky, painting the afternoon with hues of amber and crimson as Ledger stood on the porch of his family home. The familiar sights, the swaying palm trees, the rustle of leaves, and the vibrant flowers in Clara's garden, now felt bittersweet as the day of departure drew near.

A sense of urgency and nostalgia filled the air as friends and family gathered for one last evening together. The clearing that had been a sanctuary for meetings and discussions now transformed into a space teeming with laughter, shared stories, and the bittersweet pang of impending farewells.

"I can't believe this day has finally come," Wizen remarked, looking up at Ledger with wide eyes. "Are we leaving? What will it be like?"

Ledger knelt beside his son, a bittersweet smile playing on his lips. "It is a big world out there, my boy. We will find new opportunities, new friends, and new adventures. But home will always be in our hearts."

"And we'll make new friends, right?" Eliza chimed in, her small hands clasped with excitement.

"Absolutely," Ledger assured them. "And remember, we're doing this for a better future for all of you."

Rising to his feet, Ledger spotted Clara moving gracefully through the crowd, her hands skillfully preparing a final feast for their loved ones. The rich aroma of roasted meats, warm bread, and spiced vegetables drifted through the air, blending with the hum of laughter and conversation that brought the space to life.

"Clara!" Ledger called out, his heart swelling with pride as he watched her tend to the gathering with grace. "Do you need help?"

"I'm good!" she replied with a bright smile, her cheeks flushed with warmth from the heat of the kitchen. "Just making sure everyone has enough to eat before we leave. It is a celebration, after all!"

At that moment, an air of camaraderie enveloped them all. Ledger stepped back to take it all in, the children running and playing, the adults sharing stories from their past, and the elders recounting tales of resilience and hope. It was a tapestry of memories stitched from years together, and Ledger could not help but feel an ache in his heart. They were saying goodbye to not just a place but to a chapter of their lives.

As twilight descended, the flickering lanterns lit up the clearing like stars. Ledger gathered everyone around, the laughter quieting as he prepared to share his thoughts. "Thank you all for being here this evening," he began, the weight of emotion pressing against his chest. "Tonight, we not only celebrate our past but also the future we will build together in a new land. Your support has meant everything to my family and me."

"We'll miss you, Ledger," Thomas, an elder and mentor, said from the front. "You are a part of this community, and no distance can change that. Just remember that what you do, what we all do, will inspire others."

Ledger nodded, feeling tears well in his eyes. "I promise to carry a piece of St. Barthélemy with me wherever I go. This place shaped who I am, its spirit, its people, and its struggles will forever be a part of me."

Around him, many were visibly moved, some wiping away tears as they exchanged meaningful glances, knowing the bond they shared would transcend the physical distance.

As the night wore on, stories poured out with growing emotion, each memory stirring laughter and warmth. Clara gently prompted the children to share their favorite moments, and with every tale, their bond with loved ones deepened.

Finally, Ledger caught Clara's eye, and they shared a moment of understanding. She walked over, intertwining her fingers with his.

"We're embarking on a new adventure together," she whispered, her voice filled with hope. "We're not losing this part of our lives; we're simply carrying it with us."

"You're right," Ledger replied, squeezing her hand. "Together we will create another chapter, one filled with resilience and hope. I trust that we will continue to uplift one another, no matter where we find ourselves."

The evening waned slowly, and just before the stars began to dot the sky, Ledger called for one final toast. "To family and friendship," he held up a glass, the light catching in his eyes, "to the journey ahead, and to the unbreakable bonds we share! May we always remember our roots, no matter how far we go!"

As everyone raised their glasses in response, cheer, and warmth flooded the gathering, infused with precious memories and collective dreams. Somewhere in the distance, the ocean's waves lapped against the shore, a reminder of the land they were leaving behind. Together, Ledger and his family stood in that moment, fortified by love and purpose, ready to embrace the unknown that awaited them on their journey of migration.

The morning sun rose over the harbor, casting a bright shimmer across the water as Ledger and his family stood among the throng at the dock, their hearts heavy with a mix of anticipation and sorrow. The wooden pier creaked underfoot, resonating with the buzz of activity and the mingled emotions of those gathered. Families were hugging tightly, tear-streaked faces intermingling with smiles of encouragement, forming a tapestry of human experience that mirrored both hope and despair.

"Are you sure about this?" Clara asked softly, glancing around at the swirling crowd. The nearby dinghies took them out to the steamship and bobbed gently in the waves, and as Ledger took her hand, he could feel the tremor of uncertainty ripple through her.

"It's what we've decided," he replied, squeezing her hand. "We'll find our place in the new world, together."

In front of them, Ledger spotted a family prepared to board the vessel as well. It was the Gagnon family, neighbors they had known for years. Marie, the mother, was saying goodbye to her sister, tears brimming in her eyes. "You're making a mistake, Marie!" her sister cried, voice breaking as she clutched her. "You do not know what awaits you over there! What if it is worse?

But Marie shook her head, determination shining through her grief. "I must go for my children sake. We cannot keep living on this precipice! St. Thomas holds a chance for all of us."

Ledger swallowed hard, the unspoken tension growing heavier as he watched the sisters part ways. He could not help but wonder if they would ever find the same sense of belonging in their new home, aware of the sorrow that came with leaving loved ones behind.

Nearby, a group of men huddled together, their voices strained with frustration. "So, you're just going to abandon us at the time we need strength the most?" one man, Jacques, shouted, his face flushed with indignation. "Those who stay will fight for what we deserve! Your departure is a betrayal of everything we have built!"

Another man beside him nodded in agreement, jaw clenched. "You might find St. Thomas is just as dangerous as here. You are trading one form of oppression for another!"

Ledger's heart sank at the tension rising around him, the divide between those who sought to flee from danger and those who believed in standing firm. It was a microcosm of a broader struggle, and he felt the weight of their critical gazes upon him and his family.

"We're not abandoning anyone!" he finally interjected, his voice rising over the din. "We are seeking a way to ensure our children have a future. Sometimes change is necessary, and it can take many forms."

Clara stepped closer to him, her eyes scanning the crowd. She sensed the brewing discontent and wished to quell the anger simmering in the air. "We believe in our community," she added, her tone steadier. "We will never forget where we came from. This decision is for survival, nothing more."

The escalating argument quieted down momentarily as Ledger and Clara's firm voices cut through the tension. Some people from the crowd nodded, their expressions softening, while others remained entrenched in their uncertainty.

A soft voice broke through the larger scene, Louisa, clutching her favorite seashell, tugging on Ledger's side. "Daddy, when can we go? I am ready for the adventure!" Her innocent excitement cut through the tension like a breath of fresh air, and Ledger felt a rush of pride wash over him.

"Soon, little one. Be patient," he replied, ruffling her hair. He turned to Wizen, who stood wide-eyed, absorbing the clashing arguments with confusion. "Just remember, we're heading toward a new beginning together!"

As the moments dragged on, families shared final farewells filled with laughter, tears, and promises to write. Ledger looked out at the sea stretching ahead, the waves glimmering under the sun, reminding him that uncertainty lay ahead but so did hope.

With one last look at the faces of those who stayed, some supportive, some angry, and others filled with unspoken worry, Ledger took a deep breath, feeling the weight of their community's collective grief and hope resting on his shoulders.

"We'll keep our hearts tied to St. Barthélemy," he murmured to Clara as they stepped onto the small boat taking them out to the steamship, the boat rocking gently as they boarded. "No matter where we go, we carry our love for this place with us."

As the boat pulled away from the dock, the vibrant colors of the houses faded into the distance, but the complex tapestry of emotions, the love, anger, sadness, and determination, swirled around them, anchoring Ledger's resolve as they embarked on their journey toward the unknown.

***

The salty breeze whipped through the air as Ledger stood at the edge of the deck, watching the shoreline of St. Barthélemy gradually disappear in the distance. The decision to migrate by boat had been both a necessity and a leap of faith, reflecting the geographical realities of their island life and the challenges that came with it.

The steamship was no grand vessel, but a reliable one, built to brave the restless waters of the Caribbean. Ledger felt the gentle roll beneath his feet as the engine throbbed steadily, pushing them forward. Around him, a handful of families huddled close, united by shared hopes and quiet fears. The air buzzed with anticipation, though a somber weight lingered, each of them aware of the uncertain journey ahead.

"It's hard to believe we're leaving everything behind," Clara said softly, standing beside him and clutching her children close. The realization settled thickly between them, weighing on his chest, a bittersweet mixture of hope for the future and sorrow for the past.

Traveling by boat in the 19th century was fraught with dangers that loomed ominously in Ledger's mind. The waters between the islands could be unforgiving, unpredictable storms threatening to whip the sea into a frenzy. Each wave crashed against the hull with a force that now felt both exhilarating and terrifying. Ledger remembered the tales of past crossings, warnings from fishermen of hidden reefs, and currents that could pull even the sturdiest ship under.

"I hope the weather holds," he muttered, casting a wary glance at the horizon where dark clouds loomed, a stark contrast to the bright blue sky. A storm could come swiftly, turning their journey from routine to perilous in the blink of an eye.

"We'll be alright," Clara reassured him, her voice steady despite the uncertainty etched on her face. "We have to believe that."

Ledger nodded, but the unease lingered. He had heard stories of pirates who roamed these waters, taking advantage of vulnerable vessels. While the stories often felt rooted in folklore, he could not shake the image of bandits attacking and plundering small boats, leaving nothing but wreckage in their wake. He cast a careful eye along the side of the ship, his protective instincts flaring.

As the ship made its way across the waves, Ledger took in the passengers around him. Some families were filled with chatter, their excitement palpable, while others remained reserved, gazing out at the swirling blue depths, lost in their thoughts. Each person and family represented a different story, all converging on this moment, bound by the same desperation for a new start.

"I wonder what we'll find in St. Thomas," Wizen said, standing on tiptoe to peer over the edge of the ship. He always had an adventurous spirit, and Ledger admired his capacity for hope even amid uncertainty.

"Treasure, maybe!" Louisa chimed in, her eyes sparkling. "And maybe magic!"

"Sure, little one, treasure in the form of new beginnings," Ledger replied with a playful smile despite the weight on his mind. "We will find our fortune through hard work and resilience. That is the real treasure."

The children's laughter momentarily brightened the mood, but Ledger felt the tension lingering, especially from the adults on board. Conversations about the challenges ahead flowed with the tide, some families discussing the struggles of finding jobs while others speculated on the conditions in St. Thomas.

One woman, her voice husky with emotion, leaned against the railing, speaking to a group of mothers. "I heard that the labor situations are tough. Men are losing jobs, and it seems like people are more desperate now than ever."

Another man replied sternly, "That is why we left! We would rather face the unknown than stay back and drown in uncertainty. If we all work together, we can find a way to rebuild. We must believe there's hope on that shore!"

As the ship veered just slightly, sending a shudder through the passengers, Ledger felt both the vessel's vulnerability and its strength. While this mode of travel lacked the stability and safety features of modern boats, it was resilient like the families onboard, carrying hopes across the turbulent sea.

He turned to Clara, a sense of resolve firming within him. "Whatever waits for us out there, we will face it as a family. The risks we take now are part of a greater journey toward our future."

Born from their desire for safety and prosperity, Ledger's determination solidified as they pressed on through the undulating waves. Each swell of the sea became a rhythm to their new beginning, a reminder that although the voyage was uncertain, the promise of change was worth the risk.

***

As the steamship churned deeper into the Caribbean Sea, the horizon began to blur, and a sense of unease settled over the passengers. Ledger felt the familiar tug of worry. The journey would take several days, and with the unpredictable nature of the open water, danger lurked beneath the ship's surface like a predator waiting for the right moment to strike.

That first night, an unseasonably cool breeze slipped through the deck's cracks, carrying with it a haunting chill. Ledger had barely shut his eyes when the ship lurched violently, the engine roaring in protest the waves. A chorus of creaks and groans echoed around him, jolting him upright in sudden alarm.

"Clara!" he exclaimed, grabbing her hand as he glanced around the dimly lit cabin, where the children slept fitfully on makeshift beds. Eliza stirred, her small face creased with confusion.

"What's happening?" she mumbled, rubbing her eyes. The ship pitched violently again, and the whispers of fear passed through the cramped quarters like a chilling breeze.

"Just a little storm," Ledger assured her, his voice steadier than he felt. "We'll be fine."

Wizen sat up suddenly, his face pale. "It is too bumpy! I do not like it!" he cried, voice rising above the tumult. Clara looked as if she were on the verge of tears, yet she held her chin high, trying to mask her fears for the sake of the children.

Just then, Ledger noticed the other children peering wide-eyed from their own corners of the cabin. Petronel sat next to Julien, her little hands gripping his arm tightly. Dfriel and James were huddled on the floor, shivering, while Louisa clung to Koie and Nerisa, doing her best to soothe them by whispering comforting words. Nerisa, and Koie, the youngest set of twins, clutched a small rag dolls to their chest, their eyes glistening with tears.

"What's wrong with the boat?" Nerisa asked, her voice small and trembling as she glanced at Ledger, clearly searching for answers.

"Just some waves, sweetie," Ledger replied, kneeling to meet her gaze. "But we need to stay brave. We are together, and we will be all right."

Julien, always eager to distract himself from fear, piped up, "What do you think is happening outside? Are there sea monsters?" His attempt at humor drew a few nervous giggles, providing a brief respite from the tension.

"No sea monsters, just some big waves!" Clara said, putting on a brave smile. Wizen, still anxious, buried his face into his mother's side.

"Let's see if we can all stay calm together," Ledger suggested, attempting to rally the small group. "If we stick close, we can help each other."

Clara nodded. "We'll form a circle right here." She motioned for everyone to come together, creating a small enclave of support amidst the chaos. As they huddled, the ship rocked again, and the sound of the waves crashing against the hull echoed around them.

"What if we tip over?" James whimpered, his face paling at the thought.

"We will not tip over! The grown-ups know what to do, and we have been on a boat before, remember?" Louisa said firmly, trying to offer some reassurance to her siblings.

The moment of unity was short-lived as the ship pitched again, the violent sound of groaning wood causing everyone to shuffle closer together. Ledger felt the weight of responsibility profoundly as he observed the fear in each child's eyes.

"Stay close! We will protect each other!" he shouted over the noise, feeling a surge of resolve. He glanced out the cabin door toward the deck, where shouting and commotion echoed, the crew working to secure the ship against the rough waves.

With a final look at his family, Ledger steeled himself. "We need to get back on deck. We cannot stay cooped up here. Let us show them we are brave."

As they emerged into the frantic night, the chaotic scene greeted them, rain lashed against the deck, and the wind howled, whipping through the children's hair. Ledger's heart raced at the sight of the ship battling the elements, but he kept his focus on his family. They huddled together; Clara leading the little ones while he kept a protective arm around Wizen.

As they clung together, Ledger found solace in their shared bravery. In the face of the storm, they would face the unknown as a family, holding tight to one another against the howling winds and surging waves. Each gust felt like a challenge, but together, they formed a resilient front. The children's frightened faces illuminated briefly by the flashes of lightning reminded Ledger that the bond they shared could withstand even the fiercest of storms.

"Look!" Wizen called out suddenly, pointing to a distant silhouette on the horizon, a cliff that jutted from the sea, half-hidden in mist and rain. "What's that?"

Ledger squinted against the sheets of water cascading down, momentarily distracted from the chaos around them. "It might be St. Thomas!" he shouted back, though a sense of caution pulled at him. "We still have a long way to go!"

"Can we make it?" Eliza's wide eyes searched his, teeming with both curiosity and fear.

"We have to," he replied, trying to instill a sense of hope. The sight of land, even if it were only a shadow, stirred something deep within a sense of purpose and a reminder of why they had embarked on this perilous journey in the first place.

As the storm raged on, Ledger glanced at Clara beside him. She squeezed his hand tightly, her eyes reflecting a blend of worry and determination. "No matter what happens, we stick together, right?" she reminded him, her strong spirit anchoring him amidst the turmoil.

"Always," he affirmed, feeling the warmth of her presence in the chilling air.

The children hung on every word now, their fear easing as they found comfort in their parents and one another. Koie quietly reassured her twin sister Nerisa, spinning stories of daring pirates and secret treasures. Between the booming thunder, and her lighthearted tales gave the younger children a welcome distraction from their fear.

As they pressed on through the night, the rhythmic pounding of the waves became a percussive symphony, urging them forward. The ship swayed violently, but Ledger focused on the warmth of bodies around him, his family's presence acting like a lifeline.

Then, with a sudden jolt, the ship spun, heaving violently to one side as another wave crashed against the hull. Ledger felt his heart leap into his throat. "Hold on tight!" he yelled, bracing himself against the railing while keeping his arms protectively around the children.

The storm reached its zenith; rain lashed against them like icy needles, and the wind screamed with furious intensity. For a moment, Ledger feared what he could not see, a capsize, a lost hold on the safety of their little group. But as he gripped Clara's hand tighter, he felt her return the pressure, a silent promise that together they would weather this storm.

In that harrowing moment of commitment and resolve, Ledger took a deep breath, grounding himself in the love and strength that radiated from his family. They might be tossed about in the chaos of the storm, but together, they would navigate their path through it, each wave they overcame bringing them one step closer to the safety of that distant shore and the promise of a new life waiting for them in St. Thomas.

***

As the steamship continued its relentless journey across the turbulent sea, Ledger found himself caught in a swirl of emotions. Each swell of the waves mirrored the tumult within him, a constant reminder of the life they had left behind. The scent of saltwater mingled with the lingering aroma of home in his memory, warm afternoons on their porch, the laughter of neighbors, and the familiar trails woven through the hills of St. Barthélemy.

Leaving behind their home was an emotional burden that weighed heavily on his heart, and he could sense this struggle reflected in Clara's eyes and the furrowed brows of his children. As he stood on the deck, he watched the horizon blur once more. Each passing moment felt like a tug of war between anxiety and the flickering hope of what lay ahead.

"What's wrong, Daddy?" Eliza's soft voice broke through his thoughts, her small hand reaching for his. She had climbed up beside him, curiosity lacing her innocent inquiry. He noticed the shadow cast across her face by the clouds above, a mirror of his unease.

"Just thinking about everything we've left behind," he replied, trying to choose his words carefully, not wanting to add to her confusion. "But also, about what we might find on the other side of this journey."

"Like treasure?" Her eyes sparkled for a moment before she added, "I miss our house."

Those words struck Ledger like a cold wave crashing over him. He inhaled sharply, memories flooding back—dinner around their table, the warmth of the sun filtering through their window as he read stories to Wizen, Petron, Louisa, Eliza, and Julien. "I miss it too," he admitted softly. "But remember, home is not just a place; it's people, it's us, and we're together."

But as he spoke, Ledger felt a flicker of doubt creep in. Would this new place truly feel like home? The thought of uncertainty gnawed at him, and he could see Clara wrestling with similar fears as she stood by, watching their children with a wistful look.

"I can't stop thinking about everyone we left behind," Clara finally confessed, her voice barely a whisper above the wind's howling. "What if they need us?"

"I know," Ledger replied, his throat tightening. He wanted to reassure her, to share in her burden, but the truth was that those feelings of sadness and anxiety weighed them equally. "But we had to believe there was no other choice. We are doing this for them, too, to find a way to help everyone we love more than we ever could if we stayed.

Clara's eyes glistened with unshed tears, and Ledger could see the pain of their decision etched into her features. He wrapped his arms around her shoulders, pulling her close as the ship dove into a particularly vicious wave.

Ledger stole a glance behind him, seeing the children clustered together, their earlier confidence dissolving into quiet uncertainty. Julien, typically full of life, now seemed small and vulnerable against the chaos of the sea. Dfriel and Koie clung to each other, while Petronel and Wizen gently coaxed Louisa and James into soft, distracted games. But the fear remained, thick and suffocating, settling over them like a fog.

"You know," Clara said, pulling away slightly, "this journey is changing us all." Her voice was tinged with realization. "We aren't just leaving our home; we're stepping into the unknown together."

Ledger nodded, feeling the truth of her words settle within him. "That is what makes it so hard. There's so much fear mixed with this hope for a better life. It is a heavy burden to carry."

The ship lurched again, and Ledger gripped the railing tightly, grounding himself in the moment. "But we're not alone," he said, looking around at their little group, the warmth of Clara and their children anchoring him amid the emotional storm.

As the clouds above shifted and the winds howled, Ledger took a deep breath, clinging to the sliver of hope that there would be moments of joy ahead as well—new friendships for the children, work opportunities, and even a place to call their own. "We have to stay strong, for each other," he said softly, his heart swelling with love for his family.

"And for those we left behind," Clara added, her expression softening.

That shared affirmation forged a bond stronger than any storm that might come their way. With that connection, they found the strength to navigate their feelings of anxiety and sadness, holding the hope of brighter days together like a guiding star in the night sky.

His resolve solidified as they pressed on, the emotional toll of leaving their home beginning to transform into a commitment to forge a new life together. With their heads held high and the strength of their unity coursing through them like a steady current, Ledger felt ready to face whatever challenges lay ahead. They were no longer merely survivors of circumstance; they were pioneers of their destiny, ready to write the next chapter of their lives in this new land. Together, they would build something meaningful, anchoring their hearts in the mind of hope, faith, and resilience, no matter the storms that threatened to arise on their journey.

**

As the steamship arrived in St. Thomas, Ledger's heart swelled with an ambiguous mixture of hope and trepidation. The promise of new beginnings was enticing, yet it came entwined with the harsh reality of societal repercussions that awaited them in their new home. Migrating from one island to another would not just be a physical journey; it would also challenge the very essence of their identities.

The stories he had heard from relatives who had made similar crossings echoed in his mind. Many spoke of the skepticism they faced upon arriving in new communities, where the scars of past migrations lingered like shadows. "They'll look down on us," he recalled one cousin warning. "Those who leave are often seen as weak or desperate."

Ledger turned his gaze toward Clara, watching her comfort the children with soft words. He, too, felt that unspoken fear simmering beneath his bravado. They were stepping into an unfamiliar land, and they would have to confront not only the pounding waves of the sea but also the waves of judgment from a society that often held tight to its traditions and expectations.

"What if they don't want us?" Wizen's small voice broke through his thoughts. The boy had been unusually quiet during the trip, absorbing everything around him. Now, Ledger quickly knelt beside him, catching his worried gaze.

"What do you mean, son?" Ledger asked gently.

"What if the people there think we are not good enough? What if they do not like us?" His eyes brimmed with uncertainty, reflecting a fear that had burrowed deep within the hearts of each family member.

Ledger felt a pang in his chest. "Every new place has its ways, and not everyone will welcome us with open arms," he acknowledged carefully, glancing at Clara's face for her reaction. "But we must remember that we are a family. We are strong together, and we will build our lives with our own hands."

Clara nodded in agreement, though her expression remained serious. "We may face skepticism, Wizen, but sometimes people just need time to see who we truly are."

Ledger's senses were flooded by the vibrant atmosphere; the air was rich with the scents of saltwater, blooming tropical flowers, and the mouthwatering spices drifting from nearby food stalls. Children's laughter rang through the streets, their playful shouts blending with the cries of vendors selling fresh fruits and handcrafted goods.

"Look, Daddy!" Eliza squealed, tugging at his hand as she pointed to a group of children splashing in the shallows. Their laughter echoed like music, drawing in Ledger's attention and easing the weight of apprehension resting on his shoulders.

He glanced around, taking in the vibrant hues of the buildings—shades of blue, green, and yellow that seemed to dance in the sunlight. Everything felt alive, teeming with stories waiting to be discovered. "It's beautiful," Clara whispered beside him, her eyes shimmering with a mix of excitement and uncertainty.

They moved cautiously down the pier, stepping onto the bustling cobblestone streets of Charlotte Amalie. As they navigated through the throngs of people, Ledger felt both exhilarated and anxious. This was a new world, vibrant yet unfamiliar.

They wandered deeper into the town's heart, where a kaleidoscope of activity consumed every corner. A group of musicians played lively calypso tunes, creating an infectious rhythm that made it hard not to sway. A vendor beckoned them closer, showcasing an array of exotic fruits, their colors richer than anything Ledger had ever seen.

"What's that?" Wizen asked, his eyes wide as he pointed to a large, prickly fruit.

"That's a soursop," the vendor replied with a warm smile. "It's delicious, try it!"

They sampled the fruit as the vendor sliced it open, the sweet and tangy flavor bursting on their tongues. Ledger savored the moment; the laughter, the music, and the taste of the unfamiliar fruit began to unravel the knots of anxiety in his chest.

Moments later, Ledger noticed a group of families gathered around a large table filled with handmade crafts—woven baskets, colorful textiles, and intricate jewelry. The sense of community was palpable, a blend of cultures and stories threaded together.

"Everyone here seems so friendly," Clara remarked, her apprehension easing as she observed a woman teaching her daughter how to weave a basket.

"Yeah, it feels… welcoming," Ledger responded, his heart swelling with hope. He could see the laughter in the eyes of those around them, a reflection of shared experience and resilience.

As they continued to explore, Ledger felt the initial wave of anxiety start to transform into quiet confidence. They were here now, taking their first steps toward building a new life. Each friendly exchange, every smile shared, served to remind them that they were not alone in their journey; they were part of something larger.

With each passing moment, they began to embrace the realization that St. Thomas was not just a place to find shelter. It was a canvas waiting to be filled with their stories, hopes, and dreams. And with that understanding, Ledger took a deep breath, ready to dive into the vibrant waters of this new chapter.

***

As they made their way through the vibrant town, Ledger caught snippets of conversation. Some residents were curious about the newcomers; others exchanged skeptical glances. A few people whispered to one another, eyes narrowing as they observed Ledger's family trudging through the throng of bustling locals.

"Look at those. Think they can just waltz in here?" Ledger heard one woman murmur to her friend, casting a judgmental glance in their direction. Her voice dripped with a mix of derision and pity, and Ledger's heart sank at the weight of her words.

The sense of exclusion was almost palpable. Despite the warmth of the tropical sun, Ledger felt a chill seep into his bones, an instinctive reaction to the unmistakable stigma that clung to them like mist.

"Ignore them," Clara urged softly as she noticed his expression darken. "We cannot let their judgments shape us. We are here to find our place and build our future. They do not know our story."

"You're right," Ledger replied, trying to summon a sense of strength for their family. "We will have to prove ourselves—show them that we belong here. We will work hard and integrate into this community. We can overcome their skepticism."

His resolve solidified, determination rising as they ventured deeper into the streets of St. Thomas. They would need to navigate the complexities of starting over, working tirelessly to carve out a place for themselves in a community that might view them with suspicion.

With every step, Ledger felt the weight of the challenges ahead—securing work, forming new connections, and overcoming the judgment they would face. Yet beneath it all, there was a growing energy, fueled by the certainty that they were seizing control of their future. Together, they would rewrite their story, courageously stepping into this new chapter of their lives.

"We will make them see us," he declared, his voice steady with conviction. "We will show them that we are not just outsiders; we are people with dreams, talents, and stories to share. Our journey here is about hope, resilience, and the strength of our family."

As he spoke, Ledger's determination seemed to resonate, igniting a spark of courage in Clara and the children. He could see their spirits lifting, an unspoken solidarity forming in their hearts.

"We've faced storms before," Clara said, her eyes shining with unwavering support. "This is just another challenge to show who we truly are."

"Yeah! And if they do not like us at first, we will just keep being nice!" Wizen added, his youthful enthusiasm shining through the clouds of uncertainty.

"Exactly, Wizen!" Ledger replied, smiling at his son. "The more they get to know us, the more they'll see that we belong here, just like everyone else."

Nerisa, still clutching her doll, piped up, "And we can make friends! I want to find a new friend to tell about my seashell!" Her innocence injected a sense of optimism into the moment, the small child's wonder cutting through the tension.

"We'll find new friends," Ledger assured her, feeling a new sense of warmth wash over him. "This land is full of possibilities, and I believe we'll build our community here, one step at a time."

With renewed purpose, they continued to walk through the bustling marketplace, Ledger absorbing the sights and sounds around them. Vendors called out, attempting to lure in customers with their fresh produce and vibrant textiles. The sun hung high in the sky, casting golden rays that lit up the colorful stalls and infused the atmosphere with life.

Yet amidst the liveliness, Ledger remained acutely aware of the gazes that followed them. Each sideways glance hinted at questions and doubts about their presence. As they passed an open-air tavern, a group of men paused their laughter to scrutinize the newcomers, their whispers sharp and laden with judgment. Ledger felt his stomach twist, but he reminded himself that perception could change.

"Let's find a place to settle, a place we can call home," Clara suggested, her voice resolute despite the undercurrents of anxiety. "We need to create our welcome."

"Agreed," Ledger replied, taking a deep breath. "We will look for work and start laying down roots. We could even set up a small market stall—something that speaks of who we are and what we can offer."

Ideas began to swirl, forming the outline of a new future as they walked. They discussed potential trades—Ledger's experience with fishing, Clara's skills in cooking, and the children's eagerness to learn. Each child contributed to the conversation, weaving in their aspirations, and for the first time since their departure, Ledger felt a glimmer of excitement puncture the veil of their worries.

"If we work together and support each other, we can build something special here," Ledger said, feeling the warmth of optimism envelop them. "We may face challenges, but as long as we stand together, we can overcome anything that comes our way."

With newfound resolve, they traversed the vibrant streets of St. Thomas, ready to confront the episodes of skepticism that lay ahead. They were determined to make their mark, not just as migrants but as a family with roots worth planting in new soil. The journey was uncertain, but as they held on to one another, Ledger realized that their strength, love, and resilience were the real treasures they carried with them. Together, they would face the world and show it who they truly were.

***

In St. Thomas, the sun greeted Ledger's family with a warm embrace, its golden rays spilling over the vibrant buildings that lined the harbor. The scent of saltwater mingled with the sweet aroma of tropical fruits, while the sounds of laughter and conversation bubbled around them, enveloping them in the energy of this bustling new world.

Ledger felt an exhilarating mixture of apprehension and excitement welling up inside him. This island was alive with color and sound, a stark contrast to the quiet familiarity of their former home. The marketplace thrived with a diverse population engaged in animated exchanges, where English, Spanish, and Creole blended into a captivating chorus that spoke of the island's rich history and cultural tapestry.

"Look at all the different people!" Eliza exclaimed, her eyes wide with wonder as she observed a group of children playfully chasing one another while local vendors called out, showcasing their wares. Brightly-colored fabrics fluttered in the breeze, and the vivid fruits—mangoes, papayas, and coconuts—were piled high, tempting passersby with their vibrant hues.

"It's like a festival every day!" Wizen added, his earlier anxieties fading as curiosity took hold. He tugged gently at Ledger's arm, urging him to explore the crowded stalls.

The family moved forward into the heart of the marketplace, where the energy was infectious. It was a melting pot of cultures, with people who had migrated from various parts of the Caribbean and beyond, each bringing their customs, traditions, and stories. Ledger noted how different the atmosphere was from St. Barthélemy—this was a place where diversity flourished and where the blend of backgrounds formed a rich cultural mosaic.

As they navigated through the throngs, Clara leaned closer to Ledger, her voice low. "This is incredible. Look at how everyone interacts—so lively and welcoming." A warmth spread through her words, infusing their surroundings with a sense of belonging that Ledger had begun to crave.

They paused at a food stall, where a woman with curly hair and a radiant smile served spicy fish tacos. The enticing aroma wafted through the air, drawing them in. "Try some, it's the best on the island!" she called out, her voice full of enthusiasm.

"We'll take a few!" Ledger replied, reaching into his pocket for coins. As they sampled the food, the flavors exploded in their mouths—spicy, tangy, and vibrant, just like the community around them.

As the family found their footing in the rhythm of exploration, Ledger sensed the uncertainty that had weighed on them begin to fade. The warmth and openness of the people around them were like a balm, soothing the ache of leaving their old home behind. Though they were still newcomers, there was a silent bond among many—a shared understanding, as if each person's story, woven from their journey, contributed to the island's collective fabric.

"We should find a place to live," Clara suggested after they finished their tacos, glancing at their children who were eagerly pointing out different stalls.

"Yes, let's do that," Ledger agreed, feeling the weight of responsibility shifts back onto his shoulders. Finding suitable shelter would give them a sense of stability, a place to truly call home in this new land.

They wandered through the streets, passing homes of varying sizes, some quaint and colorful, while others bore remnants of colonial architecture. Along the way, they chatted with residents, learning about the neighborhoods and hearing snippets of life in St. Thomas.

As the sun began to set, casting a soft orange glow over the island, they stumbled upon a small community of houses nestled away from the busier streets. One home painted a cheerful blue, caught their eye. It had a modest front yard with bright flowers blooming around the edges.

"What do you think?" Ledger asked, glancing at Clara, who nodded enthusiastically.

"It feels inviting," she said, her face lighting up. "I can see us here."

With the children darting around, already imagining their new adventures, Ledger felt a surge of hope. They inquired about the property, and as fate would have it, the owner—a kind elderly man—was eager to rent it to a family like theirs.

They signed the agreement, and Ledger felt a sense of relief wash over him. It was not just a house; it symbolized stepping into a new chapter of their lives. They were becoming a part of something greater, making their presence known in this lively, diverse community.

As they settled into their new home, Ledger could not help but marvel at how quickly they were adapting. They began embracing the local customs, joining in community events, and making friends with neighbors. His children thrived, absorbing the rich tapestry of cultures around them and forming bonds with kids from diverse backgrounds.

"Look at us!" Clara exclaimed one evening as they enjoyed a meal on their porch, laughter echoing through the air. "We've started to find our place here."

Ledger smiled, watching as their children recounted tales of their day, filled with new friendships and experiences. "Yes, we have. This place is starting to feel like home."

And with each passing day, altogether, rant sunsets painted the sky in hues of pink and gold, they solidified their roots in St. Thomas, confident that no matter the challenges they might encounter, they were building a future together—a future that embraced both their past and the exciting possibilities of their new beginning.

***

The first rays of dawn spilled through the curtains of Ledger's modest home, casting a warm glow across the room. He stirred awake to the distant sound of roosters crowing and the gentle hum of the island coming to life. The invigorating scent of salt air wafted through the open window, reminding him that today was the day for adventure. He resolved to explore St. Thomas with his entire family—his parents, Clara, their nine children, and even Clara's parents—together to discover their new home.

After a quick breakfast filled with fresh tropical fruits and warm bread from a nearby bakery, the family gathered at the door, ready to embark on their journey. The eldest twins, James and Dfriel, playfully teased each other while the younger twins, Koie and Nerisa, tugged at their parents' skirts, eager to join in.

"Where to first, Daddy?" Wizen asked, his big brown eyes sparkling with curiosity as he tugged at Ledger's sleeve with excitement.

Ledger smiled down at him, taking in the eager faces of his children. "Let us head toward the harbor! I hear there is a market bustling with treasures from all over the Caribbean!"

As they walked, the sun climbed higher, bathing the narrow streets in vibrant hues. Every step felt significant, and the cobblestones beneath their feet whispered of generations that had walked this path before.

"Look at all the colors!" Eliza exclaimed, pointing toward the brightly painted houses lining the lanes. The yellows, blues, and reds seemed to glow, reflecting the life and energy that filled St. Thomas.

"Just think, there are stories behind every single door," Clara added, walking hand in hand with her children.

The family was enveloped by the rich sounds of St. Thomas—laughter spilled from nearby homes where children played, and the air buzzed with excitement. Vendors were setting up their stalls, arranging an array of goods that sparkled in the sunlight.

"Look! Over there!" Petronel exclaimed, pointing excitedly at a booth bursting with bright fabrics. The vibrant patterns danced in the breeze, each one a piece of art waiting to be appreciated.

"Let's take a closer look!" suggested Louisa, her keen eye already sizing up the colorful textiles.

With eager hearts, they approached the stall. The vendor, a middle-aged woman with kind eyes, noticed their interest. "These are made right here on the island," she said, her accent rich with the local dialect. "Each piece has its own story, woven by the very hands of our artisans."

"They're beautiful!" Eliza exclaimed, her eyes widening with wonder as she ran her fingers over the soft, intricate fabrics.

"Every pattern has a meaning; it tells a tale," the woman explained, her passion evident. Ledger leaned closer, captivated not only by the textiles but also by the warmth and community spirit radiating from the vendor.

Carrying on, the family strolled further through the market, their laughter punctuating the air. All around them, the rich aromas of fried plantains, spicy jerk chicken, and sweet conch fritters filled their senses, making their mouths water. Ledger's stomach grumbled appreciatively, prompting Clara to nudge him playfully.

"You're not the only one hungry!" she teased with a grin.

They came to a food stall overflowing with steaming dishes. A jovial man behind the counter offered a wide, welcoming smile. "Welcome! Come try my special today—curried goat with rice and peas!" he announced, waving them over.

Ledger glanced at Clara, who nodded with enthusiasm. They each ordered plates, savoring the explosion of flavors that danced on their tongues.

"This is the best food I've ever eaten!" Wizen exclaimed, his face smeared with sauce, making everyone laugh.

The camaraderie continued as the whole family shared the delicious bites, enjoying the warm atmosphere around them. With their bellies full and spirits high, they moved deeper into the market, observing community members embracing one another joyfully, children chasing one another, and vendors bantering with familiar ease. Ledger felt an undeniable spark: this was where they belonged.

Nearby, a musician began strumming a guitar, his soothing voice ringing out sweetly into the busy marketplace. The infectious rhythm drew people in, creating an atmosphere ripe for celebration.

"Shall we dance?" Clara asked, her eyes sparkling with mischief.

"Yes!" the children cheered, their energy uplifting.

Ledger chuckled as Clara took Wizen's hand, pulling him into a spontaneous dance. Petronel, Julien, and Louisa instantly joined in, twirling and laughing, while James and Dfriel attempted to outdo one another in exaggerated dance moves. The vibrant energy of the market enveloped them, and the children's unrestrained joy drew the eyes of passersby, some smiling while others clapped along to the lively tune.

Koie and Nerisa watched from the sidelines, their faces alight with delight as they cheered for their siblings. "We want to dance too!" they called, bouncing on their toes. At that, Clara beckoned her twins over with open arms, and soon Koie and Nerisa were swept up into the swirling circle, their laughter intertwining with the music.

Ledger's heart swelled with joy as he stepped back to take in the scene. Watching his family embrace their new surroundings, he felt a deep sense of contentment. Clara spun the children in her arms, her laughter ringing out like a bell, while the elder twins struck playful poses, bursting into giggles.

As the rhythm of the guitar quickened, Ledger could not hold back. He joined the dance, lifting Eliza high into the air as her delighted squeals filled the air. In that moment, surrounded by the warmth of their happiness, all his worries seemed to melt away.

With each spin and twirl under the warm Caribbean sun, there was a liberating sense of freedom. They were not merely witnesses to this vibrant life; they were part of it, becoming woven into the rich fabric of the community.

The crowd grew, drawn in by the lively spirit of the dancing children. Adults began to sway to the rhythm, clapping their hands and shaking maracas. Ledger exchanged delighted glances with other families, their shared smiles brimming with acceptance and joy. He felt as if the island was welcoming them with open arms, each note of music resonating with the promise of new beginnings.

As the song reached its crescendo, he saw Clara, her hair dancing in the breeze, and the children flushed with excitement, spinning and laughing in a blissful whirl. Ledger's heart soared as he realized they had taken their first real steps into this new life, richer than he had ever imagined. With every laugh and every joyous movement, they were etching their story into the rhythm of St. Thomas—a dance of belonging, community, and love that would last long after the music faded.

The warm rays of the Caribbean sunbathed Rothchild Francis Market Square in golden light, illuminating the vibrant array of stalls that lined the bustling area. Shouts of excitement and laughter mingled with the rich scents of spices and fresh produce, creating a lively atmosphere that thrummed with energy. As Ledger and his family approached their small stall adorned with beautiful produce they had carefully packed from St. Barts, he felt a rush of excitement that mingled with a nagging nerve.

"Okay, Ledger," his father Elijah said, adjusting his straw hat as he set the last basket of fresh mangoes in place. "This is your chance to learn how to sell. Remember, customer service is key." His father's encouraging tone grounded him amidst the whirlwind of emotions churning in his stomach.

Ledger took a deep breath, taking in the sights of the market around him—the bright colors of fruits and vegetables, the hum of language as people bartered and chatted, and the laughter of children darting through the crowd. But despite the vibrant scene, his mind raced with thoughts on how to engage prospective customers and make a good impression.

"Okay, I can do this," Ledger whispered under his breath, glancing around at the other stalls. He tried to identify what made their displays appealing and how vendors caught the attention of passersby. The lush greens and vibrant reds of his family's produce were certainly beautiful, but they needed to shine among the competition.

He turned to his younger siblings, who were busy arranging the colorful fruits and vegetables. "Help me set this up perfectly! The more inviting we look, the more likely we will sell." His brother Pierre and sister Margot, looked up at him eagerly, their eyes bright with excitement, and immediately began to arrange the mangos, papayas, and pineapples into pleasing formations.

As they worked, Ledger's mind spun with ideas. Should he greet each customer with a smile? Offer samples? A little bit of humor would lighten the mood. He imagined what it would be like engaging the faces of customers and win them over with his charm.

"Don't forget to talk about the flavors!" Clara chimed in; her enthusiasm infectious. "People want to know why they should buy from us rather than someone else."

"Right!" Ledger nodded, feeling the weight of the moment. He would need to not only present their wares but share the story behind them—the care they had taken to select the ripest fruits from their home on St. Barts, the sun-soaked slopes where they had grown.

His father caught the thoughtful expression on his face and spoke again, "And if someone is not interested, do not take it personally. Just move on to the next customer and keep smiling. It might just be that they are looking for something different today."

With the stall set up, Ledger took a step back, surveying their display. The vivid colors of their produce created a delightful visual feast. "I think we're ready!" he declared, a mix of determination and nervousness fluttering within him.

As the market square buzzed to life, Ledger turned to his family and said, "Let's show St. Thomas what we've got!"

They all nodded eagerly, ready to pull together as a family. Ledger hovered near the front, waiting for the first customer to approach as his siblings began chatting amongst themselves and helping one another.

A woman meandering nearby caught his eye.

"Excuse me, ma'am! Would you like to try some of our fresh mangoes?" he called out, drawing on the customer service skills his father had mentioned. The woman turned to him, intrigued by the enthusiastic invitation.

"Fresh mangoes, you say? I would love to!"

As she stepped closer, Ledger felt a surge of excitement. This was his moment to engage, to learn, and to uncover opportunities that extended beyond the stall. He let the nervousness fade, replaced by a growing curiosity about the world around him and the potential waiting just outside the confines of the market.

With each interaction, each conversation, Ledger knew he would find his way not only into the rhythm of market selling but into the larger tapestry of life in St. Thomas. This, he realized, was just the beginning of something remarkably new.

***

As the sun dipped low over the horizon, casting a golden hue across the bustling streets of St. Thomas, Ledger sat on the porch of their modest home, watching the distant waves crashing against the shore. The vibrant life of the island stirred with energy, but his mind was in turmoil, swirling with thoughts of opportunity and uncertainty.

As they settled into their new home, Ledger and his family began to see that they had arrived in a land full of promise. St. Thomas was more than just a refuge—it was a vibrant crossroads of trade, commerce, and opportunity. Each day, as they explored the market and engaged with the locals, it became clear that seizing these economic changes was essential to building a better future.

The family gathered around the dining table one evening, an array of fresh produce from their stall scattered before them. Clara's parents, joined by Ledger's mother and father, discussed what they had learned about the marketplace.

"The market is bustling, but the competition is fierce," Elijah observed, leaning back in his chair with a thoughtful look. "We'll need to find ways to stand out."

Ledger nodded, recalling how their charming stall had caught the eyes of customers but felt a flicker of doubt. "What if we expanded beyond just fruits? We could sell baked goods or local crafts. Something unique," he suggested, the idea forming like a stream of inspiration.

"I love that idea!" Clara chimed in, her excitement was evident. "We could incorporate recipes from St. Barts, maybe our grandmother's famous coconut bread!"

As they brainstormed, the conversation flowed from various unique ventures they could explore. They considered moving into selling prepared meals, blending flavors from their homeland with local Caribbean influences, or even hosting tasting events to engage the community and draw in more customers.

However, beneath the excitement lingered the weight of their past—the memories of St. Barthélemy, where the gentle waves had whispered comfort and the sun had kissed their skin in a familiar embrace. Ledger's heart ached at the thought of the idyllic life they had left behind, but each idea they discussed nudged him toward understanding that this was their new reality. They had to carve out a future for themselves and navigate the challenges that lay ahead.

With a newfound sense of purpose, Ledger set out the next day, determined to explore employment opportunities. He wandered through the bustling streets of Charlotte Amalie, the capital, where the air was thick with the scent of spices from nearby market stalls and the lively calls of vendors echoing all around. It was a vibrant tapestry of life that both energized and unnerved him.

"Maybe I can find work in a local bakery," he mused aloud to himself, his mind racing with possibilities.

As he walked past shopfronts adorned with hand-painted signs, he spotted a bustling café brimming with customers. The warm glow of the interior called to him, and with his heart pounding, he stepped inside, seeking out the owner.

"Excuse me," he approached a middle-aged woman arranging pastries behind the counter. "I am Ledger, and I am looking for work. I have experience in helping my family's produce stall and can bake a bit, too."

The woman looked him over, assessing the sincerity in his eyes. "We could use extra hands during the mornings. Are you available?"

Relief washed over him as he nodded emphatically. "Yes! I am ready to start right away."

With newfound purpose, Ledger felt he was beginning to weave into the fabric of St. Thomas, carving a niche for himself that offered the potential for growth and stability. He left the café with a spring in his step, eager to share the news with his family.

Upon returning home, he found them engaged in conversation about their ventures. Clara and her parents had taken the initiative to organize a workshop, teaching locals how to make St. Bart's-inspired dishes. They envisioned a small community gathering, where families could come together, learn, and enjoy good food.

"This could open doors for us in the community!" Clara exclaimed, her enthusiasm lighting up the room.

Ledger felt inspired by his family's determination. In this flourishing environment, he could contribute not only through his work in the café but also by supporting Clara's endeavor.

As the days turned into weeks, the family found unique ways to capitalize on their skills and experiences. Petronel and Louisa began crafting handmade jewelry from seashells, while Julien and Wizen took on odd jobs in the neighborhood, helping locals with errands and chores. Everyone was pulling their weight, determined to establish a foundation in their new home.

Yet, as every opportunity presented itself, Ledger could not shake the bittersweet nostalgia for St. Barthélemy.

The lively hum of Charlotte Amalie echoed around Ledger as he strolled back from the café after his morning shift. He wiped his brow, the warmth of the Caribbean sun already beginning to bear down on him. In the weeks since arriving at St. Thomas, he had developed a routine that felt both familiar and exhilarating. The rhythm of waking early to prepare fresh coffee and pastries, serving locals and tourists alike, had filled him with a sense of purpose.

Today, however, felt different. In his hand, Ledger held a small slip of paper from the café owner, outlining an opportunity to help at a food festival celebrating local cuisines. The owner had spoken with passion about the flavors of St. Barthélemy, recognizing in Ledger both his enthusiasm and his ability to promote the culinary traditions of both islands.

Ledger's heart raced as he approached the lively market square, where colorful stalls lined the streets, buzzing with the energy of vendors and customers. He spotted Clara, surrounded by a group of local women, her laughter bright among their chatter as they skillfully prepared dishes for an upcoming community event.

"Ledger! Come help us!" Clara beckoned; her face radiant as she rolled out dough for her grandmother's coconut bread.

He stepped up to the bustling group and grabbed an apron, feeling the camaraderie envelop him. "What's the plan today?"

"We're prepping for the cooking demonstration on Saturday," she replied. "I am so excited! I cannot believe how many people have signed up to learn!"

With a smile, Ledger fell into step beside her, rolling and cutting dough, the scent of coconut filling the air. Around them, the laughter of neighbors rose and fell like waves on the shore. It was moments like these that reminded him of his family's spirit back on St. Barthélemy, and he felt a bittersweet pang for the memories—yet a charming warmth for the new moments they were creating.

As the afternoon sun began to dip, the group of women around them shared stories about growing up in St. Thomas, their faces glowing with nostalgia. Ledger listened intently, feeling a deeper connection forming with the community. There were experiences here, of hardships and joys, that mirrored his own.

Suddenly, Clara's mother stepped forward, her hands dusted with flour as she looked at Ledger with pride. "You know, Ledger, I have been meaning to tell you how much we appreciate everything you have brought to this family—and the community. Your energy and willingness to jump in has invigorated us all."

Flushing slightly, he shrugged off the compliment. "I just want to help. We are all in this together."

"Exactly," Clara said, her smile warm. "And things are truly beginning to take shape!"

At that moment, Ledger felt the fabric of their new life in St. Thomas come together. They were not just building a new existence; they were weaving connections, cultivating a sense of community, and rediscovering who they truly were.

"So, what's next?" he mused aloud as they cleaned up, a spark of curiosity igniting within him. "How do we take this to the next level?"

"We've been thinking about a community pop-up dinner," Clara's older sister, Adele, chimed in while tying her hair back. "A night where we showcase local dishes, combining all our families' recipes. We can have music, storytelling, everything!"

Ledger's excitement grew. "That sounds amazing! I could help with the promotion through the café. We could even have a guest chef experience the charm of both islands."

Clara nodded fervently. "Yes! It would bring everyone together strengthening our roots here and honoring where we came from."

At that moment, Ledger realized that they were not just navigating opportunities; they were melding their past with their future. They were embracing St. Thomas while allowing the spirit of St. Barthélemy to shine through in each initiative they undertook.

As dusk fell across the market, casting shadows that danced on the cobblestones, Ledger felt a growing sense of belonging. The laughter that filled the air was not just background noise; it was the heartbeat of their community, welcoming him and his family into its fold.

"Let's get to work, then," he declared, looking at Clara and the rest of their family with fierce determination. "We've got a lot to do, and every step we take will be filled with flavor and love."

With hands busy and hearts full, they dove into the preparations, a collective passion weaving through them as they began mapping out plans for their pop-up dinner, confident that this was just the beginning of a vibrant chapter in their lives. Ledger felt a delightful thrill course through him as ideas bounced among the family—a cornucopia of possibilities. They considered local ingredients worthy of showcasing, herbs and spices they could source from nearby vendors, and the unique ways to blend traditional recipes with their own creative twists.

"We can create a tasting menu that tells a story," Clara suggested, her eyes sparkling with inspiration. "Each dish can represent a different part of our journey—from St. Barthélemy to here."

"And we can incorporate music from both islands," Petronel added eagerly, envisioning a fusion of sounds that would bring everyone together. "Local musicians can set the mood while we cook!"

"What if we invited some of our neighbors to join in as well?" Julien chimed in, gesturing excitedly. "We could have them share their own culinary stories and recipes, making it a true community celebration."

The thought of including others infused Ledger with a warm sense of belonging. This was not just about their family anymore; it was about creating a tapestry of flavors, traditions, and experiences that embraced everyone who had been a part of their journey.

With the sun descending further, painting the sky in hues of orange and purple, they worked late into the evening, laughter and chatter spilling out of the small kitchen. They crafted a detailed action plan, assigning roles to each family member with excitement. Clara would lead the kitchen, while Louisa and Eliza focused on decorations, infusing the space with colors reminiscent of sunset over the sea. Wizen and Dfriel volunteered to help with outreach at the cafe, ensuring everyone in the community knew about the event.

As Ledger jotted down ideas, he could not shake the warmth settling in his chest. He thought of all the faces they would soon welcome—friends, neighbors, and newcomers—each bringing a piece of their own stories to the table. His heart swelled at the possibility of blending not just cultures but lives and histories.

In that moment, surrounded by love, laughter, and the clattering of utensils, Ledger felt a profound sense of gratitude for the experiences that led them to this vibrant corner of St. Thomas. Their past may have been filled with uncertainties, but the richness of life ahead, bursting with opportunity and connection, painted a bright path forward.

"This is going to be special," he announced, looking around at the eager faces of his family. "Let's make it a night to remember."

With renewed energy, they dove back into plans, each heartbeat resonating with the rhythm of hope and possibility—laying the foundation for the lives they were building together in this new home.

***

Ledger Philogene gazed out over the coastal vista of St. Thomas, where the sapphire waters danced in the sunlight and the gentle swell of the ocean felt like a heartbeat beneath the vibrant island. This was no longer just a new home; it had become a canvas where he would paint a brighter future. However, as they sought to carve their place in this rich and tumultuous land, the journey of his family also unfolded layers of hardship, strength, and transformation.

Each day in St. Thomas revealed itself as a unique challenge, layered with opportunities they had yet to unearth. The initial excitement of their migration had masked the deeper complexities they encountered. As Ledger dove into his new role at the café and participated in planning their community pop-up dinner, he increasingly recognized the resilience required to adapt to their surroundings.

From the first day they set foot on the island, Ledger's family faced subtle reminders of the societal upheaval that led them to seek refuge. The whispers of loss and nostalgia lingered in their conversations, unearthing the bittersweet memories of life on St. Barthélemy. The shadows of their past life crept closer each time they encountered residents who were unable to fully embrace the changing tides of life, showcasing the struggles inherent to change and recovery.

The marketplace was both a wellspring of inspiration and a battleground for belonging. On some days, vibrant exchanges flowed effortlessly; on others, the fierce competition among vendors thickened the air with tension. Ledger often watched the locals as they navigated these shifts, balancing the pursuit of stability with the openness to new possibilities. These moments became a mirror for his own family's journey—navigating uncertainty while chasing their dreams.

As Ledger dug deeper into his work at the café, he learned not just the intricacies of customer service but the importance of community relationships. The connections he forged there extended beyond mere transactions; they grew into a network of mutual support in a world still healing from upheaval. Regular customers became friends who shared snippets of their lives, shaping Ledger's understanding of resilience. Their stories inspired him, igniting a spark and affirming that he was not alone on this path.

Meanwhile, the plans for the pop-up dinner began to take shape. Each gathering was more than an event; it was a testament to the strength of communities intertwined by shared experiences. Clara infused the menu with traditional recipes, melding flavors from St. Barthélemy with local ingredients, while their siblings contributed their unique talents, creating a tapestry of cultural dialogue. Ledger reveled in this collaborative spirit, feeling the ties of family grow tighter as they worked toward a common goal.

But amid the excitement, the specter of doubt sometimes loomed. Ledger often grappled with the fear that their efforts might not be enough. He worried about whether he could truly create something sustainable, something that honored both their past and future. As he often turned introspective during moments of solitude, Ledger understood that those anxieties were part of the journey—a testament to their resilience, a reflection of their desires to succeed not only for themselves but for their entire family.

Through these trials, Ledger's identity began to evolve. He was no longer just the boy from St. Barthélemy; he was becoming a bridge, connecting the histories of the islands. In conversations with locals, he found purpose in sharing his experiences, fostering understanding and collaboration that transcended differences. The memories of his past no longer felt like a burden; instead, they transformed into a source of strength, propelling him forward.

The path ahead remained uncertain, filled with both challenges and opportunities. But Ledger felt bolstered by the growing sense of community and kinship he had cultivated in St. Thomas. The island had already begun to shape him, forging a new identity that embraced the complexities of his journey.

As Ledger helped finalize preparations for the pop-up dinner, anticipation bubbled within him. He envisioned vibrant conversations, shared laughter, and the joy of people coming together to celebrate not just food, but the resilience born from their collective experiences. This dinner would be a turning point, a tribute to the journey they had endured, and a beacon of hope for what lay ahead.

Ledger understood that his migration to St. Thomas was not merely a physical movement. It was a transformational odyssey—one that invited him to embrace his power, to adapt amid a sea of change, and to become an architect of his destiny. With each step forward, he found the courage to redefine who he was, carrying the lessons of his past while fully embracing the opportunities of his present and future. This was his path forward—an intricate dance woven with resilience, strength, and the unyielding spirit of family.

಄

Chapter Three: Life In St. Thomas

The air in St. Thomas buzzed with a restless energy, a mélange of voices and sights that seemed to pulse with the rhythm of life itself. Ledger Philogene stepped cautiously onto the cobblestone streets, the vibrant surroundings stirring a whirlwind of emotions within him. This was a bustling port town of the mid-19th century, sunlight glinting off the harbor's waters while vendors called out their wares, and the scent of spices wafted through the air. Although St. Thomas promised new beginnings, the deeper complexities of its history loomed, casting long shadows over the vibrant landscape.

As Ledger made his way through the winding alleys, he marveled at the rich blend of cultures around him. People from various backgrounds—Africans, Europeans, Indigenous peoples—mingled in a tapestry of tradition and innovation. The lively marketplace was alive with the sounds of haggling, laughter, and music, reflecting the island's diverse heritage. Yet, Ledger's heart carried a heavy weight; he was acutely aware of the enduring scars left by colonialism and the struggle for identity that still lingered in the air.

The island's history was woven with complexity, its scars left by colonizers still visible in the remnants of plantations and the lingering effects of slavery. Ledger watched as some locals moved through their lives with vibrant optimism, while others carried a more restrained air, quietly striving to break free from the shadows of a painful past. He could not help but reflect on how their resilience mirrored his family's own journey, finding strength in the shared experience of hardship and hope.

With determination, Ledger sought employment, his mind set on building a foundation for his family in this promising landscape. Guided by recent interactions in the local café, he made his way toward various stores and establishments, hoping to find work that would support his family's endeavor. His heart raced with anxiety at each encounter; what if he did not meet their expectations? What if he was turned away? But as he spoke with shop owners, he adopted a newfound confidence, sharing his story and skills honed while working at the family stall.

During his search, Ledger encountered a shopkeeper named Mr. Ainsworth, a weathered man with sharp eyes and a kind smile. His emporium was stocked with goods from across the Caribbean, each item representing a world far beyond the horizon. "What do you have to offer?" Ainsworth asked, assessing Ledger with curiosity.

"I have experience with customer service and selling produce," Ledger replied, nerves creeping into his voice, but he pressed onward, fueled by the desire to make his family proud. "My family runs a market stall, and I've learned to engage customers in ways that create community."

Mr. Ainsworth nodded, his expression shifting to intrigue. "That is good to hear. We need someone who can manage inventory and interact with the locals. Can you start tomorrow?"

The rush of relief that followed felt like the warm sun breaking through a stormy cloud. Ledger accepted the position with gratitude, knowing this opportunity was a key step toward stability. The thought of contributing to his family's future and the greater community filled him with a sense of purpose he had not felt since arriving.

With that small victory, Ledger returned home to share the news with his family. Excitedly relaying the details, he found their small kitchen bustling with activity as they prepared for their upcoming pop-up dinner. Clara and Louisa were already hard at work assembling decorations, creating a vibrant atmosphere that echoed the island's lively spirit.

"We can't wait to showcase our flavors!" Clara beamed, wiping flour from her hands. "It's going to be a night to remember."

Despite the preparations, Ledger felt a nagging uncertainty about the challenges that lay ahead. While he embraced the warmth of his family's enthusiasm, he could not ignore the broader societal issues that loomed over them. The remnants of colonial rule often shaped the experiences of those living on the island; echoes of inequality and injustice resided under the surface, threatening to disrupt the harmony they hoped to create.

As days passed, Ledger immersed himself in his new job, getting to know the shop's clients and adapting to the various needs of the community. He witnessed the struggles of many, whose stories intertwined with the vibrant life of St. Thomas. Some customers faced economic hardships that echoed the historical exploitation of the islands. Yet, through resilience and camaraderie, he saw how they found ways to support one another, forming a resilient network against adversity.

Each evening, Ledger returned home, fatigued but invigorated by the day's interactions. His experiences led him to contemplate the future of his family. What would their legacy be on this island? He envisioned a workspace filled with opportunities, empowering them not just to survive but to thrive. Ledger knew that his migration was just one story in the greater narrative of St. Thomas—one deeply tied to the struggles and triumphs of countless others who had embarked on similar journeys.

As the sun set at the end of another day, Ledger found himself lingering on the porch, the golden light casting long shadows on the ground. He pondered the path that lay ahead for his family. Could they build a life that honored their heritage, while simultaneously embracing the rich culture of St. Thomas? Could they not only find their footing but uplift others along the way?

In the warmth of the Caribbean night, as the sounds of music floated through the air, Ledger felt a resolute sense of hope. There was beauty in the challenges they faced and in the union of cultures that surrounded them. They would navigate this new reality together, shaping their future against the backdrop of St. Thomas—a life woven through resilience, adaptation, and an unwavering quest for opportunity.

***

The sun had just begun to rise over St. Thomas, casting soft golden hues over the bustling harbor. Ledger Philogene stood at the edge of the docks, inhaling the briny air that carried the scents of fish and fresh bread from the nearby market. The morning chatter of merchants and sailors was already a symphony of activity. Wooden carts rumbled across cobblestones, and the sound of waves lapping against the hulls of anchored ships provided a soothing backdrop to the organized chaos.

Ledger felt a thrill course through him as he observed the daily ritual of commerce unfolding. Each ship that docked bore treasures from distant lands, their sails billowing like white clouds against the vivid blue sky. As he watched stevedores unloading crates filled with exotic fruits, spices, and textiles, he could not help but be captivated by the vibrant energy that permeated the docks.

"You are there! Philogene!" a voice bellowed, snapping Ledger from his reverie. It was Mr. Ainsworth, the shopkeeper who had offered him a job. He strode over, his weathered face sporting a grin that crinkled the corners of his sharp eyes. "Get over here! We need an extra hand today."

Eager to prove himself, Ledger quickly obliged and fell into step beside his new employer. "What do you need me to do?" he asked, the excitement bubbling within him.

"We have a delivery of spices coming in—cinnamon from St. Croix, cardamom from India—and they will be arriving shortly. I want you to help sort them out when they arrive. We cannot let them get mixed up; quality is everything in this trade. Mr. Ainsworth nodded toward a bustling cargo ship slowly making its way toward the dock, a plume of white smoke trailing after it.

As they neared the ship, Ledger's heart quickened. The crew was already skillfully tossing ropes, securing the vessel, and readying for the unloading. The dock buzzed with the shouts of sailors, laughter mixing with the creaking wood and the rhythm of crashing waves, a vivid testament to the cultural blend that shaped island life. Ledger could not help but marvel at the diversity around him, watching workers from all backgrounds collaborate effortlessly.

Soon enough, with a loud clang, the ship was secured, and the unloading began. Crates labeled in a multitude of languages—from Dutch to Spanish—were lowered, revealing the treasures inside. The vibrant hues of spices and the fragrant wafts enveloped him as they opened the crates. There, he witnessed firsthand the melding of cultures and the stories each shipment carried.

"This is where the magic happens," Mr. Ainsworth declared as they began sorting through the goods. "Every shipment is a connection to someone far away. This is not just trade; it is a journey."

Ledger nodded, fully engaged. He sorted the spices with meticulous care, taking in every detail—the deep brown of the cinnamon, the bright green of the cardamom pods. With each crate he opened, he felt more grounded in this world; he was part of something larger than himself.

Amidst the frenzy, Ledger struck up conversations with the crew unloading the ship—a group of men from various islands, sharing stories of their travels, their faces lighting up with pride as they recounted tales of their home islands. He heard snippets of different languages blending into the air, and with each exchange, he felt his own consciousness expand.

"You're new here, aren't you?" one sailor asked, a grin revealing missing teeth. "You should come to the docks more often! There is always something new to see—or trade."

"Absolutely! I want to learn everything," Ledger replied, trusting the sincerity of his words. The island thrummed with possibilities, and he felt driven to explore every avenue.

As the sun climbed higher in the sky and shadows grew shorter, Ledger helped move crates into Mr. Ainsworth's shop, the tactile nature of the work grounding him. The occasional shout from a fellow merchant reverberated like a heartbeat, guiding him deeper into the pulsing life of the harbor. This was a world of relationships and exchanges, built on years of shared history—of hardship, resilience, and dreams.

Eventually, they finished unloading the last crate, and Ledger stood back, surveying the small mountain of spices stacked neatly on the floor of the shop. He felt a bubbling excitement in his chest; this was only the beginning. He was no longer just an outsider navigating the streets; he was becoming part of the intricate web that defined the island's economic heartbeat.

"Well done!" Mr. Ainsworth said with approval, clapping Ledger on the shoulder as they stepped back to appreciate their handiwork. "Next time, you will be doing this on your own. Get ready to take charge of the goods, and soon, you will be an expert in trade in no time!"

A swell of pride filled Ledger as his thoughts turned to his family's vision for the future. They had embarked on this journey in search of a better life, and each day brought fresh connections and opportunities. The hum of activity at the docks called to him like a siren, drawing him further into the vibrant pulse of St. Thomas, where he believed their dreams could take root and flourish. Amid the wharf's energetic chaos, Ledger found himself standing on the edge of an exciting new chapter, ready to embrace every moment.

St. Thomas buzzed with the hum of commerce, a dynamic crossroads that connected nations and cultures through the vibrant pulse of trading. Ledger Philogene stepped onto the bustling docks of Charlotte Amalie, where the salty breeze mingled with the rich aroma of spices and the distant echoes of merchants hawking their goods. This lively atmosphere thrummed with energy, a vivid reminder of the opportunities the island offered to those willing to embrace its rhythms.

The docks, lined with ships from across the Caribbean and beyond, were a testament to St. Thomas's significance as a hub of trade. Vessels from France, Denmark, the Netherlands, and even as far as Africa filled the harbor, their sails puffed against the horizon like flags of hope. Merchants exchanged stories and goods of all kinds—silks, coffee, sugar, rum—while Ledger's gaze swept over the bustling marketplace, where the colors and sounds blended into a rich tapestry of life.

Ledger felt a magnetic pull toward this commercial world, teeming with possibilities for financial security. The economic landscape, shaped by its colonial history, was evolving; the islanders were beginning to reclaim their agency, crafting livelihoods that celebrated their unique strengths amidst the lingering shadows of the past. In this setting, Ledger saw not just the bustle of trade but an opportunity for his family to establish roots and flourish.

As he navigated the crowded streets toward his job at the shop, Ledger marveled at the rich array of cultures around him. He spotted a vendor from Senegal selling handmade textiles, each piece telling a story through vibrant patterns and colors. Nearby, an elderly woman from Puerto Rico expertly prepared empanadas, while the fragrant scent of spices enveloped the air like a warm embrace. These diverse markets reflected the island's melting pot, where the exchange of goods was paralleled by the exchange of traditions and identities.

The lively chatter of merchants created a vibrant backdrop to Ledger's thoughts on commerce. In his mind, he began to imagine the potential for his family's place in this growing economy. What if they hosted pop-up dinners showcasing their traditional recipes, turning their home into a unique culinary destination? Or if they partnered with local farmers to supply fresh, organic ingredients, tapping into the island's agricultural roots? The possibilities ignited a fire within him, the vision of a thriving business lighting his way forward.

After a long shift at the shop, where he engaged with customers and helped manage inventory, Ledger stepped outside, heart filled with purpose. He found himself drawn to the harbor once more, letting the salty air fill his lungs as he watched the rhythmic sway of the ships. Over the past weeks, he has gained hands-on experience in retail, learning the ins and outs of inventory management and customer service. Each interaction taught him something new—not only about business but about the resilience of the people around him.

That evening, Ledger joined Clara and their siblings on the porch, sharing the bubbles of excitement that had surfaced during his day. "You won't believe the ideas I've been having," he started, practically bouncing in his seat. "The market is full of opportunities! What if we connect with local farmers to source fresh produce for our dinners? And we can create a menu that highlights their ingredients!"

Clara leaned in, her eyes sparkling with enthusiasm. "That is brilliant! We could attract tourists while also supporting the local economy. It is a win-win!"

Ledger's heart swelled as he observed the flicker of inspired ideas passing between them. The relentless warmth of their family bond reinforced their sense of purpose. They were not merely trying to survive; they were laying the groundwork for something meaningful—something that would blend their heritage with the vibrant culture of St. Thomas.

As the night deepened and the stars blanketed the sky, Ledger pondered the challenges that lay on this trading path. He sensed obstacles rooted in history; the specter of colonialism still loomed in the socio-economic divisions that colored daily life. Competition among merchants was fierce, making it challenging for newcomers to stake their claim. He worried about how they could find their place among established businesses while also respecting the journeys of the people who had worked hard to build a life here.

Yet, within those concerns lived a flicker of hope. Ledger saw the changing tides: community members were beginning to prefer local goods over imported ones, recognizing the importance of supporting their homeland. He had overheard conversations in the marketplace about how essential it was to uplift local agriculture and traditional crafts, and it stirred something deep within him—a shared spirit of resilience and renewal.

With his heart resolute, Ledger committed himself to understanding this evolving landscape. He would learn from the merchants around him, the farmers whose produce had nourished generations, and the workers whose stories intertwined with the very fabric of the island. St. Thomas was not just a place to build a business; it was a living, breathing entity, rich with history and resilience. Each interaction would serve as a lesson, shaping his understanding of both the marketplace and the people within it. Ledger envisioned himself as an integral part of this community, not merely a newcomer seeking profit but as someone who could contribute to a legacy.

By fusing the culinary traditions of St. Barthélemy with the vibrant influences of St. Thomas, Ledger envisioned creating something unique—an experience that celebrated their heritage while embracing the island's diverse cultures. With his family by his side, he hoped to build a business that mirrored the spirit of the island, fostering connections that transcended cultural boundaries and weaving their own story into the rich fabric of St. Thomas's evolving history. With each passing day, his confidence grew, and he became increasingly certain they could thrive here—not merely survive—rekindling the hope that had led them across the sea.

As the days turned into weeks, Ledger Philogene quickly acclimated to his new life in St. Thomas. With the exhilaration of his first day at Mr. Ainsworth's shop still fresh in his memory, he found himself immersed in the local economy, embracing the roles that came with the bustling hub of trade. Each morning, he arrived at the shop promptly, ready to manage inventories and assist with customers, but he soon learned that his responsibilities extended well beyond mere transactions.

Working alongside Mr. Ainsworth, Ledger not only sorted goods and stocked shelves but also gained insight into the nuances of trade. He watched carefully as his employer negotiated with suppliers, making deals that allowed the shop to stay stocked with the freshest goods. Mr. Ainsworth's seasoned expertise was evident in his flair for conversation and his instinct for business. Ledger absorbed these lessons like a sponge, eager to imprint every detail into his understanding of commerce.

"The key to this business," Mr. Ainsworth remarked one day as they sorted through a bound shipment of spices, "is knowing your customers. They are not just buyers; they are your community. Talk to them, learn what they want and need."

Those words stuck with Ledger as he began to build relationships with regular customers at the shop. He made a point to remember their names, their preferences, and even their stories. A cheerful woman named Antonia from across the bay frequented the shop for fresh limes and tomatoes for her famous salsas. "You always know just what I need, Ledger!" she would say with a smile, and he felt a sense of pride in being able to serve her, knowing he played a small part in her culinary creations.

Beyond the shop, Ledger began assisting established merchants in the area, broadening his understanding of the various economic roles interwoven throughout the island. He joined Mr. Ainsworth on excursions to the docks, where he helped unload ships laden with goods from distant lands: grains from the Americas, textiles from Europe, and tropical fruits from the surrounding islands. Each turn of the day brought opportunities to learn from seasoned merchants, whose stories were riddled with advice and experience.

One afternoon, Ledger found himself working alongside a merchant named Elias, an older man with deep lines etched into his sun-kissed skin. Elias was renowned for his vast assortment of imported goods and had built a reputation as a respected trader. "You'll learn more from these docks than any book, man," he advised as they hoisted heavy crates from a ship. "Watch how people bargain. The best deals are made with both respect and cunning."

Ledger soaked up every ounce of wisdom, often reflecting on the intricate dance of negotiation that unfolded before him. He observed how merchants gauged the emotions of their customers, employing charm and wit to strike deals. Focusing intently on these interactions, he realized that commerce in St. Thomas was about more than just buying and selling; it was about building trust and relationships.

His time spent in these various roles began to shape his understanding of the economic fabric of the island. Ledger witnessed trade not only as an exchange of goods but to uplift the community. He saw how established merchants supported local farmers, ensuring their produce made its way into shops across the island, thus creating a cycle of sustainability that benefitted everyone involved. This sense of responsibility inspired him to consider how his family could contribute to this economic ecosystem through their upcoming pop-up dinner.

Amid the excitement, Ledger also confronted the challenges of his new roles. Some days were grueling, filled with long hours and strenuous work as he navigated the physical demands of unloading ships and managing crates. There were moments when doubt crept in, especially when competing with experienced traders for customers' attention. The pressure to succeed was relentless, and he often found himself questioning whether he was truly cut out for this life in commerce.

But Ledger's resolve drove him onward; he was determined to carve a niche for himself and his family in this vibrant economy. He noticed that while some merchants stood firmly in their ways, others were willing to adapt, blending traditional practices with innovative ideas to connect with their customers. This adaptability resonated with him, sparking the vision of integrating his family's culinary heritage into the local food scene.

As Ledger's experience deepened, he began to apply what he had learned. He attended local gatherings, where merchants shared their products and customers discussed their needs. These events illuminated how interconnected everyone was, each person playing a part in the delicate web of trade. Ledger realized that if he and his family presented their pop-up dinner not just as a business but as a community event, they could build meaningful relationships with their neighbors and customers.

When he returned home each evening, Ledger eagerly shared stories of the day's transactions and the lessons he picked up. His family listened intently, their excitement palpable as they planned how to market their dinner and engage with the community. They began brainstorming potential themes for the event, focusing on the cultural tales they could tell through their food, combining flavors and experiences from their heritage with those of the island's diverse culinary landscape.

Ledger found comfort in knowing that the path ahead was illuminated by the knowledge gained from working in this robust economy. His roles had forged connections throughout the island, deepening his appreciation for the resilience of the community.

As he settled into his growing responsibilities, Ledger felt himself evolving. The weight of uncertainty began to lift, replaced by a sense of belonging and purpose. St. Thomas was more than a mere backdrop for their new life; it was the very fabric of their family's future. With every passing day, Ledger felt assured that he was preparing not just for a pop-up dinner, but for the dawning of a bright and sustainable life on this beautiful island—one woven with opportunities, relationships, and the spirit of resilience that defined commerce in St. Thomas.

The sun hung high in the sky, casting a warm glow over the vibrant marketplace of Charlotte Amalie. Ledger Philogene meandered through the bustling stalls, the cacophony of voices weaving together with the calls of merchants hawking their goods. Today was not just another day at the shop; it was an opportunity for Ledger to connect with the community he had grown increasingly fond of.

With a small notebook tucked under his arm, Ledger wandered from stall to stall, observing the ebb and flow of commerce around him. The colorful displays of fruits and vegetables caught his eye, each stall more inviting than the last. He paused to admire a stand overflowing with ripe mangoes, their golden skin glistening in the sun.

"Looking to try some fresh mango?" a cheerful voice interrupted his thoughts. Ledger turned to see a young woman with a wide smile standing behind the counter, her hair adorned with bright flowers.

"Absolutely! They look delicious," Ledger replied, stepping closer and appreciating the fragrance wafting from the fruits.

The woman, introducing herself as Isela, deftly picked a mango from the pile and handed it to him. "This one is especially sweet. Trust me; you will not regret it!"

As Ledger took the mango, he felt compelled to ask, "How do you choose the best ones? What should I look for?"

With enthusiasm, Isela explained the subtle signs of ripeness, gesturing toward the faint blush of color and the slight give to the fruit when squeezed. "It is all about the feel and smell. You will know when they are perfect!" Her passion for her craft shone through, and Ledger found himself drawn to her bubbly energy.

Encouraged by the connection, Ledger decided to share a few details about his family's plans for a pop-up dinner. "We're planning to showcase local ingredients and recipes from St. Barthélemy, and I'd love to use some of your mangoes in a dish!"

Isela's eyes lit up. "That sounds like a wonderful idea! Supporting local and sharing our flavors, what is not to love? You should come by for some of my herbs and peppers, too. They will add a kick to your dishes!"

Eager about the possibilities, Ledger paused to jot down Isela's recommendations in his notebook. Their conversation flowed naturally, each of them exchanging stories and learning from one another. Isela shared the rich history of her family in St. Thomas, their roots deeply connected to the land and its abundance.

"I believe food connects us all," she said thoughtfully. "Every dish has a story, just like every person in this market. We all contribute to this vibrant community."

As Ledger listened, he felt a sense of purpose swell within him. This moment perfectly epitomized the relationships he was eager to cultivate in his new life. He realized that expanding his business would require more than just the right ingredients; it would necessitate partnerships built on trust and shared experiences.

After purchasing a few ripe mangoes and a small bundle of fresh herbs—feeling grateful for the introduction and help from Isela—Ledger thanked her wholeheartedly. "I will be back. I would love to keep this conversation going. Your insights are invaluable!"

Isela waved goodbye, her bright smile lingering like sunshine. "We are all in this together, Ledger! Do not hesitate to ask if you need anything else!"

As he walked away, Ledger felt invigorated. The marketplace buzzed around him, each stall a reminder of the interconnectedness that defined St. Thomas's vibrant economy. Each merchant had a story, and each transaction was a chance to forge relationships rooted in respect and mutual benefit.

With his mangoes and herbs in hand, Ledger moved through the market with renewed purpose. He envisioned his family's pop-up dinner coming to life, not as a standalone effort but as part of a larger community narrative—a celebration of flavors, culture, and the bonds that united them all.

This experience, simple yet profound, solidified what he had learned about the importance of networking. He understood now that creating a successful venture would mean nurturing these relationships, connecting with others who shared his passion for their heritage, and being responsive to the needs of the community.

In that moment, Ledger felt a surge of optimism. With every step he took through the marketplace, he recognized that he was not merely an outsider trying to make his way; he was becoming a part of the very fabric of St. Thomas. Each interaction was a thread sewing him closer into the community, and he was eager to see how these connections would help shape his and his family's future on the island.

In the vibrant and bustling environment of St. Thomas, Ledger Philogene not only embraced the opportunity to work and earn a living but also discovered a wealth of invaluable skills crucial for his future endeavors. With each day spent in the local economy, he learned the ins and outs of commerce, honing abilities that would prove essential as he navigated the complexities of trade, negotiation, and community building.

As Ledger settled into his role at Mr. Ainsworth's shop, he quickly realized that effective communication was key to every successful transaction. What began as simple exchanges with customers soon evolved into opportunities for negotiation. He watched closely as Mr. Ainsworth navigated discussions about pricing and inventory with a blend of authority and warmth. Ledger absorbed every detail, noting how tone and body language could influence a customer's decision.

One sunny afternoon, a local farmer named Benjamin entered the shop carrying a basket filled with freshly harvested vegetables. "I'm hoping we can talk about getting these into your shop," he said, displaying his produce with pride. Ledger watched as Mr. Ainsworth engaged Benjamin in conversation. Rather than immediately discussing prices, Mr. Ainsworth inquired about the quality of the harvest and how much effort was involved in reaching this yield.

"You've got an impressive crop this season," Mr. Ainsworth complimented, his authoritative yet friendly tone putting the farmer at ease. "How do you see these selling in the market?"

Ledger marveled at how Mr. Ainsworth's questions served a dual purpose: they showcased a genuine interest in Benjamin's work while opening the door for negotiation. It was about building trust, Ledger realized, and he vowed to adopt this approach in his interactions.

As the conversation unfolded, Ledger observed how both men navigated the delicate dance of pricing—offering a fair deal that would sustain Benjamin's livelihood while ensuring the shop remained profitable. Mr. Ainsworth eventually made an offer, one that Ledger mentally noted, understanding how important it was to balance profitability with community support.

With each encounter like this, Ledger practiced his negotiation techniques, becoming increasingly comfortable with discussions that had once made him anxious. He began taking small initiatives, like approaching customers to discuss bulk purchase discounts or suggesting complementary products that could enhance their shopping experience. His confidence grew as he discovered how friendly banter could ease negotiations and create a positive shopping atmosphere.

Networking quickly became another essential skill for Ledger on the island. He observed the web of interconnected relationships between merchants, farmers, and customers, realizing that who you know could be just as valuable as what you sold. One afternoon, at a local festival, he joined Mr. Ainsworth at a community event where vendors displayed their goods.

"This is where the real magic happens," Mr. Ainsworth said, gesturing toward clusters of merchants chatting amicably, exchanging ideas and contacts. Ledger saw families mingling with merchants, forging connections that would facilitate trade not just today but into the future.

Inspired, Ledger approached a woman selling handmade pottery, admiring her craftsmanship. After discussing her work, she introduced him to a musician nearby, which would later lead to an opportunity for Ledger's family to feature live music during their pop-up dinner. In those moments, he learned that networking was not merely about building contacts; it was about fostering relationships that could lead to mutual support and collaboration.

As these connections flourished, Ledger also recognized the importance of financial management. His initial role at the shop involved recording daily sales and tracking inventory, which brought him front-row seats to the economic pulse of the business. He learned to use simple accounting practices to manage cash flow, preparing him for the financial realities of running his own venture someday.

One afternoon, as Ledger sorted through receipts, Mr. Ainsworth sat down next to him, ready to discuss the shop's finances. "Understanding the numbers is crucial, Ledger," he explained, his fingers tracing over the accounts. "You want to know where your profits are coming from, where they are going. It is the backbone of every business."

As Mr. Ainsworth explained profit margins, Ledger found himself engrossed in the details. He grasped how to evaluate costs versus sales and how every small decision could impact the bottom line. This financial literacy soon became an integral part of his skill set, blending seamlessly with the people-centric dynamic Ledger was working to develop.

Days turned into weeks, and Ledger's confidence flourished. He participated in more complex negotiations, managed his own small projects at the shop, and cultivated relationships with suppliers. He even began to think critically about pricing his family's upcoming pop-up dinner, understanding the delicate balance between what customers were willing to pay and the costs involved in serving high-quality dishes.

Ledger found joy in these interactions, recognizing that learning was unfolding all around him. He understood that every conversation was an opportunity for growth, not only for his own skills but for the well-being of the community. The vibrant life in St. Thomas was like a tapestry, woven from countless threads—each representing a merchant, a farmer, or a customer—all linked by their shared stories and experiences. Ledger realized that the knowledge he gained through negotiation, networking, and financial management was not just for personal gain; it was a way to weave his family's dreams into the larger narrative of the island.

Whenever Ledger returned home at the end of the day, he shared his experiences with Clara and their siblings, fueling their collective dream of the pop-up dinner. He spoke passionately about the importance of connecting with people, listening to their needs, and building a business that honored both their heritage and the island's diverse cultural influences. These discussions filled their home with laughter and ideas, each family member contributing their own vision and creativity.

As they began to formalize their plans, Ledger saw the fruits of his labor in action. He recognized the opportunity to combine the culinary traditions of St. Barthélemy with the local flavors of St. Thomas, crafting a menu that highlighted the island's bounty while paying homage to his family's roots. Inspired by the interwoven relationships he observed in the marketplace, Ledger envisioned the pop-up not just as a meal but as an event that celebrated community—a gathering place for friends and neighbors to share stories, laughter, and, of course, good food.

Motivated by this vision, Ledger and his family started reaching out to local farmers and artisans, seeking partnerships that could enrich their event. He helped Clara negotiate for the freshest ingredients, encouraging her to incorporate the advice he had gleaned from Mr. Ainsworth and his experiences at the shop. They would visit markets together, maintain warm relationships with the vendors, and ensure that their offerings were both unique and accessible.

As Ledger's skills flourished, he felt an undeniable connection to St. Thomas forming in the fabric of their lives. He began to see himself as an integral part of the local economy—a contributor rather than merely a participant. The notion that he could honor the legacy of his family while embracing the vibrant culture of his new home filled him with a profound sense of purpose.

Through navigating the commercial landscape, Ledger was not only laying the groundwork for his family's future but also discovering that economic literacy and human connection were pillars of success in St. Thomas. Each day offered him fresh lessons, and with every interaction, he felt more equipped to build a business that would thrive on the island's dynamic energy. With his heart full of hope and enthusiasm for the journey ahead, Ledger stepped boldly into the next chapter, eager to transform their shared dreams into reality.

***

As the sun set on another bustling day in St. Thomas, Ledger Philogene walked home, his thoughts swirling amidst the backdrop of laughter and lively chatter from the nearby shops and stalls. While he had taken great pride in the relationships he was building with merchants and customers alike, a lingering shadow accompanied his every step: the remnants of the island's colonial past continued to cast a pervasive influence over its social dynamics. Despite the vibrant economy, Ledger often found himself grappling with the subtle, yet pervasive, discrimination that lingered like a specter.

The sun dipped low in the sky, painting the cobblestone streets of Charlotte Amalie in hues of orange and pink, but Ledger could feel the weight of unease settling on his shoulders. He had learned valuable skills in negotiation and networking, yet he noticed an invisible barrier that separated him from some of the more established merchants and influential players in the trade community. It was a realization that made him question his place in the carefully woven fabric of the marketplace.

Entering the shop, Ledger was greeted by Mr. Ainsworth, who was busily tallying up the day's sales. "You did well today, Ledger! Customers love your approach," his boss praised, clapping him on the back. Ledger managed a smile, appreciating the kind words but increasingly aware that acknowledgment did not always extend beyond the walls of the shop.

Outside, in the broader trade circles, Ledger often faced skepticism that seemed rooted not in merit, but in the legacy of colonialism that lingered within the community. Descendants of enslaved Africans populated the island, yet many influential merchants were of European descent—families that had established their legacies long before the arrival of newcomers like himself. When mingling at community events and gatherings, Ledger sometimes felt the unwelcome gaze of those who viewed him through a lens of historical bias.

One evening, at a local festival where merchants gathered to showcase their products, Ledger eagerly promoted his family's pop-up dinner. He and Clara had set up a vibrant booth adorned with posters showcasing their culinary offerings—local ingredients blended with the distinct flavors of St. Barthélemy. As they presented their dishes and sparked conversation, however, Ledger could not help but overhear whispers from some of the established merchants nearby.

"What do they know about real cooking?" he overheard one man scoff, eyes scrutinizing Ledger and Clara's booth. "They think they can just come here and set up shop?"

The words stung, and for a moment, Ledger felt his chest tighten with frustration. He turned to Clara, who was busy chatting with a potential customer. "Did you hear that?" he muttered under his breath, trying to mask the hurt.

"Ignore them. Let us show them what we can do," Clara replied, her determination shining through. Ledger admired her resilience, but the comment lingered in his mind like a cloud.

He knew that the economic opportunities presented by St. Thomas were often tinged with an unspoken hierarchy—an invisible line that separated those who had deep-rooted connections from newcomers. Ledger's heart raced as he remembered moments of resistance he had encountered while trying to network within certain circles. Despite his growing repertoire of skills, he faced subtle dismissals and sidelong glances, others fully engaged in their conversations while he floated at the edges, an outsider in his own pursuit.

In conversations with Clara after long days at work, Ledger expressed his concerns. "Sometimes, I feel like no matter how hard I work, there is this barrier I cannot get past. They look at me and see someone who does not belong."

Clara sighed, her eyes reflecting understanding. "It is the legacy of what has come before us. I see it too, Ledger. But do not let it deter you. We have a gift to offer, and we are part of this community now. We just need to keep pushing through."

With Clara's encouragement, Ledger sought to forge bonds with locals beyond just economic transactions. He frequented community events, aimed at building a broader sense of belonging. He approached vendors, learned about their journeys, and listened to their stories in the hope of building rapport and trust.

In time, he discovered pockets of acceptance among those who appreciated the blending of cultures. A farmer named Helena shared the importance of collaboration and invited Ledger to source ingredients from her organic farm, insisting that they work together for the benefit of all. "This island thrives on unity," she said emphatically, reinforcing Ledger's belief in the power of community.

Despite these moments of solidarity, vestiges of bias still lingered. Ledger caught himself scrutinizing the dynamics of conversations, identifying patterns of exclusion that stifled collaboration. It was a reminder that while the economy thrived on trade, it continued to be interwoven with historical prejudices that shaped social hierarchies.

One afternoon at the shop, Ledger overheard a conversation between Mr. Ainsworth and another merchant. Their tones were hushed, yet Ledger's sense of injustice flared as he perceived the underlying threads of discrimination woven into their dialogue. "You know how these newcomers are. They come in, thinking they can disrupt our way of life," the merchant remarked dismissively.

Ledger forced himself to stay focused on his tasks, but anger bubbled beneath the surface. He understood that while he was carving a niche for himself through hard work, he was also navigating a complex structure that favored established, historical connections over merit.

Yet his resolve only grew stronger. A deep sense of purpose stirred within him, extending beyond his family to encompass the community that had embraced him. Bolstered by a growing network of support, Ledger began to see how he could channel his experiences into advocating for equity and inclusivity.

With the pop-up dinner on the horizon, he determined to showcase not just their culinary skills, but also a celebration of shared heritage and the vibrant tapestry of St. Thomas' history. This moment of defiance against the social hierarchies that governed the community was his opportunity to invite others into a conversation about collaboration, unity, and the shared joys of food.

The weight of the past served as both a challenge and a catalyst for transformation. As Ledger stepped onto the path of building a new legacy for his family, he understood that confronting discrimination meant creating spaces where everyone's voice could be heard. He was committed to not just being a participant but a facilitator of change—transforming the dialogue around commerce and community in St. Thomas. Ledger envisioned his family's pop-up dinner as a platform, not only to showcase their culinary talents but also to foster inclusivity and unity among the island's diverse residents. He wanted it to be more than just an event; he aspired for it to be a gathering that celebrated the rich histories and contributions of all cultures represented on the island.

With this vision in mind, Ledger poured his energy into planning the event. He reached out to other local chefs and artisans, hoping to collaborate and create a menu that honored the flavors of St. Thomas while incorporating elements from St. Barthélemy. Through these collaborations, he fostered relationships with individuals from various backgrounds, each bringing their own perspective and expertise into the fold. Every conversation became an opportunity not only to share culinary ideas but to weave a broader narrative that transcended barriers.

Determined to highlight the importance of community connections, Ledger planned to include stories from each collaborator in the dinner, ensuring that guests could appreciate the diverse tapestry that made up their island identity. He began inviting local musicians to contribute traditional music, knowing that music has a powerful way of bringing people together and igniting a sense of shared experience.

As the date of the pop-up approached, Ledger's excitement surged, but so did the anxiety tied to the potential challenges ahead. He knew that there would be those who might resist this notion of unity, who would cling to outdated hierarchies—even within their own communities. He feared the possibility of negative reactions from members of the more established merchant circles, wary of newcomers, and any changes to the status quo.

But Ledger pushed aside his doubts, reminding himself that adversity often led to growth. He drew strength from the stories of those he had met, inspired by their resilience in building lives amidst historical injustices. Every person he worked with added depth to the event, reinforcing his belief that St. Thomas belonged to everyone who called it home, no matter their past or the color of their skin.

The transformation was not solely for himself or his family; it was for the community, a shared journey toward understanding and acceptance. Ledger's commitment to creating an inclusive space became a driving force, guiding him as he organized the details of the dinner. He envisioned a long central table adorned with the vibrant colors of local produce, where people from all walks of life could gather, share food, and engage in meaningful conversations about their shared future.

The evening of the pop-up arrived, and the air buzzed with anticipation. Guests began to filter into the makeshift dining space, their expressions a mix of curiosity and excitement. Wooden tables, adorned with colorful tablecloths and local flowers, created an inviting atmosphere. Ledger's heart raced as he welcomed each person, mindful of the diverse stories they brought with them.

As conversations flourished and laughter filled the air, Ledger finally felt the weight of the past begin to lift. That night was more than culinary exploration; it was a celebration of resilience—a reflection of collective experiences that bound them together. He observed as neighbors—once strangers—shared plates and exchanged stories, crafting new narratives of acceptance.

In that moment, Ledger understood that he was not just building a legacy for his family but also sowing the seeds of change for future generations. As he looked around the table, he saw a microcosm of hope. He realized that confronting the inequalities of the past meant embracing the richness of the present, weaving a future where diversity, camaraderie, and understanding prevailed. The road ahead might be long, but with each meal shared and each voice uplifted, he was forging a path toward a more equitable community that celebrated everyone's contributions—a true legacy of transformation.

The evening air was sweet with the scent of grilled fish and freshly chopped herbs as families and friends trickled into the colorful courtyard transformed for the night. Lanterns hung from the trees, casting a warm glow over the long tables adorned with vibrant tablecloths and shining utensils, each carefully placed to create an inviting atmosphere. Ledger Philogene stood near the entrance, his heart racing with anticipation as guests began to arrive for the pop-up dinner that he and his family had worked tirelessly to organize.

"Look how beautiful everything turned out, Ledger!" Clara exclaimed, adjusting a basket of fresh bread on the table. The aroma of garlic and rosemary wafted through the air, tantalizing the senses. She grinned at her brother, her excitement infectious. "I can't believe we actually pulled this off!"

Ledger took a moment to soak in the scene, a kaleidoscope of colors and sounds around him. Families of all shapes and sizes mingled their laughter ringing like music. He felt a surge of pride at the sight of their community coming together, sharing not just a meal but an experience that honored their diverse backgrounds.

"You did it, Clara," he replied, the knot in his stomach loosening as he caught sight of their first guests—Isela from the market, her eyes sparkling with delight as she spotted Ledger.

"I wouldn't miss it for the world!" she said, stepping forward to hug him. Her presence reassured him, and he recognized how important it was to have her energy at the table. They exchanged smiles as she admired the arrangements, her endorsement further solidifying their collective commitment to creating something special.

Soon, the air was filled with the sound of music. A local band made up of musicians Ledger had met during preparations, began to play traditional tunes that captured the island's vibrant cultural heritage. The gentle strumming of guitars and the rhythmic pulse of drums invited guests to dance, turning the courtyard into a lively celebration of joy.

As the festivities unfolded, Ledger roamed through the gathering, stopping intermittently to engage with guests and ensure everyone was enjoying the experience. He poured drinks, offered tastes of their carefully crafted dishes, and found joy in watching strangers become friends, united over shared plates and stories.

"This fish sautéed in mango sauce is incredible!" a woman exclaimed as she took her first bite. "Where did you learn to cook like this?"

"My family hails from St. Barthélemy," Ledger explained, his voice steady with a newfound confidence. "We have combined some of our traditional recipes with fresh local ingredients. It is a way to honor both our heritage and this beautiful island."

Encouraged by their laughter and enthusiasm, he moved on to the next table, where an older gentleman named Mr. Thompson sat chatting with Helene, the farmer who had brought tomatoes and herbs for the dinner. Their discussion about sustainable practices and supporting local growers felt enriching and grounded Ledger in the very purpose of the evening.

As the sun dipped below the horizon, painting the sky in deep purples and oranges, Ledger gathered everyone's attention, feeling both nervous and empowered. "Thank you all for being here tonight," he said, his voice slightly shaking but resolute. "This dinner is a celebration of our community's diversity—a gathering of flavors, stories, and shared experiences. We can create something beautiful together, to connect and learn from one another."

There was a ripple of applause, and Ledger smiled, heartening his resolve. He introduced Clara and their siblings, and one by one, shared anecdotes about the dishes prepared that night, weaving together the history of their family and the ingredients sourced from local vendors. This was not just a meal; it was a culinary tapestry that spanned generations and cultures.

As the night continued, Ledger watched guests intermingling, forming connections for which he had hoped. Conversations flowed, with people exchanging recipes and stories of their own backgrounds. A sense of camaraderie enveloped the courtyard, erasing any barriers that once divided their social hierarchies.

In a surprising moment, Ledger caught sight of Mr. Ainsworth across the courtyard, deep in conversation with Helen and Isela, their laughter ringing out in the night air. It was a turning point—seeing established merchants embrace the newcomers and recognize their contributions. Ledger felt a surge of exhilaration, realizing that their collective efforts had nurtured an environment of acceptance.

Later in the evening, Ledger had the chance to speak with Mr. Ainsworth privately. The seasoned merchant leaned against the wooden railing, watching the celebration unfold with a thoughtful expression. "You have done something remarkable tonight, Ledger. I did not grasp how committed you were to weave everyone together."

All are part of this community, no matter where we come from. Food has a way of connecting people on a deeper level, you know? **

Mr. Ainsworth nodded, a hint of a smile creeping across his face. "Indeed, it does. I have been watching you, Ledger. You are not just carving out a space for yourself; you are inviting others in. That is a rare quality, especially in a marketplace like ours."

Feeling a mix of pride and humility, Ledger continued, "I have learned so much from everyone—the farmers, artisans, and the customers. This dinner was just the start. I hope we can all support each other more moving forward."

"You're planting seeds for change, Ledger," Mr. Ainsworth replied, straightening up and meeting Ledger's gaze. "But it will not be easy. Some will still resist this new narrative."

Ledger felt a flicker of anxiety. "I understand. But tonight, it has shown me that there is a lot of support out there. If we can keep this momentum going, if we can continue to encourage conversations, we can chip away at those hierarchies."

"You're right," Mr. Ainsworth said thoughtfully. "Change is not instantaneous. It takes persistence, collaboration, and passion. You have what it takes to challenge the status quo."

As they spoke, Ledger looked out over the courtyard, where laughter and conversation danced in the air among new friends. He felt a warmth spread through him, realizing just how far he had come since first arriving on the island, uncertain and searching for his place. Now, he was not just a participant in the community's economy but a catalyst for growth and unity.

Just then, a burst of laughter echoed from a nearby table, drawing Ledger's gaze. Clara had joined a group of guests, engaging them in a lively discussion about cuisine, her enthusiasm for the infectious dishes. Watching her effortlessly connect with others, Ledger's mind sparked with an idea—this dinner could be the first of many, a series of communal gatherings that celebrated collaboration among the diverse voices of St. Thomas.

Turning back to Mr. Ainsworth, Ledger felt a renewed sense of determination. "What if we organize more events like this? A monthly dinner, perhaps? We could feature different themes, highlighting local ingredients and inviting various chefs to collaborate."

A thoughtful look crossed Mr. Ainsworth's face, and he folded his arms, pondering the suggestion. "That is ambitious, Ledger. But I think it could work. It would take effort to coordinate, but if you are willing to lead the charge, I would be glad to help. You have the community's ear."

Ledger's heart raced with excitement. "I would love that! We could even involve schools, encouraging children to learn about cooking and local history. We could invite everyone to share their recipes, their stories."

The vision of these gatherings ignited something deep within him, a sense of purpose beyond merely being a merchant—he could be a bridge, connecting varied pieces of the community puzzle. The conversations that would stem from those dinners could lead to collaboration in commerce, art, and culture, weaving a tighter tapestry for St. Thomas.

"This is just the beginning, Ledger," Mr. Ainsworth said, clapping him lightly on the shoulder. "You are onto something powerful. But remember, it is all about patience and consistency. Build those relationships, nurture them, and in time, the barriers will begin to fade."

As the night wore on and the stars twinkled above the courtyard, Ledger felt invigorated. The dinner had been a resounding success, but beyond the delicious dishes and splendid décor, the real accomplishment lay in the connections made, the stories shared, and the barriers broken.

With a renewed commitment to his vision, Ledger returned to the gathering, his heart full. He joined Clara and their guests, eager to hear more stories and thoughts on how to move forward together. The pop-up dinner had transformed into an experience of community solidarity, and he was determined to keep that energy alive.

As laughter echoed around him and the music swayed with the rhythm of the evening, Ledger realized that he was no longer just an outsider. He was becoming an integral part of the fabric of St. Thomas— part of something larger than himself, one that promised hope, resilience, and unity amidst the legacies of the past. The road ahead would have its challenges, but with each shared meal and every connection forged, he felt confident in the journey they were beginning together.

***

Ledger Philogene stood at the bustling harbor of Charlotte Amalie, the salty breeze tousling his hair as he watched local fishermen unload their catches for the day. He had grown fond of the sights and sounds of St. Thomas—the vibrant colors of the boats bobbing in the water, the enticing aroma of spices and fresh produce wafting from nearby stalls, and the lively banter of merchants negotiating prices. Yet beneath this surface of excitement lay a persistent struggle, one that played out daily as he navigated his cultural identity amid the island's rich tapestry of influences.

Ledger took a deep breath, feeling the warmth of the Caribbean sun on his skin. When he first arrived in St. Thomas, he had dreams of building a future for his family, but he soon realized that realizing that dream required a careful balance between honoring his roots and embracing the new culture around him. As a migrant from St. Barthélemy, he was keenly aware of how the legacy of colonialism shaped the way people viewed him. His heritage was deeply intertwined with a history marked by the blending of European and African influences, and he felt the weight of that legacy pressing on him.

At home, he held tight to the traditions his family had passed down—recipes from his mother, stories from his grandparents, the rhythm of their native tongue. They were threads that anchored him to a past he cherished, yet St. Thomas offered a vibrant array of new experiences that beckoned him to adapt and grow. Cultural events on the island showcased a mix of island-style festivities, music, and cuisine, and while Ledger was eager to take part, he often felt like an outsider.

One evening, after a day at the shop, he attended a local festival celebrating the island's heritage. The air hummed with energy as Steel Pan bands played lively tunes and dancers in colorful costumes twirled to the rhythm of laughter and song. Ledger joined in the festivities, his heart swelling at the jubilant atmosphere, yet he could not shake the feeling of being caught between two worlds.

As he actively participated, Ledger felt a pull to both join the celebration and stand apart, reflecting on the cultural practices of his own family on St. Barthélemy. The vibrant food stalls offered dishes rich with spices and flavors that reminded him of home, yet when he tasted some of the offerings, he found they had been adapted to local preferences and ingredients.

"You should try this conch fritter!" a local vendor exclaimed, gently urging him to sample her creation. "Best on the island!"

Taking a bite, he savored the familiar spices intermingled with a different flair. "It's delicious!" he replied with a smile, but a part of him longed for the traditional recipes he remembered from his childhood—different fish, unique techniques that his family had perfected over generations.

As the evening wore on, Ledger found himself engaging in a captivating conversation with a group of festivalgoers. They shared stories of their families and traditions, revealing the mosaic of influences that defined their cultural identities. He felt a yearning to connect on a deeper level, to share his own heritage and invite them to understand the journey that shaped him.

As Ledger shared his background, he could sense a momentary pause in their reactions. Some responded with polite nods, while others seemed unsure of how to engage with the intricacies of his history. It was a stark reminder that, as a migrant, his identity was often seen through the lens of colonial legacy. A heaviness settled in his chest, torn between celebrating the richness of blending cultures and the ever-present reminder of how colonialism colored their perceptions.

The duality of his identity—both as a resident of St. Thomas and as a descendant of a lineage shaped by colonialism—triggered an internal conflict. He cherished the strength of his cultural heritage but also felt pressure to conform to the expectations of those around him. To embrace new customs and ways of life, he pushed himself to adapt, but each effort seemed to chip away at a part of him that longed to remain authentically connected to his beginnings. The challenge of navigating this duality weighed heavily on his heart, leaving him uncertain of his place in this intricate cultural web.

As Ledger sat at the table with Clara and their siblings, he felt the stark contrast between the warmth of family bonds and the coldness of societal expectations. "I sometimes wonder if I have to choose one over the other," he confessed, his voice barely above a whisper. "Will embracing St. Thomas mean letting go of who I am?"

Clara reached across the table, placing her hand on his. "You do not have to choose Ledger. Our culture is a part of us, and it evolves with where we are. You can take your past with you, letting it influence how you move forward.

Her words resonated with him, igniting recognition that adapting did not mean abandoning his roots. Instead, it could mean weaving his unique experiences and heritage into the vibrant fabric of St. Thomas. There was a way to celebrate both identities, allowing them to coexist in a harmonious blend that reflected his journey.

Later that week, experiencing a moment of inspiration, Ledger rummaged through old family photographs and letters passed down through generations. Each image was a snapshot of his lineage—festivals in St. Barthélemy, family gatherings where traditional recipes were passed around like treasured heirlooms, laughter echoing across sunlit beaches. As he held the worn photographs, he felt a surge of pride. His history was rich and multifaceted, and it deserved to be honored.

Eager to honor the fusion of his identities, Ledger resolved to weave his cultural heritage into the next pop-up dinner. He imagined a menu that celebrated local ingredients while also featuring family recipes, each dish reflecting the flavors that had shaped his upbringing. As he carefully curated the offerings, the combination of ingredients—like fresh conch paired with the bold spices of St. Barthélemy—became a reflection of his journey, a tribute to both his history and the new life he was building.

During this creative process, he invited Clara to join him in experimenting with flavors. Together, they cooked in the evenings, laughter rising along with the fragrant steam from the stovetop. They incorporated their family's recipes while letting the island's fresh ingredients inspire them. Clara was thrilled to blend their culinary heritage with local produce, and Ledger felt a renewed excitement for what lay ahead.

One afternoon, as they prepared dishes side by side, Ledger voiced a thought. "What if we invite some of our local friends to join us in the kitchen? It could be a chance to share our culture directly while learning from them too."

"That's a fantastic idea!" Clara replied, her eyes sparkling with enthusiasm. "It would create space for dialogue, a chance to build bridges while sharing our culinary traditions."

They quickly organized a cooking session, reaching out to local friends and vendors in the community. The response was overwhelmingly positive, and soon they had gathered a small group ready to come together in the spirit of collaboration.

When the day arrived, Ledger felt a mix of excitement and nerves. He wanted to create an environment where everyone felt welcome to share their stories, recipes, and knowledge. As their friends arrived, he greeted them with gusto, introducing them to the vibrant array of ingredients laid out on the kitchen counter.

"Today," Ledger said with a smile, "we are not just cooking; we are sharing stories and traditions. What we create here is a blend of all our cultural backgrounds. Let us honor that by lifting each other's recipes and flavors."

With the sounds of laughter and lively conversation filling the kitchen, the group dived into the cooking process. They exchanged cooking techniques, each person offering insights from their heritage as they diced, sautéed, and sampled each dish along the way. Ledger felt the barriers that once seemed daunting begin to dissolve in the heat of collaboration.

As they worked, stories flowed naturally, enriching the experience with personal histories. One of the local cooks shared tales of family gatherings around similar dishes, recounting how food had been an essential part of their identity and culture—a reminder that despite their different backgrounds, they all understood the unifying power of shared meals.

That evening after hours spent bonding over spices and simmering pots, they finally sat down to share the fruits of their labor. The table was spread with an array of dishes—a conch stew infused with local herbs, a St. Barthélemy-style grilled fish seasoned to perfection, and colorful salads bursting with island flavors. As they clinked glasses and dug into the meal, Ledger felt a deep sense of belonging wash over him.

"This is what it's all about," he thought, watching his friends engage over the table, the laughter a harmonious backdrop to the clinking of forks and the fragrant aroma of their shared meal. Each bite told a story, a celebration of both their origins and the vibrant future they were crafting together. In that moment, Ledger felt the warmth of connection envelop him, a feeling that seemed to transcend the complexities of his dual identity—a blend of his heritage and the culture blooming around him.

As plates were passed around and stories flowed freely, he realized how deeply the act of sharing food could forge bonds and foster understanding. It was a reminder that their identities could coexist, each bringing unique flavors and narratives to the table. Here, at this moment, was a perfect reflection of their intertwined experiences—a true fusion of cultures.

"This fish is incredible!" one of his friends exclaimed, taking another bite. "You must share the recipe, Ledger. It is unlike anything I have tasted before."

Ledger smiled, feeling a rush of pride as he thought of the recipe his mother had taught him. "It's a family recipe," he explained. "We use local spices from St. Barthélemy, but here, I wanted to incorporate the flavors of St. Thomas. It is perfect for a celebration like this."

The evening unfolded with warmth and camaraderie, as the group lingered over shared dishes and laughter. Conversations deepened, touching on personal histories and cultural roots. When someone inquired about Ledger's arrival in St. Thomas, he spoke openly of his hopes, the hardships he had overcome, and the understanding he had gained along the way. In telling his story, Ledger felt a quiet affirmation take root—his voice not only heard but valued. The act of sharing became a bridge, connecting his journey to those around him in a meaningful and lasting way.

"You know," one friend said thoughtfully, "your journey is not just your own. It resonates with many of us who have found ourselves navigating multiple cultures. We are all blending our pasts into something new."

Ledger nodded, feeling a sense of collectivity in their experiences. "Exactly! It is about embracing our individual histories while also recognizing how they intertwine with our community.

As the evening wound down, Ledger glanced around the table, struck by the tapestry of faces—each represented by distinct heritages, now intertwined in laughter and camaraderie. He found solace in knowing that while the struggles with his identity had been real, they were also part of a larger narrative. One that reflected the beauty of migration, history, and the hope for a better tomorrow.

"I think we should do this more often," Clara suggested, breaking through his thoughts. "Maybe we can create a series of these cooking nights—a way to keep building connections through food."

The idea sparked a wave of excitement among the group, and Ledger felt the energy surge once more. "I love that! We can highlight different themes and dishes from our cultures, share stories, and learn from one another.

The room buzzed with enthusiasm, and Ledger's heart swelled with hope. He knew this was just the beginning. By creating a space where everyone could feel free to share their traditions and histories, he could help foster a sense of belonging that had once felt out of reach.

As the evening ended and guests began to depart, a feeling of unity hung gently in the air, hinting at the possibility of more shared moments coming. Ledger felt a weight lift from his shoulders, the questions surrounding his cultural identity no longer felt heavy. He had come to realize that honoring his roots did not mean resisting change. Instead, the merging of his past and present was not a conflict to resolve, but a truth to embrace—one that defined his evolving sense of self.

Before the evening ended, Ledger turned to his friends, gratitude spilling from his heart. "Thank you all for being part of this. Your stories and your presence mean more than you can imagine. Together, we can create something beautiful here."

As the last goodbyes rang out and the kitchen quieted, Ledger felt a renewed sense of purpose surging through him. He would continue to explore the depths of his identity while building bridges within the diverse community of St. Thomas. The journey might be complex, but it was a journey worth embracing—a journey that promised to lead to connections, understanding, and a celebration of all that made them uniquely whole.

***

The moon hung high over St. Thomas, spilling silvery light across Ledger's modest kitchen as he leaned against the counter, the remnants of the evening still fresh in his mind. The earlier sounds of laughter and conversation had faded into a gentle hush, replaced by the occasional rustle of palm leaves swaying in the soft island breeze. He looked around the kitchen, now quiet but still holding onto the warmth of the gathering that had just unfolded.

Leftover dishes were artfully arranged on the table, where friends had shared not just food but also pieces of themselves. The aroma of spices lingered in the air, a tantalizing reminder of the vibrant meal they had crafted together—a blend of St. Barthélemy influences and local St. Thomas flavors. Ledger felt a deep sense of satisfaction wash over him as he recalled each moment—the sound of clinking forks, the bursts of laughter, the shared stories weaving together their diverse backgrounds.

He moved to the table and picked up a half-empty pitcher of rum punch, pouring himself a small glass. As he settled into a chair, he reflected on how the evening had unfolded. "This is what community feels like," he murmured to himself, recalling the way his friends had engaged, eyes bright with enthusiasm and curiosity.

Despite the initial nervousness he had felt at sharing his heritage, Ledger found it heartening to see how his story resonated with others. The gentle way his friends had responded to his experiences— nodding in understanding when he spoke of his journey—had sparked a sense of connection he had not felt in a long time.

"I shouldn't have doubted the impact of sharing," he thought, taking a sip of the punch. The sweet tang of the drink settled warmly in his chest, just like the feeling of camaraderie that had enveloped him throughout the evening. Ledger was reminded that while navigating the complexities of cultural identity could be overwhelming, there was beauty in vulnerability.

Tonight, had been more than an event; it had been a cultural exchange—a way to elevate the voices often hidden beneath the weight of history. "I want to create that space again," he mused, envisioning future gatherings where stories could flow as freely as the rum punch had. The idea of regular cooking nights ignited a spark in him, a vision of the transformative power of food and shared experiences.

With a smile creeping at the corners of his mouth, Ledger remembered the moment when one of the local cooks had excitedly shouted across the kitchen, "This fish is incredible! You must share the recipe, Ledger!" It was a stark contrast to the feeling of isolation he had often grappled with—an affirmation that his contributions were valued and recognized.

Inspired by Clara's suggestion to host more gatherings, Ledger felt a growing desire to plant deeper roots in the community—not just as a trader seeking his livelihood, but as a storyteller adding to the cultural fabric of St. Thomas. He imagined each event as an opportunity to build stronger bonds, bridging diverse traditions and nurturing mutual understanding across cultural lines.

Yet even as he relished this newfound sense of purpose, a flicker of concern tugged at his mind. "What about those who resist this blending?" he wondered, a weight settling in the pit of his stomach. He could already hear the whispers of doubt he had encountered before—those who held tightly to the islands' traditional hierarchies, resistant to the idea of change. "Will they accept me and my heritage?"

But as he sat in the silence of his kitchen, Ledger felt the stirring of determination outweigh those fears. He recalled the conversations he had shared tonight, the stories that had floated across the table, mingling with the aromas and laughter. They had each shared their histories, interwoven by common threads of struggle and resilience. Weaving his story into that tapestry had not diminished his identity; it had strengthened it.

He set the glass down and stood up, glancing at the remnants of the evening, a colorful mixture of dishes, plates scattered with bits of food, and laughter echoing in his mind. Ledger felt invigorated by the possibilities ahead, envisioning how his role could evolve within this community.

"I'll keep pushing forward," he promised himself, a renewed spark igniting in his chest. "This is my home now, and I can honor my past while embracing the present." Ledger felt a wave of excitement swell in him—a commitment to not just exist within the community but to actively shape it, inviting others to celebrate their identities alongside him.

With newfound resolve, he began tidying the kitchen, a smile lingering on his lips. The journey ahead was still unclear but tonight had shown him the power of connection and the enduring strength of cultural identity that could flourish in a multifaceted environment. Each dish washed, each utensil returned to its place, felt like an affirmation of his commitment to foster inclusivity, and celebrate diversity. He felt lighter as he wiped down the kitchen counter, his thoughts racing with ideas for future gatherings.

Night had fully settled over St. Thomas, and the sky twinkled like the vibrant lights strung across the courtyard where they had gathered. Each star seemed to pulse with possibilities, mirroring the energy he felt inside. "I can do this," he whispered to himself, thinking not just of the dinners, but of the relationships he could nurture and the stories waiting to be shared.

As he finished cleaning, Ledger paused, staring out the window at the moonlit harbor. Waves lapped softly against the shore, a soothing rhythm that echoed the heartbeat of the island. It was a reminder of how deeply intertwined his own life was with the currents of those around him. The thought filled him with gratitude. This island, with its histories marked by colonial struggles and vibrant cultural exchanges, was becoming a part of him as he was becoming a part of it.

He turned back to the kitchen, running a hand through his hair. "What if I create a storytelling night?" he thought, the idea crystallizing in his mind. He could invite friends to not only cook but also share tales from their cultures—stories of joy, hardship, and resilience. A night focused on the art of storytelling could emphasize the richness of their experiences, creating a safe space for everyone to feel heard.

Each new idea sparked a fresh surge of energy within him. He imagined an evening where children explored their roots through stories and flavors, while adults shared memories and aspirations under starlit skies. It was a dream that wove together the essence of his dual heritage—merging the soul of St. Barthélemy with the spirit of St. Thomas into one unified, living story.

As he put the last dish away, he felt an exhilarating sense of purpose solidifying within him. He would lead discussions that celebrated their complexities and shared the joy of different cultures mingling beautifully together. He could even weave in moments of history, honoring the enduring struggles that had brought them all to this point—an acknowledgment that could foster deeper understanding and connection.

Lost in thought, Ledger turned off the kitchen lights, the light from the moon casting a soft glow across the room. He felt a sense of fulfillment knowing he was beginning to carve out a legacy for his family and for himself, one that embraced all the vibrant aspects of life on the island.

With a final glance around, he felt at peace. There would be challenges ahead—questions of acceptance, resistance from some community members, and the inevitable struggle that came with blending traditions. But he was ready to face each one, equipped with the support of friends who had now become family through their shared stories and experiences.

"Tomorrow, I'll start reaching out," he resolved, heading to bed with dreams of future gatherings dancing in his mind. He envisioned dialogues that crossed cultural lines, tables bursting with food, laughter echoing in the night, and connections deepening with each shared moment.

As Ledger lay down to rest, the weight of uncertainty that once pressed upon him lifted, replaced by the prospect of change—a change he was determined to be a part of. No longer just a lone vessel navigating the murky waters of identity, he felt empowered to shape his reality and inspire others through the power of connection and cultural celebration. Tomorrow would be the first step, and he was ready to embrace it with open arms.

The sun rose brightly over the turquoise waters of St. Thomas, casting a warm glow across the bustling harbor. Ledger Philogene stood on the bustling dock, watching fisherman unload their catches of the day, the aroma of saltwater mixing with the fresh scent of the sea. But beneath the vibrant surface lay an intricate web of economic challenges that often stifled the dreams of migrants like him.

Despite his enthusiasm for his new life on the island, Ledger had come to realize that pursuing his entrepreneurial aspirations was far from straightforward. Each day brought the stark reality of economic limitations into sharper focus. As a newcomer, he was acutely aware of how access to resources was essential for starting a business, yet deeply entrenched barriers often left him feeling powerless.

The local market buzzed with seasoned vendors—many from families who had traded there for generations, often reaping the lingering advantages of colonial-era favoritism. Ledger had witnessed the dynamics up close: customers gravitated toward familiar stalls, credit flowed more freely to the well-established, and newcomers were left to navigate the system without the safety net of longstanding connections.

In his small shop, which he had set up with the modest savings he had gathered from his family's support and occasional odd jobs, Ledger often felt the pressure of competition pressing down on him. His offerings of traditional dishes inspired by his heritage competed against well-established brands, many of which had the backing of local families whose roots run deep in the cultural fabric of St. Thomas.

"You can't compete with what they have," a vendor had said to him during one of their encounters at the market, shaking his head. "They have everything—resources, connections, and customers. You must find a different angle."

Ledger had nodded, masking his frustration with a knowing smile. But the weight of those words lingered, pushing him to confront the daunting reality that his ambition faced. Finding a unique angle wanted to solve a puzzle with missing pieces, especially when the very foundation of competition rested on deeply entrenched economic disparities.

Over the next few days, Ledger explored ways to expand his offerings while grappling with questions of how to access the capital necessary to do so. A few conversations with fellow merchants at the market revealed a familiar story: many had struggled to secure loans or investments due to a lack of collateral or established credit history. He wondered how he could overcome these hurdles when his very existence felt overshadowed by the privileges of others.

As he strolled through the market, the vibrant colors of fruits, vegetables, and handcrafted goods around him painted a picture of possibilities, yet also encased the challenges that made them feel out of reach. Small, family-run businesses thrived next to stalls owned by well-connected merchants who offered items at prices he could not compete with. The thought gnawed at him, fueling a mix of frustration and determination.

One afternoon, Ledger decided to visit a local bank to inquire about a small business loan. He touched the worn wooden door of the bank building, which had stood the test of time, much like the established merchants he had seen thrive. As he entered, he was greeted by the cool air inside, a stark contrast to the sticky humidity outside. He waited patiently for his turn to speak with a loan officer, his heart racing as he planned how to articulate his vision.

When it was finally his turn, a middle-aged man greeted him with a polite smile. "How can I help you today?" he asked, flipping through a file as Ledger laid out his ambitious plans for his shop—all the ways he intended to blend his cultural heritage into a culinary experience.

As he spoke, Ledger noticed the officer's polite expression beginning to fade. The man leaned back in his chair, crossing his arms as he looked at Ledger. "Well, Mr. Philogene, you've got some great ideas here, but to obtain a loan, you'll need collateral, and frankly, your credit history isn't strong enough to warrant much trust."

Ledger felt a sinking sensation, his hopes deflating in the face of the officer's words. "But I have plans to grow my business, to contribute to the community," he pleaded, his voice rising slightly in frustration.

The officer waved a hand dismissively. "That is all well and good, but without collateral, I cannot approve anything. The reality is the market is tough; you will need a full track record of success to prove you can sustain operations.

As Ledger stepped out of the bank, frustration tightened in his chest. *"How am I supposed to prove myself if no one will take a chance on me?"* The sunlight struck his face, but he barely noticed it, his mind spinning with disappointment. He paused on the busy street, drawing a deep breath and squaring his shoulders to steady himself. Though the usual clamor of the market buzzed around him—vendors shouting, children laughing—it all felt strangely distant. The vibrant vision he held for his business dimmed beneath the weight of financial obstacles that now felt impossible to overcome.

"There has to be another way," he muttered under his breath, the determination igniting within him. He knew he could not give in to despair; he needed to think strategically. If traditional paths to capital were blocked, he could find alternative routes or creatively leverage his community connections.

As he walked along the market, ideas began to swirl in his mind. "What if I collaborated with other local vendors?" he pondered, catching sight of a nearby stall run by a woman named Rosalinda, who sold vibrant handmade crafts inspired by Caribbean culture. She had often expressed admiration for Ledger's cooking, and he wondered if there was mutual ground to explore.

"Hey, Rosalinda!" he called, approaching her stall. The sunlight danced through her colorful fabrics, illuminating her cheerful smile as she welcomed him.

"Ledger! How are you?" she replied, wiping her hands on a cloth as she stepped forward.

"I'm good, just trying to think of ways to grow my business," he admitted, his voice tinged with earnestness. "I think collaboration could be key. What if we worked together on something that highlights both our crafts—like a market event?"

Rosalinda's eyes lit up at the prospect. "You mean like a food and crafts night? Oh, I love that idea! We could invite other vendors too. The more, the merrier!"

Ledger's heart raced with excitement. This was it—an opportunity to create a community event that brought together local businesses and showcased their strengths. "Exactly! We could set up a series of evenings where people can sample local dishes and see handmade crafts at the same time. It will create a unique experience for everyone," he explained.

The idea blossomed between them as they envisioned themed nights—one dedicated to traditional island flavors and another showcasing cultural crafts from across the Caribbean. They could even incorporate storytelling sessions where vendors shared the histories behind their crafts and cuisine, creating a richer experience for attendees while drawing the community closer.

"But we'll need some support," Rosalinda interjected, her brow furrowing slightly. "Getting the word out and managing logistics will take a lot of coordination."

They spent the next hour brainstorming logistics—how to approach other vendors, promote the event on social media, and coordinate with local artists and musicians to enhance the atmosphere. As they spoke, Ledger felt the weight of his recent disappointment lifting, replaced by a renewed sense of purpose and the realization that community collaboration could amplify their chances of success in the competitive landscape.

Later that evening, Ledger sat at the small kitchen table, still buzzing from the day's discussions with Rosalinda. He took out a notebook and began to outline their ideas, jotting down payment options for vendors, potential dates, and creative ways to attract attendees. The excitement of working alongside others gave him energy, a feeling of shared investment that stoked the fire of his aspirations.

"This could work," he thought, glancing up at the fading light outside. "If we rally together and create something unique, it could draw in a crowd that values local culture and community." He began to see a blueprint for resilience, where every vendor could contribute their niche while pooling resources—a shared marketing strategy that would help them all flourish together.

He knew the process would not be straightforward; there would be challenges along the way, particularly with establishing credibility among customers and gaining genuine support from the island's residents. But he felt more motivated than ever, ready to tap into the communal spirit of St. Thomas and its rich cultural heritage.

The next day, Ledger reached out to other local vendors, buoyed by the enthusiasm Rosalinda had shared. As he met with them one by one, he found a community willing to collaborate. Faces that had once seemed solely competitors transformed into partners in vision—each vendor eager to contribute their flair and stories to the event.

With every meeting, Ledger's confidence grew. There were still many logistical hurdles ahead, from securing a venue to managing promotional efforts, but he felt the thrill of working toward a collective goal. What he had once perceived as personal limitations began to shift, morphing into opportunities for collaboration that allowed everyone to rise together.

As he returned home each evening, Ledger felt a renewed sense of hope. He had moved beyond the isolation of navigating his entrepreneurial dreams alone—he was now forging bonds that would help him break down the economic barriers that had loomed over him.

"If we take care of our own," he thought, reflecting on the importance of community, **"we can create a thriving economy that honors all our heritages and dreams."** The words resonated deeply within him as he envisioned a future where interconnectedness formed the backbone of their local economy—a tapestry woven from the diversity of their cultures and experiences.

As he prepared for the upcoming event, Ledger immersed himself in every detail, energized by the collective enthusiasm of the vendors around him. He coordinated meetings, designed promotional materials, and even created a social media campaign to generate buzz about their collaborative food and crafts night. Each step felt like a small victory, a defiance against the solitary struggles he had endured earlier.

The day of the first event arrived with a sense of anticipation tinged with nerves. Ledger arrived early at the venue, a spacious community center that reflected the colors of the island—bright blues and greens, adorned with local art hanging on the walls. He and Rosalinda had spent the previous day decorating the space, filling it with the warmth and vibrancy reminiscent of St. Thomas itself.

As vendors began to set up their stalls, Ledger could not help but feel a swell of pride for what they were creating. The air was alive with energy—laughter mixed with chatter as people prepared to showcase their crafts and culinary delights. Ledger moved from stall to stall, helping his fellow vendors arrange their displays, ensuring everything was right.

"This is amazing!" he exclaimed to Rosalinda as they surveyed the room, now filled with the aromas of freshly cooked dishes and the vibrant hues of handmade crafts. "Look at how everyone is coming together."

She smiled, her eyes sparkling with excitement. "I cannot believe we pulled this off! I feel like we are creating something special."

Soon, the doors opened, and the first guests trickled in, greeted by the enticing smells wafting through the entrance. As the evening progressed, more and more people arrived, their laughter filling the space. Ledger stood at his cooking station, ambitiously preparing a traditional dish that he hoped would spark interest—an aromatic fish stew inspired by recipes passed down through his family.

As guests began to sample the dishes, Ledger felt a newfound surge of confidence. He engaged with attendees, sharing stories behind his recipes, and inviting them to connect with his heritage. The conversations flowed effortlessly, punctuated by compliments on the food.

"This is delicious!" a woman said, her eyes lighting up after tasting a bite of the stew. "What is in this? It tastes so vibrant!"

"It's a blend of spices from St. Barthélemy mixed with some local ingredients," Ledger explained, feeling a sense of pride in his roots, eager to share his culture with others. "I'm glad you enjoy it!"

As the night wore on and the crowd continued to grow, Ledger watched in awe as attendees mingled among the stalls. Vendors exchanged smiles and stories, their fears and reservations melting away in the face of community support. The bonding over shared experiences created an atmosphere of belonging that Ledger had long been yearning for.

Behind a stall filled with colorful crafts, a group of children clamored for attention as they checked out the displays. Rosalinda took a moment to engage them, showing them how to create small crafts while smiling broadly. The laughter of the children was infectious, lifting Ledger's spirits even more.

"We've done something incredible here," Ledger thought, glancing around at the vibrant activity. With each person who tasted his dish or admired the crafts, he felt the barriers that had once seemed so daunting begin to crumble.

He caught sight of a familiar face among the crowd, the loan officer from the bank. Ledger felt a surge of determination. He was no longer merely the ambitious migrant struggling against economic limitations; he was part of a flourishing community that transcended those very barriers.

As the evening wound down, Ledger took a moment to step away from the bustle. He leaned back against a cool wall, allowing himself to absorb the sounds of joy, hope, and connection that had filled the room. Every voice, every laugh, was a reminder that they were all striving together toward a shared dream—a thriving economy rooted in mutual support and respect.

"If we can keep this momentum going," he mused silently, "we can change the narrative. We can cultivate an ecosystem where resources are shared, opportunities explored, and everyone lifts one another up."

With renewed purpose, he returned to the crowd—a smile dancing on his lips. He was part of something transformative, a movement dedicated to building a future that honored their diverse heritages while embracing the collective strength of their ambitions. This community was more than just a collection of individuals; it was a living, breathing organism based on trust and unity—a mosaic of cultural identities merging into something beautiful.

As the night concluded and attendees slowly began to leave, Ledger felt a sense of fulfillment wash over him. The event had not merely showcased their crafts and cuisine; it had forged connections and sparked a dialogue that would ripple through the community long after the last dish was served. He watched as friends exchanged phone numbers, promising to stay connected, and as families carried home bags filled with local goods, their excitement palpable.

The vendors began to pack away their unsold items as the final guests trickled out. Ledger helped Rosalinda and the others clean up, their conversations punctuated by laughter and reflections on the night.

"I can't believe how many people showed up!" Rosalinda exclaimed, her eyes shining with excitement. "We should do this again next month!"

Ledger nodded, his mind racing with ideas. "And we can invite more vendors! There are so many talented people in our community who would love to participate." He was already envisioning how they could expand the event, incorporating local musicians for entertainment or even workshops where guests could learn to cook or craft alongside the vendors.

"This momentum can't stop here," he said, galvanizing the group around him. "We need to keep this energy alive. It is about building something lasting."

As they finished tidying up, Ledger felt a sense of camaraderie, unlike anything he had experienced in his journey so far. The shared struggles had transformed into a celebration of resilience and creativity. They packed away sculptures, pots, and pans, but the spirit of the evening lingered in the air, vibrant and hopeful.

Later, as he strolled home under the blanket of stars, Ledger reflected on the shift within him. The night had proven that the barriers he faced did not have to define him or limit his ambitions. He felt empowered by the support of those around him, buoyed by the realization that he was not alone in his aspirations. Together, they could challenge the established order with their collective strength— serving as a testament to the fusion of cultures and the power of community.

Arriving at his small apartment, he opened the door and stepped inside, still riding the high from the evening's success. He made his way to the kitchen, where remnants of his fish stew still lingered in the air, an aromatic reminder of what had come to life less than an hour earlier.

Sitting at the table, he grabbed his notebook, still filled with notes from the planning sessions and ideas for future events. He flipped it open, adding fresh notes. "Next Event Ideas:" he wrote at the top of the page before jotting down his thoughts—more vendors, workshops, musicians—each bullet point sparking excitement as he envisioned the possibilities.

He paused, then added a final line: "Keep building community connections."

At that moment, Ledger realized that the path forward was not a solitary one; it was a shared journey. The fabric of his dreams intertwined with the hopes of others, demonstrating that together, they could create economic opportunities that would uplift them all.

With a sense of gratitude filling his heart, Ledger placed the notebook down and stepped to the window, looking out at the shimmering lights of the harbor. The water glistened under the moonlight, a representation of the flow that had begun to infuse his life with vibrant possibilities.

As he settled into bed, Ledger let the sense of hope wash over him, the belief that he could play a role in shaping a brighter future for himself and his community. "Tomorrow is a new day," he thought, closing his eyes with a smile. "And with it, more opportunities to create—together."

The afternoon sun poured through the open window of Ledger's small apartment, casting a warm glow over the modest living room. Ledger sat at the table, a stack of papers strewn in front of him, his brow furrowed in concentration. The aroma of home-cooked food wafted in from the kitchen, where his mother, Clarissa, prepared dinner, her movements filled with the rhythm of familiarity.

"Are you sure about this, Ledger?" Clara's voice broke the silence, as she leaned against the doorway, arms crossed. She had that look, the one that conveyed both support and concern.

Ledger's gaze lingered on the papers before him, filled with scratch notes and the layout of his business plan. "I must try, Clara. I cannot keep holding back. If I want to grow my shop, I need capital to invest in more inventory—and even to expand the menu."

"I understand that, but banks can be tricky. You know they want guarantees, collateral. They might not see the potential in what you are trying to build," she replied, stepping further into the room, the warmth of her presence grounding him.

He sighed, running a hand through his hair, frustration creeping in. "That is just it! How can I show them my potential when I do not have the resources to prove it? It feels like I am trapped in this cycle."

Clarissa entered the room, wiping her hands on a towel and setting a dish of stewed vegetables down on the table. She glanced between her son and Clara, sensing the tension in the air. "What's this about the bank?" she asked, concern creasing her brow.

"I'm thinking of applying for a loan to help expand the shop," Ledger replied, his voice steady but filled with underlying anxiety. "But I am worried about getting approved. What if they turn me down?"

Clarissa moved closer, placing a comforting hand on his shoulder. "Ledger, you are brave for wanting to take that step. But you must go in prepared. Have you thought about how you will present your proposal and what you need to ask for?"

"I've been drafting a plan," he admitted, revealing the papers slightly, "but the idea of sitting in front of a banker just... I do not know. What if I am not persuasive enough? Or worse, what if they laugh in my face?"

Clara stepped forward, her expression firm. "That is not going to happen. You have a vision; you have worked hard. You just must talk about your plans confidently. Tell them about the community events you want to start, and how you want your shop to be a part of St. Thomas's culture. Show them that it is more than making money."

Ledger nodded slowly, soaking in her words. "It's about connecting with people," he murmured, feeling the weight of her encouragement. "But the economic limitations here… it is all so daunting. The established businesses have the upper hand."

Clarissa chimed in, her voice was soft yet firm, "You cannot let that deter you, mom chéri. Many successful businesses started with little more than a dream and hard work. If you believe in yourself and your vision, others will be able to see it too."

Her words fueled a flicker of determination within him. "But what if I do not have enough collateral? What if they need references I just cannot provide?"

"That's why you need to highlight what you do have," Clara encouraged. "Talk about community support, your unique background, the culinary experiences you bring to the table. They might not be able to ignore someone passionate and committed."

As he looked at the papers again, Ledger felt the fear begin to ebb, replaced by a renewed sense of hope. "I'll focus on the strength of my vision, the connections I've already built," he said, the words crystallizing into resolve. "If I can show them that I have a plan, maybe they'll take me seriously."

Clara smiled, her body language relaxing. "That is the spirit! And remember, you are not alone in this. We are all rooting for you."

Clarissa leaned in to give Ledger a reassuring hug, warmth wrapping around him like a comforting quilt. "Just be honest and passionate. You have so much to offer, and you should not be afraid to ask for what you need."

They gathered around the table, Ledger feeling a wave of nurturing energy from both Clara and Clarissa as they flipped through his notes together, brainstorming ways to present his shop's vision. The cozy atmosphere filled with the scents of dinner and the gentle sounds of their encouragement pushed away the lingering doubts.

"So, are you ready to give it a shot?" Clara asked, her eyes sparkling with confidence.

With a deep breath, Ledger nodded. "Yeah. I am ready. I will go to the bank tomorrow."

A sense of purpose took root in him, reinvigorated by their unwavering support. He had a plan, a family who believed in him, and a fierce determination to overcome the economic limitations that had once seemed so daunting.

As they gathered around the table, Ledger found himself leaning into the moment, fueled by the collective strength of his family's support. The atmosphere was filled with the comforting sounds of familial chatter and the clatter of cutlery as they began to serve dinner. Clarissa placed a hearty portion of rice and beans on each plate, the steam rising fragrant and inviting.

"Before we dig in, let's toast to new beginnings," Ledger suggested, lifting his glass of sweetened iced tea, his earlier doubts muted by the warmth enveloping him. Clara and Clarissa raised their glasses, their smiles bright and encouraging.

"To new beginnings!" they chorused, their voices melded into one harmonious note that stirred something powerful within Ledger.

As they settled back to their meals, Ledger could not shake the feeling of possibility that buzzed in the air. With each bite, he felt stronger, picturing the bank meeting ahead, the firm but hopeful words he would present. "You know," he said, breaking the comfortable silence, "this is more than just getting a loan; it is about taking control of my future. It is about using what I have learned from both of you and sharing my culture with the community."

Clarissa nodded, her eyes reflecting pride. "That is the spirit, my son. And remember it is not just about the monetary support; it is about the validation that you can succeed despite the odds.

Clara added, "Even if things do not go as planned with the bank, you will know you have tried, and that is worth its weight in gold. You are building something that matters, not just for yourself, but for others too."

The conversation flowed effortlessly after that, weaving through stories of past family struggles and triumphs that had molded them into who they were today. Clarissa shared tales of her early days as an immigrant, her journey marked with countless obstacles against which she had fought tirelessly to establish a life for her family.

"I once stood in line at government offices, hoping for any kind of assistance," she recounted, her voice tinged with nostalgia. "But those hardships taught me resilience. They showed me that every setback is just a setup for a comeback."

The strength conveyed in her tone stirred something deep within Ledger. "I never thought of it that way," he mused, absorbing her words. "Maybe this isn't just about me trying to get a loan; maybe it's about setting an example for others who are following in my footsteps."

Clara, full of enthusiasm, leaned in. "Absolutely! You are not just navigating this for yourself. You are paving the way for future generations, not just in our family but for others in this community. It is about embracing our roots while building a new legacy."

Inspired by their discussions, Ledger recalled conversations he had had with other vendors at the market. He knew many of them faced barriers like his. "What if I could organize workshops for other aspiring entrepreneurs, and share what I learn about the business side of things? I could help them navigate these same challenges!"

"That's a fantastic idea," Clara said, her eyes lighting up. "If more people can start their own businesses, we can create a ripple effect. You would be contributing to a thriving local economy."

Clarissa chimed in, "And you would be further strengthening our cultural community around food and craftsmanship. Just look at how vibrant our gathering was with the vendors last week.

Both women nodded in agreement, and Ledger felt a renewed sense of determination bloom within him. "I'll present that tomorrow too—that if they back me, I can help lift others up as well."

With the dinner ending, they transitioned to desserts. Clarissa's signature coconut tart arrived at the table, its sweet scent wrapping around them like a familiar hug. As they enjoyed the delicious treat, the room filled with laughter, stories, and a sense of belonging that fueled Ledger's hope.

Finishing the last bites, he felt an overwhelming sense of gratitude for the support system surrounding him. The fear that had shadowed him earlier in the day began to dissolve. "Thank you both for believing in me," he said earnestly, looking from Clara to Clarissa. "I couldn't have come this far without you."

"We believe in you because you're worthy of belief," Clara replied softly, her sincerity warming his heart.

As they cleaned up together, Ledger had a profound sense of purpose. "No matter what happens tomorrow, I'm ready," he thought, glancing at his family as they laughed together, sharing stories that passed seamlessly from one to the next. "I am ready to make my mark, to honor our past while daring to dream for the future."

Tomorrow there will be a new chapter in his journey. Ledger finished tidying up the remnants of dinner before heading to his bedroom, the gentle echoes of laughter still resonant in his ears. He lay in bed that night, staring up at the ceiling, mentally rehearsing his presentation for the bank.

"Focus on the vision, Ledger," he whispered to himself, feeling a mix of excitement and anxiety. He envisioned his shop, bustling with customers savoring his dishes, surrounded by a community thriving on cultural exchanges and mutual support. He thought of all the stories he wanted to share, how each dish represented not just a meal but a part of his identity.

Finally, sleep began to claim him, a blend of anticipation and optimism swirling within his mind. Just as he drifted off, he resolved to embrace the day's challenges head-on—regardless of what the bank decision would be, he would stand firm in his beliefs and dreams.

The next morning dawned bright and warm, the sun casting cheery golden rays into his apartment. Ledger woke early, enthusiasm coursing through him as he prepared for the day ahead. He dressed carefully, opting for a crisp white shirt and dark jeans, wanting to make a good impression. His reflection in the mirror showed a young man filled with a new determination and purpose.

A few days later, as Ledger made his way back to the bank, a bubbling mix of excitement and apprehension surged inside him. The vibrant streets of St. Thomas were alive with energy; vendors were already setting up their colorful stalls, and the enticing aroma of freshly baked bread filled the air. Each friendly wave and smile from passersby reinforced his determination. *"This is my community,"* he thought, feeling a deep sense of belonging wash over him. *"I want to contribute to our cultural tapestry."*

Upon arriving at the bank, he paused outside briefly, taking a deep breath to calm his racing heart. The ambient sounds within—murmured conversations, the rustle of papers, and the rhythmic click of keyboards—created a familiar atmosphere. *"You've got this, Ledger,"* he whispered to himself, steeling his resolve before pulling open the door and stepping inside.

The bank's interior greeted him with warm light reflecting off polished wood furniture and soft carpeting. The receptionist welcomed him with a polite smile, gesturing for him to take a seat. As he settled into the chair, a flutter of nerves danced in his stomach. He gripped the meticulously prepared papers in his hands, ready to convey all he had practiced with Clara and Clarissa.

Minutes felt like hours as he waited, his mind racing with outcomes. Just when doubt began to creep in, the loan officer finally emerged, a more familiar face this time. "Mr. Philogene?" he called, waving Ledger over with a welcoming nod.

Ledger rose, smoothing his shirt and taking a deep breath before approaching the desk. "Hello," he replied, his voice steady despite the adrenaline bubbling inside him. "Thank you for meeting with me."

The officer gestured for him to sit, his expression warm but professional. "Of course. I wanted to talk with you about the recent event I attended," he began, a spark of recognition lighting his features. "Your vision for the culinary shop truly resonated with me. The atmosphere was vibrant, and I could see the sense of community you described."

Ledger's heart raced with hope as he realized the impact the event had had had made. "I appreciate that you could attend," he said, eager to hear more.

The officer continued, "Witnessing the connections you fostered at that gathering solidified my belief in your project. After reviewing your application and considering what I saw, I am willing to proceed without requiring collateral.

Shock and relief washed over Ledger. "Really?" he asked, his voice scarcely above a whisper.

"Yes," the officer confirmed, nodding kindly. "You've made a compelling case, not just on paper but in person as well. I believe in your commitment to creating a positive impact."

A smile spread across Ledger's face as the weight of anxiety began to lift. "Thank you so much! This means the world to me," he exclaimed, barely able to contain his exhilaration.

As the officer continued, they discussed the steps forward, the barriers of doubt crumbling under Ledger's renewed determination. What had begun as a nervous pitch evolved into a collaborative dialogue, weaving the foundation for potential approval.

By the time they wrapped up the meeting, Ledger was overflowing with a sense of accomplishment. The path ahead still held challenges, but for the first time, he felt that he was moving toward the future he envisioned, his dreams no longer mere whispers in the wind. As he gathered his papers, the officer offered an encouraging smile.

"I will be in touch soon, Mr. Philogene. We are excited to help you get started," he said with genuine enthusiasm.

"Thank you for your trust and support," Ledger replied, a grateful smile breaking across his face. The surge of energy coursing through him was palpable, a renewed sense of possibility pulsing in his veins.

Stepping out of the bank, the hustle and bustle of St. Thomas enveloped him like a warm blanket. He paused on the steps, inhaling deeply the rich aromas of the island, the warm bread from nearby vendors, and the sweet, salty breeze rolling in from the sea. It was as if the world were alive with vibrant colors, each hue a reminder of the community he sought to uplift.

"I'm doing this for us," he thought, picturing the faces of the people he hoped to inspire. His resolve solidified further; it was about more than just his shop. It was about creating opportunities, breaking cycles of exploitation, and redefining what success meant in his community.

As he walked through the streets, Ledger noticed people animatedly chatting, sharing laughter and stories. Their joy lifted his spirit even higher families gathering, vendors showcasing their goods, and children playing freely. *"This is the tapestry of life I'm part of,"* he reflected, his heart swelling with pride at the thought. With every step, confidence flourished within him. He envisioned the shop he wanted to build, a vibrant space buzzing with energy and creativity, where locals would come together to share their culinary heritage. He imagined hosting workshops that would empower others with the knowledge and skills they needed to pursue their own dreams while fostering a sense of community interconnectedness.

Lost in these thoughts, he barely noticed the familiar figure waving to him from across the street until Clara's voice rang out. "Ledger!" she called, her arms waving excitedly as she made her way toward him.

A buoyant smile crept onto his face as he approached her. "It went wonderfully! The loan officer attended the event, and after seeing everything in action, he is on board," Ledger said, his eyes sparkling with anticipation.

"That is amazing! I knew you could do it!" Clara replied, her face lighting up with excitement. She reached out to hug him tightly, and he felt a surge of warmth and support feeding his resolve.

"Not only that, but he said he could move forward with my application without needing collateral. I cannot believe it!" The relief in his voice was palpable, a weight slowly lifting off his shoulders.

"This is incredible news, Ledger! Just imagine what you will create. This community is starving for spaces like yours—where culture can thrive and be celebrated," Clara enthused, her eyes twinkling with shared dreams.

He nodded fervently, a vision blooming in his mind. "Speaking of cultural celebration, I want to host events in the shop—culinary nights showcasing local talent and flavors. We could involve other vendors too! It could become a gathering spot for everyone."

Clara's jaw dropped in delight. "That is a fantastic idea! You will create a vibrant hub for everyone to come together. We need to involve more people—let us plan market days, workshops... the possibilities are endless!"

As Clara and Ledger brainstormed ideas, a sense of energy surrounded them, igniting their passion and excitement. The sun hung low in the sky, casting a golden hue over the town, accentuating the atmosphere of newfound beginnings.

For the first time in his life, Ledger felt empowered not just by the promise of financial support, but also by the realization that he was no longer just a passive recipient of his family's legacy. Instead, he was stepping boldly into his own narrative, determined to create meaningful change in a world shaped by the complexities of history and culture.

With Clara by his side, the future now shimmered before him—a vibrant tapestry of endless possibilities, ready to be woven into reality. Each step he took was no longer heavy with the weight of inherited guilt but buoyed by hope, determination, and the unwavering support of those who believed in his vision.

In the weeks that followed his successful meeting at the bank, Ledger felt an energetic shift in his life. With the approval of his loan looming closer, he realized that while his culinary shop was a crucial part of his vision, so too was the community he aimed to foster around it. Inspired by this, Ledger increasingly sought out connections with other migrants in St. Thomas, eager to build a network of support and collaboration.

The local community center served as a vibrant hub for various migrant groups, bustling with life and stories waiting to be shared. Ledger arrived one sunny afternoon, the warm breeze rustling through the palm trees and inviting him into space alive with animated chatter and laughter. As he entered, the comforting scent of spices and simmering pots wafted from the kitchen, beckoning him toward a room filled with enticing aromas.

He began to scan the room, his eyes landing on a cluster of people gathered around a long table, each engaged in a lively discussion. Creating connections had always felt daunting, but Ledger took a deep breath and approached the group.

"Hello, everyone! I am Ledger Philogene," he introduced himself, his voice steady despite the flutter of nerves in his stomach. "I'm in the process of opening a culinary shop to celebrate our local culture."

The group turned to him, curiosity piqued. A woman with bright eyes and a warm smile stepped forward. "I am Maria, and I manage a small bakery in the market. It is great to meet you, Ledger!" She gestured for him to join them, and he felt immediate warmth radiating from the group.

As they began to share their stories, Ledger discovered that many of them had embarked on similar journeys—each looking to create new lives in a land of opportunity while grappling with the challenges brought on by their pasts. He listened intently as Maria spoke about her struggles and triumphs, her resilience mirroring his own aspirations.

"Starting from scratch is daunting, isn't it?" Maria said, her voice tinged with nostalgia. "But we have each other to lean on, and together, we can thrive."

From that moment, a sense of camaraderie blossomed among them. As the afternoon went on, they exchanged ideas about sourcing local ingredients, collaborated on recipes, and discussed ways to market their unique culinary offerings. Each person brought something valuable to the table—knowledge of traditional techniques, insights into customer preferences, and the collective strength to navigate the complexities of their new surroundings.

Throughout the following weeks, Ledger found himself returning to the community center often. There, he connected with artisans, farmers, and fellow culinary enthusiasts, each encounter solidifying the foundation of a robust support system. He formed partnerships with Maria and others, planning shared events to showcase their diverse culinary backgrounds. They discussed the possibility of hosting a cultural fair at Ledger's future shop, where guests could experience a taste of various dishes from their homelands, creating a tapestry of flavors and stories.

One evening, as Ledger and a few others gathered to discuss the impending event, they shared laughter and dreams. "Imagine the joy on people's faces when they taste a dish from their homeland!" Maria exclaimed, her enthusiasm contagious.

"We can create a space where everyone feels at home, even in a new place," Ledger added, his voice brimming with excitement. Ideas flowed freely; each suggestion was met with encouragement and build-up, igniting a fire of creativity among them.

The event not only promised to showcase their culinary talents but also represented a union of their journeys—not just as individuals, but as a community working together toward a common goal. They spoke of their hopes, of breaking down barriers and uniting through food, laughter, and shared experiences.

As the weeks progressed and the fair drew closer, Ledger felt a sense of belonging that had once seemed elusive. The connections he cultivated not only supported his entrepreneurial aspirations but also nurtured the bonds of friendship and solidarity among the group. No longer were they merely fellow migrants; they were a collaborative force, united in their mission to carve out a new existence that honored their past while looking toward a hopeful future.

Through these relationships, Ledger came to realize that success was not solely defined by the success of his own business—it lay in the strength of the community he fostered, in the resilience they built together, and in the new lives they all sought to create amidst the challenges that lay ahead. He envisioned a culinary shop that would not only serve delicious food but also become a hub of connection, empowerment, and culture—a place where every flavor had a story, and every story celebrated the vibrant fabric of their shared experiences.

That Saturday, Ledger stood at the community center, his heart racing with excitement. The group had agreed to host an informal gathering aimed at strengthening their connections and discussing potential collaborations. As he set up tables and chairs, he looked around at the vibrant decorations that adorned the walls—colorful fabrics representing the diverse cultures of the attendees. The atmosphere was charged with anticipation.

He was grateful for the support of his friends, Maria, and Prudina, who helped him prepare for this event. They had worked tirelessly to spread the word, ensuring that everyone felt welcomed and encouraged to share their experiences. The smell of fresh pastries filled the room, courtesy of Maria's famous baked goods.

"You've really outdone yourself with these," Ledger said, glancing at the assortment of treats. "I can already tell they'll be a hit!"

"Just wait until they taste the guava tarts," Maria replied with a proud smile, as she arranged the pastries on a table. "I think they'll sell like hotcakes!"

As guests began to trickle in, Ledger greeted each person with enthusiasm. Familiar faces began mingling with new ones, and he felt a palpable sense of camaraderie as the room filled with laughter and chatter. It was the perfect setting for forging connections.

"Hey Ledger, how's the shop planning going?" Prudina asked, her eyes sparkling with curiosity as she joined him at the registration table.

"It is coming along! I am just trying to figure out how to combine everyone's talents and make something that represents us all," he replied, excitement evident in his voice. "Today's gathering is a step in that direction."

More and more attendees arrived, and soon, the room vibrated with energy. After a brief welcome speech, Ledger invited everyone to share their stories about food, culture, and their dreams for the future. He noticed how these tales sparked a sense of connection among the group. As each person spoke, their passion for their heritage and culinary traditions permeated the air.

One participant, a woman named Amara, shared her journey of creating spices from her homeland, a process that had been passed down through generations. "I want to introduce these flavors to the community," she said, her voice steady but emotional. "They deserve to be celebrated and enjoyed."

Another participant, a young man named Bruce, who had recently started growing his own vegetables, spoke about his aspirations to provide fresh produce to local restaurants. "I know how hard it is to get good ingredients, especially if you're on a budget," he shared, gesturing to everyone in the room. "That's why I want to help everyone gain access to affordable, quality food."

Ledger felt his heart swell with pride at the way stories intertwined, creating a rich tapestry of shared purpose. Each narrative echoed his own, highlighting the struggles and triumphs of those who sought to carve out a place for themselves in this new environment.

"What if," Ledger interrupted gently, "we could create a space together? A market that showcases all our skills and products, where we could support one another?"

The room fell silent for a moment and then bursts of conversation filled the air as people began to consider the idea. Views clashed, but with each opinion voiced, optimism grew. Slowly, reactions turned from uncertainty to excitement, as people began to envision the possibilities together.

"I love the sound of that," Maria agreed, bobbing her head. "It would be like a family reunion, but with food!"

Bruce added, "We could design cooking demonstrations and teach each other recipes. It would be awesome to show what we can do with these amazing ingredients.

As discussions flourished, Ledger saw sparks of inspiration igniting among the group. People began brainstorming ideas for a potential gathering where food could be intertwined, celebrating culinary heritage while uplifting each other.

"Maybe we can set a date for a community culinary fair!" Amara suggested, her eyes bright with enthusiasm.

What started as a simple gathering was blossoming into something far more impactful. Ledger smiled, buoyed by the energy in the room. As laughter and chatter echoed off the walls, he knew this event was more than just another meeting; it was the birth of a movement.

As the evening ended, Ledger thanked everyone for their participation and vulnerability. "Together, we can really make a difference. Let us keep this momentum going, and turn our dreams into reality," he encouraged, his voice filled with determination.

When the last guests left, and the laughter faded into the twilight, Ledger felt a sense of fulfillment wash over him. He and his friends began the process of cleaning up, sharing their hopes for what lay ahead.

As Ledger's network of connections among fellow migrants flourished, so too did his ambitions. Inspired by the vibrant culinary exchanges and the shared stories of resilience, he began to contemplate exploring new avenues for trade within the Caribbean market. The more he engaged with local food producers and vendors, the more he recognized the untapped potential that lay within the region's commodities, particularly tropical fruits and spices that thrived in the lush Caribbean climate.

One sun-drenched morning, Ledger set out to visit a local market. He had heard raving reviews about a vendor known for his exquisite selection of tropical produce. As he wandered through the bustling stalls, the air was alive with the fragrance of ripe fruits and aromatic spices. Vendors called out to passersby, their lively banter mingling with the sounds of laughter and conversation. It was a scene that invigorated him, and he felt inspired to immerse himself deeper in this world.

Approaching a stall brimming with vibrant mangoes, pineapples, and bananas, Ledger struck up a conversation with the vendor, an elderly man with a weathered but kind face. "These fruits are beautiful! Where do you get them?" Ledger asked, admiring the luscious produce.

"All from local farms!" the vendor replied with a smile, his pride evident. "We source everything fresh each morning. It is the best way to ensure quality while supporting our local economy."

The vendor's words resonated with Ledger, and he felt a surge of ideas taking shape in his mind. He imagined sourcing these fruits not only for his culinary shop but also for potentially establishing a venture that could bridge local agriculture with broader markets. "Have you ever thought about expanding your distribution?" Ledger inquired, curiosity was driving him forward.

The vendor chuckled, shaking his head. "It can be a complex, young man. The market is competitive, and the logistics are tough. But if you have the passion and drive, anything is possible."

Deeply inspired, Ledger thanked the vendor and continued his exploration of the market. He was captivated by the variety of produce on display—exotic fruits, fragrant spices, and artisanal goods. Each stall represented a story, an opportunity to connect with the richness of Caribbean heritage.

As he walked, Ledger began to sketch out ideas in his mind, considering how he could create a business model that both supported his family and elevated local producers. He envisioned launching a trade enterprise that would not merely serve his own needs but foster collaboration among local farmers, creating a network where they could collectively flourish. This venture would enable him to showcase the best of Caribbean agriculture while also championing the importance of sustainability.

What if he could secure direct contracts with farmers to source their goods and supply them to local restaurants or even export them to international markets? The thought excited him, and each bold idea sparked another. He pictured a business that encompassed not just the culinary shop, but also an agricultural trade platform that would empower others while strengthening the local economy.

Returning home that afternoon, Ledger sat at his kitchen table, the sunlight streaming through the window, illuminating the notepad in front of him. He began jotting down thoughts furious ideas for a business plan, potential partnerships with local farmers, and strategies for marketing Caribbean produce. He felt invigorated by the prospect of establishing a venture that would not just support his family but also lend a hand to the community.

"What if I host workshops for local farmers on best practices for sustainable farming and marketing?" he pondered aloud, envisioning a cycle of education that could uplift those around him. He realized that this would not only enhance the quality of the produce but also empower farmers to thrive in the competitive market.

Over the next few weeks, Ledger continued to explore these ideas, reaching out to fellow migrants and locals alike. He gathered information about trade regulations, potential buyers, and best practices in sourcing and distribution. Each conversation further fueled his ambition, unveiling opportunities he had never considered.

The more he delved into the world of trade, the more convinced he became that the path he was envisioning could be viable. He could create a business that fused his passion for culinary arts with a commitment to supporting local agriculture, crafting a model that demonstrated how commerce and community could converge.

As he continued to develop his concepts, Ledger's aspirations began to crystallize into a clear vision—an enterprise that would celebrate the richness of Caribbean culture and contribute to the economic vitality of his community. The thought of all he could achieve, not just for himself but for those around him, ignited an unwavering passion within him.

His dreams of culinary excellence were no longer singular; they had expanded to include the vibrant ecosystem of trade and agriculture that surrounded him. With each step forward, Ledger felt himself becoming not just a creator of culinary delights, but also a catalyst for change in the Caribbean, a force committed to uplifting his community and fostering resilience among local farmers and artisans. He envisioned a network of collaboration where farmers could thrive, consumers could access fresh and flavorful produce, and the rich tapestry of Caribbean culture could be showcased and celebrated. Each conversation he had with other migrants and local stakeholders deepened his understanding of the interconnectedness of their struggles and aspirations.

With his sights set on marrying culinary creativity with agricultural sustainability, Ledger began to develop plans for a community initiative—a farmers' market that would serve as a platform for local producers to sell their goods directly to the public. He imagined vibrant stalls brimming with tropical fruits, colorful vegetables, and fragrant spices, all accompanied by cooking demonstrations that showcased how to utilize these ingredients in delicious, culturally relevant dishes.

In his mind, this market would not just be a venue for selling food; it would be a hub for sharing knowledge, culture, and community spirit. Workshops could teach residents about nutrition, cooking techniques, and the benefits of supporting local agriculture. The relationships forged through this initiative would strengthen the bonds among community members, empowering them to take pride in their heritage while embracing new opportunities.

As Ledger contemplated the future, he felt an electrifying blend of purpose and excitement. This was not merely about profit; it was about creating a legacy that enriched the lives of those around him. He pictured himself standing at the market, surrounded by vibrant produce, laughter, and the chatter of families celebrating food in its purest form. He envisioned the buzz of activity, the sounds of music playing in the background, children running joyfully, and the aromas wafting through the air as satisfied customers sampled fresh fruits and dishes inspired by their diverse heritages.

He knew that such an initiative would require dedication, hard work, and the cooperation of many in the community, but Ledger was undeterred. The connections he had made with fellow migrants and local producers were already paving the way for collaboration, and he felt the weight of responsibility transform into motivation. With each passing day, he became increasingly determined to cultivate a space where everyone could participate in elevating Caribbean produce, emphasizing not only the importance of fresh ingredients but also the rich cultural narratives behind them.

And so, driven by this newfound sense of purpose, Ledger began reaching out to local farmers, chefs, and members of the community. He organized informal gatherings to discuss his vision, eager to gather input and inspire collective action. Ledger shared his hopes and dreams, listening intently as others expressed their own ideas and aspirations. It became clear to him that this journey was one of co-creation, where their voices mattered in shaping a future that reflected their shared experiences and dreams.

With each collaboration and conversation reaffirming his resolve, Ledger felt a surge of optimism. His dreams were no longer just lofty ideals; they were becoming tangible goals grounded in community and collaboration. He realized that, through this venture, he was not just seeking to build a business; he was igniting a movement—one that would redefine success in the Caribbean as not simply striving for individual gain but aspiring for collective prosperity.

A few days later, Ledger sat at his modest dining table, surrounded by a whirlwind of notes, sketches, and a local map that sprawled across the surface. The sun filtered through the window, casting a warm glow on the papers as he traced potential routes to connect with local farmers and producers. His mind buzzed with ideas—ideas that could expand into something substantial if nurtured with care.

With a coffee in hand, he picked up his phone and dialed Maria. He could hardly contain his excitement as the phone rang. When she answered, her cheerful voice filled him with motivation.

"Hey, Ledger! Checking in on your plans?" she asked, clearly able to sense the enthusiasm in his tone.

"Absolutely! I have been doing some research on local farms, and I think we could start with a few key producers for our market," Ledger replied, his voice steady with resolve. "If we can establish direct relationships with them, it would not only provide us with fresh ingredients but also foster a sense of community."

"That sounds fantastic! I know a couple of farmers at the Saturday market who might be interested in collaborating." Maria's voice brimmed with excitement. "Let's go visit them together this weekend."

Ledger felt a thrill at the thought of taking that next step. "Perfect! I will prepare a proposal outlining how this market can help tap into their potential while ensuring a steady income stream for them."

They discussed details about the farmers they could approach, exchanging names and experiences. After hanging up, Ledger felt invigorated. It was time to bring his ideas to life, to transition from contemplation to action.

The following Saturday, the vibrant market was bustling as usual, filled with locals browsing the myriad of stalls. The lively atmosphere was intoxicating. As Ledger and Maria made their way through the crowd, Ledger felt energy surging within him. This was the pulse of the community, an embodiment of what he aimed to cultivate—a dynamic network in support of local producers.

After perusing some of the stalls and greeting familiar faces, they arrived at a small booth adorned with fresh vegetables and herbs. The vendor, a stout man with laughter lines etched across his face, looked up and offered them a warm smile.

"Ah, Ledger! Maria! Good to see you both," he greeted, extending his hand. "What brings you to my humble stall today?"

"We're hoping to discuss potential collaborations." Ledger's voice was confident as he shared his vision of the Caribbean Culinary Celebration and the opportunity for local farmers to showcase their produce directly while receiving fair compensation.

"You know, I've been thinking about these connections ourselves," the vendor replied, nodding thoughtfully. "There has been talk about establishing a more local network, but it has not taken off. Your idea could be just the catalyst we need!"

Encouraged, Ledger continued to explain his plan, emphasizing how the market would benefit not only the vendors but also strengthen community ties. He shared stories from other attendees at the community center gathering, highlighting the importance of cultural pride and local food.

As Ledger spoke, the vendor's expression transformed from curiosity to earnest interest. He began nodding along, envisioning the possibilities that Ledger was laying out before them. "This could really meet a need in the community while celebrating our heritage. I would love to be a part of it."

Once they wrapped up their conversation and exchanged contact information, Ledger felt a surge of hope. They shared the number of other farmers they needed to contact, and as they walked away, Maria looked at him, her eyes brightening. "You saw the impact that had on him, right? This could be the start of something special!"

"I can feel it," Ledger replied, the weight of possibilities settling comfortably on his shoulders. They continued to wander the market, his mind racing with new ideas and potential partnerships.

They eventually approached another stall, run by a young woman selling tropical fruits. After a brief introduction, Ledger laid out his proposal once more. This time, the woman's enthusiasm matched his own.

"I have always wanted to connect more with my community through food. Count me in!" she exclaimed, her voice brimming with excitement.

With each conversation, Ledger witnessed his vision gaining momentum. Each vendor they spoke to add another layer to the collaborative network he imagined. By the time their market tour concluded, he felt vibrant energy in the air, a palpable sense of hope and shared purpose.

As they headed home, Ledger glanced at Maria, whose smile mirrored his own. "We did good today," he said, exhilarated by their progress.

"This is just the beginning," Maria replied, her spirited enthusiasm infectious. "You're not just building a business, Ledger; you're creating a movement."

Her words hung in the air like a promise, and Ledger felt a swell of hope and determination surge within him. He turned to her, a smile breaking across his face.

"A movement," he echoed, the term resonating with him in a way he had not anticipated. "I like the sound of that."

As they walked along the lively street, Ledger envisioned the butterflies that danced among the blooms nearby, drawing nectar from local flowers. He felt invigorated—each connection he made was like a seed sown, ready to blossom into a supportive network that would not only push his culinary dreams forward but also empower others to share their stories, flavors, and heritage.

As they walked, Maria continued to share her excitement. "Imagine the impact we could have! Families supporting families, collaborating instead of competing… It is just so powerful!"

He nodded, already picturing a vibrant market brimming with fresh produce, delicious food, and laughter—a celebration of their rich culture and shared experiences. Ledger could see the joy on people's faces, reveling in the authenticity of the ingredients and recipes they represented.

"We need to start reaching out to the others, too," he said, his voice filled with urgency. "The more we can get involved now, the more momentum we'll build."

Maria agreed, and as they brainstormed who to approach next, Ledger's mind began to contemplate the larger vision: combining trades, art, and music into a cohesive experience that honored their Caribbean heritage. They were moving beyond just food; they were crafting an entire experience that would resonate deeply with the community.

"What about inviting local musicians to perform?" Maria suggested enthusiastically. "We could integrate music and dance, even have cooking demonstrations alongside the performances! It would create a lively atmosphere that people would want to come back to."

Ledger nodded vigorously. "Yes! It could become a festival, a true celebration of what we represent as a community. We can showcase our artists and talents and give them a platform to shine."

Fueled by their conversations, they decided to make an impromptu stop at a local café known for its cozy ambiance and community vibe. As they settled into a corner booth with their drinks, Ledger pulled out his notepad, scribbling down ideas furiously.

"We should come up with a rough schedule for the event," he suggested, his pen flying across the page. "We can theme different days around various culinary traditions, maybe one day focused on seafood, another on fruits, and so forth."

Meanwhile, the café around them buzzed with local patrons, chatting and sharing stories, embodying the same spirit they sought to cultivate. Ledger paused, soaking in the atmosphere. He thought about how vital it was to center the event around interaction and connection, providing a space for people to engage with each other, share food, and build relationships.

"And we can add cooking workshops where people can learn how to cook traditional dishes from their cultures," Maria added, brainstorming alongside him. "They'll walk away not just with a full stomach but new skills and memories, too."

They continued to refine their ideas at the café, envisioning every aspect of the event—how to approach local businesses for sponsorship, engaging local schools, and utilizing social media to bring out a crowd. The excitement between them blazed like a warm summer sun, and as they jotted down ideas, Ledger looked out the window and saw the vibrant life outside—the laughter of children playing, the warmth of neighbors greeting each other, and the sense of community thriving.

"This is more than just a market," Ledger said, his voice filled with conviction. "It's about creating lasting relationships, supporting each other, and redefining what success looks like in our community."

The afternoon sun began to set, casting a golden glow through the windows of the café, as he savored this moment of clarity; he felt certain they were onto something monumental. Here they were, two-spirited individuals on a mission to illuminate the rich tapestry of their culture, nurturing not only their dreams but also those of everyone around them.

"Together, we can change the narrative," Maria said softly, her eyes alight with excitement as she gave Ledger a reassuring pat on the hand.

"Let's start planting the seeds, then," Ledger grinned, ready to embark on the journey ahead, a journey of empowerment, celebration, and community that would blossom into something remarkable.

The sun rose over St. Thomas, casting a golden hue that danced on the turquoise waters. Ledger stood on the balcony of his small apartment, listening to the gentle rustle of palm fronds swaying in the breeze. Each morning brought him a renewed sense of purpose, a reminder that he was carving out a new life for himself and his loved ones. But as the days turned into weeks, another thought began to take root in his mind—a desire for permanence, a place to call home.

As he sipped his morning coffee, Ledger reflected on the changes that had unfolded since moving to the island. The vibrant community he was building, the friendships he was cultivating, and the culinary ventures blossoming around him filled him with hope. Yet, a nagging thought lingered in the back of his mind: the desire to create a solid foundation for his extended family.

His thoughts turned to his parents, his wife Clara, and their nine children, as well as his siblings, younger cousins, aunts, and uncles, each one of them having faced long struggles and heartaches. They had supported one another through difficult times, united by dreams of a brighter, more stable future. Ledger felt a deep sense of love and responsibility for his entire family. He envisioned them all together in a warm, welcoming home, filled with laughter, cooking, and shared stories—an anchor amidst the rapid changes and challenges of life.

"A home," he whispered to himself, envisioning a place where everyone could thrive, free from the burdens of their past—a place where his younger cousins could find educational opportunities, where his mother could rest and feel secure, and where they could all gather for joyous celebrations.

Determined to explore this vision, Ledger reached for his notebook and jotted down thoughts and ideas. He began sketching plans for a cozy family home that would be large enough to accommodate everyone but still manageable and rooted in the community he loved. A garden in the backyard to grow the herbs and vegetables he cherished from his childhood, a kitchen that welcomed everyone to cook together, and a living room where laughter would resonate high above the waves outside.

He envisioned creating a space that embraced their heritage, highlighting Caribbean culture with vibrant colors and art created by local artists. The style would reflect their history—open spaces that allowed the sea breeze to flow freely, large windows that offered breathtaking views, and comfortable nooks for storytelling and shared moments.

However, the reality of this dream weighed heavily on him; he knew it would take more than just wishes and sketches to make it happen. He would need stability—financial stability, resources, and a solid plan. Ledger understood that to lay down roots, he had to build his culinary venture and network further, strengthening community ties and finding ways to bring income into the family.

As he organized his notes, he made a list of avenues for income: expanding his market ideas, embracing the culinary festival, and even potentially teaming up with others in the community to start a cooperative business where vendors could thrive collectively. Each idea only reaffirmed his belief that, by providing for his loved ones and uplifting others, he could create a future grounded in security and stability.

Inspired by this new perspective, Ledger felt a surge of motivation rush through him. He envisioned the discussions he would have with his family—dreaming together about how they could build this new life and investing not only in material things but in nurturing one another's hopes and aspirations. They had always been there for each other, and now, he hoped to offer them a sense of belonging, a permanent base from which they could flourish.

Later, he called Maria, excited to share his thoughts, I have been thinking about the future—about my family." He started, unable to contain his enthusiasm. "What if we could create a space where everyone could come together, a home that nurtures our culture and preserves our memories?"

Maria listened intently, a bright smile spreading across her face. "That sounds incredible, Ledger! It is exactly what we all need. A place to cultivate our dreams while holding onto our roots."

Her support bolstered his excitement, and they discussed locations for the future home, ideally close enough to the culinary market where he could keep his business thriving while also being near the community he valued so much. They brainstormed how to combine their efforts to create a family-centric initiative, supporting each other in their dreams.

"We could even have a community garden as part of the home," Ledger proposed, envisioning a lush space filled with local plants, where everyone could gather to grow food and bond together. "Everyone can contribute, and we could host workshops on how to cook with what we grow. It would be a way to strengthen both family and community ties."

Their conversation crescendo with ideas and inspirations, each suggestion igniting further visions of the future they could cultivate together. Ledger realized that he was not just dreaming about a home for himself; he was envisioning a legacy—a sanctuary where love, laughter, and culture flourished amid the gentle waves and rolling hills of St. Thomas.

As he hung up, Ledger felt a renewed sense of purpose enveloped him. He knew building a permanent home would not happen overnight, but with every step he took forward, every connection he made, and every plan he laid out, he felt more confident in the possibility of achieving this vision. His family had faced so much, and now it was time for them all to grow, together in a space that reflected their resilience, hopes, and love.

With each passing day, Ledger committed himself to nurturing not only the dream of a home but the community around him, understanding that the two were inexorably linked. The more he engaged with local vendors and farmers, the more he realized that in sowing seeds of collaboration, he was also planting the roots for his family's future.

Over the next few weeks, the idea of establishing a family home turned into action. Ledger dedicated himself to searching for properties that could accommodate not only his immediate family but also future generations. He scoured local real estate listings, made calls, and sought advice from friends in the community. Every lead he pursued felt like a step closer to materializing his dream.

One afternoon, Ledger decided to take a break from the hustle of his search and visit a local farm, which he had learned was run by a woman named Elise, known for her sustainable practices and dedication to community engagement. As he walked the well-trodden path between trees laden with mangoes and papayas, he was reminded of the lush landscapes of his childhood. The fragrance of tropical fruits was intoxicating, bringing back memories of family gatherings back home, where fruits were abundant, and laughter echoed under the shade of big trees.

When he arrived at the farm, Elise welcomed him warmly, her hands dusty from harvesting. "It is good to see you, Ledger! How can I help you today?"

"I've been thinking about expanding my network and supporting local agriculture," he explained, eager to share his vision. "And honestly, I also want to learn from you. I believe that by connecting growers and local businesses, we can create something that will benefit us all—and even help me lay down some roots for my family."

Elise nodded, clearly intrigued. "That is a noble ambition. Community is everything here. If you are interested in collaboration, we could offer workshops for families to learn how to grow their own food. It would be a great way to empower them and teach them the importance of sustainability."

The idea struck a chord with Ledger. "That is exactly what I am looking to create—a place that fosters learning, connection, and resilience. We could even hold these workshops where I eventually plan to establish my family home, intertwining our visions."

The conversation flowed easily, and as they discussed shared goals, Ledger felt a growing sense of camaraderie. They talked about the potential for farmers' markets, where local growers could sell their produce and tell their stories, inviting others to be part of the vibrant tapestry of community life. Each idea generated more ideas, like ripples in the water, expanding their shared vision.

"Let us plan a community event. We can introduce families to the benefits of local produce, and you could showcase your culinary skills as well," Elise suggested, her enthusiasm matching his own.

With their plans set, Ledger spent the following days gathering resources and engaging fellow community members. As he shared his dream of building a home alongside a thriving community initiative, he felt the excitement build around him. The enthusiasm was infectious, and people began to contribute their ideas and resources, wanting to take part in this blossoming vision.

Before long, they organized a community gathering at the farm, which they named the "Roots and Fruits Festival." It would celebrate local culture and food, inviting families to learn about sustainable gardening and cooking. Ledger envisioned it not just as an event, but as a crucial step toward the permanence he craved for his family. He sketched out a loose schedule filled with workshops, cooking demonstrations, and even a small space for local artists to showcase their work—all the while preparing a dish that highlighted the produce grown right on Elise's farm.

As the day of the event drew closer, Ledger's anticipation grew. He spent long nights preparing, blending culinary creativity with his desire to uplift the community. With each moment spent organizing and collaborating, he felt more certain that he was on the right path.

On the day of the festival, the atmosphere was electric. Families gathered, laughter and chatter filling the air as children ran around, their faces painted with excitement. Ledger set up a stall decorated with vibrant tropical fruit and colorful signage, showcasing fresh ingredients ready to be transformed into delicious dishes.

As he looked around at the smiling faces—a tapestry of cultures and stories interwoven together, he saw pieces of his dream beginning to materialize. Conversations flowed, and neighbors shared their favorite recipes, bonding over flavors and memories. Ledger moved from group to group, engaging, sharing ideas, and absorbing the energy that enveloped him.

When it was time for his cooking demonstration, Ledger felt a rush of adrenaline. He stood before the crowd, sharing not just recipes but also the vision behind the gathering—how every meal, every ingredient, woven into the fabric of their community, had significance. When it was time for his cooking demonstration, Ledger felt a rush of adrenaline. He stood before the crowd of eager faces, the vibrant colors of produce surrounding him, and he could sense the collective anticipation in the air. As he began to prepare the ingredients—juicy tomatoes, fragrant herbs, and the fresh catch of the day, he shared his personal stories of growing up, where meals had served as the heart of family gatherings.

"Food is more than sustenance," he said, stirring a pot as the aromatic scent of sautéing onions filled the air. "Every meal we create reflects our culture, our struggles, and our triumphs. Each ingredient carries stories that connect us to our heritage and one another."

As he spoke, Ledger moved seamlessly through the process, demonstrating techniques and encouraging participation. He invited children to help slice vegetables and asked families to share their favorite seasoning tips. Laughter rang out as he playfully narrated how his mother used to cook, how she would remind them to taste and adjust until it was right.

"Imagine this dish being served at our family table," he continued, gesturing to the colorful spread before him. "Picture all of us gathered—sharing stories and creating new memories. That is what we are building here today—a space where we can celebrate not just food, but our community."

The crowd leaned in, captivated by his passion. Ledger could see nods of agreement, faces lighting up as families connected over their own stories, recalling how meals had bonded them during tough times. It was becoming evident that the festival was achieving more than he had imagined—it was fostering connections, not just among strangers but among family and community.

Once he plated the final dish—a colorful, aromatic seafood stew—he presented it to the audience. "This," he declared, "is a representation of us: vibrant, diverse, and full of flavor. I invite you all to taste it and to think about what it means to you."

As people sampled the dish and reacted with delight, Ledger reveled in their shared joy. The atmosphere was electric, filled with conversation, laughter, and the clinking of utensils. He felt a sense of fulfillment wash over him. He had not only demonstrated a recipe; he had sparked a movement, reigniting the importance of food as a means of connection and celebration.

By the end of the demonstration, families gathered around him, exchanging recipes and tips, and fostering new relationships that would last long after the festival ended. Ledger stepped back, taking in the scene—the energy of the crowd, the smiles of his neighbors, and the blossoming sense of community around him.

That day, he felt the seeds of his dream taking root. Each shared dish, every story exchanged, and every echoing laughter was a step toward building the home he envisioned—a home where love and culture would thrive, where stability could be forged in the embrace of family and community. As the sun began to set, casting a warm glow over the festival, Ledger knew he was on the right path to realizing his vision of not just a house, but a true home for his family.

The day of the Roots and Fruits Festival dawned bright and clear, with the sun shining down on the lush landscape of St. Thomas. Ledger arrived early at Elise's farm, his heart racing with excitement. Colorful banners fluttered in the breeze, and the scent of fresh produce filled the air as vendors set up their stalls, showcasing vibrant fruits and vegetables alongside handmade crafts and locally inspired delicacies. Musicians were tuning their instruments nearby, and the sound of laughter and chatter seemed to hum through the atmosphere.

Clara and their nine children joined him, each buzzing with anticipation. Wizen, the eldest at fifteen, helped Ledger unload baskets of ripe tomatoes, tender okra, and fragrant herbs from their van while Petronel, Louisa, and Eliza darted around, enthused about the activities planned for the day. Julien, the adventurous spirit of the family, raced after the two youngest sets of twins, Koie and Nerissa, who squealed with delight as they chased butterflies fluttering through the wildflowers.

"This is amazing," Clara said, beaming as she took in the vibrant scene. "I can feel the energy of the community already! It is going to be a special day."

Ledger took a deep breath, savoring this moment together. "I cannot wait to share the seafood stew on which I have been working. I want everyone to feel that connection to our culture and the memories we share through food."

As he began to set up his cooking station beneath a large, sun-soaked tent, Clara and the children helped arrange the fresh ingredients, preparing for the demonstration. The sight of the bright produce stirred memories of Ledger's own childhood, recalling cozy family gatherings where food brought them together, and stories were meant to be shared. This festival was an opportunity to honor those memories while creating new ones with the community he cared so much about.

"Ledger! Over here!" called Maria, waving enthusiastically as she approached her own stall, filled with vibrant sauces and spice blends. Her energy was contagious as she joined Clara and the children, who were already bustling with excitement.

"Isn't this amazing?" Maria remarked, glancing around at the animated scene unfolding. "I can feel the excitement in the air!"

"It's incredible," Ledger replied, arranging the last of the produce. "I really want to show everyone that food can connect us, not just with our meals, but with our histories."

As the clock ticked closer to the event's start, families began to gather near the main stage. Musicians began playing lively island tunes, and children twirled joyfully in the sun-drenched grass, laughter echoing around them like the music itself. The atmosphere was electric, igniting connections and strengthening bonds—this festival was a celebration of togetherness, a reflection of their shared hopes and dreams.

As families arrived at his stall, Ledger noticed Wizen stepping forward, taking on a supportive role by assisting his father. "Welcome! I will be preparing a seafood stew that celebrates the flavors of our island. Feel free to join us as we cook!"

Eyes sparkled with curiosity as they gathered around. Ledger felt a rush of energy as he began chopping vegetables, inviting everyone to participate in the process. "Help me with simple tasks! We will make this stew together!"

"I want to hear your stories as we cook," he said, his hands deftly working at the cutting board, while Koie and Nerissa wandered close by, fascinated by the colors and smells. "What does food mean to you?"

A woman stepped forward, her voice warm and enthusiastic. "Food means family! I remember my grandmother making her famous conch fritters every Sunday. It was always about gathering."

Ledger smiled, nodding in agreement. "Exactly! Each dish we prepare contains the essence of our roots and the stories we carry."

As the group lent a hand in preparing the stew, Ledger encouraged them to share their culinary experiences, weaving a tapestry of tradition and memory into the fabric of the demonstration. When it was time to add the fresh seafood to the bubbling pot, he spoke passionately about the importance of supporting local fishermen and sustainable practices. "This isn't just about the food; it's about our community, our past, and our future," he emphasized, stirring the pot as the delightful aromas wafted through the air, drawing more people in.

The laughter and chatter around him swelled into a vibrant chorus of connection. He glanced at Clara, who was managing the younger children as they explored the nearby stalls. Watching Petronel and Louisa playfully engage with other kids made his heart swell with pride. The festival was transformed into a tapestry of stories interwoven by shared heritage, resilience, and joy.

As the stew simmered, Ledger began to plate the first servings, filling each bowl with the fragrant mixture that had brought so many together. He smiled as he invited everyone to come forward. "You're not just tasting my dish today; you're tasting the stories of our island," he declared, urging them to reflect on the flavors and connections they had made throughout the day.

Wizen stood beside him, proudly handing out the steaming bowls of stew to eager families. "Here you go! This is a taste of our culture," he said, passing a bowl to a little boy with wide eyes.

As families sampled the stew, smiles spread across their faces, each spoonful rich with connection. "This is delightful!" one of the children exclaimed, his voice slicing through the ambient chatter. Cheers of approval rippled through the crowd, and Ledger felt the warmth of satisfaction swell within him.

Before long, Ledger had a line at his stall, families eager to sample the dish he had put together with such love and intention. Each bowl of stew not only offered a taste of culinary tradition but also engaged people in a collective experience. Laughter echoed, and stories were exchanged as everyone gathered around the warm pot, their senses engaged in a lively dialogue of aromas and flavors.

Meanwhile, Clara was busy entertaining Nerissa and Koie, who were enthralled with the colorful crafts at a neighboring stall. Louisa and Eliza joined them, chattering excitedly about the art projects, their creativity mirrored in the laughter of other children making their own festive crafts. They were having the time of their lives, and Ledger felt a deep sense of gratitude for this moment, the mingling of family and community, the shared joys of cooking and creation.

As the afternoon wore on and the sun began to dip lower in the sky, casting a golden light across the festival grounds, Ledger took a moment to observe the scene before him. Wizen was engaging with a group of kids, teaching them how to make simple dishes with the produce they had just picked up, while Julien showcased some of the other local dishes scattered throughout the festival. Clara moved among the stalls, chatting with neighbors and helping others in the community. The sense of belonging swelled in Ledger's chest, and he could not help but smile.

"This is what it's all about," he thought to himself, thrilled at the sense of unity that filled the air. Everyone was contributing to a shared experience that transcended food; it was a celebration of life, culture, and community spirit.

Just then, an older gentleman approached his stall, reminiscent of Ledger's own father. He leaned in, inspecting the stew with an appreciative smile. "This smells heavenly, son," he said, his voice warm and encouraging. "What's your secret?"

Ledger chuckled, feeling a kinship with the man. "It is simple—love and a touch of heritage. Every ingredient has a story."

The gentleman nodded thoughtfully, then took a bowl from Wizen. "A good meal is like a good story. It brings people together."

After tasting the stew, his eyes lit up. "You have created something special here. You are honoring your roots beautifully."

Encouraged, Ledger turned to face the crowd, raising his bowl slightly. "This festival is our opportunity to celebrate who we are and where we come from! May our dishes, stories, and laughter continue to strengthen the ties that bind us as a community!"

Cheers erupted in response, and Ledger's heart soared as everyone around him echoed their agreement, celebrating the bond they were building through food and shared experiences.

As the last rays of sun dipped below the horizon, painting the sky with vibrant hues, Ledger felt a sense of fulfillment wash over him. This festival had become a tapestry of connections—a creating of shared stories that intertwined the past with the present. They were nurturing not just culinary traditions but a sense of belonging and purpose that enriched their lives, ensuring that all children— his own and those of the community—would take pride in their heritage.

In that moment, Ledger knew that together they were cultivating not just food, but dreams, resilience, and hope. Each shared laugh, story, and bowl of stew was a step toward crafting a legacy—one that celebrated their unity and the journey they would take together, all under the warming embrace of a St. Thomas sunset.

As the sun dipped below the horizon, painting the sky in shades of pink and orange, Ledger sat on his balcony and gazed out at the shimmering ocean. The vibrant festival earlier that day had fueled his optimism, but now, as twilight enveloped the island, the harsh realities of his dreams crept back into his thoughts. Although he longed for a permanent home to gather his family and cultivate their future, he knew that the journey to achieve this vision was fraught with challenges.

The first hurdle that weighed heavily on his mind was the question of land ownership. Ledger was acutely aware of the complexities surrounding property acquisition in St. Thomas; the legacy of colonialism still loomed large, casting long shadows over the availability and accessibility of land. Many locals, including their own family members, struggled to secure affordable housing, often facing steep prices or complicated legal barriers. He could not help but wonder if he would be able to find a suitable parcel of land where he could build the home of his dreams, a place that could offer stability and security for his extended family.

He began researching available plots, seeking guidance from local real estate experts and other community members. He learned that much of the land on the island was owned by absentee landlords or corporations, driving prices up and making it difficult for locals to invest. The thought of navigating the bureaucratic labyrinth that often-accompanied property purchases was daunting. Ledger felt a growing sense of urgency; he needed to act swiftly before opportunities slipped away, but the weight of uncertainty loomed large.

Another significant obstacle lay in accessing the resources he needed to build a home. Ledger knew that creating a welcoming and sustainable space would require not only financial investment but also a steady supply of materials. He envisioned incorporating local resources, such as timber and stone, but he quickly realized that securing these materials could be a challenge. The economic disparities in the region meant that smaller, local suppliers often struggled to compete with larger companies. This system leaned heavily on chains of global supply that compromised not only quality but also the potential for community engagement in his project.

Alongside these logistical challenges, the socio-economic conditions on the island made the pursuit of his dream even more complicated. The lingering effects of colonialism had created a socio-economic landscape that was riddled with inequities. Many families faced barriers to stable employment, and the high cost of living often meant that necessities overshadowed aspirations for home ownership. Ledger understood that many in his community bore the same burdens—dreams of permanence overshadowed by the realities of limited resources and opportunities.

As he reflected on these issues, Ledger felt a surge of responsibility to not only consider his family's future but also the wider community's well-being. He thought of the connections he had forged during the festival and the collaborative spirit that had emerged. If he wanted to create a legacy, he knew he had to channel that spirit into something actionable, using his experiences and relationships to advocate for broader change. He began to develop ideas about forming a cooperative with other families facing similar challenges to pool resources and share knowledge.

The more he pondered these hurdles, the more he realized that he had to engage with local leaders and activists who were already working to address land reform and economic inequities. He started attending community meetings, listening to the voices of others who had weathered these storms, and absorbing the wisdom shared by those dedicated to making a difference. By aligning himself with these efforts, Ledger believed he could not only fortify his own aspirations but also contribute to dismantling the barriers that had long restricted growth for many families in the region.

Despite the overwhelming challenges ahead, Ledger understood that building a permanent home meant more than just having a physical structure. It was about fostering a culture of resilience, collaboration, and empowerment. He envisioned a community where families could thrive together, sharing resources and support, and breaking free from the limitations imposed by the past.

With a newfound determination, Ledger began mapping out a plan that integrated both his dream for his family and his commitment to his community. He jotted down potential partnerships, explored communal land trusts, and envisioned workshops to educate families on home-building practices and sustainability. Each step would not only move him closer to his vision but also empower others in the process.

As the stars twinkled above the calm waters of St. Thomas, Ledger felt a renewed sense of purpose. The journey toward permanence would indeed be rife with challenges, but he believed that together, they could rewrite their narrative. With every obstacle they faced, they would only grow stronger, bound by a common goal of creating a secure, nurturing environment for their families, one where the joys of laughter, culture, and love could flourish for generations to come.

Life in St. Thomas serves as both an opportunity for growth and a reminder of the complexities that come with migration, particularly in a post-colonial context. For Ledger Philogene, every day in this vibrant yet challenging landscape encapsulates the resilience of individuals navigating the intricate web of identity, acceptance, and economic mobility. The island, with its breathtaking beaches and lush valleys, is a place of beauty but also a stark reminder of its colonial past that still casts a long shadow over its present.

As Ledger walked through the bustling streets of Charlotte Amalie, he felt a mixture of hope and trepidation. The marketplace was alive with vibrant colors, aromas drifting from food stalls, and the chatter of locals exchanging news. Yet beneath this lively surface lay a complex interplay of histories, cultures, and aspirations. Ledger understood that to thrive, he needed to navigate this landscape skillfully, forging connections that were both personal and professional.

His thoughts often drifted to his roots—his family's journey from St Barts to St. Thomas. While his parents had sought new opportunities in the hopes of starting anew, the scars of their migration story shaped real challenges in their lives, such as discrimination and economic hardship. Ledger felt the weight of this legacy. Their experiences fueled his determination to create a stable and nurturing environment for his own family.

Amidst the backdrop of shifting socio-economic structures and lingering inequities, Ledger recognized the importance of community. As he engaged with fellow vendors at the festival, he shared not only recipes but also stories from his past—memories imbued with the rich traditions of his heritage. He found strength in these connections, discovering a shared commitment among community members to uplift one another. Each conversation underscored the importance of collective resilience, giving him a sense of belonging and purpose that had often felt elusive.

As he continued to set his commercial ambitions in motion, Ledger began exploring opportunities to support local farmers and artisans. He envisioned a cooperative where aspiring entrepreneurs from the community could share resources and knowledge, forging a path toward economic mobility that honored the island's culture and unique identity. This idea had taken root during the festival, where he had witnessed the power of collaboration. In each shared dish and every storytelling moment, he saw the potential for a more sustainable future.

Yet, the landscape was not without its hurdles. The complexities of migration and post-colonial dynamics cast long shadows over the ambitions he held dear. Ledger grappled with feelings of inadequacy, wondering if he could truly carve out a future that honored both his aspirations and the realities of his past. The dreams of stability and prosperity for his family were continually challenged by the stark inequalities he observed, from limited access to resources to systemic barriers that stifled growth.

Ledger found strength in the stories of his community, drawing inspiration from those who had navigated these challenges before him. He regularly attended local meetings, engaging with leaders who spoke of community-based initiatives aimed at fostering equality. He sought out mentors who had succeeded in carving a niche for themselves, asking questions, and absorbing their insights. With each conversation, he fortified his understanding of the land where he sought to build his dreams.

In quiet moments, Ledger often reflected on the duality of his existence in St. Thomas. On one hand, he felt the thrill of opportunity—an endless horizon of possibilities beckoned him. On the other hand, echoes of history reminded him of the complex path that had led his family here. He yearned to create a legacy that encompassed both his French and European heritage and his life on the island, where the past could inform the present in a meaningful way.

As Ledger laid the groundwork for his future, he focused on balancing ambition with the realities of his surroundings. He discovered that his entrepreneurial ventures could be woven into the community fabric; he did not have to pursue progress in isolation but could instead build a network of support and collaboration. In the process, he learned to value the stories of others, understanding that their journeys intertwined with his own.

In the end, Ledger's experiences in St. Thomas reflect the intricate tapestry of life within a post-colonial context—one where resilience must meet adaptability. As he forged connections, explored his commercial ambitions, and came to terms with his identity, he was shaping a future that embraced the complexities of his journey. He realized that each step forward was not just about building a better life for himself and his family, but about contributing to a community that was resilient, vibrant, and deeply intertwined with the legacies of its past.

Chapter Four: Return to St. Barthelemy

After a decade of building a life in St. Thomas, Ledger Philogene stood on the brink of a momentous decision: he would return to his roots in St. Barthélemy. This journey, however, was not merely a physical return; it represented a profound emotional and psychological exploration of identity, belonging, and the legacy his family had woven over generations. As he prepared to finalize the sale of his family's estate, memories began to flood back—each one a thread pulling him toward a deeper understanding of his past and the costs of migration.

In the quiet moments leading up to his departure, Ledger found himself grappling with conflicting emotions. Excitement mingled with a sense of inevitability, and nostalgia washed over him like the gentle caress of ocean waves. The vibrancy of St. Thomas, alive with its culture and community, had been his home for so long, but the pull of St. Barthélemy whispered to him, tempting him to reckon with the history and heritage that lay there.

As he recalled his childhood home, memories of laughter and family gatherings danced in his mind. The estate—nestled among fragrant hibiscus and towering palm trees—had been the gathering place for countless family celebrations. It had echoed with the voices of ancestors, the warmth of shared stories lighting up the dark nights. The estate was more than just a building; it was a repository of memories, dreams, and the weight of his family's legacy. To finalize the sale wanted to sever a vital connection to his heritage, yet Ledger knew it was a necessary step in his journey toward reconciliation with his past.

Ledger's decision was underscored by the changes he observed in St. Barthelemy during his years away. The island had evolved, reshaped by the tides of globalization and tourism that had swept through its shores. He envisioned an island that had grown in stature and complexity, its cultural fabric interwoven with layers of new influences. Yet, he also feared that the essence of what had once made his homeland special might be fading in the rush toward modernization.

As he prepared for the journey, Ledger reflected on the personal costs of migration—the sacrifices he and his family made for a chance at a better life. St. Thomas had offered opportunities for growth and connection and yet, in many ways, it had also drawn him away from his roots. He pondered the paradox of seeking a better future while feeling increasingly disconnected from the land and people that had shaped his early years. Each journey, he realized, had come with its own set of trade-offs, the vibrant tapestry of experience woven from the threads of belonging and separation.

The plane ride was filled with contemplation. Looking out at the clouds, Ledger felt a mix of anticipation and apprehension. The rhythmic pulse of the engine reminded him that he was moving not just across distance, but also through time. He was journeying back to reclaim the parts of himself that had lain dormant since he left. Would he find the island he remembered, or would time have rewritten the landscape entirely? Would he be welcomed back as a son of the soil, or would he feel like a stranger in his own homeland?

Upon landing, the familiar scent of salt air and vibrant flora washed over him, stirring memories buried deep within. The island felt both a foreign and familiar reminder of his childhood and the life he had left behind. As he made his way to the estate, his heart raced. This was more than just a house; it symbolized the dreams of his ancestors, a testament to their perseverance and love. As he approached the home, he imagined his family gathered around the dining table, laughter bubbling over as they shared stories late into the night.

As he stood before the grand entrance, Ledger's hand hesitated over the weathered wooden door. It felt surreal to be here, confronting the legacy that had shaped him. The estate, with its cracked paint and wild overgrowth, showed signs of age—a stark reminder of the passage of time and the life he had lived elsewhere. Yet it still held an undeniable charm, a nostalgic echo of home that tugged at his heart.

In this moment of homecoming, Ledger was not just returning to a physical place; he was engaging in an emotional pilgrimage. The walls held the whispers of his ancestors, and the land beneath his feet carried their stories. This journey would force him to confront the complexities of his identity, to reconcile the years spent away with the profound connection he felt to his heritage.

As he stepped inside the estate, the coolness enveloped him, bringing back floods of memories, the clink of cutlery during family meals, the sound of his parents' voices floating through the corridors, and the warmth of family gatherings. Each sound reverberated in his mind, reminding him of the legacy that defined him. Here, within these walls, existed the essence of who he was—a tapestry woven with threads of joy, struggle, and resilience. The air was thick with the past yet tinged with a sense of possibility for the future. As Ledger moved deeper into the estate, he took slow, deliberate steps, allowing the echoes of his childhood to wash over him. Each room he passed was a focal point for myriad memories—sights and sounds so vivid that they momentarily transported him back in time.

In the dining room, sunlight filtered through the dusty windowpanes, casting a golden hue on the long, polished table where countless meals had been shared. He recalled festive dinners, lively discussions filled with laughter, families, and friends gathered close, feasting on his mother's prized recipes. The smell of her homemade dishes lingered in aromas that spoke of home and safety. Now, the table sat empty, its surface polished but longing for warmth and connection.

In the living room, remnants of the past played out like a slideshow in his mind. He could almost hear the conversations swirling around him, the laughter of siblings and cousins intermingling with the gentle strumming of his father's guitar. The walls, adorned with family photographs, told stories of love and legacy, but they were also reminders of the lives that had been lived and the moments that had passed.

Ledger took a deep breath, centering himself amidst the nostalgia. It all felt bittersweet—a reminder of what he had cherished and what he had lost. As he strode into the kitchen, he could almost see his mother bustling around, her apron tied at her waist, a pot simmering on the stove as she sang softly to herself. The kitchen had always been the heart of the home, a sacred space where flavors mingled, and relationships deepened. But now, it felt abandoned, a vessel of memories awaiting rejuvenation.

He opened a cabinet, smoothing his palm over the worn wood, remembering how they would gather there to bake together, learning family recipes handed down through generations. The sound of laughter echoed in his ears again, but now it was just him, standing in the silence left behind.

"What will become of this place?" Ledger wondered, letting his thoughts inch closer to the realities of his decision. He could sell the estate—turn a profit and finally close this chapter of his life. But was he truly ready to let go? Would the act of selling sever the ties to his roots, leaving pieces of his identity scattered like autumn leaves in the wind?

Each corner of the estate urged him to reflect on the family legacy, the sacrifices of his ancestors, their dreams, and their hopes. He could feel their presence as if they lingered in the very air he breathed. Ledger understood that his journey back to St. Barthélemy was not just about revisiting old spaces; it was a quest for understanding and reconciliation. It was an opportunity to explore his identity in a way he had never fully embraced.

As he wandered through the hallways, past the photographs that bore witness to decades of family history, he felt the desire to make this place a vibrant part of his life once more. The estate could become more than a remnant of the past; it could be a bridge to a future that honored both his heritage and the life he had built in St. Thomas.

With renewed resolve, Ledger began to imagine how he could revitalize the estate. It had the potential to be a retreat, a gathering space for family and friends, reconnecting them to their roots while welcoming new influences. It could become a cultural center that highlighted the traditions of St. Barthélemy while fostering discussions about the complexities of migration and identity that permeated his life.

As the idea crystallized, Ledger also recognized that returning home would require an emotional reckoning. He would need to confront the bittersweet truth of letting go of both the estate and his old way of thinking. Emotion swelled within him as he considered the cost of his migration journey, the steps he had taken to forge a new life, but also the connection he yearned to maintain with his roots.

Outside, the sun dipped lower, casting long shadows across the yard, where vibrant bougainvillea clung tenaciously to the wrought iron fences. Ledger stepped outside, breathing in the salty breeze as he considered what it meant to be home. The island—the land of his ancestors—was an integral part of his identity, yet his experiences in St. Thomas had shaped him into the man he had become.

For Ledger, homecoming was not merely about returning to a place; it was about reconciling the many parts of himself—the son of the soil found in St. Barthélemy, the father and community member thriving in St. Thomas, and everything in between. It was about weaving together the legacy of his family with the man he was today, acknowledging the complexities of migration while honoring each journey's unique story.

As the evening settled in, Ledger stood at the edge of the estate's expansive garden, watching the sky transform into an artist's palette of oranges, purples, and deep blues. The air felt thick with memories, tinged with the scents of jasmine and the salty ocean breeze. He let himself be absorbed by the beauty of the moment, a quiet acknowledgment of the depths of his journey and the myriad feelings that accompanied his return.

In the growing twilight, he could almost hear his mother's voice, soft and reassuring, guiding him through the complexities of life. "Home is where your roots are planted, my son," he imagined her saying. The teachings of his parents began to resonate anew, urging him to embrace both the heritage that shaped him and the new life he had built elsewhere. This homecoming was an opportunity to blend the past and present purposefully, to create a future that honored both paths.

As night began to blanket the estate, Ledger found solace in the familiar sounds surrounding him, the distant lull of waves crashing on the shore and the rustling of palm fronds swaying gently in the breeze. He stepped further into the garden, drawn to a particularly vibrant cluster of hibiscus flowers, their bold colors glowing in the fading light. They symbolized resilience, thriving amidst the tropical sun and occasional storm. Just like his family.

"Can this estate be a symbol of rebirth?" he wondered, a vision forming in his mind—one where community and heritage converged into a hopeful future. "What if I turned the estate into a place where stories are shared, where cooking classes celebrate our culinary traditions, and where the island's youth can be inspired to create their own paths?"

Ledger was filled with newfound determination. The road ahead might not be easy transforming the estate into a cultural hub would require effort, resources, and support. Yet this was not just about revitalizing a house; it was about nurturing a community—a space where his children and their peers could reconnect with their roots while facing the realities of a changing world.

Inspired, he felt a rush of motivation. The estate could be a gathering place, a sanctuary that provided shelter not just from the elements but also from the harsh realities many faced in a rapidly changing economic landscape. By fostering connections through heritage, he could weave new stories into the fabric of his family legacy.

As he stood amidst the blooms of his childhood garden, Ledger felt a flicker of hope that life would flourish again within these walls. He could see children running through the yard, laughter echoing as families gathered to celebrate their identities and histories. The estate could be alive with all the sounds of joy he had once known—an extension of his family's legacy reimagined for the present moment.

Just then, the stars began to twinkle above, speckling the darkening sky with the shimmering reminders of generations that had come before him. In that stillness, Ledger found peace. This was not just a farewell to a place but a heartfelt embrace of his journey and the promise of a new beginning.

He took one last glance at the estate, its silhouette framed against the starlit sky. No matter what the future held, he was determined to cultivate the roots of its legacy while nurturing the branches of progress. It was time to merge the past with the possibilities of the future, creating a home that honored his family's history and welcomed the next generation into a world of growth and connection.

With that thought firmly planted in his heart, Ledger turned back toward the house, ready to make his way inside. It was time to breathe life back into his family's legacy—to usher in a new chapter that reflected not only his past but also the bright possibilities that lay ahead. Homecoming was not merely a return; it was a rebirth.

Ledger stood in the grand foyer of his family estate, the echo of his footsteps resonating in the quiet space. Dust motes floated lazily in the light filtering through the tall windows, illuminating the faded grandeur of the place that had borne witness to generations of his family history. With each step he took, the weight of emotion pressed heavily on his heart—a tide of nostalgia tugging at his awareness as he prepared to finalize the sale of the plantation that had long been a symbol of both his heritage and the complex history of colonialism.

The decision to sell had not come lightly to him. It felt bittersweet, a culmination of years spent wrestling with the implications of ownership—a verb that carried its own burden, especially for an estate like this one, steeped in the legacy of colonial exploitation. Ledger understood that the plantation had once thrived on the backs of enslaved people, their labor crucial to the wealth it generated. For his family, it had served as both a source of sustenance and a reminder of a painful past. It had held the laughter of family gatherings, the joy of triumphs, and the sorrow of losses. Letting go was an act filled with reverence and responsibility.

As he prepared to meet with the prospective buyers—the local developers whose plans for the estate would shift its purpose from a familial legacy to a commercial investment—Ledger reflected on the contradictions inherent in his decision. Selling the estate would signify the end of an era, yet it also represented a unique opportunity to secure a stable future for his family in St. Thomas. With the resources gained from the sale, he could launch his vision of creating a community center that honored the cultural ties of their heritage while fostering new economic possibilities.

With this weighing on his mind, Ledger felt a mix of pride and sorrow. He no longer saw the estate solely as a relic of his family history; he recognized it as a profound responsibility to honor the past while pivoting toward the future. He wanted to approach this transition with full intention, ensuring that it would benefit not only his family but also the broader community from which they hailed.

The clock ticked closer to noon, and Ledger noticed the way the sunlight shifted, illuminating different parts of the estate in varying hues. He brushed his fingers across the wooden banisters that spiraled up the staircase, feeling the decades of history embedded in its surface. He could almost hear his father's voice resonating, guiding him, reminding him that home is not just a place but a feeling—a sense of belonging rooted in love and connection.

As he gathered his thoughts, the sound of a car rolling up the gravel path interrupted his moment of reflection. Ledger could see the buyers stepping out of their vehicle, their confident strides exuding ambition and forward-thinking. This was the moment he had been preparing for, the culmination of discussions that had begun months ago.

Looking back at the estate one last time, Ledger whispered a quiet farewell to the ghostly echoes of his ancestors before moving toward the front door. Steeling himself, he stepped outside to greet the visitors with a warm but collected demeanor.

"Welcome to the Philogene estate," he said, extending his hand to them. The buyers introduced themselves, all too eager to discuss their vision for the property. As they walked through the expansive grounds, Ledger felt the pangs of nostalgia wash over him with every crumbling stone and fading wall.

"We envision transforming the estate into a boutique hotel and cultural center," one of the buyers explained, gesturing widely as they strolled through the verdant landscape now speckled with wild blooms. "It has great potential with its rich history and proximity to local attractions. Imagine how much life and tourism this could bring to the area!"

Ledger nodded, but his heart conflicted with enthusiasm and apprehension. He had spent countless hours imagining other futures for this space—a place to gather and cultivate community, a center for education, and a tribute to their heritage. While he could see the appeal of revitalizing the estate into a commercial venture, he hesitated at the prospect of losing the soul of what the plantation represented for him and his family.

As the buyers continued outlining their plans, Ledger remained engaged yet contemplative, considering the implications of their proposals. Memories flooded his mind—summer afternoons spent running through the garden, the warmth of family reunions, and the quiet strength of his ancestors whispering stories that taught resilience and perseverance. Could their plan honor these memories while also propelling the family into a new chapter?

Eventually, the conversation shifted to the matter of finances, and Ledger listened as they discussed offers and potential timelines. Each figure mentioned felt like a tangible step toward the future he sought to create—the foundation for the community center he envisioned in St. Thomas, a place where culture could thrive alongside economic growth.

But as the numbers rolled off their tongues, the emotional weight of his decision circled back to him like a tide, challenging his resolve. Ledger felt the tightness in his throat as he considered the impact of the sale—not just in terms of profit but in what this decision symbolized. He could see the potential for change, but could he fully release this part of his heritage, this place that had been an integral thread in the tapestry of his life?

As the buyers continued to present their case, Ledger found himself silently grappling with the deeper implications of letting go of the estate. Would it still belong to him if he relinquished ownership? Would it lose its essence—the lifetime of love and memories stitched into its very foundation? He thought back to the stories shared over family dinners, the lessons learned in the shade of the sprawling trees during lazy afternoons, and the whispered echoes of his ancestors who had labored and dreamed of freedom.

"This estate means more than just a financial opportunity," he finally spoke up, interrupting their enthusiastic pitch. The buyers paused, their expressions shifting to intrigue, even confusion. "It has been the heart of my family for generations. Selling it would not only change its purpose but also redefine my connection to my heritage."

The developers exchanged glances, and Ledger could sense the air thickening with the weight of his words. He continued, "I have a vision for this property, one that honors its history and provides a space for community enrichment. I want it to remain a place that reflects who we are and where we come from, a gathering spot for celebrations and shared stories."

The lead buyer, a sharp-looking woman in her forties, looked at him intently. "We understand that history is important. Our goal is to enhance the property while preserving its essence. We can work together on this—create a design that honors the estate's legacy. Imagine a hotel that incorporates the story of your family and the island's culture. It could be a destination that brings people in, educates them about the past, and uplifts the community."

Ledger met her gaze, torn between skepticism and genuine curiosity. Could a commercial venture truly honor the history he cherished? Could it stand alongside the memories of laughter and love that echoed through the walls? With a mix of resolve and uncertainty, he asked, "How can you ensure that the narrative of my family's legacy isn't lost in your plans?"

The woman nodded, a sign of respect for his concerns. "We are committed to working with local historians and community leaders. We can create educational programs and events that celebrate the estate's history. This way, it will not just be a hotel; it will be a place where all visitors learn about and honor the culture."

Ledger took a deep breath, feeling the wheels turn in his mind. The possibility of merging his desire for preservation with a new vision intrigued him. "I would need to see a comprehensive plan before agreeing to anything," he cautioned, holding firm to his principles. "If I'm to part with this place I love, it must be on grounds that honor the Philogene name."

With a tentative agreement in place, the conversation shifted back to the logistics of the sale, numbers now flowing positively as Ledger weighed the potential benefits this decisive step could bring him and his family. While Margaret, the lead buyer, spoke about timelines, Ledger could not shake the bittersweet feeling that accompanied each exchange, like a heavy yet beautiful anchor holding him to the past.

As the meeting concluded, Ledger stood looking at the estate, now just a backdrop to a business transaction—yet still pulsing with history and memory. The buyers departed, buoyed by the prospect of a fruitful endeavor, while he remained, leaning against a weathered column, contemplating the magnitude of what lay ahead.

At that moment, he understood that this was not just a decision about buildings or dollars and cents; it was about continuity, representation, and the delicate balance between embracing change and honoring tradition. With the sale of the estate, he was not simply cutting ties to his past—he was actively engaging in a dialogue between old and new, past and future.

Ledger realized that any potential future for his family would require a commitment to acknowledging where they had come from while forging ahead with purpose. Selling the estate might signify an end to one story, but it also opened the door to a new chapter one he could shape, one in which he would strive to nurture a legacy that would continue to resonate through time.

As he turned away from the estate for the last time, Ledger felt a renewed sense of purpose settled over him. The journey ahead would require courage and determination, but it also held the promise of growth and transformation—an opportunity to weave a brighter future for himself, his family, and his community, all while ensuring that their heritage remained alive and celebrated in a new, meaningful way.

As Ledger prepared for the journey of finalizing the sale of his family estate, he was acutely aware of the weight of his family's legacy bearing down on him. The plantation, which had stood for generations beneath the Caribbean sun, was more than just an inheritance; it was a symbol rich with the stories of his ancestors—their struggles, sacrifices, hopes, and dreams etched into its very walls. Each room held the echoes of laughter and tears, a tapestry of family history woven from threads of resilience and endurance.

Yet with this wealth of memories came a profound complexity that Ledger could no longer ignore. He grappled intensely with the duality of their history, the paradox of wealth that was built on a foundation of exploitation and human suffering. This estate, where children had played amidst the flowers and where family meetings had been held, also stood as a stark reminder of an era marked by inequality and injustice. The contradictions weighed heavily on him, eliciting feelings of both pride and sorrow.

As he moved through the rooms, caressing the rustic furniture and allowing the weight of memories to envelop him, Ledger fluctuated between moments of reverence and reflection. In the dining room, he could still see his family seated around the table, their animated conversations, their shared meals, a space of love and unity. But overlaying those joyful memories was the unsettling reality of the land's past, the very soil that had sustained their livelihood steeped in a darker history of colonial exploitation.

"How do I honor this legacy?" he pondered, feeling the tension ripple through him. The wealth generated from this property had indeed provided his family with opportunities and security, but it had also come at a cost that could not be overlooked. Ledger recognized that their prosperity was interwoven with the shadows of the past—an inheritance that was both a blessing and a burden.

He closed his eyes, leaning against the window frame that framed the estate's sprawling gardens. He envisioned the hands that had toiled in the fields, the lives sacrificed for profit, and the stories that had been erased from the narrative of this land. For every family meal shared, there was a history of labor and loss that had built the very foundation he now prepared to leave behind.

But Ledger also felt a sense of pride—the pride of knowing that his ancestors had overcome immense hardships. They had fought for their place in history, carved lives for themselves amid adversity, and passed down a legacy of resilience. They were not just figures of a painful past but also champions of survival. They had laid the groundwork for him to stand here today, poised to make decisions that could positively impact future generations.

With each step through the estate, Ledger sought balance—the recognition that both pride and sorrow could coexist and inform the way forward. He realized that his journey was not just about selling a property; it was about embracing the entirety of his heritage. It was about acknowledging the complexities, understanding the nuances of what it meant to inherit such a place, and, more importantly, what responsibilities came with that inheritance.

As he prepared for what lay ahead, Ledger envisioned ways to keep the stories alive. He wondered how he could shape the narrative—not just for himself, but for future generations, ensuring that their family history, with all its layers, was honored and remembered. Could he turn the new direction into an opportunity for education, awareness, and healing?

Reflecting on his vision, he considered transforming the estate's potential into a catalyst for conversations about the past. "Perhaps I could establish a community program that teaches local history," he mused, picturing workshops, storytelling sessions, and culinary classes that celebrate the culture and contributions of those who had come before him. He wanted to create spaces where people could gather, learn, and connect, fostering a sense of community that echoed the ties that bound his family together through generations.

In these moments of reflection, Ledger also thought about his children and the generations that would follow him. What would he tell them about this place? How could he instill in them a sense of pride while also ensuring they understood the historical context of their inheritance? He envisioned nights spent around dinner tables, sharing stories of their family's journey, imparting the lessons learned from both triumphs and trials, so they could carry forth their family's resilience and commitment to justice.

As the afternoon sun cast long shadows across the estate, Ledger felt a renewed sense of purpose wash over him. The sale of the plantation held bittersweet implications, but within that transition lay the opportunity for growth, understanding, and healing. He could reconcile pride and sorrow, embracing the duality of his family's legacy as he sought to create a future that honored the past while paving the way for a more equitable tomorrow.

With the echoes of his ancestors swirling in his heart, Ledger stepped out into the gardens one last time. The scent of blooming hibiscus wafted around him, and the memories of family gatherings filled his mind, each vivid image imbued with both joy and bittersweet longing. The vibrant colors of the hibiscus pay homage to the lively spirit of his ancestors—flowers that had thrived against the odds, much like the family they represented. As he walked among the blossoms, he could almost hear their laughter, feel the warmth of their presence, and sense the strength that had been cultivated here over generations.

The garden, now a patchwork of color and life, was a testament to determination and resilience. It had flourished despite the ravages of time and change, reflecting the enduring nature of family and heritage. Ledger paused by the old mango tree, its branches heavy with ripe fruit, and he recalled the summer days spent here as a child, climbing its sturdy trunk, and sharing sweet mangoes with cousins. The tree had stood as a symbol of growth and stability, a link to the roots that anchored him to this place.

"What will happen to this garden?" Ledger wondered aloud, the question mingling with the gentle rustle of leaves. As he stood there, he felt an overwhelming desire to ensure that the essence of this estate—and all it represented—was not lost in the sale. He wanted to carry forward the lessons of his ancestors: resilience, love, and an unwavering commitment to family.

He envisioned maintaining a piece of the garden even after the sale, by proposing a cooperative effort with the new owners to create a public garden that would serve as both a tribute and an educational space. It could be a sanctuary, where future generations could gather to learn about the history of the land, the stories of those who had come before them, and the importance of nurturing their roots, even in a changing world.

With renewed determination, Ledger walked back toward the estate's entrance, the sun now beginning to sink lower in the sky, casting a golden hue across the gardens. He felt a determination stirring within him, the weight of history guiding his aspirations for the future. Ledger understood that the sale of the estate did not signify forgetting; rather, it represented an evolution—an opportunity to transition from mere ownership to stewardship, fostering a legacy that included lessons of the past alongside visions for the future.

Coming full circle, he found himself back in front of the estate, staring at its familiar silhouette. The decision to sell might be the hardest thing he had ever done, but he realized that it was also a path forward. By embracing the complexities of his family's legacy, he could create possibilities that honor their struggles while also promoting inclusivity and growth for the broader community.

As he reflected on the responsibilities that accompanied this legacy, Ledger realized that he wanted to shape not only his children's understanding of their heritage but also the community's connection to it. He envisioned programs that would invite local schools to engage with the estate's history, hosting workshops where the stories of their ancestors could be shared, celebrated, and taught.

He could see it now—a space alive with activity, where the local community would come together to explore the rich culinary traditions inspired by the land, participate in art and craft workshops that echoed the creativity of their forebears, and host events that honored the essence of their history. Each gathering would strengthen communal bonds and reaffirm the importance of remembering their roots even as they progressed.

The sun dipped below the horizon, painting the sky in hues of lavender and gold. With a deep breath, Ledger made a silent promise to his ancestors—a vow to honor their struggles and to amplify their voices, ensuring their stories would resonate long after he was gone. He decided he would document his family's history, sharing it with his children and the community, illuminating the complexities of their journey—so that they could learn from it, grow from it, and weave it into the tapestry of their futures.

As darkness began to settle around the estate, Ledger felt an overwhelming sense of clarity. He would finalize the sale, but he would also shape a future that honored the heritage of his family. This was not just about the physical transfer of land; it was a profound opportunity to affirm what it meant to be Philogene—a lineage marked by resilience, rooted in love, and intertwined with a rich, intricate history.

With these thoughts warming his heart, Ledger turned away from the estate for the last time. He carried with him not just the weight of his family's legacy but the promise of a brighter future—a future that would recognize the duality of their history and strive to bridge the past with the aspirations they dared to dream. His heart swelled with hope as he ventured toward the horizon, eager to establish connections that would transcend generations and keep the spirit of his ancestors alive.

As Ledger boarded the seaplane bound for St. Barthélemy, a rush of mixed emotions surged through him. The familiar scent of the ocean breeze wafted in as he settled into his seat, the rhythmic hum of the engine resonating with the beating of his heart. The years passed quickly, yet here he was about to return to the island he had called home for the first part of his life. Each mile brought him closer, but it also amplified the weight of memories—joyful and painful—that had shaped his identity.

Looking out the window, the azure waters of the Caribbean unfolded below, dotted with emerald islands basking under the sun. Memories from his childhood flooded his thoughts, almost tangible in their clarity. He could feel the warmth of the sun on his skin, hear the laughter of his siblings, and recall the sounds of family gatherings echoing across the estate's garden. He imagined his mother dancing in the kitchen, stirring a pot of fragrant stew while his father strummed softly on his guitar, the melodies weaving through the air like an embrace.

"Home," he whispered to himself, a deep yearning swelling within him for the simplicity and warmth of those days. The buoyancy of childhood felt like a distant echo, starkly contrasted by the complex emotions now swirling in his heart. The island that was once his paradise now bore the weight of its turbulent history, a history that Ledger could not ignore.

As the seaplane descended, Ledger's excitement mingled with apprehension. He was returning to a cherished place that had changed significantly during his time away, where development and tourism had begun to reshape the landscape. Yet he knew that beneath those changes lay the very essence of the culture he loved—the music, the food, and the vibrant spirit of its people.

But as the plane touched down on the water and he stepped onto the floating dock, bittersweet pangs of nostalgia surged anew. The beauty of the land was marred by the pain of colonialism; the scars of exploitation and suffering were forever etched into the soil. The ancestral trauma echoed in his mind, intertwining with joyful memories of his upbringing.

"What is the cost of this beauty?" he pondered as vibrant colors of the island's flora greeted him, flowers bursting with life and resilience. Ledger understood that those blooms came from a history marked by profound grief, a history that could not be erased. This juxtaposition troubled him. Could he truly embrace the cultural richness of his homeland while acknowledging the painful histories tied to its roots?

As he made his way through the bustling seaport, he felt the warmth of the local people around him, their radiance and openness inviting him to reconnect. Yet, accompanying that warmth was an undercurrent of sorrow—a reminder of the division that colonialism had wrought, both in his family and the fabric of the island's identity.

Walking through the vibrant market stalls that lined the streets, Ledger was greeted by wafts of spices, lively music, and the vibrant colors of textiles, but his heart felt heavy. Families at the market laughed and shared stories, yet he could not shake the stark contrast between the joy he remembered and the haunting legacy of a painful past.

A memory surfaced a faded photograph of his great-grandparents, their serious expressions revealing the weight of their experiences. They had endured unspeakable hardships, and in their struggle, they had birthed a legacy of strength and resilience. Yet, the implications of their past loomed over him like storm clouds, dampening his nostalgic celebration.

Passing by a group of children playing soccer in a nearby field, he felt a pang of longing. These were the moments he had cherished as a child, where carefree laughter mingled with the salty breeze. Yet he recognized that beneath such joy lay the reality of an island that continued to grapple with its colonial history and systemic injustices.

"How do I reconcile these memories?" Ledger questioned, both grateful and sorrowful as he walked the familiar streets of his youth. "How do I embrace my past while pushing for a better future?"

With each step toward the estate, nostalgia tugged at him, the anticipation tinged with the tension of unresolved pain—pain felt not only by those who lived on the island but by his ancestors, whose struggles formed the foundation of his identity. He longed for a way to honor their legacy while addressing the deep scars of division that had persisted.

Arriving at the estate, he paused momentarily before the grand entrance. The familiar silhouette towered above him, a magnificent structure weathered by time. It was a symbol of his family's history, yet it bore witness to the island's complex saga. As he stood there, raindrops began to fall, blurring the lines of his memories while refreshing the air.

"What does this estate mean to me now?" Ledger asked himself, reflecting on the convergence of his memories and the weight of history pressing in on him. Would it simply stand as a relic of a privileged past, or could it evolve into something transformative, something that honored both his family's legacy and the island's troubled history?

The raindrops fell softly around him, each one tapping a gentle rhythm on the tiled roof of the entrance, blending with the nostalgic echoes of laughter and joy that had once filled these halls. The estate stood firm, weathering storms for generations, much like his family, who had persevered through trials and tribulations over the years. Yet, as he looked at the intricate wooden doors and the aged stone walls, he felt the weight of unaddressed pain lingering within their confined stories untold, experiences buried beneath the guise of privilege.

He stepped inside, the heavy wooden door creaking its welcome as he crossed the threshold. Instantly, he was enveloped by the rich scent of aged wood and the coolness of the tiled floors. Each room was like a snapshot of his past, an invitation to explore both joy and sorrow amid the textured history of his ancestors. As he moved through the great hall, he could almost hear the echoes of family gatherings, the clinking of glasses, the sounds of warmth and belonging, and the music that had always filled the air, reminding him of the nights they celebrated their culture with fervor.

Every photograph on the walls seemed to gaze at him with expectation as if they knew their stories were waiting to be retold. Ledger felt the stirrings of nostalgia well up within him, coupled with the heavy reality of the complexities of colonial history that hovered like a specter in the corners of every cherished memory. "How can I carry forward what they have given me while acknowledging the sacrifices made?" he pondered, grappling with this duality.

He found himself standing in the dining room, the long oak table still set as if awaiting the return of loved ones. In his mind's eye, he could see his mother at the head, her laughter ringing out like music as she served traditional dishes from the family recipe book—a mix of vibrant spices and deep-rooted culture. Those gatherings had been filled with love, the shared stories that bridged generations, creating a tapestry of connection woven with celebration and belonging.

Yet, amidst the joy, the absence of those no longer with him loomed large. He could feel the weight of lost voices, the stories not told, the laughter once shared, a haunting reminder of pieces of his family history that had been silenced. The painful truths of colonialism lingered, echoing in the spaces between those joyful moments, a reminder of the scars borne by his ancestors.

"How can I celebrate our culture while acknowledging the struggles intertwined with it?" Ledger mused, contemplating the delicate balance he needed to strike. He realized that moving forward would not mean erasing the past but instead integrating its lessons into a narrative where love, resilience, and community could coexist alongside sorrow and grief.

In the living room, Ledger gazed at the old family portraits hanging on the walls, each face a testament to resilience. They seemed to call to him, urging him to honor their legacy through action. "Their stories deserve to be told," he thought. They were more than just figures in history; they were representations of strength and endurance, of a lineage that had endured so much, and he felt compelled to ensure those stories did not fade into obscurity.

He could almost hear his ancestors urging him on, compelling him to weave these narratives together—to embrace both the joy and the pain and transform it into a tapestry of healing. It was a responsibility he felt keenly, a call to ensure the past was recognized without allowing it to define the future.

As he moved toward the garden, the sound of raindrops softened into a gentle patter, mingling with the whispering leaves, a reminder of nature's renewal. Here, in this precious space where he had once sought solace amid the chaos, Ledger envisioned it as a sanctuary of possibilities, a place to cultivate growth, both for himself and for the community around him.

He knelt beside a patch of wildflowers, their colors vibrant against the backdrop of the storm clouds. This garden could become a metaphor for resilience; just as the flowers thrived despite their environment, Ledger saw the potential for his community to flourish, even amid the complexities of their history.

With a renewed sense of purpose building within him, Ledger envisioned a future where this estate would act as a hub for community engagement, a place for dialogue and healing, and where the voices of the past could be honored while paving the way for a unified future. He imagined workshops on heritage crafts, cooking classes that celebrated traditional recipes, and storytelling nights where people could share their own family narratives, creating connections that would bridge generations and foster understanding among community members. As he pictured each event, he felt a wave of excitement wash over him—a burgeoning hope that this estate could inspire healing and collaboration in a place still grappling with the shadows of its past.

"This could be a sanctuary," he thought, "a place where we can embrace our collective history and create something beautiful." Ledger envisioned children and adults alike gathering in this space, hands covered in flour as they cooked together, laughter filling the air as they shared recipes passed down through generations. He could see the faces of his neighbors, their eyes lighting up as they reminisced about childhood meals, tales of their grandparents, and the rich flavors that formed the heart of their culture.

He envisioned the nights spent in the garden or under the grand old trees, where chairs would be set out as families and friends sprawled in an atmosphere of camaraderie. As the sun dipped below the horizon, the flicker of lantern light would dance on the faces of storytellers, their voices rising and falling in rhythm with the excitement of the listeners. The stories shared would not only recount the joy of life on the island but would also honor the struggles and resilience that had paved the way for their present.

"Every story matters," Ledger reflected, acknowledging each account, each struggle, each act of courage from those who had come before. He understood that embracing the entirety of their history would allow his community to heal, evolve, and find strength in unity. Gathering these stories and sharing them would help build bridges, not just among neighbors but with the land itself—becoming stewards together, acknowledging the remnants of pain while celebrating the profound beauty that remained.

Walking around the garden, he imagined planting a community patch, a space where everyone could contribute—a representation of growth that echoed the shared labor and nurturing it would take to foster resilience. His vision expanded: he could invite local artisans to teach their crafts, reviving skills that had once flourished but were now at risk of fading away. Together, they could create a cause that would lighten the weight of sorrow, providing new narratives that honor the island's vibrant spirit.

His imagination carried him further, envisioning collaborations with local musicians who would fill the estate with the sounds of island rhythms and melodies. They could create a series of cultural festivals where the past and present mingled, where young musicians could be inspired by their elders, thus preserving traditions while innovating new expressions of their identity.

"Music and art—they're the heart of our story," he mused, excitement bubbling within him. Each note played, and each brushstroke applied would weave a narrative that not only embraced the past but also articulated hopes, dreams, and aspirations for the future.

Yet as the vivid pictures of joy, community, and culture blossomed in his mind, correct reflection brought with it the shadows of history. He knew that as he pursued this mission, he would confront the remnants of colonial scars that still lingered. Ledger understood that engaging deeply with this past was essential to create an environment where his plans for the community could truly thrive.

"We must address this together," he whispered under the rustling leaves, absorbing the gravity of his intentions. By bringing people together to reflect on the pain of the past, they could transform it into a source of strength. Ledger envisioned a council of community members—elders, activists, artists, and youth who could guide and participate in these discussions, ensuring that everyone's voice was not only heard but respected.

With that thought, Ledger stood up from the garden bed, determination igniting within him. He would take the time to seek out those who might feel apprehensive about discussing their histories openly, assuring them that vulnerability would foster connection, not division.

"This estate is a place for healing," he reassured himself. "A safe space to unpack the burdens we have inherited, to share the victories and share the grief. Every voice must be part of this conversation."

As the sun began to set, casting a warm golden light on the garden, Ledger felt a sense of urgency rising within him. The vibrant blooms and lush greenery were a testament to resilience. Just like those flowers, he believed that the community could thrive in even the most difficult environments if they worked together in nurturing one another, carrying forth the stories of those who came before while making way for new voices to emerge.

With newfound clarity, he turned back toward the estate, the silhouette of the building now radiant against the colorful sky. "This is our chance," he thought, conviction strengthening within him.

As he reentered the estate, he was resolved that his imagination would transform into reality. Ledger was ready to commit himself fully—to honor the legacy of his ancestors, weave together stories of joy and grief, and build a future forged from love and resilience that would vibrate with the pulse of a shared, unified community that celebrated their diverse histories while fostering understanding and collaboration, a community where every voice mattered and all stories had a place, creating a rich tapestry of resilience, hope, and shared dreams for generations to come.

The rippling waves of the Caribbean Sea danced beneath the seaplane as it soared toward St. Barthélemy. The unmistakable scent of saltwater wafted through the cabin, mingling with the warmth of the tropical sun that filtered through the windows, transporting Ledger back to a time and place entwined with his childhood. Each gentle bump in the air felt like a reminder of the deep well of memories contained within him, stirring emotions that surged as powerfully as the ocean below.

As the seaplane glided forward, Ledger pressed his palms against the cool metal of the armrest, feeling the wind rush past him as the plane picked up speed for the descent. The physical sensations were vivid; he imagined the saltwater showering down like the tears of those who had once stood on the shore, watching their loved ones set sail in search of a better life. He was acutely aware that this journey echoed the earlier migrations of his ancestors—individuals who had traversed great distances in the hopes of finding freedom, opportunity, and a place to call home.

"What does home mean to me now?" he pondered, gazing out at the horizon where the sea met the sky in a seamless embrace. Time seemed to stretch and contract in the span of a heartbeat, evoking the passage of years marked by growth and change. He felt a connection to the countless others who had embarked on similar journeys—voices of his ancestors whispering Each rise and fall of the seaplane reminded Ledger of the turbulent history of his family. It was not just the aircraft that carried him over the water; it was the collective weight of their stories—their struggle not only for prosperity but also for acknowledgment, recognition, and healing. The turbulence of the flight mirrored the emotional currents roiling within him as he reflected on the meaning of home.

As the seaplane gently rocked in the air, he was transported to memories of his mother's soothing voice, calming his fears during fierce storms—her laughter filling the space with warmth, reminiscent of home, each jolt of the plane echoing the joy beneath the palm-shaded kitchen. Yet interwoven with that warmth was the stark reality of loss and division that his family bore as a legacy of their colonial past. The complexities of his heritage flooded his thoughts as he navigated these waters, grappling with the blend of joy and sorrow that defined his journey.

For too long, Ledger had compartmentalized these feelings—sectioning off nostalgia from sorrow, pride from grief—as if they were distinct entities. Yet, as the seaplane glided through the wind, it became increasingly clear that this emotional landscape was layered, and each experience shaped him more profoundly than he had previously acknowledged.

With every jolt of the plane going through turbulent clouds, he felt the weight of the past pressing down on him, mingling with a sense of urgency. What would he do upon arriving at St. Barthélemy? How would he engage with the history that shaped his family? As they neared the island's coastline, the lush greenery beckoned him, a reminder of the beauty that existed alongside the legacy of pain inherent to the island's journey.

As the seaplane landed and approached the dock, Ledger was enveloped by a rush of feelings, the sweet thrill of familiarity, and the aching bittersweet quality of memories past. He recalled his departure from this island years ago, a young man filled with dreams and uncertainties, eager to forge a new path through life's uncharted waters. Now, he returned with a deeper understanding of what he had left behind, the layers of his family history blending into a richer narrative.

The grand old palm trees lining the shore seemed to salute him, their fronds waving in the wind as the boat slowed to a stop. The sound of waves lapping gently against the hull reminded him of family gatherings, laughter echoing in the sunshine, the simple pleasures of life on the island. Yet, he could not ignore the undercurrents of loss threaded through the memories. Those moments were interlaced with stories that spoke to the struggles of his ancestors—the fight for identity, survival, and dignity in a land that held the weight of colonial history.

As Ledger disembarked, he felt the solid ground beneath his feet—a grounding reminder of where he had come and all that had led him back. The island welcomed him with open arms, but it also challenged him to confront the complexities residing within its beauty. He took a deep breath of the warm, fragrant air, feeling the tension in his shoulders ease slightly while recognizing the emotional challenge that lay ahead.

Walking along the familiar path to the estate, he recalled the long walks he had taken with his family, threading through the same trees, feeling rooted in their collective history. Each step felt like a pilgrimage—a return to something sacred, a re-engagement with the land that had once nurtured its ancestors. Ledger understood that this journey was not just a return to a physical place but a reclamation of his identity, one that would require courage and introspection.

As he walked, the landscape unfolded around him like a living tapestry, vibrant and full of potential. The lush greenery of banana plants and bright tropical flowers swayed gently in the breeze, whispering secrets of the past—the laughter of children, the stories shared under starlit skies, the tears shed in times of hardship. Each rustle of the leaves called his name, urging him to remember not just the joy but the struggles that had shaped this land.

With every step, the emotional weight of his journey pressed upon him. Memories flowed like the gentle current of the nearby river, cutting through the terrain, carving a path that mirrored his own—winding, sometimes turbulent, yet leading toward clarity. Ledger felt a deep connection to the generations that had walked this path before him, their footprints embedded in the earth, a reminder of their presence and the resilience they had embodied.

As he approached the estate, its majestic façade rose before him, a guardian of secrets and history. The worn stones called to him, inviting him to touch them, to honor the legacy that had been built upon the very ground he now stood on. Raising his hand, he brushed the cool surface of the wall, feeling its texture beneath his fingertips. It was a connection to his ancestors, to their dreams and struggles, a tangible reminder of not just what they had endured but also what they had achieved.

"This is more than just a building," he whispered, stepping forward. "It's a testament to resilience." The estate was not simply a place of wealth and comfort; it was steeped in stories of sacrifice, a site where love and loss had danced together through time. Ledger felt a swell of determination to preserve that legacy and to act as a steward of their narrative.

Stepping into the courtyard, he heard the familiar chirps of the birds that inhabited the trees nearby; their songs were a symphony that wrapped around him, echoing the harmony of his childhood. But even in the beauty of the moment, Ledger felt the shadow of the past lingering—whispers of the countless lives who had been tied to this land, lives that had borne the brunt of exploitation and suffering.

He took a moment to breathe in the rich, earthy scent of the soil, allowing the lush surroundings to ground him. "How do I honor these lives?" he questioned inwardly, knowing that the way forward required an acknowledgment of all aspects of history—the painful and the beautiful.

With renewed resolve, Ledger began to formulate ideas, envisioning a project that would bridge the divide between the estate's heritage and the present. He could create a space for education, a center where stories of the past would be celebrated and explored. He imagined workshops focused on traditional crafts, storytelling sessions featuring descendants sharing their ancestors' trials and triumphs, and community gatherings that would foster connection and healing.

The notion that this estate could serve as a healing ground resonated deeply within him. It would be more than a tribute; it would be a living, breathing space of reconciliation, where the past could be confronted with honesty and respect, and futures could be built on shared understanding. Ledger felt excitement mingle with his emotions as he envisioned how he might nurture the connections between the island's history and the culture flourishing today.

As he stepped inside the estate, memories wrapped around him like a favorite blanket—both comforting and challenging. The rich timber of the walls bore the weight of family gatherings, and the photographs of ancestors watched over him from their frames, their gazes inviting him to reflect and remember.

"I am here to carry your stories forward," he vowed silently, standing in the entryway. Inside these walls, he felt the responsibility to ensure that the voices of the past were not silenced as time moved on. Ledger understood that healing required courage—to confront the shadows, honor the truth, and create a foundation for future generations to build upon.

As the golden light of the setting sun streamed through the windows, painting the interior in warm hues, Ledger felt a sense of clarity wash over him. This was not just a return; it was a reclamation of his identity, rooted in the realization that home was not merely a physical location but an intricate weave of memories, struggles, and aspirations of those who had come before him.

He resolved to embrace the challenges ahead, knowing that the journey would not be easy. Building a future that acknowledged the complexities of the past would be a monumental task, but it was one he was willing to undertake. With courage kindling within him, Ledger took a deep breath and stepped further into the estate, ready to honor his heritage and forge a path forward, one grounded in love, resilience, and hope for a brighter tomorrow.

Upon arriving in St. Barthélemy, Ledger felt a rush of mixed emotions as he stepped off the seaplane and onto the dock. The familiar scent of the salty sea air wrapped around him, but as he looked out over the landscape, he was struck by the profound transformations the island had undergone over the past decade. The vibrant colors of the buildings and the lively chatter of locals filled his senses, yet beneath the surface, he could feel the remnants of colonialism, a weight that lingered in the atmosphere.

Strolling through the streets, Ledger's heart raced at the sight of the changes around him. The bustling crowds were filled with new faces—tourists and expatriates intermingling with long-time residents, a blend that had begun to reshape the social dynamics of the island. The shops that had once displayed local crafts now showcased designer boutiques and the air was filled with the sounds of multiple languages intertwining, a reminder that St. Barthélemy's identity was evolving. Yet, he could not shake the disquieting feeling that these developments came at a cost.

As he wandered further into the heart of the island, Ledger observed how the islanders forge a new identity, driven by a desire for progress yet firmly grounded in their rich history. Young people mingled with elders, conversations overlapping as they shared stories and aspirations for the future. There were signs of community art projects celebrating the island's heritage, murals depicting historical events, and cultural icons that honored their ancestors.

Yet, even during this vibrancy, Ledger was aware of the palpable shadows of the past. The scars from colonialism whispered among the palm trees and echoed through the conversations of those who had lived through it. While some welcomed the influx of tourism and development as a means of economic growth, others expressed concern that their cultural identity was becoming diluted.

"How do we balance progress with preservation?" he wondered, contemplating the complexity of the island's evolving narrative. Witnessing the local cafés bustling with patrons, he recognized both the excitement of innovation and the apprehension that came with change. How could they ensure that the authenticity of St. Barthélemy was not lost in the pursuit of modernity?

As he turned a corner, the vibrant market came into view, filled with stalls adorned with fresh produce, local crafts, and the melodies of island life. Ledger's heart lifted at the familiar sights and smells—spices, tropical fruits, and the laughter of children playing nearby. Yet, he could see how much had changed; the market that once felt like a unified gathering space now showed signs of gentrification, with many vendors displaced by new developments eager to cater to tourist tastes.

Standing amid the vibrant chatter, Ledger felt the weight of responsibility settle on his shoulders. The island's history was not just in the past; it was woven into the very fabric of the present, shaping the lives of its people today. "What is my role in this?" he pondered, a sense of urgency igniting within him. How could he contribute to the ongoing narrative of his homeland, honoring its legacy while supporting its evolution?

As he made his way through the market, Ledger began to formulate a vision of how the islanders could celebrate their identity amid the changes. He envisioned community gatherings that highlighted the richness of their cultural heritage—events where local artisans could showcase traditional crafts, live music could echo the rhythms of their ancestors, and storytelling could reconnect people with their roots.

"This is not just a return for me," he mused, eyes scanning the faces in the crowd. "It's an opportunity to engage, to listen, and to promote unity in the face of change." The journey to understanding his place within this transforming landscape was just beginning, but he felt a burgeoning sense of hope—a hope that together, the people of St. Barthélemy could navigate the complexities of their past while building a resilient future.

Stepping back into the vibrant flow of the market, Ledger embraced the mosaic of culture, heart, and history that encapsulated St. Barthélemy. For every change that tugged at the essence of the island, he recognized a corresponding strength in its people, a resolve to redefine what it meant to belong. And as he soaked in the lively atmosphere, he felt that this was the beginning of something transformative—a fresh chapter that had been written long before him, one in which he was now ready to actively participate.

As Ledger approached the family estate, a sense of reverence washed over him, juxtaposed with an unsettling heaviness in his heart. The grand structure stood resolutely against the backdrop of a brilliant blue sky, its weathered facade a testament to both the passage of time and the vibrant history it encapsulated. This place, once filled with laughter and life, now felt like a shadow of its former self, a remnant of a bygone era that clung to the land—a mighty fortress of memories waiting to be revisited.

Stepping through the large wooden doors, Ledger was met with a familiar yet haunting stillness. The scent of aged wood and polished furniture filled the air, whispering stories of ancestors long past. Each room he entered seemed to hold its breath, as if waiting for him to unlock the memories contained within their walls. Gazing around, he could almost see the flickering candlelight at family dinners, feel the warmth of shared moments—a paradise that had, over time, morphed into a monument of history.

Yet, as he walked through the halls adorned with portraits of his forebears, Ledger was acutely aware of the weight of legacy pressing upon him. These faces, caught in mid-laughter or reflection, held the dreams of those who had come before him—dreams of prosperity, respect, and cultural identity forged out of the tumultuous tides of colonialism. Ledger understood that he had inherited not just their aspirations but also their mistakes. Each photograph felt charged with emotion, a reminder of the successes achieved, but also of the struggles endured by his family and the innocent lives affected by decisions made generations ago.

In the parlor, where family gatherings had once pulsated with energy, Ledger felt a torrent of conflicting emotions. There was pride in the resilience of his family, but also frustration at their complicity in the very systems that had marginalized others. "What does it mean to inherit such a legacy?" he wondered, confronting the questions that nestled deep within him. The thrill of reclaiming a heritage was intertwined with the burden of reckoning with its complexities.

He wandered into the garden that had once been a vibrant oasis, imagining the laughter of his children echoing among the flowers, but now it felt overgrown and neglected. Wild vines had begun to weave through parts of the estate, reclaiming the land. While nature's encroachment illustrated the passage of time, it served as a metaphor for the unfinished business of his lineage. Ledger knelt in the soil, feeling the rough earth in his palms, a visceral connection to those who had come before and to the land itself that bore witness to their triumphs and failures.

With each memory that surfaced, Ledger grappled with his role in shaping a new future for his family. "How do I honor their dreams without perpetuating their mistakes?" he pondered, fully aware that the narratives of his ancestors should not define him but rather guide him as he sought to carve out a path for himself and his descendants. The importance of understanding their history weighed heavily on him; it was both a gift and a challenge.

As he stood amidst the remnants of his family's past, Ledger felt an urgent sense of responsibility. He wanted to create a bridge between the past and the future—an active engagement with the stories and lessons that had been passed down to him, ensuring they were not relegated to silence. "We have the power to create something new," he resolved, envisioning a legacy built not only on their achievements but also on empathy, inclusivity, and collective healing.

Leaving the garden, Ledger paused at the entrance of the estate, absorbing the grandeur that had once defined his family. He understood that walls could not contain the weight of history, nor could they shield him from the necessary confrontations with the past. His journey was about acknowledging the tapestry of existence that linked him to his ancestors while embracing the possibilities of a future yet untold.

"Who am I in this narrative?" he asked himself, committed to threading the lessons learned from the past into the fabric of his own life. The estate might stand as a testament to a certain history, but it was now also an invitation—a call to action for him to engage with both the beauty and the darkness of the legacy he had inherited. He felt the pulse of responsibility resonate within him, inspiring him to transform this inherited weight into a source of strength and vision for the generations to come. As he departed, Ledger carried with him not just the echoes of his ancestors, but also the promise of a new story waiting to be written—one that embraced the complexities of their past while forging a path toward healing and understanding for the future.

As Ledger prepared for the visit from his old friend Thomas, he felt a mixture of excitement and apprehension swirl within him. Their friendship had blossomed in childhood, nurtured by shared adventures, laughter, and the innocence of youth. However, years of separation and the complexities of adulthood have created a palpable distance between them. Thomas had stayed behind in St. Barthélemy, while Ledger pursued his dreams in St. Thomas, and the contrasting paths they had taken weighed on his mind.

As he awaited Thomas's arrival, Ledger found himself reflecting on what their friendship represented. The memories flooded in—carefree days spent exploring the island, fishing off the rocks, and sharing secret dreams as they lay under the stars. Those moments had been foundational, shaping his understanding of home and belonging. Yet, as he laid those memories alongside his current reality, he realized how much he had changed and how much the island itself had transformed in his absence.

When Thomas finally arrived, Ledger felt an initial rush of nostalgia, but it was quickly overshadowed by the reality of their different experiences. He could see the traces of the years etched on Thomas's face, a mix of wisdom and weariness that spoke of struggles faced at home. They exchanged heartfelt embraces, but beneath the surface lay an undertow of unspoken questions about their diverging paths.

Over coffee, they began to share stories, a dance of familiarity and newness. Thomas spoke of the changes on the island, the new developments, and the challenges faced by locals as they adapted to shifting socio-economic dynamics. In contrast, Ledger recounted his experiences in St. Thomas—the opportunities he had seized, the connections he had made, and the personal sacrifices that had accompanied his journey.

"I've missed this place," Ledger confessed, his voice thick with emotion. "But it feels different now. I feel different."

Thomas nodded, a knowing look in his eyes. "We all evolve, you know? But the island is still a part of us. It is just… complicated now."

Their conversation danced around the themes of identity and belonging, veering toward the essence of what it meant to call St. Barthélemy home. Ledger found solace in the fact that he could share his struggles with Thomas—the loneliness that accompanied his achievements, the moments of doubt, and the pain of separation from his roots.

In that exchange, he confronted a raw reality: despite the opportunities he had found, his migration had come at a great personal cost. The friendships that once fueled his spirit were now strained by distance, and the emotional connection he craved felt tenuous. Each of them had navigated their own paths, and in doing so, they had both experienced loss—of dreams, of connections, of the innocence of youth.

As the visit ended and Thomas prepared to leave, Ledger felt a deep sense of gratitude for their time together. It was a reminder that while their journeys might differ, the essence of their friendship had not faded. They were still two boys who had grown up under the same sun, bonded by a shared history that transcended physical distance.

Standing at the doorway, Ledger felt an echo of hope. While the costs of migration were real and painful, the visit had also illuminated the potential for reconnection—both with Thomas and with the island. The path forward involved not only reflecting on the sacrifices made but also actively weaving those threads of connection back into his life. As he watched Thomas walk away, Ledger felt a renewed commitment to bridge the gap between his past and present, honoring both the struggle and the friendship that had shaped him.

As Ledger settled into the quiet of his room in the family estate, he took a moment to reflect on his decade spent in St. Thomas. The memories flowed like the tides, bringing with them both the buoyancy of opportunity and the weight of sacrifice. While his time on the island had been marked by growth, new friendships, and career advancements, he could not ignore the personal costs that accompanied his migration. The bright lights of St. Thomas had shone a path toward success, but they had also cast long shadows over the connections he once held dear.

During the quiet moments, Ledger often found himself grappling with a profound sense of isolation. The external beauty of his new life had been intoxicating at first—the vibrant community, the sun-soaked beaches, and the rhythmic pulse of island life. Yet, beneath the surface, he felt a disconnection from his heritage, a loneliness that crept in at times when he least expected it. Despite the friends he had made, no one could fill the void left by family and the familiarity of home.

Often, he would hear his mother's voice echoing in his mind, urging him to remember where he came from. In St. Thomas, he had reinvented himself in many ways—a professional, an islander, a friend—but the journey had come with the struggle of establishing an identity that felt authentic. He was balancing the expectations placed upon him by a new community while wrestling with the longing for the roots he had left behind. The blend of cultures that surrounded him was enriching, yet it sometimes left him feeling like an outsider—a participant in life, but never fully immersed.

In those moments of solitude, he found himself yearning for the connections that had once grounded him in St. Barthélemy. The tastes of local dishes that his mother had prepared, the stories passed down through generations, the laughter shared over bonfires beneath the stars—all these memories felt like distant echoes of a life that he could not fully reclaim. The sacrifices he made for economic stability created an ache in his chest, a bittersweet longing for the simpler moments spent with loved ones against the backdrop of his childhood home.

Reflecting on the choices that had led him to this point, Ledger recognized the delicate balance between ambition and connection. He was proud of the professional success he had achieved in St.

Thomas—opportunities and experiences that many could only dream of—but he could not ignore the emotional toll it had taken. Each promotion, each network he built, came at the expense of family gatherings and celebrations. The big moments, the ordinary days filled with love and laughter, were sacrificed on the altar of self-sufficiency.

As the sun began to set outside, casting golden hues through his window, Ledger acknowledged that the loss he felt was not merely personal; it was interwoven with the larger story of his community. So many had made similar choices, leaving their homes in search of better lives, only to navigate the rocky terrain of longing and disconnection. The sacrifices for survival were often silent struggles, woven into the fabric of their new identities, unnoticed amidst the busyness of daily life.

"Am I still connected to my roots, or have I lost them forever?" he pondered, the question echoing in his mind. His heart ached at the thought that by pursuing his dreams, he may have contributed to the very struggles that plagued his homeland. Ledger understood that while he could forge a new path for himself, he must also remain committed to preserving the bonds that tied him to his past.

It was in this reflection that an idea began to take shape—a desire to reconnect not only with his roots but also to find ways to bridge the gap between the lives he lived in St. Thomas and St. Barthélemy. He envisioned initiatives that could strengthen ties among those living away from home, creating opportunities for dialogue and support, and fostering shared dreams rather than isolating them in silence.

The journey would not be easy, nor would it erase the scars of separation. But Ledger resolved to embrace the entirety of his experience—both the growth and the grief—determined to transform his longing into something constructive, a conduit for connection rather than a reminder of separation. As he sat in the soft glow of twilight, he felt a flicker of hope ignite within him, a conviction that he could reclaim his narrative and contribute to building a future in which loss and sacrifice became a source of strength rather than sorrow.

That evening, Ledger found solace in the quietude of the family estate, the fading light of dusk casting long shadows across the floors. As the warmth of the sun dipped below the horizon, he sank into an old wicker chair on the veranda, a cherished spot overlooking the garden that had once flourished under his grandmother's careful tending. The air was thick with the fragrant scent of jasmine, a perfume that held memories of laughter and love—a stark contrast to the pangs of loss and sacrifice that had filled his earlier thoughts.

As he watched the sun set behind the hills, Ledger felt a wave of nostalgia wash over him, mingled with the bittersweet taste of reality. This was a moment for reflection, a time to sift through the conflicting emotions that had accompanied his journey. He thought of the sacrifices he had made in pursuit of a better life. While the accomplishments he achieved in St. Thomas had come with opportunities, they had also exacted a heavy toll: distance from family, the chasm of isolation, and the feeling of being adrift, even amidst the successes.

"What have I truly gained, and at what price?" This thought echoed in his mind like an unsettling refrain. Had he traded the warmth of familial connections for fleeting gains that felt increasingly hollow in the stillness of his heart? He could not shake the feeling that every triumph had been shadowed by a profound sense of separation from those he loved most.

As twilight deepened around him, Ledger began to confront the emotional weight of his choices. Distant memories floated to the surface—his mother's laughter, the joyous gatherings of relatives, and evenings spent sharing stories beneath a canopy of stars. For every opportunity he had sought, there had been a counterweight, a silent sacrifice made by those who had supported him from afar. How had they borne his absence?

His mind now raced to the faces of his family. They were not just figures from his past; they were a vital part of his present, each one shaping who he was becoming. The realization struck him: his journey had not merely been about his own growth but also about how his path had impacted the lives of those still rooted in St. Barthélemy.

In that moment, Ledger understood the importance of reconciling the past with the future. He could not carry the weight of his decisions in solitude; he needed to weave the threads of his journey with the stories of those who had remained. His family's resilience resonated with a powerful reminder that their struggles and sacrifices deserved acknowledgment, that they too were pivotal characters in the narrative he was crafting.

"I cannot let my journey sever the bonds of our shared history," he resolved quietly, feeling the stirrings of a new commitment take form within him. Rather than seeing his migration as a departure, he could envision it as the beginning of a new chapter, one that would honor his roots while actively engaging with the lives of his loved ones.

As Ledger paused to gather his thoughts, the first stars began to twinkle in the indigo sky, casting gentle light upon the garden. He envisioned a future filled with possibilities—a future where he could not only reclaim his narrative but also foster connections that would bridge the distance created by his choices. He could create spaces for dialogue, rekindle memories, and build something meaningful that would enrich both his life and theirs.

Feeling a surge of clarity, he allowed himself to dream of gathering his family, of sharing the rich tapestry of experiences that had shaped him and inviting them to be part of his journey forward. They could navigate this evolving definition of family together, honoring the past while embracing the future.

By the time the stars were bright in the night sky, Ledger understood that though loss and sacrifice were complex parts of his story, they could also serve as the foundation for a renewed commitment to family. This new clarity opened pathways in his heart—pathways to regeneration and connection, pathways that would encourage growth both for himself and for those who had stood by him through it all. He felt an excitement building at the thought of reshaping his identity, not just for himself, but for his family, forging a legacy built on love, resilience, and shared stories.

As the last rays of sunlight dipped below the horizon, casting a warm glow across the garden, Ledger found himself lost in thought, reflecting on the future of his family. The legacy of those who had come before him weighed heavily on his mind, but it was the impact of his own journey that loomed largest. Moving to St. Thomas had been a decision borne of necessity, a drive to seek opportunities and build a better life. Yet, in that pursuit, he could not ignore the subtle but profound ways this choice had reshaped not only his identity but also the identities of those he had left behind.

In the quiet solitude of the estate, Ledger remembered the faces of his relatives—cousins, aunts, uncles—those who had remained in St. Barthélemy while he sought fortune elsewhere. His migration had ushered him into a new world filled with possibilities, but he knew that it also cast ripples through the lives of his family. They were left to navigate their own paths, their own challenges, as he carved out a space for himself among the palm trees and cerulean waters of St. Thomas.

His thoughts drifted to family gatherings, the laughter that had once filled their home, and the collective spirit of shared dreams and celebrations. He considered how his decision had altered the dynamics of their relationships. In seeking his place in a new community, had he inadvertently created distance within his own? Did they view his absence as a rejection, or could they see it as an opportunity for growth, both for him and them?

"What does family mean in this context?" he pondered, wrestling with the question. Was it simply the people who shared his blood, or did it extend to those who had shaped his experiences and growth? The bonds formed through shared history and time spent together were precious, yet the definition of family was evolving, shaped by the realities of migration and modernity.

Ledger recognized that the concept of home was not solely tied to physical locations. It was a tapestry woven from shared experiences, emotions, and memories, an intricate design that spanned across distances. His new life in St. Thomas had allowed him to redefine what it meant to belong, but it had also posed questions about how to maintain and nurture the connections that stemmed from his origin.

As he reflected on his role within this shifting landscape, Ledger felt a developing desire to bridge the gap between his two worlds. He envisioned ways to cultivate a sense of unity among his family, regardless of where they resided. This could manifest through regular gatherings that celebrated their heritage—a mix of both local traditions and the new experiences he had gained. Two worlds, he realized, could coexist; they could inform and enrich one another rather than remain in conflict.

"How can I create spaces for dialogue and connection?" he wondered, exploring potential initiatives that could bring family together, whether through digital family reunions or planned visits back to St. Barthélemy. He could be the conduit for sharing stories, for fostering understanding, and for sustaining ties that might otherwise crumble under the weight of distance.

The reality of his choices had painted the canvas of their lives differently. Each stroke was colored by the necessity of change, and he was determined to help his family navigate this new narrative together. He wanted to ensure that while he carved out a place for himself away from home, he would not leave behind the essence of what it meant to be a family bound by shared dreams.

Feeling a renewed sense of determination, Ledger stood and gazed out over the fading twilight, imagining the possibilities for the future. He could be an architect of connection, a storyteller who honored their history while inviting them to be part of the future he was building. The nostalgia that once weighed heavily on him now transformed into an inspirational vision—a commitment to redefining family, not as a static entity, but as a dynamic, evolving community that embraced change while honoring its roots.

"We are stronger together," he affirmed quietly to himself, feeling a sense of clarity wash over him. The sacrifices made in pursuit of a better life need not sever the ties to his past; instead, they could inspire a deeper appreciation for the relationships that shaped his journey. In carving his own path, Ledger now saw an opportunity to uplift his family, forging connections that would last through generations, binding them together in a shared narrative of resilience and love. With that newfound understanding, he felt a swell of hope for what lies ahead, both for himself and his family, a vibrant future waiting to be embraced.

The journey back to St. Barthélemy felt surreal, each heartbeat resonating with the significance of what it represented. For Ledger Philogene, this trip was far more than a mere transaction to finalize the sale of the family estate; it was a profound exploration of identity, legacy, and the intricate costs of migration. As he navigated the familiar yet transformed landscapes of his childhood, Ledger found himself grappling with the complexities that came with returning home—an experience that shimmered with the duality of nostalgia and discomfort.

As his plane descended toward the island, the breathtaking views of emerald hills and turquoise waters reached out to him, drawing memories from the depths of his consciousness. Yet even the beauty of the landscape could not mask the weight of his reflections. Ledger's thoughts were pulled in a myriad of directions, each tethered to his past and the echoes of colonialism that had marked the island's history. He could hear the voices of his ancestors whispering through the winds, reminding him of the struggles they endured and the resilience they embodied.

Those reflections became more vivid as he set foot on solid ground. The familiar warmth of the sun against his skin stirred a rush of emotions, both welcome and disquieting. Here was a place rich with its history, but it was also a landscape that bore the scars of colonialism, of lives disrupted and dreams deferred. Ledger had left St. Barthélemy seeking opportunity and stability, yet the journey had drawn him into a broader conversation about belonging and what it meant to be shaped by the legacies of a turbulent past.

Walking through the streets, now punctuated by new developments and international influences, Ledger observed how the island was evolving. Different faces went about their daily lives, and the vibrant culture he remembered was simultaneously preserved and transformed. This duality brought with it a sense of dislocation, as he sensed both the warmth of familiarity and the sharp edges of change. How could he reconcile his love for this island with the recognition of its complexities? The ongoing narrative of his homeland, woven together by both colonial shadows and emerging resilience, continued to unfold dynamically around him.

"This isn't just my story," he mused, absorbing the bustling atmosphere filled with laughter and chatter—an amalgamation of cultures layered atop one another. "This is the story of everyone who calls this place home." The realization hit him: in his quest to lay claim to his identity, he also needed to Honor the collective experience of all who had endured the trials of migration, displacement, and transformation. He felt an urgency to advocate for understanding, empathy, and a renewed commitment to the cultural heritage that defined the island.

As he approached the family estate, the towering structure loomed before him, both a monument to his ancestral roots and a poignant reminder of the sacrifices made. Here, Ledger stood at a pivotal crossroads, faced with the weighted history and the possibilities for the future swirling within him. The decisions he made moving forward would not only sculpt his narrative but also influence the stories of future generations. He felt the responsibility of reshaping that narrative, to infuse it with hope, and to ensure that the legacy he carried was one of acknowledgment and resilience rather than silence and shame.

Entering the estate, the familiar scents and sights washed over him, igniting memories that breathed life into the stillness. The peeling walls and faded photographs whispered the stories of those who had come before. Each room was a repository of dreams and struggles, a testament to their endurance in the face of unimaginable circumstances. Ledger understood that honoring their sacrifices meant confronting the complexities of his own choices, the migration driven by necessity that separated him from the people and places he held dear.

With every step through the house, he reflected not only on the financial implications of selling the estate but also on the emotional and cultural impact of such a decision. The potential sale represented a severing of ties to the physical space, but it could also symbolize an opportunity for renewal—a chance to forge connections between past and present, to create pathways for dialogue between generations. What if the sale could enable him to invest in initiatives that supported the community, promoting sustainability and growth rather than erasure?

As he stood in the family parlor, Ledger felt an unwavering determination grow within him. He envisioned organizing community events that celebrated their shared heritage, workshops that educated young islanders about their history, and platforms for storytelling that honored the struggles and triumphs of their ancestors. This was not merely about preserving the legacy of his family; it was about cultivating a collective narrative that transcended individual experiences, creating a tapestry of resilience woven from the threads of each person's journey.

"I can reclaim this narrative," he whispered to himself, feeling the surge of purpose eclipses the doubts that had simmered beneath the surface. "I can honor their struggles and elevate my family's legacy in ways that reflect our shared humanity." As he looked out the window toward the horizon, Ledger knew he had a long road ahead, filled with both challenges and possibilities. This homecoming was not just a return but an awakening and a call to action, an invitation to engage with the past while embracing the complexities of the present.

With a heart full of resolve, Ledger stepped away from the shadows of nostalgia and into the light of hope and possibility. He was prepared to weave together a new chapter one that honored those who had shaped him and charted a course for his family's future, where the legacies of resilience and strength would shine brightly amidst the evolving landscape of St. Barthélemy.

ॐ

Part Two: New Beginnings

Chapter Five: Journey to Dominica

After finalizing the sale of the family estate in St. Barthélemy, Ledger Philogene's return to St. Thomas felt like a pivotal moment—a bridge between the life they knew and the future that beckoned with promise. The sale had marked the end of an era, yet rather than lingering on what was left behind, Ledger was filled with a renewed sense of hope. This was not just a closing chapter; it was the key to unlocking a fresh start for his family.

As he contemplated the possibilities, the idea of migrating to Dominica began to take root in his mind. The island represented more than just a new home; it embodied opportunity, potential, and a chance to build a better life for Clara and their children. It was a place where they could set down new roots, surrounded by a vibrant community that thrived on the spirit of resilience and togetherness. Ledger envisioned the lush landscapes, the welcoming smiles of the locals, and the rich cultural traditions that would envelop his family in warmth and belonging.

Introducing this vision to Clara and the children was both exciting and daunting. Ledger understood the weight of such a decision, aware that change often brought with it uncertainty and sacrifice. He reflected on the comfort of the life they had established in St. Barthélemy—the familiar faces, the rhythm of daily life, the memories woven into their surroundings. Yet, he felt a call to something greater, something that could not be ignored.

As he gathered his family around the table, Ledger sensed the mix of emotions swirling among them—curiosity, apprehension, and a glimmer of hope. He recognized that for Wizen and Julien, the thought of leaving friends behind might bring sadness, while for Clara, practical concerns about the logistics of migration and the challenges of starting fresh could overshadow the allure of new beginnings. Yet, there was also an undeniable excitement in the air as they discussed the possibilities that lay ahead.

In sharing his vision, Ledger felt the weight of his responsibility to lead his family into the unknown. He wanted them to see that this journey could be the catalyst for transformation, offering them the chance to redefine their identity and aspirations. He was determined to foster a sense of adventure and resilience in them. The prospect of a new life, with all its challenges and triumphs, could become an indelible part of their collective story.

Reflecting on that pivotal conversation, Ledger understood that their migration was not just about moving to another island; it was about embracing change as a family and nurturing the bonds that held them together. The hope and aspirations they harbored could only flourish in the fertile ground of love and support, no matter where they found themselves.

As they began to envision their future in Dominica, Ledger felt a deep sense of gratitude wash over him. He was grateful for the courage of his family to explore this journey with him, for the strength they drew from one another, and for the connection they shared with their extended family who might join them in this venture. Together, they could face whatever lay ahead, grounded in the love they had for each other.

In this moment of reflection, Ledger knew that the transition would be challenging, but he believed in the resilience of the human spirit. This chapter was not merely an end; it was an invitation to write a new narrative—one filled with hope, community, and the promise of a brighter future in Dominica.

In the year 1809, at the age of forty-two, Ledger stood at a significant crossroads in his life, contemplating a decision that would alter the trajectory of his family's future. After much reflection and heartfelt discussions with his wife, Clara, and their nine children, he concluded that migrating to the lush, inviting landscapes of Dominica was the best path forward. The decision was not taken lightly; it was the culmination of thoughtful conversations about their aspirations, the opportunities that lay ahead, and the promise of a new beginning.

The sound of laughter trickled through the Philogene home as the children played together in the living room, the familiar chaos a comfort to Ledger and Clara. It was an ordinary evening, yet a palpable current of anticipation hummed in the air as they prepared for an important family discussion. After the sale of the family estate in St. Barthélemy, the gravity of their next steps weighed heavily on their hearts.

Seated at the dining table, Ledger looked across at Clara, whose expression mirrored his own mix of excitement and anxiety. They had long discussed the prospect of a new beginning since returning, but now it was time to solidify their decision. The proceeds from the sale weighed heavily on their minds, symbolizing both a closure and a doorway to new possibilities.

"We need to talk about Dominica," Ledger began, his voice steady yet thoughtful. "I believe it offers us a chance to build a better future—a nurturing environment for our children."

Clara nodded, her brow furrowed as she considered the implications of such a move. They had discussed this briefly before. "I can see the appeal, Ledger," she replied carefully, "but we must be certain. This is not just about us; it is about the kids and their future."

"Exactly," he agreed. "Leaving St. Thomas and the shop for Aunt Marie to manage was a big step. It means we are letting go of a lot, but we have an opportunity to create something new in Dominica."

The idea of leaving their property in St. Thomas, managed by Aunt Marie—his father's sister—was both comforting and concerning for Ledger. He trusted her completely, knowing she would take care of the shop and uphold the family legacy while allowing them to focus on starting anew. But the thought of abandoning the family business still stirred a sense of loss within him.

"What if we're sacrificing too much?" Clara asked softly. "What if Dominica doesn't fulfill our expectations?"

"Every decision carries risk," Ledger replied, leaning forward, his eyes earnest. "But we must look beyond just escaping the past. We need to think about stability, the community we can build, and the nurturing environment our children deserve. Dominica has so much potential."

He continued, outlining the aspects of the island that had drawn him to the idea of moving: the vibrant culture, friendly community, and beautiful landscapes that offered opportunities for adventure and growth. "We can also foster connections with nature, embrace a slower pace of life, and ensure our children grow up in an environment rich with resources and support."

Clara listened intently, her heart swelling with both hope and fear. She thought of their children—Wizen, Petronel, Julien, Eliza, Louisa, James, Dfriel, Koie, and Nerisa—and all they had experienced. "They deserve a place where they can flourish," she acknowledged. "But what about our roots? St. Barthélemy has been home for so long."

"Home is where we choose to build our lives," Ledger replied gently. "We are not abandoning our roots; we are expanding them. We can integrate our heritage into our new life, sharing our culture and stories while embracing the new."

Clara looked around the room, at the children now playing together and laughing, their joy infectious. She could see the potential for Dominica to be a foundation upon which they could build their family's legacy—a space that could be filled with love, laughter, and shared experiences.

"You're right," she finally said, her voice steadying with resolve. "If we are going to do this, we need to make it a family decision. The kids should have a say in this transition too."

Ledger smiled, grateful for Clara's willingness to open the conversation to their children. "Let us gather them and share our thoughts. Their voices matter in this decision."

Moments later, the children, still energized from their play, gathered around the table, eyes wide with curiosity. Ledger and Clara exchanged glances before begin recounting their journey—the sale of the family estate and the potential move to Dominica. Ledger shared his vision for life in Dominica, where fertile soil and rich resources promised agricultural prosperity. He spoke passionately about the land's beauty, the chance to establish a stable home, and the possibilities for their children to thrive in a new environment.

Wizen spoke up first, his excitement bubbling over. "Is it true? Are we moving to a new place? Is it like a big adventure?"

Ledger smiled, recognizing the spirit of adventure in his son. "Yes, Wizen. It can be an adventure. We see it as a chance to start fresh, but we want to hear what you all think."

Petronel's eyes sparkled. "Will there be beaches? I want to see the ocean!"

Eliza jumped up, her face glowing with excitement. "And will there be places to explore? I want to go on hikes and see all the animals and plants!"

Clara could not help but smile at their enthusiasm. "Yes, Dominica is known for its beautiful landscapes, including rainforests, waterfalls, and beaches. There are so many adventures waiting for you all."

Julien, who had been listening intently, asked, "What about our friends here? Will we have time to say goodbye?"

Ledger's heart ached at the mention of their friends. "Moving does mean saying goodbye to some people we care about, but we will also have a chance to make new friends. And you can stay connected with your old friends through letters and phone calls."

Koie and Nerisa, ever curious, looked at their parents with wide eyes. "Can we visit the beach every day?" they both asked in unison, their innocent excitement infectious.

"We can certainly go as often as we can," Clara promised, her heart swelling with tenderness as she observed their youthful enthusiasm.

"I want to catch crabs," Dfriel piped up, his eyes wide with mischief. "Can we do that?"

"Of course! And we can go on boat rides, explore the mangroves, and even snorkel," Ledger added, his excitement mirroring theirs. The kids' faces lit up at the thought of exploring the wonders of nature.

James chimed in, his adventurous spirit shining through: "I want to try surfing! Is there a chance we can learn to surf?"

The energy around the table was electric, and Clara took a moment to savor the laughter and excitement filling the room. With each question, she felt the possibility of this new beginning weaving a rich tapestry of opportunity for their family.

"We'll find people who can teach us—people who know the best places to go," Ledger assured them, envisioning not just a move to a new country but an integration into a community filled with adventure and culture.

After a spirited discussion, Clara brought the focus back to their decision. "It sounds like you are all excited about the move, but we must recognize this change will come with challenges too. We will be leaving our home in St. Thomas behind and starting fresh in a new place."

Wizen nodded, thoughtful. "It will be different, for sure. But can we do it together? As a family?"

"Absolutely," Ledger affirmed, overwhelmed by pride in how hearty and resilient his children had become through this process. "Every adventure we face will be together. We will be a team, supporting each other every step of the way."

Eliza glanced at her siblings, and with a hint of determination, she said, "If we ask, our friends will visit us in Dominica! We can show them all the cool things there!"

"That's a great idea!" Petronel agreed. "We can have a welcome party!"

The room erupted into discussions about who they would invite and what they would do with their friends when they arrived in Dominica.

"So, are we ready to make this decision as a family?" Clara asked, her voice was steady and warm.

Ledger had a feeling of pride as he witnessed his children embracing the change with courage and excitement. After sharing nods and murmured affirmations from the younger ones, Wizen declared, "Yes! I think we should do it if we have each other!"

Clara reached out to hold Ledger's hand, their fingers intertwining. "Then it's settled," she said softly. "We move to Dominica."

As they all shared in the excitement of their new journey, Ledger felt a profound connection to his family. It was a collective decision that transcended mere practicality. This move was not just about leaving behind their past but about building a vibrant and hopeful future together.

With children chattering animatedly about new adventures and the promise of tomorrow, Ledger knew they were making a move toward stability, nurturing relationships, and a family-centered lifestyle filled with possibilities. He envisioned a welcoming space where traditions would be honored, enabling them to create a tapestry of experiences as a family in their new home.

Before making a final decision, Ledger knew it was essential to involve his parents and siblings in the discussions about their move to Dominica. His parents had devoted their lives to building the family business and honoring that legacy was of utmost importance to him. He gathered everyone for a family meeting, where he expressed his deep gratitude for the sacrifices they had made and shared his vision for the future. Ledger reassured them that Aunt Marie, his father's sister, would take over the reins of the business, ensuring it remained a staple in their community. This arrangement would allow them to maintain their roots while exploring new opportunities.

The heartfelt discussions that unfolded in their living room were a blend of nostalgia and ambition. Ledger's parents listened attentively and recognized the potential benefits that migration to Dominica could bring to their family. They believed wholeheartedly in their ability to flourish in this new environment. With their support and encouragement, Ledger felt a renewed sense of resolve and excitement about the journey ahead, knowing he had the blessings of his entire family behind him as they embarked on this new chapter together.

That night, as they gathered in the living room, Ledger reflected on the dreams they had shared. Their laughter echoed off the walls, mingling with the sounds of lighthearted play. This was the essence of what they were carrying with them—a love that would continue to thrive regardless of where they planted their roots.

The journey ahead would hold challenges and uncertainties, but together, as a family, Ledger felt they were embarking on a captivating adventure, one filled with promise, growth, and shared experiences. As the evening shadows deepened and the stars began to twinkle outside the window, he felt a surge of hope envelop them. This was more than just a move; it was a chance to rediscover what it meant to be a united family, and they would navigate every twist and turn together.

The sun had begun to dip low in the sky, casting a warm golden hue across St. Thomas as the Philogene family tackled the daunting task of packing. Each box and suitcase were a vessel holding memories, filled with the tangible remnants of their life in this cherished paradise. Laughter mingled with the sounds of shuffling boxes, but an undercurrent of anxiety rippled through the air, a reminder of the monumental change that lay ahead.

Clara and Ledger stood side by side in the living room, sorting through their possessions. "Do we really need all of this?" Clara asked, holding up a pair of summer dresses that had seen better days. She tilted her head thoughtfully, contemplating the items that filled their home.

"Maybe not," Ledger replied, taking the dresses from her and placing them in a donation box. "Let us keep just what we need and what brings us joy. We are starting anew, after all."

As they continued to sort through clothes, toys, and keepsakes, each item sparked a memory—holidays spent with family, birthdays celebrated with friends, quiet evenings spent by the water. The nostalgia was bittersweet, pulling at their hearts and reminding them of all the moments that had defined their lives in St. Thomas.

In the nearby children's room, the sounds of laughter echoed as the kids scoured through their toy bins, trying to decide what to bring along. Wizen, Petronel, Eliza, and Julien combed through their treasures, intensely debating their choices.

"I'll take my soccer ball!" Wizen shouted, holding it high with pride.

Petronel clutched her art supplies close. "And I am taking my sketchbook! I want to draw everything in Dominica!"

Eliza looked around, her brow furrowed in concentration. "What about my stuffed bear? I cannot sleep without him!" She hurriedly shoved the bear into her backpack.

As the evening wore on, Clara moved to the kitchen and opened the cupboards, glancing over jars of spices and favorite cookware. She hesitated, her heart heavy. "Do you think we'll find the same ingredients in Dominica?" she mused aloud, imagining the flavors and smells that had permeated her home.

"We can find similar ones, or even discover new ones," Ledger replied, stepping in to help. "Cooking is one constant we can always carry with us. We will make it work."

The practicalities of moving to a new country hung in the air, each decision layered with meaning. Amid the excitement that tinged their preparations, the emotional weight loomed large; they were not just packing belongings but also leaving behind familiar places and beloved friends. The thought of saying goodbye cut deeper than any box they filled.

Through the process, Ledger felt the unmistakable weight of responsibility pressing down on him. He often stepped outside into the evening air to clear his head, feeling the warm breeze against his skin—a bittersweet reminder of the home they were preparing to leave. With each breath, he acknowledged the sacrifices they were making for the sake of their children's futures.

"This isn't just about us leaving," he whispered to himself. "It's about building a new life where they can thrive." He knew that this step meant not only uprooting their family but also stepping into a world filled with uncertainties. Nevertheless, he felt a thrill at the prospect of new beginnings, shaking off the nagging doubts that whispered in the back of his mind.

As the packing continued, social gatherings turned into bittersweet farewells. Clara organized one last get-together with close friends, knowing that they needed a proper goodbye before the journey to Dominica. The laughter bubbled forth, brightening the atmosphere, but the undertone of emotion was palpable.

Friends quickly visited, bringing homemade dishes and heartfelt gifts, tokens of their affection, and well-wishes. Clara's best friend, Lila, wrapped her arms around her tightly. "I'll miss you so much," Lila said, her voice thick with emotion. "You're going to do amazing things in your new home."

"I will miss you too! Promise you will visit us?" Clara replied, tearfully laughing as she clutched a small charm Lila had given her—a reminder of their friendship.

As they said their farewells, Ledger found himself reflecting on the people and places that had shaped their lives. The life they had crafted together was anchored in these connections, filled with laughter, friendship, and support. "It's just goodbye for now," he assured their friends, his heart both heavy and hopeful. "We'll make new memories, and we want you to be a part of our journey."

The sun hung low in the sky, painting the St. Thomas harbor in warm hues of gold and amber as the Philogene family gathered at the bustling dock for their farewell. The sounds of laughter and chatter filled the air, mingling with the gentle lapping of waves against the boat's hull. The steamboat stood ready to take them to their new life in Dominica, but the weight of parting from their home felt heavy in their hearts.

Ledger stood with Clara and their children, taking in the scene around them. Friends and neighbors had come to bid them farewell, many holding homemade signs and gifts—tokens of appreciation for the years they had shared in their community. He could see Lila across the dock, waving enthusiastically, with tears glistening in her eyes.

"I can't believe this is happening," Clara said softly, squeezing Ledger's hand. She was trying to be brave, but he could feel her emotions simmering just below the surface.

"We'll come back to visit," Ledger reassured her, looking into her eyes. "And we'll keep everyone updated on our adventures."

The children ran to their friends, embracing them tightly, tears mixing with the joy of their shared memories. "Promise to write!" Petronel called, her voice breaking slightly as she clutched her best friend's hand.

Koie and Nerisa bounced up and down. "We will send you postcards! And pictures!" they chimed in unison, their youthful excitement shimmering through the bittersweet atmosphere.

"Just come to visit us in Dominica!" Wizen shouted, his mature voice full of conviction. He threw his arms around his friends, trying to soak in every moment before they left.

Amid the chaos of farewells, Ledger's parents arrived, their faces lighting up with a blend of pride and excitement, mingled with the bittersweet emotions of leaving their longtime home. They had decided to migrate to Dominica alongside the family, eager to support their children as they embarked on this new adventure. Ledger stepped forward, enveloping his mother in a heartfelt embrace. "We've been waiting for you," he said, his voice thick with emotion. "We didn't want to leave without you."

His father nodded, emotion shining in his eyes. "We believe in you, Ledger, and we are thrilled to be joining you on this journey. This is just the beginning for all of us, and your dreams are worth pursuing."

As they pulled away, Clara stepped in to give Ledger's parents a heartfelt hug. "We are so glad you decided to join us on this journey. It would not be the same without you. And we can always count on Aunt Marie to manage the family business," she reassured them.

Together, they felt the weight of the moment—leaving behind their familiar home while looking forward to the promise of new beginnings in Dominica.

As the time for departure drew near, Ledger glanced at the horizon, where the sunlight was beginning to wane. The boat's crew was preparing to cast off the lines, and he felt a tightening in his chest. "Let's gather for one last picture!" he called to the family and friends, wanting to capture this moment forever.

They huddled together, arms around each other, smiling through the tears. Clara stood with Ledger at the center, the children flanking them, and their friends rounded the group. The camera clicked, freezing a snapshot of love and hope against the backdrop of their beloved home.

Just as they started to disperse, a soft voice broke through the noise. "We'll miss you all!" Lila called out, her voice filled with warmth. "Do not forget to keep us posted! We will be waiting to hear all about your adventures!"

"And we'll have stories to share!" Ledger replied, his heart was swelling with gratitude. He waved to everyone as the boat slowly drifted away from the dock, the first wave of separation washing over them.

The children pressed their noses against the railing, staring back at the familiar shores they had called home. Tears shimmered in their eyes as they caught glimpses of their friends waving goodbye. Koie began to sing a song they had learned together, her sweet voice ringing out against the gentle churning of the water:

"Goodbye, St. Thomas, we will see you soon,

Our hearts will carry you, beneath the moon."

Her siblings joined in, their voices intertwining in a melody that filled the air, soothing their hearts. And as the boat pulled farther away, Ledger felt the stirring of hope begin to replace the ache of leaving. They were on the cusp of a new adventure, propelled not just by the wind in their sails, but by the love and support of their family and friends left behind.

As the shoreline of St. Thomas became a memory fading into the distance, Ledger stood with his family, hearts united in purpose, ready to embrace whatever awaited them in Dominica.

The morning air was thick with anticipation as the Philogene family stood at the docks, gazing at the brightly painted steamboat that awaited them. The sea glimmered under the sun, vast and inviting, a reminder of the journey they were about to embark on. Ledger's heart raced with a mix of excitement and nostalgia; he could not help but recall their first sea voyage—the one that had brought them from

St. Barthélemy to St. Thomas—years ago. This new journey to Dominica, however, felt refreshingly different.

"Look at those colors!" Eliza exclaimed, pointing at the boat's vibrant hull, painted in shades of turquoise and coral.

"It's beautiful!" Petronel added, her eyes wide with wonder.

As they boarded, Ledger took a moment to observe the vessel. The upgraded steamboat was a far cry from the small, cramped ferries of his past—a more comfortable and spacious craft, built for carrying families and cargo across the Caribbean waters. It promised a smoother ride, with amenities that would keep their spirits high during the voyage.

Once on board, the family found a cozy spot on the upper deck, allowing for breathtaking views of the surrounding sea. They settled in, children clamoring for the best seats, and Ledger could not help but smile at their energy.

"Remember, we need to stay together," Clara reminded them, her voice steady yet excited. "This journey is a new beginning for all of us."

As the boat pulled away from the dock and the shoreline of St. Thomas faded into the distance, the thrill of their adventure surged through them. The gentle rocking of the boat was comforting, as Ledger took in the expanse of water opening before an emblem of their transition from the familiar to the unexplored.

They settled in for the crossing, the rhythm of the boat lulling the children into a sense of adventure. Ledger leaned back, looking out over the waves as they glimmered under the sun. Clara joined him, grasping his hand. "This is it, Ledger," she said, her voice full of promise. "We're really doing this."

"We are," he replied, squeezing her hand gently. "The future is right in front of us."

As the voyage progressed, the family began to share stories—memories of their time in St. Thomas and the dreams they held for their new life in Dominica. They spoke of places they wanted to explore, the foods they hoped to try, and the friendships they anticipated forming.

Wizen was the first to break the surface of nostalgia. "Remember our fishing trips?" he asked, eyes shining with enthusiasm. "We should do that again in Dominica!"

Petronel clapped her hands. "And I want to find new things to draw! There will be so much inspiration there."

Julien, who had been captivated by the view of the sea, chimed in, "And I can write stories about our adventures! What if I write about the animals we see?"

Clara looked at her children, warmth filling her heart at their excitement. "Those are beautiful ideas. We can create a family journal to capture all our memories."

As they spoke, Ledger noticed the camaraderie growing stronger among his children. They were bonding not just as siblings but as fellow adventurers looking forward to the possibilities ahead. Together, they shared laughter and dreams, weaving a tapestry of hope against the backdrop of the shifting waters.

The sea was unpredictable; at times, the waves swelled, and the boat rocked gently, yet it only amplified their adventure. With each passing moment, Ledger felt a growing sense of freedom—freedom from the weight of leaving their past behind, and freedom to embrace the uncertainty of the future.

"The water reminds me of life," he said, contemplating aloud. "It can be tumultuous at times and serene at others. But it always keeps moving forward."

Clara nodded thoughtfully. "It's a good reminder," she replied. "We need to be like these waves—adaptable and ready for what's next."

As they journeyed deeper into the Caribbean Sea, the sun began to dip below the horizon, painting the sky vibrant hues of orange and pink. The beauty of the moment captivated them, casting a spell of wonder as they all turned their attention to the horizon. The promise of their new life shimmered in the fading light—a bright beacon calling them forward.

The children were enthralled, pointing at the clouds and the colors, their excitement infectious. "Look at how beautiful it is!" Koie said, her voice laced with awe.

**"I've never seen anything like it I've never seen anything like it!" Koie exclaimed, her eyes wide with wonder as she pointed toward the horizon. The sun had dipped lower, casting a stunning array of colors across the sky—rich oranges and fiery reds blending into soft purples and deep blues, reflecting beautifully on the water's surface. The breathtaking view mirrored the excitement coursing through the family's veins, an intoxicating blend of adventure and possibility.

Julien leaned forward, captivated by the scene unfolding before them. "It's like a painting," he whispered, as if afraid to break the spell.

Ledger smiled at his children, feeling a wave of pride wash over him. "It really is something special, isn't it? Just like our journey, filled with unexpected beauty."

Clara wrapped her arm around his shoulder, sharing in the moment. "We are leaving one world behind but look at what awaits us! This is just the beginning."

As they continued to sail on the gentle waves, Ledger felt a sincere connection forming among them. They were navigating not just through physical waters but through the emotional currents of change, exploring the depths of their hopes and dreams. Each wave that splashed against the hull of the boat felt like a call to embrace the unknown with open hearts.

The children began to share their own dreams for the new life waiting for them. "I want to learn how to swim in the ocean!" Petronel announced enthusiastically.

"And I want to find all the cool animals!" Eliza added, her eyes sparkling with excitement.

"What about me? I will be the best fisherman in Dominica!" Wizen declared, puffing his chest out proudly. Laughter erupted among the siblings, everyone buoyed by the thrill of their combined aspirations.

As they gazed out at the captivating sunset, Ledger exchanged knowing looks with Clara. He was reminded that this journey was not just about geography, but also about forging deeper family bonds amidst the changes ahead. Together, they would encounter challenges and discoveries, each moment combining to create the rich tapestry of their new life.

The boat continued gliding forward, powered by the steam that billowed from its stacks—symbolic of their own intent to move forward, leaving behind the remnants of their past while embracing the promise of the future. "Let's make a pact," he said, raising his voice over the sound of the waves. "No matter what happens in Dominica, we'll face it all together, as a family."

"Together!" they echoed, their voices ringing with determination and unity as the sky darkened above them, the stars beginning to twinkle like beacons of hope. At that moment, they knew that their journey was only beginning, their hearts open to whatever lay ahead in their new home.

The journey had been long and filled with the rhythmic sway of the sea, but as the steamboat approached the island of Dominica, excitement coursed through the Philogene family like the cool breeze cutting through the salty spray. The once-distant outline of the island began to transform into a lush, vibrant landscape, dotted with green hills and cascading waterfalls. The sun hung high in the sky, casting a warm golden hue over the emerald terrain.

Ledger leaned against the railing, his heart pounding with anticipation. "Look at that!" he exclaimed, pointing toward the shore. Clara, standing beside him, squinted against the sun and smiled as the first glimpses of their new home became clearer.

"It's beautiful," she replied, her voice filled with awe. The verdant mountains seemed to rise dramatically from the crystal-clear waters, creating a breathtaking backdrop for their arrival.

Wizen and Koie scrambled to the front of the boat, their eyes wide with wonder. "I can see the houses!" Wizen shouted, bouncing on his heels. "They look different from St. Thomas!"

"Everything looks different," Koie chimed in, trying to spot the colorful markets and the swaying palm trees that lined the shores. The island's vibrant colors seemed to pulse with life, and the children could barely contain their excitement.

As the steamboat pulled closer to the port at the Old Market Square, the sounds of the vibrant marketplace reached their ears—lively chatter, the calling of vendors, and the distant rhythm of calypso music filled the air. A sweet, fragrant breeze carried the smell of fresh fruits and spices, tantalizing their senses.

"We're nearly there!" Clara called out, her eyes shining with emotion. She glanced back at Ledger, who stood transfixed, his gaze locked on the approaching land. This was a new beginning for them, and the weight of it settled over him like a warm embrace.

The crew began preparing to disembark, and Ledger turned to his family, gathering them close. "Are we ready for this?" he asked, a mix of nerves and exhilaration bubbling within him.

"Absolutely," Clara replied, squeezing his hand tightly. The children, their faces full of joy, nodded enthusiastically, eager to set foot on this new land.

As the boat finally docked with a gentle thud, a sense of excitement crackled in the air. Ledger led his family down the gangway, each step echoing the anticipation of what lay ahead. They stepped onto the sturdy wooden planks of the dock, and Ledger took a deep breath, inhaling the rich scents of the market mingled with the salty breeze.

The Old Market Square buzzed with life. Brightly colored stalls stretched across the square, overflowing with ripe bananas, juicy mangoes, and spices that ignited the senses. The chatter of the locals blended with the calls of street vendors, creating a lively atmosphere that wrapped around them like a blanket.

"Welcome to Dominica!" shouted a vendor, his arms wide as he waved at the new arrivals. "Come have some fruit!"

Ledger felt a smile break across his face as they stepped further into the square. Everything felt vivid and alive, a sharp contrast to the familiar comforts of St. Thomas. The children darted toward a stall, mesmerized by the display of tropical fruits, while Clara took Ledger's hand.

"This is just the beginning, isn't it?" she said, her eyes sparkling with excitement.

"Yes, it is," Ledger replied, his heart swelling with hope. This was more than a journey; it was a chance to discover new opportunities and to build a life full of adventure. They were here—together—ready to embrace whatever awaited them in the heart of Dominica.

As they ventured further into the colorful market, Ledger could not help but think that this was where their new story would begin, rooted in the warmth of the island and the love of family. The sights, sounds, and smells of this bustling hub filled him with optimism for the future. Here, surrounded by life and color, they would craft a new story together. This island, with its rich culture and dynamic spirit, beckoned them forward into a bright, uncharted horizon. With every step they took deeper into Roseau, Ledger's resolve grew stronger; they would embrace all that lay ahead, ready to weave the next chapter of their lives into the vibrant fabric of their new home.

Upon arriving in Roseau, Ledger and his family were immediately struck by the bustling atmosphere of the capital. The vibrant streets surrounding the Market thrummed with energy, alive with the sounds of merchants calling out to passersby, their voices a melodic blend of English and Creole. The air was thick with the enticing scent of spices and tropical fruits, mingling in sweet bursts that made their mouths water.

Stalls overflowing with bright, colorful produce lined the streets—plump avocados, glossy tomatoes, and bundles of fragrant herbs created a visual feast. Local artisans showcased their crafts, from intricately woven baskets to vibrant paintings that captured the spirit of the island. Ledger's heart raced with excitement as he took in the rich tapestry of life in Roseau, each detail a stark contrast to the quiet that had surrounded their former plantation home.

"Look at all the colors!" Clara exclaimed, tugging at Ledger's sleeve as they navigated through the crowd. A nearby vendor was displaying freshly picked pineapples, their golden skin glistening in the sunlight. Ledger could not help but grin at her enthusiasm.

"It's incredible," he replied, glancing down at Nerisa and Koie, who were wide-eyed with wonder. Nerisa pointed toward a vendor selling bright red sorrel drinks, and Koie eagerly tugged on Ledger's arm.

"Can we try some?" he asked, his voice barely containing his excitement.

"Of course! Let us find out what it tastes like," Ledger said, happy to indulge his children. They edged their way through the throng of locals and tourists, laughter and lively conversations swirling around them. The atmosphere pulsated with life, every corner promising new discoveries.

As they approached the vendor, Ledger could not help but marvel at the warmth of the people. The vendor, an elderly woman with a brilliant smile and eyes that sparkled like the sea, eagerly poured the sorrel drink into small cups. "Here, taste this! It is refreshing!" she said, her voice rich with the lilting accent of the island.

The children took cautious sips, then erupted with delighted laughter. "It's sweet!" Clara exclaimed, her face lighting up as she took another drink. Ledger joined in, savoring the cool, tangy flavor, feeling energized by the new experience.

Further down the street, a group of musicians played lively calypso tunes, their rhythm infectious. Ledger felt his spirit lift as he watched people sway and dance, lost in the music, their faces full of joy. He could not help but smile, feeling the excitement wrapped around him like a warm embrace.

"I can't believe how alive it is here," Clara said, her eyes sparkling as she took it all in. "This is nothing like St. Thomas."

"And that's a good thing," Ledger replied, feeling a rush of optimism. They were stepping into a world filled with possibilities, and the pulse of Roseau echoed his own heartbeat—a vibrant call to adventure.

As they continued to explore, the rich culture enveloped them. The laughter of children playing on the streets, the chatter of neighbors greeting each other, and the hustle of merchants inviting them to browse their wares created a symphony of life.

Ledger glanced at his parents, who were admiring the scene with a mix of pride and hope. This was their new home. He could feel the weight of that realization settle over him, both heavy and exhilarating.

"Let's take a moment to just absorb it all," he suggested, leading his family to a shaded area near the bustling market. They gathered, looking out over the vibrant street, their hearts swelling with the promise of the life they would build in this lively capital.

At that moment, Ledger realized that this journey was more than just a physical move; it was a chance to weave their story into the vibrant fabric of Roseau. And as they stood together, united and hopeful, they knew the adventure had only just begun.

In Roseau, The Philogene family decided to seek temporary accommodations at the Green Parrot Inn while they searched for permanent dwelling in Roseau. Nestled just a short walk from the bustling market, the inn offered a warm welcome with its vibrant exterior and lush garden filled with tropical flowers. Ledger and his family felt a wave of relief and excitement as they approached the Green Parrot Inn. Nestled amid a riot of lush greenery, the quaint guest house exuded charm with its vibrant wooden façade, inviting verandas, and the sweet scent of tropical flowers wafting through the air. The sound of birds chirping and leaves rustling in the breeze added to the welcoming atmosphere, easing the family's worries as they stepped into this new chapter of their lives.

Clara looked around, absorbing the beauty of the gardens and the relaxed, friendly vibe. The owner, an elderly woman named Madame Renaud, greeted them with a warm smile, her eyes twinkling with kindness. She quickly ushered them inside, embracing their children with affectionate pats on their heads. The inn was cozy and filled with rustic wooden furnishings that whispered stories of travelers who had come and gone. Sunlight streamed through the open windows, casting a golden glow over the colorful carpets that adorned the floors.

They were shown to their rooms, which were simply yet tastefully decorated, each one featuring soft linens and wooden shutters that opened to the gardens outside. "It feels like a dream," Clara said softly, her heart buoyed by the vibrant surroundings. Ledger smiled, admiring her enthusiasm. Despite the trials of their journey, this moment felt like a welcome embrace from the island itself.

After settling in, the family gathered on the expansive wooden veranda that was wrapped around the inn. They sank into the comfortable wicker chairs, weary from their travels yet grateful for the opportunity to pause and enjoy their surroundings. As the sun dipped lower in the sky, the golden hues of dusk illuminated the gardens, where colorful blossoms swayed gently in the evening breeze.

Dinner was served that first night, a delightful introduction to the local flavors of Dominica. Madame Renaud prepared a feast of fresh fish, seasoned with herbs and spices sourced from the market—its flaky texture and vibrant taste captivated both Ledger and Clara. The children eagerly munched on plantains and rice, their faces lighting up with every new flavor. Around the table, laughter and chatter filled the air as they savored the meal, grateful for the hearty food that tasted like home, even in a new place.

As the week unfolded, they began to form a routine. The mornings were spent exploring Roseau, visiting the bustling Market Square to soak in the vibrant life around them. The children delighted in the sounds of merchants calling out their wares and the sheer variety of fruits and crafts available. Clara reveled in the community spirit, often chatting with other shoppers, and gathering new recipes to try, while Ledger took in the political discussions that animated the air, feeling increasingly engaged in the local culture.

Afternoons were blissfully spent lounging on the inn's veranda, where Ledger would share stories with their children about the importance of family, hard work, and the new opportunities that awaited them. Clara occasionally joined in, recounting their journey and the dreams they held for their future in Dominica.

By nightfall, they returned to the inn, where laughter rang among the guests as they shared in the communal atmosphere cultivated by Madame Renaud. With each passing day, the Green Parrot Inn felt more like a home place filled with connections, laughter, and the promise of new friendships. As the week ended, Ledger felt assured that they would find a dwelling of their own soon, but part of him longed to extend their stay in this little oasis that had welcomed them with open arms.

The Green Parrot Inn encapsulated the spirit of Roseau—warm, inviting, and full of life—just as Ledger and his family were discovering their own roles within this flourishing community. Together, they forged memories in that tranquil spot, laying the foundation for their new beginnings in a land that was slowly beginning to feel like home.

As the Philogene family settled into their temporary accommodations at the Green Parrot Inn, they eagerly set out to explore the local culture that defined Dominica. The streets of Roseau were alive with a rich blend of Carib, African, and European influences, each contributing unique flavors and traditions that made the island vibrate with cultural richness. Ledger felt a sense of wonder as he walked among the people, absorbing the sights and sounds around him. Colorful parades celebrating local festivals filled the streets, while artisans showcased their crafts—handmade jewelry, intricately woven baskets, and vibrant textiles that reflected the island's spirit. The murals adorning the walls tell stories of the island's history, weaving together the narratives of its diverse inhabitants. Metered by the rhythm of calypso music echoing from nearby stalls, Ledger was captivated by the sense of belonging that permeated the air; it was as if the island welcomed him with open arms.

Clara, while embracing the vibrancy of their new home, found herself facing the challenges of adapting to a new environment for her family. The lively festivities, though enchanting, also felt overwhelming at times. As she watched the bustling community navigate the streets with ease, she could not help but feel a twinge of anxiety about their place in it. Clara immersed herself in the local culture, attending cooking classes that introduced her to the fusion of flavors found in Dominican cuisine, but she struggled with feelings of homesickness and the weight of responsibility to create a sense of stability for her children. Despite the challenges, she made a conscious effort to engage with the locals, forging friendships with other mothers who shared their experiences and wisdom. Each interaction reaffirmed her resolve to build a new life in Dominica, weaving her family's story into the vibrant tapestry of traditions that surrounded them—even as she navigated the complexities of this transition. In the moments of laughter and joy shared with their new neighbors, Clara found small pockets of comfort that rekindled her hope for the future.

In the moments of laughter and joy shared with their new neighbors, Clara found small pockets of comfort that rekindled her hope for the future. The warm smiles of the local mothers at the market, as they exchanged recipes and stories, began to ease her apprehension about their fresh start. One afternoon, while sharing the recipe for a tangy peppered sauce, a neighbor named Miriam invited Clara to a traditional cooking circle they held every Saturday. Clara could feel the pull of community, a realization that she was not alone in this new journey. The promise of friendship and connection became a soothing balm for the uncertainty that had clouded her initial days in Dominica.

As Clara immersed herself in the rhythm of daily life in Roseau, the bustling sounds of the market became a reassuring background melody. She reveled in the vivid experiences—teaching the children how to pick ripe mangoes at the vendor's stall and laughing together as they dodged chickens wandering the streets. Each small interaction slowly built her confidence, and she began to cherish the beauty of local life. Clara also discovered the island's rich heritage through conversations with the elder members of the community, who shared tales of the Carib Indians and the diverse traditions woven into the fabric of Dominica. These moments offered Clara not just insight, but a sense of belonging that felt both refreshing and familiar, bridging the gap between the past they had left behind and the future they were creating together.

In this vibrant tapestry of culture, Clara found a renewed sense of purpose. She began to envision a home where her children could grow and flourish, surrounded by a community that embraced diversity and shared a love for life. Weekly dances under twinkling lights at the local community center became a cherished tradition for Clara and her family, allowing them to celebrate their new beginning while nurturing the connections they were forming. With each smile exchanged and every flavorful dish shared, Clara felt her worries begin to fade, replaced by the promise of a brighter future in this lively island paradise.

As Ledger and his family navigated the lively streets of Roseau, he began to recognize the wealth of economic opportunities the city offered. The capital pulsed with activities that revolved around trade, agriculture, and emerging industries, creating an environment ripe for entrepreneurial endeavors. Merchants, farmers, and artisans filled the marketplace with vibrant goods, from fresh produce to handcrafted souvenirs, each stall a testament to the island's rich resources and industrious spirit. Ledger watched closely as traders negotiated prices, their animated discussions punctuated by laughter and friendly banter. This lively atmosphere ignited a spark of inspiration in him; he could envision a future where he not only supported his family but also contributed to the thriving community around him.

Ideas began to take shape in Ledger's mind as he considered the possibilities for establishing a new venture. He noticed the growing demand for locally sourced products, particularly in sustainable agriculture and eco-tourism—sectors that aligned well with the island's innate charm and beauty. He imagined opening a small shop that could showcase handmade crafts, organic fruits, and vegetables, even creating a space where locals and tourists could come together to appreciate the island's culture and heritage. Conversations with local vendors revealed a network of relationships he could tap into, fostering collaboration and community spirit. With each passing day, Ledger felt more and more determined to seize this opportunity and build a business that not only supported his family but also integrated them into the heart of Roseau, allowing them to become part of the fabric of this vibrant city.

With each passing day, Ledger felt more and more determined to seize this opportunity and build a business that not only supported his family but also integrated them into the heart of Roseau, allowing them to become part of the fabric of this vibrant city. As he explored the streets, the rhythmic hustle of commerce sparked ideas, and soon, Ledger found himself sketching out a plan for a small market stall that could showcase both locally sourced goods and crafts created by the talented artisans he had begun to meet.

He envisioned a space where visitors could experience the true essence of Dominica, sampling fresh produce and discovering handmade treasures crafted by the skilled hands of local makers. Ledger approached local farmers about sourcing their organic fruits and vegetables, his enthusiasm earning nods of encouragement. They shared stories of their own struggles and successes, further igniting his desire to foster a community-centered business. He began to map out the logistics, envisioning how he could incorporate elements of eco-friendly practices—promoting sustainability not only in his sourcing but also using biodegradable packaging and support for local artisans.

As Ledger roamed the streets, he also seized every opportunity to gather knowledge. He engaged with seasoned entrepreneurs at local cafés, soaking up advice from those who had navigated the island's unique challenges. Their insights about marketing to tourists and the importance of community partnerships proved invaluable. Each conversation left him feeling energized and inspired, reinforcing his belief that he could carve out a place for his family in this dynamic environment.

By the end of the week, Ledger had created a rough business plan that he began sharing with Clara. He painted a vibrant picture of their future, describing how their market stall could become a gathering spot for the community, a place where stories were shared over hearty meals made from local ingredients. Clara listened intently, her excitement mirroring his own as he spoke about introducing a "Taste of Dominica" sampler event, where locals could showcase their culinary talents alongside their goods.

This vision of a collaborative, community-driven space began to take root, a dream that aligned perfectly with their aspirations for a new life in Roseau. Ledger saw not only a way to support his family but also a chance to build lasting relationships and contribute to the city's economic growth. With their dreams intertwined in this vibrant backdrop, Ledger and Clara stepped forward, excited to discover all the possibilities that lay ahead. The future felt hopeful, and the pulse of Roseau resonated with promise, beckoning them to embark on this new adventure together.

Adjusting to life in Roseau meant that the Philogene family needed to adapt to a new rhythm, one that pulsed with the vibrant energy of the capital. Ledger, eager to establish their roots, devoted his days to seeking work and exploring the array of economic opportunities that Roseau presented. He juggled various tasks—visiting local merchants to pitch his ideas, networking with potential partners, and even securing part-time jobs to help ease the family's financial strain in the transition. Each day brought new challenges, but Ledger was fueled by the thought of building a more secure future for Clara and their children.

Meanwhile, Clara embraced her role within the household, finding ways to contribute as she managed the day-to-day responsibilities of their family amidst the bustling new life. With her heart set on creating a warm home, she began to establish routines that would nurture the children—early morning lessons under the shade of a mango tree, afternoons spent exploring local parks, and evenings filled with family meals cooked from the fresh produce Ledger brought home. Clara instinctively connected with other mothers in the neighborhood, forming a support network that not only provided her with friendship but also helped her feel more integrated into the community. Sharing stories and tips, they bonded over the shared challenges of parenthood and adapting to the fast-paced lifestyle of Roseau.

Despite their efforts, the family faced hurdles in securing a permanent dwelling. Finding suitable housing in such a vibrant area proved more complicated than they had hoped. They explored various neighborhoods, visiting modest homes and apartments, but many were either too expensive or not right for their needs. Ledger and Clara navigated the rental market with determination, attending community meetings and speaking to locals who might know of available homes. Each setback tested their patience, but they leaned on each other, determined to find a place where they could plant their roots and truly feel at home.

As they settled into the rhythm of Roseau's daily life, the family began to recognize the beauty woven into the island's diverse social fabric—something far richer than they had ever experienced. They attended local festivals that celebrated the island's history and culture, immersing themselves in the music, dance, and culinary delights that filled the streets. Ledger and Clara felt themselves becoming part of a larger story, as the welcoming smiles of their neighbors and the laughter of their children echoed through their days. Slowly but surely, the Philogene family was building their new life in Dominica, one marked by resilience, unity, and the thrill of embracing the unfamiliar.

In those early weeks, despite the challenges, Clara's heart swelled with hope as she envisioned the possibilities ahead. They were not just surviving; they were beginning to thrive amid the vibrant chaos of Roseau. Each new connection made, and every small triumph felt like a step closer to fulfilling their dream of establishing a happy, stable life in this beautiful island paradise. As they faced the unknown together, Clara and Ledger's bond grew stronger, solidifying their resolve to create a home filled with love, laughter, and a deep appreciation for the rich tapestry of their new surroundings.

Eventually, Ledger and his family found a cozy dwelling on Hanover Street in Roseau, a location that perfectly balanced accessibility and community spirit. This vibrant street pulsed with life, reflecting the essence of Roseau, characterized by friendly neighbors and the rhythmic buzz of daily activities. The house itself was a charming two-story structure, painted in warm, inviting colors that blended seamlessly with the surrounding architecture. Large windows filled the interiors with natural light, creating ample space for comfort and connection. A small garden in front offered a touch of greenery, providing a perfect backdrop where Ledger could watch his children play and thrive.

The dwelling's proximity to several educational institutions was a major advantage for the family. Just a short walk away was Convent High School, known for its strong academic reputation and nurturing environment. Nearby, St. Mary's Academy stood as a respected institution for young male students, also within easy reach. Families appreciated the convenience of having both Convent Primary School and Dominica Grammar School close by, ensuring that quality education was always just around the corner.

Ledger found joy in taking leisurely strolls to the market, immersing himself in the community's daily rhythm. The market was a bustling hub filled with fresh produce, local crafts, and the enticing aroma of street food. It was a place where neighbors caught up, vendors shared stories, and the spirit of camaraderie was palpable. Each visit turned into an opportunity to connect with the locals, fostering a growing sense of belonging in his new environment.

One day, while exploring the vibrant stalls, Ledger encountered an elderly woman who was selling freshly caught fish alongside baskets of ripe tomatoes and aromatic herbs. With a warm smile, she invited him to sample her wares and engage in conversation. As they chatted, she shared stories of her family's history, and the cherished recipes passed down through generations. Intrigued, Ledger listened intently, captivated by her tales of traditional cooking methods and the significance of certain dishes in their community.

Seeing his interest, the woman offered to teach Ledger how to prepare a beloved dish from her childhood—Callaloo Soup. Excited at the prospect of learning something new, Ledger gladly accepted her invitation. She brought him over to her stall, where she gathered fresh callaloo leaves, coconut milk, spices, and local seasonings.

As she demonstrated the preparation techniques, she fondly recalled her own memories of cooking with her mother, her eyes sparkling with nostalgia as she mentioned the laughter that filled their kitchen. With each step, she instilled in Ledger not just the recipe but also a sense of cultural pride and a connection to the island's rich culinary traditions.

Through this shared experience, Ledger developed a deeper appreciation for local cuisine and the stories woven into it by those who came before him. This encounter not only enriched his understanding of the island's food culture but also fostered a strong sense of community. Ledger realized that every recipe carried with it a piece of history and identity, creating bonds between people that transcended generations. In that moment, he felt more than ever that he was not just a visitor in Roseau; he was becoming an integral part of its vibrant tapestry.

As Ledger and Clara walked hand in hand through the bustling streets of Roseau, the vibrant colors and sounds enveloped them like a warm embrace. The aromas of fresh fruits and spices danced through the air, drawing them toward the lively marketplace that had become a central point of their exploration. Vendors called out to passersby, showcasing their goods with pride—ripe mangoes, fragrant herbs, and handmade crafts that told stories of the island's diverse culture.

"Look at those bananas, Clara! They are huge!" Ledger exclaimed, pointing to a stall bursting with tropical fruits. Clara laughed, nodding enthusiastically. "And those papayas look ripe enough to eat! We should pick some up for breakfast."

As they selected their fruits, Ledger struck up a conversation with the vendor, a middle-aged man named Solomon with a warm smile and an easy manner. They chatted about the challenges of farming in the tropics, the importance of sustainability, and how the community was coming together to support local agriculture. Solomon's insights sparked something in Ledger, a realization that the struggles of local farmers mirrored his own quest for stability and success in this new environment.

Meanwhile, Clara wandered to a nearby stall where an Indigenous woman was weaving intricate baskets from the Roseau reeds. Clara admired the craftsmanship, her fingers lightly tracing the patterns of a particularly colorful basket. "How do you make these?" she asked, genuinely intrigued.

The weaver, a vibrant woman named Etta, looked up with a broad smile. "It takes time and patience, but every basket tells a story," she replied, her hands deftly continuing her work. "This one here represents the morning sun, while that one symbolizes the ocean waves. Weaving is like life; it is all about creating connections."

As Clara listened, she felt a sense of belonging bloom within her. Here, among the locals, she saw glimpses of the resilience and artistry that defined Roseau. They were not just strangers; they were individuals with their own unique histories, intertwined in the rich tapestry of the island's culture.

After a while, Ledger and Clara regrouped, their arms laden with fresh produce and handwoven crafts. "Did you see how passionate Solomon was about farming?" Ledger mused, his thoughts still lingering on their conversation. "He really cares about his community and what he's growing."

Clara nodded, her excitement bubbling over. "And Etta's weaving! I think I might try my hand at it. It felt good to learn how each basket has its own significance. There is so much we can connect with here."

Their interaction with Solomon and Etta not only deepened their appreciation for the local culture but also stirred a burgeoning sense of commitment within them. They left the market not just with groceries and crafts, but also with a newfound understanding of how integral community and culture were to their experience in Roseau.

As they made their way back to their temporary home, Ledger's mind raced with thoughts about how these personal connections could inform his business ideas. Inspired by the presentations of effort and creativity he had witnessed, he felt a growing urge to engage deeply with this community—to give back as much as he had received. They were starting to settle into life in Roseau, and as much as it was about finding their place, it was equally about weaving themselves into the stories of those around them, laying the foundations for a life full of purpose and interconnectedness.

On a sunny Sunday morning, the Philogene family prepared for a visit to the Roseau Cathedral, a majestic structure that towered over the vibrant streets. The cathedral's stained-glass windows shimmered in the sunlight, casting colorful light across the cobblestone courtyard where families gathered in cheerful groups. The air felt charged with anticipation as they joined the crowd, the welcoming sounds of laughter and animated conversation enveloping Ledger, Clara, and their children.

As they entered the grand nave of the cathedral, Ledger marveled at the intricate wooden beams that supported the lofty ceiling. The atmosphere was filled with the rich scents of incense and polished wood, which mingled harmoniously with the soft murmur of the parishioners. The family found a pew toward the front, and Ledger gently guided his children to sit without fuss. Clara tucked a loose strand of hair behind her ear, her eyes sparkling as she looked around, taking in the reverent atmosphere.

Father Michael Monaghan, the priest, stood at the altar, warmly greeting everyone with a smile that radiated kindness. He was a seasoned figure in the community, known for his compelling sermons and deep compassion for his congregation. Today, as he began the service, his voice resonated like a gentle wave, carrying a sense of peace that washed over the gathered families.

"Welcome to our Sunday service," Father Michael said, his tone warm and inviting. "Today, we gather to give thanks for the many blessings in our lives and to seek guidance in our journey together."

Ledger felt a deep sense of connection as the congregation joined in hymns, their voices rising together in beautiful harmony. He watched as the children leaned into the music, their faces filled with wonder and joy. Clara, holding the youngest ones, encouraged them to sing along, fostering a sense of unity and belonging within their family.

As the service progressed, Father Michael shared a thoughtful message about community and compassion. He spoke of the importance of supporting one another, especially during challenging times. "We are all threads in the rich tapestry of life," he said. "Each of us has a unique story and purpose, and when we come together, we strengthen our bonds and uplift those in need."

Ledger's heart swelled with pride as he listened, the words resonating deeply with his ambitions for his own family and the community. The notion of collective action reaffirmed his commitment to being an advocate for social justice and community support. He glanced at Clara, who exchanged knowing looks with him, both inspired by the message.

Later in the service, the congregation took part in a moment of prayer, offering heartfelt intentions for the well-being of loved ones, the community, and the world beyond. Ledger closed his eyes, reflecting on the challenges they had faced since moving to Roseau, but also the joy and connection they had discovered. In this sacred space, he felt a surge of gratitude for the opportunities they had been given and the bonds they were forging with their neighbors.

As the service concluded, Father Michael invited newcomers to introduce themselves. Ledger felt a mix of nervousness and excitement as he stood with Clara and the children, introducing the Philogene family to the parish. "We are grateful to be part of this vibrant community," he said, his voice steady and sincere. The warm applause from the congregation filled him with encouragement and affirmation.

After the service, the family mingled with other parishioners, greeting friendly faces and sharing stories over cups of coffee and homemade treats prepared by the church community. The sense of camaraderie was palpable, and Ledger felt invigorated by the supportive environment that thrived within the church. His children eagerly chatted with their new friends, forging connections that would only strengthen their roots in Roseau.

As they departed the cathedral, Ledger took a deep breath, soaking up the warmth of the sun and the camaraderie of their newfound community. The church service had not only provided spiritual nourishment but had also gently reminded them of the power of unity and compassion. With Clara and their children by his side, Ledger felt a renewed determination to engage further in community advocacy, inspired by Father Michael's words and a deepening understanding of the role they could play in shaping a brighter future for themselves and their neighbors.

As Ledger settled further into the rhythm of life in Roseau, he soon discovered that the city was not only a bustling center of commerce but also a focal point for political activity. The streets buzzed with spirited conversations about governance and social justice, and Ledger found himself drawn to these discussions, eager to understand the issues shaping his new home. It was not long before he attended his first community meeting, held at a local church, where citizens gathered to discuss pressing matters concerning the island's future. Ledger listened intently as residents voiced their concerns about the rising cost of living, the environmental policies affecting local agriculture, and the need for better support for small businesses.

Engaging with the local community allowed Ledger to grasp the complexities of the political climate in Dominica. He learned about the history of activism that had helped shape the island's governance, particularly among the various ethnic groups that had come together to fight for their rights and recognition. The intertwining discussions of governance, societal expectations, and collective action became not just topics of interest, but a call to participate in the unfolding narrative of Roseau. Inspired by the passion of his neighbors and the realization that their voices could collectively influence change, Ledger began considering his role in advocating for the rights and well-being of his family and community.

The importance of community engagement resonated with him as he witnessed the power of collaboration. He saw how local leaders organized initiatives to improve education, healthcare, and housing, emphasizing that individual efforts contributed to a stronger, more united community. Ledger felt a growing sense of responsibility; it was not enough to seek personal success through his business aspirations. He wanted to uplift those around him and stand alongside his neighbors in addressing the challenges they faced together. Discussions with Clara opened pathways to collaboration as well; she expressed a desire to support local causes, especially those focused on children's education and health.

As the weeks went by, Ledger became more actively involved, attending meetings and volunteering for community initiatives. He found himself joining a group advocating sustainable agriculture practices, understanding that protecting the environment was essential for the future of Roseau. This involvement deepened his connections with local leaders and residents, allowing him to hear their stories and struggles firsthand. Through these interactions, Ledger developed a clearer vision of how he could blend his entrepreneurial ambitions with a commitment to social responsibility, creating a business that not only thrived economically but also served the greater good.

The political climate of Roseau became a catalyst for change not just in the community but within Ledger himself. With each decision and action, he felt a growing conviction to champion the rights of his family and neighbors, recognizing that their collective strength was vital in navigating the complexities of their environment. Ledger's journey of adapting to Roseau transcended personal aspirations; it became a shared mission to advocate for a brighter, more equitable future, ensuring that as they built their new life, they also contributed to the enduring legacy of resilience and unity in their community.

Ledger's journey of adapting to Roseau transcended personal aspirations; it became a shared mission to advocate for a brighter, more equitable future. He began to recognize that their success as a family was intrinsically linked to the well-being of those around them. Each conversation and collaborative effort reinforced the idea that they could not only carve out a space for themselves in this island community but also uplift their neighbors who faced similar struggles. Ledger envisioned a life where local voices were amplified, where collective action could reshape the narrative of Roseau into one of progress and inclusivity.

With Clara's support, Ledger started organizing community workshops that addressed issues ranging from financial literacy to environmental sustainability. They invited local experts and activists to share knowledge and resources, fostering a culture of empowerment and participation. Ledger witnessed the palpable enthusiasm from his neighbors, who were eager to take part and contribute their own expertise and experiences. The workshops quickly became a hub of ideas, sparking discussions about entrepreneurial opportunities, community gardening, and the preservation of cultural heritage. As he stood before the group, watching faces light up with hope and determination, Ledger felt a profound sense of purpose surge within him.

The community's response was invigorating and heartwarming. Neighbors began to transform their idle conversations into action, creating a ripple effect that inspired even more residents to join in. Together, they focused on issues like establishing a farmers' market to support local agriculture, advocating for cleaner public spaces, and addressing the needs of vulnerable populations within the community. Ledger found himself collaborating with local leaders to petition for improved public services, helping to raise awareness about the social injustices that many faced. They spoke openly about the challenges of accessing healthcare, housing, and quality education, ensuring that their voices were heard by local governing bodies.

Through this engagement, Ledger learned about the interconnectedness of individual and collective aspirations; he recognized that lasting change required persistent effort and unwavering solidarity. As the Philogene family weaved themselves further into the fabric of Roseau, they found themselves an integral part of a growing movement. Clara, energized by the newfound purpose, organized volunteer events for the children, instilling in them the importance of community service and social responsibility. Ledger's business vision began to incorporate elements of this collaboration, shaping a model that prioritized not just profit but also social impact—an enterprise that gave back to the community and welcomed them with open arms.

As Ledger looked around at the workshops filled with laughter, passion, and a shared commitment to progress, he felt an overwhelming sense of gratitude. They were not just adapting to life in Roseau; they were actively shaping it. Together, they were forging a neighborhood defined by resilience and unity, a place where every voice mattered, and every individual had the opportunity to contribute to the growth and development of their community. This collective spirit became the foundation upon which Ledger and Clara would continue to build their lives, ensuring that their journey in Roseau would resonate far beyond their own family and create a legacy of hope for generations to come.

As Ledger and Clara settled into their new life on Hanover Street, they made their children's education a top priority, recognizing it as essential to breaking the cycle of hardship they sought to escape. For them, knowledge was the key to unlocking a future filled with opportunities, and they were determined to provide that for Wizen, Julien, Petronel, Eliza, Louisa, James, Dfriel, Koie, and Nerisa.

The couple embarked on a thorough search for the best local schools and educational resources, driven by their desire for the children to thrive in a society that placed high value on education. They visited St. Mary's Academy, where Wizen and Julien would attend. The school's reputation for nurturing young minds through a balanced curriculum—focusing not just on academics but also on character development—impressed Ledger and Clara. Meeting the dedicated teachers, who spoke passionately about empowering students to realize their potential, further solidified their choice.

Meanwhile, Petronel and Eliza were enrolled at Convent High, a school renowned for its academic excellence and supportive community atmosphere. Ledger and Clara appreciated that the school encouraged girls to pursue their passions, whether in the arts, sciences, or athletics. They felt a sense of assurance knowing their daughters would be in an environment that celebrated and nurtured their unique talents.

The youngest children, Louisa, James, Dfriel, Koie, and Nerisa, attended the Roseau Boys and Girls School, where the strong emphasis on foundational learning, respect, and friendship resonated with Ledger and Clara's values. This vibrant school provided ample opportunities for exploration and discovery, allowing the children to develop their interests in a safe and engaging environment. Clara frequently volunteered at the school, helping with arts and crafts projects, where she delighted in seeing the children express their creativity.

Their evenings were transformed into dedicated family sessions, where Ledger and Clara facilitated homework and reading time. They shared stories and lessons about perseverance and the importance of education, discussing how their children could carve out paths that would one day lead to diverse opportunities in the future. Each child's individuality shone through in these sessions, as Wizen and Julien tackled math problems with newfound enthusiasm, while Petronel and Eliza immersed themselves in science projects that ignited their curiosity about the world.

In addition to traditional education, Ledger and Clara sought out local resources that enriched their children's learning experiences. They discovered community centers offering after-school programs, workshops in technology, and weekend classes in music and art. These opportunities added depth to their children's education, fostering a love for lifelong learning and exploration. They envisioned crafting a well-rounded experience for their children—one that equipped them with the skills and confidence needed to navigate the complexities of the world around them.

As the months passed, Ledger and Clara felt a growing sense of pride as they witnessed their children flourish. The classroom achievements and newfound friendships enriched their lives, while the family's commitment to education helped solidify strong connections to the community. Each academic milestone reached—whether passing a challenging exam, performing in a school play, or excelling in sports—felt like a victory not only for the children but for the entire family. Ledger and Clara knew they were on the right path to securing a brighter future for their children, building a life grounded in knowledge and opportunity that would ripple through generations to come.

The migration to Dominica signifies a profound turning point for Ledger Philogene and his family. Stepping into the bustling capital of Roseau has washed over them like a tide—bringing with it both exhilarating opportunities and daunting challenges. As they acclimate to their new environment, their aspirations for a better future ignite within them, fueled by a collective determination to forge a life that honors their past while embracing new possibilities.

In these early days, the complexities of establishing a new life weigh heavily upon them. Ledger reflects on the trials they have faced—navigating unfamiliar systems, juggling school schedules for the children, and finding a sustainable means of income. Yet amidst these challenges, he finds a deep well of resilience. Each small victory, whether it is helping Wizen and Julien with their homework or attending a lively community gathering, serves as a reminder that they are not facing this journey alone.

The Philogene family's embrace of community shines brightly during this transformative time. They actively seek connections, weaving their lives into the rich tapestry of Roseau's culture. The warmth of the marketplace, the shared laughter with neighbors, and the heartwarming messages from Father Michael at Sunday services all contribute to a growing sense of belonging. Ledger recognizes that it is through these interactions and relationships that their story begins to intertwine with that of this vibrant island community.

As he watches Clara nurture their children's education and talents, he feels a swell of hope. They are not just building a home; they are cultivating a strong foundation for future generations. This commitment to resilience and community invigorates Ledger's spirit, allowing him to dream beyond immediate challenges. He envisions a future where his children can thrive, unencumbered by the hardships that constrained their past.

Reflecting on their journey so far, Ledger understands that migration is not just a physical relocation; it is an evolution of the heart and spirit. In embracing their new life in Dominica, the Philogene family is learning to face adversity with courage and to see opportunity in every challenge. They are transforming their aspirations into actions, driven by a shared resolve to create a brighter future.

Amidst the lush landscapes and welcoming streets of Roseau, they are discovering their place in this new world. Determined to weave their story into the fabric of their home, Ledger and his family embrace every moment, knowing that their journey of resilience and community has only just begun. As the sun sets on this chapter of their lives, they step forward with renewed purpose, ready to navigate whatever lies ahead.

CB

Chapter Six: Life In Roseau

Having settled in the vibrant capital of Roseau, Ledger Philogene, and his family stood on the precipice of opportunity, ready to carve out their new lives in this lively island community. The transition had not been without its challenges; however, the Philogene family quickly adapted to the rhythm of life in Dominica. Each day brought fresh hope, new experiences, and a renewed commitment to integrate into their surroundings.

The streets of Roseau buzzed with energy as Ledger walked through the market, a familiar warmth enveloping him. The colorful stalls brimmed with produce, spices, and handmade crafts, creating a vivid tapestry of the island's agricultural bounty and rich culture. As he navigated the bustling pathways, Ledger was not just an observer; he was determined to intertwine his story with that of the community.

With a keen eye for business honed during his time in St. Thomas, Ledger began to explore trades that could help support his family. He spoke with local vendors and gauged their needs, eager to find ways to contribute and thrive. The experience of negotiating deals and understanding market dynamics came naturally to him, yet he remained humble, aware that every interaction was an opportunity to learn and grow.

One market day, he conversed with Amélie, a vivacious woman who sold locally sourced spices. Her laughter was infectious as she shared stories about her upbringing in Roseau. "You must try my ginger balm," she insisted, handing him a small jar. "It is good for the soul and even better for sore muscles after a long day. You will find it helps you blend in with the locals faster than anything else!" Ledger chuckled, thanking her for her kindness and wisdom. This interaction sparked a budding friendship that would later open doors to deeper connections within the community.

Realizing that mere trade was not enough to make a lasting impact, Ledger also sought to engage in local politics. Conversations around the market square often revolved around pressing issues—land rights, education reforms, and the island's quest for greater autonomy. Encouraged by the spirit of activism that echoed through the streets, Ledger felt a strong calling to contribute his voice to these important discussions.

He began attending town hall meetings, where community members gathered to voice their concerns and share visions for the future. The air buzzed with passion and determination, and Ledger found himself inspired by the fervor of his new neighbors. Drawing on his previous experiences in St. Thomas, he approached these discussions with a sense of purpose, committed to advocating for the needs of his own family while also championing the collective aspirations of the community.

As he listened to the thoughts of his fellow islanders, Ledger recognized the significance of blending his perspectives with theirs. He learned to navigate the complexities of culture, balancing his own background while honoring the traditions of those who had lived in Roseau for generations. Gradually, he found common ground with his new friends, sharing insights, exploring solutions, and celebrating their shared identity.

Back home, Ledger shared tales from the market with Clara and the children around their evening meals. He painted vivid pictures of the spirited exchanges and the dreams of the people he had met, igniting their imaginations and instilling in them a sense of pride in their new home. Clara, always supportive, encouraged him to continue pursuing his passion for community engagement, recognizing the importance of belonging and contributing to the fabric of Roseau.

As days turned into weeks, Ledger began to envision a future where his family thrived—where Wizen Julien, James, and Dfriel would play football in the sun-drenched fields, and Nerisa and Louisa would chase after butterflies in the lush gardens. It was a future filled with promise, one where their contributions could cultivate not just their success but the prosperity of the entire community.

With renewed determination, Ledger stepped into this new chapter, ready to face the complexities of life in Roseau head-on. The journey to integrate into their new surroundings had begun, and he was committed to making the most of every opportunity that lay ahead, confident that they would weave their story into the vibrant tapestry of Dominica for years to come.

As the sun rose over Roseau, painting the sky in hues of gold and pink, Ledger Philogene set out to explore the bustling market that lay at the heart of the capital. With his previous experience in the commercial sphere of St. Thomas fresh in his mind, he felt ready to navigate this vibrant new landscape. Here, the market was not merely a place to buy and sell; it was the pulse of the community, a dynamic hub of trade, culture, and connection.

The air was alive with the sounds of vendors setting up their stalls and shouting friendly greetings to each other as they unpacked their goods. Ledger marveled at the colorful array of produce, spices, and handcrafted items that filled the market. Ripe bananas hung in clusters from wooden stands, while trays of vibrant fruits—mangoes, passion fruits, and guavas—beckoned invitingly to passersby. The rich scents of freshly cooked local dishes wafted through the air, mingling with the earthy aroma of spices that brought a sense of warmth and familiarity to this new environment.

Stepping confidently into the market, Ledger set out to establish relationships with local suppliers and merchants. He knew that to thrive, he needed to understand not just the goods available but also the people who produced them. Drawing on his prior experiences, he crafted a strategy to engage with local vendors. As he meandered through the aisles, he introduced himself, explaining his background and his interest in forming mutually beneficial partnerships.

At a table adorned with an assortment of spices, Ledger struck up a conversation with a wiry man named Marco, who was eager to share his knowledge of the market. "You'll find that the key to success here is understanding the dynamics," Marco explained, his hands animated as he gestured toward the bustling crowd. "Everyone knows each other, and trust is everything. If you can build the right relationships, opportunities will come."

Ledger listened intently, appreciating Marco's candor and insight. Drawing on his own experience, he began to share his vision of connecting local products with broader markets, envisioning how he could help promote their goods beyond Roseau. As their conversation unfolded, Ledger invited Marco to collaborate on a small venture—introducing unique spices and sauces to nearby islands, tapping into new clientele who craved the rich flavors of Dominica.

Encouraged by the promising exchange, Ledger continued to explore, seeking out other vendors and establishing contacts with merchant associations. He found himself at another stall run by Patricia, a spirited woman who sold vibrant crafts that showcased the artistic heritage of Dominican culture. Ledger admired the intricately woven baskets and beautifully painted ceramics, feeling a spark of inspiration as he discussed collaborations. "Let's feature your crafts in the markets of St. Thomas," he proposed. "People there would love to invest in the beauty of our island's culture."

Patricia's eyes lit up. "You really think so? I have always wanted to share our work with a wider audience. But how do you think it would work?"

With a warmth that made her feel at ease, Ledger detailed a plan to create special showcase events, featuring local artisans and their crafts. He envisioned marketing these events with the authenticity and creativity that Roseau exuded, transforming the way locals approached trade.

As the market bustled around him, filled with the vibrant chatter of families and friends connecting, Ledger began to identify potentially lucrative opportunities with keen insight into the market dynamics. He noted the fluctuation of goods, seasonal trends, and the increasing demand for locally sourced products in the surrounding islands. Leveraging his background, he recognized the chance to create a distribution network that would not only benefit him but elevate the efforts of many small vendors eager for wider recognition.

Over the following days, Ledger worked tirelessly to formalize his connections. He joined local merchant associations, attending meetings that enabled him to tap into the collective knowledge of the community. These gatherings were filled with spirited discussions on commerce, community interests, and even matters of governance, all of which reflected the shared dreams and aspirations of those in attendance.

One evening, Ledger sat at the local café after a meeting, reflecting on how quickly relationships had begun to flourish. He sipped his coffee, savoring the rich, nutty flavor while watching the ebb and flow of people in the market. He no longer felt like an outsider; he was evolving into a valued member of a place that promised new beginnings.

As the days turned into weeks, Ledger's reputation grew, and his efforts proved fruitful. He secured agreements with local suppliers, amplifying their voices while ensuring they received fair compensation for their goods. His ability to connect the dots between local artisans and broader markets began to cultivate a sense of excitement within the community, fostering a spirit of collaboration that invigorated Roseau.

With each handshake and shared smile, Ledger felt more rooted in this vibrant landscape. Through trade and community engagement, he was not just building a business; he was helping to weave together the fabric of Roseau, a place where dreams flourished and where he, Clara, and their children could truly belong. The future glimmered with promise, and Ledger embraced the challenge of navigating these new waves, ready to harness the power of partnership and community.

As Ledger Philogene settled into the rhythm of life in Roseau, he quickly realized that the key to his success would lie in leveraging the skills and knowledge he had developed in St. Thomas. Armed with a keen understanding of negotiation, inventory management, and customer relations, he set out to carve a niche for himself in the bustling local market.

Drawing on his previous experience in trade, Ledger took a pragmatic approach. He started small, focusing on the sale of fresh produce and textiles sourced from local farmers and artisans. He visited nearby farms, establishing relationships with growers who shared his vision for creating a sustainable local economy. With each interaction, he embraced the wisdom of the island's agricultural practices while also introducing strategies he had learned back home.

At the market, Ledger set up a modest stall adorned with the vibrant colors of fresh vegetables, ripe fruit, and handwoven textiles. The eye-catching display drew inquisitive customers, and Ledger greeted them with enthusiasm, showcasing the quality of his goods. "Try these mangoes!" he urged a passerby, offering a sample. "They're ripe and juicy, straight from the farm down the road."

His genuine approach, coupled with his understanding of customer relations, helped forge connections with the local clientele. Ledger learned to listen intently to their needs and preferences, an invaluable skill that deepened his rapport with the community. As he engaged in conversations about the produce, he also discovered the stories behind the textiles, learning about the artisans who crafted them and the heritage each piece embodied.

Over time, Ledger's small stall began to attract attention. Word of mouth spread through Roseau, and the locals appreciated his commitment to quality and fair pricing. They admired his ability to negotiate with local suppliers, ensuring that both parties benefited from their transactions. Ledger's approach emphasized collaboration and mutual respect, solidifying his reputation as a trustworthy vendor.

With his small venture gaining traction, Ledger recognized that expanding his inventory was the next logical step. He began incorporating a wider variety of products, such as specialty sauces, local spices, and handmade crafts. His previous experiences enabled him to analyze market trends effectively, keeping an eye on what items resonated with consumers.

One afternoon, Ledger spotted an opportunity while mingling with other vendors at the market. A lively discussion unfolded around the growing demand for organic produce and eco-friendly products. Seeing a gap in the offerings, Ledger decided to explore this niche, reaching out to local farmers who practiced sustainable agriculture. He shared his vision of bringing greener lifestyles to the community, enhancing the narrative of health and environmental consciousness that resonated with the islanders.

Ledger's negotiation skills came into play as he proposed partnerships with these farmers. He assured them that by working together, they could not only reach a wider audience but also contribute to a healthier, more sustainable future for Roseau. Seeing his genuine passion and commitment, several farmers expressed interest, leading to agreements that would mutually benefit their operations.

As days turned into weeks, Ledger continued to expand his network, attending local meetings organized by the merchant association. These gatherings served as a cornerstone for building relationships with other business owners and entrepreneurs in Roseau. Ledger shared his insights from his experiences in St. Thomas, emphasizing the importance of collaboration and community support.

His involvement in these discussions showcased the value of his background, earning him respect within the local business community. Ledger's perspective added depth to conversations about economic growth and sustainable practices, and he was often invited to present ideas on how to improve trade strategies among the merchants.

Through his unwavering commitment and dedication, Ledger established himself not just as a vendor but as an influential member of the community. He understood that the success of his venture was tied to the overall prosperity of Roseau, and he was determined to contribute to that shared vision.

Slowly but surely, Ledger's small stall transformed into a thriving business, and he soon garnered enough capital to secure a larger space in the market. This new location allowed him to showcase a wider variety of products and engage with even more customers. His ability to negotiate deals, manage inventory effectively, and maintain strong customer relations had paid off, setting him on a path to success.

With each passing day, Ledger felt increasingly integrated into the fabric of Roseau. He no longer viewed himself as an outsider; he was part of a thriving community, working together to build a promising future. The challenges of starting anew were far from over, but Ledger embraced them with confidence, believing that his journey in Roseau had just begun.

As he looked around the bustling market, filled with laughter and life, Ledger knew that he was leveraging not just his skills but also the spirit of collaboration and camaraderie that defined this vibrant island. With fresh opportunities ahead and a growing network by his side, he was ready to face whatever challenges lay ahead, fully committed to his family and the community that had welcomed them so warmly.

As Ledger's business flourished in the vibrant marketplace of Roseau, he began to realize the profound impact of sourcing local products on both his financial standing and the community at large. Driven by a commitment to fostering relationships with local producers, he sought to showcase the rich agricultural and artisanal heritage of Dominica. His efforts were not just about profit; they were about revitalizing the local economy and celebrating the craftsmanship that defined this beautiful island.

One sunny morning, Ledger set out on an exploration of the countryside to meet local farmers and artisans. Armed with a notepad and a discriminating eye, he was eager to find unique products that would resonate with his growing customer base. His first stop was the Colihaut area, where he was thrilled to discover an abundance of corn, Red beans, and sorrel being cultivated. The farmers he met were deeply passionate about their crops, sharing stories of their sustainable farming practices and the pride they took in their produce.

"Corn from Colihaut is the best on the island," a farmer named Joseph boasted, pulling a few ripe ears from his cart to display. "And the sorrel? It makes the finest drinks, especially around the holidays," Our red beans are a standout ingredient in our signature dish, and Joseph starts sharing with Ledger the details of that recipe: dumplings, red beans, and pigs' snout (gel Cochon).

Ledger nodded appreciatively, understanding that these local specialties could be a highlight of his offerings. "I can help you reach more customers," he said enthusiastically. "Let us make sure your produce shines in the market. I will promote it as locally sourced and organic."

Joseph's face brightened at the prospect of collaboration. "I would like that. The more people appreciate our crops, the more we can improve our lives here."

From Colihaut, Ledger continued to the Carib villages, where he sought out the Indigenous people known for their beautiful Carib baskets. These baskets were not merely functional; they were works of art, each telling a story through intricate patterns and vibrant colors. Ledger met Sangrina, a skilled weaver, in her small workshop surrounded by raw materials.

"Each basket holds the history of our people," she explained, her fingers deftly weaving strands of palm. "They are made with love and tradition. I would be honored to see them appreciated outside our community."

Understanding the value of her craftsmanship, Ledger proposed a plan. "I will showcase your baskets in my stall and share their story with my customers. Let us celebrate this tradition and your heritage together."

In the coming weeks, Ledger returned to Roseau with a treasure trove of products—colorful baskets and fresh produce that reflected the island's bounty. He arranged his stall to highlight these items, creating visually captivating displays that drew customers in. Hand-painted signs proudly proclaimed, "Locally Sourced," and he shared stories of the farmers and artisans with anyone who stopped by.

Business boomed as more residents began to recognize the importance of supporting local craftsmanship and agriculture. Word spread quickly: Ledger's stall was not just a place to shop; it was a celebration of Dominica's rich culture and community spirit. His approach resonated with the growing desire among the people to stay connected to their roots while supporting one another in economic pursuits.

The local market became a gathering point, where neighbors exchanged recipes using the fresh produce from Colihaut and discussed the beauty of the Carib baskets from Sangrina. Ledger also hosted tasting events, inviting locals to sample sodas made from fresh sorrel and other delicacies crafted from the vibrant produce he sourced. For the first time, he witnessed the community coming together—a unified spirit bolstered by shared pride in what they could create.

His efforts did not go unnoticed. As Ledger's stall gained popularity, other merchants began to take notice of his approach to business. Many approached him to learn how they could incorporate local products into their own offerings. Ledger was more than willing to share his knowledge, emphasizing the importance of collaboration and community support.

"By valuing what we have here, we can all succeed together," he often told them, encouraging a culture of unity in trade rather than competition. "Let's uplift each other and make Roseau a beacon of local pride."

Over time, Ledger's economic contributions bolstered the local economy, creating a ripple effect that reached every corner of the community. Farmers like Joseph found themselves selling out their best produce, and artisans like Sangrina enjoyed newfound recognition for their craftsmanship. This interdependence sealed their relationships, fostering a network of trust and collaboration that flourished beyond mere transactions.

As he stood behind his stall, watching families leave with bags filled with goods from local farmers and artisans, Ledger felt a deep sense of fulfillment. He had created not just a successful business but a thriving community of producers and consumers who were empowered to take pride in their heritage.

With each sale, he celebrated not just financial gain but the tangible impact of supporting those around him. He understood that true wealth was measured not only in profits but also in the strength of community bonds and the shared resources among the people of Roseau. Ledger's growing business had become a conduit for the stories, talents, and dreams of his neighbors. Each day, as he exchanged goods for currency, he witnessed the tangible connections it fostered—friendships that blossomed over shared meals, laughter exchanged between families, and artisans taking pride in their crafts being appreciated by others.

In Ledger's eyes, every basket woven by Sangrina, every ear of corn harvested by Joseph, and every bottle of sorrel drink purchased contributed to a tapestry that represented the collective spirit of the island. Their shared successes created a cycle of encouragement and support, inspiring others to follow suit and invest in local labor and craftsmanship. He envisioned a future where the vitality of Roseau was anchored in its people—where growth was measured not just in financial terms but in the resilience and pride of a united community.

Reflecting on his interdependence during quiet moments at his stall, Ledger made a resolve to continue nurturing these bonds. He began organizing community events that showcased local talent—craft fairs where artisans could display their work, harvest festivals that celebrated the agricultural bounty of the island, and workshops that promoted traditional skills. These gatherings not only highlighted the richness of Dominica's culture but also reminded everyone that they were part of something much larger than themselves.

As these initiatives took shape, Ledger found himself at the center of a movement that began to shift the way people perceived their economic landscape. More residents of Roseau became advocates for local products, taking pride in the heritage and quality of their own goods rather than relying on imports. Stores began to feature locally made products, and community members discussed and promoted Roseau's offerings at neighboring islands.

Through the friendships he had cultivated, Ledger witnessed the blossoming of a spirit of collaboration that extended far beyond the market. It was a sense of unity ignited by shared goals—the pursuit of local sustainability, the empowerment of artisans, and a collective commitment to uplift one another. The pride in one's work turned into pride in one's community, and Ledger found joy in knowing that his small actions were part of a greater tapestry of change.

In the evenings, as Ledger sat with Clara and their children at their humble home, surrounded by the familiar sounds of laughter and the scent of fresh meals, he realized that this life was far richer than anything he had previously experienced. They were not only building their future but also contributing to a legacy that would resonate in Roseau for generations to come.

As he watched Wizen, Julien, James, Dfriel, and Koie play football outside, their laughter mingling with the vibrant sounds of the market, Ledger felt a profound sense of purpose. He was committed to nurturing the fabric of this community and ensuring that its heart continued to beat strong. With each interaction, each relationship forged, and each product sold, he was weaving together a narrative of hope and resilience—a narrative that spoke of the true essence of wealth in Roseau, defined by community, collaboration, and shared dreams.

During the late 19th century, Dominica was governed as a British crown colony, with the British governor serving as the head of administration. This colonial structure often marginalized the voices of the local population, limiting their influence over the governance of their own lives. Amidst this backdrop of colonial rule, the people of Dominica began to actively engage in discussions about governance, rights, and community responsibilities, seeking to assert their identity and advocate for change. As Ledger Philogene immersed himself in this political landscape, he recognized the importance of civic engagement and became determined to understand and contribute to the aspirations of his new community.

In addition to his business pursuits, Ledger Philogene began to take notice of the political landscape in Dominica. As he spent more time in the bustling market and engaged with the diverse populace of Roseau, he became increasingly intrigued by the vibrant discussions that surrounded him—conversations that delved deep into governance, rights, and the responsibilities each citizen held toward their community.

At first, Ledger observed from the sidelines, absorbing the passionate debates that erupted among marketgoers. He listened intently as locals discussed the latest developments in politics, from the push for greater autonomy from colonial powers to the issues surrounding land rights and local representation. The energy in the air was palpable, filled with a sense of urgency and a collective desire for change. This lively atmosphere ignited a spark within him; Ledger recognized that to truly integrate into his new community, he needed to engage with these vital discussions.

With a resolve to understand the needs and aspirations of his fellow islanders, Ledger began attending town hall meetings, where residents gathered to voice their concerns and share visions for the future. These meetings were often standing-room-only affairs, filled with passionate speeches and animated exchanges. Ledger was struck by the diversity of perspectives and ideas that flowed through the room, revealing a community deeply committed to shaping its own destiny.

"Power belongs to the people," one community leader proclaimed, her voice strong and unwavering. "We deserve a say in the decisions that affect our lives!"

Ledger felt the weight of her words resonate within him. He realized he shared the responsibility to contribute to this dialogue. Stepping forward, he was eager to lend his voice to the people's voices—to advocate for their rights and support initiatives that could foster positive change.

With each meeting, Ledger absorbed the complexities of local governance and the issues facing Dominica. He learned about the struggles of his neighbors, particularly regarding access to education, healthcare, and economic opportunities. Many spoke passionately about the challenges of colonial influence and the urgent need for autonomy, echoing sentiments that resonated deeply with his own experiences from St. Thomas.

Ledger began engaging more actively in these discussions, sharing insights from his own background, and fostering connections with other community members who shared his commitment to advocacy. He was not there just to listen; he wanted to contribute meaningfully to the conversations that would shape the future of Roseau.

One evening, as he returned home from a particularly invigorating town hall meeting, Ledger shared his thoughts with Clara. "There's so much passion in this community for change. It is inspiring," he said, watching the stars twinkle above them. "I feel like I have to be a part of it, to help amplify our voices."

Clara smiled, sensing his enthusiasm. "You have always been committed to advocating for what is right. We have a chance to make a difference here, Ledger. Your business can be a platform for that."

Emboldened by Clara's support, Ledger immersed himself further in local political matters. He began volunteering with grassroots organizations focused on civic education and engagement, helping to facilitate workshops that encouraged residents to understand their rights and navigate the political system. His background in negotiation and community building proved invaluable, allowing him to connect with individuals who were previously disengaged or unsure about how to participate in the democratic process.

As he ventured deeper into the political landscape, Ledger found himself accompanying community leaders to meet with local government officials, advocating for policies aimed at improving the lives of the island's residents. He discovered that the obstacles facing the community were not insurmountable; with the right coalition of voices, they could effectively demand change and secure the resources needed to elevate their quality of life.

His involvement in local politics also strengthened the bonds he had formed through his business. The merchants and producers he worked with began to see him not only as a trader but also as an advocate for their interests, someone committed to amplifying their concerns. Ledger became a catalyst for dialogue, encouraging others to express their views on how they could collectively shape a brighter future.

Through his experiences, Ledger developed a deeper understanding of civic engagement and the importance of being an informed and active participant in the community's governance. He learned that political awareness was not merely an interest but a necessity for those who wished to foster growth and progress.

As the political climate in Dominica continued to evolve, Ledger stood at the intersection of commerce and advocacy, ready to play his part in helping to elevate the voices of the community. With every meeting he attended and every discussion he engaged in, he felt not only a growing connection to Roseau but also a sense of purpose that would guide him through the challenges ahead. Empowered by the desire to make a difference, Ledger knew that his journey was just beginning—a journey where he could contribute to the vibrant tapestry of life in Dominica and help shape the collective aspirations of its people.

As Ledger Philogene settled into life in Roseau, he recognized that cultivating a strong sense of community was as vital as his business success. Eager to connect with his new neighbors and understand their concerns, he began attending town meetings and community gatherings, immersing himself in the local culture and politics. These gatherings were vibrant affairs, filled with passionate discussions on issues affecting daily life and the future of Dominica.

At one of the town hall meetings held at St Gerard's Hall, Ledger was struck by the energy in the room. Locals of all ages gathered, eager to share their ideas and express their concerns. As speakers took to the floor, delivering impassioned speeches about education, public health, and access to resources, Ledger listened intently, absorbing the diverse perspectives shared by the community members. Among them, he heard echoes of his own experiences as an immigrant, which allowed him to empathize with the struggles many faced.

Over the following weeks, Ledger made it a point to attend every meeting he could, eager to engage in the discussions. He began to introduce himself to local leaders—individuals who had been at the forefront of community advocacy for years. Their dedication was inspiring, and through these interactions, Ledger learned about the cultural, social, and economic issues that shaped the lives of Roseau's residents.

During one meeting focused on youth education, Ledger felt compelled to contribute. Drawing on his experiences from St. Barthelemy and St. Thomas, he shared strategies that had successfully integrated local cultures into educational programs. "If we teach our children about their heritage early on, we empower them to take pride in who they are," he proposed, earning nods of agreement from many in the audience.

His insights resonated with both local families and fellow migrants, bridging gaps between their experiences. Many were drawn to his genuine care for community issues and his willingness to advocate for solutions that would benefit everyone. Ledger's commitment to representing diverse interests helped establish him as a budding leader in the community, someone who could inspire collaboration and dialogue among the residents.

Encouraged by the positive responses to his contributions, Ledger continued to engage in conversations about pressing issues, such as access to healthcare and the need for improved infrastructure. He organized informal get-togethers after-town meetings, where locals could discuss their ideas and concerns in a more relaxed setting. This initiative fostered camaraderie and deepened the bonds between neighbors, allowing him to further understand the challenges they faced.

One evening, he arranged a community picnic at the Botanical Gardens, inviting families and residents to come together for food, games, and conversation. The atmosphere was lively, filled with laughter and the warm scents of traditional dishes. Ledger watched as children played together while parents exchanged stories about their lives and aspirations. It was a beautiful tapestry of the community, and he felt a profound sense of fulfillment witnessing people connect on a personal level.

Through these gatherings and discussions, Ledger earned the trust of many community members. They began to reach out to him for support, seeking guidance on navigating local issues and advocating for their needs. Ledger found himself increasingly drawn into the complexities of local politics, understanding that his voice could help amplify the concerns of those who felt unheard.

As his involvement grew, Ledger collaborated with established local leaders to organize forums that allowed residents to discuss important matters more openly. These events helped demystify the political process, empowering locals to understand their rights and their ability to drive change in their community. Ledger emphasized that collective action was the key to addressing the issues that mattered most to them.

Throughout this journey, Ledger learned that building community connections was not merely about networking; it was about fostering relationships rooted in respect and shared purpose. He celebrated the diverse voices within Roseau and recognized the strength that came from collaboration, paving the way for a united front in advocating for the community's interests.

With each meeting he attended and every connection he made, Ledger felt increasingly integrated into the heartbeat of Roseau. He was no longer just a newcomer; he was becoming a vital part of the community's narrative, championing the dreams and aspirations of those around him. Establishing himself as a leader in a once unfamiliar place, Ledger was determined to help craft a brighter future for all, ensuring that every voice was heard and valued in the chorus of community life.

As Ledger Philogene immersed himself further into the political landscape of Roseau, he quickly realized that advocating for community issues was not without its challenges. While many residents welcomed his insights and enthusiasm, he also encountered resistance from established local leaders who were skeptical of newcomers like him. These leaders had devoted years to their causes and often viewed outsiders with caution, fearing that Ledger's fresh perspectives might disrupt the delicate balance they had fought to maintain.

At a town hall meeting focused on local economic development, Ledger noticed the skepticism firsthand. During discussions about enhancing access to markets for small businesses, one of the senior leaders, a seasoned merchant named Mr. Raphael, voiced his concerns. "We have our ways of doing things here," he said, his tone rigid. "We have built this community through years of hard work. Why should we listen to someone who just arrived?"

Ledger felt the weight of the room shift at those words. The air thickened with tension as other leaders exchanged wary glances. However, instead of retreating, he knew this moment demanded his diplomatic skills. He took a deep breath before responding. "I understand the value of tradition and the hard work that has brought us here," he began carefully. "But I believe that by combining our experiences, both new and old, we can elevate our community even further. Together, we can tap into new opportunities while respecting our history."

Though Ledger's words were met with silence, he could sense that some in the audience were reflecting on what he said. Navigating this political landscape required him to be both resilient and strategic. He understood that establishing trust and credibility would be essential if he wanted to make a meaningful impact in Roseau.

Determined to break down the barriers between himself and the established leaders, Ledger focused on building alliances. He reached out to individuals who had influence and respect within the community, hoping to find common ground and build rapport. He invited them to his market stall, where they could discuss ideas over fresh produce and local dishes. Through these informal discussions, he shared his visions and sought their insights on pressing issues, making sure they felt valued and heard.

During one such meeting, Ledger spoke with Astrid, a respected community activist known for her tireless work in advocating for youth education. "I admire your dedication to our children's future," he said genuinely, having learned of her initiatives to improve after-school programs. He spoke of his own experiences in St. Thomas and how education had played a pivotal role in transforming lives, emphasizing that together they could expand those opportunities in Roseau.

Astrid listened thoughtfully, appreciating the respect Ledger showed for her expertise. "If you genuinely want to make a difference, it's critical to engage with people and listen to their needs," she advised. "Change requires patience and persistence. You must show them you are here for the long haul."

Taking her advice to heart, Ledger remained committed to demonstrating his dedication to the community. He sought opportunities to participate in local initiatives, volunteer for events, and support causes that resonated with residents. By doing so, he built credibility and began to earn the respect of those who were initially hesitant about his involvement.

Over time, small shifts began to occur. Mr. Raphael, noticing Ledger's unwavering commitment, invited him to join a committee focused on local business development. It was a significant step that signaled a willingness to collaborate, but Ledger knew he had to tread carefully. He listened intently during meetings, ensuring established leaders felt their voices were prioritized while subtly introducing new ideas when the moment felt right.

However, resistance still lingered. Some community members were hesitant to embrace change, fearing the loss of traditions they held dear. Ledger often found himself caught between his desire to push for progress and the need to respect the values held by others. It was a delicate balance, and he sometimes felt the weight of these challenges pressing down on him.

In one particularly heated discussion about updating local trade regulations, Ledger proposed a model based on successful practices he had observed in other islands. Yet he was met with fierce opposition from a group of merchants, their voices rising in anger. "We don't need outsiders telling us how to run our businesses!" shouted one, and Ledger could sense the frustration simmering beneath the surface.

Frustrated but undeterred, Ledger remembered Astrid's words about patience. He took a step back and reframed his approach. Instead of solely presenting new ideas, he began facilitating open dialogues where community members could voice their opinions and concerns. These conversations allowed him to identify common goals and gradually build consensus, helping others see that his advocacy was about enhancing their community, not undermining it.

Through persistence, mutual respect, and an unwavering commitment to collective efforts, Ledger gradually gained the trust of those who had once viewed him with skepticism. His journey through the political landscape was fraught with obstacles, but he understood that true advocacy necessitated collaboration. With each shared experience and connection forged, Ledger was laying the groundwork for a more inclusive and engaged community.

As he navigated the complexities of local politics, he remained hopeful that he could unite the voices of both seasoned leaders and newcomers alike, paving the way for positive change in Roseau. In this journey, each challenge was an opportunity—a lesson in patience, respect, and the enduring power of community connection.

For the Philogene family, moving to Dominica marked the beginning of an exhilarating journey into a world rich with cultural dynamics, but it also presented a set of challenges they had not anticipated. The vibrant tapestry of local traditions, music, and languages enveloped them as they settled into their new home, offering a vivid landscape teeming with opportunities for discovery. However, the transition was not without its hurdles; adapting to a new social environment came with its own set of complexities.

As Ledger immersed himself in the local marketplace and political scene, Clara focused her energy on creating a nurturing home for their children, Wizen, Petronel, Julien, Eliza, Louisa, James, Dfriel, Koie, and Nerisa. She was eager to instill in them the values and practices from their home in St. Barthelemy while embracing the rich culture around them. However, she quickly realized that balancing their family's customs with local traditions was a nuanced task, one that would require sensitivity and openness.

The local community was full of warmth and individuality, each family holding their own traditions dear. Clara frequently attended gatherings hosted by other mothers, hoping to build connections and find common ground. At one such gathering, the lively sound of laughter filled the air as children played in the yard, and the aroma of traditional Dominican dishes wafted from the kitchen. Clara found herself both enchanted and intimidated by the lively atmosphere.

"Welcome! I am Marissa," one mother said cheerfully, extending her hand. Clara smiled, grateful for the warm introduction.

"Clara," she replied, shaking Marissa's hand, feeling a mix of excitement and nervousness.

As the conversation flowed, Marissa shared stories about local customs, family traditions, and the annual festivals that were staples in the community. Clara listened attentively, eager to learn but aware of her own family's different practices. As the mothers discussed their own experiences with schooling and childcare, Clara felt the weight of cultural differences pressing upon her.

Gone were the familiar rhythms of life she had known in St. Barthelemy; here, she faced different expectations and norms that sometimes clashed with her own beliefs. For example, while the local customs on celebrations differed from her family's traditions, Clara wanted to honor both her roots and the local way of life, a delicate balance that required careful navigation.

When the topic of school came up, Clara felt a pang of anxiety. Should she enroll Wizen and Julien in local schools, where they would be immersed in Dominican culture, or should she seek out private institutions that might align more closely with her values? The fear of their potential alienation in new environments wrestled with her desire for them to embrace their heritage.

Determined to find a path forward, Clara decided to invite a few mothers over for coffee, hoping to foster relationships that could bridge their different backgrounds. As they chatted in the cozy comfort of her home, she shared stories from St. Barthelemy, emphasizing the beauty of their traditions while expressing her eagerness to learn about Dominican customs. This gesture of openness sparked lively discussions, and soon they were sharing recipes and stories from their respective cultures.

"Let's have a potluck!" Marissa suggested enthusiastically. "We can each prepare a dish from our culture. It would be a great way for our children to learn about each other!"

The idea resonated with Clara, and she quickly agreed. The potluck became a melting pot of flavors and stories, showcasing the diversity of the community. On the appointed day, families arrived with dishes that represented their heritage; Clara prepared djon djon rice, a beloved recipe from St. Barthelemy, while her neighbors brought conch fritters, callaloo soup, and plates of spiced chicken.

As the children played together, Clara felt her initial apprehension begin to melt away. Watching Wizen and Julien eagerly interact with their new friends, she realized that cultural integration did not mean losing one's identity. Instead, it was an opportunity to share and blend traditions, fostering a sense of belonging for her family and those around them.

Over time, Clara became more involved in school activities, joining the parent-teacher association and volunteering for arts and crafts projects. This involvement gave her a deeper insight into local customs while allowing her to contribute her skills and experiences to the school community. She began organizing art days where children could explore both Dominican and St. Barthelemy's artistic traditions, painting murals that told stories from their diverse backgrounds.

Through these connections, Clara not only strengthened her own sense of community but also forged friendships that transcended cultural boundaries. Other mothers began to seek her out for advice on activities that merged different cultural practices, and together they created a supportive network that celebrated both heritage and innovation.

As the months passed, the Philogene family grew more comfortable in their new environment. Clara learned to navigate the complexities of relationships and found joy in immersing herself in the local culture while honoring her traditions. She embraced the lively rhythms of Roseau, the vibrant colors of its festivals, and the welcoming spirit of its people, all while maintaining the essence of her family's heritage.

Through her journey of cultural integration, Clara discovered that adapting to change could be both beautiful and challenging. It was a path filled with learning, growth, and resilience. By embracing the richness of both cultures, she found a way for her family to remain true to their roots while flourishing in their new surroundings. Together, they were not just living in Roseau; they were becoming an integral part of its ever-evolving story—a testament to the enduring strength of community and the power of connection.

As the Philogene family settled into life in Roseau, Ledger, and Clara's children—Wizen sixteen, Petronel fourteen, Julien thirteen, Eliza twelve, Louisa eleven, James ten, Dfriel ten, and the youngest twins, Koie and Nerisa seven—found themselves grappling with complex cultural challenges. Each of them was at a different stage in life, processing their identities as newcomers while trying to embrace the vibrant tapestry of Dominica's society.

For Wizen, the eldest, the stakes felt particularly high. At sixteen, he was acutely aware of the social dynamics at play in his new high school. His thick accent and distinct Caribbean style set him apart from his classmates, many of whom were deeply immersed in Dominica's local customs and traditions. Wizen often felt torn between wanting to fit in and the desire to honor his heritage. During discussions in class about local history and culture, he found it difficult to share his own experiences from St. Barthelemy without feeling alienated. He noticed how his peers would nod and discuss familiar legends and stories, while his voice felt almost foreign when he introduced tales from his home.

Petronel, at fourteen, experienced a similar struggle. She had always been passionate about fashion, often mixing bold colors and designs reminiscent of her family's Caribbean background. But at school, she noticed a different style prevailing among her classmates, more subdued tones, and mainstream trends. Determined to blend in, Petronel felt pressured to change her wardrobe. Yet, when she wore her vibrant prints, she received mixed reactions. Some classmates admired her uniqueness, while others whispered among themselves, making her question whether her heritage was something to be celebrated or concealed.

During these struggles, Julien, who was thirteen, took a different approach. Although he too felt the weight of cultural expectations, he immersed himself in Dominica's customs, eager to explore this new environment. He found himself drawn to local music and dance, participating in school performances and showing his classmates his enthusiasm. Yet when he spoke of his experiences from St. Barthelemy, he noticed his peers occasionally shift their focus, making him feel as if they were not fully engaged in understanding his background. Julien cherished his Caribbean identity but grappled with feelings of inadequacy when sharing it with others.

Meanwhile, Eliza twelve, and Louisa eleven navigated their own challenges. They noticed the camaraderie among local girls and longed to join them. Eliza, bold and outgoing, quickly approached her peers, eager to make friends. However, she often faced awkward moments when local customs differed from her own—simple gestures like greetings or expressions of affection. Louisa, more reserved, admired her sister's confidence but felt overwhelmed by the pressure to adapt. Sometimes, she would retreat to her room, feeling lost between the vibrant rhythms of Dominica and her own quieter heritage.

James and Dfriel, both ten years old and filled with childlike curiosity, embraced their surroundings with a mix of excitement and apprehension. They were eager to play with local children and join in games, yet they occasionally felt the pull of difference. They were reminded of their past experiences on St. Barthelemy, where their local customs were the norm, while here, they were still learning the local dialects and traditions. James, the more outgoing of the two, often tried to bring his friends into his playtime stories about his heritage but sometimes felt the disappointment of not being understood.

Koie and Nerisa, the youngest at seven, were still processing the various cultures swirling around them. With innocent curiosity, they quickly noticed the language and customs, joining in with local children in their games. For them, the struggles around identity were less pronounced. Still, they occasionally sensed the confusion on their parents' faces when trying to explain aspects of their upbringing. They often ended up intertwining local customs and their own traditions, creating a delightful mix that delighted their peers but baffled older siblings trying to define their identities more clearly.

Together, the Philogene siblings formed a tight-knit support system as they navigated their combined struggles with identity in their new environment. They often gathered to share experiences, talk about their day, and reflect on their feelings of belonging—or the lack thereof. During one of these family nights, as they shared a meal prepared with love by Clara, Wizen opened. "Sometimes, I feel like I don't belong anywhere," he confessed, his voice low. "When I talk about home, I can see people's faces. It feels like they do not really understand."

Petronel nodded, "I get that. I love our heritage, but I do not want to be seen as 'different' either. I just want to fit in." Her vulnerability resonated with the others, and they began sharing their own feelings of being caught between their familial expectations and their need to adapt.

Encouraged by their shared struggles, Julien suggested they celebrate both their heritage and the new traditions they discovered. "Let us have a cultural day! We can invite some friends over and show them our favorite aspects of St. Barthelemy. We can make food, play games, and even do some dance. It will help them learn about us, and we will learn about them too!"

The room was buzzed with excitement at the idea. It was a plan that allowed each sibling to express their cultural identity in a way that could bridge the gap between their heritage and their new life.

In the days leading up to the cultural day, the Philogene siblings rallied together, combining their strengths to prepare. They shared recipes, learned new songs, and practiced traditional dances from both their heritage and Dominican culture. Their enthusiasm transformed the experience into a celebration of connection and learning.

When the day arrived, they welcomed their friends with open arms, excited to showcase their traditions. As the laughter filled their home, and the delicious smells wafted throughout, it became clear that the cultural struggles they faced could coexist with the beauty of incorporation and connection.

Through this celebration, Wizen, Petronel, Julien, Eliza, Louisa, James, Dfriel, Koie, and Nerisa began to realize that their identities were not merely defined by their past experiences or their new surroundings. They were uniquely woven together, creating a rich tapestry that honored both their Caribbean heritage and the vibrant culture of Dominica.

In that moment of unity, the Philogene siblings felt a sense of belonging wash over them; they understood that they could embrace their roots while forging a new identity, one that honored both the challenges and the gifts of being part of a diverse and dynamic community. Together, they would continue to navigate the intricate pathways of identity, pooling their strengths to celebrate the beauty of their shared journey.

Recognizing the importance of forging connections in their new home, Ledger and Clara Philogene took it upon themselves to actively seek out community events, festivals, and cultural celebrations in Roseau. They understood that participating in these gatherings would not only help their family immerse themselves in the local culture but also provide an opportunity to share aspects of their own Caribbean heritage.

As they explored the vibrant streets of Roseau, the family encountered a colorful tapestry of activities that highlighted the island's rich traditions and communal spirit. One weekend, they attended the annual Carnival celebration, where the air buzzed with excitement, pulsating with the rhythms of calypso and Soca music. Dancers donned vibrant costumes adorned with feathers and beads, twirling joyously to the beat, while vendors served local delicacies. Clara's eyes sparkled as she watched her children take part in the revelry, their laughter mingling with the sound of steel pans and drums.

"Can we dress up like that next year?" Julien asked, eyes wide with wonder as he pointed to a group of children in dazzling outfits. The rest of the family buzzed with excitement, and Ledger nodded enthusiastically. "Absolutely! We can start planning our costumes right away," he replied.

Later that evening, the family returned home, their hearts full of joy and inspiration. The children, still buzzed from the festivities, gathered around the dining table, eager to discuss their experience. "Everyone seemed so welcoming!" Eliza exclaimed. "It felt good to be part of something so big."

Feeling invigorated, Clara suggested, "Why don't we host a small gathering at our home to celebrate Carnival together? We can invite our neighbors and share some of our traditions, too." The children cheered at the idea, excited about the prospect of blending their experiences with the local culture.

In the following weeks, the Philogene family worked together to prepare for their gathering. They brainstormed ideas for food, music, and activities that would reflect both their Caribbean roots and the vibrant customs of Dominica. Clara planned to cook traditional dishes like djon rice and fried plantains, while Ledger organized a small performance showcasing traditional Caribbean dance, hoping to engage both their family and the neighborhood.

When the day of the gathering arrived, the Philogene home buzzed with energy, filled with the enticing aromas of cooking and the sounds of laughter. Neighbors began to trickle in, some curious about the Philogenes and others eager to celebrate. The children waved enthusiastically at their friends from school, who arrived with smiles and open minds.

The diverse crowd mingled easily, allowing everyone to share stories and experiences. Ledger started the afternoon by explaining the significance of Carnival—how it symbolized freedom, creativity, and community spirit. Petronel took the opportunity to showcase her artistry, introducing a craft station where children could create colorful masks adorned with feathers. The table quickly filled with laughter and chatter as guests delighted in expressing their creativity.

As the evening progressed, Clara invited everyone to join in a dance lesson, teaching a few traditional Caribbean moves. Some guests hesitated, but with encouragement from Wizen and Julien, the floor soon filled with laughter and twirling bodies. In a heartwarming display of cultural exchange, the guests attempted to mimic the dance, blending elements of Dominican dance with Caribbean rhythms. The joy was palpable, transcending any initial reservations.

In a significant moment of connection, one neighbor, Ms. Renée, stood up to share a story about her own experiences during Carnival as a child. "We all have our own stories, our celebrations," she told the crowd, smiling as she gestured to the dancing children. "It's beautiful to see how our traditions can come together." Her words resonated with many, bridging the gaps between their different backgrounds as stories flowed freely.

Encouraged by the warmth of acceptance, more of the Philogene family's neighbors began to share their own cultural practices. From cooking demonstrations to folk songs, the evening quickly transformed into a vibrant tapestry of shared experiences. Dfriel and James led a group of children in a game they had learned back in St. Barthelemy, weaving in elements of local flavor that their friends enjoyed.

By the end of the night, the guests left with full bellies, happy hearts, and newfound friendships. As the laughter died down and the last guests departed, Clara and Ledger gathered their children to reflect on the evening.

"That was amazing!" Julien said, his face glowing with excitement. "I didn't expect everyone to get so into it!"

Petronel nodded in agreement. "We showed them that we are proud of our culture, and they shared theirs too. It is like we all learned something new."

Inspired by the success of their gathering, the Philogene family committed to becoming active participants in their community's ongoing events. They began attending local farmers' markets, artisan fairs, and community workshops, embracing opportunities to interact with their neighbors while enjoying the vibrant displays of local produce and crafts. Ledger found himself drawn to the stories behind each stall, eager to learn about the artisans and farmers who poured their hearts into their work. Clara enjoyed connecting with fellow parents as they exchanged tips on everything from gardening to child-rearing, forging friendships that transcended cultural boundaries.

The family's participation in these events allowed them to showcase their traditions while appreciating those of others. At one farmers' market, they set up a stall featuring dishes from St. Barthelemy alongside local favorites. The response was overwhelmingly positive; attendees were intrigued by the unique flavors, and many local families relished the opportunity to sample something different. Clara shared the stories behind the dishes, explaining the significance of each ingredient and how they were prepared during family gatherings back home.

In turn, the Philogene children began to meet peers who were equally curious about their experiences and heritage. Wizen found friendships budding as he became involved in a youth soccer league, where the focus on teamwork transcended cultural differences. Through sports, he built camaraderie with teammates while honoring the skills and techniques he had learned in St. Barthelemy.

Julien and Eliza formed a small art club at school, encouraging their classmates to explore various artistic expressions from both Dominican and Caribbean influences. They organized collaborative projects that celebrated colors, designs, and motifs from their diverse cultures. The excitement of creating art together helped dissolve any lingering barriers of misunderstanding, making it easier for everyone to appreciate the beauty in cultural diversity.

As the year progressed, the Philogene family established themselves as active contributors to their community, and with each passing event, they were able to bridge more gaps and foster stronger bonds among their neighbors. They even experienced the sweetness of cultural integration firsthand during a local festival that celebrated both Dominicans and their traditions.

That day, the Philogene family proudly wore brightly colored attire that represented both St. Barthelemy and Dominica. Clara and the children prepared a delightful feast of local delicacies while Ledger organized an impromptu cultural showcase, inviting attendees to share performances that celebrated their traditions. It became a vibrant celebration of unity and diversity, as people from all walks of life joined together to dance, sing, and share stories.

By the end of the festival, Ledger and Clara looked at their children with pride, recognizing the embrace of their culture and the seamless blend of traditions that had begun to form in their community. "We've come a long way," Ledger remarked to Clara, feeling a swell of gratitude for the important connections they had forged.

Clara smiled back, her heart full. "It is incredible to see how our family has woven our heritage into the fabric of this community. Together, we have created a space where everyone can share their stories."

The Philogenes had succeeded in building community bonds that celebrated both their Caribbean roots and the beauty of the Dominican culture. In doing so, they not only carved out a place for themselves in Roseau but also enriched the lives of those around them, demonstrating that through shared experiences and mutual understanding, everyone could feel a sense of belonging, bridging cultures and uniting them in the celebration of life.

As they headed home, conversation buzzing with excitement, the Philogene family felt a profound sense of home—not only within their house but in the community that now embraced them. It was a comforting revelation that together, they could foster a sense of belonging in a place rich with tradition, all while planting the seeds for a deeper understanding and appreciation of cultural diversity. Their journey of building community bonds had only just begun, and the road ahead promised even more opportunities for connection, understanding, and celebration.

As the Philogene family continued to immerse themselves in life in Roseau, they quickly recognized that navigating a new environment came with its own set of challenges—from adapting to different social norms to understanding the local education system. In response to these challenges, they began actively building a support network that included both other migrant families and residents, creating a community that would help them through the ups and downs of their new journey.

Clara took the lead in establishing connections and attending gatherings and meetings for migrant families organized by local organizations. At one of these meetings, she met other mothers who were also seeking support as they acclimated to life in Dominica. Among them was Maria, a kind-hearted mother from Venezuela, who had just moved with her two children. They quickly bonded over their shared experiences of uprooting their lives for a better future.

"Sometimes, it feels overwhelming," Maria confessed as they sat together during a coffee break at the meet-up. "I miss my home, but I want my children to thrive here." Clara nodded empathetically, understanding the weight of those words. They exchanged stories about their experiences and the challenges they faced in raising their children in a new culture.

Recognizing the importance of mutual support, Clara proposed an idea to Maria and a few other mothers she had met: "What if we start a support group? We could meet regularly to share advice, challenges, and resources. Sometimes, it helps just to know you are not alone."

The initiative gained traction quickly, and soon the group expanded to include other families—migrants from Haiti, Cuba, and even some Dominican locals who offered valuable insights into the community. They met bi-weekly at Clara's house, rotating who hosted, and the gatherings quickly became a cherished staple of their lives.

During these meetings, they shared tips on navigating local schools, finding jobs, and understanding cultural practices. They also celebrated one another's successes, whether it was a child excelling in school or a parent landing a new job. The emotional support within this network grew deeply, forming connections that were grounded in shared experiences and resilience. Meanwhile, Ledger also realized the significance of fostering relationships within the local community. He attended town hall meetings and connected with local leaders, advocating issues relevant to both the migrant community and long-standing residents. Ledger often invited his new acquaintances to family events, introducing them to the Philogenes' unique blend of Caribbean and Dominican traditions.

At community events, such as the local festival showcasing indigenous crafts and music, Ledger sought out opportunities to introduce the Philogene family to residents. "This is my children's first festival in Roseau," he would say with a smile, his pride evident as he pointed out Wizen, Julien, and the others as they engaged with their new neighbors. "We love the cultural exchange happening here."

Slowly but surely, bridges were built. Neighbors began volunteering to help the Philogenes with various tasks, whether it was assisting with school applications, translating documents, or sharing insights about local customs and traditional practices. In turn, the Philogene family contributed to the community by hosting events that celebrated the cultural diversity of both migrants and locals.

One afternoon, Clara organized a family potluck for the support network. As the aroma of stews and baked goods filled their home, laughter and chatter blended into a beautiful symphony—the sound of connection. Each family brought a dish that represented their culture, and the table overflowed with a feast that showcased the vibrant influences of the Caribbean and Latin America.

As the families sat around the table, they engaged in meaningful conversations. "We should start a neighborhood group centered around local traditions," one mother suggested. "We can share our culinary skills and even learn some traditional dances together."

This idea was met with enthusiasm, and soon they began planning workshops that would allow families to share their heritage. They would teach each other recipes, songs, and dances, nurturing an environment where everyone felt valued, heard, and connected.

Back at school, Wizen, Petronel, and Julien joined forces with other migrant children, who shared many of the same struggles. They quickly became inseparable friends, keeping each other motivated in their studies and encouraging one another to navigate social dynamics. Wizen, who had previously shied away from speaking up in class, found newfound courage from the support of his peers. They celebrated each other's successes and commiserated over challenges, forming a tight-knit group of allies who felt empowered by their shared experiences.

Koie and Nerisa thrived in this environment as well. With family and peers surrounding them, they began participating in smaller school events, eagerly sharing their heritage through art projects and presentations. The support network created not only joy but also a sense of safety. They knew that whatever challenges they faced, they had a community behind them.

The emergence of this support network significantly eased the transition for the Philogene family, providing them with crucial emotional support, practical assistance, and a sense of belonging that they had not expected to find so rapidly in their new environment. As they navigated the complexities of settling in, the friendships cultivated within this network helped mitigate feelings of isolation and anxiety.

Clara found comfort in confiding in the other mothers about her parenting experiences and sharing laughs over the challenges of raising children in a different culture. Maria and the others provided valuable insights into their own journeys, allowing Clara to see that the challenges she faced were not hers alone. They guided her through the maze of local customs, school systems, and even the nuances of grocery shopping at local markets, where she learned to find ingredients, she once thought she would have to forgo.

Ledger benefited from the support network as well. Through the connections he made with local leaders, he was able to access resources for job opportunities, mentorship, and community engagement initiatives. He participated in local forums that focused on the needs of both migrant families and long-standing residents, fostering conversations that echoed the values of inclusion and collaboration. The more he engaged with the community, the more he saw the impact of shared experiences in fostering cohesion.

As the seasons changed, the Philogene children blossomed within this nurturing environment. Wizens found himself thriving academically and socially, boosted by the encouragement of both his family and his friends. The support network helped him transition from a sense of being an outsider to feeling like an integral part of the community. Petronel and Julien flourished as well, participating in after-school programs alongside their peers and bringing home stories of shared projects that blended their different cultures.

Eliza and Louisa found themselves especially connected to the other migrant children. They participated in art classes where they could explore their creative spirit while sharing their own unique styles inspired by their Caribbean heritage. The friendships they developed fostered a sense of security as they celebrated their differences together.

Even the youngest members of the family, Koie and Nerisa, thrived amid the vibrant interactions within the support network. They engaged in playdates organized by the other parents, discovering new friendships with local children. Their laughter rang out at neighborhood gatherings, and they learned songs and games that blended their Caribbean background with Dominican customs, creating a playful fusion of cultures.

In a heartfelt moment, the Philogene family hosted an end-of-year celebration that brought together all the families from their support network. The evening transformed into a beautiful melding of tastes, sounds, and joyous spirits as families celebrated not only their uniqueness but also the shared experiences that had united them. As the sun set and the stars began to twinkle above Roseau, Clara stood at the forefront, glancing around at all the friends they had made.

"Gather around everyone!" she called out, her voice filled with emotion. "Tonight, we celebrate not just our cultures, but the strength of this community we have built together. We have shared our meals, our traditions, and our stories, creating something incredible."

Applause resonated throughout the gathering, and Ledger added, "In a world that often feels divided, we have found family and kinship in one another. This is just the beginning of our journey together."

As the evening unfolded with music, dancing, and storytelling, the Philogene family felt an overwhelming sense of gratitude for the connections they had forged. The emergence of this support network had not only eased their transition into Roseau but also provided a solid foundation for building lifelong relationships that would weather the storms of change.

Reflecting on their experiences, the Philogenes recognized that their new life in Dominica was not merely about adjusting to a new place; it was about embracing a shared story, one where each culture contributed to a deeper understanding of the human experience. They had woven their heritage into the vibrant fabric of their new community, transforming challenges into celebrations of unity and resilience.

Together, they stepped confidently into the future, equipped with the knowledge that they were not just adapting to their new home—they were actively shaping it, fostering a community that embraced diversity and uplifted one another. As the stars twinkled brightly above Roseau, the Philogene family knew their hearts had truly found a home.

Understanding that a solid education would be fundamental to their children's success in Dominica, Ledger, and Clara Philogene made it a top priority to find local schools that offered a quality curriculum suitable for their diverse families. They knew that navigating this new educational landscape was crucial not only for academic growth but also for social integration.

The search for the right school began with extensive research and conversations with both local families and other migrant families in their support network. Clara spoke passionately about her goal of finding a school that would provide an inclusive environment, promoting both learning and the appreciation of different cultures. Ledger shared her enthusiasm, recognizing that the right school could fulfill their desire for their children's education to reflect their Caribbean heritage while also embracing the local Dominican culture.

After numerous visits to various schools, they settled on a public institution with a strong reputation for academic excellence and a welcoming attitude toward multicultural families. The school celebrated diversity in its curriculum, introducing students to a range of perspectives and histories. It was precisely what the Philogene family was looking for—an environment where their children could thrive academically while also making friends from different backgrounds.

Once enrolled, Wizen, Petronel, Julien, Eliza, Louisa, James, Dfriel, Koie, and Nerisa embraced this new chapter of their lives with excitement and hesitance. The older children were particularly aware of the changes, feeling the weight of expectations in a new academic setting, while the younger ones adapted with the natural resilience of childhood curiosity.

To help their children acclimate, Ledger and Clara became actively involved in the school community, attending parent-teacher meetings consistently. They understood that being engaged not only demonstrated their commitment to their children's education but also allowed them to connect with other families and educators. During one such meeting, they discussed curriculum updates, and the various extracurricular activities offered, which excited the children immensely.

"Mom, can we join the art club?" Eliza asked during dinner one night, enthusiasm bubbling in her voice after hearing about the options at the meeting.

"Of course! And I think joining the soccer team would be great for you, too, Wizen," Ledger replied, keenly aware of the importance of both physical activity and socialization in their adjustment to life in Dominica.

Petronel chimed in, "I hope they have a music program! I want to learn to play the steel drum." The parents exchanged glances, recognizing that their children's eagerness to participate signaled budding friendships and a desire to connect with their peers.

In the spirit of mutual engagement, Clara decided to organize a parent workshop that would offer insights into best practices for supporting children through their educational journeys. She reached out to other moms from their support network and was thrilled at the enthusiastic response. The planning sessions became an opportunity for bonding among parents, creating a united front that could support the children's academic and social development.

During the workshop, parents shared experiences and strategies, while local educators offered insights into the Dominican schooling system, emphasizing the importance of parental involvement. Clara and

Ledger learned that fostering relationships with teachers could create a positive reinforcement loop for their children's learning experience.

The Philogene family made it a point to consistently communicate with their children about school life. During family dinners, they opened the floor for discussions about everyone's day—homework assignments, exciting projects, and even the challenges faced in navigating new friendships. This dialog encouraged the children to express their feelings, easing any anxiety about being in a new environment.

One evening, after a particularly spirited family discussion, Julien said, "I love hearing everyone's stories! It makes me feel like we are all on this adventure together." His comment sparked smiles all around the table, reinforcing the idea that they were truly a team on this journey.

As the school year progressed, the Philogene children began to find their footing. Wizen, having embraced soccer, developed friendships with teammates, many of whom shared his passion for sports. Julien thrived in his art class, and Eliza's enthusiasm propelled her to take the lead in school performances. Petronel's talents with the steel drum flourished, and she even organized a small performance that showcased various cultural influences. These experiences bolstered their confidence as they paved their way in their new environment.

Encouragingly, the family continued to maintain a strong line of communication with teachers, reinforcing the idea that education was a collaborative effort. At every parent-teacher meeting, Ledger and Clara actively participated, asking questions and offering insights into their children's strengths and areas where they could use additional support. The teachers welcomed their involvement, appreciating the Philogene family's genuine interest in fostering a nurturing learning environment.

As the academic year ended, the Philogene children had settled well into their respective classes, excelling in both their studies and social lives. The family celebrated their achievements during a fun-filled family outing, where they shared highlights of the year while reassured that they were making significant progress in their new lives. They visited one of Dominica's stunning natural attractions, the Emerald Pool, basking in the beauty of the island's lush landscapes. The cool, clear waters were a refreshing retreat from the humid afternoon heat, and the sounds of nature around them seemed to echo the joy they felt in their hearts.

As they settled by the pool, Ledger initiated a round of appreciation, encouraging each family member to share their proudest achievement from the school year.

"I think I've improved a lot in math," Wizen started a shy smile on his face. "I even helped some classmates with their homework!" His siblings cheered, proud of their elder brother's effort to integrate.

Petronel added, "I was the soloist in our school assembly! I sang a song from home, and everyone loved it."

"You were amazing!" Julien exclaimed, pretending to swoon. "I can't wait for the next one!" Everyone echoed their support, their laughter mixing with the sound of splashing water.

"I won the art competition!" Eliza announced, her eyes sparkling. "My painting was inspired by our Carnival celebration. I was so nervous, but it felt good to share our culture."

"That's awesome, Eliza!" Louisa said, her voice filled with admiration. "I want to paint something too!"

James and Dfriel exchanged proud glances, then said in unison, "We made new friends this year!" Their excitement was contagious, and everyone burst into cheers.

Koie and Nerisa, slightly quieter than their siblings but equally enthusiastic, chimed in with their highlights as well. "We learned a new song in school!" Koie said, clapping his hands.

Nerisa added, "And we made friendship bracelets for our classmates!" Clara nodded approvingly, delighted by her younger children's engagement and social connections.

As the sun began to set, casting a golden hue over the landscape, Clara spoke up, her voice filled with emotion. "I think what I am most proud of is how you all faced this transition together. You supported one another and made the most of every opportunity. It is not just about school achievement; it is about how you bonded as a family and embraced this new environment.

Ledger nodded, feeling a wave of gratitude wash over him. "I could not agree more. You have not only adapted; you have thrived. More importantly, you have all created a beautiful support system among yourselves, which will serve you well in life."

With their hearts light and spirits high, the Philogenes decided to cap off their day with a family swim in the Emerald Pool, splashing and laughing together. They played games, dove into the water, and floated on their backs, shrouded in the tranquility of the moment.

Later, as the sun dipped below the horizon and painted the sky in shades of pink and orange, they gathered on the bank to enjoy a picnic Clara had prepared. The food was simple yet flavorful—jerk chicken, rice, and fresh fruits—but it tasted exceptional amid their laughter and shared stories.

"Let's make this outing a tradition," Ledger suggested as they finished their meal. "At the end of every school year, we can celebrate together like this, reflecting on all we've accomplished while planning for the new adventures ahead."

"Absolutely!" exclaimed Petronel, her enthusiasm infectious. "Next year, we should bring musical instruments and have a mini concert here!"

With that idea, the evening became a celebration not only of their achievements but also of their growing bonds as a family. The journey had been filled with challenges, but they had navigated it together, and now they looked forward with hope and excitement to the future.

As they packed up their things and headed back to their car, Clara felt a surge of pride. This family outing symbolized the warmth and resilience that defined the Philogene family. They had effectively laid a foundation for their children's education in a new culture, demonstrating that family support, community engagement, and a commitment to learning could transform challenges into opportunities.

With laughter trailing behind them as they walked, Clara and Ledger knew that together, they were not just adapting to a new life; they were forging a new path filled with endless possibilities for their family.

Throughout the challenges of adapting to life in Dominica, Ledger's determination and resilience shone brightly. He was keenly aware that their new environment, while vibrant and promising, came with its own set of hurdles—cultural differences, educational adjustments, and the weight of leaving behind their familiar home. Yet, no matter how daunting the obstacles seemed, he remained unfalteringly focused on his family's future, striving to create a nurturing environment where his children could flourish.

In the early days, as they settled into their new routines, Ledger often reflected on the sacrifices they had made to come to Dominica. Each struggle they faced served as a reminder of their strength. When the children encountered difficulties at school—whether grappling with language barriers or feeling out of place—Ledger was there to encourage them. "Every challenge is just a steppingstone to something greater," he would tell them. "You're building resilience, and that will serve you for the rest of your lives."

His unwavering optimism resonated with his children, helping to instill a sense of hope even during tough moments. When worries crept into their minds, Ledger encouraged open conversations. They would gather around the dinner table, where he would invite them to share what was troubling them. "Let's work through this together," he would say, creating an atmosphere of trust and support that allowed his children to voice their feelings without fear of judgment.

For example, one evening, Wizen expressed frustration about a group project at school where he felt marginalized. "I don't think they see me as part of the team," he confessed, his voice heavy with concern. Ledger leaned in, offering his full attention. "Have you talked to them about it?" he asked gently, guiding Wizen to articulate his feelings. "Sometimes, it takes a little effort to bridge that gap. Let them know how much you want to contribute."

With his father's encouragement, Wizen reached out to his classmates and shared his ideas, becoming a valued member of the group. Ledger's approach reinforced the spirit of resilience; he taught his children not to shy away from challenges, but to face them head-on, armed with determination and the knowledge that their family stood firmly behind them.

In the meantime, Clara was equally dedicated to nurturing their family dynamics. She and Ledger worked as a team, sharing their experiences and supporting one another through emotional or logistical hurdles. They would hold hands as they planned budgets or discussed potential career opportunities for Ledger, always reminding each other of the vision they had for their family's future.

As they continued to adapt to new routines, Ledger also took time to connect with other fathers in the community, exchanging insights about parenting and the unique experiences of raising children in a foreign land. This camaraderie allowed him to forge connections that further deepened his sense of belonging. He began to realize that he was not alone in facing these challenges; many families were navigating similar paths.

Through the lens of resilience, Ledger recognized the importance of celebrating even the smallest victories. He established a routine where they would reflect on their week every Sunday evening. As they sat together, he encouraged each family member to share one success or positive experience. Whether it was receiving praise from a teacher, making a new friend, or simply overcoming a small fear, these moments of acknowledgment became a source of motivation that filled their hearts with hope.

During one of these reflections, Louisa exclaimed, "I was nervous about presenting in front of the class, but I did it, and everyone clapped for me!" The room erupted in cheers, and Ledger beamed with pride. "You, see? That is what resilience looks like! Every time you conquer a fear, you are building a stronger version of yourself."

As the months passed, the struggles they faced only strengthened the Philogene family's bond. The shared experiences deepened their understanding of one another, allowing them to develop empathy and patience. Together, they became a buffer against uncertainties, always reminding each other of the beauty that comes from overcoming challenges.

Spring arrived, bringing with it a sense of renewal and hope. Ledger took the opportunity to gather the family for a picnic at the botanical gardens—a local haven filled with blooming flowers and lush greenery. As they spread out the blanket and shared homemade sandwiches, Ledger felt a sense of calm wash over him.

Looking around at his children, who laughed and played together, he realized that their journey was about more than just adapting to a new environment. It was about coming together as a family, learning, and growing stronger through every obstacle. "We've faced a lot this year, but look at how far we've come," he said, his voice steady. "Let's continue to embrace the challenges ahead, knowing we're in this together."

Clara added, "Resilience is not just about enduring; it is about thriving. And that is exactly what we are doing. Every day gives us a chance to create new memories and to learn something about ourselves and each other. With each challenge we face, we are not just surviving, we are building a legacy of resilience and hope for our children."

The children, taking in their mother's words, nodded in agreement. Each one felt the weight of those statements, understanding that their family history was being rewritten with every new experience. As they played together in the gardens, their laughter echoed through the air, a harmonious reminder that joy could be found even amid uncertainty.

"I want to help others too!" Eliza shouted, her excitement bubbling over as she ran over to her father. "We can organize a 'welcome picnic' for new families moving to Roseau, just like ours. We can show them around and help them feel at home."

Ledger smiled, his heart swelling with pride. "That is a fantastic idea, Eliza! It is a great way to give back and build community bonds," he encouraged, exchanging a proud glance with Clara.

At that moment, the Philogene family realized that their journey was not just about their own integration into Roseau but about cultivating relationships that could potentially uplift others in similar situations. They began brainstorming ways to contribute positively to their community, channeling their experiences into assistance for newly arrived families.

As they finished their picnic, Ledger took a deep breath of the fresh, fragrant air. "I think we should make this a special tradition," he suggested, gazing at the vibrant blooms surrounding them. "Every year, we can celebrate how far we have come while welcoming those who are just starting their journey. It is a way to remind us that while challenges are inevitable, hope is always within reach.

The children cheered in agreement, their faces aglow with excitement over the plan. As Ledger looked at Clara, he felt the warmth of their shared vision—one where resilience and hope could help bridge the gap between cultures, creating a community that was stronger together.

Days turned into weeks, and during their family meetings, they began to plan the details of the welcome picnic. They collaborated on the logistics, from creating flyers to inviting other families to the support network. Wizen even immersed himself in designing a program filled with fun activities and games, ensuring that everyone who attended would feel the joy that their family had experienced.

As the date of the picnic approached, anticipation buzzed in the air. The Philogenes felt a renewed sense of purpose, knowing they were not just creating an event but fostering a welcoming space for others.

On the day of the picnic, as families began to arrive, Ledger marveled at how the community he once viewed as foreign was now a mosaic of faces familiar to him. From the Venezuelan family they had met at the first support meeting to Dominican neighbors who had joined their efforts, the gathering was a beautiful blend of cultures, experiences, and stories.

As everyone settled in, Clara welcomed the attendees, her voice warm and inviting. She spoke of the importance of community, resilience, and hope, urging everyone to share their journeys, however challenging or uplifting. As different families opened about their experiences, it became clear that each story mirrored their own—that of struggle followed by triumph, of fear replaced by friendship.

Throughout the day, laughter echoed as children played, parents connected, and a sense of belonging filled the air. As he watched his children interact with others, Ledger felt a profound sense of fulfillment. They were not just creating memories for themselves; they were contributing to a larger story, one that wove their lives into the fabric of Roseau and beyond.

As the sun began to dip on the horizon, casting a golden light over the gathering, Ledger reflected on the journey they had taken to get to this moment. Every challenge, every moment of doubt had led them here—to a place of resilience, hope, and community.

The Philogene family had not only embraced their new life; they had transformed it, becoming beacons of hope for others experiencing their own transitions. With hearts full of gratitude and a renewed commitment to each other and their community, they looked ahead optimistically, ready to face whatever challenges awaited them.

In that moment, surrounded by laughter, friendship, and love, they understood that they were crafting their legacy—one of resilience, hope, and unwavering connection that would carry them forward as they continued to build a brighter future together.

Life in Roseau is a tapestry woven from both challenges and opportunities for Ledger Philogene and his family. Each day unfolds as a unique thread, forming a vivid portrait of their experiences and growth within this vibrant community. The adjustments they face, whether they are adapting to local customs, navigating new educational environments, or learning the intricacies of local commerce and politics—have become essential elements of their journey.

Ledger's active involvement in trade and local affairs is a testament to his commitment to contributing positively to Roseau. He not only seeks to provide for his family but also to engage with his neighbors and business partners to foster an inclusive and supportive economic environment. Through his efforts, he embodies the spirit of resilience that defines his family, striving to build bridges between cultures while honoring their own unique heritage.

As they immerse themselves in their new life, Ledger and Clara have embraced the idea that adapting to a new culture is not merely about survival; it is a way to redefine who they are as a family. Their experiences of struggle and triumph have nurtured a profound strength in their bonds, allowing them to draw closer together as they navigate the complexities of their circumstances.

Each member of the Philogene family has begun to flourish, discovering new passions, friendships, and avenues for growth. The children are becoming engaged citizens, aware of the world around them, and eager to participate in shaping their futures. With each new experience, they are cultivating a rich identity that blends their Caribbean roots with the colorful tapestry of life in Roseau.

Understanding the significance of these transitions, Ledger and Clara lay the groundwork for their evolving identity and aspirations. They set intentions for their family, encouraging their children to embrace new beginnings with open hearts and minds. In doing so, they serve as pillars of support, nurturing dreams and ambitions while instilling the values of empathy and community engagement.

As they move forward, the Philogene family recognizes that their journey is framed not just by the challenges they face, but by the opportunities for connection, growth, and meaningful contributions to their new home. With every interaction and shared experience, they craft a narrative rich in resilience and hope, reflecting their determination to thrive in this beautiful, diverse community.

In the embrace of Roseau, they find not only a new home but a canvas for their dreams—a space where they can bloom, evolve, and redefine what it means to be a family in a world of constant change. As they continue to navigate the complexities of their life together, they remain committed to building a brighter future, one thread at a time. The promise of new beginnings lies ahead, guiding them ever forward on this journey of discovery, integration, and belonging.

 CB

Chapter Seven: Transitioning To Grand Bay

After several months of navigating the bustling streets of Roseau, Ledger Philogene began to feel the weight of city life pressing down on him. While the vibrant energy of the capital had provided numerous opportunities for professional growth and cultural engagement, he recognized an urgent need for a quieter existence, one that aligned more closely with his family's aspirations for stability and self-sufficiency. The frenetic pace of urban living, coupled with the complexities of commerce and local politics, led him to reconsider what was essential for his family's well-being.

Ledger spent many evenings reflecting on their journey. He envisioned a life that embraced simplicity, allowing his children to connect with nature, learn the value of hard work, and cultivate a sense of community in a more tranquil setting. He often recalled the stories his parents shared about farming in Haiti—the rhythms of the seasons, the satisfaction of growing one's food, and the strong bonds formed among neighbors working the land together. These revelations stirred a deep-rooted desire within him, illuminating the path toward a new dream.

With this vision in mind, Ledger began exploring the possibility of relocating his family to Grand Bay, a picturesque rural community known for its lush landscapes and agricultural potential. He was drawn to the idea of establishing roots in a place where fresh air and wide-open spaces could replace the hustle and bustle of city life. In his heart, he believed that a rural setting could provide the ideal backdrop for his children to thrive—immersed in the natural world, learning the importance of sustainability, and growing together as a family.

Once the decision to move was made, Ledger shared the news with Clara, who listened attentively as he expressed his aspirations. "Imagine the kids having space to run around to plant and harvest their own food," he said, excitement evident in his voice. "They would learn about the land and where their food comes from. It is an opportunity for them to connect with their roots."

Clara considered his words. While she appreciated the allure of a simpler life, she also understood the challenges that lay ahead. "It sounds wonderful, Ledger, but farming can be unpredictable," she cautioned. "We have experienced challenges before in the city. What if we face setbacks again?"

Ledger nodded, acknowledging her concern. "I know it will not be easy, but I believe we can make it work together. We have built resilience as a family, and if we embrace this new chapter with the same spirit, I am confident we can succeed.

With their shared resolve solidified, the family began preparing for the transition. They packed their belongings, into a truck, and bid farewell to the bustling streets of Roseau. As they traveled to Grand Bay, the landscape shifted from concrete and asphalt to rolling hills and verdant greenery. A sense of calm enveloped them, a tangible excitement tinged with the unknown.

Settling into their new home proved to be an adventure. The rustic charm of their new dwelling—a modest but cozy house surrounded by rich soil—filled them with hope. Ledger envisioned plots of land ripe for cultivation, where they could plant root vegetables, herbs, and fruits. The family began to map out their aspirations for a small-scale farm, eagerly discussing what crops they might grow and the sustainable practices they wished to implement.

Despite the optimistic outlook, Ledger soon faced the harsh realities of rural life. Establishing agricultural roots proved to be a formidable challenge. The first few months required intensive labor as they cleared the land and prepared for planting. Ledger worked tirelessly, often rising before dawn

179

to till the soil and plant seeds. The physical demands of farming took a toll on his body, but he pushed through, motivated by the vision of nurturing a fruitful homestead for his children.

As Ledger delved deeper into farming, he found himself confronting not only the physical labor but also the mounting economic uncertainties that plagued the agricultural sector. Weather patterns were unpredictable, and unforeseen challenges such as pest infestations or poor soil conditions loomed constantly. Even as the family celebrated small victories—like the first sprouts of green emerging from the ground or the sweet aroma of herbs ready for harvest—he could not shake the worry about their long-term viability.

In quiet moments, Ledger would sit on the porch, overlooking their fledgling plot of land and allowing the weight of his aspirations to settle in his mind. He often contemplated the fine balance between hope and fear, success, and struggle. Farming, he realized, was a continual cycle of renewal and resilience—a reflection of the very journey his family was undertaking in this new chapter of their lives.

As Ledger grappled with the various challenges that farming presented, he also found comfort in the beauty of the land around him. The sun rising over the hills each morning served as a reminder of opportunities yet to come, and each evening setting behind the trees invited quiet reflection. Through this transition, he discovered that every seed planted represented not just a future harvest but also a step toward grounding their family's identity in a way that honored their heritage while embracing the promise of new beginnings.

As Ledger Philogene settled into the rhythm of life in Roseau, he could not shake the feelings of restlessness that simmered beneath the surface. While the bustling capital had presented plentiful opportunities for commerce and political engagement, a deeper yearning for a different kind of life began to take hold. Ledger envisioned a lifestyle that emphasized peace, a slower pace of living, and a deeper connection to the land.

Every day, as he navigated the busy streets of Roseau—filled with honking cars, crowded markets, and the incessant buzz of city life—Ledger felt a growing disconnect. He often found himself reminiscing about the stories his parents had shared of their lives in St Bart's, where the days started with the rising sun, chores were accomplished by the light of day, and life centered around family, community, and agriculture. He craved a space where his children could experience that same connection to nature, understanding the cycles of growth and harvest, and developing a respect for the earth.

In his heart, Ledger dreamed of a home surrounded by rolling hills, lush gardens, and the sounds of nature. He imagined waking up each morning to the chorus of birds, feeling the warmth of the sun on his face while tending to his land. He hoped to cultivate a small, sustainable farm that would not only provide food for his family but also serve as a tranquil sanctuary where they could bond and learn together.

Ledger envisioned his children growing up away from the chaos of urban life, nurturing a close-knit family dynamically rooted in nature and agriculture. He could see Wizen learning how to plant seeds and understanding the hard work that goes into growing food. He could picture Eliza picking ripe tomatoes from the vines, feeling the satisfaction of harvesting what they had nurtured. The idea of teaching Petronel and Julien how to care for animals and tend to the land filled him with hope, and he imagined family gatherings around a table filled with fruits, vegetables, and meals crafted from their labor.

As he mulled over his desires, Ledger shared his thoughts with Clara one evening after dinner. The two of them sat on their porch, watching the sun dip below the horizon, and he could feel the weight of his aspirations in the air. "Clara," he began, hesitating slightly as he considered how to articulate his vision, "I have been thinking a lot about our life here. It feels as though we're caught in a whirlwind, and I can't help but wonder if there's a better way for us to live."

Clara turned to him, her expression attentive. "What do you mean?"

"I want us to find a place where we can breathe," he continued, his voice earnest. "A place where our children can grow up in nature, where we can cultivate our own food and live more simply. I want them to experience the land in a way that connects them to themselves, each other, and our heritage."

Clara considered his words, feeling a mix of excitement and apprehension. "It sounds beautiful, Ledger. But you know the challenges that come with farming and living off the land. Are we ready for that?"

"I believe we are," he replied, his eyes shining with conviction. "We have faced so much already. This could be a new beginning for a chance to reclaim some of what we have lost in the chaos. We could create a life filled with purpose, teaching our kids the importance of hard work, community, and sustainability."

Clara smiled and reached for his hand, feeling the passion in his words. "You have always had a way of seeing the potential in things. If we do this, we need to approach it with clear eyes. It will require dedication, but I believe in us, and I want to support your vision. Let us research our options and see what we can find."

With Clara's encouragement fueling his desire for change, Ledger began to map out their next steps. He explored the surrounding areas for potential farmland, learning about the challenges and rewards of agricultural life. As he delved deeper into his research, he connected with local farmers who shared their insights, experiences, and wisdom gained from years spent cultivating the earth.

During his visits, Ledger found himself fully immersed in conversations about sustainable farming practices, crop rotation, and the importance of community-supported agriculture. The more he learned, the more certain he became that their family could thrive in this new lifestyle, away from the distractions of the city.

Through these interactions, Ledger discovered that the spirit of community in rural areas was profoundly different from what he had known in Roseau. Neighbors shared resources, helped each other in times of need, and celebrated each other's successes. This sense of togetherness resonated deeply with him, reaffirming his desire to cultivate not only crops but also relationships based on trust and mutual support.

As days turned into weeks, the vision of a rural life grew clearer. Ledger began preparing the family for the potential transition, engaging the children in conversations about their future. He painted a vivid picture of life in a peaceful landscape, where they could explore the outdoors, play freely, and be part of something bigger than themselves.

"Imagine waking up to the sun shining and going outside to help me feed the chickens, or picking fresh fruit from the trees," he said, his excitement contagious.

With a sense of anticipation bubbling inside him, Ledger Philogene prepared for the trip to Grand Bay. It was time to see for himself the place that had captured his imagination, the rural community that represented everything he hoped for in a new beginning. As Ledger and Clara embarked on their journey, he could not help but envision a future filled with possibility—lush fields, vibrant gardens, and a close-knit family thriving together in harmony with the land.

As they drove along the winding roads toward Grand Bay, they were greeted by breathtaking views of rolling hills, dense trees, and sweeping vistas of the Caribbean Sea. The sharp contrast between the urban sprawl of Roseau and the tranquil beauty of Grand Bay was exhilarating. With each passing mile, Ledger felt his excitement grow, a sense of hope swelling within him. This was a place filled with potential, a canvas on which they could paint their dreams.

Upon arriving, they caught sight of small farms spread across the landscape, each with its own personality—some with crops bursting from the earth, others with livestock grazing nearby. The air was thick with the scent of rich soil and blooming flowers, a stark reminder of the life they could cultivate here. Ledger and Clara stepped out of their vehicle, inhaling deeply, feeling the peaceful ambiance enveloped them.

With directions from friendly locals, they made their way to the community center, where a gathering of farmers was taking place. Ledger felt a rush of excitement as they approached, knowing that this was the heartbeat of the community, the place where knowledge and support flowed freely among those passionate about agriculture.

As they entered the center, they were greeted by warm smiles and hearty handshakes. The community was a patchwork of diverse backgrounds, with seasoned farmers, enthusiastic newcomers, and families who had been cultivating the land for generations. Ledger and Clara felt instantly welcomed, their presence embraced as if they were already part of the fabric of Grand Bay.

"Welcome!" an older gentleman named Mr. Ruiz said, his voice resonating with warmth and authority. "We are gathered here today to share our harvest stories and exchange tips for the upcoming planting season. You are just in time to join us!"

Feeling a surge of gratitude, Ledger and Clara took seats among the group, eager to listen and learn. As various farmers shared their experiences, it became clear that there was a strong sense of camaraderie in the room. They spoke passionately about the challenges they faced, unpredictable weather, pests, and fluctuating market prices—but they also celebrated their successes, the rewards of hard work, and the joy of sharing the fruits of their labor.

During the meeting, Ledger took meticulous notes, absorbing the wealth of knowledge being shared. The discussions ranged from practical gardening techniques and organic pest control to the concepts of crop rotation and sustainable farming practices. The more he learned, the more convinced he became that this community was precisely what he and his family needed.

After the meeting, Ledger approached Mr. Ruiz, his heart pounding with both excitement and nervousness. "I'm Ledger Philogene, and this is my wife, Clara," he introduced himself. "We are considering moving to Grand Bay and starting a small farm. Are there any opportunities to learn more about farming here?"

"Of course!" Mr. Ruiz beamed, extending his hand to Ledger. "Many of us would be delighted to share our knowledge with you. Farming is about community, after all. If you are willing to put in the hard work, we would be happy to help you settle in and get started."

The warmth of Mr. Ruiz's welcome struck a chord in Ledger. He could feel the support of the community already forming around him, a key piece of the puzzle he had been searching for. As they spoke, Ledger learned more about local resources, farming initiatives, and even cooperative programs that could help get newcomers up to speed.

As the conversation continued, Clara felt a wave of reassurance wash over her. The uncertainty that had hovered over the decision to move began to dissipate, replaced by a sense of belonging that was hard to ignore. She listened intently, envisioning their children playing alongside other kids in the community, running through fields, and exploring the wonders of nature right outside their doorstep.

After their enriching discussion, Ledger and Clara took a walk through the surrounding fields with Mr. Ruiz. They passed rows of crops bursting with life, colorful flowers, and the occasional friendly animal peering through fences. The landscape was undeniably fertile, and Ledger's heart soared at the possibilities that lay ahead. Here, they could grow everything they had hoped for—vegetables, herbs, and even some fruit trees.

"See that field over there?" Mr. Ruiz pointed. "The owner will be retiring soon, and he is looking for someone to take over the land. It might be an excellent opportunity for you if you decide to move here."

Ledger's eyes widened at the prospect. The idea of taking over a farm felt like a dream coming to life. The potential was immense, and he could already visualize the fruits of their labor flourishing in that very field. He exchanged glances with Clara, who mirrored his excitement, her own hopes igniting at the thought of establishing roots in such a welcoming environment.

"What would it take to maintain the land?" Ledger asked, his curiosity piqued. "And what kind of support is available for new farmers?"

Mr. Ruiz nodded, appreciating Ledger's enthusiasm. "It is a big commitment, but it can be done with dedication and the right resources. Many of us here have been through similar transitions. We hold workshops and have mentorship programs for newcomers to help them get started. Plus, we often share tools and resources amongst ourselves. You will not be alone in this."

"With such support, it seems like a wonderful opportunity," Clara added, her voice steady despite the whirlwind of thoughts racing through her mind. "It could be the fresh start we've all been yearning for."

Feeling invigorated, Ledger envisioned long days spent planting crops alongside his children, teaching them about the land and the importance of caring for it. They could cultivate the very soil that would nourish their family—a tangible connection that would bind them not only to each other but also to the land they chose to call home.

As the sun began to set, casting a golden hue over the lush landscape, Ledger and Clara took a moment to absorb their surroundings. The light gently illuminated the ocean in the distance, and the evening breeze filled the air with the scents of fresh earth and blossoming flowers. It felt as if nature herself was encouraging them to leap.

That night, Ledger and Clara found a small inn in Grand Bay to stay overnight, allowing them to reflect on the day's experience. As they settled in, Ledger could not contain his excitement. "This could be our future," he said, a sense of possibility dancing in his voice. "I cannot help but feel this is where we belong. We could cultivate not just crops but a whole new way of life."

Clara smiled at him, feeling the connection to this place grow stronger. "We would be investing in our family's future," she replied. "It's touching to think that our children could learn the values of hard work and community from such an early age."

"We've faced our fair share of challenges, but what if we turned those into opportunities?" Ledger mused. "If we commit to this, we could create a sustainable livelihood while teaching them the importance of resilience and the fruits of labor."

As they prepared for bed, Ledger's mind raced with ideas and plans. He imagined ways they could lay out their future farm—where to plant vegetables, which animals they might raise, and how to build an efficient irrigation system. The visions were vibrant and detailed, painting a picture of a life rich in purpose and fulfillment.

The following morning, they woke early, energized by their discussions and the serene beauty that surrounded them. After breakfast, Ledger suggested they return to the community center to meet more farmers and gather additional insights before heading back to Roseau. Clara readily agreed, feeling the stirrings of excitement bubbling within her.

At the community center, they saw familiar faces from the previous day—farmers eager to share more about their lives and their ongoing challenges. Ledger felt a rush of gratitude for the openness and support offered by this community. As he spoke to others about the opportunity to take over the field, he felt their encouragement as a warm embrace; seasoned farmers were ready to help him navigate the initial hurdles he would face.

"Starting is always the hardest, but we're here to help each other," one farmer said, patting Ledger on the back. "Once you get into the rhythm of the land, you'll find your way."

By the time they left Grand Bay, Ledger and Clara had gathered valuable knowledge and inspiration. They returned to Roseau filled with renewed purpose and enthusiasm. The decision to move began to crystallize in their minds, and Ledger felt more certain than ever that this was the path they were meant to pursue.

As they navigated back through the bustling streets of the capital, exchanging excited glances and ideas, Ledger knew that the opportunity for change was within their reach. Grand Bay represented not just a new home, but a promise of growth—a chance to cultivate a life steeped in connection, community, and sustainable living. With each passing mile, his heart raced with the potential of what lay ahead, the vision of their rural dream growing clearer, more attainable, and irresistibly inviting.

As the decision to relocate to Grand Bay solidified, the Philogene family plunged into the bustling preparations for their move. The once-quiet home in Roseau burst into activity, filled with the sounds of sorting, packing, and animated discussions about the future. Each family member found their own way to contribute to the transition, driven by a mixture of excitement, anxiety, and anticipation.

Ledger took charge of the larger items and furniture, carefully labeling boxes and brainstorming how they would arrange their new home in Grand Bay. He envisioned a cozy space filled with warmth and love, where every corner would reflect their journey and aspirations for a sustainable lifestyle. He could picture fresh flowers on the kitchen table, vibrant artwork from the kids adorning the walls, and shelves stocked with tools and seeds for their new farming venture.

Meanwhile, Clara focused on the smaller possessions, guiding the children in categorizing their belongings. "Let's divide everything into keep, sell, and donate," she suggested, her tone encouraging yet practical. The children eagerly agreed, and soon the living room filled with piles of clothing, toys, and books.

"Look at this!" Julien exclaimed, holding up a dusty soccer ball that had seen better days. "Remember when we played in the park? We should keep this!"

Nerisa chimed in, her eyes sparkling with nostalgia. "And my drawing of the park! It should go in our new house!" She rushed to retrieve the framed artwork from the wall, visualizing how it would add personal warmth to their new space.

Ledger watched as his children reminisced about the home they were leaving behind, feeling both a pang of sadness and immense pride. Although they were saying goodbye to a familiar environment, he found solace in knowing that they were moving toward something profoundly transformative.

As the process unfolded, Clara seized the opportunity to engage the children in conversations about dreams for their new life in Grand Bay. "What are you most excited about?" she asked, her voice gentle and inviting.

"I want to have my own garden!" Nerisa declared enthusiastically. "I'll plant flowers and vegetables and make it beautiful!"

"That's a great idea," Clara encouraged. "And what will you grow?"

"Tomatoes! And herbs! And even blueberries!" Nerisa replied, her mind racing with the possibilities.

Julien, feeling inspired, added, "I want to help Dad with the farm. I want to learn how to plant and take care of the animals! We can have chickens!"

Ledger beamed at his son's aspirations, envisioning the day when they would work side by side on the farm, teaching him the skills he had come to cherish. "Absolutely, Wizen. You will be my right-hand man," he replied, a sense of purpose lighting up his heart.

James and Dfriel, although younger, quickly jumped into the conversation, inspired by their siblings' excitement. "Can we have a treehouse?" Julien asked with wide eyes. "I want to climb trees!"

"Of course! And we will make it a place for all of us to play and read," Clara promised, feeling her own anticipation grow as they painted a vivid picture of their rural life together.

As they continued to sort through their belongings, mixed emotions swirled among them—there was excitement for what awaited in Grand Bay and nostalgia for memories made in Roseau. They shared stories of their experiences in the capital, talking about the friendships they had formed, the adventures they had embarked on, and the lessons they had learned along the way.

Amid the laughter and heavy lifting, Ledger felt moments of anxiety creeping in. Was this the right choice? What challenges would they face as they transitioned to farm life? He reminded himself that these feelings were natural, a part of the process. Embracing change was never easy, but it was often where growth happened.

Clara, sensing Ledger's tension, offered a reassuring smile. "We'll figure it out together," she whispered. "This is an adventure for all of us, and we'll support each other through whatever comes our way."

Taking her hand, Ledger nodded, grateful for her unwavering support. They were embarking on a journey that would redefine their lives and bring them closer together. "You are right. We will take it one day at a time."

As the packing progressed, the living room transformed into a maze of cardboard boxes, each labeled with care. They rallied together, engaging in discussions about the logistics of moving, from scheduling the truck to organizing a farewell gathering with their friends in Roseau. Ledger took the lead on reaching out to neighbors and organizing a small get-together, a chance for the family to say their goodbyes while expressing gratitude for the connections they had made.

The night before the big move, the family gathered for a final dinner in their Roseau home. They shared a meal filled with laughter, discussing their favorite memories from their time in Roseau. Clara prepared a feast of dishes that had become family staples—rice and peas, jerk chicken, and a fresh salad drizzled with vinaigrette. The aroma filled the air, creating a warm ambiance that wrapped around them like a comforting embrace.

"Remember that time we got caught in the rain at the market?" Wizen laughed, his eyes glinting with nostalgia. "We ended up soaking wet but still bought those lemons for lemonade. Dad said it was the best lemonade he had ever tasted!"

Ledger chuckled, shaking his head. "You had a knack for finding trouble, didn't you? And still, we had such a great time that day."

Petronel chimed in, "And there was that festival with the music and dancing! I want to find a festival like that in Grand Bay!"

"Yes!" Eliza agreed, clapping her hands excitedly. "We can dance in the fields if they have music! Imagine all the flowers around us!"

Clara smiled as she listened to her children recount their cherished moments, grateful that they could reminisce about both the joyful and the silly adventures they had experienced together. It was in these shared stories that she saw the foundation of lasting bonds being forged—a reminder of the love and laughter that had filled their home.

"Every place we've lived has its own spirit," Clara said, her voice softening. "And while we will always treasure our time here in Roseau, I know Grand Bay will offer us a different kind of beauty and opportunity. Just think of the memories we will create there!"

After dinner, they gathered in the living room to look through old photographs, reminiscing and laughing as they flipped through albums full of moments frozen in time. The room echoed with joy, but underneath it all was a bittersweet sense of closure. They were preparing to say goodbye to not just a house, but the memories stitched into the very walls they had called home.

As the evening wore on, Ledger noticed the flicker of emotion in Clara's eyes. He reached for her hand and squeezed it gently, silently acknowledging the changes ahead while also celebrating their shared journey. "No matter where we go, as long as we're together, we can build new memories," he reassured her, aware that the thrill of their new adventure would also bring challenges.

Feeling the warmth of her hand in his, Clara smiled back, her heart steadied by his words. "And we'll always carry a piece of Roseau with us in our hearts."

The children, sensing the introspective atmosphere, chimed in, "And we'll bring the best of Roseau to Grand Bay!" Wizen declared. "Our new adventure will start with the feelings we have now."

As they exchanged excited and hopeful chatter, the family discussed their plans for settling into Grand Bay—what vegetables to plant first, which animals to raise, and the layout of the farm. With each idea, their anticipation grew, brightening even the most bittersweet moments of the night.

Eventually, they moved the conversation back to practical matters, making a list of things to bring and things to leave behind. Clara suggested a family tradition: every year, they would revisit some of their favorite moments from Roseau, by cooking familiar dishes or reenacting fond memories, ensuring that those cherished times remained alive in their hearts.

Finally, as night fell, they snuggled together on the couch, wrapped in blankets, sharing their hopes and dreams for the future. Each expressed what they were most looking forward to be it gardening, exploring the surrounding nature, or simply having space to play and connect as a family.

In that moment, Ledger felt a swell of gratitude for the strength of their family. The obstacles they had faced in Roseau prepared them for this new chapter, and he knew that by working together, they would rise to meet whatever challenges awaited them in Grand Bay.

As the stars twinkled outside, he gathered his family closer, sharing a heartfelt promise. "Let us be brave together, work hard, and create a beautiful life in Grand Bay. No matter what, we will always have each other."

And with that, a sense of peace washed over them, as they closed that chapter in their lives and embraced the possibilities that awaited. Ignited by dreams and united in love, the Philogene family felt ready to take their next steps into the world ahead of them.

Arriving in Grand Bay filled the Philogene family with a sense of excitement and possibility. The air was fresher, the landscape more vibrant, and the rhythm of life slower—not unlike the peaceful dreams they had fostered during the preparations for the move. As they stood in front of their new home, Ledger took a deep breath, feeling a wave of gratitude wash over him. They finally had a chance to begin anew.

After unpacking their belongings and settling into their modest but cozy house, Ledger and Clara gathered the children on the porch to discuss their next steps. "Today marks the beginning of our farming journey!" Ledger announced, his eyes shining with enthusiasm. "We will plant crops that will thrive in this Caribbean climate. Who is ready to get their hands dirty?"

"Me! I want to plant tomatoes!" Eliza exclaimed, jumping up and down with excitement.

Wizen nodded vigorously. "And I want to raise chickens! Can we start with a coop?"

Clara smiled at their enthusiasm. "Absolutely, but we need to plan carefully. We will need to learn together and support each other."

As they set out to prepare the land, Ledger leaned on the knowledge he had gained from his previous ventures in trade. He knew the basics of supply and demand, understanding what crops were popular and how markets worked. However, he quickly discovered that farming required a unique set of skills, patience, perseverance, and a deep understanding of the land.

The first task was to clear the overgrown fields around their home. Armed with hoes, rakes, and shovels, Ledger, Clara, and the children worked side by side, sweating under the Caribbean sun. They laughed, chatted, and encouraged one another as they transformed the land. Working as a family on the earth felt like a rite of passage; they were no longer just dreamers, they were farmers, shaping their future.

Once the land was cleared, Ledger gathered the family to discuss what to plant. He pulled out a notebook where he had jotted down a list of crops suitable for the climate. "We can start with root vegetables like sweet potatoes and cassava, and we should also consider tomatoes, peppers, and some leafy greens," he shared.

"Don't forget the fruit!" Eliza piped up. "Can we plant mangoes and papayas?"

"Great idea!" Clara added enthusiastically. "Fruits will not only provide us with delicious snacks but might be a good source of income too once we establish the farm."

Ledger smiled at their eagerness and encouraged them to share any ideas they had. They laid out a plan for the garden, designating areas for each crop, including a small space for family herbs, where they would grow basil, thyme, and cilantro.

After producing the plan, the family set out to procure seeds and gardening supplies. They visited the local agricultural shop in Grand Bay, where the community warmly greeted them. Mr. Ruiz, the farmer from the community center, was there to lend a hand, offering advice on soil management and pest control.

"The soil here is very rich—perfect for growing," Mr. Ruiz explained, introducing the family to the variety of seeds available. "Starting with food crops that are well-suited for this area will ensure a good yield. Make sure to rotate your crops to maintain the soil's health."

After loading their truck with seeds, tools, and organic fertilizers, the family returned home with a sense of purpose. The children were buzzing with excitement, eagerly anticipating the planting. They spent the following days digging rows, planting the seeds, and watering them carefully, constantly checking back to see if anything had sprouted.

Ledger enjoyed applying his trade knowledge, devising a plan to sell their excess produce at the local market once they had a good harvest. However, he quickly learned the importance of patience in farming. The days stretched on, and waiting for seedlings to emerge tested his resolve.

"Can we check how the plants are doing again?" Wizen asked one afternoon, looking a bit anxious as they stared down at the freshly planted rows.

Ledger chuckled gently, kneeling beside him. "You will learn, son. Plants take time. Just like we need time to adjust to our new life here, they need time to grow. Let us check back in a few days."

During this waiting period, Ledger also prioritized family bonding. They spent evenings at home sharing stories, playing games, and exploring the nearby forest. Nature became their playground, with the children discovering hidden paths, colorful birds, and interesting plants. It was a time of connection, both to nature and one another, renewing their spirits as they settled into this new chapter.

Weeks passed, and soon small green shoots began to break through the soil, signaling the fruits of their labor. The sight filled Ledger with pride. Their hard work and patience were beginning to pay off, and he felt a wave of relief wash over him. Each tiny sprout represented not just their efforts but the promise of a bountiful harvest and the life they envisioned in Grand Bay.

"Look!" Eliza exclaimed one sunny morning, bounding excitedly toward Ledger and Clara as they inspected the garden. "The tomatoes are growing! Can we pick them now?"

Ledger knelt beside her, eyes sparkling with encouragement. "Not just yet, but soon! We need to let them develop fully so they will be juicy and perfect for our meals. But we can check on the others."

He watched as the children eagerly pointed out the various plants, each observing the small progress with wonder. Wizen had taken on the role of their little farmer, clutching a tiny hoe he had fashioned from scraps, pretending to tend to the sickly seedlings that had not yet emerged.

"Let us give them a little more time, friend. Remember the importance of nurturing things before they bloom," Ledger said, noticing the impatience in his son's brows. Wizen nodded, his understanding deepening with each lesson learned on the farm.

On more than one occasion, the family collaborated on tasks to improve their growing space. They built simple trellises for the climbing beans, mulched around the plants to retain moisture, and even experimented with natural pest deterrents made from garlic and hot pepper, inspired by advice shared at the community center.

As they devoted themselves to the farm, Ledger found that he was constantly learning—about soil, weather patterns, and the intricate balance of nature. He began keeping a journal, noting observations and insights while experimenting with different planting techniques.

"Farming is not just about hard work; it's about listening to the land," he mused one evening after another satisfying day in the garden. Clara nodded thoughtfully, her hands busy preparing dinner with freshly picked herbs. "What are you thinking about planting next?" she asked.

"Maybe we should consider some beans," Ledger replied, his mind racing with ideas. "They fix nitrogen in the soil, which will help our other plants, and they're a great source of protein."

"That's perfect!" Clara said her enthusiasm was infectious. "We will have to involve the kids in planting them, too. They love helping!"

Ledger reveled in their teamwork, appreciating the unity that blossomed alongside their crops. Each day brought them closer as a family, working side by side under the warm sun, sharing laughter, fending off frustrations when things did not go as planned, and celebrating small victories.

Then came the day when they could finally harvest their first crop—plump, ripe tomatoes glistening in the sun. Eliza squealed with joy as she plucked them from the vine, giggling and handing them to her brothers. "Look what we did!" she shouted, her glee contagious.

Gathering their bounty, the family came together to create a simple meal—fresh tomato salads garnished with herbs from their garden, alongside grilled chicken that Clara had prepared. As they sat down together at the table, Ledger could not help but beam with pride. The colors on their plates were vibrant, reflecting the efforts of their labor and the dedication they had poured into this new life.

"This is amazing," Wizen said, biting into a slice of fresh tomato. "It's so sweet!"

"Sweet like the memories we're building," Ledger replied, feeling a surge of gratitude to have his family gathered around him, joy radiating from their faces.

As they savored the fruits of their labor, Clara raised her glass in a toast to their new life. "To new beginnings," she proclaimed, her voice filled with warmth. "May we continue to grow, learn, and thrive together."

And with that toast, the family sealed their commitment to this journey. Although challenges lay ahead, they understood that each obstacle was but a steppingstone on the path to establishing themselves in Grand Bay—a journey filled with hard work, togetherness, and the nurturing of both their crops and their bonds.

As the sun dipped below the horizon, casting a golden glow over the fields, Ledger settled into the comforting realization that they were becoming more than just farmers; they were part of a community, an evolving legacy rooted deeply in the land they now called home. The adventure had just begun, and he was ready to embrace every moment.

As the days turned into weeks in Grand Bay, the Philogene family immersed themselves in the laborious yet rewarding task of building their farm. Each member of the family took on roles that suited their strengths and interests, creating a collaborative spirit that transformed hard work into a shared adventure. Ledger, Clara, and the children worked side by side, turning their vision into reality while deepening their connection to the land and to one another.

The early mornings became a cherished routine. Ledger, filled with energy and purpose, awoke the family with the rising sun. "Today is another day to nurture our farm!" he would call out, his enthusiasm infectious. With a hearty breakfast fueling them, they donned their work clothes and set out to tackle the various tasks that awaited them.

Ledger focused on teaching his children the fundamentals of farming, instilling lessons that would serve them for a lifetime. He started by explaining soil health, the foundation of effective farming. "Healthy soil grows healthy plants," he told them one morning as they gathered around a section of their land. He showed them how to perform soil tests, looking for moisture content and nutrient levels, and the children eagerly followed his lead, feeling the earthy particles between their fingers.

"Look how dark and rich this soil is! It is full of life," he said, his voice filled with excitement. Wizen knelt beside him, poking at the ground curiously, while Eliza gathered small samples in her hands, captivated by the vibrant world beneath their feet.

"Can we add compost to make it even better?" Eliza asked, her eyes wide with curiosity.

"Absolutely! Adding compost is a great way to feed the soil and the plants," Ledger replied, thrilled by their enthusiasm. That day, they all pitched in to create their compost pile, gathering kitchen scraps and yard waste.

As they built the compost, Ledger explained how the scraps went through a transformation, enriching the soil over time. "Just like us, the land needs to be fed to grow strong," he emphasized, imparting the values of patience and care that farming required.

Meanwhile, Clara embraced her role in cultivating the gardens surrounding their home. With a keen eye for beauty and function, she designed a space that not only provided food but also reflected their commitment to this new lifestyle. While Ledger taught the children about the intricacies of soil and planting, Clara worked alongside them, convincing the kids to help her plant colorful flowers that would attract pollinators to the garden beds.

"Look at how many different colors we can use! We can plant sunflowers over here and zinnias over there," she encouraged, her hands eagerly sifting through vibrant flower seeds. "Creating a beautiful garden will be just as important as growing our food crops. It is all part of our life here."

Amidst laughter and playful banter, the Philogene children loved helping their mother. They learned to seed the beds alongside the vegetables, turning the garden into a tapestry of colors that brightened their property. One afternoon, while they carefully placed the last flower seeds, Eliza asked, "How can we make sure the flowers grow strong like the vegetables?"

Clara smiled, impressed by her daughter's curiosity. "Just like vegetables, flowers need water, sunlight, and nutrients from the soil. They will thrive if we take care of them."

Together, Clara and the children developed their watering schedule, turning their daily check-ins into quality family time. They joyfully discussed which flowers bloomed and which vegetables blossomed, creating a bond that tied them closely to their emerging farm.

As the weeks went by, Ledger and Clara recognized that building a functional farm was an evolving process. They needed structures for their crops and a shelter for any animals they intended to raise. Weekend mornings found them gathering wood and materials, building raised planting beds, and reinforcing the chicken coop, a priority for Wizen.

"Can I help with the coop, Dad?" Wizen asked one Saturday, his excitement palpable.

"Of course! Let us measure the wood and hammer together," Ledger replied, demonstrating the proper techniques while emphasizing safety. With each swing of the hammer, Wizen's confidence grew. He was proud to be contributing to their new farm, and Ledger could not help but smile as he watched his son tackle each task with determination.

Underneath the warmth of the tropical sun, Ledger shared more than just practical skills that day. He explained the importance of sustainable farming practices, such as rotating crops and utilizing companion planting to promote growth and ward off pests naturally. "We have to respect and nurture the land, so it can give back to us for years to come," he said, imparting lessons that extended beyond farming and into the core values of hard work and stewardship.

The entire family worked hard to create a thriving environment that would sustain them. As the seasons changed, Clara added fruit trees to their growing farm, envisioning a future filled with lush orchards that would provide shade, beauty, and a bounty of delicious treats. She carefully selected varieties that thrived in the Caribbean climate—mango, guava, and papaya—and enlisted the children to help with planting and caring for the young trees.

On one particularly sunny afternoon, she gathered Wizen, Eliza, Petronel, and Julien in the back of their property, where a soft breeze swayed the palm fronds overhead. "Today, we're going to plant our first fruit trees!" Clara announced, holding up a young mango sapling. "Can anyone tell me what we need to do to help them grow strong?"

"They need water and sunlight!" Eliza shouted, her face beaming with excitement.

"Exactly!" Clara smiled, then continued, "And we need to dig a good hole, making sure to give them plenty of space. Let us work together, and in time, we will have our very own mangoes to enjoy!"

With shovels in hand, the children dove into the task, learning how to prepare the soil properly and ensuring each tree was planted at the right depth to support growth. As they finished planting the last sapling, Clara reminded them, "This is just the beginning. These trees will take time to grow, just like everything else on our farm."

"Will it take long until we can eat the fruit?" Julien asked, his brow furrowed with concern.

"Yes, it will take a couple of years," she replied, kneeling beside him. "But remember, we will nurture them and watch them grow. And when they finally bear fruit, it will be such a wonderful reward for all our hard work!"

As the days became longer and warmer, Ledger spent time expanding their farm by building a small greenhouse to start seedlings earlier in the season. The children loved the idea of having a special space where they could watch the plants grow from tiny seeds to healthy sprouts. "Let's decorate it!" Eliza suggested, envisioning a colorful space full of life.

Armed with paint, ribbons, and colorful stones, the family transformed their greenhouse into a vibrant hub of activity. They painted butterflies, flowers, and sun motifs on their walls, reflecting the joy they felt in their hearts as they embarked on this journey together. With each stroke of the brush, they infused the space with their hopes and dreams, turning it into a symbol of their new life.

Throughout the season, Ledger continued to teach his children about the importance of nurturing the land while explaining farming techniques that balance productivity with sustainability. They learned to plant cover crops to enrich the soil, manage irrigation efficiently, and recognize beneficial insects from harmful pests. Ledger encouraged them to keep a farm journal, where they documented their progress, challenges faced, and the lessons learned—an invaluable resource for their shared journey ahead.

One evening, while enjoying the glowing light of the setting sun over their plot, Ledger reflected on how far they had come. Their efforts were beginning to yield results—vibrant vegetables and fragrant herbs flourished, their fruit trees established roots, and the garden had become a flourishing ecosystem buzzing with life.

Clara joined him on the porch, a contented smile on her lips as she admired their work. "I can't believe how much we've accomplished in such a short time," she said softly, resting her head on Ledger's shoulder. "Our little farm is becoming a reality, and I love how we're building it together."

"Yes, it's amazing what hard work and love can create," he replied, wrapping her in his arms. "I am proud of how we have all come together. It was a leap of faith to start this journey, but it is already bringing us closer."

As the sun dipped below the horizon, the shimmering colors of the sky mirrored their family's journey. It illuminated the farm, casting a warm glow over the plants, animals, and the home they were cultivating together.

In those moments of tranquility, with healthy crops surrounding them and laughter from the children wafting through the air, Ledger felt the weight of worry lift from his shoulders. They had committed wholeheartedly to this farming life—carving pathways not just in the earth but in their hearts, where the joys of family and the lessons of the land would intertwine beautifully.

As they sat together under the stars, Ledger and Clara held hands, promising to nurture their dreams, cultivate their relationships, and harvest the rich life that lay ahead. They were leaping into a beautiful future built by their own hands—a future filled with endless possibilities rooted in love and resilience.

As the Philogene family settled into their new life in Grand Bay, they quickly realized that farming was not just an individual endeavor but a communal one. The resilience of the land they worked, and the success of their crops were intimately tied to the wisdom and support of those who had come before them. Eager to delve deeper into the farming community, Ledger and Clara sought connections with their neighbors, recognizing the value of shared experiences and collective knowledge.

One bright Saturday morning, Ledger discovered that the local community garden was hosting an open day, inviting new and veteran farmers alike to come together. Excitement bubbled within him as he gathered the family. "Today is an opportunity to learn from others, share what we have started, and strengthen our ties here. Who wants to join me?"

"Me! I want to see everything!" Eliza chimed in, clapping her hands.

"I'm in," Wizen added, leaning over the kitchen table, his eyes sparkling with enthusiasm. Petronel and Julien nodded in agreement, eager to be part of something bigger than themselves.

At the community garden, the Philogenes were welcomed with open arms. Rows of healthy, vibrant plants stretched across the landscape, and the air was filled with the earthy scents of fresh soil mingled with the sweet fragrance of blooming flowers. They were greeted by Mr. Ruiz, who had offered them invaluable advice during their initial days of planting.

"Welcome, Philogene family!" Mr. Ruiz exclaimed, his warm smile matching the sun overhead. "I am so glad you could join us. Today, you will have the chance to tour the gardens and learn about the projects we are working on.

As they walked through the garden, the Philogenes met fellow farmers who shared their experiences and tips on various crops. A woman named Lila demonstrated her method for planting and cultivating okra, explaining how she prepared the soil to promote thriving crops. "Cultivating healthy soil is essential for keeping pests at bay and ensuring good growth," she advised, showing them how to mix compost into the earth.

"Can we try?" Wizen asked, his curiosity piqued, and Lila gladly allowed him to help.

"I see you've got a knack for it!" she encouraged as he carefully dug into the soil, mixing the rich compost. He beamed with pride, feeling more confident in his skills.

Meanwhile, Clara joined a group learning about companion planting. A seasoned farmer named José explained how certain plants thrive when grown together, enhancing each other's growth and minimizing pests. "For example, planting basil near tomatoes can keep aphids away," he shared, his voice full of wisdom.

"That's incredible!" Clara exclaimed, jotting notes in her book. "We've started growing both—imagine how well they'll do together!"

After the demonstrations, the community gathered for an informal lunch—potluck style—where they shared dishes prepared with their harvests. Clara brought a fresh salad topped with herbs from their garden, proud to contribute to the meal. The warmth of camaraderie forged through shared food and stories warmed their hearts as they sat and talked with new friends.

Over heaping plates of food, Ledger sat with other farmers, discussing their experiences in the field. He listened intently as they shared valuable tips on sustainable practices, such as crop rotation. "Rotating your crops isn't just good for the soil, it helps keep pests from settling in and reduces diseases," one farmer shared.

"That makes perfect sense! We have already begun with tomatoes, peppers, and beans; I will ensure we rotate them seasonally," Ledger noted, feeling more grounded in his understanding of farming.

As the sun began to dip, casting a warm golden hue over the gathering, Clara joined Ledger, her eyes alight with excitement from the interactions and knowledge they had gained. "I feel like we've just touched the tip of the iceberg," she said, her voice brimming with enthusiasm. "These connections could be pivotal for us as we grow."

"Absolutely," Ledger agreed, feeling invigorated by the sense of community they had found. "Not only are we learning practical things, but we're also building relationships that will help us establish our place here in Grand Bay."

That sense of belonging grew stronger in the following weeks. The Philogene family continued to partake in community meetings and workshops, eager to absorb as much knowledge as possible. They joined a local co-op that pooled resources to help new farmers access seeds, tools, and materials, further deepening their connections within the community.

Through their involvement, Ledger and Clara also discovered a community youth program that taught local children about sustainable farming practices, instilling the importance of caring for the environment. Recognizing a fantastic opportunity to blend their values of family and community, they both volunteered to help mentor the children in practical farming activities.

"Engaging with the kids is a great way to solidify our place here," Clara said, her eyes shining with enthusiasm. "Not only can we share what we have learned, but we can also learn from them. They have a deep connection to this land and different insights we can benefit from."

Ledger nodded in agreement. "Absolutely. We can inspire them while also cultivating friendships. Our children need to connect with other kids who share similar interests. This will enrich all our lives."

As the Philogenes began participating in the youth program, they quickly found joy in working alongside the local children. Every Saturday, a group of eager young learners gathered at their farm, ready to get their hands dirty. The air was filled with laughter and excitement as Ledger and Clara led them in a variety of activities, planting seeds, tending to the garden, and even building small compost bins.

On one Saturday, Ledger organized a planting demonstration. He encouraged the kids to try their hand at planting new seedlings. "Remember what we talked about last week? Every plant has its favorite space in the garden, just like you each have your favorite spot to play," he instructed, showing them how to dig holes for the seedlings.

Eliza took charge, helping her peers carefully place their seedlings on the ground. "This one's a tomato; it needs a lot of sunlight!" she exclaimed, sharing her newfound knowledge with confidence. She beamed as she watched the younger children surround her, eager to absorb every bit of information.

Clara, meanwhile, gathered the kids for an impromptu lesson on the importance of pollinators. "Without bees and butterflies, we wouldn't have as many fruits and vegetables to enjoy," she explained, showing them how to create a simple bee hotel using recycled materials.

As they worked, Clara encouraged the children to think about ways to make their own gardens more inviting to pollinators. "What flowers can we plant next to our crops?" she asked, prompting discussions filled with creativity and curiosity.

"Sunflowers!" shouted one child, excitedly waving his hands. "They'll attract the bees!"

"Yes, and marigolds too!" another chimed in, and soon a buzz of ideas filled the air, each child eager to contribute. From building habitats to planting a wide variety of flowers, their suggestions fostered teamwork and shared visions for their community garden.

As spring melted into summer, the Philogene family began to feel the positive effects of their community connections. Not only did their knowledge about sustainable farming grow, but they also formed lasting friendships, creating a support system woven into the fabric of Grand Bay.

They began attending local farmers' markets, where Ledger and Clara showcased their produce alongside their new friends. The hustle and bustle of the market became a weekly highlight for the family, filled with vibrant colors, the sound of laughter, and the aroma of fresh, local food. There, they mingled with fellow farmers, exchanging tips and celebrating each other's successes, all while introducing their children to the joy of community engagement.

"I love coming here!" Eliza exclaimed one Saturday as she helped arrange their fresh tomatoes and herbs at their market stand. "It's like a big party with so much food!"

Ledger smiled, watching as his children embraced the lively atmosphere. They worked together, packaging their goods, chatting with customers, and sharing stories about their farming journey.

"Remember," Clara reminded them, "selling at the market is not just about selling. It is about sharing what we grow and building relationships with the people who live around us."

As they packed up at the end of the market day, the Philogene family celebrated their successes, both big and small. They returned home, tired but fulfilled, knowing they were not just growing crops— they were cultivating a sense of home.

In the following months, their farm became a sanctuary, a space not only for growing food but also for nurturing friendships and learning together. The bonds forged with neighbors and community members transformed the Philogene family's experience in Grand Bay into a tapestry of shared memories, knowledge, and love.

Through engaging with the local farming community, Ledger and Clara found their place within Grand Bay, solidifying their commitment to a lifestyle rooted in sustainability and connection. They were thankful not just for the soil beneath their feet but for the community that embraced them—a community that helped them grow as individuals and as a family.

Together, the Philogene family thrived, and as they looked out over their blossoming farm, they knew they had found something truly special: a home.

The Philogene family quickly discovered that transitioning to rural life meant embracing a new way of living, one dictated by the rhythms of farming. Gone were the lazy Sunday mornings and late nights with friends; instead, their days became structured around the sun and the cycles of growth beneath their care. As the weeks turned to months, they adapted to this demanding yet fulfilling routine.

Each day began with the sunrise. The rooster from across the field would crow, breaking the silence of dawn and signaling the start of their day. Ledger would often be the first to rise, relishing the tranquility of the early morning. He experienced a sense of peace while sipping his coffee on the porch, the warm light spilling across the land, illuminating the rows of young crops that they had lovingly planted together as a family.

"Good morning, Dad!" Eliza chirped as she joined him, blinking sleepily against the brightness of the day.

"Good morning! Ready to help with the farm?" Ledger asked, his heart swelling with pride as he watched his daughter's eyes light up.

"Yeah! What are we doing today?" she replied enthusiastically.

As day broke, Clara joined them, and soon the house erupted with the sounds of breakfast preparation. The children scurried around the kitchen, their excitement infectious as they packed lunches for their time in the fields. They relished the fresh fruit from their own trees, slicing juicy mangoes and sweet papayas while discussing plans for the day ahead.

After breakfast, the family gathered their tools and headed out to the fields, where they quickly fell into a rhythm. Early mornings were dedicated to the most strenuous tasks: tilling the soil, planting new seeds, and tending to their budding crops. Each family member had a role—Ledger focused on planting and harvesting, Clara managed the flower and vegetable gardens, while the children learned their chores, slowly becoming more adept at tasks like watering, weeding, and gathering the essential tools.

As the sun climbed higher in the sky, the heat became palpable. The physical toll of farm work was relentless; sweat dripped from their brows as they toiled in the sun. Yet through the labor, they began to develop resilience. Ledger reminded the children often, "This is hard work, but it teaches us perseverance. When we see the fruits of our labor, it will be all worth it.

In the afternoons, Clara often implemented a break to combat the midday heat. She prepared simple, refreshing meals using items harvested from their growing garden—salads, fresh fruit, and sandwiches that revitalized their energy. They gathered under the shade of a nearby tree, stealing moments of rest while sharing stories or playing games to keep spirits high.

After lunch, they returned to work, and as the temperatures cooled in the late afternoon, they would finish the day's tasks by taking care of winding-up chores. This often involved watering the plants, checking for pests, and ensuring all tools were cleaned and stored properly.

One evening, as the sun set over the horizon, casting vibrant hues of orange and pink across the landscape, Ledger sat on the porch with Clara while the children played nearby. "This is what I always wanted for us," he said, watching their kids laugh and chase each other. "A life connected to nature and to each other."

Clara smiled. "But it's not without its challenges," she replied thoughtfully, observing the fatigued smiles on their children's faces. "Some days I wonder if we're doing too much."

"We are building character as much as a farm. Each day brings new lessons, and they are learning the value of hard work," Ledger reassured her, recognizing the toll their new lifestyle could have on the children.

The days softened into weeks, and though both Ledger and Clara occasionally felt the fatigue of long hours, they also felt rejuvenated at the back of their minds by their family's progress. They implemented evening routines to take care of their combined well-being. After dinner, the family would gather for story time, reading together under the stars or recounting their favorite moments from the day. It became a cherished practice, fostering a sense of belonging and togetherness.

As they adjusted to their new routine, both parents took care to ensure that their children were not overwhelmed. They introduced play breaks, dance-offs in the kitchen, or nature walks through the nearby woods, fostering joy amidst the hard work. Eventually, their days blended seamlessly into a rhythm that honored both the laborious and rewarding aspects of farming life.

On weekends, they often ventured into the Grand Bay community, participating in local events or taking the time to exchange ideas with fellow farmers. These outings provided essential social connections and nurturing friendships that counteracted the physical toll of their new life.

One afternoon, while attending a seasonal festival in the town square, Ledger watched Eliza and Wizen dance joyfully among other children. He felt a wave of contentment wash over him as he observed the pure joy radiating from their laughter. The festival was bustling with life, filled with vibrant colors, the rich aromas of local foods being cooked in the open air, and the sounds of lively music resonating through the crowd. Families gathered, mingling together while sharing stories of their farming successes and challenges.

"Look at them!" Clara exclaimed, her eyes sparkling as she caught Ledger's gaze. "I cannot believe how much they have settled in. They really belong here."

Ledger nodded, feeling the warmth of pride swell in his chest. "This place is becoming our home, and it's wonderful to see them so happy."

As the couple watched the children dance, they could not help but recall their first days in Grand Bay—the uncertainty, the challenges, and the hard work that had brought them to this place. Now, the energy of the community, combined with their efforts, had created a sense of belonging for which they had longed.

Later, as the sun began to set, painting the sky in strokes of deep orange and lavender, they found themselves strolling together through the festival booths. Clara encouraged Ledger to sample a bowl of fresh coconut ice cream, and they laughed at the way he held the bowl with both hands, savoring each scoop as his children insisted on sharing their favorite treats.

"Here, try this!" Eliza said excitedly, handing Ledger a piece of fresh mango sticky rice from a nearby stall.

"Delicious! You two are fantastic taste testers," Ledger replied, grinning as he watched their faces light up at the array of flavors.

Clara leaned in closer to Ledger, her voice soft amid the festivities. "You know, we are really starting to mesh with the community. People are recognizing us, and we are forming friendships."

"Definitely," he agreed, taking in the overall atmosphere of joy and togetherness. "It takes time, but with every event, we're building connections that strengthen our roots in this place."

As twilight descended, the organizers prepared for the festival's final event—a dance performance celebrating local culture. Families gathered around, and Ledger took Eliza by the hand while Clara held Wizen's. They settled onto a blanket, the children eagerly anticipating the spectacle.

When the dancers appeared, adorned in colorful costumes, the audience gasped in awe. The rhythm of the drums pulsed through the air, and the children leaned forward, entranced by the movements and stories depicted in the traditional dance.

"This is amazing!" Wizen whispered, his eyes wide. "I didn't know people could move like that!"

Eliza nodded vigorously, her face alight with excitement. "We need to learn how to dance like that!"

With the performers twirling and weaving stories through their movements, Ledger felt a stirring sense of unity enveloping the crowd, everyone clapping, laughing, and cheering together. The sense of community had grown stronger, and he realized that this festival was more than just entertainment; it was a celebration of their shared lives and experiences.

As the last dance wrapped up and the audience erupted into applause, Ledger felt a renewed sense of determination. The adjustments to their new routine had provided not just a new way of life, but also a newfound appreciation for the relationships they were cultivating.

As they gathered their belongings and headed home, Clara took Ledger's hand, squeezing it tightly. "We have come a long way. I cannot believe how well we are adjusting. I sometimes worry about the kids and the workload but seeing them so happy reassures me."

"They're thriving because we're all in this together," Ledger replied, glancing back at Eliza and Wizen, who were chattering excitedly about the dances they had seen. "And they're learning the value of hard work and community."

That night, long after the festival lights dimmed and the sounds of joy faded, the Philogene family returned home exhausted yet elated. They settled in for the evening, recounting their favorite moments from the day and soaking in the feeling of connection that enveloped them.

In the days that followed, the rhythm of farm life continued to shape their new existence. Early mornings and late afternoons became ingrained in their routine as they invested time and effort into their agricultural ambitions. The challenges were still there, but now they faced them together stronger and more united than ever.

As the crops grew taller in the fields and the children flourished in their new environment, the Philogene family found not just the physical adjustments to rural life, but also the emotional anchors that would bind them to Grand Bay for years to come. They understood that adjusting to their new routine meant creating a life rich with purpose, laughter, and love—one that they would cherish as they continued growing and nurturing each other, and their little piece of paradise.

As summer settled over Grand Bay, the Philogene family found themselves navigating both the joys and struggles of rural life. While they had made significant strides in building their farm, the challenges of farming were far from over. Each day brought new tests that were not always predictable, forcing them to adapt and find resilience in the face of adversity.

The sunny days that had nourished their crops took a sharp turn when a sudden tropical storm rolled in off the coast. Ledger stood on the back porch, eyes scanning the quickly darkening sky, tinges of anxiety rippling through him like the wind racing through the trees. The forecast had hinted at rain, but the ferocity of the storm caught everyone off guard.

"Ledger, we need to secure everything!" Clara called as she rushed outside, her voice firm. "We can't let our work be washed away!"

"Grab the tarps! We must cover the seedlings!" he shouted back, adrenaline flooding his system. The children scrambled to help, their faces reflecting the urgency of the moment.

They rushed to protect what they could, frantically covering young fruit trees, securing bundles of vegetables, and moving equipment and tools to higher ground. Despite their best efforts, the storm unleashed heavy rains and gusting winds that threatened to undo weeks of hard work.

As the storm raged outside, Ledger could not shake the sinking feeling in his stomach. "What if we lose everything?" he whispered to Clara, fear creeping into his voice as they huddled together under the porch.

"It is okay. We have prepared for storms before, and we will recover if we lose some crops," she reassured him, though her heart raced at the thought as well. "It's an obstacle, and we'll face it as a family."

When the storm finally subsided, the damage was evident. They ventured out to assess the extent of the destruction, and Ledger felt his heart drop as he looked at the flooded fields and uprooted plants. The reality of their situation weighed heavily on him, and doubt began to creep in—a feeling he had tried to keep at bay.

"It's going to take a lot of work to get back on track," he said, running a hand through his hair, frustration alive in his eyes. "I thought we were doing everything right, but now…"

"Let's focus on what we can fix," Clara interrupted gently, placing a steady hand on his arm. "We can replant what we can and salvage the healthy crops. We will figure this out together—just like we always do."

Ledger nodded, but the pressure to provide for his family loomed larger than the storm clouds that had just passed. With each passing day, he felt the tension build as uncertainty hung over their farming efforts.

Days later, while he was trying to establish a plan of action, he learned of yet another challenge—a pest invasion had emerged, an army of aphids and caterpillars attacking their perfect rows of crops. Frustrated and overwhelmed, Ledger found himself grappling with feelings of inadequacy.

"Why is everything so hard?" he vented to Clara one evening, sitting at the kitchen table, his head in his hands. "I thought this was going to be a life worth living for us, yet it feels like we can't catch a break."

Clara, who had been washing vegetables from their garden, paused and looked at Ledger with compassion. "Farming is unpredictable. It comes with its challenges, and the key is how we respond to them. We need to seek solutions instead of being overwhelmed by the problems," she replied, her voice steady.

With her encouragement, they decided to reach out to fellow farmers in the community for advice. That weekend, they attended a local farmer's meeting focused on pest management strategies. Listening to seasoned farmers share their experiences, Ledger felt a glimmer of hope amidst his doubts.

One farmer, Mrs. Thompson, spoke passionately about integrated pest management (IPM). "It is about understanding the pests and creating a balance. You can use natural repellents or attract beneficial insects," she said, her voice clear and unwavering. "Do not be afraid to experiment. Nothing is perfect, but perseverance will get you through."

Inspired by her words, Ledger approached her after the meeting. "We have been dealing with a pest invasion, and I am worried about the impact it will have on our crops. What should we do?" he asked, vulnerability creeping into his tone.

Mrs. Thompson shared her tips and resources, encouraging him to utilize neem oil and plant companion crops to deter pests naturally. "Start small, test what works for you, and adjust as needed. Every farm is unique," she advised, her smile warm and encouraging.

Returning home, Ledger felt a renewed sense of purpose. He relayed the information to Clara and the children, who were eager to help him implement the new strategies. They gathered in their small kitchen, maps, and diagrams of their fields spread out across the table, excitement replacing some of the earlier tension.

"Okay, team," Ledger said, tapping the map with his finger. "Mrs. Thompson suggested we start by planting some companion crops between our vegetables to help repel pests. We will also create a natural spray with neem oil to protect our plants."

Eliza raised her hand, her eyes sparkling with enthusiasm. "I want to help with the neem oil! Can I mix it with the water?"

"Of course! That is a great job for you, Eliza," Ledger smiled, grateful for her eagerness. He turned to Wizen next. "And I need your help collecting herbs from the garden. We will mix those in too; they can act as natural deterrents for the pests."

"You can count on me, Dad!" Wizen replied, racing outside to gather basil and garlic, convinced they could take on any pest that threatened their crops.

Clara joined in the planning, noting, "Let us make sure we pick companion plants that thrive alongside what we already have. Sunflowers and marigolds are perfect for attracting beneficial insects, and they will add beauty to our fields."

With a clear plan of action in mind, the family set out to rejuvenate their farm. The atmosphere was invigorating, filled with a shared sense of purpose. They worked side by side, planting seeds and nurturing their seedlings while singing songs and sharing laughter amidst the labor.

Days turned into weeks, and with each passing day, their crops gradually flourished. Ledger marveled at how, despite the setbacks, the plants seemed to respond positively to their efforts. The routine of farming had transformed once more, with new rhythms emerging learning, and experimenting became part of their daily life.

However, just as things were improving, the unpredictability of farming struck again. During a visit to the market, Ledger overheard several farmers discussing significant market fluctuations affecting prices for produce. Anxiety gnawed at him as he realized that while their crops were thriving, the financial aspects of farming remained precarious.

"This year's been tough for everyone," a farmer lamented. "Prices are dropping across the board; it's going to be hard to make ends meet."

Later that evening, Ledger sat down with Clara, sharing his concerns about the potential economic impact of the market instability on their farming ambitions. "What if we can't sell our crops for what we need?" he asked, his brows furrowing. "What if all this hard work doesn't pay off?"

Clara took a deep breath, her expression thoughtful. "We will find a way to adapt, just like we always have. We need to diversify our offerings and reach as many markets as we can." She paused, then added, "We could think about creating value-added products—things like salsa or pickles with the tomatoes and peppers we have grown. That could help us maintain stability."

"Brilliant idea," he said, nodding in agreement. "We have the resources; we just need the right strategies."

That night, the couple brainstormed potential products they could create. They spent hours researching recipes, mapping out their strategy to tap into local markets, and how to package their goods attractively. The prospect ignited a spark of excitement in Ledger, pulling his focus away from the looming uncertainties.

As their plan took shape, they decided to make their first batch of salsa using the surplus tomatoes they had harvested. The children stood along the kitchen counter, tearing the tomatoes and chopping herbs, reveling in the creation of something new. Together, they crafted a flavorful mixture, fermenting it with a homemade label that read, "Philogene's Fresh Garden Salsa."

Days later, at the market, they launched their first product. As customers sampled their salsa, Ledger felt a swell of hope return. People enjoyed the taste, asking for more, while bright ingredients from their farm turned into tangible items they could sell.

Rediscovering their resilience through these challenges fostered a renewed sense of community. They received support from fellow farmers who offered advice on pricing and marketing, reinforcing the spirit of cooperation that defined their town.

While the unpredictability of weather, pests, and market fluctuations continued to loom over their heads, Ledger realized something vital along the way. Adaptability and camaraderie were not important; they were necessary for survival in this world of farming—traits woven into the very fabric of the community and, more importantly, their family.

Though challenges would always be a part of their journey, the Philogene family learned how to face them together, drawing strength from one another as they continued to evolve alongside the land they cherished. As each day ended, Ledger found solace in the love that surrounded him—the love that had anchored them during unpredictable storms and paved the way through uncertain futures. It was this bond and determination that would guide them through whatever obstacles lay ahead.

As the weeks rolled into months, the Philogene family faced each challenge with unwavering support for one another. Though the unpredictability of their new lifestyle was daunting—like the quick changes in weather patterns or unexpected pest invasions—they learned to approach uncertainty with creativity and resilience. Each hurdle became an opportunity to adapt, innovate, and strengthen their family ties.

They continued refining their salsa recipe and eventually expanded their line of products, creating vibrant pickled vegetables and fresh herb blends. With each successful batch, their confidence swelled. They poured their hearts into their creations, hand-labeling each jar with cheerful designs that reflected the spirit of their farm.

The local market became a vibrant hub for the family. With each weekend, more customers came by to taste their latest offerings, and word spread quickly about the delicious products from the Philogene family. With each sale, Ledger felt a renewed sense of hope, realizing they were building not just a farm but a community of supporters who appreciated their hard work.

Yet the unpredictability of farming was ever present. On one particularly hot afternoon, Ledger noticed signs among their crops that made his heart sink. The tomato plants were showing signs of blossom end rot, a common issue caused by inconsistent watering and nutritional imbalance.

"We need to act fast," Ledger said, his brow furrowing with concern as Clara joined him in the garden. "If we don't correct the pH of the soil, our harvest will be ruined."

Clara knelt by the plants, examining them closely. "Let us test the soil and add the necessary amendments. We can bring in compost and ensure we provide consistent water. It will not be easy, but we can fix this."

That evening, they conducted research together, gathering the data needed to adjust their approach. The children watched as they collaborated, taking notes and offering ideas. "We can make a watering schedule," Eliza suggested. "And if we all take turns, it won't be too much work!"

Wizen chimed in, "What if we create a fun chart to track our plants? We could draw happy faces when they are healthy!"

Inspired by their children's enthusiasm, Ledger and Clara decided to implement those ideas. They created a colorful watering chart to keep track of the plant's needs while explaining the importance of balanced care and sustainability to their children.

As the family worked together to amend the soil and set a watering schedule, Ledger found comfort in the shared labor. Even amid the pressures of farming, the children's laughter, and eagerness to help brought lightness to the arduous tasks. It was a reminder that they were working toward a common goal—a life they cherished together.

Through trial and error, unwavering support, and the realization that challenges were part of their journey, the Philogene family flourished. Every setback became a lesson learned, fostering not just growth in their crops, but also growth within each other. They discovered that it was okay to have doubts, but those doubts could be transformed into motivation.

One afternoon, as autumn crept in, Ledger stood in the field, contemplating the once-barren ground that had been transformed into a place of life. The crops were healthy once again, ripening under the golden sun, and the knowledge they had gained hung like a beautiful tapestry around them, reflecting their journey so far.

"Hey, everyone!" Ledger called his voice echoing through the fields. "Come check this out!"

Clara and the children rushed over, curious. He pointed toward a section of the garden overflowing with vibrant tomatoes, peppers, and herbs. "Look at the results of our hard work! We did this together!"

Eliza squealed with delight, rushing to the bountiful plants, while Wizen knelt to inspect the ripening vegetables. The sense of accomplishment electrified the air, and Ledger felt a powerful wave of pride. All the challenges they had faced had only solidified the foundation of their family.

As dusk settled in, casting a warm glow over their farm, Ledger gathered his family for a moment of gratitude. "You know," he began, looking each of them in the eye, "this journey has not been easy.

We have faced storms, pests, and setbacks, but we have come through it together. Our bond has made us stronger."

Clara squeezed his hand, her eyes reflecting shared understanding. "And each challenge has made us better at what we do. We live and learn together."

"Together," the children echoed, their voices bright as the stars began to twinkle above them.

In that moment, surrounded by the fruits of their labor and the love they shared, Ledger realized that the challenges of farming could never overshadow the joy they brought into their lives. As they walked back toward the house together, under a sky painted with stars, they felt ready to embrace whatever lay ahead confident that together, they could overcome any obstacles that came their way. The air was crisp and filled with the earthy scent of freshly turned soil, hinting at the promise of tomorrow. They chatted excitedly about plans for the next day: setting up their booth at the local farmers' market, experimenting with new salsa flavors, and planting more vegetables for the upcoming season.

As they reached the porch, Ledger paused to look back at the fields, glowing softly under the moonlight. The quiet hum of nature surrounded them, a symphony that marked the end of another day infused with both challenges and triumphs.

"Tomorrow," Ledger said, turning to his family, "we will put in the final touches for our market display. I am going to make sure our products stand out even more. What do you all think?"

The kids chimed in. "We could make colorful signs!" Eliza suggested. "And I want to help with the taste samples!" Wizen added, bouncing slightly on his feet, excitement radiating from his small frame.

Clara smiled, feeling pride swell within her. "And I can create a fun flyer to showcase our new products! We will get this right."

In the days that followed, the Philogene family poured their energy into their preparations. Each evening after dinner, they gathered around the table to craft beautiful signs, experiment with their recipes, and talk about their experiences in farming. Laughter filled their home, mingling with the aroma of fresh herbs from the garden, creating an atmosphere of creativity and collaboration.

By the time Saturday arrived, their excitement was palpable. As the family loaded the truck with their carefully prepared goods—jars of salsa, pickles, and bundles of fresh vegetables—the sun rose over Grand Bay, casting a warm golden light across the landscape.

At the market, vibrant booths lined the streets, and the energy was electric. Ledger felt a mix of nerves and exhilaration as they set up their stand. Clara arranged their colorful products attractively, while the children busily created their eye-catching signs and prepared samples for eager customers.

"Look at our setup!" Eliza exclaimed, her eyes wide as she stepped back to take it all in. Each jar sparkled in the sunlight, and the banners they had made were filled with cheerful colors and inviting words.

As customers began to trickle in, Ledger felt a sense of pride swell within him. This was not just about selling their goods; it was about sharing a piece of their journey and hard work with the community. With every interaction, he emphasized their story—how they had navigated storms, pests, and market fluctuations together, each experience only forging their resolve to succeed.

"Would you like to try our fresh garden salsa?" Clara offered to a couple browsing their booth, her smile warm and inviting. "It's made with tomatoes and herbs from our farm, and we're excited to share it with the community!"

As tastes were sampled, Ledger could see the delighted reactions on people's faces. The flavors danced on their tongues, and the smiles that appeared were like sunlight breaking through clouds. Sales began to pour in, and soon their table was lined with empty sample cups and happy customers chatting about their favorite flavors.

"This is amazing!" Wizen exclaimed, handing out more samples to enthusiastic passersby. "We're going to sell out!"

And sure enough, as the sun dipped low in the sky and the market began to wind down, the Philogene family found their table nearly cleared of products. Ledger felt a rush of gratitude wash over him. They had not only survived the setbacks but had also built something beautiful, a thriving business rooted in love, hard work, and the support of their community.

As they packed up for the day, Ledger took a moment to reflect on how far they had come. The challenges they faced had tested their limits, forcing them to adapt, learn, and grow together. With every hurdle, they had emerged stronger and closer, threading their experiences into a tapestry of resilience that defined their family.

Under the fading light, Ledger gathered his family close, and with his heart full, he proclaimed, "No matter what challenges we face in the future, I know we will tackle them together. We have proven time and again that if we stick together, we can overcome anything.

Clara's eyes sparkled in agreement, and Eliza and Wizen nodded vigorously. "Together!" they echoed again, their voices ringing out in unison.

As they headed home, tired but triumphant, Ledger looked ahead with unwavering determination. The path of farming would always hold its uncertainties, but their love and commitment to one another would be their guiding stars, lighting the way through any storm. That night, as they gathered on the porch to watch the stars twinkle above, they realized that the adventure was just beginning. Together, they would embrace every twist and turn, ready to forge their own story in the heart of Grand Bay.

As the sun sank into the horizon, casting golden hues across the Philogene farm, Ledger leaned against the barn's weathered wood, arms crossed tightly over his chest. He listened to the familiar sound of crickets chirping, but tonight, the soothing rhythm failed to calm his racing thoughts. Economic uncertainties loomed large over their newfound life, casting a long shadow that felt as heavy as the crops that thrived under summer sunlight.

Despite the joy of watching their plants grow, Ledger could not shake the pressure that accompanied their agricultural venture. Every season brought hope, but it also came with significant financial challenges. The investment in equipment, seeds, and soil amendments weighed heavily on his mind, and the inconsistent revenue from their harvests gnawed at his confidence.

"Ledger?" Clara's soft voice cut through the evening silence, and he turned to see her approaching with a slight frown etched on her brow. "You have been quiet. What is on your mind?"

He hesitated before finally voicing what had been troubling him. "I am just worried about our financial situation. Even though we are selling some products at the market, and the crops look good now, what if we have a bad harvest? Or what if the prices drop again? With all the capital we have invested, I feel like we are treading water. What if I cannot provide for our family?"

Clara moved closer and placed a hand on his shoulder, sensing the weight of his concern. "We are doing our best, Ledger. Farming is full of unpredictability, but I believe in what we are building here. The community appreciates our hard work, and that counts for a lot."

He sighed, looking away from Clara, frustrated, bubbling beneath the surface. "But it is not just about the work we are doing. It is about sustainability. What if we cannot make ends meet? What if this does not work out? What if we fail?" His voice cracked slightly, revealing the vulnerability he had been trying to hide.

"Failure is a possibility in any venture," Clara replied, her tone firm yet compassionate. "But it does not define us. We can adapt and learn. Together."

A moment of silence passed between them, the night growing thicker as the fireflies began to twinkle in the surrounding fields. Clara's reassurance helped, but Ledger could not escape the sense of impending doom that hung over him like dark storm clouds on the horizon.

The next morning, Ledger resolved to act. He gathered his notebook and sat at the kitchen table, determined to create a budget that accounted for their farming expenses and projected income. As he scribbled numbers, he was both hopeful and anxious, weighing their costs against what they might earn at the market.

Yet each calculation felt like a gamble. Due to pest invasions and erratic weather, their crops had not been as productive as he had hoped. Market prices fluctuated dramatically, often leaving him pinned against the wall with the reality that they were not guaranteed a stable income.

Moreover, unexpected expenses cropped up—equipment that needed repair or new seeds that had to be purchased. Ledger felt his heart sink as he added up the columns, finding themselves in the red month after month.

"Ledger?" Clara's voice called out, breaking through his concentration. She peeked around the corner of the kitchen. "You have been working on the budget for a while. How is it looking?"

"It's... complicated." He exhaled sharply. "We are not where I thought we would be. I just do not know how to turn this around. I wish I could ensure our future, but I do not have all the answers."

Clara sat down across from him, concern etched on her face. "Have you thought about reaching out to other farmers? Sometimes they have ideas or resources that could help you weather these uncertainties."

Ledger considered this. He had been so focused on doing everything himself that he had not fully tapped into the community around them. "You are right. I guess I have been too proud to ask for help."

As the days passed, propelled by Clara's encouragement, Ledger began to attend local farmer meetings more regularly. The atmosphere was friendly and supportive, filled with farmers willing to share their experiences and challenges. He listened intently as others recounted their own struggles with crop yields, unpredictable weather patterns, and market fluctuations. Their honesty gave him hope and reminded him that he was not alone in his anxieties.

One evening, a seasoned farmer named Mr. Hargrove approached Ledger after the meeting. "You don't know what you don't know," he said, chuckling warmly. "But that is all right. It is a learning process. Why don't you come by my farm tomorrow? I can show you some practices that might help improve your yields and efficiency.

Grateful for the offer, Ledger's spirits were lifted as he realized that he did not have to navigate this journey alone. The weight on his shoulders felt a little lighter, fueled by the prospect of learning from someone with more experience.

The next morning, Ledger arrived at Mr. Hargrove's farm, greeted by the sight of thriving crops organized in rows. The vibrant greenery energized him, and he felt like a student ready to absorb all the knowledge he could.

"Welcome, Ledger!" Mr. Hargrove called out, wiping his hands on his overalls as he approached with a friendly smile. "I am glad you came by. Let us get to work!"

As they walked the fields together, Mr. Hargrove shared valuable insights about crop rotation, pest management strategies, and soil health. "It's all about balance," he explained as they crouched beside a row of peppers. "You want to create an ecosystem that supports your crops rather than fights against pests. Have you considered planting cover crops during the off-season?"

Ledger took notes, soaking up every bit of information. "I have not... I did not know those could be useful for a farm like ours," he admitted, feeling a tinge of hope spark within him.

"Absolutely! Cover crops can improve soil structure and nutrient content while also helping to suppress weeds. Plus, it will save you some money on fertilizers in the long run." Mr. Hargrove continued guiding him through various techniques and practices, each revelation filling Ledger with excitement.

After hours of discussion and hands-on learning, Ledger felt empowered. "Thank you for all this, Mr. Hargrove. I cannot tell you how much I appreciate your guidance. I have been so focused on just making it through each day that I did not see the bigger picture."

"Anytime! We are all in this together. Farming is tough, but the community should support each other. Let me know how it goes. I am just a phone call away if you need help," Mr. Hargrove replied, patting Ledger on the back.

As he drove home that day, Ledger could not help but feel a renewed sense of determination. Armed with new strategies and backed by a supportive community, he realized that while the uncertainties of farming would always exist, he could face them with knowledge and resilience.

That evening, he gathered Clara and the kids on the porch. "You won't believe what I learned today!" he exclaimed, brimming with enthusiasm.

Clara leaned in, her eyes twinkling in the warm dusk. "Tell us everything!"

With animated gestures, Ledger shared the techniques Mr. Hargrove had taught him. The children listened intently, their faces lighting up with curiosity and excitement. "And guess what? We are going to start planting cover crops! They will help our soil and make our next harvest even better," he added, looking deep into Clara's eyes. "I feel like I can actually take control of this situation."

"That sounds incredible!" Clara responded, her relief palpable. "We'll work together to implement these changes."

Inspired, they spent the next week preparing their fields, implementing crop rotation and planting cover crops that would enrich the soil while preparing it for the next planting season. The family worked hard, but with the newfound hope transformed labor into something more rewarding.

As they toiled in the fields together, Ledger found comfort in their shared effort. There were still tough days when stress crept in, but as they took small steps forward, there was an undeniable shift. Ledger began to see their farm as not just a source of financial responsibility but as a legacy they were creating together.

One evening, as the sun set behind the mountains, painting the sky in hues of pink and gold, Ledger sat with Clara and the children. "I've learned that we can't control everything in this business, and that's okay," he said pensively. "What matters is how we respond to the challenges we face. And I know we will find a way forward together."

Eliza nodded. "We are a good team, Dad! We can beat anything that comes our way!"

"Absolutely! And we are building something great here," Wizen chimed in, looking proudly at the rows of seedlings stretching across their fields.

Clara squeezed Ledger's hand, a knowing smile breaking through. "We may face economic uncertainties, but we have each other. Together, we are resilient."

As they shared laughter and stories, Ledger realized that while the road ahead was uncertain, it was not one he had to walk alone. With newfound knowledge, the support of their community, and the unwavering bond of their family, they were ready to face whatever challenges the future held.

Over time, Ledger came to understand that these uncertainties were part of the journey they had chosen. With every lesson learned and every obstacle overcome, they were writing their own story—one filled with resilience, love, and hope that would carry them through the trials of farm life. Each setback became a steppingstone, shaping not just their agricultural practices but also their family's identity. They were more than just farmers; they were a team, building a life together against the backdrop of the vast fields that surrounded their home.

As the weeks turned into months, Ledger felt a new rhythm settling into their lives. The pressures of inconsistent revenue from crop yields still hovered in his mind, but the knowledge he had gained from Mr. Hargrove and the camaraderie of the local farming community offered him a sense of stability he had not anticipated.

As they implemented their new practices, Ledger and Clara noticed the results: healthier plants, improved soil quality, and a promising yield that gave them renewed confidence. Each harvest brought a mix of excitement and anxiety, especially as market fluctuations continued to challenge their financial stability.

One crisp autumn morning, they prepared for the seasonal harvest festival. It was an important opportunity to showcase their crops and sell their products, drawing in local customers eager to buy fresh produce. The children buzzed with excitement about the upcoming event, dreaming about their booth that would be filled with jars of salsa, pickles, and vibrant vegetables.

"Let's make this festival really special!" Eliza said, bouncing on her toes. "We can decorate the booth with flowers and colorful ribbons!"

"Great idea!" Clara replied, jotting down all the details they needed to consider. "And we'll create some taste-testing stations to encourage people to try everything."

Ledger felt the familiar blend of excitement and anxiety as they prepared. "We need to ensure we have enough products to meet demand," he reminded Clara, furrowing his brow. "We've been working hard, but I want to make sure we don't run out."

"We'll work together, just like always," Clara reassured him, placing a comforting hand on his back. "No matter what happens, we'll give it our best shot."

The day of the festival arrived, bright and filled with promise. Their booth glimmered under the autumn sun, adorned with colorful flowers, and tastefully arranged products that boasted the fruits of their labor. As they set up, Ledger could not help but feel a swell of pride—this was more than just a market day; it was a celebration of what they had built together as a family.

As customers poured in, smiles spread on their faces, and Ledger felt the warmth of connection in each interaction. They handed out samples, laughed with familiar faces, and shared stories about their farm journey. The community's support was palpable, and with each jar sold and each positive comment received, a burden lifted from Ledger's heart.

"Your salsa is amazing!" a local woman said, her eyes lighting up as she took her first taste. "I can't wait to buy a few jars for my family!"

Word spread quickly, and soon their booth became one of the most popular spots at the festival. Eliza and Wizen delighted in helping customers, sharing their favorite flavors, and proudly representing their family.

As the sun began to set, casting a golden glow over the festivities, Ledger looked around at the bustling community that had rallied behind them. "We're doing it, Clara," he whispered, a sense of disbelief washing over him. "We're really building something here."

Clara smiled back at him, her eyes sparkling with happiness. "Yes, we are. It is all thanks to our hard work and willingness to adapt. We have turned challenges into opportunities, and our family is stronger for it."

Just as they were about to pack up, a local chef known for her influence in the culinary scene approached their booth. After sampling their salsa, she exclaimed, "This is fantastic! We need to feature your products in my new farm-to-table restaurant. Can we collaborate?"

Overwhelmed with excitement, Ledger could not believe what he was hearing. "Are you serious? That would be incredible!" A wave of joy washed over him as he realized this could open new doors for their family's farm.

"That's the magic of community," the chef smiled, sensing his enthusiasm. "You're doing something special here, and I want to support it."

As the festival ended, Ledger and Clara packed up their remaining products, but not without an impressive number of sales already behind them. The unexpected collaboration left them buzzing with excitement and anticipation for what lay ahead.

Days later, as they gathered around the kitchen table, Ledger reflected on the remarkable turn of events. "I never imagined we would be at this point. Fostering connections and partnerships can lead to opportunities we did not see coming," he said, feeling the weight of doubt begin to lift.

Clara nodded, pride filling her heart. "We are ready to grow, Ledger. We have learned to face the uncertainties together, and now we can embrace the possibilities."

Their story continued to unfold with each hard-working day, each shared laugh, and every obstacle they tackled together. With the success of the harvest festival and the exciting collaboration with the local chef, Ledger and Clara's determination reignited. They had proven to themselves that hard work and resilience could lead to meaningful connections and opportunities.

As days turned into weeks, their routine settled into a delightful rhythm. Mornings were filled with the sounds of roosters crowing and the sun peeking over the horizon, beckoning them to the fields. The kids helped tend to the crops, learning firsthand about sustainable farming practices as they split their time between schoolwork and farm chores.

Ledger and Clara worked tirelessly, refining their processes and expanding their product line to include herb blends, pickled vegetables, and even dried fruit snacks. They focused on quality and sustainability, knowing that these values resonated with their customers. The collaboration with the chef became a partnership that opened new avenues—she featured their products on her menu, providing a platform that showcased the freshness and quality of their farm.

Word of mouth spread quickly, and soon customers from neighboring towns flocked to their booth at the market, eager to try their handmade offerings. "I've been hearing so much about your salsa!" a customer exclaimed one sunny Saturday morning. "I had to come to see what all the hype was about!"

As Ledger saw the joy in their customers' faces and the excitement surrounding his family's hard work, he felt a renewed sense of purpose. The pressure that once burdened him began to lift, replaced by a growing confidence in their path.

However, the road was still not without its bumps. The unpredictable nature of farming remained, with various challenges and uncertainties lurking around every corner. A late frost threatened their spring crops, and drought conditions raised concerns about watering and fertilization practices. But instead of succumbing to anxiety, Ledger leaned on the connections he had forged in the community. He reached out to fellow farmers for advice and gathered insights on managing the growing conditions.

With guidance from others, he embraced the idea of crop diversification. "If one crop fails, we can rely on another," he shared with Clara one evening after dinner. "I think adding more variety to our farm might cushion us against unforeseen challenges."

"I think that's a brilliant idea," Clara replied, her eyes gleaming with enthusiasm. "Let us map out what we could plant for the next season. It could lead to even more opportunities!"

Together, they sat at the kitchen table, sketching out a plan for their upcoming planting season. They brainstormed new vegetables, herbs, and fruits that would complement their existing crops and cater to their customers' tastes. With every addition to their plan, Ledger felt a sense of excitement, as if they were crafting a recipe for success together.

As the seasons shifted, they continued to adapt and innovate. The farm became a testament to their growth not only as cultivators of the land but also as a family. They invited friends and neighbors over for harvest dinners, showcasing dishes made with ingredients from their farm, fostering a deeper sense of connection with the community.

One evening, Ledger noticed the enthusiasm in his children as they eagerly prepared for the gathering. Eliza and Wizen set the table, excited to show off their family's bounty to their friends. On the menu were dishes featuring their colorful vegetables, flavorful salsas, and fresh herbs—a reflection of their hard work, creativity, and the love they nurtured throughout the year.

As the sun dipped below the horizon, casting warm orange and pink tones across the sky, family and friends gathered for an enjoyable evening. Laughter and camaraderie filled the air as people shared stories, relished the delicious food, and grew aware of the journey the Philogene family had embarked upon.

"Your salsa is incredible!" one neighbor enthused, dabbing his finger into the bowl of fresh salsa. "You've truly hit a home run with this—how do you do it?"

Clara and Ledger exchanged proud smiles, the fruits of their labor showcased at that very moment. "It's all about finding the right ingredients and the love we put into it," Ledger replied, feeling fulfilled.

As the gathering wound down and the stars illuminated the night sky, Ledger found himself standing on the porch, silhouetted against the soft glow of the kitchen lights. Clara joined him, snuggling close. "Tonight was perfect," she said, her voice a tender whisper.

"It really was," he agreed, his heart swelling with gratitude. "I've learned that, despite the uncertainties, we have each other—and that makes all the difference."

"Together, we've built something beautiful," Clara affirmed, her hand resting on his shoulder with a peace that radiated from her presence.

With their family surrounding them, Ledger felt a renewed sense of hope. Their journey was ongoing, filled with both dreams and challenges, but they faced it together, side by side. Each day brought new opportunities to grow, adapt, and evolve. As the seasons turned, Ledger understood that the heart of their farm was not just in the soil they tended but, in the resilience, they cultivated within their family and community.

With the spring planting season fast approaching, Ledger eagerly applied the lessons he had learned over the past year. He and Clara attended local workshops, diving deeper into organic farming practices and innovative techniques for pest management. Together, they experimented with companion planting, utilizing vibrant marigolds to ward off pests and inviting the beneficial insects that would improve their crop yields.

"Look at those peppers!" Clara exclaimed one sunny afternoon as they inspected their thriving plants. "They're looking healthier than ever!"

"They really are," Ledger replied, a grin spreading across his face. "And I think the new irrigation system we installed is helping too. We have avoided the dry patches we struggled with last year."

The combination of new practices and their willingness to adapt made a tangible difference. Their crop yields improved, and as harvest time approached, Ledger felt a sense of pride in what they were accomplishing as a family. This year, their hard work was beginning to pay off in a more significant way.

As they prepared for the summer harvest, anticipation tingled in the air. The community they had built around their farm expanded, and more locals began showing up at their booth, eager to buy their vegetables and homemade products. The collaboration with the chef continued to flourish, and Ledger found himself increasingly involved in producing recipes for her restaurant, which featured their harvest prominently.

One day, as they sorted through freshly picked tomatoes for a special order, Clara paused and turned to Ledger, her expression serious. "We should think about expanding our reach even more. Have you considered creating an online store for our products? It could help us reach customers beyond the market."

That idea sparked a fire in Ledger. "You know, that could open whole new avenues for us! We have built such a strong local following; I bet we could find demand beyond our town."

Motivated by Clara's suggestion, they dedicated time to building an online presence and crafting a website that showcased their story, values, and farm-fresh offerings. The kids excitedly helped with the logistics, creating colorful marketing materials and even shooting photos of their harvest that burst with color and freshness.

With the website up and running, Ledger felt a renewed sense of purpose. The possibilities felt endless, and soon, orders began to trickle in from customers who had discovered their products online. Each notification of a new sale brought a thrill of excitement and validation that their hard work was bearing fruit.

Yet, with this growth came new challenges. Managing an online store required meticulous attention and time, and Ledger felt the pressure of balancing the farm's day-to-day operations with the new venture. Some days, doubt crept in, and he wondered if they had bitten off more than they could chew.

One evening, sitting at the kitchen table surrounded by papers, Clara noticed the tension in his shoulders. "You're working too hard again," she said gently, placing a comforting hand on his. "We are in this together. If it is too much, we can adjust our approach."

"I just want to make sure we do this right," Ledger admitted, rubbing his temples. "What if we can't keep up?"

Clara leaned closer, meeting his gaze. "Remember, we are on this journey together. We can reassess our priorities and delegate some of the tasks. We can involve the kids more and teach them about managing the online side. They love being involved, and it could be a great learning experience for them."

He sighed, her words washing over him like a soothing balm. "You are right. I cannot do this alone, and I should not have to."

Taking Clara's advice to heart, Ledger began to involve Eliza and Wizen more in their business. He worked with them to create an easy inventory system, teaching them how to use the online platform while also instilling a sense of responsibility within them. Sharing these tasks not only lightened his load but also deepened the bond they shared as a family.

"Look, Dad! I just sent out our first order!" Wizen declared one evening, his face alight with excitement as he pressed the keyboard, confirming the shipment.

"Way to go, buddy!" Ledger replied, beaming with pride. "See? We are building this together!"

As the summer days passed, the farm flourished with fresh growth, and their collective efforts began to pay off in myriad ways. They reached a broader audience as customers continued to discover their online store, and the Philogene family was bustling with energy and excitement.

One balmy afternoon, Ledger found an email in his inbox that made his heart race. The local food magazine had reached out, expressing interest in featuring their story for their upcoming issue on innovative local farms. They wanted to highlight families like the Philogenes who redefine farming through community engagement, sustainable practices, and innovative approaches to local agriculture were. As Ledger read the email again, a thrill of disbelief washed over him. This was an incredible opportunity to share their journey and inspire others who might be facing similar challenges in the farming world.

"Clara! Come read this!" Ledger called out, practically bouncing in his seat. Clara appeared from the kitchen, flour dusting her apron, and leaning over his shoulder to read the email. Her eyes widened with excitement, and she clasped her hands together.

"This is amazing! We must do it! This is our chance to share our story with so many more people," Clara said, her enthusiasm infectious.

"I know! But what if we are not ready? What if they come out and see that we are still figuring things out?" Ledger's excitement was laced with anxiety, the pressure of perfection creeping in again.

Clara smiled, her expression unwavering. "They want to highlight our journey, not just our success. Everyone knows farming comes with complexities—embracing those challenges is what makes us relatable. And besides, we have come so far already!"

Feeling the certainty in Clara's words, Ledger took a deep breath and nodded. "You are right. We need to be authentic and share what we have learned—the triumphs and the trials. It is about our family, our community, and the lessons we have gained along the way."

Over the next few weeks, they prepared for the feature, setting aside time to organize their thoughts and present their story clearly. Ledger spoke with the magazine's writer, sharing not only their successes but also the struggles that had tested their resolve. He recounted the challenges of inconsistent crop yields, the moments of doubt, and the importance of community support.

Throughout the process, Clara and the kids contributed their thoughts and insights, encapsulating the family dynamic that made their farming journey unique. They all took turns reflecting on what the farm meant to them, sharing heartfelt anecdotes about their daily lives, the joy of harvests, and the laughter that resonated around the dinner table.

One afternoon, while the photographer captured images of the family working in the fields, Ledger reveled in the sense of unity. The children scampered through the rows of vegetables, laughing as they helped to harvest ripe tomatoes and peppers. Clara was nearby, her hands skillfully preparing samples of their salsa for the photoshoot, her smile radiating warmth and pride.

As the photographer snapped away, Ledger felt a deep appreciation for this moment—a realization that their collective efforts had turned their dreams into reality. They were a family thriving in the face of uncertainties, standing together against the odds.

The magazine issue featuring the Philogene family hit the stands a month later, and the excitement in their small town was palpable. Ledger and Clara watched as friends and neighbors gathered around the local shops, flipping through pages filled with vibrant photos and an inspiring story of resilience and community.

"Look at this!" Clara exclaimed, pointing to the magazine cover showcasing their family amidst a lush backdrop of crops. Ledger felt a rush of pride and disbelief. "Our journey is out there for everyone to see!"

As customers continued to trickle into their booth at the farmers' market, Ledger noticed a newfound interest in their products. "I read about your farm in the magazine!" one customer said, holding up a copy proudly. "Your story really inspired me."

With every interaction, he realized that their narrative was not just about their farming journey; it was a testament to the connections they had forged within their community. People began to understand the thoughtfulness and effort that went into each jar of salsa or bundle of vegetables.

"Thank you for sharing your story," another customer said, inspecting a jar. "I feel like I know you all now."

At that moment, Ledger understood that they were not just selling produce; they were building relationships. They were proud representatives of a community that believed in supporting one another through the ups and downs of life. The magazine not only elevated their profile but strengthened the bonds they had with neighbors, friends, and local customers.

As the culmination of their hard work and resilience, they embraced the opportunities that lay ahead. This journey was far from perfect, but it was filled with love, laughter, and lessons learned side by side. With Clara and the kids by his side, Ledger felt ready to confront whatever challenges the future might bring, their hearts brimming with hope and determination.

The Philogene family continued to grow, explore new ideas, and expand their farm, knowing that with each lesson learned, they were building a legacy that would last for generations to come. With every jar of salsa sold, every harvest shared, and every story told, they wrote their own narrative, one grounded in resilience, love, and the unwavering support of their community. As Ledger looked toward the horizon, he knew that their journey was just beginning.

In the heart of Grand Bay, where rolling fields of corn swayed gently in the wind and barns stood tall against endless skies, the spirit of community ran deep. The rural fabric of this small town was woven with threads of shared experiences, challenges, and triumphs among its residents, especially among the farmers who called it home. For Ledger Philogene, the camaraderie of local farmers became an invaluable lifeline as he navigated the unpredictable world of agriculture.

From the moment he and Clara set foot on their new farm, they were welcomed with open arms by their neighbors. It did not take long for Ledger to realize that the bonds formed under the vast expanse of the Appalachian sky were not only supportive; they were vital to survival in such a demanding profession. Early on, he was introduced to an informal network of farmers who met regularly to share knowledge, tools, and even anecdotes of their journeys, both heartbreaking and uplifting.

One crisp autumn morning, Ledger attended the monthly gathering of the Grand Bay Farmers' Association, which met in the barn of a local veterans' hall. As he entered, a chorus of familiar voices filled the air, laughter bouncing off the wooden beams overhead. The faces that turned toward him were warm and inviting—some were weathered by years of hard work, others filled with youthful excitement, reflecting the blend of experience and fresh energy that characterized their community.

"Ledger! Right on time!" called out Mr. Hargrove, waving him over to a long table laden with coffee and pastries baked by the local women's group. With a smile, Ledger accepted a cup of steaming coffee and settled into a chair beside Clara, who had joined him to learn more about local farming practices.

As the meeting began, the farmers discussed pressing matters: crop reports, weather forecasts, and upcoming events. They shared stories of recent wins—a successful harvest festival, a new cooperative grocery opening in town selling local products, or collaboration ideas that had blossomed among farms in the area. Each success reinforced the strength of the community.

"Last year was tough all around, but with teamwork, we're back in action," Mr. Hargrove noted. "I say we should celebrate our harvests and bring the community together again. How about another autumn festival?"

Cheers of agreement erupted around the table. The thought of another festival stirred Ledger's heart. "It is a great idea! It was a wonderful way to merge our efforts with the community last time," he chimed in, feeling the warmth of belonging swell within him.

Clara leaned closer to Ledger, her excitement palpable. "We could do tastings of all the local products again! Maybe even host some cooking demonstrations."

As they brainstormed ideas, Ledger listened to his fellow farmers share their challenges as well. The conversation turned to a drought that had affected several farms. Local farmers voiced their concerns, but rather than despair, there was a noticeable resolve in their voices, a collective hope that the community would rise together.

"Last month, I had a few fields that were really hurting," said Mary Jenkins, a newer farmer in the area. "But with the support of my neighbors, I borrowed some equipment they were not using and managed to resurrect a portion of my crops. It is incredible how we can help one another."

Ledger nodded in agreement. "That is what got me through last year. Having the community behind you makes such a difference. I do not know what I would have done without the guides and assistance of all of you."

By the end of the meeting, plans were set into motion for the autumn festival, and Ledger left with a sense of contentment growing in his chest. As he and Clara drove home, she turned to him with a radiant smile. "Did you see how everyone rallied together? It is beautiful how supportive they are of one another—even with their own struggles."

"Absolutely," Ledger replied, warmth flooding back to him. "I feel grateful to be a part of this. It is not just about farming; it is about family and community."

Over the next few weeks, as preparations ramped up for the festival, the sense of unity among the local farmers blossomed. They shared equipment, knowledge, and even labor when needed. As the festival date approached, Ledger found himself not just prepping his own farm products but also getting involved in the collective efforts of the community.

One bright Saturday morning, a group of farmers gathered at Ledger's farm for a communal harvest, picking tomatoes, squash, and peppers that would be showcased at the festival. Laughter echoed across the fields as friends worked side by side, forming an unbreakable bond through the simple act of working together.

"This is what it's all about!" Mr. Hargrove exclaimed as he tossed a freshly picked tomato to Ledger. "No better way to strengthen our friendship than to come together like this!"

With each basket filled, Ledger felt the burdens of the past year begin to lift, replaced by an overwhelming sense of purpose and belonging. Each ripe tomato and vibrant squash represented not just the fruits of their labor but also the network of support that surrounded them. As laughter and conversation flowed freely among the group, Ledger was reminded that he was part of something much bigger than just his own farm.

As the sun climbed higher in the sky, sweat glistened on their brows, but spirits remained high. Clara moved through the rows, encouraging the kids to help, teaching them how to identify the ripest fruit, and ensuring they felt included in every task. Ledger watched their joy, their laughter mingling with the camaraderie of the adults, and he could not help but smile.

"Hey, Ledger!" Mary called out from across the garden, holding up a particularly large tomato. "This one is a real beauty! Let us make sure it goes to your salsa!"

"Absolutely! That will be the star of the festival!" Ledger shouted back, feeling a rush of excitement. It was these little moments of shared purpose and collaboration that cemented his love for their town and the community that formed the backbone of his farming experience.

As they gathered to take a break, Ledger set out cold drinks and snacks he had prepared. The group lounged on hay bales scattered around the barn, their chatter a comforting hum amidst the countryside's peace.

"This festival is going to be huge!" Eliza chimed in, her energy is contagious. "I can't wait to show everyone the salsa we made together!"

"Me too! And our farm's colorful veggie baskets!" Wizen added, his eyes bright with anticipation.

With each joyful remark, Ledger felt a swell of pride in what they were building, not just a farm but a way of life woven into the fabric of Grand Bay. He took a moment to appreciate the efforts, the smiles, and the welcome distractions that united them.

Returning to the conversation, Mr. Hargrove leaned back, a satisfied grin on his face. "You know, if we keep this up, we might just draw more people to our town. The festival could become a tradition that not only showcases our farms but also the spirit of Grand Bay."

"Exactly!" Clara added, her enthusiasm reflecting in her radiant smile. "This is about showcasing who we are. Our food, our families, our culture—everything!"

It was a sentiment that resonated deeply with everyone present. They knew that their stories intertwined, with each farm contributing to the rich tapestry of the community.

By the end of the day, their baskets brimmed with the colors of the harvest: deep reds, bright yellows, and rich greens. As they looked over the impressive bounty, Ledger could not help but feel a sense of gratitude wash over him. Hand in hand, these farmers shared not only tools and seeds but also dreams and aspirations—a testament to resilience in the face of uncertainty.

The days leading up to the festival passed in a flurry of activity. Ledger and Clara worked late into the night, preparing their products and finalizing arrangements. They collaborated with their neighbors, ensuring that every detail was attended to. They even exchanged recipes and ideas, blending flavors and traditions that represented the heart of Grand Bay.

On the day of the festival, the sun shone brightly, and the air buzzed with excitement. Children ran through the rows of booths and adults mingled, sharing stories and laughter. The scent of grilled vegetables and fresh salsa wafted through the air, mingling with the sound of local musicians providing an upbeat soundtrack to the festivities.

When it was time for Ledger to showcase their products, he felt a rush of nerves and excitement. Stepping up to the booth adorned with vibrant banners and colorful displays, he and Clara welcomed the community, eager to share what they had worked so hard to create.

"Welcome, everyone!" Clara beamed to the crowd. "We're so excited to share our farm's offerings with you today!"

As the foot traffic increased, Ledger felt the warmth of the community envelop him. Neighbors came by, excited to try the salsa he and his family had crafted together. Children lined up, delighting in samples of everything from spicy tomato salsa to tangy pickled vegetables.

"This is incredible!" someone called out, after sampling a spoonful of their famous salsa. "You've outdone yourselves this year!"

With every positive comment and encouraging smile, Ledger's heart swelled with gratitude. He took a moment to glance around at the vibrant energy of the festival—families laughing, children playing, and farmers forging connections that would last well beyond the event.

"Thank you for supporting local farms, everyone! We are so grateful to be part of this wonderful community," Ledger said, his voice steady and full of genuine appreciation.

As he surveyed the crowd, he saw Mr. Hargrove nearby, hearty laughter spilling forth as he shared stories with other farmers, their camaraderie evident. There was a certain magic in the air, a sense of unity that enveloped the entire festival. Ledger's heart swelled as he witnessed the community thriving together, a living testament to what they had built collectively.

Mr. Hargrove caught Ledger's eye and raised his glass of freshly brewed lemonade to him, a sign of solidarity and shared joy. "This is what it's all about!" he called out, his voice booming over the sounds of laughter and music. "Celebrating our hard work and the spirit of Grand Bay!"

Feeling invigorated by the moment, Ledger waved back, his spirit buoyed by the knowledge that he was truly a part of this community, woven into the very fabric of rural life. It did not matter how tough times had been; what mattered was the support and encouragement that surrounded them.

As the day progressed, Ledger engaged with various visitors, from curious newcomers to long-time residents, each interested in hearing about the Philogene family farm. "What's your secret?" a local chef asked as she sampled their salsa, her eyes lighting up with delight. "It's bursting with flavor!"

"Every jar is made with love and local ingredients," Ledger replied, smiling proudly. "We have been experimenting and learning from our neighbors along the way. Farming is a constant journey!"

As the sun began to dip toward the horizon, casting a warm golden glow over the festival, Ledger gathered Clara and the kids for a moment of reflection. Together, they watched the crowd, soaking up the vibrant atmosphere. Dance music filled the air as young and old broke out into cheerful routines, children darting between booths with sticky fingers and beaming smiles.

"Look at all of this," Clara said, her voice filled with wonder. "We couldn't have imagined it would come together like this when we first started."

"It's amazing," Ledger agreed, taking a deep breath. "Every challenge along the way has led us to this moment. I am grateful for all of it—the hard work, the support, the friendships we have built."

Just then, Wizen tugged on his father's shirt. "Can we go join the dance, Dad? Everyone is having so much fun!"

"Sure! Let us join in," Ledger said, glancing at Clara, whose eyes sparkled with approval.

The four of them made their way into the midst of the crowd, joining in as people danced and celebrated life together. Laughter echoed around them as Ledger felt the joy flow through him. This was what community was all about supporting one another through thick and thin, celebrating the good times, and creating lifelong memories.

As the night wore on, the festival reached a crescendo, with music coaxing everyone into a joyful dance under the vast starlit sky. Ledger felt alive, embraced not only by his family but by the entire community. It was these moments that would fuel him through any challenges that lay ahead.

Eventually, as the music softened and laughter began to fade, Ledger and his family started to pack up their booth, another successful festival behind them. His heart was full as he observed the scene around him—families exchanging hugs, local vendors chatting enthusiastically about the day's events.

"Today was incredible," Clara said, her voice warm with satisfaction. "I think we've made some lasting connections."

"Definitely. It is clear we are part of something special," Ledger replied, feeling a sense of hope wash over him. "This community has shown us what it means to stand together and support one another."

That night, as they gathered around the kitchen table with remnants of the day still buzzing in their minds, they could not help but smile and share stories about their favorite moments from the festival. Eliza talked excitedly about the dance-off between local youths, while Wizen recounted how the mayor had stopped by their booth and complimented their salsa.

"Can we do this again next year? I want to make sure we have an even bigger part!" Eliza suggested, her passion was shining through.

"Oh, absolutely. This could be our tradition," Ledger affirmed, excitement in his voice. "We'll continue to strengthen our bonds as a family and with our community."

As the kids chimed in with ideas for next year's festival and new products they could introduce, Ledger realized that they were all on the same page, driven by the same vision of resilience and shared hope.

In Grand Bay, he had found more than just a place to cultivate crops; he had found a family—a community tied together by respect, trust, and mutual support. Together, they would weather the storms of life, constantly growing and nurturing not just their farms but the relationships that fueled their spirits.

As they cleared the table, Ledger caught Clara's eye, and they exchanged a knowing look. With each passing day, each shared experience, they were weaving their place into the rich tapestry of Grand Bay, a tapestry vibrant with colors, stories, and the hard-earned lessons of life. Ledger could feel a deep sense of belonging forming, a connection to the land and the people that went beyond mere survival. It was about thriving, too, and sharing in the joys and trials that came with being part of such a close-knit community.

In the weeks following the festival, their farm blossomed in more ways than one. The community spirit continued to flourish, inspiring Ledger and Clara to deepen their roots in Grand Bay. They began to participate more actively in local events, from potluck dinners at the church to volunteering for cleanup efforts at the town park. Each engagement brought them closer to their neighbors, solidifying friendships that would stand the test of time.

One evening, as they gathered on their porch, Ledger and Clara watched Eliza and Wizen chase fireflies through the fields. The sun dipped low on the horizon, casting a soft golden hue across the landscape.

"I've been thinking," Clara said softly, her gaze lingering on the children playing. "What if we started a community garden at the edge of our property? It could be a place for everyone to contribute and learn from one another, especially those who might not have their own space to grow."

"That's a wonderful idea!" Ledger replied, the gears in his mind was already turning with possibilities. "We could host workshops, teach them about sustainable farming practices, and share the joy of cultivation. It would reinforce our connections even more."

The more they discussed it, the more excited they became. They envisioned workshops led by local farmers, teaching skills like planting techniques, pest management, and crop rotation. They imagined a space where families could come together, share knowledge, and nurture plants while building friendships.

With their idea taking root, they organized a meeting at the community center, inviting farmers and townspeople alike. As Ledger spoke passionately about the potential of the community garden, he saw nods of agreement from familiar faces in the audience.

"We all know that farming can be isolating at times," he said, his voice steady. "Sharing this space could not only provide knowledge and resources but also strengthen the bonds between us all. Imagine a garden where every plant represents a story, a family, a connection."

After the meeting, many expressed their enthusiasm and interest in participating. Mary Jenkins stepped forward, eager to lead a workshop on organic gardening, while Mr. Hargrove offered to contribute seeds from his heirloom vegetable collection.

In the following weeks, excitement spread through Grand Bay like wildfire. Families began working together, clearing the chosen plot of land, and preparing the soil. Laughter echoed in the air as children helped dig and plant, while adults shared tips and stories about their personal farming experiences.

As the garden began to take shape, Ledger marveled at how it became a symbol of resilience and community. Each row of newly planted seeds represented hope, connection, and the idea that together they could achieve something greater than what they could do alone.

Ledger and Clara hosted regular workdays, inviting everyone to come and dig deeper into the roots of farming in Grand Bay. With each gathering, the community garden became a living tapestry of their collective efforts—colors bursting forth as flowers bloomed, vegetables ripened, and friendships flourished.

"Mom, look at this!" Wizen exclaimed one day as he pulled a bright red tomato from the vine. His laughter was contagious as he showed it off to Ledger, who could not help but beam at his son's excitement.

"That's a fantastic tomato, buddy!" Ledger replied, bending down to inspect the fruit. "You and Eliza worked hard on these plants. Your effort is really paying off!"

Eliza, busy gathering herbs nearby, piped up, "And we can make our salsa with all these tomatoes! It will be the best salsa we have ever made!"

"Absolutely! We will have a huge feast to celebrate the harvest," Clara added, her joy palpable. "This garden has brought us all together, and there's no better way to enjoy it than through a great meal!"

As the harvest season approached, anticipation and excitement built within the community. Families began sharing recipes, planning potlucks, and envisioning a grand feast that would highlight the fruits of their collective labor.

On a warm evening, Ledger found himself sitting around a long table outside, adorned with colorful dishes made from ingredients harvested from the garden. The mingling of flavors and scents filled the air, and laughter floated up like a sweet melody against the backdrop of the sunset.

"To community!" Mr. Hargrove toasted, his glass raised high. "For the friendships we have built, the challenges we have faced, and the ways we continue to support each other! May this garden grow as strong as our bonds!"

As glasses clinked and voices cheered, Ledger glanced around at the faces illuminated by the warm glow of string lights overhead, each one a cherished part of his life and the journey they had collectively embraced. The joy radiating from the gathered friends and neighbors filled him with a profound sense of gratitude and belonging. The laughter and chatter blended into a beautiful symphony of connection, echoing the very essence of Grand Bay—tightly knit and resilient.

As he took in the scene, Ledger felt a rush of emotion. This was what he had dreamed of when he and Clara first decided to pursue their farming venture: a place where they could not only cultivate crops but also foster community, love, and understanding. Their farm was no longer just a piece of land; it was a vital part of a flourishing network, a living testament to the heart and soul of the people who inhabited it.

Clara caught his eye and smiled, her gaze sparkling with joy and pride. She nodded slightly as if sharing his thoughts without words. With her by his side, they had transformed not just their lives but the lives of those around them.

"Alright, everyone!" Clara called out, her voice cutting through the festive noise. "Let us dig into this feast and share our favorite memories of the garden! What is the best thing you have grown this season?"

One by one, stories spilled forth. A family recounted their first successful carrot harvest; another shared the delight of discovering the perfect balance for growing herbs. Each anecdote illuminated the personal victories and unexpected challenges they had all faced together, weaving layers of rich experiences into the fabric of their shared community.

"I've never felt more connected to my neighbors," a woman said, her eyes bright with enthusiasm. "This garden has been a blessing for my family. We have learned so much together."

"And the salsa we made!" chimed in another farmer, waving a jar adorned with a bright label. "My kids cannot get enough of it! I have even had to hide the last few jars to save some for us!"

Laughter erupted, and Ledger could see the pride etched on the faces of everyone around the table, pride in their achievements and the community they had cultivated.

As the evening progressed, music filled the air, and more hands joined in the jubilant celebration. People began dancing under the twinkling lights, couples swinging each other around while children twirled with wild abandon. The atmosphere buzzed with camaraderie and warmth, a beautiful reminder of how far they had come together.

Ledger could not help but grin as he watched Eliza and Wizen join their friends in a makeshift dance circle, their laughter ringing out like joyous bells. He exchanged a glance with Clara, both feeling the magic of the moment wash over them. They had created an environment where their children could thrive alongside their neighbors, fostered by shared goals and mutual love for the land.

Eventually, the night began to end, and the last remnants of the feast dwindled away. Ledger stood, feeling a sense of fulfillment. "Thank you all for being here tonight and for being part of this journey. The success of our garden pales in comparison to the friendships we have built, and I could not ask for a better community to share this with.

Applause erupted, and Ledger felt a lump form in his throat. These people had encouraged him during the toughest times; they had rallied by his side when he felt unsure. It was more than just farming; it was about standing together through the highs and lows of life.

As the warm evening air settled around them, Ledger gazed confidently at the stars beginning to twinkle overhead. He realized they were surrounded not merely by crops but by a community grounded in resilience and hope. The beauty they shared extended far beyond the garden; it bloomed in the relationships forged, the lessons learned, and the love deepened through each shared experience.

In that moment, he knew that no matter what challenges the future might hold—weather uncertainties, economic strains, or personal struggles—they would face them together. They had each other's backs. They belonged, and together, they would nurture this thriving community for years to come.

As the last of the songs echoed into the night and goodbyes were exchanged, Ledger took a deep breath, feeling both satisfied and excited for the future. This was their home; this was their life—and it was more beautiful than he had ever envisioned. Grand Bay, with all its challenges and triumphs, had woven the Philogene family into the rich tapestry of its vibrant existence. And Ledger felt ready to embrace whatever came next, alongside his cherished community.

As the colorful hues of fall began to paint the landscape of Grand Bay, the Philogene family found themselves swept up in the vibrant cultural traditions that defined their new home. The arrival of autumn heralded not only the change of seasons but also a series of cherished local festivals and celebrations that brought the community together. For Ledger, Clara, and their children, these events became opportunities to immerse themselves fully in the traditions of their new environment while also sharing pieces of their heritage.

The first major event on the horizon was the Harvest Festival, an age-old celebration marked by the culmination of the season's hard work. The local community center transformed into a warmly lit hub of activity as families prepared to showcase their bounty. Ledger and Clara eagerly gathered their prized vegetables, ready to share their farm's yield with the community.

"Can you believe it's already time for the Harvest Festival?" Clara said her excitement was infectious as she sorted through their produce. "I love how this celebration brings everyone together."

"It's amazing," Ledger agreed, feeling a swell of gratitude for the seamless integration of their family into the community. "Events like this make me appreciate the richness of our new home—and the traditions that bind us all."

As they headed to the community center, Ledger spotted familiar faces from the farmers' association. The warmth and camaraderie were palpable as neighbors greeted one another, exchanging stories and excited chatter about their gardens and cooking preparations for the evening's festivities.

Inside, the hall was adorned with hay bales, handmade decorations, and booths filled with an assortment of colorful produce. The clamor of children's laughter mingled with the sweet sounds of local musicians setting up for a night of celebration. Ledger felt a familiar thrill; this was more than just a gathering; it was a celebration of community and culture.

"Table six is where we'll set up our booth!" Clara exclaimed, guiding the kids to an empty spot. "Let's get everything organized before the festivities start."

While Clara arranged their offerings, Ledger stepped outside for a moment to admire the surroundings. The air was crisp, filled with the scent of fresh apples and warm, spiced cider. Anticipation hung in the atmosphere, electrifying the connection between neighbors and friends. He spotted Mr. Hargrove, who waved him over.

"Ledger! Great to see you! We are low on volunteers for tonight's apple bobbing contest. Think you and the kids could help?" Mr. Hargrove's eyes twinkled with enthusiasm.

"Absolutely! We are in!" Ledger replied, feeling a sense of belonging deepen with each interaction. The spirit of community wrapped around him like a comforting blanket, letting him know he was no longer an outsider.

As evening fell, families gathered in anticipation of the festivities. The Harvest Festival kicked off with spirited games: sack races, pumpkin bowling, and, of course, the ever-popular apple bobbing. Laughter burst forth as children splashed water everywhere, their joy resonating among the crowd.

When it was time to share food, Ledger and Clara presented their renowned salsa along with jars of pickled vegetables, proudly labeled with colorful tags crafted by Eliza and Wizen. Local families flocked to their booth, eager to taste what the Philogenes had created.

"Your salsa is the talk of the town!" said Mary Jenkins, beaming as she sampled their latest creation. "It's fresh and flavorful—you've captured the essence of Grand Bay!"

"Thank you! We are so happy to share it with everyone," Ledger replied, beaming with pride. He glanced at Clara, who was engaged in conversation with another family about their favorite harvest recipes. It filled him with joy to see their connection to the community blooming.

As the night progressed, Clara spoke with several families about incorporating traditions from their culture into their celebrations. Inspired by their vibrant history, she invited neighbors to join them for a cultural exchange dinner at their farm in the coming weeks. "We'd love to share some of our family recipes with you if you're interested," she said enthusiastically. "It would be great to blend our traditions with yours."

The idea sparked interest, leading to exciting conversations about various dishes and cooking techniques. Clara looked at Ledger with a hopeful smile, and he could not help but feel thrilled at the prospect of deepening their bonds while sharing their heritage.

After a long evening of festivities, the crowd began to disperse, tired but happy from the communal celebration. As they packed up their booth, Ledger and Clara reflected on the connections they had forged.

"Watching everyone come together tonight was amazing," Ledger said, gazing at the excited chatter of families starting their long walk home. "I love how we can celebrate our traditions while embracing those that are unique to this community."

"Yes! I feel like we are contributing to a beautiful tapestry," Clara agreed as she carefully secured the last of their produce in a sturdy box. "Each event we participate in makes our connections deeper and richer. It is incredible how sharing our culinary traditions can enhance the vibrant culture here.

Relieved and satisfied with the evening's success, they exchanged smiles before heading home. The car ride was filled with the children's animated chatter about the games they had played, the delicious food they had sampled, and the new friends they had made.

"Did you see when Wizen bobbed for apples? He was a champion!" Eliza laughed, leaning against her brother, who looked both proud and slightly damp from his earlier antics.

"Next time, I'll make sure to win," Wizen proclaimed with determination, his eyes sparkling with the competitive spirit that characterized their family.

As they pulled into their driveway, Ledger reflected on the joyful experience of the festival, and how it served as a reminder of the importance of culture and community. They had established roots in Grand Bay, and with each festival, every shared meal, and every new friendship, they were weaving their family story into the larger narrative of the town.

The following weeks brought additional opportunities to celebrate their newfound community. Clara's dinner invitation was met with enthusiasm, and soon, families from the festival RSVP'd. As the date approached, Ledger and Clara discussed their plans, eager to share their favorite recipes and introduce their neighbors to the traditions that constituted their family's identity.

"Let's make the gumbo recipe my grandma taught me," Clara suggested one evening as they prepared dinner. "It's a huge part of our heritage and has always been a favorite in our family."

"And I think we should also make some sweet potato pie. It was a Thanksgiving staple back home," Ledger added, recalling warm memories of family gatherings filled with laughter and good food.

With a plan in place, they began preparing for the dinner. The Philogene home buzzed with excitement as they decorated their dining room, setting the table with colorful linens and vibrant centerpieces made from the autumn harvest. Floral arrangements crafted from fresh wildflowers and delicate herbs from their garden adorned the tables, adding a touch of warmth and hospitality.

On the evening of the cultural exchange dinner, the aroma of gumbo simmering on the stove filled their home, mingling with the scent of freshly baked sweet potato pie. Their neighbors arrived, bringing with them their own culinary creations, eager to share and learn from one another.

As family after family filed in, the energy in the room grew palpable. Clara and Ledger greeted everyone warmly, encouraging them to mingle and explore the spread of food laid out beautifully on the table.

"Wow! Everything looks amazing!" exclaimed Mary Jenkins as she surveyed the array of dishes. "I can't wait to try it all!"

They gathered around the table, leaving plenty of space for food and conversation. Clara welcomed everyone and shared her excitement about this gathering. "We are so grateful you all could join us tonight. We look forward to sharing some special family recipes and learning about yours!"

As they shared stories and laughter over delightful dishes, Ledger realized that this was more than just a meal; it was a celebration of blending cultures. Neighbors boldly shared their culinary techniques and traditions, each story laced with personal anecdotes that made their food come alive.

An older couple shared the history of a classic dish passed down through generations, while a younger family demonstrated how to incorporate local ingredients into traditional recipes. Each new flavor and story added another layer to the tapestry of their community, one woven from diverse threads of experience.

"Can I help with the gumbo, Clara?" Eliza asked, her eyes widened with excitement.

"Of course! Let us teach everyone how to make it together," Clara replied, motioning for Eliza to join her in the kitchen.

As they cooked, the kitchen filled with the comforting sounds of chatter and laughter. Ledger took a moment to step back from the heat of the stove, surrounded by a bubbling atmosphere of companionship. He felt a profound sense of fulfillment watching everyone come together—friends, neighbors, and family contributing to something bigger than themselves.

When the time came to serve the meal, everyone gathered around the table, and Ledger raised a glass. "To the community," he began, his voice steady with emotion. "To the friends we've made, the lessons we've learned, and the traditions we share and create together!"

Glasses clinked in enthusiastic agreement, followed by hearty cheers and laughter. Each family embraced the spirit of camaraderie, adding their stories to the rich culture of Grand Bay.

As the evening unfolded, plates were filled with delicious food, stories flowed freely, and connections deepened. Ledger glanced around the table, feeling a sense of pride swell within him. This new chapter of their lives was not just about farming; it was about cultivating relationships and embracing the vibrant tapestry of cultures that enriched their lives.

When dessert was served, the children delighted in sweet potato pie, their smiles brightening the room as they savored each sweet, spiced bite. Laughter bubbled up, mixing with the sounds of contented sighs as everyone enjoyed the fruits of their collective labor. The sweet potato pie—golden and flaky with the warmth of cinnamon and nutmeg—was a hit, and it felt like a gentle bridge between their past and present.

"Can we have this every week?" Wizen asked, belly full, his eyes sparkling with enthusiasm. "I love everyone being here! It is like one big family!"

"Absolutely! This should be a tradition!" Clara exclaimed, glancing around at the smiling faces around her. "We can rotate houses and keep exploring each other's culinary traditions. There is so much we can learn from one another."

The idea of regular cultural dinners sparked excitement among the guests, with people nodding and sharing their own thoughts on how much they treasured the evening. Mary Jenkins settled comfortably in her chair and raised her hand for attention. "I would love to host next month! My husband and I make a great potato salad that is a staple at all our gatherings. Plus, we could feature some local music to kick things off!"

"Count us in!" Mr. Hargrove added, looking delighted. "And I'll bring some freshly baked bread—best in town if I say so myself!"

With each suggestion, the energy in the room shifted, bursting with ideas, laughter, and plans for future gatherings. Ledger and Clara exchanged proud smiles, gratified to see their initial dinner bubbling into a monthly tradition that would help stitch the community even closer together.

"I could throw in some dance lessons!" Eliza exclaimed, her eyes alight with excitement. "We can invite everyone to teach their favorite local dance. It will be like a big party and—"

Her enthusiasm was infectious, prompting everyone to throw out suggestions on how to add elements of fun and engagement to the next gathering.

Amidst the chatter, Ledger felt a deep sense of fulfillment wash over him. They had created something special, a safe space for everyone to share their roots and revel in each other's cultures. It was harmonious, like a well-crafted melody, where every family added their notes to the beautiful song of Grand Bay.

As the night began to wind down, families began to gather their belongings, reluctant to part ways but filled with warmth from the evening's connections. The Philogenes offered a heartfelt farewell to their neighbors, with promises of future gatherings fluttering in the air.

Once the door closed and the last of the laughter faded into the night, Clara looked around their home, a satisfied smile spreading across her face. "I cannot believe how wonderful tonight was. It felt like we truly became part of this community."

Ledger wrapped an arm around her shoulders, pulling her close. "Because we are. We leaped by sharing our traditions, and in return, this town embraced us. It is not just about farming for us anymore; it is about weaving our lives into the colorful fabric of Grand Bay."

As they cleaned up together, their conversation flowed easily, filled with reflections on the evening and dreams for the future. The joy of sharing food and stories had not only brought them closer to their neighbors but also closer as a family—a blend of new experiences providing invaluable lessons and cherished memories.

In the days that followed, the Philogene family continued to build upon what they had started. They welcomed new neighbors, explored local farms, and dove deeper into the lore of Grand Bay. They visited other cultural events—music festivals, craft fairs, and seasonal parades—always eager to learn and partake, infusing their activities with the warmth of their own heritage.

Spring brought with it a renewed sense of hope and fresh opportunities. As Ledger watched the bulbs bloom and vibrant colors emerge from the earth, he felt revitalized. This was their home—each day, they cultivated not just crops but connections that enriched their lives.

Eventually, as the Philogenes settled into their routine of blending traditions and practices, Ledger reflected on the growth they had experienced. Every dinner they shared, every festival they attended, and every story they exchanged was a thread weaving their family deeper into the tapestry of Grand Bay.

"I can't wait for the summer festival next month," Clara said one evening, her voice buzzing with excitement. "I heard there's going to be a big cook-off, and I think we should enter."

Without hesitation, Ledger nodded, a smile spreading across his face. "Getting to showcase our farm's bounty and represent our cultural traditions? I am all in!"

As they drew closer to summer, the anticipation of future celebrations only fueled their passion for their farm and community. Day by day, the Philogenes became more than just farmers; they became integral threads in the colorful fabric of Grand Bay, a community bound together by shared experiences, love, and a commitment to honor both their own traditions and those of their neighbors. Each festival, dinner, and gathering was a testament to the strength of their connections, a living acknowledgment that they all contributed to a vibrant narrative woven through the heart of Grand Bay.

As summer rolled in, the town prepared for its biggest celebration of the year—the Grand Bay Summer Festival. Excitement buzzed through the community as preparations unfolded, and Ledger felt a rush of anticipation at the thought of participating alongside their friends and neighbors.

"Can you believe how quickly this year has gone?" Clara remarked one evening as they tended to the farm. "It feels like just yesterday we were nervous newcomers at the Harvest Festival."

"Now look at us!" Ledger replied laughter in his voice. "We are part of the planning committee for the Summer Festival! Who would have thought?"

They had indeed come a long way. The Philogenes had not only embraced their cultural roots but also woven them into the fabric of Grand Bay's celebrations. They collaborated with local farmers to organize a "taste of Grand Bay" showcase, where people could sample diverse dishes representing the myriad backgrounds of the community.

As the festival approached, Ledger and Clara rallied families to contribute their best recipes. Clara spent evenings testing flavors in the kitchen with Eliza and Wizen, excitedly preparing their entries— gumbo, sweet potato pie, and even a spicy salsa that had become a local favorite.

When the day of the festival finally arrived, the town square transformed into a kaleidoscope of colors. Booths lined the streets, filled with offerings from bakeries, farms, artisans, and crafters. The sweet smell of homemade pies mixed with the earthy aroma of fresh vegetables, as festive music played in the background, inviting people to dance and celebrate.

"Look at all the people!" Clara exclaimed, eyes wide as she took in the bustling scene. Families gathered, children played games, and friends exchanged hugs and laughter, all reveling in the sense of joy that the festival brought.

"Let's find our booth!" Ledger encouraged, guiding his family toward their designated spot. As they set up their table adorned with colorful banners and tables filled with their dishes, they felt prideful knowing they were representing both their heritage and the community they now called home.

As the day unfolded, Ledger welcomed visitors, sharing stories about the ingredients and cultural specialties they had brought to the festival. "This gumbo recipe is my grandmother's," he explained to a curious onlooker while scooping a generous portion into a tasting cup. "It has been passed down for generations and holds a piece of our family history."

Meanwhile, Clara discussed the significance of each dish, connecting the flavors to her own childhood and emphasizing the importance of cultural exchange. People sampled, chatted, and returned for seconds, delighted by the flavors that celebrated their community's diversity.

"Your salsa is out of this world!" someone exclaimed with a wide grin after sampling their spicy salsa. "I could eat this every day!"

As dusk began to settle, families settled on blankets in the park for a communal dinner under the stars, sharing the bounty of the festival. Ledger glanced around at the gathered community—neighbors who had become friends—and felt a deep contentment wash over him. They had built something beautiful here, transforming their farm into a vital component of life in Grand Bay.

The festival culminated in a lively dance and music showcase, where musicians filled the air with lively tunes, drawing everyone into an impromptu dance circle. Eliza and Wizen laughed as they twirled and twirled, their joy radiating like sunlight. Ledger joined them, abandoning any hesitation, swept up in the merriment and warmth of the moment.

As stars twinkled brightly above, Ledger held Clara close, wrapping his arm around her shoulders as they watched their children play. "We did it," he murmured softly, taking a moment to soak in the simplicity of happiness. "We made a place for ourselves in this community."

"We did," she replied, her eyes shimmering with emotions. "And it's only the beginning."

With the rhythmic beat of the drums echoing around them, Ledger silently vowed to continue nurturing the bonds they had formed with their neighbors. They would cultivate their farm together, share meals and laughter, and ensure that the experiences they all treasured would thrive through generations.

As the festival lights danced in the distance, Ledger felt invigorated by the possibilities ahead. They had become more than just a family of farmers; they were part of a living, breathing tapestry woven from the threads of love, shared experiences, and a profound commitment to celebrating the rich cultural heritage that made Grand Bay an extraordinary place to call home.

As spring blossomed into summer, the Philogene family settled into a rhythm on their farm, a rhythm that intertwined hard work, community support, and the steady progression of their dreams. Ledger stood at the edge of the fields one sunny evening, watching the golden light of the setting sun cast long shadows across the crops. The sight filled him with a sense of pride and accomplishment. Their farm was beginning to flourish, but not without a fair share of challenges.

From the outset, Ledger had known that establishing roots in Grand Bay would require resilience. The season had thrown its fair share of hurdles their way—unexpected frosts that threatened their early crops, late rains that made the soil too soggy for tilling, and annoying pests that seemed determined to enjoy their hard work as much as they did. But each challenge only strengthened their resolve.

"Remember when we thought the potatoes were a total loss from that frost?" Clara remarked one evening as they reviewed their weekly progress after a long day in the fields. She smiled at Ledger, her eyes reflecting both the weariness of the day and the spark of determination that had become their family's signature.

"Yeah, but we did not give up. We reworked our plans, adapted their planting schedule, and now look at them!" Ledger replied, flipping through their farm journal. It was a record of both triumphs and setbacks, a testament to their journey of resilience. "We're getting close to a solid harvest this season."

"We're learning so much along the way," Clara added, a gleam in her eyes as she recalled the late nights spent researching best practices for their crops, often with Eliza and Wizen snuggled in their reading nook nearby. "This farm is becoming part of us, and we're becoming part of it."

That sense of belonging to both the land and the community was becoming increasingly palpable. Ledger had spent hours engaging with his neighbors, learning from them, and sharing his insights. Mr. Hargrove had become a mentor, often quickly visiting to check their progress or lend equipment when needed.

"You've got a good handle on those crops, Ledger," Mr. Hargrove said one day as he leaned against the wooden fence that separated their properties. "But do not forget to take breaks. Burnout will not do you or your family any favors."

"It's easy to forget that" Ledger admitted, wiping the sweat from his brow. "But I see what you mean. Balance is key, isn't it?"

"Absolutely," Mr. Hargrove affirmed with a nod. "This farm life is a marathon, not a sprint. Just make sure you are planting seeds of rest along with your vegetables."

Over the following weeks, Ledger began to embrace the importance of pacing himself. Inspired by Mr. Hargrove's words, he initiated family game nights and cooking sessions together. These moments of respite allowed them to unwind and strengthen their family bond, reminding them that their journey to establish roots was about more than just successfully running a farm—it was about nurturing their love for one another.

One Friday evening, after a particularly taxing week of planting and fussing over seedlings, they gathered in the backyard for a casual barbecue. The children excitedly prepared veggie skewers made from everything they had harvested: sweet peppers, zucchini, and cherry tomatoes.

"This is going to be the best dinner ever!" Eliza declared as she helped her mother season the vegetables. James, eager to contribute, danced around their patio, twirling and singing a little tune he had made up about summer fun.

As they feasted on the vibrant skewers grilled to perfection, Ledger could not help but marvel at how far they had come. Through adversity, they had cultivated more than their crops—each challenge they faced had served to strengthen their unity and deepened their understanding of hard work.

After dinner, as twilight settled over Grand Bay, they spread a blanket on the grass and sat together, listening to the soft chirping of crickets. Ledger turned to Clara, a content smile on his face. "The farm is thriving, and so are we. Every challenge we have faced has only made us stronger."

Clara nodded knowingly. "And it is more than just us. The community has taken notice of our hard work and resilience. I have seen so many neighbors stopping by lately to check in or help—it is heartwarming."

Inspired by this community spirit, the Philogenes decided to invite their neighbors over for a Farm Day, where families could learn about what they were growing, help with various tasks, and enjoy a meal together. They put up colorful signs around town, eager to share their journey with the community that had embraced them.

On the day of the event, as families arrived with smiles and friendly waves, Ledger felt a rush of excitement. The children dashed around, enthusiastic to show their friends the crops they had helped plant and tend to over the seasons. Eliza proudly pointed out the rows of tomatoes, their vibrant red hues glistening in the sunlight. "Look at these! They are almost ready to pick!" she exclaimed, grabbing Wizen's hand and leading their friends toward the garden beds.

"Can we help?" one of the neighborhood kids asked, eyes wide with curiosity.

"Sure! Come on!" Wizen beamed, and soon a small group of children was bent over the tomatoes, giggling as they compared sizes and discussed how they would use them in salsa and sauces. The sight warmed Ledger's heart; it was moments like these that transformed their farm into a hub of connection and learning.

Meanwhile, Ledger and Clara set up a series of activities for the adults, including demonstrations on composting and organic pest management. Local farmers shared their wisdom alongside Ledger, creating a rich atmosphere of camaraderie and knowledge exchange.

"Remember, this is about sharing what we've learned with each other," Ledger addressed the gathering crowd. "Farming is an art of resilience, and the more we support one another, the stronger we all become."

As everyone looked on, Clara led a group in making a batch of fresh salsa, using the tomatoes, peppers, and herbs harvested that morning. The aromas wafted through the air, drawing everyone toward the outdoor kitchen setup, where they chipped in, chopping and mixing with laughter.

"Who knew farming could be this much fun?" one neighbor exclaimed, dipping a chip into the vibrant salsa, savoring the fresh flavors. "I think I might need to start my own garden!"

By midday, the sun shone warmly overhead, and every inch of the farm teemed with life and activity. Families enjoyed a potluck lunch spread on picnic tables decorated with wildflowers, exchanging stories and recipes as they feasted on hearty dishes, each infused with the unique flavors of their diverse heritages.

Watching everyone gathers, Ledger felt a sense of fulfillment wash over him. They had built something beautiful here—a community. The challenges they once faced had not only tested their strength but forged strong relationships with those around them.

As the afternoon wore on, Clara proposed a friendly competition inspired by a local fair tradition— a vegetable growing contest. "Why don't we all bring our biggest veggies next week and see who can win the Grand Bay Blue Ribbon?" she suggested excitedly.

The crowd buzzed with enthusiasm over the idea, and Ledger watched as neighbors nodded in agreement, already eager to showcase their best produce. The friendly rivalry would bring everyone back together, a reminder of the shared goals that united them.

That evening, as the sun dipped below the horizon, the Philogene family gathered among the remnants of the day—scattered laughter, half-finished plates, and a myriad of voices still echoing in the air. The warmth of community filled their hearts, and the stars began to twinkle above, offering a quiet backdrop to their reflections.

"I can't believe how much today inspired everyone," Clara said, leaning contentedly against Ledger as they watched the kids play tag in the fading light. "The support we've received is incredible."

"I feel like we're weaving our fate into the very fabric of this community," Ledger replied, his eyes shining with optimism. "Each step forward reinforces our place here, and with every challenge, we're only growing stronger and more unified."

Days turned into weeks, and the excitement surrounding the upcoming vegetable contest lingered in the air. Ledger dedicated time to mentoring new gardeners and extending guidance to anyone willing to learn. He helped neighbors select seeds and offered his tools whenever needed. Every interaction deepened their ties, fortifying the network of support that formed around the farm.

As the contest day approached, Ledger found himself marveling at the lush green fields that had transformed under their care. The rows of crops stood tall and proud, showing the fruit of their labor and the unwavering commitment to nurture their land.

On the day of the contest, families arrived armed with their finest vegetables, eager cheers, and friendly banter filling the atmosphere. The Philogene property transformed into a lively fairground complete with judging tables, picnic blankets, and laughter that echoed across the fields.

Ledger marveled at the vibrancy surrounding him, the colors of the produce, the joy reflected in the smiles of his friends, and the sense of fulfillment radiating from Clara and their children.

As the judging commenced, Ledger could not help but feel proud of what they had all achieved. Resilience and adaptation had carved a path through the difficulties they faced, guiding them toward this moment of connection, collaboration, and joy. Each contestant represented not just their success but also the growth and unity of the community they had nurtured together.

Having built their farm from the ground up, the Philogenes were no longer just inhabitants of Grand Bay. They were key players in a thriving tapestry woven from the threads of hard work, shared experiences, and communal support. Their efforts had nurtured not only a successful farm but also lasting friendships and connections that transcended individual challenges and cultural boundaries.

As the day progressed, anticipation filled the air for the results. Families mingled, children raced about, and the aroma of dishes prepared for a gathering filled the space—a feast made not just of food but of shared effort and love. Everyone was eager to celebrate each other's successes, no matter what the outcome of the contest.

During the judging, Ledger watched as neighbors offered cheers and encouragement to one another, genuinely celebrating not only their wins but the collective hard work put forth throughout the season. It was a powerful reminder of their journey together, emphasizing that in unity, they were all stronger.

Finally, as the sun began to dip low in the sky, Clara gathered everyone around the central table, which displayed the impressive bounty of vegetables. The judges, a friendly panel of seasoned farmers from the community, examined each entry, offering compliments and insights.

"With great joy, we declare the winners of the Grand Bay Vegetable Contest!" Clara announced, her voice brimming with enthusiasm. "And remember, every entry was a testament to your hard work and creativity!"

As the crowd erupted in applause, Ledger felt a swell of pride for each person who had leaped to grow, share, and connect. The judges called out the winners, and although Ledger's heart raced, he knew that no matter the results, they all shared in the joy of the day.

When their family's tomato entry was announced as the winner of the "Best in Show," cheers erupted from their friends and neighbors, many rushing forward to congratulate them. Ledger, with Clara and the kids at his side, grinned as he accepted the ribbon, a physical reminder of their commitment, hard work, and the community that had supported them every step of the way.

"This is amazing! We did it!" Eliza shouted, jumping up and down in excitement.

Wizen gleefully declared, "Next year, we'll grow even bigger ones!"

As the celebration continued, Ledger looked around at the faces of their friends and family, lighting up with joy and camaraderie, and he felt an overwhelming sense of gratitude. Each person gathered each vegetable entered, and each friendly competition spoke to the resilience they had cultivated—individually and as a community.

Eventually, night blanketed the fields, transforming the festival into an enchanting evening under the stars. Lanterns flickered to life, and tables were filled with delicious food, laughter, and spirited conversations. The air buzzed with stories of shared experiences and new possibilities.

As they gathered around the fire pit for s'mores and storytelling, Ledger realized that this was more than just a day of friendly competition; it was a celebration of the journey they had embraced together. It was a testament to the power of resilience, the capacity for adaptation, and the deep-rooted connections they were forging with those in Grand Bay.

"We've created something beautiful here," Clara whispered to Ledger as they watched the children roast marshmallows, their faces aglow with the flickering firelight. "Every hardship we faced was worth it to be part of this."

"Absolutely," Ledger replied, squeezing her hand. "This community, our farm—it's a reflection of all the hard work and love we've poured into it."

With renewed hope filling his heart, Ledger imagined a future brimming with potential—a future where they could continue to nurture their land, build upon the lessons learned, and strengthen the bonds they had formed. The Philogene family had become integral to the Grand Bay community, their lives intertwined with those around them.

As they celebrated, Ledger knew they were not just cultivating crops; they were nurturing a legacy of resilience and unity, a legacy that would endure through generations. The tapestry of Grand Bay was more vibrant with each passing season, and together, they would continue to sow the seeds of a hopeful future, reaping the rewards of hard work, determination, and a shared commitment to one another.

The transition to Grand Bay represents a significant change for Ledger Philogene and his family as they navigate the challenges of establishing agricultural roots in a rural setting. Leaving behind their former lives, they embraced the uncertainty of farming, trading the familiar rhythms of urban life for the unpredictable cycles of nature. As they encountered obstacles—unexpected frosts, pest infestations, and the steep learning curve of agricultural practices, they faced the real trials that came with cultivating a new life.

Yet, within these challenges lay opportunities for growth and transformation. Ledger's commitment to the land deepened, revealing the profound connection between farmer and field. Each seed planted symbolized not only the potential for a bountiful harvest but also the hope of a future built on resilience and hard work. His family, too, evolved alongside him, embodying adaptability in their shared commitment to overcoming difficulties.

Through evenings spent in the garden, cooking together in the kitchen, and engaging with their neighbors, the Philogenes began to weave themselves into the fabric of the Grand Bay community.

The relationships they forged became a source of strength, illustrating that farming is not merely an individual endeavor, but a collective journey powered by teamwork and support. Their involvement in community events and the spirit of camaraderie fostered a profound sense of belonging.

This journey of transformation reflects their unwavering commitment to resilience and adaptability. It highlights how the challenges of farming prompted them to draw upon their inner strengths and enlist the help of their neighbors, reminding them that they are never alone in their pursuits. The tapestry of their lives became more vibrant as they integrated their personal history with the new experiences found in Grand Bay.

Ledger's reflection on this pivotal experience reveals a deeper understanding of what it means to create roots in a new place. It signifies that the pursuit of a fulfilling life—grounded in family and the land—can thrive even amid uncertainty and strife. With every passing day, the Philogene family honors their commitment to each other, their community, and the land that binds them together, paving a path toward a hopeful future filled with new possibilities and shared dreams.

ᘓ

Part Three: Challenges and Choices

Chapter Eight: Death Of Ledger Father

The call came early on a gray morning, the kind of day that felt heavy even before the news arrived. Ledger stood in the kitchen, a steaming mug of coffee cradled between his hands when his phone rang. His heart sank as he recognized the number of the hospital. "This can't be good," he thought, bracing himself for the worst.

His father's voice echoed in his mind, filled with warmth and sage advice from countless conversations over the years. "You must learn to live off the land, Ledger. It is where you will find your strength and purpose," he had often said, wisdom that had resonated through their journey to Grand Bay. But now, that voice would be silent, taken too soon by an unexpected illness that had crept in like a thief in the night.

The news shattered Ledger's world, leaving a profound emptiness where guidance, love, and shared laughter once flourished. He felt as if a vital part of his identity had been stripped away, the anchor that had grounded him in the tumultuous waters of life was now gone. As he stared out the window at the fields he had nurtured, their vibrant green seemed dulled by the weight of grief.

The weeks following his father's death were shrouded in sorrow. Ledger struggled with waves of emotion that crashed over him unexpectedly. Memories of his father flooded his mind: teaching him how to till the soil, instilling the values of hard work and integrity, and those quiet evenings spent discussing dreams and ambitions while the stars glimmered overhead. Those moments felt both distant and achingly present. They shaped Ledger into the man he was and losing that guiding light left him adrift.

Clara stood beside him during those dark days, a steadfast presence as they both navigated their grief. She understood the depth of Ledger's loss, having witnessed firsthand the bond between father and son—a bond steeped in tradition, love, and reliance. "Your father believed in you, Ledger," she reminded him one evening as they sat on their porch, shadows enveloping them. "He would want you to carry on his legacy, to keep those traditions alive."

As the days turned into weeks, Ledger found himself reflecting on what that legacy meant. His father had dreamed of thriving off the land in Colihaut, a vision that, while not yet fully realized, had been passed down through generations. Ledger now carried that torch. He was not just a farmer in Grand Bay; he was a custodian of his family's history, history entwined with the future aspirations he nurtured for his children.

But with the weight of this legacy also came responsibility. Ledger began contemplating the opportunities that lay ahead in the agricultural region of Colihaut, where the land was rich, and the traditions ran deep. Would he expand their efforts in Grand Bay, or should he explore connections in Colihaut that could lead to a broader reach in sustainable farming? The choices felt monumental, yet each possibility tugged at the threads of his father's dream, urging him to honor it as he charted his own path.

His thoughts were often interrupted by moments of introspection, where Ledger would catch himself imagining his father's advice with newfound appreciation. "Adapt and evolve, son. That is how we survive." It resonated more profoundly than ever—a reminder that growth comes from both surpassing obstacles and embracing change. Now, more than ever, Ledger needed to draw on that resilience.

As the harvest season approached, Ledger returned to the fields, his hands working the soil as they always had, but now infused with a sense of purpose fueled by both remembrance and anticipation. With each seed he planted, he felt as if he was sowing pieces of his father's spirit into the land, nurturing the roots of the future while honoring the past.

Ledger found himself enveloped in the rhythm of farm life again, pulling away from the abyss of grief to focus on the essence of what truly mattered: family. He drew closer to Wizen, Petron, Eliza, Julien, Louisa, James, Dfriel, Koie, and Nerisa, sharing stories about their grandfather and ensuring that the values he had instilled in Ledger would carry through to the next generation. He encouraged them to explore their interests in agriculture, to imagine the possibilities that awaited them, and to nurture the connection to their heritage and the land.

In the evenings, as they gathered for dinner, Ledger and Clara would reminisce about their shared experiences with his father. They would discuss how his father had tended to his garden with care, how he had cultivated relationships with neighbors, and how he had approached each challenge with unwavering determination. Those conversations became a nourishing balm for Ledger's soul, a way to keep his father's memory alive while forging ahead as their own family unit.

The local community offered immense support during this time as well. Neighbors showed up to lend a hand in the fields, bringing meals, sharing stories, and comforting the family in their time of sorrow. This outpouring of love reminded Ledger that he was part of a larger network that transcended immediate grief. As he observed the kindness from those around him, he felt the seeds of hope beginning to take root—the knowledge that even amid loss, bonds could be strengthened and legacies upheld.

As the vibrant colors of fall began to replace the greens of summer, Ledger stood at the edge of his fields once more, feeling an unexpected sense of calm enveloping him. He began to envision his future in a clearer light—a blend of his father's dreams and his own aspirations. The agricultural riches of Colihaut beckoned to him, a new chapter waiting to be written.

With the echoes of his father's wisdom enveloping him, Ledger decided. He would honor his father by embracing the opportunities ahead, expanding his horizons while keeping the family legacy intact. Ledger resolved to reach out to agricultural cooperatives in Colihaut, exploring possibilities that could benefit not only his farm but also the community. He recognized that the potential for collaboration could open doors for innovation and sustainability, allowing them all to thrive together.

Driven by a renewed sense of purpose, he began the process of networking. Ledger reached out to old friends, former colleagues of his father, and local agronomists, eager to learn about cutting-edge practices and sustainable farming methods that could integrate seamlessly into their existing operations. He sought ways to diversify their crops, introduce new practices that honored the land, and create an ecological balance that would ensure future generations could inherit a vibrant legacy.

In conversations with Clara, Ledger often shared his visions and the excitement burgeoning within him. "We can build something here that combines the best of both worlds—our roots in Grand Bay and the potential of Colihaut," he said one evening as they studied maps together on the dining table. "I want our children to grow up knowing they can thrive here and make their own mark."

Clara nodded, her eyes alight with understanding. "Your father would be so proud of this direction. He always believed in finding ways to adapt and grow. It is our turn to keep that spirit alive, for both him and our family."

Through shared determination, they collaborated to plan their next steps. Ledger involved the children as well Wizen and Petronel spent afternoons researching sustainable farming practices and engaging with the community to understand their needs and aspirations. They cultivated a sense of ownership and responsibility, feeling the weight of their family's legacy while also carving out their paths.

As the harvest season progressed, Ledger's heart felt a renewed warmth in the knowledge that he was honoring his father not just in memory but in action. Each time they gathered at the end of the day, bringing in the fruits of their labor, he felt his father's presence among them—a guiding spirit, encouraging them to push forward with hope.

In a pivotal meeting with local farmers from Colihaut, Ledger presented ideas for a cooperative initiative that would allow them to share resources, knowledge, and markets. "There's strength in unity," he emphasized to his neighbors. "Together, we can cultivate not only our own farms but the community's prosperity. We can attract new families, share our traditions, and inspire one another."

The response was overwhelmingly positive, with many expressing a desire to join forces, share their experiences, and work collaboratively. Ledger felt a rush of excitement sweeping through the room, resonating as a signal that their shared vision was not just a dream but a burgeoning reality.

As winter approached, Ledger observed changes not only in the landscape but within himself. He was beginning to integrate the lessons from his father's life more deeply into his own leadership style—valuing the wisdom of community, embracing challenges, and pursuing growth with determination.

This chapter in their lives was a testament to the endurance of legacy, a fluid conversation between past and present, interwoven with hope for the future. The Philogene family had faced profound loss, but from that sorrow, they were drawing strength and inspiration, cultivating a vision that would honor their past while laying the groundwork for the possibilities ahead.

Ledger's heart swelled with pride as he envisioned a future where his children would carry the torch lit by their grandfather. The legacy of love, dedication, and resilience would continue to thrive through them, each harvests a reminder of the journey they had embarked upon together.

Now, standing amongst the remnants of their bountiful fields, Ledger understood that while his father's physical presence was gone, his spirit would forever engage with the land and the community that had been built alongside it. And in that profound realization, Ledger felt a renewed commitment to embrace the opportunities that lay ahead, expanding his horizons while keeping the family legacy alive in every seed sown, every relationship nurtured, and every challenge faced with unwavering resolve.

The news of Ledger's father's death sent shockwaves through the family, reverberating in a way that felt both immediate and disorienting. From the moment the phone call ended, a heavy silence enveloped the Philogene household, each family member grappling with the reality of their loss in their own way. Ledger stood in the kitchen, the mug he had been holding slipping from his fingers and shattering on the floor, a reflection of the shattered world he felt beneath his feet.

As disbelief washed over him, Ledger battled a torrent of emotions—grief, anger, and deep sorrow. He had been prepared for life's uncertainties, but this… this was different. The loss resonated deeply, resonating like an echo in his heart, leaving him feeling unmoored. A father's love, wisdom, and presence are fundamental structures in a person's life, and Ledger felt that foundation crack as he recalled the lessons imparted by his father over the years.

Memories flashed through his mind: sunlit afternoons spent in the fields, learning the intricacies of farming; long heart-to-heart conversations that stretched late into the night, filled with advice about hard work and integrity; and joyous family gatherings filled with laughter, where his father took every opportunity to emphasize the importance of family ties. Each memory served as a reminder of the values his father had instilled in him and a stark realization of how profoundly those lessons would now shape his role as the new patriarch of the family.

"Dad was always there," Ledger whispered to Clara, tears forming in his eyes as they sat together, their hands intertwined. "He was my guide, my anchor in everything. Now I feel... so lost."

Clara's heart ached for Ledger as she listened. "It's okay to feel that way," she reassured him softly. "You are still carrying his legacy with you. He is a part of who you are, and that will never change."

Yet, even with her comforting words, a sense of vulnerability enveloped Ledger, intensifying with the realization that he must now navigate his own role as the head of the family without the steady presence of his father. How could he honor the family traditions while also forging his own path? The pressure of this new title weighed heavily on him, a mantle he had never expected to wear so soon.

In the days that followed, Ledger found himself engulfed in a quiet grief that was profound and expansive. The farm, once a place of growth and possibility, now felt somber, mirroring the loss that hung in the air. Mornings bled into nights as he worked the fields out of habit, yet each task felt laden with the memory of his father's presence—every seed planted, every weed pulled a poignant reminder of all he had learned from him.

"Dad always said farming was like life—it's about being rooted and adaptable," Ledger thought, reflecting on the very lessons that drove their family's legacy. But even as he recalled these teachings, he grappled with his own insecurities—was he truly capable of embodying those values? Could he lead his family the way his father had?

The first family gathering following his father's passing was bittersweet. The dinner table, typically filled with laughter and light-hearted banter, felt unusually quiet. As they sat together, Ledger observed the silent grief etched on Clara's face and the somber expressions of Eliza and Wizen. He realized that the impact of their loss stretched beyond his own heart—it resonated throughout the family. They were all grappling with the absence of the patriarch, each carrying their sorrow as they faced the uncertainties of the future.

In a moment of vulnerability, Ledger spoke up, breaking through the thick silence. "Dad taught us to lean on each other," he began, his voice breaking slightly. "We are a family, and now more than ever, we need to stay connected. I know it is hard, but we need to talk about what we are feeling—honor Dad's memory in the process."

Eliza nodded, her young face serious. "I miss him," she confessed quietly, her voice trembling. "He always listened when I wanted to tell him about my day."

Wizen added, "Can we tell stories about Grandpa? I liked it when he told us about his farm and how he built it."

Ledger felt a lump form in his throat as the floodgates opened, and the family began sharing their memories. They talked about his father's humor, his tireless work ethic, and his unwavering love for them. With each story shared, tears flowed freely, but so did laughter—filled with love and nostalgia, the memories weaved together into a tapestry that honored their father's life.

As they grieved together, Ledger began to feel a sense of clarity emerge through the haze of sorrow. While the loss of his father was a deep wound, it also reminded him of the strong family ties that had been built over generations. Their shared laughter and tears highlighted the very essence of what it meant to be a Philogene—a legacy grounded in love, dedication, and perseverance.

That night, as Ledger lay in bed, he felt a flicker of hope amid the overwhelming grief. He realized that navigating this new role did not mean he had to do it alone; he had a family that stood with him, ready to face the future together. And while his father would no longer be there to offer guidance in person, Ledger understood that his father's wisdom would always be a part of a voice echoing through his thoughts and decisions. The lessons learned and the values instilled would guide his actions as he took on the mantle of leadership, and it was up to him to keep those teachings alive.

With this realization, a sense of resolve began to take root within Ledger. He recognized that honoring his father's legacy meant embracing the responsibilities that came with it, nurturing not only the land but also the family that depended on him. No longer would he dwell solely on the loss; instead, he would channel his grief into purpose—transforming his sorrow into a commitment to create a future that reflected their shared dreams and values.

The days turned into weeks, and Ledger found himself deep in thought about the next steps for his family and their farm. He decided to bring everyone into the process, inviting Eliza and Wizen to share their ideas on how they could move forward together. They gathered in the kitchen, a place that had always been filled with warmth and laughter.

"Let's plan a new planting season together," Ledger proposed, his eyes sparkling with renewed determination. "We can choose what to grow and how we want to honor Grandpa's memory through it."

Eliza's face lit up. "We could plant sunflowers! He always said they are happy flowers, and they would look so beautiful in the fields!"

Wizen chimed in, "And tomatoes! Grandpa loved to make sauce with his tomatoes! We can sell some at the market and even donate to charity."

Ledger listened intently as their enthusiasm made its way into the room. For the first time since their father's passing, he felt a shift—a sense of healing in building something together, a project that honored their grandfather while embracing the future.

Over the following weeks, the family worked side by side, reclaiming not only the land but the joy they felt in each other's company. They planted sunflowers and tomatoes, cultivated vegetables, and prepared the earth for the coming season. With every seed they placed into the soil, they were weaving the fabric of their legacy even tighter, ensuring that their family story would continue to flourish.

Amidst the physical labor, Ledger found moments to reflect on his father's life—the challenges he had faced, the dreams he had chased, and the ways he had cultivated both land and family. As he tended to the plants, he often imagined his father beside him, providing encouragement and practical tips about caring for the soil.

"Just like farming, life has its cycles," he thought, clutching the dirt in his hands. "There will be seasons of growth and seasons of rest. It is okay to feel sadness, but it is also important to celebrate life."

As they prepared for the first harvest, Ledger made a point to commemorate their progress. He suggested they set aside a special evening to share a meal made from the bounty of their labor, a way to celebrate both their past and the bright future ahead.

On the night of their harvest dinner, the table was adorned with fresh vegetables, homemade pasta, and sunflowers that spread cheer across the room. As they sat down together, Ledger looked around at his family and felt gratitude swell within him.

"Tonight, we celebrate not just our harvest but also the spirit of our family and our Grandpa," he started, voice steady but filled with emotion. "He taught us about hard work, integrity, and the importance of sticking together. Let us carry those lessons forward, ensuring that our roots grow deep and strong."

Eliza raised her glass, her smile wide. "To Grandpa! And to our family!"

Wizen followed suit, his youthful joy lighting up the room. "And to make more delicious memories!"

As they all cheered and clinked their glasses, Ledger felt an undeniable sense of healing wash over him. The vibrant gathering served as a reminder that while grief may flow like a river through their lives, they were not alone in navigating its depths. Together, they would honor their patriarch's memory by forging ahead with resilience, love, and hope.

In the days that followed, as Ledger embraced the role of family leader and nurtured the bonds that held them together, he understood that grief would always be a part of his journey. Yet, it was also through that grief that he found clarity and purpose. He was determined to cultivate a legacy rooted in love—one that would carry on the values of integrity and hard work while allowing his family to flourish as they honored the past and embraced the future together.

Each day on the farm became a step forward—a testament to the Philogene spirit, living through the land and in the hearts of those who remained. As he plowed the fields, Ledger felt a blend of sadness and hope, realizing that while the path ahead might be fraught with challenges, it was also ripe with possibility, and he was ready to embrace whatever lay ahead. Each furrow he carved into the earth was both a tribute to his father's legacy and a commitment to forging a new chapter for his family. The rhythmic motion of the plow became a meditative act, allowing Ledger to process his emotions while immersing himself in the tangible connection to the land they had nurtured together.

As he worked, the warmth of the sun broke through the clouds, bathing the fields in golden light. Ledger paused for a moment, taking in the vibrant landscape that stretched before him—the freshly tilled soil, the sunflowers swaying gently in the breeze, and the promise of new crops thriving under their care. This was more than just a farm; it was a living testament to resilience, a microcosm of family, memory, and hope.

In the quiet moments following his father's passing, Ledger found himself enveloped in a profound sense of reflection. As sunlight streamed through the windows of their family home, he often sat alone in his father's old armchair, staring out at the fields sprawling beyond—the life he had once shared with his dad now felt both vibrant and laden with memories.

Each passing day brought new insights into the legacy his father had left behind. Ledger contemplated his father's life as a farmer: a life devoted to nurturing the land, working tirelessly from dawn until dusk and finding joy in the cycle of sowing and reaping. His father had embodied the resilience that farming demanded, teaching Ledger that success often stemmed from hard work and unwavering dedication.

As he looked back on those formative years, Ledger recalled countless lessons imparted under the vast sky, where his father had shared wisdom about the importance of integrity and honesty. "A man's word is his bond," his father would often say, instilling in Ledger the idea that trust and character were foundational in both farming and life. These principles not only shaped Ledger's identity but also defined the way he interacted with the world around him.

The weeks that followed his father's death were marked by a growing recognition of the responsibility he now carried. Ledger understood that it was not merely about maintaining the farm or honoring his father's memory; it was also about ensuring that his children, Eliza and Wizen, understood their heritage. He felt a deep urgency to pass on the values that had been woven into the fabric of their family life.

During the evenings, Ledger began a new tradition—family gatherings where stories of their grandfather were shared, echoing the warmth of his presence. He wanted Eliza and Wizen to appreciate the legacy embedded in their family history. They would sit around the dinner table, and he would recount tales of his father's youth, his work ethic, and the countless sacrifices made to provide for the family. Every shared story served as a bridge connecting the past to the present, reminding them of the strength and resilience that defined their family.

"Your grandpa loved this farm," Ledger told them one night, his voice a mixture of pride and melancholy. "He believed in the power of hard work and community. It is up to us now to continue that legacy, to ensure it grows."

Eliza listened intently, her eyes wide with curiosity. "What was his favorite thing about farming, Dad?" she asked.

Ledger smiled, recalling the joy that lit his father's face while tending to the fields. "He loved watching things grow, seeing the fruits of his labor come to life, and sharing that bounty with others. He believed it was like sharing a piece of yourself."

Wizen, who had remained quiet, suddenly spoke up. "Can we plant some of his favorite crops this year? I want to help!"

"Yes! That is a wonderful idea," Ledger encouraged, his heart swelling with pride. "Planting the things he loved will keep his spirit alive in these fields."

Through these conversations, Ledger began to see the ripple effect of his reflections. He understood that the legacy left behind by his father was a living entity, one that thrived in the stories told and the values upheld. It was about more than just the land; it was about instilling a sense of purpose and identity in future generations.

As the days turned into weeks, Ledger dedicated time during the weekends to engage with Eliza and Wizen in the fields. They would plant crops together, eagerly discussing everything from the best planting techniques to tales of their grandfather's gardening tricks. He watched as his children cultivated their connection to the earth, planting roots both literally and metaphorically.

"Dad!" Eliza exclaimed one sunny afternoon as they worked together, dirt smudged on her cheeks. "I want to learn everything about farming—just like Grandpa did! I want to make him proud."

As her voice filled the air, Ledger felt a wave of emotion wash over him. Her enthusiasm and determination mirrored his father's spirit, and in that moment, he understood that the legacy would indeed endure. By nurturing their curiosity and instilling a sense of responsibility, he was ensuring that their family traditions would be carried forward and woven into the next generation.

The process of grief mixed with purpose transformed Ledger's understanding of legacy. It was a responsibility he embraced—not as a burden but as an honor. Every conversation, every crop planted, and every story shared became a thread in the tapestry of their history, creating a vibrant narrative that not only honored his father but also celebrated the family they were building together.

As the seasons changed and the farm began to yield its bounty, Ledger found solace in the knowledge that he was carrying his father's torch while crafting his own path. He envisioned a future rich with possibility, where his children would grow up with a deep appreciation for the land, the values of hard work, and the importance of family. Ledger dreamt of a home filled with laughter, where Eliza and Wizen would gather at the dinner table to share stories of their daily adventures, filled with the same warmth that had surrounded him during his own childhood. He imagined them running through the fields, not just as a playground but as a canvas for their dreams, learning to cultivate the earth just as their grandfather had taught him.

As the harvest season approached, Ledger felt a sense of excitement blossoming alongside the crops they had planted together. The preparations for the upcoming harvest festival took on a life of their own. He wanted to create an event that would not only celebrate their hard work but also freeze a moment in time—one that connected the community and honored their heritage.

"Let's invite everyone from the market," Ledger said one evening after dinner, looking at Clara, Eliza, and Wizen as they cleared the table together. "We can have a festival where we showcase the produce we have grown, share food, and tell stories about Grandpa. It will bring everyone together, just like he always envisioned."

Clara smiled, her eyes shining with support. "That sounds wonderful, Ledger. It could really deepen those connections within the community, just as your father would have wanted."

With newfound enthusiasm, Ledger and his family began planning the festival, pouring their energies into organizing activities that reflected the spirit of cooperation and togetherness that his father had always emphasized. Eliza took charge of creating colorful decorations, while Wizen eagerly volunteered to help set up games for the kids. Together, they put flyers to distribute around the market, inviting everyone to join in the celebration of the harvest and their community.

As the day of the festival drew closer, the anticipation grew along with the harvest. Ledger watched Eliza and Wizen become increasingly engaged, their eyes sparkling with joy and determination. They crafted a large banner adorned with sunflowers and colorful drawings, proclaiming, "Harvest Festival: Celebrating Our Family and Community!" The sense of pride he felt as they worked together further solidified his commitment to ensuring that his children understood not only the value of hard work but also the beauty of connection.

On the day of the festival, the once quiet fields transformed into a vibrant celebration filled with laughter, music, and the mouthwatering aroma of freshly prepared dishes. Neighbors and friends arrived, bringing their produce and sharing stories with one another. Ledger felt a deep sense of fulfillment as he watched his children interact with the community, spreading happiness while recalling stories of their grandfathers.

"Look, Dad!" Wizen exclaimed as he led a group of children to a game of sack races they had set up. "We're having so much fun!"

As Ledger joined him, he could not help but think about how the festival reflected the very essence of his father's legacy, that joy in simple moments, and the importance of togetherness. This was the beginning of something beautiful, a fulfillment of the ideals his father had championed throughout his life.

As evening fell and the sun dipped below the horizon, casting a golden glow over the gathered crowd, Ledger took a moment to breathe deeply, soaking in the atmosphere of connection and community. It was everything he had hoped for and more. The laughter, the shared stories, and the celebration of the harvest came together to form an enduring tapestry—a reflection of their past, present, and future.

Standing alongside his family, Ledger felt a comforting presence wash over him. He imagined his father observing the scene, a smile on his face, pride swelling within him as he saw the legacy continue to thrive through his son and grandchildren.

At that moment, Ledger understood the true essence of legacy was not merely about maintaining traditions; it was about breathing life into them, allowing them to evolve, and witnessing how they could bring joy to future generations. He knew his father's spirit would always remain a guiding force, encouraging him to grow, nurture, and connect.

As the festivities continued, the colors of the sunset painted the sky with shades of orange and pink, mirroring the vibrant life of the Philogene family. Ledger felt a renewed commitment to uphold the values instilled in him by his father, ensuring that Eliza and Wizen would carry those lessons forward—farming, family, and community intertwined as they embraced the endless possibilities that lay ahead.

From that day forward, Ledger made a silent promise to his father: to honor his legacy by not only cultivating the land but also nurturing the bonds that tied their family together. And as he envisioned the future, he saw not only the hard work of the present but also the blossoming hopes and dreams that would continue to thrive in the hearts of his children.

With each passing season and every new harvest, Ledger and his family would flourish, carrying forward the love, dedication, and spirit of their patriarch—transforming grief into growth, memories into traditions, and legacy into a living testament of hope.

In the days following the funeral, the weight of loss hung heavy in the air, permeating the rooms of the Philogene home. The silence was both comforting and suffocating, a constant reminder of the absence left by Ledger's father. In those moments of grief, Ledger found solace in the company of Clara, whose presence offered a steady anchor amid the emotional turmoil.

As they sat together on the porch one evening, the sun dipped low in the sky, casting a warm golden hue over the fields, Ledger turned to Clara, who seemed lost in thought. "I've been thinking a lot about Dad and how he would want us to move forward," he began, his voice softer than usual. "He dedicated his life to this land and our family. How do we honor that?"

Clara nodded, her gaze fixed on the horizon as if searching for answers. "It is important that we keep his spirit alive by remembering his values—hard work, integrity, and the importance of family. But we also must find a way to adapt those values to our lives today." She paused, glancing at Ledger. "What do you think?"

"I agree," Ledger replied thoughtfully. "It feels like he built a foundation for us to stand on, but it is up to us to decide how to build on that. I want our children to understand their roots, to feel connected to their grandfather's spirit." The thought brought a mixture of warmth and sorrow, but Ledger was determined to turn that grief into something meaningful.

Clara placed her hand on his, her eyes shining with understanding. "We can create new traditions that reflect not only his legacy but also our vision for the future. Let us involve Eliza and Wizen in this process, help them understand the significance of what their grandfather built—the lessons he taught us about work, family, and community."

The idea sparked something within Ledger. "We could start by organizing gatherings where we share stories about him, what he meant to us, and the values he stood for. Family dinners, even a small tree-planting ceremony to commemorate him and our growth as a family. Each year, we could do something to remember him."

"I love that," Clara said, her enthusiasm growing. "We could even invite neighbors and friends from the community. He knew so many people who loved him—this could be a great way to honor him together."

As they spoke, the conversation flowed seamlessly, weaving a tapestry of shared vision and hope. They began discussing their plans, speaking about how to cultivate not just the crops on their land but the relationships and traditions that defined their family. With each idea exchanged, Ledger felt a sense of purpose returning to him, fueled by Clara's unwavering support and encouragement.

"We should also focus on expanding our farming practices to honor what he believed in, to involve the community in new ways," Ledger suggested, growing more animated. "He always wanted to help others—from sharing what we grew to teaching people about sustainable farming. What if we created workshops? We could show others what we have learned."

Clara beamed at the idea. "That is perfect, Ledger! Your father would have loved that. Imagine how many people we could connect with and inspire through their love of the land, just as he did. We could even create a special day dedicated to teaching kids about farming, just like you learned from him."

The thought of sharing their knowledge rekindled a light within Ledger, and as their conversation drifted into the night, he realized that one of the greatest gifts they could give their children was a sense of belonging to something larger than themselves. By continuing their father's legacy, they could instill in Eliza and Wizen not only the importance of their history but also the desire to create a better future.

As the stars began to twinkle overhead, Clara leaned back in her chair and sighed contentedly. "You know," she said quietly, "I have always admired how your father kept the family together. We have that same opportunity now let us make the most of it."

Ledger gazed at the stars, contemplating her words. "Yes, we have a chance to shape our family's story. We are not just preserving his legacy; we are making it our own."

In the days that followed, Ledger and Clara began implementing their ideas, turning their conversations into action. They organized family dinners, inviting not only Eliza and Wizen but also friends and neighbors who had known Ledger's father. By sharing stories and laughter, they created a space filled with warmth, where memories flowed like the sweet tea, they passed around the table.

They worked on their plans for the community workshops, reaching out to farmers' networks and local schools to invite participation. Ledger felt an invigorating sense of anticipation, knowing that as they opened their doors to others, they were also opening the door to new relationships, experiences, and opportunities for growth. Each interaction held the potential to weave new threads into the rich tapestry of their family legacy, connecting them with others who shared a love for the land. Ledger imagined the sound of laughter, the shared knowledge echoing through the fields, and the community coming together to celebrate the values his father had embodied.

As the weeks passed, the preparations for the workshops and family gatherings took shape. Ledger and Clara worked tirelessly, drawing up plans and organizing materials. They decided to host the first workshop in early spring, focusing on sustainable farming practices that combined traditional methods with modern techniques. Ledger felt thrilled at the thought of sharing his skills and knowledge while involving Eliza and Wizen in every aspect, encouraging their curiosity and deepening their connection to the family farm.

The day of the workshop arrived, filled with vibrant sunshine and a steady breeze that carried the fragrant scent of blooming flowers. The Philogene farm was alive with energy as neighbors, local farmers, and families arrived with bright smiles and open hearts. Ledger stood at the entrance, welcoming each guest, his heart swelling with pride as he saw the community come together.

"Thank you all for joining us today!" he announced, glancing around at the familiar faces. "We're excited to share what we've learned here on our farm, and we hope to inspire each of you to keep our connection to the land strong."

As the workshop began, Ledger led the group through practical demonstrations of planting techniques, composting, and pest management. Eliza and Wizen eagerly assisted, their enthusiasm contagious as they engaged with attendees, answering questions and sharing anecdotes about their grandfather's wisdom. The workshop became a lively exchange—a beautiful blend of knowledge and experience shared among friends and families.

Later in the afternoon, Clara organized a break filled with homemade snacks and refreshments, featuring ingredients from the farm. They gathered around picnic tables under the shade of sprawling oak trees, laughter echoing as stories flowed freely.

"Your father was one of a kind," a neighbor remarked to Ledger as they munched on freshly baked bread. "He had a gift for bringing people together. It is wonderful to see you continuing that tradition."

The compliment warmed Ledger's heart, and he smiled, thankful for the support of the community that had rallied around them. "It means a lot to us," he replied sincerely. "We want to make sure that his spirit lives on in everything we do. He loved this land and the people in our community, and we are excited to share that love."

As the sun began its descent, painting the sky in hues of orange and pink, Ledger and Clara gathered everyone for a final circle. They shared a few words of gratitude, reflecting on the day's success and the connections made.

"Today was just the beginning," Clara said, beaming as she looked out at the gathering. "These workshops will not only share knowledge but foster relationships that will help our community and family grow stronger together."

As the evening settled in and the stars began to appear, Ledger felt a renewed sense of hope. He glanced at Clara, their shared vision transforming into reality before their eyes. It was clear they were not only honoring the past but also actively shaping their future—a future built on the foundation laid by Ledger's father and enriched by new relationships and opportunities.

The success of the workshop instilled a bubbling energy in the Philogene household. In the months that followed, they continued to hold workshops, hosting farm-to-table dinners, and community potlucks where everyone brought their own dishes made from locally sourced ingredients. Each event brought people closer together, reinforcing the importance of family, friendship, and support.

Ledger watched his children thrive in this environment, their love for the land blossoming alongside their understanding of the values passed down through generations. Eliza began to cultivate her own small garden plot, while Wizen took the lead in helping organize the children's activities during the workshops, proudly carrying on his grandfather's legacy of teaching and sharing knowledge.

One evening, as they cleaned up after a delightful potluck, with the last rays of the sun filtering through the trees, Ledger reflected on how far they had come. With Clara by his side, they had managed to weave together the past and present, forging a path filled with growth and connection.

"There's something beautiful about how our community has embraced these gatherings," Clara remarked, wiping her hands on a cloth. "Every time we come together, I can almost hear your father's laughter echoing through the fields."

"And I can feel his presence guiding us," Ledger replied, a soft smile emerging. "I believe he'd be proud of what we're creating here—a place where values are honored, traditions are cherished, and new memories are made."

As the moon rose high, casting a gentle glow over the farm, Ledger felt a deep sense of peace settles within him. He knew that by keeping the doors of their home and hearts open, they would not only honor his

Father's legacy also cultivates a nurturing environment for future generations—a space where love, learning, and community thrive. It was a promise he made to himself and to his children: to foster connections that would withstand the test of time, just as the roots of the plants they tended together grew deeper with each passing season.

As he and Clara stepped inside their home, still filled with the echoes of laughter from the evening's gatherings, Ledger felt a renewed sense of purpose. There was something profoundly fulfilling about working alongside his family, creating new traditions that celebrated their past while welcoming new possibilities. The legacy of his father was alive in every decision they made, in every seed they planted, and in every relationship they built.

In the quiet moments before bed, while the children drifted off in their rooms, Ledger and Clara sat together on the porch, cradling warm mugs of tea. The night was still, the stars twinkling brightly above them like distant lanterns illuminating the path they were on.

"I've been thinking about all that's happened since Dad passed," Ledger confessed, gazing up at the vast sky. "It has been hard, but it has also allowed us to explore so much more than I imagined. I feel like we are even closer to the community than before.

Clara nodded, her expression soft with understanding. "Grief has a way of opening our eyes to what truly matters. It has pushed us to act, to connect not just as a family but as part of something larger. It is a reminder of how precious life is, and how important it is to nurture what we have.

"Do you think he's watching over us?" Ledger asked, curiosity threading through his voice.

"I do," she replied thoughtfully. "He is proud of us, seeing how we are keeping his spirit alive through love and action. We are honoring his memory in ways he would have wanted us to—by bringing people together, sharing knowledge, and passing down values."

A comfortable silence settled between them as they sipped their tea, each lost in thoughts of the future. Ledger felt a warmth spread through him, a reassurance that they were on the right path. They had transformed their grief into a powerful motivation to embrace life fully, to create an impact not only in their own lives but also in the lives of others.

Over the following months, the workshops grew more popular, drawing participants from nearby towns and strengthening ties within the community. Ledger and Clara collaborated with local farmers, inviting them to share their knowledge and showcase their produce. The farm, once a solitary space of hard labor for Ledger, had blossomed into a vibrant hub of shared ideas, laughter, and connection.

Ledger began to see the farm as a living legacy—a place where the essence of his father lived in the rhythms of planting, nurturing, and harvesting. Together with Clara, Eliza, and Wizen, they created a space that embodied the values of hard work, integrity, and community. Each gathering, and each lesson taught, added another layer to the rich history of the Philogene family.

As they hosted community events and workshops, Ledger also took time to reflect on his own growth. He realized that he was becoming not only a better farmer but a better father and husband. He embraced the challenges of leadership with a heart full of generosity, motivated by the desire to foster connections, much like his father had done.

And with every laugh shared at the dinner table, every story told, and every seed planted in the earth, Ledger felt a profound sense of gratitude for the journey ahead. His father's spirit remained a guiding light, urging him forward as he forged a path that honored the past while embracing the endless possibilities of the future.

As Ledger and Clara sat on the porch, the soft hum of crickets filling the air, they understood that the life they were building together was not just a tribute to their father's legacy, it was a celebration of love, family, and the collective strength of community. They had opened their doors, invited others in, and in doing so, had created a home where heart and heritage flourished, and where the spirit of the past, present, and future intertwined gracefully.

As the days turned into weeks after his father's passing, Ledger found himself in a constant state of reflection. Each morning, as he stood at the edge of the fields, he felt the weight of his loss settle upon him, mingling with a budding sense of purpose. The sun would rise with the promise of a new day, illuminating the lush landscape of Colihaut—its fertile soil spreading before him, ripe with potential.

While his grief was a heavy cloak draped over his shoulders, Ledger began to recognize the opportunities lying in wait in the very land he stood upon. The agricultural region of Colihaut had long been known for its capacity to yield bountiful harvests. The rich, dark earth, coupled with the favorable climate, made it an ideal setting for farming—a gift that had sustained generations. His father had nurtured this land with care, and now it was Ledger's turn to continue that legacy.

Sitting on the porch one evening, Ledger grabbed his notebook, the one filled with his father's sketches and handwritten notes about farming techniques, crop rotations, and community ties. He flipped through the pages, each one telling the story of a life dedicated to cultivating both the earth and the bonds of family. As he read, inspiration sparked within him. Now was the time to not only honor his father's memory but to also embrace the possibilities that lay ahead.

With a clear focus in mind, Ledger began to assess how he might expand their farming efforts. The farm had always produced staple crops, but he sensed there was room for growth—an opportunity to build a sustainable livelihood that could benefit his family and the community. He envisioned diversifying their crops, incorporating more vegetables, herbs, and even fruits that could thrive in the fertile soil of Colihaut.

As he sat there, he made a list of potential crops to explore—a mix of traditional staples and innovative choices. "We could grow more tomatoes, peppers, and squash," he mused aloud. "And consider some fruit trees—avocados, mangoes, and even passion fruit. They could thrive in our climate!"

But Ledger knew that diversification would not just enhance their offerings; it would also provide resilience against the uncertainties of farming. He recalled conversations with neighboring farmers who had shared stories of the unpredictable weather affecting crop yields. By expanding their harvest variety, they could mitigate risks and ensure a more stable income.

Energized by his ideas, Ledger decided to take a walk through the fields, breathing in the fresh air and allowing the beauty of the land to inspire him. As he walked, he carefully surveyed the soil, the sunlight gleaming on the rich earth, and the native plants that thrived in the surrounding areas. He could see the potential not just for additional crops but also for sustainable practices that could help preserve the land for generations to come.

He imagined implementing techniques such as crop rotation, companion planting, and organic pest management, all practices he had learned from his father and read about since. These methods not only improved soil health but also reduced the reliance on chemical fertilizers and pesticides, aligning with his desire to farm responsibly.

"I want to leave this land better than I found it," Ledger whispered to himself, feeling a burgeoning sense of responsibility. He envisioned the farm thriving as a sustainable entity, capable of supporting their family while also contributing positively to the local ecosystem and community.

As he walked back to the house, Ledger's thoughts turned to the community of Colihaut itself. The interconnectedness of the farmers, the markets that featured local produce, and the cooperative spirit that had always been a part of their way of life filled him with hope. He realized he could not only expand their farming efforts but also collaborate with others in the area—sharing resources, knowledge, and ideas.

The following day, Ledger began reaching out to neighboring farmers and local agricultural groups, proposing the idea of cooperative workshops focused on sustainable practices. "What if we came together to share what we know?" he suggested during a community meeting. "We could learn from each other, diversify our crops, and ultimately strengthen our collective efforts to adapt to the changing landscape of agriculture."

The response was overwhelmingly positive. Farmers from nearby farms expressed excitement about the opportunities to collaborate, sharing ideas for new crops, techniques, and practices that had worked in their own fields. Ledger felt a surge of optimism as he realized that they were all striving for the same goal: to keep Colihaut strong and vibrant.

As the conversations continued, Ledger began to feel not just the weight of his grief but the power of shared purpose—a reconnection to his father's legacy, a commitment to the land, and a renewed drive to embrace the future. The workshops flourished, bringing farmers together to explore new methods, host seed swaps, and cultivate both the soil and their relationships.

With each passing day, Ledger's vision of a sustainable and flourishing farm began to take root in his heart and in the fertile ground of Colihaut. The community workshops were a resounding success, each gathering filled with laughter, shared stories, and a wealth of knowledge exchanged between seasoned farmers and eager novices. As they explored innovative methods, framed by a foundation of traditional practices, excitement rippled through the community.

Word began to spread, and more neighbors joined their efforts. Ledger saw families come together, bringing their children to learn about farming, pest management, crop health, and the importance of preserving the environment. He watched as Eliza and Wizen eagerly helped set up the demonstrations, their youthful enthusiasm contagious, reminding Ledger of the joy that came from nurturing the land.

They experimented with new crops, some emerging from the collective dreams of the community. Together, they decided to try growing heirloom varieties that had been forgotten, reviving recipes and flavors that linked them to their heritage. As Ledger walked through the rows of vibrant vegetables and blossoming fruits, he felt a renewed sense of purpose, knowing he was not only honoring his father's legacy but also creating something meaningful for the future.

Ledger also began implementing practices such as permaculture, which emphasized working with nature rather than against it. He transformed parts of their land into a lush garden filled with native plants that attracted beneficial insects and pollinators. His heart swelled with pride when he witnessed the vibrant landscapes and the creatures that now thrived alongside their crops.

Recognizing the economic potential of this approach, Ledger began to think beyond simple crop sales. He envisioned a farm that could offer tours, workshops, and educational programs focused on sustainable agriculture and environmental stewardship. The idea of welcoming visitors and teaching them about the significance of farming and local ecosystems filled him with excitement. "We could build a future where people come to connect, to learn, and to appreciate the land," he envisioned.

Ledger discussed this idea with Clara one evening, as they sat on the porch enjoying the sunset. "Imagine families coming here to learn about farming, to experience the beauty of the land, and to take a piece of that back home with them," he said, his eyes bright with enthusiasm. "It could create a new revenue stream for us while fostering a deeper appreciation for sustainable practices."

"I love that idea," Clara replied, her smile widening. "It aligns perfectly with what we are trying to achieve. It could engage the community and inspire a whole new generation to care for the land. Plus, it would reflect your father's passion for teaching and sharing.

Over the next few months, they worked tirelessly to bring his vision to life. Together, they planned educational programs and constructed a welcoming space for guests. They set up shaded areas for workshops, created paths through the gardens, and built a small outdoor kitchen for cooking demonstrations featuring seasonal produce.

The meticulous planning paid off when they officially launched the first "Colihaut Farm Experience" in early summer. Flyers filled with colorful images of cheerful vegetables and enthusiastic children graced the local market, creating buzz around town. On the opening day, Ledger watched as families arrived, excitement palpable in the air.

As the sun rose, shedding golden light across the farm, Ledger felt a mix of nerves and excitement. He greeted visitors with Clara and the children by his side, explaining the layout of the farm and what they could expect to learn throughout their visit. He led them through the fields, teaching them about organic methods of cultivation, the importance of biodiversity, and how every action on the land had a ripple effect on the environment.

He was met with curious questions and eager faces, all soaking in the information and sharing their own ideas. It reminded him of the gatherings he had as a child with his father, and he could feel his father's spirit watching over them, encouraging him in his new role as teacher and guide.

As the day progressed, Ledger felt an overwhelming sense of fulfillment wash over him. He watched Eliza helping younger children plant seedlings, their laughter echoing across the field, and Wizen demonstrating irrigation techniques to interested families. He realized that the farm had transformed into a space that was not only productive but also a sanctuary for learning and connection.

When the day ended, Ledger and Clara stood together, watching the sunset casting long shadows over the fields. Their hearts were full, and Ledger felt gratitude wash over him for the journey they had undertaken together. "This is just the beginning," he said, a smile spreading across his face. "I can feel it. We are building something truly special here, something that honors Dad's legacy and shapes our future.

Clara nodded, her eyes reflecting the colors of the sunset. "We are not just farming; we are cultivating community, love, and sustainability. It is more than I ever imagined."

As they embraced the cool evening air, Ledger knew that the journey ahead would be filled with challenges and triumphs. But with each passing day, as their farm continued to thrive and their family grew stronger, Ledger felt a deepening sense of hope and resilience. The laughter of Eliza and Wizen echoed through the fields, intertwining with the rustling leaves and the soft cooing of doves that nested nearby. Each morning brought new challenges, but with them came opportunities for creativity and collaboration.

With the success of their first farm experience, Ledger and Clara set their sights on expanding their offerings. They started planning seasonal festivals that would celebrate not only the harvest but also the rich culture and traditions of Colihaut. These events would feature local artisans, musicians, and vendors, transforming their farm into a community gathering space where people could share their crafts, stories, and seasonal delights.

"Imagine a Harvest Festival with games, food stalls, and music!" Clara exclaimed one evening over dinner, animatedly sketching ideas on a napkin. "We could invite everyone to bring a dish made from their favorite local ingredients, turning it into a potluck celebration."

"Yes! And we can showcase different crops and how they are grown," Ledger replied, excitement bubbling within him. "We could organize workshops, demos, and even a small farmers' market. It would be a fantastic way to bring the community together and include everyone in our journey."

As they discussed the details, Ledger's vision expanded beyond the farm itself. He dreamed of creating a network of local farmers dedicated to sustainable practices, where knowledge could flow freely, and resources could be shared. He thought about how they could organize meetups to learn from each other and promote their products collectively.

Inspired by these ideas, Ledger reached out to various farmers in the region, proposing a monthly gathering to discuss challenges, successes, and strategies for sustainable farming. The response was enthusiastic; farmers who had been struggling in isolation were eager for the chance to connect and collaborate. Each meeting fostered a sense of camaraderie, turning mutual struggles into collective solutions. They exchanged knowledge about pest management, soil health, and innovative crop techniques, further enhancing the agricultural landscape of Colihaut.

As the seasons changed, so did their farm. With each new crop, Ledger saw a reflection of the love and commitment they poured into the land. The diverse array of crops not only enriched the soil but also captured the hearts of local families, who eagerly anticipated the fresh produce available at the farmers' market. The farm was buzzing with life, transforming into a vibrant ecosystem where flora and fauna flourished side by side.

But amidst the excitement of growth and opportunity, Ledger still grappled with moments of grief. He would often find himself standing alone in the quiet of the fields, feeling the absence of his father acutely. In those moments, he would touch the earth, absorbing the wisdom it held, and remember the lessons his father taught him about patience, resilience, and the unyielding spirit of the land. Those memories became a source of strength, allowing him to honor his father through every plant nurtured and every relationship cultivated.

One day, while working alongside Eliza in the garden, she paused and turned to him. "Dad, do you think Grandpa would like what we're doing?" her eyes wide with curiosity.

Ledger knelt beside her, holding a seedling gently in his hands. "I think he would be proud, Eliza. He always believed in sharing knowledge and connecting with others. We are continuing that spirit by bringing everyone together to learn about the land and each other."

"Do you think he's here with us, watching?" she asked, her voice soft.

"I'd like to believe he is," Ledger replied, smiling as warmth spread through his chest. "He may not be here in the way we want, but his spirit lives on in this land and us. Every time we plant a seed, every laugh we share, he is a part of it."

As the sun began to set, painting the horizon with hues of orange and purple, Ledger felt a deep sense of fulfillment. The farm had become more than just a livelihood symbolizing resilience, unity, and the continuity of tradition woven together with innovation. Each day brought new challenges but also new ways to grow—not just in crops but in relationships, understanding, and community ties.

With each passing day, as their farm continued to thrive and their family grew stronger, Ledger realized they were not merely surviving; they were creating a life full of purpose and connection, honoring the past while building a future steeped in hope. In the heart of Colihaut, amidst the rhythm of seasons and the laughter of loved ones, Ledger found solace and strength. He knew that their journey was just beginning, and as they looked toward the future, they would carry the legacy of love and resilience with them in every step they took on the land they cherished.

With a renewed sense of determination coursing through him, Ledger spent the next few weeks immersing himself in the agricultural landscape of Colihaut. He understood that to truly honor his father's legacy and build a sustainable future for his children, he needed to grasp not only the nuances of their own farm but also the broader context of the community in which they lived.

One early morning, Ledger set out with a notebook in hand, eager to explore the avenues available to him. He knew that Colihaut was blessed with fertile soil and a favorable climate, but he sought to understand the specifics—the unique crops that thrived, the challenges farmers faced, and the opportunities ripe for the taking.

As Ledger drove along the winding roads flanked by fields, he marveled at the lush greenery surrounding him. The hills rolled gently, dotted with fences and barnyards, and the scent of damp earth filled the air after an overnight rain shower. It was a comforting reminder of the life he was committed to nurturing and strengthening.

His first stop was a local market bustling with activity. Farmers set up their stalls, displaying vibrant vegetables, fresh fruits, and artisanal products. Ledger approached a vendor selling heirloom tomatoes, their colors a dazzling array of reds, yellows, and greens.

"Good morning! Those tomatoes look amazing," he said, nodding toward the display. "How do you grow them?"

The vendor, a middle-aged man with sun-worn skin and a welcoming smile, brightened at the compliment. "Thanks! We grow them using organic methods—no chemicals. The warmth from the sun and our rich soil really helps them thrive. Would you like to know more about our techniques?"

Ledger eagerly agreed, and as they talked, he took detailed notes about crop rotation, heirloom varieties, and the importance of soil health. The vendor emphasized the need for patience and observation in farming, stressing that every season brought its lessons.

Inspired by their conversation, Ledger moved on to visit several other vendors, each sharing their insights on crops like sweet potatoes, okra, and various herbs that flourished in Colihaut's climate. He learned about the importance of diversifying crops to minimize risks, especially with the unpredictable weather patterns that had begun to emerge over recent years.

One farmer, an elderly woman named Miss Clara, caught his attention with her enthusiasm. "You can't just grow what everyone else is growing; you need to find your niche!" she advised, her eyes sparkling with wisdom. "Consider what the market needs and how you can fill that gap. We are fortunate here; the soil is forgiving, and we can try different things if we are mindful of what is already thriving."

Ledger took her words to heart, pondering how he could apply them to his own farm. He jotted down notes on potential niche crops that could be incorporated into their operations, like specialty herbs and unique vegetables that might draw the interest of local chefs or health-conscious consumers.

As he continued his journey, he stopped to speak with small-scale farmers and backyard garden enthusiasts, asking about the community structure and existing support systems. He learned about local cooperatives that aimed to promote sustainable agriculture and how many farmers were already collaborating to share resources, equipment, and market access.

Eventually, Ledger made his way to a local cooperative meeting, where he met farmers from various backgrounds interested in sustainable practices. The energy in the room was electric as participants discussed collective initiatives, ranging from community-supported agriculture (CSA) programs to educational workshops for aspiring farmers.

Listening to their stories, Ledger felt a deep connection to this community's spirit—everyone was eager to learn and help one another thrive. Inspired by their camaraderie, he shared his vision for expanding their family farm, proposing collaborations that could benefit everyone.

"What if we organized farm tours or popular events to showcase what we're doing here?" Ledger suggested, enthusiasm bubbling in his voice. "It could bring additional revenue to all of us, and we can promote eco-friendly practices at the same time."

The room erupted with nods of agreement, and discussions blossomed around the idea. It was clear that the farmers were excited about solidarity and the potential of working together. By the end of the meeting, Ledger felt invigorated, knowing that he had found kindred spirits who could help him turn his vision into reality.

Over the following weeks, he dedicated time to visiting local schools and community centers, where he shared what he had learned with families interested in agriculture. Ledger spoke passionately about growing their own food, practicing sustainable methods, and understanding the importance of supporting local farmers. Each encounter deepened his resolve to create a future where his children would have access to fresh, healthy food and a strong connection to the community that surrounded them.

As Ledger returned to his own farm at the end of each day, he felt a profound sense of purpose. He envisioned how their land could evolve, filled with vibrant crops and dedicated spaces for learning and collaboration. He imagined fields bursting with color, each section representing a different crop, carefully cultivated to thrive in Colihaut rich soil. His mind wandered to the possibility of community events—festivals celebrating the harvest, workshops teaching sustainable farming techniques, and family gatherings that brought everyone together to share in the bounty of the land.

With every conversation he had with local farmers, Ledger's ideas for his own farm continued to flourish. He thought about introducing a section dedicated to educational gardens—areas where children and adults alike could learn hands-on about the planting process, the importance of biodiversity, and the value of organic methods. He could see school groups wandering through the fields, eyes wide with curiosity as they participated in planting and harvesting.

The farm, he envisioned, could serve as a living classroom—an oasis of knowledge where families could reconnect with the land, understand sustainable practices, and appreciate the hard work that went into producing the food they often took for granted. He found himself sketching out plans for the layout, illustrating not just rows of crops but spaces for workshops, open-air events, and even a small market stall where they could sell produce and other local goods.

"Dad always said that the land gives back tenfold," Ledger thought to himself as he circled back to his original goal—securing a better future for his children. He wanted to create a legacy that would not only honor his father's commitment to farming but also ensure that Eliza and Wizen would grow up with a deep appreciation for the earth and the community surrounding them.

He knew that achieving this vision would require hard work and dedication, but he felt a growing sense of excitement. The possibilities were endless. Each farmer he spoke to fuel his determination, showcasing the resilience of those who came before him and inspiring him to forge new paths.

One evening, while sitting on the porch after a long day of planning and research, Ledger shared his vision with Clara. The sky was painted in hues of orange and pink as the sun dipped below the horizon. A gentle breeze rustled the leaves of the trees, creating a soothing backdrop to their conversation.

"Imagine transforming our farm into a hub of education and sustainability," Ledger proposed, his eyes bright with passion. "We can have workshops, invite schools, and connect with local businesses. We could be leading an initiative that brings people together, all while promoting the health of our community and our land."

Clara leaned back, absorbing his enthusiasm. "I love that idea," she replied thoughtfully, resting her hand on his knee. "We could really make a difference, not just for us but for everyone around us. Providing that connection to the land is so important."

"We will teach people how to grow their own food, the importance of healthy eating, and how to respect the environment. It is a win-win for everyone," Ledger continued, feeling the synergy of their ideas.

As the weeks passed, Ledger began to act on his vision, starting with small steps. He launched a monthly community day at the farm, inviting families to come out for hands-on activities such as planting seeds and learning about sustainable practices. The response was overwhelming: families, children, and neighbors who once only shared polite land acknowledgments were now coming together, eager to learn and connect.

With each event, Ledger and Clara nurtured a strong sense of community, transforming their farm into a lively gathering place filled with laughter, learning, and connection. Children scampered through rows of sunflowers, parents picked herbs, and elders shared stories of days gone by, weaving a rich narrative that celebrated their agricultural heritage.

Through these initiatives, Ledger's dream began to materialize; the farm was evolving into more than just a business—it was becoming a vital part of the community fabric. It was a place where values of sustainability, education, and connection thrived side by side.

As he watched his children flourish amid the vibrant culture they had cultivated, Ledger felt a profound sense of fulfillment. With each interaction, each seed planted, and each community event, he was not only honoring his father's legacy but also forging a new path—one filled with hope, possibility, and a deep commitment to the future of their family and the land they cherished.

As Ledger sat on the porch of the family farmhouse, the evening sky blanketed the horizon in hues of deep blue and soft purple, a stark contrast to the internal struggle brewing within him. The decision to expand their operations into Colihaut and relocate the family was resting heavily on his mind. He gazed out at the rolling fields that had been in his family for generations, feeling both a rush of excitement and an undercurrent of fear swirl within him.

The farming community in Colihaut was thriving, replete with opportunity. Ledger's recent exploration of the area had unveiled a landscape ripe for growth—untapped markets for fresh produce, a supportive network of farmers, and sustainable practices that aligned with his vision. However, he was acutely aware that expanding their operations came with significant risks which he could not ignore.

He pulled out his notebook, now filled with observations, sketches, and market analyses. As he flipped through the pages, his thoughts danced between the potential rewards and the uncertainties that lay ahead.

The warm glow of the setting sun filters through the kitchen window, casting a golden hue over the table where Ledger sits. In front of him lies a notepad filled with a jumble of thoughts and aspirations, surrounded by scattered notes—each one a fragment of his vision for the future. Clusters of scribbled ideas, diagrams of crops, and sketches of potential layouts for their farm create a tapestry of his dreams and plans. Ledger's brow is furrowed in concentration, the long hours spent poring over every detail evident in the slight weariness of his eyes. He knows that this moment is crucial, a steppingstone toward something greater, but the weight of uncertainty presses down on him.

Clara enters the kitchen, wiping her hands on a towel after finishing the day's chores. As she notices Ledger's focused demeanor and the scattered papers, she senses the heaviness in the air. Leaning against the counter, she crosses her arms and studies him for a moment before speaking. "You have been at this for hours. What have you so deep in thought?" Her voice is gentle yet concerned, a reminder of their shared journey and the goals they hold dear. She knows that the weight of responsibility often falls heavily on Ledger's shoulders, and in this quiet moment, she hopes to draw him out, to share in whatever burden he carries.

Ledger looks up, meeting Clara's gaze as a soft smile breaks through the intensity of his concentration. He glances briefly at the notes scattered before him, his mind still buzzing with ideas, before returning his focus to her. Here is the anchor he needs, the partner who shares his dreams and understands his struggles. "I've been thinking about how we can make the most of our land," he admits, his voice steady but infused with passion. "I want to create a farm that truly reflects who we are and our vision for the future." As he speaks, the weight of his thoughts begins to lighten, energized by Clara's presence, and he feels ready to share his dreams and collaborate on the path ahead.

"I've been weighing the rewards and risks of moving into Colihaut," Ledger said, his voice steady but laced with the gravity of his thoughts. He flipped to a fresh page in his notepad and began writing, outlining the key points he had been considering. "There's so much potential, but I can't ignore what's at stake." As his pen glided across the paper, the words began to take form, echoing the careful deliberation that had occupied his mind for hours. He understood that embarking on this journey would require not only hard work but also a calculated approach to the uncertainties that lay ahead.

"Like increased crop diversity," he continued, enthusiasm creeping into his tone. "Colihaut's soil is rich—heirloom tomatoes, specialty herbs, you name it. We could diversify what we offer and really appeal to a broader customer base." Each point he wrote down felt like a steppingstone toward a new reality, invigorating him with possibilities. The thought of growing unique varieties and attracting a wider clientele sparked his imagination, painting a vivid picture of bustling farmers' markets and thriving partnerships with local restaurants.

Intrigued, Clara approached the table, leaning in to get a better look at his notes. "That sounds promising," she replied, her excitement palpable. "More options mean more income, right?" Her voice carried an infectious enthusiasm, and she felt a surge of optimism at the prospect of expanding their horizons. Clara knew that diversifying their crops could stabilize their income, reducing reliance on any single crop and helping to cushion them against unpredictable market fluctuations.

As Ledger scribbled down ideas, Clara envisioned the potential impact on their lives: not just financial growth but the chance to create a vibrant, dynamic community around their farm. "Imagine the flavors we could experiment with and the recipes we could share," she mused, her mind racing with possibilities. The thought of showcasing their unique offerings at local events thrilled her, further fueling the fire of ambition that had always burned brightly in both. Together, they could cultivate not just crops, but a thriving enterprise that celebrated their shared vision for a sustainable, fulfilling life in Colihaut.

"Exactly!" Ledger exclaimed, his excitement palpable as he continued to outline the benefits of their potential move. "And there is the community support. The farmers I met during those workshops are eager to collaborate and share knowledge. We could pool resources, mitigate some risks, and foster sustainability among us." He ran a hand through his hair, the gesture a reminder of the weight of his current responsibilities, but also a sign of his growing energy as he envisioned the possibilities ahead. He could see clearly now—the local farming community coming together, sharing tools and techniques, and creating a network of mutual support that would not only enhance their enterprises but also strengthen the agricultural landscape of Colihaut.

As he spoke, Ledger's animated demeanor drew Clara closer, captivated by his vision. "I also envision creating educational programs for families and schools," he continued, his voice rich with enthusiasm. "Imagine our farm as a hub where people come to learn about sustainable practices! It could encourage more visitors and provide us with some financial stability." The idea of turning their farm into a place where knowledge and community could intersect brought a sparkle to his eyes. He pictured children running through the fields, learning to plant seeds, and families gathering for workshops on composting and permaculture. This initiative could cultivate a sense of stewardship for the land while simultaneously generating income through entrance fees and donations.

Clara's mind raced alongside his, inspired by the thought of transforming their farm into a vibrant center for education and collaboration. "That sounds incredible, Ledger. We could create something truly special—a space where people not only appreciate the beauty of nature but also gain the skills to protect it. Her words had a confidence that mirrored his enthusiasm, and together they began to sketch ideas for workshops, hands-on experiences, and community events that could take root alongside their crops. With each idea shared, their vision of the future became clearer, solidifying into a shared dream that was both ambitious and attainable.

Clara's eyes brightened at the idea, considering the possibilities with enthusiasm. "That would be amazing! A way to engage families in our work and create a community space," she said, her voice infused with excitement. The thought of children laughing and playing among the crops filled her with joy, and she envisioned vibrant community gatherings, workshops, and events that could bring people together in meaningful ways. Creating a hub of activity would not only elevate their farm but also foster connections between families, encouraging a deeper appreciation for agriculture and sustainability within their community.

However, as Clara painted a picture of this lively future, Ledger's expression shifted subtly, a hint of worry creeping in. "And we can't forget the emotional aspect," he replied, his tone becoming more serious. "A lively, engaging environment for Wizen, Petronel, Julien, Eliza, Louisa, James, Dfriel, Koie, and Nerisa would be incredible. They could learn about the land, growing food, and community collaboration." His words carried a weight that tempered Clara's enthusiasm, as he considered what it meant for their children to grow up surrounded by nature and the values of hard work and cooperation. Ledger envisioned Eliza and Wizen working alongside them, cultivating a love for the earth and a sense of responsibility toward the community that supported them.

He paused, letting the weight of his concerns settle in the air as the vibrant possibilities began to clash with the realities of their endeavor. The room grew quiet, the atmosphere heavy with contemplation as he shifted his focus to the potential risks that lay ahead. With a heavy hand, he wrote down his worries—financial instability, unpredictable weather patterns, and the pressures of maintaining a business amid fluctuating markets. Each word felt like a hammer striking against the enthusiasm they had just shared, reminding him that while dreams of growth and community engagement sparkled brightly, they were also fraught with challenges that required sober reflection and careful planning.

He sighed, the sound heavy with the weight of his thoughts. "But with those rewards come some daunting risks," he continued, his eyes cast down at the notepad filled with hopes and ideas. "Expanding means significant financial investment—land, equipment, infrastructure. I must assess our current financial situation carefully." The reality of their ambitions settled on his shoulders like a heavy cloak, reminding him that dreams can often come with a steep price. Ledger understood that every decision they made would have far-reaching implications, not only for their farm but for their family's future. Balancing the allure of a thriving business against the risks of overextension was no small feat.

Clara's brow furrowed as a serious tone slipped into the conversation. "Overextending ourselves could jeopardize everything we've built here," she added, her voice steady but filled with concern. She knew all too well how long they had fought to establish their farm, nurturing it through countless challenges. The stakes felt high, and she understood the fragility of their success. While the prospect of growth was exhilarating, Clara remained grounded in the reality of the hard work and sacrifices that had brought them this far, her instincts urging caution and careful consideration.

"Right," Ledger responded, nodding in agreement. "And then there's market uncertainty. Agriculture is volatile, influenced by everything from weather patterns to consumer trends. What if we invest in crops that fail?" He cast a fleeting glance out the window, the setting sun painting the sky in shades of orange and pink, but his expression was visibly troubled. The thought of failure loomed large in his mind, and he felt the tension of the unknown tugging at him. It was one thing to dream big, but another entirely to navigate the unpredictable waters of the agricultural market. Ledger knew that they needed more than just passion and ambition; they required a solid plan and a willingness to adapt in the face of potential setbacks. The path before them was fraught with uncertainty, and he understood that careful deliberation would be crucial to protect what they had built together.

"Then there's relocation," Ledger added, his voice softening as he considered the implications. "Uprooting our family from this home—so many memories of Dad are tied to this place. What emotional toll would that take on Wizen, Petronel, Julian, Eliza, Louisa, James, Dfriel, Koie, and Nerisa, even you?" The weight of those words hung heavily in the air, a palpable reminder of the past that was woven into every corner of their farm. Ledger felt a deep ache in his chest as he remembered his father, who had poured his heart and soul into nurturing this land. It had been a sanctuary of love and family, and the thought of leaving it behind wanted to peel away a part of their identity. He worried about how such a change could affect their children, who were still navigating their grief after losing their grandfather.

After a moment filled with heavy silence, Clara reached out and placed a hand on his shoulder for reassurance, her warmth grounding him. "I've been worried about that too," she confessed, her voice steady but colored with concern. "Changing their environment after losing their grandfather could be tough." Clara understood how profound the impact of such a loss could be, especially for the children. Their home was not just a physical space; it was filled with echoes of laughter, lessons learned, and the bonds of love that had been forged over the years. The thought of uprooting Eliza and Wizen from a place so rich with memories felt daunting, and they both recognized the delicate balance between moving forward and honoring the past.

Ledger turned to look at her, vulnerability in his eyes, seeking comfort in her presence. It was in moments like this, sharing fears and uncertainties, that he felt the strength of their partnership. "I just want to make the right decisions for them," he murmured, the weight of responsibility heavy on his shoulders. He knew they had to consider more than just financial implications; they had to protect their children's emotional well-being too. Together, they stood at a crossroads, knowing that whatever choice they made would shape not only their future but also the legacy they were building for Eliza and Wizen. The path forward was unclear, but in this shared moment of honesty, Ledger felt the power of their unity—their ability to face challenges together, whether in laughter or in trepidation.

"And lastly, community acceptance," Ledger continued, his brow furrowing as he spoke. "Just because I have felt welcomed," does not guarantee that they will embrace us once we move. Trust takes time, and a misstep could sour everything for which we have worked." The reality of their situation weighed on him as he contemplated the dynamics of a new community. While the connections he had made so far felt promising, he knew that relationships were fragile and required consistent effort to cultivate. He feared the potential repercussions of a poor first impression or an ill-timed decision that might alienate them from the very people whose support would be crucial for their success.

Clara squeezed his shoulder gently, her touch conveying a sense of solidarity that momentarily lightened the heaviness in his heart. "I understand," she replied softly, her voice steady amidst the uncertainty that enveloped them. The thought of navigating the complexities of a new social landscape was daunting, but Clara also recognized the importance of being proactive in addressing these concerns. "So, what do we do now?" she asked, a hint of determination coloring her words. "Do we push forward, or take a step back?"

Her question hung in the air, an invitation for Ledger to explore their next steps together. Clara's presence was a reminder that they did not have to face these fears alone; they were partners in this journey. Ledger took a moment to consider their options, weighing the potential for growth against the risks they had just outlined. "Maybe we can take a more gradual approach," he suggested thoughtfully. "We could make smaller commitments and engage with the community more before diving in fully. Building those relationships could help us ease into the transition and allow us to understand the needs and values of the people in Colihaut."

Clara nodded, her expression shifting from concern to thoughtful contemplation. "That sounds reasonable," she agreed. "We can invest our time in understanding the community while slowly integrating our vision for the farm." The prospect of taking small steps felt reassuring and practical, allowing them to assess their surroundings without losing sight of their goals. Together, they began to formulate a plan—a way to honor their roots while exploring the promise of a new beginning. In that moment, they united with renewed focus, ready to face whatever challenges lay ahead, side by side.

Taking a deep breath, Ledger gathered his thoughts as he looked at Clara, sensing the weight of their conversation. "I think we need to balance ambition with caution," he said, his voice steady and resolute. "Let's research more about Colihaut, talk to the farmers again, and involve our children in these discussions." His mind raced with the potential strategies they could employ, the conversations they could initiate, and the knowledge they could gain. Involving their children in the process felt especially important; it would not only help Eliza and Wizen understand the changes but also make them feel like active participants in their family's journey. Ledger's determination grew as he realized how they could turn uncertainty into a shared adventure, fostering a sense of ownership and responsibility among all of them.

As he met Clara's gaze, a spark of determination ignited between them, illuminating the path forward. "We owe it to ourselves and our family to consider all angles before jumping in," he continued passionately. "It's about honoring the past while striving to create something meaningful for the future." This dual focus reminded him that their roots would always be important, but it was equally essential to cultivate a space where new memories could blossom. The idea of intertwining their history with future aspirations filled him with purpose, as he envisioned how their farm could evolve into a thriving hub that embraced both the legacy of his father and the dreams they held as a family.

Clara nodded in affirmational silence, her expression glowing with support and understanding. She felt a swell of admiration for Ledger's vision and a renewed sense of hope for their journey ahead. They sat together at the table, united in their resolve and purpose, ready to face whatever challenges lay ahead. Each heartbeat echoed their commitment to one another and their shared dreams, reinforcing the bonds that had been forged through countless trials. In that moment of quiet strength, they knew they had taken the first steps toward building a future that respected the past while embracing new possibilities, and together they felt ready to navigate the path that awaited them.

Torn between the potential for a flourishing future and the fear of instability, Ledger felt the familiar pang of grief tugging at him. Losing his father had thrown him into a whirlwind of uncertainty, and the thought of forging ahead without the guidance and wisdom he had once relied on was daunting.

Taking a deep breath, Ledger decided to write down his thoughts, forcing himself to articulate his fears and hopes clearly. On one side of the page, he wrote "Rewards," listing the opportunities and dreams he envisioned. On the opposite side, he wrote "Risks," detailing every concern that weighed him down.

After an hour of contemplation, Ledger leaned back, taking in the stillness of the evening. He began to see patterns emerging. *What if he approached this decision methodically?* Rather than acting impulsively on excitement or fear, he could create a plan to mitigate the risks while maximizing the rewards.

He could secure financing through grants and loans designed for sustainable agriculture. Doing thorough research on crop viability in the new area may provide insight into market demands, allowing them to tailor their offerings. He could engage with community members one-on-one, fostering relationships gradually to build trust and ensure smoother integration into the Colihaut farming scene.

Finally, as for the emotional aspect, Ledger felt it was essential to honor his father's memory in the process, by preserving aspects of their old home in meaningful ways. He could still involve Wizen, Petronel, Julien, Louisa, Eliza, James, and Dfriel, in farm traditions, ensuring they retained a sense of continuity amid change.

With a renewed sense of clarity and purpose, Ledger realized that he could frame this decision as not just a move but a natural evolution of their family legacy. It was not about abandoning the past; it was about honoring it by striving to thrive in an uncertain world. Ledger understood that while the decision to move into Colihaut would require change, it also offered an opportunity to build upon the foundation his father had laid. It was about creating something new and vibrant while carrying forward the values of hard work, resilience, and community that had shaped his upbringing.

As the last slivers of sunlight faded and stars began to twinkle in the night sky, Ledger felt a sense of resolve building within him. This decision was not merely about the physical act of relocation; it symbolized a shift in perspective—a chance to innovate, adapt, and grow amidst uncertainty. By embracing the future, he could cultivate a legacy that honored his father's memory while providing his children with a bright and hopeful future.

He envisioned his father standing at the edge of the fields, an encouraging smile on his face, urging him to leap. The conversations they had shared about farming—about the importance of planting seeds, nurturing the soil, and patiently waiting for the rain—flashed through his mind. Each of those lessons resurfaced now, serving as a guiding light as he weighed the options before him.

The next morning, Ledger woke early, renewed by clarity and purpose. With the stars still shimmering in the sky, he crafted a plan. He would reach out to several farmers in Colihaut to discuss potential partnerships and opportunities to collaborate without fully committing to a permanent move just yet. He would also investigate grants and resources available for first-time farmers wanting to expand, ensuring they had a firm financial foundation.

As he drank his morning coffee, the aroma mingling with the brisk air of dawn, Ledger's thoughts shifted to his children. Their perspectives mattered in this decision, and he wanted them to feel involved and heard. He resolved to sit down with Eliza and Wizen and explain his ideas, asking for their input and thoughts on what they envisioned for their future. After all, this would be their home, too.

Armed with determination, Ledger took a moment to write down his key points, solidifying his thoughts before discussing them with Clara. He wanted her perspective, as her insights would be crucial in navigating this transition. More importantly, he felt the need for her support, as they needed to stand united in a decision that would affect their entire family.

When Clara joined him in the kitchen, he greeted her with a warm smile. "I've been thinking about the move to Colihaut and what it could mean for us," he began, pulling out his notes. "There are so many opportunities there for us to explore, but I want to balance that with the risks involved."

As he laid out his ideas, Clara listened intently, nodding along with his thoughts. Together, they weighed the pros and cons, focusing on how they could integrate their love for their current land with the potential of something new. As they talked, Ledger felt the weight of uncertainty lifts slightly; they were no longer alone on this journey but partners navigating the path together.

"Let's involve the kids in this," Clara suggested, her eyes sparkling. "They have a stake in it, too, and it could help them process everything that is happening. It is a big change, and we should do it as a family."

"Absolutely," Ledger replied, feeling the warmth of possibility spreading through him. "We can share our plans with Eliza and Wizen, get their input, and encourage them to think about what they want in their lives. This is not about us; it is about the legacy we are creating for them.

With a renewed sense of purpose and excitement, Ledger and Clara planned a family meeting for the next evening, eager to include their children in this pivotal moment. By acknowledging their feelings and dreams, Ledger hoped to create an atmosphere of unity and purpose—a shared vision of the future that honored their past while embracing the unknown.

As the day progressed, Ledger found himself buoyed by the potential ahead. They had much to consider, but they were ready to face the challenges together. The future remained uncertain, but as he looked out over their steadfast fields, he felt an unwavering commitment to nurture not only the land but also the love and strength that came from family.

At that moment, he understood that the essence of farming was not just about cultivation and harvest; it was about resilience, growth, and adaptation. With this realization, Ledger stepped forward into the unknown, prepared to navigate the risks and rewards that lay ahead, ever rooted in the values that had been passed down to him—an unwavering dedication to honor the past while striving to create a bright future for the generations to come.

The morning sun streamed through the kitchen window, casting a warm glow over Ledger as he stood by the sink, washing the remnants of breakfast ware. The rhythmic sound of running water offered a moment of peace amid the whirlwind of thoughts swirling in his mind. Today felt pivotal—a day when he could either retreat into comfort or embrace the uncertainty of change.

As he scrubbed a stubborn dish, Ledger's thoughts drifted back to his father, a man whose life had been a testament to dedication and hard work. He could almost hear his father's voice drifting through time, echoing lessons that had been etched into his heart.

"There are no shortcuts, Ledger. Every seed we plant requires care and effort."

These words resounded, grounding him as memories flooded his mind: long days spent working alongside his father in the fields, the smell of freshly tilled earth, and the satisfaction of a day's toil. He recalled how his father had shown him the significance of resilience—the way he had faced harsh seasons, bent but never broken. "We adapt; we overcome," his father would say, determination shining in his eyes.

A smile crept onto Ledger's face as he remembered the community gatherings—the laughter and camaraderie shared among neighbors on long summer evenings, the mutual support offered during harvest season when hands joined together to gather the fruits of their labor. This spirit of community was an integral part of who they were and formed the very fabric of the farming life he cherished.

Setting aside the last dish, Ledger leaned against the counter, letting these thoughts settle. It was clear: if he intended to guide his children through the potential turmoil of relocating and expanding their farm into Colihaut, he needed to embody the values his father had instilled in him.

These principles would be the cornerstones of their future—a guiding light through the uncertainty that lay ahead. He envisioned how these values would influence not only their farming practices but also their family's interactions with the new community they hoped to join.

With renewed conviction, he walked to the window and gazed outside at the fields that spread before him, shimmering in the morning light. The rows of crops were thriving, a testament to the hard work and care poured into each season. It was here, in this very place, that he had learned the importance of nurturing both the land and his family.

"I want to teach Eliza and Wizen what it means to work for something worthwhile," he murmured, his resolve deepening with every word. He envisioned the conversations they would have about the integrity of farming, instilling in them the same pride he felt when he put his hands in the soil, connected to the earth that had sustained generations.

As he prepared for the day, Ledger considered inviting his children out into the fields to help him. He could share the simple but profound joys of planting seeds, nurturing plants, and watching them grow. He wanted them to feel the richness of their heritage, the bond that came with understanding the trials and triumphs of farming life.

Taking a moment to gather his thoughts, Ledger felt a surge of commitment wash over him. Moving to Colihaut could be the genesis of an exciting chapter for their family, but it would be dangerous to embark on this journey without the solid foundation of values that had shaped him.

After dressing, he made his way toward his children's rooms, eager to wake them for their day's tasks. As he entered Eliza's room, he found her comically tangled in her blankets, her hair a wild mess of curls.

"Rise and shine, sleepyhead," he said with a chuckle, seating himself at the edge of her bed. "Today, we're going to spend some time in the fields."

Eliza blinked sleepily, hiding her face under her pillow for a moment before peeking out. "What are we doing there, Dad?" she asked, her curiosity piqued.

"We're going to plant some seeds," he replied, a feeling of anticipation swelling in his chest. "I want to show you how to care for the crops, just like Grandpa taught me. It is important work, and I want you to feel the meaning behind it."

"Can Wizen come too?" she asked, sitting up, her expression brightening.

"Of course," Ledger said, his heart swelling with pride. "The more, the merrier. This is something we will do together as a family."

Moments later, he gathered Wizen from his room, herding both children toward the back door, excitement evident in their eyes. Out in the sunshine, with the vast landscape before them, Ledger felt a renewed sense of purpose.

As they stepped into the golden light, he gathered his children close. "I want to talk about something important," he began, his voice steady but warm, as he knelt to meet their eyes. "This isn't just about planting seeds in the ground today; it's about lessons that come from the earth and the hard work that goes into growing those seeds."

Eliza and Wizen exchanged curious glances, their attention fully captured.

"This farm has been in our family for generations," he continued, gesturing toward the fields. "Your grandfather worked tirelessly to make it what it is today, teaching me that real success comes from effort, dedication, and resilience. It is about facing challenges head-on and never giving up, no matter how tough things get.

Wizen tilted his head, processing his words. "But why do we have to work so hard, Dad?" he asked, his youthful innocence shining through.

Ledger smiled softly, appreciating the question. "Hard work teaches us responsibility. It helps us understand what it takes to create something beautiful and meaningful. When we plant seeds today, it is not just about crops; it is about nurturing them, caring for them, and watching them grow. It is a journey, just like life."

Eliza's eyes sparkled with determination. "I want to grow the biggest tomatoes," she declared, her usual enthusiasm bubbling to the surface.

"And I want to grow herbs!" Wizen exclaimed, his face lighting up in excitement.

"That's the spirit!" Ledger chuckled, feeling the warmth of their enthusiasm inspired him further. "And while we are doing this, we will also think about how we can be part of our new community in Colihaut. Just like your grandfather did, we will help each other, learn from one another, and create connections. That is what makes us stronger."

Ledger stood up, motioning for them to follow him toward the rows of untouched earth, fresh and ready for planting. "So, let us make a deal. Today, we are planting not just seeds, but traditions. Together, we will honor the values that have brought our family this far: hard work, resilience, and the importance of community."

As they walked toward the field, the children nodded, filled with purpose. The sun was bright above them, and the day stretched wide with possibility.

After selecting seeds from the storage shed, Ledger showed Eliza and Wizen how to prepare the soil, their hands digging into the earth alongside his. They laughed and chatted, absorbing the lessons woven into the fabric of their activity. With each seed they planted, Ledger felt the bond among them deepen, a tangible connection enriched by shared experience.

Throughout the afternoon, as sweat dripped from their brows and the gentle winds rustled through the crops, Ledger repeatedly reflected on his father's timeless lessons. He encouraged the children to share what they envisioned for the future, prompting them to dream big and consider their roles in the journey ahead.

"We'll face challenges, but just like the crops," he urged, "we must be resilient. And remember, it is not just about being successful; it is about enjoying the process and growing together.

As the sun began to set, casting a warm golden hue over the farm, Ledger stood back to admire the small plot they had cultivated. Eliza and Wizen, tired yet exhilarated, looked up at him, their faces glowing with pride.

"Today was amazing, Dad," Eliza said, wiping her hands on her overalls.

"It was!" Wizen added enthusiastically, his eyes bright with excitement. "Can we do this again?"

"Every chance we get," Ledger promised, his heart swelling with hope for their shared future.

Together, they stood in that moment of quiet satisfaction—a family united, grounded in the values that would guide them through their next chapter. The farm was not just a piece of land; it was a legacy, and now, more than ever, Ledger was committed to honoring that legacy, moving forward with love, strength, and a determination to thrive.

The air was thick with the rich scent of earth and the sounds of laughter as Ledger parked his truck in the bustling town square of Colihaut. The first community gathering he was attending—a farmer's market—promised a blend of opportunity and social connection. He gripped the steering wheel for a moment, tension coiling in his chest. After the uncertainty of previous weeks, stepping into this new community felt both exhilarating and daunting.

As he stepped out of the truck, Ledger could see families mingling under a grove of vibrant tents. Farmers displayed their produce, showcasing an array of colorful vegetables, fragrant herbs, and homemade goods. The lively atmosphere was infectious, and he took a deep breath to embrace it.

As Ledger walked through the bustling market, he took in the vibrant sights and sounds that surrounded him: the laughter of children running between booths, the rhythmic chatter of vendors calling out to potential customers, and the rich aroma of fresh produce wafting through the air. The atmosphere was alive with energy, brimming with the promise of community connection and local flavor. He felt a sense of excitement pulse through him as he navigated the crowded pathways, eager to discover the myriad offerings that reflected the heart of this place.

His gaze was drawn to a booth laden with fresh heirloom tomatoes, their vibrant colors—deep reds, sunny yellows, and muted greens—catching his eye like jewels glistening in the afternoon sun. The temptation proved irresistible as he approached the stand, drawn by the bountiful display. A woman in her sixties, with silver-streaked hair and a welcoming smile, stood behind the booth, embodying the warmth of the community that Ledger sought to become a part of.

"Hi there! These look incredible," he said, genuine enthusiasm in his voice. "Where do you grow them?"

"Oh, thank you!" she replied, her face lighting up further at his compliment. "I grow them just a couple of miles down the road. It is the soil here perfect for tomatoes." She gestured to the rows of rich soil visible behind her booth, glowing under the mid-afternoon sun, its dark hue contrasting beautifully with the lush greens of the nearby plants. The vendor's pride in her produce was evident, and Ledger felt a spark of inspiration as he listened to her speak about the local agricultural practices.

The conversation flowed easily, allowing him to engage deeper with the community he aspired to be a part of. "Do you have any tips for growing them?" he asked, eager to soak up her knowledge. The vendor was more than happy to share her secrets, discussing the specifics of watering schedules, the benefits of companion planting, and the importance of compost. Each piece of advice felt like a building block for the future he envisioned, and Ledger could not help but imagine how fruitful collaboration with local farmers could be as he considered the possibilities for his own aspirations in Colihaut.

"I've heard that," Ledger replied, his tone hopeful as he stepped further into the conversation. "I am Ledger, by the way. I am considering moving my family here and expanding our farming operations." He introduced himself with a mix of excitement and nervousness, eager to see how the community would react to his aspirations.

The woman's eyes brightened at his words, and she leaned closer, her voice animated with enthusiasm. "Oh, you'll love it here!" she exclaimed, her genuine warmth radiating from her. "We are all about supporting one another. There is a real sense of community among us farmers. It is not just about selling; it is about sharing knowledge, too. As she spoke, Ledger felt a wave of relief washes over him, the initial apprehension he had felt about fitting into this new environment beginning to dissipate. The warmth and camaraderie she described were reassuring, painting a picture of the community he hoped to join and nurture.

Her enthusiasm ignited a flame of hope within him, a feeling that they might find a true home in Colihaut where their family could thrive alongside others. He imagined weekends spent swapping tips with neighbors, sharing crops at market stalls, and building friendships that would last through the years. "That's exactly what I'm looking for," he said, a smile breaking across his face. "We want to not only grow our farm but also connect with others who are passionate about what they do."

The vendor nodded enthusiastically, clearly pleased to hear his sentiments. "You are in for a treat. There are workshops and community events all year round. You will meet folks who have been farming here for generations, they have a wealth of knowledge! Plus, we always welcome new ideas and fresh perspectives." Ledger felt his heart race at the mention of community events and the opportunity to learn from seasoned farmers. Each revelation added to his sense of belonging, and he started to envision not just a farm, but a supportive network of friends and mentors who would lift one another up. With this newfound optimism, he felt more convinced than ever that Colihaut could be their next chapter, a canvas upon which they could paint their future.

"That's fantastic to hear," Ledger replied, his enthusiasm palpable. "I've been looking for ways to get involved and connect with the agricultural community." He felt a sense of relief wash over him as the conversation started to flow naturally, solidifying the connections he hoped to build.

Their discussion quickly deepened, encompassing a range of topics from crop rotation to pest management, each subject revealing the vendor's wealth of knowledge and experience. She spoke passionately about sustainable practices and the benefits of organic farming, sharing stories from her own successes and challenges. Ledger listened intently, scribbling down names and phone numbers, eager to follow up on her generous offers for guidance and introductions. With every new piece of information, his excitement built, transforming his initial hesitation into a fervent desire to immerse himself fully in this new chapter of their lives.

"You should come to the next farmer's cooperative meeting!" she suggested, her eyes alight with enthusiasm. "It is held every month at the community center, and you can meet all sorts of people. Everyone is eager to share experiences and best practices." The idea thrilled Ledger; it sounded exactly what he needed to jumpstart his integration into the community and learn from others who shared his passion for farming. "I would love to do that! When is it?" he asked eagerly.

As they continued talking, Ledger noticed another vendor setting up a booth beside them. The man, in his forties, overheard their conversation and joined in with a friendly smile. "Did I hear something about the farmer's cooperative meeting? That is a great way to get involved!" he chimed in, his voice warm and welcoming. Ledger felt a spark of excitement at the thought of meeting more people in this vibrant community. With each new connection, he felt the threads of belonging weave more tightly around him, reassuring him that he was on the right path. The possibility of forming friendships and collaborations in this tight-knit community was becoming not just a dream, but a tangible reality.

"You are thinking of moving to Colihaut? I cannot recommend it enough!" the man declared with excitement. "I am Ben, by the way. There is a great spirit here, especially among farmers. We look out for one another." His enthusiasm was infectious, and Ledger felt a strong sense of camaraderie as he reached out and shook Ben's hand firmly. The handshake was more than a greeting; it felt like a welcoming gesture steeped in understanding and shared experience.

"I'm Ledger," he introduced himself, a smile breaking across his face. "My family and I are excited about the potential here, but I'm still trying to navigate everything." Ledger's honesty allowed him to connect more deeply with Ben, who visibly comprehended the balancing act of moving a family and a livelihood.

Ben smiled knowingly, a twinkle lighting up his eye as he nodded in understanding. "It can be overwhelming at first," he reassured Ledger, "but believe me, once you are in, you are one of us. We have all had our struggles. Just last season, I faced a devastating blight, and the community rallied around to help. It meant the world." His words painted a vivid picture of resilience and solidarity that resonated deeply with Ledger. Hearing Ben's personal experience reminded him that every farmer had faced trials, and it was the community's support that often made the journey bearable.

As Ledger listened to the stories of mutual support and camaraderie, he felt a lifting of the weight he had been carrying since his father's passing. It was as if new roots were beginning to take hold, nurturing his spirit in ways he had not anticipated. The challenges ahead no longer seemed insurmountable; instead, they felt like shared experiences waiting to happen within a community that valued connection and compassion. Ledger left the booth with a new sense of belonging igniting in his heart, eager to forge ahead and become part of this remarkable tapestry of farmers who supported one another through thick and thin.

"That sounds incredible," Ledger replied, a sense of hope swelling within him. "It's reassuring to know we might find a network of support." He felt invigorated by Ben's words as if a bridge had been built between anxiety and possibility.

With Ben's encouragement, Ledger began moving from booth to booth, eager to absorb the stories and experiences of those he met. Each interaction deepened his understanding of the local agricultural landscape, and the warmth of shared laughter and camaraderie enveloped him like a comforting embrace. He learned about best practices in organic farming, the ins and outs of community-supported agriculture, and the importance of maintaining local traditions that had been passed down through generations. The more he listened, the more he felt inspired by the collective wisdom of the community, each tale a thread woven into the rich tapestry of Colihaut's farming heritage.

As days turned into weeks, Ledger attended more gatherings, including potlucks and seasonal festivals, immersing himself in the vibrant spirit of the community. He witnessed firsthand the vital role that the community played in shaping agricultural practices in Colihaut. Families would gather not only to celebrate their hard work but also to share challenges, brainstorming solutions together with an infectious energy that rippled through the crowd. The discussions flowed freely, often accompanied by hearty laughter, as members exchanged ideas and strategies to overcome obstacles they faced on their farms.

Each gathering felt like a celebration of resilience and interdependence, and Ledger was struck by how the community's strength stemmed from its unity. He began to envision his family at the heart of these connections, participating in monthly meetings and seasonal events. The prospect of not just growing crops but also nurturing relationships filled him with anticipation. Slowly but surely, he felt the foundations of a new home taking shape, reinforced by the understanding that they would not face their challenges alone. The sense of belonging he yearned for was no longer a distant dream, it was becoming a reality, fueled by the warmth and support of the people in Colihaut.

At a vibrant potluck, Ledger's senses were overwhelmed by the rich aroma of homemade dishes and local delicacies that filled the air. Every table overflowed with colorful plates, showcasing the best of what Colihaut had to offer. The atmosphere buzzed with laughter and chatter, creating a tapestry of sound that wrapped around him like a warm blanket. Ledger found himself seated at a table with several farmers, their faces glowing with enthusiasm as they traded stories about their crops, each tale a testament to their passion for the land.

"I have my best luck with winter squash," one farmer shared, his hands animated as he spoke. "It's a tough crop, but it pays off if you nurture it right!" He leaned in closer, eyes sparkling with excitement as he recounted the intricacies of caring for his squash plants throughout the changing seasons. It was clear he took immense pride in his work, and Ledger felt a familiar spark of motivation ignited within him.

"That's true!" chimed in another farmer, grinning broadly. "But I swear by my heirloom carrots. They take a bit longer to grow, but the flavor is unbeatable. You cannot find anything like them in the grocery stores!" His enthusiasm was infectious, and Ledger could not help but chuckle along with the group, admiring the camaraderie that encapsulated the table. Here, discussions about soil health transformed into shared laughter, and anecdotes about pests evolved into playful banter about gardening mishaps.

With each story shared Ledger felt more at home, a sense of belonging swelling in his chest. He appreciated the genuine enthusiasm these farmers exhibited, their passion deepening the connections forming in this friendly circle. For the first time in a long while, he sensed that he was not just an outsider looking in. He was becoming part of something larger, a vibrant community bound by shared experiences and a common love for the land they cultivated. This potluck was not just a meal; it was a celebration of their journey together, a reminder that they were all in this together, navigating the joys and challenges of farming side by side.

"It sounds like there's a real art to growing what works best here," Ledger remarked, his excitement bubbling to the surface. "I can't wait to delve in." The farmers nodded in agreement, their faces glowing with the same passion that ignited his enthusiasm. They understood the commitment and creativity required to cultivate their crops, and Ledger felt himself drawn even more deeply into their shared world of agriculture.

One of the farmers leaned forward, a twinkle in her eye that hinted at the insider knowledge she was eager to share. "You know, Ledger, if you're coming here to grow, you'd better be ready to try out the local crops," she said, her voice laced with enthusiasm. "You will not want to miss growing some of our special herbs. They are in high demand at the markets!" Her words piqued Ledger's interest, and he leaned closer, eager to absorb every detail she had to offer.

"Herbs?" he replied, his curiosity evident. "I would love to hear more about them. I have been thinking about diversifying our offerings." This idea resonated deeply within him. He had always believed in the importance of variety and knew that expanding beyond traditional crops could open new avenues for their farm. The prospect of growing locally sought-after herbs felt like a perfect fit for his vision.

The farmer smiled and launched into a passionate explanation of the specific herbs that thrived in Colihaut's climate—basil, thyme, and rosemary among them. She described not only the growing techniques but also the ways these herbs could be utilized in the kitchen, in artisanal markets, and even in local restaurants. As her words flowed, Ledger found himself envisioning vibrant greenery sprouting in his fields, connecting with customers who appreciated the fresh flavors of locally grown produce. The possibilities felt endless, and the more they spoke, the more he felt that he was not just entering a market but weaving himself into the fabric of this agricultural community.

"You'll find a bunch of unique varieties—everything from lemon balm to lavender," Farmer 1 shared enthusiastically. "They bloom beautifully and attract a lot of interest. Plus, it is a good way to experiment with new flavors!" Their eyes sparkled with delight as they spoke of the potential each herb held, from culinary applications to the fragrant allure they could offer at farmers' markets. Ledger nodded, envisioning the vibrant colors and delicate scents of these herbs thriving in his fields, further fueling his excitement.

As the sun began to set, casting a golden light across the gathered families, Ledger felt a profound sense of connection—not just as a newcomer, but as someone with a burgeoning place in the community. The warm hues of the sunset mirrored the warmth he felt radiating from those around him. It was a moment of realization that he was not just an outsider anymore; he was welcomed with open arms into a landscape rich with shared experiences and mutual support.

With a serious expression, Ledger turned to the group, wanting to express the depth of his gratitude. "I can't express how much this means to me and my family," he said earnestly. "Coming from where I did, I was worried about finding a place to belong. But hearing everyone's stories… it feels like there is a true spirit of collaboration here." Each word he spoke depicted the weight of fear he had carried, replacing now with hope and belonging.

The farmers smiled, their expressions warm and supportive, radiating the sense of community that defined Colihaut. They understood exactly how he felt, having navigated similar paths themselves. It was this shared understanding that fortified their bonds, and Ledger felt an overwhelming sense of gratitude wash over him. In that twilight glow, he sensed not just acceptance, but a growing connection that filled him with optimism about the journey ahead—one that he would embark on with new friends and allies by his side.

"That's exactly right," Claude chimed in, nodding his agreement. "We all have our struggles, and we are here to lift each other up. It is not just about farming; it is about rebuilding lives together, side by side. His words resonated deeply with Ledger, who sat back and absorbed the warmth and encouragement radiating from the group. It struck him how profound this sense of community could be, where the emphasis was not solely on crops but on relationships and support. He knew that his father would find solace and strength in this community, just as he was beginning to.

As the gathering continued, laughter and music mingled in the warm evening air, creating a joyful atmosphere that wrapped around everyone present. Ledger found himself swept up in the camaraderie, sharing in the collective joy that transcended the challenges they all faced. As the sun dipped lower, casting a rich purple hue over the horizon, he felt a tether forming between himself and the people of Colihaut—a connection that felt genuine and promising. He realized this was more than just an opportunity to grow crops; it was a chance to nurture meaningful relationships and build a life that honored the values he cherished most.

That night, as Ledger drove home, a smile spread across his face at the thought of sharing his newfound experiences with Clara and the kids. He envisioned their excitement about becoming part of this welcoming community, their laughter mingling with his as they dreamed about the farm and the friendships they would forge. Each turn of the road felt lighter, filled with hope and reassurance. He was not just bringing his family into a new home; he was leading them into a place brimming with possibilities, collaboration, support, and genuine connection. This was the very essence of what he had longed for in the wake of his father's passing, and the thought filled him with gratitude and anticipation for the future that awaited them all in Colihaut.

The golden rays of the late afternoon sun poured through the windows of Ledger's farmhouse, casting a warm glow over the rustic kitchen where he found himself deep in thought. He leaned against the counter, a steaming cup of coffee cradled between his hands, as he gazed out over the fields, the shadows stretching long and inviting as the day began to end.

Each filled row of crops held a story, and he felt a profound sense of responsibility to ensure that the legacy of the land—of their family—would endure for generations to come. He envisioned a future where the children would not only inherit land and crops but also an intricate tapestry of knowledge, traditions, and values that their grandfather had imparted to him.

What kind of legacy do I want to create for my children? Ledger pondered, the question swirling in his mind like the steam rising from his mug. The weight of the inquiry settled heavily on his shoulders, each thought intertwining with memories of his own upbringing. He envisioned his children navigating life, filled with challenges and opportunities, and he felt an overwhelming desire to ensure they had the tools to thrive.

With a sudden spark of inspiration, Ledger reached for his notebook, a trusted companion filled with past reflections and aspirations. Laying it on the counter, he opened the pages to a clean sheet, his pen poised and ready. He thought of the lessons his father had taught him—hard work, resilience, family unity—and how he could instill those same principles in his children. As he began to write, the words flowed easily, each one a promise to nurture these values within their family.

He considered the importance of hard work, recalling his father's hands calloused from labor but steady and sure in their guidance. Ledger wanted to teach his children that diligence and perseverance could open doors to a brighter future. The memory of family gatherings, where laughter echoed and stories were shared, reminded him of the power of unity. He envisioned creating traditions that would bring them together, instilling a sense of belonging and support that would last a lifetime.

As he filled the page, Ledger found himself contemplating the meaning of resilience, the strength to rise after each setback. He wanted his children to understand that failure was not the end but a steppingstone toward growth. Each challenge faced would be an opportunity to learn and adapt, forging their character and fortifying their resolve.

With each stroke of the pen, Ledger felt a renewed sense of purpose. This legacy he envisioned was not merely about imparting lessons but about creating an environment where his children could flourish, rooted in the values that had shaped him. And as he finalized his thoughts, Ledger realized that this was just the beginning of a journey—one where he would actively model these principles, guiding his children toward becoming the resilient, hardworking individuals he dreamed they would be.

Teach the Value of Hard Work—Ledger wrote down the first point, his pen was gliding smoothly across the page. Memories flooded back, taking him to the countless hours he had spent in the fields with his father, planting, harvesting, and sometimes weeding under the intense sun. Those were long, hot days, filled with sweat and determination, but they were also rich with lessons that transcended the physicality of the labor. He had learned that hard work was not about the toil; it was about commitment, the pride that arose from seeing a task completed, and the understanding that effort yields rewards. He wanted his children to grasp this fundamental truth, to recognize the intrinsic joy found in labor and the satisfaction that comes with a job well done.

As he continued to write, Ledger felt a surge of determination. I will involve them in every aspect of farm life, he thought, envisioning days spent in the fields alongside his children. From planting seeds to tending to animals, they would experience the rhythm of the seasons together, creating a bond through shared labor. He pictured them fanning out in the garden, hands in the soil, learning not just how to grow crops but also how to nurture patience and resilience. These lessons would be invaluable, equipping his children with a work ethic that would carry through in all aspects of their lives.

Ledger considered the beauty of watching his children take part in the harvesting process, the thrill of seeing the fruits of their labor materialize after days, weeks, and months of dedicated care. He wanted them to relish the feeling of gathering ripe vegetables, the sweet scent of fresh earth, and the sight of vibrant blooms dancing in the breeze. By actively engaging them in these tasks, he hoped they would cultivate a deeper appreciation for the land, understanding that every plant and animal requires care, discipline, and time to flourish.

He also envisioned family discussions around the dinner table, where they would reflect on their labor that day, what worked, what did not, and how to improve next time. These conversations would foster an environment of learning and growth, where mistakes were not failures but steppingstones toward success. Ledger was resolute in his mission to create a lineage built on these principles, where hard work becomes a cherished value, shaping his children into capable, confident individuals.

Share Stories of Family and History—Next, Ledger contemplated how crucial it was for Wizen, Petronel, Julien, Eliza, Louisa, James, Dfriel, Koie, and Nerisa to know not just about their grandfather's legacy but also the rich history of their family. He remembered how his father often shared stories from his own childhood, recounting the struggles and triumphs that had shaped their family's journey. Those tales had instilled a sense of pride and belonging in him, weaving a tapestry of identity that he cherished deeply. Ledger wanted nothing more than for his children to feel that same connection to their roots, to know that they were part of something larger than themselves, and to carry that legacy forward.

As he brainstormed how to incorporate storytelling into their lives, Ledger noted to himself, I could set aside time each week for family gatherings—a dedicated space to share these stories over dinner. He envisioned evenings filled with laughter and reflection, where tales of past generations would come alive around the table, fostering an appreciation for their lineage. He could already see his children's eyes lighting up with curiosity as they listened intently, hanging on every word about their grandparents' adventures and the lessons learned through hardship.

In addition to the verbal exchanges, Ledger also thought that we could even create a scrapbook or journal to preserve our family history. This would be a tangible way to keep their heritage alive, something they could revisit and cherish in years to come. Each page could be filled with photographs, handwritten stories, and reflections, creating a repository of memories that would spark conversations for generations. He envisioned a family project where each member contributed their own stories, even writing down their thoughts and feelings about what it meant to be a Philogene. This collective effort would not only preserve their history but also strengthen their bond as a family unit.

By encouraging his children to engage with their family's past, Ledger hoped to cultivate a sense of responsibility in them—an understanding that they are stewards of their legacy. As he scribbled down his thoughts, he felt a renewed commitment to ensuring that the lessons and stories of those who came before were not just echoes forgotten but vibrant parts of their everyday lives. This endeavor would serve as a foundation for his children's identities, instilling in them the importance of resilience, unity, and love as they continued their own journeys in the world.

Foster Bonds of Family—Ledger's thoughts turned to the importance of family bonds, reflecting on how vital it was to cultivate an environment where love, support, and understanding flourished among them. He recalled how his father had always emphasized the strength that came from family unity, often reminding him and his siblings to lean on one another in times of need. Those lessons had resonated deeply with him, shaping his understanding of what it meant to be part of a family. Ledger knew that nurturing these bonds would be essential in raising children who felt secure and cherished, who understood their value in the grand tapestry of their family's legacy.

We will have traditions, he scribbled down, feeling enthusiasm flow as he envisioned the possibilities. He imagined creating family farm days, when everyone would come together to tackle projects around the land, whether it was planting new crops or repairing fences. These days would be marked not just by hard work but also by shared laughter, storytelling, and an unspoken understanding of the importance of unity in achieving common goals. He could picture his children learning that teamwork was not just productive but incredibly fulfilling, forging connections that would last a lifetime.

In addition to work, Ledger thought about seasonal festivals—a chance to celebrate the fruits of their labor and the changing cycles of nature. Where we gather with friends and neighbors, he wrote, considering how these gatherings could become a cornerstone of their family life. Each season could usher in its own set of celebrations, from harvest festivals filled with delicious food, music, and dancing, to winter gatherings where they would cozy up around the fire, sharing warmth and stories. He wanted his children to see that togetherness was a source of strength and joy, a celebration of their collective journey through life.

He envisioned these traditions serving as threads that would weave the family closer together, providing a sense of continuity and belonging. Ledger wanted his children to grow up knowing that they could always rely on each other, no matter the challenges they faced outside their home. As he continued to sketch out his thoughts, he felt a swell of hope. By fostering these bonds and creating cherished memories, he could lay a foundation of love and resilience that would support his family through all of life's ups and downs, teaching his children the true value of togetherness.

Instill Resilience—Ledger understood the importance of resilience, especially in the context of farming, which was fraught with challenges. Whether it was a harsh season of drought or pests wreaking havoc on crops, farming demanded not only hard work but also the ability to adapt and persevere through adversity. He wanted his children to grasp that setbacks were an inevitable part of life, but it was their response to those challenges that defined their character and shaped their futures. He recalled moments from his own life when he had to dig deep, reminding himself that each failure was an opportunity for growth.

I need to teach them to embrace failure as a learning opportunity, he wrote fervently, envisioning a mindset he wanted to foster within his family. Ledger imagined days spent in the field discussing the difficulties they faced, not just as farmers but as individuals navigating life's complexities. Perhaps when a crop failed or a project did not turn out as expected, they could gather to analyze what went wrong. This would not only address the immediate issues but also cultivate a spirit of reflection and problem-solving, reinforcing the idea that setbacks were not the end, but rather steppingstones to success.

He also thought about how these discussions could extend beyond the farm. We can even have discussions about challenges they face at school or in life, he mused, aiming to create an open environment where his children felt comfortable sharing their own struggles. By using these moments as teachable lessons about resilience, he hoped to instill a sense of courage and determination in them. Whether it was dealing with bullying, academic pressure, or personal setbacks, Ledger wanted his children to know they could always confront challenges head-on.

Ledger envisioned a family culture where resilience was celebrated, and where failures were openly discussed without fear of judgment. He wanted them to understand that resilience was not about bouncing back but also about evolving in the process. As he penned these ideas on the page, he felt a sense of clarity and purpose; each lesson of resilience would equip his children with the tools they needed to navigate life's uncertainties. He hoped to empower them to face obstacles with grace and confidence, fostering a legacy of strength that would carry them through any hardship they encountered, both on the farm and beyond.

Encourage Community Involvement

Finally, Ledger felt an overwhelming sense of gratitude for the community in Colihaut—the friendships he had developed and the support he had encountered. He recognized that instilling the value of community in his children would be essential. They needed to understand the importance of working together and supporting others, just as their neighbors had rallied around him.

Community service projects, he thought, scribbling it down. *Let us volunteer as a family—whether it is helping at local events or contributing to local farms. Share our skills and support others. It will teach them empathy and connection.*

As Ledger looked at the list forming before him, a sense of purpose filled him. He felt invigorated by the vision unfolding on the page—a comprehensive path to forging a legacy that honored both their past and future.

That evening, after dinner, Ledger gathered the children in the living room. The ten of them settled into their cozy space, the flickering light of the fireplace casting a warm glow that made the atmosphere feel inviting and intimate. As the gentle crackle of the fire filled the room, Ledger felt a sense of anticipation rising within him.

"I have something important to share with you all," he began, an excited tone lacing his voice. Their eyes sparked with curiosity, each child leaning in just a little closer as they awaited his words. He could see the excitement building among them, amplifying his own enthusiasm for what he was about to unveil.

"What is it, Dad?" Petronel asked, tucking her legs beneath her and fixing her gaze on him, her palpable interest. Ledger smiled at her eagerness, feeling a swell of pride for each of his children, whom he regarded as the heartbeat of his aspirations.

"I've been thinking about how we can honor our family's legacy and what we want to pass down to you all," he continued, his voice filled with conviction. "I want to create a future where you not only inherit this land but also understand the stories, values, and lessons that come with it." He paused for a moment, allowing his words to sink in, watching as Wizen, Petronel, Julien, Eliza, James, Dfriel, Koie, and Nerisa leaned forward, intrigued.

Each of their faces reflected a mixture of curiosity and excitement. He knew this conversation was vital, not just for the future of their land but for the unity of their family. Ledger could sense that they were beginning to grasp the significance of what he proposed. This was about more than just farming; it was about cultivating a deeper connection to their heritage and fostering a sense of responsibility that would empower them as they grew. He envisioned weekends spent on the land, learning lessons from the earth, sharing stories around the fire, and building the bonds that would form the foundation of their family's legacy for generations to come.

Eliza's eyes brightened with curiosity. "What kind of stories, Dad? Like the ones about Grandpa?" she asked, her voice filled with eagerness. It was clear that the mention of their grandfather sparked a deep interest in her, and Ledger felt a wave of nostalgia wash over him, recalling the tales his father had shared with him.

"Exactly!" Ledger replied enthusiastically. "Your grandfather had so many experiences to share about working the land, about facing challenges, and how to never give up. You need to know those stories—to understand the hard work and resilience that built our family. He leaned forward, hoping to convey the gravity of these lessons, as he watched the children absorb his words. He wanted them to appreciate how their heritage was woven into the very fabric of the land they would inherit.

Wizen, however, furrowed his brow slightly, a hint of worry crossing his face. "But what if we don't like farming as much as you do?" he asked, his honesty reflecting a genuine concern. The question hung in the air, and Ledger admired his son's bravery in voicing his feelings.

Ledger smiled warmly, appreciating Wizen's candor. He put a reassuring hand on his son's shoulder, affirming the importance of his thoughts. "That is okay, Wizen. It is perfectly fine if you find your passions elsewhere," he replied gently. "What matters is that you will carry forward the lessons of hard work, perseverance, and the importance of community—no matter what path you choose. Our family values are not about farming; they are about facing life with courage and supporting each other, wherever that journey may lead. He hoped his words would ease Wizen's worries, reminding him that their family legacy was not confined to one pursuit but rather a way of living and loving together.

"That's okay!" Ledger reassured them, his tone warm and understanding. "It is not just about farming. It is about learning the value of hard work in whatever you choose to do. Whether it is in school, sports, or your future jobs, those lessons stay with you." He could see how his words resonated, and it encouraged him to share even more with his children about his vision for their future.

He glanced around the room, taking in the eager faces surrounding him, and a deep sense of responsibility washed over him. He wanted to instill a sense of belonging and connection, not just to the land but to their family history. "And I want you both to feel bonded to this land, to your roots," he continued, his voice steady with conviction. "I plan to set aside time each week for us to work together on the farm—planting, harvesting, just being outside. It is going to be a way for us to connect, learn from each other, and create our own stories.

As he spoke, he was aware of their initial curiosity blossoming into engagement. He could feel their excitement bubbling up as they envisioned the shared experiences that awaited them, the laughter, and challenges they would face together on the farm. This was more than just a task; it was a chance to weave their own memories into the fabric of the family legacy.

"I want us to create traditions that will bring us together," Ledger added, picturing weekends filled with planting seeds, the joy of harvesting together, and evenings spent recounting the stories of their day. "No matter where life takes you, these moments will be a part of who you are." His heart swelled at the thought, and he hoped that they would embrace the adventure ahead with open hearts, knowing they were not just inheriting land, but also the spirit of perseverance and connection.

Eliza's eyes widened with excitement, shining brightly in the warm glow of the fireplace. "Can we grow some new plants?" she asked eagerly. "Like those cool herbs from the market?" Her enthusiasm was contagious, and Ledger felt a smile spreading across his face as he envisioned the possibilities that lay ahead.

"Absolutely!" he replied, matching her excitement. "We can experiment with growing new herbs and vegetables. And we will document everything we do, even create a scrapbook of our journey together. What do you think?" The idea of capturing their experiences in a scrapbook thrilled him, and he hoped it would serve as a tangible reminder of the time they spent cultivating both the land and their family bonds.

Wizen's face lit up with a broad grin. "That sounds fun! We could draw pictures of all the plants we grow!" he suggested, his imagination clearly running wild with ideas. Ledger could almost picture the pages filled with colorful sketches, each drawing accompanied by a story that highlighted their adventures and discoveries. This project would not only be educational but also a creative outlet for his children to express themselves.

"Exactly!" Ledger replied, his heart swelling with pride. "Every plant we grow will tell a story. And beyond that, I want to establish traditions—like family dinners after harvests, where we sit together and share our best memories of the season." He loved the thought of gathering around the table, the fruits of their labor in front of them, as they reflected on the moments they cherished and looked forward to.

As he spoke, he could see the excitement building in their eyes, and it filled him with joy. These were not just plans for crops; they were seeds of connection, creativity, and shared experiences that would help cultivate a strong family legacy. Ledger felt a profound sense of fulfillment, knowing he was not only nurturing the land but also nurturing the hearts and minds of his children, creating a foundation for their future that was rich with love and shared stories.

"I also want us to be part of the community here," Ledger continued, feeling the passion for his vision pouring out of him. "We can volunteer together, help at local events, and build friendships with our neighbors. It is important to support one another—you will see how powerful that can be." He could already envision the connections they would forge, the shared efforts that would draw them closer to the people around them.

Eliza nodded vigorously, her enthusiasm radiating from her. "I like that! It sounds like we will be busy, but it will be a lot of fun if we do it together. The thought of being actively involved energized her. Ledger smiled, recognizing her eagerness and the way it mirrored his own passion for building ties within the community.

Wizen jumped in, clearly excited by the idea. "Yeah! And we can invite friends over to help too." His suggestion opened a new avenue of possibility in Ledger's mind, envisioning their friends laughing and playing alongside them as they cultivated the land, creating memories that would last a lifetime.

Ledger grinned wide, feeling a sense of fulfillment beyond measure. "Exactly! This is about more than just us. It is about creating a legacy that fills not just our lives but the lives of those around us. A legacy of hard work, love, and community." His voice was imbued with conviction, and he could see the spark ignite in his children's eyes as they grasped the bigger picture.

The fire crackled in the background, sending pops and crackles into the air, adding to the cozy ambiance of their discussion. Ledger felt an immense wave of hope wash over him, knowing that the seeds of a family legacy were beginning to take root in their hearts. The room felt alive with warmth and connection, rich with the promise of shared experiences and fulfilled dreams. He could see now that this vision was not only a way to honor the past but also a pathway to a vibrant future—one that was bound to be filled with possibilities, laughter, and the unshakeable bond of family and community.

"So, what do you say? Are you in?" Ledger asked, his heart thumping with anticipation. He scanned the eager faces of his children, hoping to see their excitement reflected on him. Eliza and Wizen exchanged enthusiastic glances that spoke volumes, and within moments, they both nodded energetically.

"We're definitely in!" Eliza exclaimed, her face lighting up with happiness. The enthusiasm in her voice was infectious, stirring a sense of pride within Ledger as he realized how fully they were embracing this vision.

"Let's make our own stories!" Wizen added, his grin wide and full of determination. It was clear that they were not just ready to join him on this journey; they were eager to contribute their own chapters to the family legacy that he had begun to outline for them.

With their resounding agreement, Ledger felt a deep sense of fulfillment settle inside him, a soothing balm that chased away any lingering doubts he had. He knew that this journey was just beginning, but together, they would cultivate not only crops but also an enduring legacy that would thrive for generations to come. It would be a legacy rooted in their family's history, where the hard work and love of those who came before them blended seamlessly with their aspirations for the future.

As he looked into the eyes of his children, Ledger felt a sense of purpose wash over him. They were embarking on an adventure filled with shared experiences, valuable lessons, and the happiness that comes from working side by side. Together, they would forge memories that would tie them to the land, to one another, and to the community that welcomed them with open arms. It was more than just a journey; it was the foundation of a life grounded in growth, connection, and a commitment to honor their roots while bravely reaching for the future.

The sun began to sink below the horizon, painting the sky in a beautiful palette of oranges and purples. Ledger stood outside the farmhouse, his hands tucked deep into the pockets of his worn jeans as he stared out across the fields. Each gentle breeze carried whispers of change, rustling the leaves of the nearby trees and sending a shiver of uncertainty through his heart.

The crossroads loomed before him—expanding their agricultural efforts into Colihaut was a decision weighed down with both promise and peril. Ledger's gaze roamed over the familiar landscape that had been his home for so long. Each furrow in the earth told a story, each patch of crops whispered memories of laughter and toil, of shared meals and long nights spent under the stars with his father.

What would it mean to leave this place? He mused, his heart heavy with the burden of that question.

With every passing day, the allure of new opportunities in Colihaut seemed to grow stronger. He had already witnessed how welcoming the community was, eager to share knowledge and resources, a stark contrast to the isolation he sometimes felt in his current position. The prospect of diversifying their crops, engaging in educational programs, and creating lasting connections filled him with excitement. Yet, the thought of uprooting his family from the land that was steeped in his father's legacy weighed heavily on him.

With a sigh, Ledger stepped inside the dimly lit kitchen, his sanctuary of sorts. The scent of his coffee lingered, mingling with the rich aroma of the earth that clung to his clothes. He pulled out a chair at the worn wooden table, resting his elbows on its surface as he stared at the half-finished notebook that detailed plans for their move—loose ideas and sketches for the farm in Colihaut hastily jotted down in the margins.

Economic stability, he reminded himself. The vision of what a successful expansion could mean for his family flickered in his mind. It held the promise of income flowing in from a diverse array of crops— vibrant tomatoes, fragrant herbs, and even a few specialty plants that could attract new customers. This could mean savings for their future, for education, for experiences that would enrich the lives of their nine children.

Yet, as he revisited these thoughts, the weight of the familiar tugged at him harder. The trees that lined the boundary of his land bore witness to years of family gatherings, of his children playing and exploring. His heart ached at the thought of leaving behind the memories that were intertwined with every inch of this place.

What about the emotional burden? He pondered, thinking of Clara, and the children. The move would require adaptation—not just for him but for his entire family. Would they mourn the loss of their familiar landscape, the childhood memories rooted in their home? Would it strain their bonds as they navigated this new life together?

He recalled his children's joy over the farm they had shared—their anticipation at planting seeds, cultivating their own little corner of the world, and creating memories intertwined with their family's legacy. How could he take that away from them?

With urgency, Ledger moved from the kitchen to the living room, pacing back and forth to channel the restlessness lodged within him. He thought about meeting with the families in Colihaut, the strength of their community pulling him in, presenting a chance to create something vibrant and new. Yet would that be at the cost of what made his family uniquely theirs?

The road ahead was murky, and as he stood at this metaphorical crossroads, mixing anticipation with trepidation, he felt the weight of the choices hanging heavily in the air.

He plopped down onto the worn couch, running a hand over his face, contemplating how he had arrived at this juncture. The decision did not just involve him but the legacy he created for his children. How would they perceive the move? Would it be an adventure, or would it be seen as a loss?

Closing his eyes, Ledger poured over the myriad of possibilities that danced before him, each one vivid and enticing. The first option was to expand in Colihaut, a vision filled with promise. The allure of economic growth beckoned him, alongside the potential for new connections and a sustainable future. He could envision the vibrant crops he would plant, leading to new customers who would appreciate the fruits of his labor. The thought of forging strong community bonds filled him with hope; neighbors would come together in times of need, providing support during challenging days and celebrating successes in brighter ones. The very idea of planting roots in a place that seemed so welcoming and full of opportunity excited him beyond measure.

On the other hand, there was the option to stay where they were—a choice steeped in familiarity and comfort. He felt a deep-rooted connection to the land that had shaped his family's history and, in many ways, defined his own identity. This choice would honor his father's legacy, maintaining the traditions that had been passed down through generations. Yet, as he contemplated the weight of this decision, he could not shake the nagging fear of stagnation. Remaining in this familiar cycle might mean trapping himself and his family in a routine that offered little in terms of growth or adventure.

The contrast between these two paths was stark, each holding its own set of risks and rewards. Staying meant clinging to the past but potentially sacrificing future opportunities. Expanding to Colihaut represented change, opportunity, and the chance to craft a new legacy, but it also came with the uncertainty and challenges that all new beginnings entail. Ledger felt the weight of this decision press heavily upon him, knowing that whichever path they chose would shape the course of their lives for years to come.

As he opened his eyes, Ledger resolved to consider not just the benefits of each choice but also the values he wanted to instill in his children—the importance of growth, community, and resilience. He knew he had to align his decision with the legacy he wished to create, one that honored the past while embracing the future. With his family's support and their shared dreams, he felt ready to navigate the complexities of this choice, believing that the right path would reveal itself in time.

As he mulled over these choices, Ledger felt the tides of uncertainty pulling at him, a gentle yet persistent wave that threatened to overwhelm him. Each option had its merits, yet each had its own shadows lurking beneath the surface.

What if the move did not yield the opportunities for which I am hoping?' he thought, anxiety creeping into his consciousness. The risk of failure loomed large, and he could easily envision the challenges of adapting to a new environment, new neighbors, and new expectations. What if the community was not as welcoming as it seemed, or if their crop yields did not meet his family's needs?

At the same time, the notion of staying felt equally daunting. There was comfort in familiarity, yes, but there was also a sense of stagnation—economic pressures that pressed down harder with each passing season. Ledger could feel the weight of his father's expectations resting on his shoulders, the silent urgency to keep the family legacy alive and flourishing amid the creeping vines of doubt.

The night sky began to blanket the farm, stars twinkling above like distant memories waiting to be recalled. Ledger stepped outside again, feeling the cool night air on his skin, grounding him. He glanced up, letting the vastness of the universe wash over him.

What would my father want? He asked himself, envisioning the reassuring smile and wise eyes of the man who had taught him the values of hard work, resilience, and perseverance. He remembered the countless nights spent on the porch, listening to his father's stories of challenges faced and overcome, leaving behind what was comfortable to seek something greater.

"Don't be afraid to take risks, Ledger," he could hear his father say. *"Sometimes the most rewarding paths are the ones that scare you the most."*

With that guiding thought, Ledger began to see the equation of his choice in a new light. It was not merely about the risks involved in moving to Colihaut or the comfort of staying where they were. This was an opportunity to grow—not just crops, but as a family. The decision embodied the very essence of resilience his father spoke of embracing uncertainty for the chance at something better.

Returning inside, Ledger felt a renewed sense of clarity. Spreading out the notes he had jotted down, he began to formulate a plan that melded both aspects of his contemplation.

What if we could start small in Colihaut? he mused. They could test the waters. They could establish a few partnerships with local farmers and gradually expand their crops, mitigating some of the risks. He could take the time to ensure that his family felt comfortable with the change before fully committing to it.

The idea glimmered to life in his mind like the stars outside. Ledger could see a path forward that honored his father's legacy while also forging new beginnings for Eliza and Wizen. It was about creating a bridge between the past and the future, merging their rich history with the opportunities that a new place could offer.

I will involve Clara in these discussions, he thought, a sense of comfort in knowing she could provide input on their family's direction. *We will approach this together, as a team, and make sure everyone is on board.*

As he finally settled into bed that night, Ledger felt a newfound resolve settling in his chest. The choices before him were daunting, but he recognized they were also ripe with potential. With his family by his side, he could navigate these uncharted waters and create a legacy that encompassed both the past and the future, an enduring testament to their journey as a family rooted in love, resilience, and the spirit of farming.

The kitchen buzzed with a familiar warmth as the rich aroma of Clara's hearty stew filled the air, wrapping the room in a comforting embrace. Ledger leaned against the counter, stealing glances at his wife as she sliced fresh bread with deft, rhythmic movements. Her hands worked skillfully, the sharp knife gliding through the crust with ease, and Ledger could not help but admire the way she turned simple ingredients into something nourishing and delicious. The clatter of dishes and the joyful laughter of the children echoed from the dining room, a symphony of sounds that created an atmosphere brimming with life and happiness.

But today felt different—the air was thick with anticipation, and important decisions loomed on the horizon. Ledger gazed out the window for a moment, watching the sun begin to set over the land they cherished so deeply. It was a beautiful sight, one that reminded him of the heritage they were nurturing together. Yet, he knew it was time to engage his family in the discussion about their future. The weight of choices ahead pressed on him, possibilities unfolding like the steam rising from the pot on the stove.

He could sense the excitement and energy in the house, and he knew that involving Clara and the kids in these discussions would strengthen their bonds and ensure that everyone felt a part of the journey. It was not about him making decisions alone; it was about weaving together their collective hopes and dreams. With every shared conversation, he felt they were crafting a family narrative that would shape their shared destiny.

As the stew simmered and the bread toasted, Ledger took a deep breath, steeling himself for the conversation. He wanted to invite his family into a dialogue that had implications for them all—a dialogue about their roots and the direction they would take. With a determined heart, he envisioned gathering everyone around the dinner table that evening, not just to enjoy Clara's meal but also to collectively dream and strategize about the future they would build together. This was a moment ripe for connection, and in the intimacy of their home, Ledger felt hopeful about the discussions that lay ahead.

"Hey, everyone! Can we gather around the table for a bit?" Ledger called, clearing his throat to gain their attention. "I'd like to chat about something important." He watched Wizen, Petronel, Julien, Eliza, Louisa, James, Dfriel, Koie, and Nerisa exchanged curious glances, their playful chatter quieting as they shuffled into the kitchen. Clara looked up from her work, an inquisitive smile spreading across her face, sensing the seriousness in his tone.

The children settled into their usual seats, the table suddenly buzzing with a mix of curiosity and warmth. Ledger took his place at the head of the table, feeling a blend of excitement and nervousness twist in his stomach. This was a moment steeped in significance—one that could shape the future of their family in ways he was just beginning to comprehend. As he looked around at the familiar faces of his loved ones, a deep sense of gratitude washed over him. They were a team, a unit that thrived on trust and love, and now, they would collectively navigate this pivotal moment.

"What's on your mind, Ledger?" Clara asked, her gentle demeanor providing the encouragement he needed to speak. The question hung in the air, heightened by the anticipation of their gathered family. He appreciated how she always created a space for open dialogue; her support reassured him as he prepared to unveil the thoughts dancing in his head.

Taking a moment to collect his thoughts, Ledger glanced around the table once more, absorbing the energy in the room, the laughter, the eyes filled with expectation, and the love that connected them all. "I've been thinking a lot lately about our future and the paths we might take," he began, feeling the weight of his responsibility as the words flowed from his heart. "There are some opportunities on the horizon, and I want us to explore them together—as a family."

As he spoke, Ledger noticed the intrigue grow in the children's expressions, each of them leaning in slightly closer, eager to hear what he had to say. He realized that this conversation was not just about decisions but about inviting them into a journey filled with possibility and connection. This was their moment to share dreams, ideas, and concerns, and Ledger felt a surge of hope building within him.

Taking a deep breath, Ledger felt the weight of his thoughts settle in as he prepared to share his vision. "I've been thinking a lot about our farming future lately, especially after meeting with the folks in Colihaut," he began, scanning the expectant faces around the table. "There are some opportunities to expand our agricultural efforts there, but it comes with big changes—and I want us to discuss it as a family." He paused, letting the gravity of his words sink in, and he could sense the children leaning in, their interest piqued. Clara's supportive nod gave him the confidence to continue.

"What kinds of changes?" Wizen asked, his curiosity evident, while Eliza's brow furrowed in thought. The atmosphere in the room shifted, charged with a mixture of excitement and apprehension. Ledger appreciated their willingness to engage in this important conversation, and he knew he had to be clear about the potential implications of his proposal.

"Do you mean moving to Colihaut?" Eliza asked, her voice filled with both hope and uncertainty. She had a way of cutting straight to the heart of things, and Ledger admired her ability to articulate the question that was on everyone's mind.

"Yes," he replied, feeling both exhilarated and anxious. "I mean considering the possibility of moving our farming operations to Colihaut, where we could take advantage of new land and opportunities for growth." As he spoke, Ledger could see the gears turning in their heads. He continued, wanting them to understand the full scope of what such a move could entail. "It could mean better crops, a chance to connect with a new community, and the potential for our family to thrive in ways we have not yet imagined. But it would also mean leaving behind what we have known, our home."

The room fell silent for a moment as the weight of his words hung in the air. Each family member processed the idea in their way, and Ledger felt a mixture of pride and fear as he laid it all on the line. He wanted to hear their thoughts, their hopes, and their worries, knowing that they were all in this together. This conversation was just the beginning, but it was a critical step toward a shared future, one that needed the voices of all its members.

"Not necessarily moving," Ledger clarified, sensing the need to ease the tension that had settled over the table. "But possibly expanding our operations there." He paused, looking into the curious eyes of his family. "I want to hear your hopes and concerns about it, so we can make a decision together." His voice was steady, but inside, he felt a mix of vulnerability and hope. This was a chance for all of them to be part of something bigger, deepening their bonds as a family.

There was a moment of silence as everyone considered the implications of his words. The weight of the conversation hung in the air, and Ledger could see the wheels turning in their minds. He smiled to himself, feeling an overwhelming sense of gratitude for having them by his side. This was what family was all about supporting one another through uncertainties and navigating challenges together.

"What would expanding even mean?" Wizen asked, his brow furrowed in concentration as he sought clarity. His question reflected the genuine curiosity Ledger admired in his son, and it opened the door for deeper exploration of the idea.

"It could mean planting new crops, using different farming techniques, or even diversifying what we grow," Ledger explained, growing more animated as he spoke. "We might work with local farmers in Colihaut to learn from their experiences, tap into new markets, or explore selling directly to customers in nearby towns. It is about finding ways to enhance what we already do, while also challenging ourselves to grow beyond our current capacity. He could see Wizen pondering this, and Ledger sensed that his son was already imagining the possibilities.

He continued, "But it also means considering how that might change our daily lives. It could require some travel to Colihaut, longer work hours during certain seasons, and potentially new relationships to build. I want you all to think about how you feel about those changes." Ledger paused, inviting them to share their thoughts and feelings about the prospect of expanding their farming efforts. He wanted them to feel invested in the future, understanding that their voices would shape the direction they would take as a family.

"It could mean new crops—different types, even herbs and vegetables we haven't tried before," Ledger shared, his enthusiasm growing as he painted a vivid picture. "There's a strong community there, and they're very supportive of new farmers." He could already envision the lush greenery of thriving plants, the vibrant colors of fresh produce, and the enriching relationships that could form in this new environment. The idea sparked excitement in him, and he hoped to share that energy with his family.

Clara listened thoughtfully, processing the possibilities with her typical grounding presence. "That does sound promising," she said slowly, "but what about our home here?" Her question was important; it reminded Ledger of the roots they had planted in their current location and the legacy they had built together as a family. He appreciated her perspective and the way she balanced his ambition with the reality of their situation.

"That's what I'd like to discuss," Ledger replied, meeting her gaze with determination. "I think we could test things out slowly—start with just a few crops in Colihaut, see how it goes before making any big decisions. We do not have to rush into anything." His tone was reassuring, hoping to alleviate any anxieties floating in the air. He wanted them to understand that this was not about abandoning their home but rather exploring new possibilities while still honoring their roots.

"The idea is to experiment and learn," Ledger continued, feeling the atmosphere shift slightly as his family mulled over his suggestion. "We can analyze what works and what does not without disrupting

274

the stability we have here. It could even enhance what we already do. If we discover new crops that thrive, it might bring us more resources and flexibility." He paused, giving them a moment to process the idea, his heart lining with hope that they would see the potential of this endeavor.

"Maybe we could even bring some of those experiences back here and enhance our methods," he added, trying to connect the two locations in their minds. He hoped this approach would frame their conversation and inspire his family to share their feelings and ideas freely, creating a collaborative spirit around their future.

Eliza nodded, her eyes lighting up with possibilities as she imagined the vibrant colors of new crops. "Could we grow the heirloom tomatoes like the ones at the market?" she asked eagerly. "They looked amazing!" Her enthusiasm was infectious, and Ledger could not help but smile. He could picture those luscious tomatoes ripening in the sun, ready to be shared at family meals or sold at the local market, and it filled him with excitement.

"Absolutely!" Ledger replied, his voice was bright with affirmation. "And we could incorporate what we learn from the farmers there into our own practices here. There is so much we could gain from this experience." He felt a surge of optimism as he thought about blending the old with the new, enriching their current approach to farming while embracing the wisdom that might come from fresh perspectives.

However, Wizen furrowed his brow, clearly deep in thought as he weighed the implications of their discussion. "But what if we do not like it? What if we miss our friends and this place?" he voiced, concern knitting his features. Ledger met his son's gaze, sensing the weight of that question and the vulnerability it carried. It was important for him to validate those feelings, recognizing that the prospect of change often brought uncertainty and anxiety.

"I understand, Wizen," Ledger said gently, leaning forward slightly as he spoke. "It is completely normal to feel that way. Our friends and the memories we have built here are important, and it is okay to be worried about leaving those behind. He wanted his son to know that he was not alone in these feelings; change can be daunting for anyone, especially for a child who has known a certain environment for so long.

"What I hope we can do is keep our roots here while exploring the possibilities in Colihaut. We do not have to sever ties; we can find ways to stay connected with our friends and community here. Perhaps even inviting them to visit us on our new adventure!" He offered this thought, hoping to inspire a sense of continuity rather than loss. Ledger had faith that their family could thrive together, no matter where their journey led them.

"That's a real fear, Wizen," Ledger acknowledged, nodding in understanding. "Change can be hard. If we do decide to expand, we will make sure to keep strong connections with our friends here and stay involved in our community. We would not just leave everything behind—we would take our roots with us." He wanted his son to know that their past and present were intertwined, and no matter what lay ahead, they could carry their memories and relationships forward.

Clara chimed in, reinforcing Ledger's words with her soothing presence. "And it is essential that we make this decision together as a family, so everyone feels heard. We can set up times to talk about how everyone is feeling whether we are in Colihaut or here." Her emphasis on inclusivity resonated deeply with Ledger. It was vital for each family member to have a voice in this journey, fostering a sense of unity and shared purpose.

Wizen, the eldest, and Eliza exchanged glances, sensing the shift in the atmosphere as the tension began to lessen. Petronel leaned in, her curiosity piqued, while Julien tapped his fingers on the table in thought. Louisa smiled encouragingly at Eliza, and James nodded in agreement, eager to weigh in. Dfriel, Koie, and Nerisa listened attentively, their expressions brightening as the conversation unfolded. Ledger noticed the warmth returning to their faces, and he felt a surge of hope at how necessary this open dialogue was. It was not about farming or moving; it was about honoring their family dynamic and ensuring that every voice was contributing to shaping their future. Together, they could build a path forward that reflected not just his aspirations, but those of the whole family.

"We're all in this together," Ledger reiterated, glancing around the table at the faces he loved most. "Every opinion matters, and it's these conversations that will help us make the best choice for all of us." He felt reassured knowing they could navigate these uncertainties collaboratively, and the prospect of involving everyone in the decision-making process only strengthened his determination. As they continued to discuss their hopes and concerns, Ledger envisioned a future that could blend the best of both worlds, rooting their family firmly in the community while exploring new growth opportunities.

"Can we also explore what it's like to live in Colihaut?" Eliza suggested, her eyes sparkling with enthusiasm. "Maybe we could visit during one of the markets!" The idea of experiencing the vibrant community firsthand seemed to resonate with everyone, and Ledger felt a spark of excitement at the thought.

"Yeah! It would be fun to see what their farms look like!" Wizen added, his expression brightening as he considered the possibilities. The idea of visiting Colihaut was gaining momentum, and Ledger could not help but smile at their eagerness. It was heartening to see his children engage so positively, their curiosity igniting new energy in the conversation.

"That's a great idea!" Ledger exclaimed, feeling a swell of pride in their collective vision. "Let us plan a visit soon. We will explore the area, meet some of the farmers, and really get a feel for the community." He could already imagine the family walking through the bustling market, vibrant stalls brimming with fresh produce, and the camaraderie between local farmers. It was a perfect opportunity to connect with potential new neighbors and gain insights that could inform their decisions.

As they discussed the details—scheduling the visit and what they might want to see— the conversation flourished, ideas flying back and forth like a lively game of catch. They talked about what crops they hoped to discover, what kinds of products might be unique to Colihaut, and even how they could document their experience to share with the rest of the family later. Ledger felt a sense of relief and excitement as he witnessed the way they united over this common goal. This was not about farming; it was about building memories together, exploring new horizons, and cultivating their bond as a family.

In that moment, Ledger knew they were taking an important step—not just toward exploring new agricultural opportunities, but also toward deepening their connection as a family. The thought of embarking on this journey together filled him with hope, and he could sense that they were all ready to embrace whatever came next.

As they finished dinner, laughter filled the space, and Ledger felt a deep contentment. The discussions had helped forge a shared purpose, allowing each family member to voice their hopes and concerns while ensuring that everyone felt invested in the direction they chose to take.

That night, as he tucked Koie into bed, he reflected on how significant this moment had been. Involving Clara and their children had strengthened their family bonds and illuminated a path where hope, understanding, and unity flourished.

With a sense of clarity wrapping around him like a warm blanket, he knew that whatever decision they made, they would face it together, united as a family—ready to embrace the challenges and joys that lay ahead.

As the night deepened, the soft glow of the table lamp cast comforting shadows around the room. Ledger sat with Clara on the couch, their hands intertwined, their hearts full after the heartfelt discussions with Wizen, Petronel, Julien, Eliza, Louisa, James, Dfriel, Koie, and Nerisa. The children had retreated to their rooms, buzzing with excitement over their upcoming plans, leaving Ledger and Clara in a quiet moment of reflection.

Clara turned to him, her voice gentle. "It is a big decision, isn't it? The possibility of expanding into Colihaut could change everything."

Ledger nodded, his mind still circling back to the various choices that lay ahead. He took a deep breath, savoring the musty warmth of the familiar farmhouse. It is big—and daunting. But the more I think about it, the more I realize that every path we take is filled with uncertainty. *Clara squeezed his hand, encouraging him to share more.*

I have always been afraid of the unknown. It is natural, given how much my father valued stability. But it is time I embraced that uncertainty instead of letting it paralyze me. *Clara's eyes sparkled with understanding.* Do you mean how he taught you to approach challenges?

Exactly! Dad faced so many uncertainties, whether it was farming through storms or dealing with setbacks. He always found a way to navigate them. That is the legacy I want to carry forward, taking calculated risks and trusting my instincts.

He leaned back against the couch, his thoughts swirling with the possibilities before him.

The idea of expanding is not about farming; it represents a leap into the future, into something new. I want to explore those risks, with my family beside me cheering me on.

Clara tilted her head thoughtfully, her expression shifting to one of pride.

That is a beautiful way to honor your father's memory. Taking those risks could lead to something wonderful for all of us.

Ledger felt a surge of gratitude for Clara's support. She had always been his rock, grounding him when uncertainty weighed heavily on his shoulders.

I want to step into the unknown but with all of us involved. We can do our research, meet new people, and test the waters together. If something does not work out, we will adapt.

With every word, he felt more resolute. His father's guiding presence enveloped him like a warm embrace, instilling confidence that the journey would not be faced alone.

We can gather feedback from the children, Clara remarked too. Their voices matter in this decision, and their enthusiasm could make a world of difference.

Ledger smiled, the thought brightening his heart. Involving everyone had already sparked excitement; it was the way forward.

Yes! And we can honor our roots while exploring new branches. It is about balance—keeping what makes us whole while allowing room for growth.

He stood up and moved to the window, looking out at the vast expanse of their fields bathed in silver moonlight. The familiar landscape brought back memories of laughter and labor, but beneath it lay the potential for new growth, both in crops and in family.

The night felt alive with possibilities. Were they truly ready to embrace what lay ahead? He believed they were. *Ledger, whispering to himself,* Embracing the unknown…

With that thought, Ledger felt a weightlift, interchangeable with a sense of freedom. The road stretched before him, and while it remained undefined, he realized he could shape it alongside his family. The fear of the unknown no longer crippled him; it invigorated him.

As he crawled into bed beside Clara, he turned to her, the warmth of their shared aspirations igniting his heart. Whatever happens next, I know we will face it together. We are a team, and that makes all the difference.

Clara smiled, and settled beside him, her presence a comfort as they drifted off to sleep, hearts intertwined. Ledger closed his eyes, ready to embark on this journey into the uncertain future that awaited them, buoyed by love, family, and the legacy that forever guided him.

ᙦ

Chapter Nine: Move to Colihaut

After reflecting on his father's legacy and the potential for a prosperous agricultural future, Ledger Philogene stands at a turning point in his life. With determination in his heart, he makes the momentous decision to purchase two properties—Au-Fonde and Lawi Dovant—in the promising community of Colihaut. This bold step is driven by his unwavering desire to secure a stable livelihood for his family through farming.

However, the initial excitement of this new venture soon gives way to the realities of rural life. As Ledger and his family settle into their new surroundings, they quickly realize that the journey will not be without its challenges. They are met with the complexities of adapting to a different community, confronting skepticism from local farmers, and grappling with the unpredictable nature of agricultural work.

As they navigate these hurdles, Ledger, Clara, Wizen, Petronel, Julien, Eliza, Louisa, James, Dfriel, Koie, and Nerisa must band together, drawing strength from each other while striving to maintain their hope for a better future. This chapter of their lives will test their resilience, but it will also illuminate the power of family unity and the enduring legacy of courage that binds them. Join them as they embark on this transformative journey, seeking to cultivate not just crops, but also a lasting sense of belonging and purpose in their new home.

The sun rose slowly over Colihaut, casting a golden hue on the rich landscape. Ledger stood at the edge of what would soon be his family's new home, his heart racing with a blend of excitement and trepidation. Before him lay two properties—Au-Fonde and Lawi Dovant—acclaimed for their fertile soil and favorable climate. He could almost envision the fields bursting with vibrant crops, thriving under the sun's embrace.

With each breath of fresh morning air, Ledger felt the enormity of his decision settles over him. Purchasing this land was not just a venture into farming; it was a leap toward securing his family's future and honoring the legacy his father had instilled in him.

He remembered sitting at the kitchen table, furiously scribbling plans while his father spoke of the resilience needed in farming.

"Farming is more than just a business, Ledger. It is about the earth, our community, and nurturing the generations that follow," his father had said, eyes sparkling with passion.

Ledger shook off the nostalgia, focusing instead on the task ahead. He pulled out his notebook, filled with sketches and notes he had compiled over the past few weeks. Calculating costs, potential yields, and the array of crops he dreamt of planting, he felt a rush of purpose.

As he walked along the boundaries of Au-Fonde, his boots sank into the dark, loamy soil, and he could not help but smile. This land was alive, brimming with possibilities. He envisioned the laughter of the children as they helped him plant the first seeds, their hands in the dirt, learning the ways of the earth just as he had.

That evening, Ledger gathered Clara, Wizen, Petronel, Julien, Eliza, Louisa, James, Dfriel, Koie, Nerisa, and His mother Clarissa, around the kitchen table. The familiar warmth of home wrapped around them like a comforting embrace as he prepared to share his news. He could feel the buzz of anticipation in the air, heightened by the scent of freshly baked bread and simmering stew. With a steady voice, he declared, "I have decided. I am going to purchase Au-Fonde and Lawi Dovant."

Wizen's eyes lit up with curiosity, his interest piqued by the mention of their potential new land. "Really? What does that mean for us?" he asked, leaning forward in his chair, eager for more information. Meanwhile, Petronel also leaned in closer, her excitement palpable as she awaited further details. The atmosphere at the table shifted subtly, charged with both intrigue and questions. Ledger could see the wheels turning in their minds as they considered the implications of this big step.

Clara smiled, her supportive presence steadying him as he continued. He knew they would all have a role to play in this journey, and he felt grateful for their willingness to embrace the unknown. As he explained his vision of what could be possible on the new land—growing diverse crops, connecting with the local community, and building a life enriched by their experiences—he watched them absorb the information, their expressions transforming from a curiosity into a shared excitement about the future. It was a pivotal moment, and he felt the weight of it settle around them, binding them together in a common dream.

"Are you certain, Ledger? This is a significant step," Clara asked, her brow slightly furrowed in concern. The weight of his decision hung in the air, and Ledger could sense the gravity of the moment. He took a deep breath, wanting to convey his conviction and reassure her.

"I believe it is the right choice for us," he replied, his voice steady. "The land has rich soil and a climate that supports a range of crops. More importantly, it is a chance for us to build stability—both financially and as a family." As he spoke, he could see Clara processing the information, her mind racing through the implications of such a move.

"I trust your judgment," she said thoughtfully. "But we must be prepared for the challenges that come with rural life." Her reflection mirrored the concerns swirling in his own heart. Ledger nodded, fully aware that they would face obstacles along the way.

"I know it will not be easy. There will be hurdles," he admitted, looking around at the faces of his family gathered around the table. "But we're in this together, and I believe we can cultivate not just crops but also a home filled with our family's legacy." His conviction echoed in his heart, and he hoped his words would inspire confidence in Clara and their children. Together, they could navigate any storm that came their way, gaining strength from one another as they ventured into this new chapter.

"Can we grow all the vegetables we talked about? Heirloom tomatoes and herbs?" Koie asked enthusiastically, his eyes shining with anticipation. His eagerness for this adventure was palpable, and Ledger found himself grinning at the thought of their potential harvests.

"And can we have a treehouse?" Nerisa chimed in, her voice filled with excitement as she pictured a little hideaway among the branches. The enthusiasm in their voices reinvigorated Ledger, reminding him of the joy that lay ahead. He smiled, envisioning the labor and love that would go into their new life—how they would cultivate not just the land but also cherished memories as a family.

Yet beneath this excitement lurked the realities they would face. Ledger knew that adapting to a new community meant navigating different customs and building new relationships with fellow farmers and neighbors. The change would come with challenges, and he could not ignore the demanding rhythms of agricultural life. The exuberance he felt at his children's dreams was tempered by the awareness that they would need resilience and hard work to make it all happen. Still, Ledger felt a renewed sense of determination; together, they could embrace the journey and overcome whatever hurdles lay ahead.

A few days later, Ledger wandered through the fields of Lawi Dovant, situated in the heart of the main village. The open expanse invigorated his imagination and filled him with both excitement and trepidation. Though he had successfully secured the properties, the weight of responsibility now rested heavily on his shoulders.

The landscape stretched out before him, a beautiful patchwork of greens and browns that seemed to go on forever. Yet, amidst its beauty, there was a humbling quality, a solemn reminder of the hard work that lay ahead. Each swaying blade of grass and every rustling leaf whispered the promise of potential, but they also echoed the challenges that would require dedication and perseverance. As Ledger surveyed the land, he felt a mix of hope and resolve, knowing he was about to embark on a journey that would shape not only the land but also his family's legacy.

He recalled the stories of his father's struggles—poor harvests, market fluctuations, and the unpredictability of nature. Each tale served as a lesson learned, a testament to resilience in the face of adversity. Ledger understood now that farming was a delicate dance with uncertainty, where every decision he made could either fortify their roots or hinder their growth. These memories lingered with him, guiding his thoughts as he prepared to navigate the challenges ahead.

That evening, as they gathered for dinner, Ledger felt a pulsing mix of excitement and apprehension buzzing through the air. The aroma of Clara's cooking wafted through the kitchen, filling the space with warmth and comfort, but it was the prospect of their upcoming trip that had everyone on edge. He could see the anticipation in Wizen's eyes and the curiosity radiating from Petronel, Julien, Eliza, Louisa, James, Dfriel, Koie, and Nerisa as they settled around the table. This was more than just a meal; it was the gateway to their future.

As they began to serve the food, Ledger broke the momentary silence with a sense of purpose. "Tomorrow, we'll visit Colihaut together as a family," he announced, his voice confident yet laced with enthusiasm. "I want us to meet the locals, understand their practices, and learn from them." Each family member responded with eager nods and encouraging smiles, the idea of this shared adventure igniting sparkles of hope in their eyes.

The implications of the visit were significant; it meant stepping into a new community, embracing unknown challenges, and rolling up their sleeves to learn. "We'll have the opportunity to see how they farm, possibly pick up some tips and tricks that could help us when we start our own journey," he continued, picturing the vibrant market and vibrant community interactions. "And who knows? We might even make some new friends along the way."

The thought of this exploration filled Ledger with optimism, and he could feel the excitement bubbling from his children. He knew they would face uncertainty and hard work ahead, but for now, they could share in the joy of discovery and possibility. Each of them had a role to play, and together they would navigate this transition, one step at a time. As they dug into their meal, the conversation flowed freely, infused with enthusiasm about the adventure awaiting them.

Clara nodded in agreement, a smile spreading across her face as she caught the infectious enthusiasm of her children. Koie and Nerisa exchanged excited glances, their eyes sparkling with the possibilities that lay ahead. The thought of embarking on this new adventure together filled them with a buoyant energy that coursed through the entire room.

"Can we bring our sketchbooks?" Nerisa asked eagerly, her voice tinged with enthusiasm. "I want to take notes about what we see!" The idea of documenting their experience inspired a wave of excitement, and Ledger could envision Nerisa sketching the vibrant colors of the market and the lush fields they would explore.

"And maybe even take some seeds back!" Koie chimed in, his mind racing with the idea of growing something unique in their own garden. The conversation ignited a flurry of imagination, each child bouncing ideas back and forth about what they might discover and bring home. Ledger could not help but feel a surge of pride as he witnessed their eager responses.

"Those are great ideas!" he encouraged, the warmth of their excitement enveloping him. "Bringing your sketchbooks can help you remember everything we learn and see. And collecting seeds would be a wonderful way to start our own garden with a touch of what we find in Colihaut!" As he spoke, he felt the bond of family grow even stronger, knowing they would navigate this journey together, united by their shared dreams and ambitions.

"Doing that will help us feel this land in our hearts," Ledger said, his voice filled with conviction. "We'll make it ours one step at a time." The sincerity of his words hung in the air, resonating with each member of the family. He could see the determination in their eyes, and it reassured him that they were on this journey together.

As dinner concluded, Ledger felt a surge of hope and purpose coursing through him. The clatter of plates and the soft laughter of his children created a symphony of life that filled the cozy kitchen. Each moment spent together reinforced his belief in what was to come. The road ahead would be arduous, with its share of challenges and uncertainties, but he was resolved in his determination to navigate it alongside his family.

This land would become their legacy—a canvas where they could paint their dreams and nurture their ambitions. Ledger envisioned a thriving homestead filled with gardens, laughter, and love, a place where each corner held memories created together. He thought of the lessons they would learn, the hardships they would face, and the abundance of joy they would cultivate, all intertwined with the teachings of the past.

With his heart full, Ledger looked around the table at the faces of his family, and he felt a renewed sense of purpose. Together, they would embrace the journey ahead, transforming the land into a home rich with their values and aspirations. This was just the beginning, and he could not wait to see what awaited them on this remarkable adventure.

The sun hung high in the sky as Ledger approached the bustling center of Colihaut, where the air was rich with the sounds of community life. With every step, he felt a swirl of anticipation and determination. Today marked the beginning of the negotiation process for Au-Fonde and Lawi Dovant, and he was ready to leverage every ounce of his experience in the trade to secure the best possible deal.

Ledger entered Kai Cocoa, the building that housed the local land authority's office. The walls were adorned with maps of the area, showcasing the vibrant farmland and tightly knit community. Upon arrival, he knocked gently and was invited inside by a stout man named Mr. Charles, the district representative.

"Welcome, Ledger! I have been expecting you," Mr. Charles said, his smile warm and inviting. "Please, take a seat."

Ledger settled into the chair across from Mr. Charles, acutely aware of the weighty conversation that lay ahead. The office was filled with the scent of polished wood and the faint rustle of papers, adding to the gravity of the moment. Although the two men exchanged pleasantries—discussing the weather and the bustling activity outside—Ledger kept his focus sharply on the task at hand. He knew there was much at stake, and he wanted to ensure every detail of the negotiation was clear in his mind.

As Mr. Charles glanced over some documents, Ledger felt his heartbeat quicken. This was not just a meeting; it was a crucial step toward realizing his and his family's dreams. The stakes were high, and he wanted to make a solid impression. He took a deep breath, reminding himself of his preparations and the vision he held for Au-Fonde and Lawi Dovant. He could not let the nerves derail his ambitions.

"Thank you for meeting with me," Ledger began, his voice steady but laced with anticipation. "I'm eager to discuss the properties Au-Fonde and Lawi Dovant and the negotiation process." He met Mr. Charles's gaze, hoping to convey his genuine interest and determination.

"Absolutely! Both parcels have much to offer," Mr. Charles replied, leaning slightly forward with an air of enthusiasm. "They've been well-maintained and, as you know, are renowned for their fertile soil." The district representative's approval reassured Ledger, igniting a sense of pride in the land he hoped to call his own.

Ledger nodded, mindful of the potential the properties held. He knew he had to approach this conversation with care, balancing his enthusiasm with the realities of negotiation. As Mr. Charles continued to highlight the advantages of the parcels, Ledger mentally prepared himself to navigate through the financial details and conditions that would follow. He understood the importance of presenting both his vision and his willingness to make a fair deal. With determination brewing within him, he reminded himself that this was not just about acquiring land; it was about his family's future and the legacy they would create together.

"I'm glad to hear that," Ledger replied, nodding appreciatively. "However, I would like to ensure that the agreement reflects the true value of the properties and the potential they hold." He leaned slightly forward, emphasizing his seriousness about the matter.

As they delved into the details, Ledger expertly articulated his points, weaving together market comparisons and potential yields to support his case. He referenced recent sales in the area, outlining how Au-Fonde and Lawi Dovant could not only sustain a family but also flourish under the right stewardship. His passion for the land shone through as he made a compelling argument for why these properties deserved a fair valuation. Mr. Charles listened attentively, nodding at various points and taking notes, clearly impressed by Ledger's knowledge and commitment.

The back-and-forth exchange became a dynamic discussion rather than just a negotiation, with Ledger demonstrating his grasp of the complexities involved. He was determined to convey his vision of nurturing the land while also building a sustainable future for his family. Mr. Charles appreciated Ledger's foresight, recognizing that his genuine interest in the properties also reflected a potential asset to the community.

As the hours passed, Ledger realized that negotiating land in Colihaut was deeply intertwined with community dynamics and unwritten rules. He began to appreciate the local culture—an intricate tapestry woven with respect for tradition and the significance of maintaining strong relationships within the community. Understanding this context shifted his perspective, encouraging him to think beyond just financial terms and consider the emotional layers involved in the negotiation.

Mr. Charles leaned back in his chair and gestured thoughtfully as he spoke. "You have a solid grasp on the market," he acknowledged, "but the previous owners have sentimental ties to these properties. They may not be willing to part with them easily." Ledger nodded, recognizing that this was an important insight. He was entering a delicate situation that required more than just strategies focused on numbers and yields.

In that moment, Ledger recalled his father's lessons about connection, empathy, and compromise. He understood that to navigate this negotiation successfully, he needed to approach the previous owners with respect for their feelings and history tied to the land. Harnessing that wisdom, Ledger began to formulate a strategy that would allow him to connect with the owners on a more personal level, creating a dialogue that honored their memories while advocating for his family's vision for the future. With this new understanding, he felt invigorated, ready to craft a proposal that would resonate with both the heart and the mind.

"That's a fair point," Ledger responded thoughtfully. "Perhaps we could frame the negotiation as a partnership rather than just a transaction. I'm not just looking to buy land; I want to build something that honors its legacy." He spoke earnestly, hoping to convey his desire to preserve the essence of what came before and ensure that the properties continued to thrive within the community context.

Mr. Charles' eyes sharpened with interest, and Ledger could see he had struck a chord. The district representative leaned forward, engaged by this new perspective. "An approach based on mutual respect could indeed soften their stance," he said, nodding in agreement. Ledger felt a surge of optimism as the conversation began to take on a more collaborative tone, opening possibilities that had previously seemed out of reach.

The idea of partnership resonated with both men, allowing them to envision a future where the land would not only serve Ledger's family but also remain a cherished part of Colihaut's heritage. Ledger could sense Mr. Charles' appreciation for this approach, as it suggested a shared commitment to the community's continuity. This newfound focus encouraged Ledger to dig deeper into the story of the properties and the families that had cared for them, further solidifying his resolve to honor their legacy as he pursued his dreams.

With a renewed strategy in mind, Ledger arranged a meeting with the previous owners, an older couple named the Marcellus. As he approached Au-Fonde, he could not help but admire the land's stunning beauty. The rolling fields, adorned with lush greenery and rich, dark soil, seemed to beckon to him, whispering promises of potential and growth. Each step he took was charged with the weight of the opportunity at hand; he felt a deep responsibility not only to his vision but also to honor the legacy of the Marcellus family. This moment held the promise of connection, and Ledger knew that if he could convey his genuine intentions, he might forge a path that respected both the past and the future of this cherished land. Au-Fonde!

The Marcellus couple greeted Ledger warmly on their porch, a charming space framed by vibrant flowering plants and the stunning landscape that stretched out beyond. As they exchanged pleasantries, Ledger could sense their deep attachment to the land; it was palpable in their stories and animated laughter. He listened intently as they reminisced about planting seasons, bountiful harvests, and cherished family gatherings that had taken place under the shade of an ancient mango tree.

Each tale painted a vivid picture of a life intertwined with the rhythms of nature, and Ledger felt the weight of their memories wrapping around him, further solidifying his resolve to honor their legacy while pursuing his own dreams. The warmth of their shared history made it clear that this was not just a piece of property to them; it was a cornerstone of their lives, and Ledger was determined to approach the conversation with the respect and care it deserved.

"I can see how much this land means to you both," Ledger began, his voice steady and sincere. "I want you to know that I don't simply wish to purchase it; I aim to honor its legacy and continue the work you've done here." The couple exchanged glances, their surprise evident as they absorbed his heartfelt words. Sensing their curiosity, Ledger took a moment to articulate his vision, detailing how this land would serve as the foundation for a stable future for his own family, filled with the same joys and traditions they had experienced.

He spoke about cultivating the fields, nurturing the relationships within the community, and ensuring that the spirit of Au-Fonde would live on through his efforts. His words flowed with genuine emotion, and Ledger hoped they could see that his intentions were rooted not only in ambition but in a deep respect for the life and history that the Marcellus couple had built on this beautiful land.

"You speak with a passion that is rare," Mrs. Marcellus remarked, her eyes shimmering with appreciation. "It gives me hope for the future of Au-Fonde." Her words warmed Ledger's heart, and he felt a spark of connection growing between them, built on a mutual respect for the land and the dreams that were so intricately woven into its very fabric. He could sense the couple's initial reservations beginning to fade, their willingness to consider his proposal shifting in the air around them.

As they continued to talk, Ledger shared more about his plans: how he envisioned preserving the heritage of Au-Fonde while integrating sustainable practices that would honor the environment. He spoke about creating a space where future generations could gather, just as the Marcellus family had done, and how he hoped to cultivate not only the land but also community spirit. The more they engaged in this dialogue, the more he could see the Marcellus couple softening, their hearts opening to the possibility that he could be a steward of their cherished legacy. This blossoming connection filled the room with warmth, a tangible sense of hope that perhaps both their stories could intertwine in a meaningful way.

"If we could agree on a reasonable price, I would also love to involve you in the transition, perhaps as informal advisors," Ledger said, his tone earnest. "Your insights could be invaluable to me as I learn the ropes." He hoped that this offer would resonate with the couple, allowing them to remain connected to the land that had been such a significant part of their lives. As he spoke, he envisioned how their guidance could not only help him understand the intricacies of Au-Fonde but also tangibly honor their legacy.

Mr. Marcellus stroked his chin, visibly considering the proposal. The silence stretched for a moment, filled with the weight of the history that surrounded them. Ledger felt a mix of anticipation and respect as he waited for the elder man's response, knowing that this decision held considerable importance for both him and the Marcellus couple. Finally, Mr. Marcellus looked up, a thoughtful expression on his face. "That could be agreeable," he replied slowly. "We want to see this place thrive, not just fade away into the hands of a stranger." His words brought a wave of relief and encouragement to Ledger, affirming that there was a path forward that respected the history of Au-Fonde while allowing for new beginnings.

After several more meetings with the Marcellus couple, Ledger returned to Mr. Charles with a proposal that deftly reflected both their wishes and his own vision for the future of Au-Fonde. He had learned to embrace the narrative of the land, recognizing that the negotiations had evolved into something far deeper than a mere transaction; they were about weaving together the stories of its past and the aspirations of its new steward.

"I believe we can reach an agreement that honors the Marcellus' legacy while supporting my goal of building a sustainable future for my family," Ledger stated confidently. He felt a sense of purpose as he outlined the proposal, emphasizing the shared vision he had developed with the couple during their conversations. Together, Ledger and Mr. Charles reviewed the terms, both men focused and engaged. As the details of the deal began to take shape, Ledger felt a surge of confidence, buoyed by the progress he had made.

With each clause discussed, he skillfully navigated through the final details, leveraging the relationships he had built along the way. The respect and trust established with the Marcellus couple proved invaluable, allowing him to present a compelling case that aligned with their hopes for the land. Through patience and empathy, Ledger had transformed a challenging negotiation into a collaboration, and now, as the agreement neared completion, he saw the fulfillment of a dream—one that intertwined his future with the enduring legacy of Au-Fonde.

Finally, the contracts were signed, and Ledger stood proudly at the edge of his new properties, a mix of relief and joy filling his heart. Au-Fonde and Lawi Dovant were now his, but they represented so much more than just land; they were a fresh start for his family, a vessel for dreams and aspirations, and a testament to his father's teachings about hard work, perseverance, and respect for the land. Every inch of soil beneath his feet carried the weight of history, and Ledger felt honored to be part of that ongoing story.

This is just the beginning," Ledger whispered to himself, his voice barely audible over the gentle breeze. As he gazed over the fields shimmering under the sun, he envisioned the possibilities ahead— lush crops, laughter-filled gatherings, and the building of a vibrant community centered around shared values and connection to the earth. Ledger felt a profound sense of hope for the future, realizing that their journey was only starting.

While challenges undoubtedly awaited, he was ready to embrace them, armed with the spirit of resilience and community that had guided him thus far. With every heartbeat, he felt his dreams drawing closer, igniting a passion within him to honor the legacy of Au-Fonde while crafting a new chapter for his family. This was more than a dream realized; it was a promise to uphold the values and connections that made the land truly special.

The sun smiled down on Ledger and his family as they arrived at Au-Fonde, its warm rays illuminating the vibrant green fields that stretched out like a promising canvas underneath the bright blue sky. Clara, Wizen Petronel, Julien, Eliza, Louisa, James, Dfriel, Koie, and Nerisa tumbled out of their truck, their eyes wide with wonder and excitement. Ledger felt a swell of pride as he watched their reactions unfold, knowing that this moment marked the beginning of a new chapter for all of them.

"Here it is—our future!" Ledger exclaimed, motioning towards the land, his voice filled with enthusiasm. The boundless beauty of Au-Fonde was a vision he had long cherished, and now it was finally a reality shared with the ones he loved. As if responding to his invitation, Nerisa darted ahead, her laughter ringing out across the fields like music, a sound that filled the air with joy and possibility. Koie followed closely behind, his curiosity piqued as he stepped cautiously into the unfamiliar landscape, his eyes scanning the horizon for adventure.

Clara walked slightly behind the group, her gaze drifting over the vast expanse with both awe and a hint of apprehension. She took in the sight of the undulating fields, the shade of the distant trees, and the promise of new beginnings, her heart a mix of excitement and uncertainty. Ledger could sense her feelings, and he approached her gently, ready to reassure her that together they would cultivate not only the land but also a sense of belonging and family. This new home, with its fertile ground and endless opportunities, was a place where dreams could take root, and Ledger was determined to nurture them alongside his family.

"It is breathtaking, Ledger. I can almost see what it will become," Clara said, her voice filled with wonder as she took in the expansive landscape before them. Ledger nodded in agreement, feeling the pulse of potential in the air. Together, they walked side by side, tracing the edges of the cultivated land that stretched out before them like a promise waiting to be fulfilled.

The earth, rich and dark, smelled sweet and fresh, a testament to the care the Marcellus couple had devoted to it over the years. Each step they took released the earthy aroma, invigorating their senses and grounding them in the moment. Ledger felt a deep connection to the land and the legacy it represented, knowing that with Clara by his side, they were ready to nurture its potential. He imagined not just fields of crops, but a place filled with laughter, gatherings, and shared dreams—a haven for their family's future.

As they examined the contours of the land, Ledger shared his ideas for what could be planted in the coming seasons, envisioning vibrant rows of vegetables and fruit trees flourishing under the sun. Clara listened intently, her apprehensions easing as she embraced the vision forming in her mind—one of growth, sustainability, and community. With every passing moment, Ledger could see her confidence blossoming, and he felt reassured that together they could transform Au-Fonde into the thriving home they both desired. Each glimpse of the horizon sparked their imagination, breathing life into their dreams and solidifying their commitment to making this land a true reflection of their family's journey together.

After touring Au-Fonde, the family made their way down to Lawi Dovant, nestled in the heart of Colihaut village. The transition from one property to the other felt significant, like crossing a threshold into new possibilities and adventures. Ledger sensed a thrill coursing through him, yet an undercurrent of anxiety lingered, reminding him of the responsibilities that accompanied this beautiful land. It was more than just an acquisition; it was a commitment to nurture and protect a legacy while forging its own path.

As they stepped onto Lawi Dovant, a breathtaking scene unfolded before them. Wildflowers danced in patches between the rows of untouched earth, their vibrant colors painting a vivid tapestry that contrasted sharply with the dark soil. The air was filled with the sweet scent of blossoms, and the gentle rustle of leaves whispered promises of growth and renewal. As they wandered deeper into the fields, Ledger could feel the land's untapped potential pulsing with life, a hidden vibrancy that beckoned them to explore further.

Each step brought new sights and sounds: bees buzzing industriously, birds flitting among the branches, and the gentle breeze carrying the distant call of nature. Ledger paused to observe his family, their faces illuminated with wonder as they took in their surroundings. He felt a mixture of excitement and responsibility weighing on him. This was not just a place to work; it was a canvas for their dreams, a living entity that would require their care, collaboration, and creativity. With each passing moment, he was reminded that, while challenges might lie ahead, the journey they were embarking on at Lawi Dovant was rich with promise, ready to unfold in ways they had only begun to imagine.

"Can we plant a garden here?" Koie exclaimed, pulling on Ledger's arm, his eyes sparkling with excitement. "Look at all this space!" The simple vision of rows filled with vibrant plants and blooming flowers ignited a passion within him, and Ledger could not help but marvel at his son's enthusiasm. As Koie gazed up at him, Ledger felt the energy of possibility radiating from the landscape around them.

Nerisa chimed in with a grin that lit up her face. "We could grow so much! Imagine having our own strawberries!" Her gleeful imagination painted pictures of juicy red berries, freshly picked and shared during family gatherings, and Ledger found himself swept up in their infectious hope. He envisioned the laughter of his children as they spent afternoons tending to their garden, each plant a new adventure, each harvest a shared celebration.

However, as much as he wanted to revel in their excitement, Ledger also felt a flicker of reality settling in, casting a shadow over his thoughts. While the idea of cultivating strawberries and other crops was exhilarating, the weight of the work ahead loomed large in his mind. There were preparations to be made, soil to be enriched, and countless hours of labor required to transform their dream into reality. He knew that the journey would demand dedication and resilience and that challenges would arise along the way.

Despite the dawning realization, Ledger could not suppress the smile that tugged at his lips. The prospect of building a life here, side by side with his family, was worth every effort. "Absolutely," he said, kneeling to meet Koie's enthusiastic gaze. "We will plant a garden—our garden. Together, we can make it thrive." Seeing the delight in his children's eyes re-energized his sense of purpose, reminding him that, although the road ahead would be demanding, it would also be filled with unexpected joys and opportunities to grow as a family.

"We can definitely plant a garden," Ledger said, his voice steady yet inviting. "But it's important to remember that farming requires hard work and commitment." He wanted to temper their excitement with some grounded realism, as he knew the journey ahead would demand more than just enthusiasm. It would take diligence, resilience, and a willingness to embrace the challenges that often accompany a life tethered to the land.

Just then, Clara joined them, kneeling beside a small patch of vibrant wildflowers that danced gently in the breeze. Her smile was warm, yet Ledger could see the shadows of uncertainty lurking in her eyes. He appreciated her presence; it grounded him, reminding him that while dreams were soaring high, the reality of their situation needed careful consideration.

"It's beautiful here, Ledger," Clara said softly, her gaze drifting over the fields, but there was a question in her tone. "But do you think we're ready for this?" Her words hung in the air, a gentle reminder of the weight of responsibility they were stepping into. Ledger knelt beside her, allowing the moment to settle between them, recognizing the sincerity in her concern.

He understood that beneath their excitement lay valid apprehensions about the heavy lifting ahead. The vision of a thriving garden and a successful homestead was enticing, but it also came wrapped in layers of responsibility that could feel overwhelming. "I believe we can do this," he replied, turning to her with a reassuring smile. "We're a team, and together we can face whatever challenges come our way." At that moment, he wanted Clara to know that her concerns were heard and that they would navigate this new journey as partners—drawing strength from one another while embracing the beauty that lay ahead.

"I believe we are ready," Ledger said, his voice steady and filled with conviction. "It will not be easy, but if we work together, we can make it work. Just like we talked about during our decision-making—the four of us can nurture this place as a family." He wanted to instill a sense of hope in them, to remind them that the strength of their bond was what would anchor them through any adversity. As he spoke, he could see the flicker of determination lighting up Clara's features, and he knew they could overcome the inevitable challenges together.

However, the reality of their task began to settle back in, and Ledger noticed Nerisa and Koie exchanging glances, their excitement momentarily muted by the weight of the questions playing in their minds. Koie finally broke the silence, his brow furrowed with concern. "What if things do not grow? What if it is too much work?" The worry in his son's voice struck Ledger deeply, grounding him in the moment.

Taking a deep breath, Ledger cherished his son's honesty, as it reminded him just how much Koie cared about this venture and their family. "I completely understand why you're worried," he replied softly, kneeling to meet Koie's gaze. "Farming can be unpredictable, and there will be hard days ahead. But it is important to remember that every challenge is an opportunity for us to learn and grow, both as a family and as farmers. He wanted his children to grasp that struggle was a part of the journey, but so was grace and resilience.

"Along the way, we'll share the work, celebrate our successes, and learn from the setbacks together," he added, hoping to instill confidence in them. "No matter what happens, we will face it all as a team." Through his gentle words, he aimed to reassure them that while uncertainty was a natural part of embarking on this adventure, his commitment to their shared dream would remain unwavering. Being honest about their fears was the first step in cultivating not just the land before them, but also a deep-rooted sense of trust and unity within their family.

"Farming can be unpredictable, but that's part of the beauty," Ledger explained, his voice calm and reassuring. "With hard work and patience, we can learn from the land and adapt to whatever comes our way. We will face challenges, but we will also celebrate our successes together." His words hung in the air, an affirmation of their collective journey and the resilience they would need to cultivate a flourishing life at Lawi Dovant.

Clara placed a reassuring hand on Koie's shoulder, her comforting gesture, a silent promise of support. Ledger noticed how his soothing tone lifted the tension, a spark of excitement flickering back in their eyes. It was a moment where doubt began to dissolve, replaced by the possibility of achievement and growth. Their worries, while valid, now felt more manageable as they united in purpose.

"Can we make a plan?" Nerisa exclaimed, her voice brimming with newfound excitement. "Like what to plant first and how to take care of everything?" Her enthusiasm sparked a wave of positive energy through the group, melting away any lingering apprehension. Ledger could see the glow of ambition igniting in their expressions, and it warmed his heart.

"Absolutely!" he replied, feeling touched by her determination. "Planning together is a great idea. It will not only help us stay organized but also solidify our bond as a family." He envisioned them gathering around a table, brainstorming ideas, sketching out their garden layout, and devising a schedule for planting and maintenance. This collaborative effort would ground them in the realities of their new life while simultaneously weaving them closer together. Together, they could transform the land into something truly special, not just through their individual efforts, but through their shared dreams and collective spirit.

"Great idea, Nerisa," Ledger said, his eyes lighting up with enthusiasm. "We can create a roadmap for our garden. It would be smart to start with things that grow quickly, like herbs and vegetables. They will give us a fast return on our efforts and help build our confidence as we learn."

As they continued walking, Ledger began outlining ideas for each parcel of land, envisioning rows of thriving plants that would soon populate their space. Each suggestion he made was infused with optimism and practicality, from vibrant basil and parsley to sturdy tomatoes and radishes.

The sound of their footsteps crunching on the gravel echoed around them, a comforting rhythm that marked their progress. With every step, they wove a tapestry of hopes and dreams, the air thick with promises of a shared future. It was more than just gardening; it was about nurturing their bonds and cultivating a sense of home together. Each idea they exchanged fueled their excitement, setting the stage for a fruitful partnership that would blossom in ways they had yet to imagine.

As the sun dipped low in the sky, painting the horizon in hues of orange and pink, Ledger gathered his family on a small rise overlooking Au-Fonde. The view was nothing short of remarkable, with rolling hills and vibrant fields stretching out before them like a canvas waiting to be filled. He felt a rush of gratitude swell within him, a deep appreciation for this new chapter in their lives.

"This is our home now, Ledger said, gazing out at the breathtaking landscape. "Together, we will nurture this land, with laughter and patience guiding us as we grow." His voice carried a conviction that resonated with the weight of his words, promising to cultivate not just the earth, but their relationships and dreams as well.

Clara leaned into him, her warmth anchoring him amidst the swirl of emotions. He could feel her steady presence, a source of strength that encouraged him to embrace the challenges ahead. The children stood side by side, their eyes filled with both wonder and determination, as they took in the beauty surrounding them. This was the beginning of a journey that would push them to their limits but also bring them closer together. Ledger realized that as they embarked on this adventure, they would not only grow crops but also forge unbreakable bonds, planting seeds of love and resilience that would flourish through every trial and triumph they faced.

"I can feel the potential here," Clara said softly, her voice a gentle melody against the backdrop of the fading day. The warmth of her words wrapped around Ledger, filling him with a sense of hope. "With time, we'll see this land flourish, and so will we." Her vision reflected not just a belief in the soil beneath their feet but also in the strength of their family unit, and it resonated deeply within him.

As day turned to dusk, Ledger felt the weight of uncertainty fades. The vibrant colors of the sunset mirrored the blossoming optimism in his heart. Together, they would tackle the challenges ahead, embracing the journey as a family united by purpose and love. He envisioned the days to come— working the fields, sharing laughter, and overcoming obstacles hand in hand.

Here, within this land, they would cultivate not just crops but a legacy that intertwined their hopes, fears, and dreams. Each seed they planted symbolized a chapter of their story, growing not only into sustenance for their bodies but also into a rich tapestry of shared experiences and cherished memories. In that moment, Ledger understood that this journey would not just transform the land; it would transform them all, nurturing their bonds and helping them to thrive together in ways they had yet to fully comprehend.

The vibrant La Place Dame of Colihaut buzzed with life, with stalls adorned with colorful produce, and cheerful vendors calling out to passersby. The air was rich with the scents of spices and fresh fruits, creating an intoxicating atmosphere that invited exploration. Ledger Philogene walked through the market at La Place Dame with Clara, Wizen, Petronel, Julien, Eliza, Louisa, James, Dfriel, Koie, and Nerisa by his side, all eager to integrate into their new community. They moved together like a small but determined unit, a mix of excitement and apprehension rippling among them. The welcoming smiles of some vendors reassured Ledger, yet he could not shake the feeling beneath the cheerful surface, there were undercurrents of tension swirling through the air—an unease that he sensed more than he could articulate.

"Look at those bananas! They are huge!" Clara exclaimed, her finger pointing eagerly toward a stall overflowing with vibrant yellow fruit. Her infectious enthusiasm ignited a spark of joy in the group. Excitement sparkled in Nerisa's eyes as she tugged on Clara's arm, inching closer to the stall, determined to get a better look at the tempting bounty. The allure of fresh produce was undeniable, and Ledger could see how it drew his family in, momentarily clouding their worries with the simple pleasures of the marketplace.

In contrast, Koie hung back, shyly scanning the crowd. The chaos of vibrant colors and animated voices seemed daunting to her, a stark reminder of how far they had come and how much they still needed to navigate. Ledger noticed his hesitance and felt a pang of empathy; he wanted to reassure him, to help bridge that gap between the energy of their new environment and her cautious spirit. As he glanced around, he realized that while they sought to embrace their new surroundings, the journey to truly belong would take time—a journey that would require courage, understanding, and the warmth of family to guide them through the vibrant chaos of their new home.

"Let's make sure to support local farmers," Ledger said, his voice steady and filled with purpose. "It's important we build connections here." He understood that establishing relationships with their neighbors would be crucial for their integration into this new community. As they approached a stall overflowing with fresh vegetables and herbs, Ledger felt a mix of excitement and trepidation. He hoped that by engaging with local vendors, they could foster goodwill and come to understand the land and its people more deeply.

As they drew closer, a middle-aged man, Mr. Telford, greeted them with a curt nod. Ledger had heard mixed opinions about him; he was respected as a dedicated farmer with years of experience yet also known for expressing concerns about newcomers encroaching on the land. The stories he had heard gave Ledger pause, but he resolved to meet the man's wariness with openness.

Mr. Telford eyed Ledger cautiously, sizing him up. "I have heard about you folks buying up the land. Planning to grow crops, I assume?" His tone was direct, laced with the skepticism of someone protective of his territory and livelihood. Ledger felt the moment hang in the air, knowing this was a pivotal opportunity to clarify their intentions. He realized the importance of transparency in forging new relationships; it was essential to communicate that they sought not to displace, but to enhance the community, rooting themselves in collaboration and mutual respect. With a deep breath, Ledger prepared to respond, hoping to turn this tentative encounter into a foundation for understanding and support.

"Yes, sir. We are excited about the opportunities here," Ledger replied, striving to convey genuine enthusiasm despite the palpable tension in the air. He could feel Mr. Telford's skepticism radiating from him like a heavy fog, and the unease settled over the marketplace like a weight. It was hard to ignore the questions lingering unspoken in the space between them, the doubts about their intentions, the concerns over their impact on the community. The air felt charged with unvoiced fears: fears of competition, of change, and of newcomers disrupting a way of life that had been carefully cultivated over generations.

"Well, you'll find it's not as easy as it looks," Mr. Telford said, crossing his arms defiantly. His body language was defensive, and Ledger recognized the challenge in his words. "Farming here, you have to respect the land and the people who've been tending to it for years." The emphasis on respect resonated with Ledger, and he admired the man's dedication to preserving the integrity of the community. But the edge in Telford's voice reminded him of the uphill battle they faced in earning acceptance.

Feeling Clara step closer to him, Ledger sensed her support and shared determination. She must have noticed the tension as well, and it heartened him to know they stood united in this moment. Ledger swallowed hard, steadying himself, and nodded in agreement, determined to respond with both honesty and humility. "We understand that, and we are committed to learning from those who know this land best. We want to honor the traditions here while also contributing positively to the community." He hoped his words would bridge the gap between them, showing Mr. Telford that they were allies rather than adversaries in the journey that lay ahead.

"I respect that completely, Mr. Telford," Ledger replied earnestly, aiming to convey sincerity with his words. "We want to learn from the land and the community. We aim to contribute, not compete." He maintained steady eye contact, hoping to dissolve the barriers between them. He could see the flicker of acknowledgment in Telford's eyes, a sign that his message was beginning to resonate.

However, Mr. Telford's expression softened only slightly; the skepticism still lingered in his gaze, a reminder that respect alone would not erase the apprehension surrounding newcomers. "Some folks are worried about new techniques. Change can be disruptive. Just be careful—you do not want to upset the balance that is worked for us," Telford cautioned, his tone now more measured but still firm. With that, he turned back to his stall, leaving Ledger with the weight of those words hanging in the air.

Ledger stood there for a moment, contemplating the meaning behind Telford's warning. It was clear that their presence had stirred something deeper within the community, and he understood the importance of approaching their new life with care and consideration. He was reminded that change, while often necessary, could also evoke fears rooted in the desire for stability and continuity. Just then, he felt Clara squeeze his hand, a silent reminder of their shared purpose and commitment to each other and their family. Her warmth provided comfort as he considered the road ahead, knowing that patience, understanding, and genuine efforts would be essential as they navigated this intricate dance of integration and growth.

Back at Au-Fonde, Ledger gathered his family in a circle, keen to discuss their first encounters with the locals. The sunlight was beginning to fade, casting a warm glow over their gathering, yet he felt the nagging tension from his conversation with Mr. Telford weighing heavily on his mind. It was crucial, he believed, that they maintained open lines of communication within the community if they were to flourish in their new home.

"We've received mixed reactions from the locals," Ledger began, addressing his family with a balance of hope and seriousness. "Some are welcoming, but others, like Mr. Telford, seem wary of us." He watched their faces, noting the mixture of curiosity and concern reflected in their expressions. He knew this was more than just a farming endeavor—it was about being part of a community and fostering trust.

Dfriel, sitting with his legs crossed, toyed with a clump of dirt in his hands, his eyes downcast as he pondered the situation. "Why don't they want us here, Dad? We are just trying to farm like they do," he asked, his voice carrying a blend of confusion and sadness. Ledger felt a mixture of pride and concern for his son; it was a valid question. Dfriel's innocence highlighted the difficulty of their position, and Ledger realized the need to explain the nuances of their new life and the fears that often accompany change.

"I know it seems unfair," Ledger replied gently, hoping to reassure him. "Change can be scary for people, especially when it feels like their way of life might be threatened. We must show them our intentions through our actions—by being respectful and understanding." He saw some of the tension ease from Dfriel's shoulders as he continued, "We are here to learn as much as we are to teach. Let us work on building those bridges together." He could see Clara nodding in agreement, her smile encouraging the spirit of collaboration they were all striving for. It was evident that open dialogue and patience would be essential in this journey, not just for their family but for fostering relationships that could blossom in the fertile soil of understanding and shared aspirations.

"It's natural for people to feel uncertain when change comes," Clara said thoughtfully, her voice a soothing balm amidst the tension. "They have been farming this land for generations. We must show them we are here to help, not hurt." Her words resonated with everyone, emphasizing the importance of empathy as they navigated their new environment. Clara's insights provided a necessary perspective, reminding the family that understanding the history and traditions of the locals was as important as their own aspirations.

Just then, Louisa's face brightened with ideas, her enthusiasm infectious. "What if we invited some of the locals over for dinner? We could share a meal and talk about our plans!" The suggestion hung in the air like a promise, and Ledger could not help but smile at his daughter's instinctive desire to connect. It was a wonderful idea, one that could foster goodwill and lay the groundwork for understanding. However, he wanted to ensure they approached this opportunity with awareness of the complexities involved.

"That's a great thought, Louisa," he replied, appreciating her enthusiasm. "Building relationships is important. We should find ways to collaborate, even learn from them before implementing new ideas." He wanted his family to grasp the significance of proceeding with caution and respecting the established practices while finding common ground. Clara nodded in agreement, a sense of resolve settling among them as they contemplated their strategy.

"Let's reach out to the community, show them our intentions," she added, her voice steady and encouraging. "We want to honor their traditions while introducing our methods gradually." Ledger felt emboldened by their collective commitment, knowing that their approach would be key to fostering a sense of belonging. He envisioned the dinner table filled with laughter and conversation, where flavor and culture intertwined, paving the way for cooperation and shared growth. This was more than about their family succeeding; it was about creating a community where everyone could thrive together.

A week later, Ledger stood in front of a brightly lit Kai cacao adorned with colorful banners. He and Clara had organized a small gathering, hoping to foster dialogue between newcomers and established residents of Colihaut. The buzz of conversation filled the air as families arrived, curiosity mingling with skepticism.

As locals began to gather, Ledger felt a mix of excitement and anxiety. Would they be receptive to this initial outreach? The room filled with sound, and Ledger took a deep breath, stepping forward to address the crowd.

Ledger addressed the audience, Thank you all for coming tonight. Clara and I are thrilled to be a part of this community. We want to learn from you and share our plans for our new farm. Your insights and experiences mean a lot to us as we settle into Colihaut.

The crowd listened intently, some nodding in appreciation while others remained cautious. He could feel a mix of curiosity and skepticism—with many eyes focused on him, he pressed on, determined to resonate with their concerns.

We recognize that change can be unsettling, especially in a place with such a rich farming tradition. That is why we are committed to respecting those traditions while exploring ways to grow together. We see incredible potential in collaboration, whether it is through sharing resources, combining efforts in crop planning, or simply learning from each other's journeys.

Ledger glanced around the room, meeting the eyes of several farmers, including Mr. Telford, who had expressed skepticism during their first encounter in the marketplace.

I know some of you have been rooted in these lands for generations, and we want to assure you that we are here to contribute positively—not to compete. We are eager to adapt our methods to better suit this community and the land itself.

He took a moment to breathe, allowing his words to settle in.

To start, we want to invite you to our farm. We would love to show you what we have in mind, listen to your thoughts, and gather your invaluable experience.

As Ledger made eye contact with a few members of the audience, he noted a subtle softening of expressions, and that fueled his confidence.

We also have plans for a community garden where everyone can participate—growing together, learning together, and celebrating the bounty of our hard work.

Wizen, Petronel, and Julien joined him, standing proudly beside their father. Petronel raised her hand slightly, a confident sparkle in her eye.

And we would like to do fun activities, like planting days and harvest celebrations!

A ripple of laughter and warmth spread through the crowd. Ledger sensed some of the barriers beginning to lower, making space for connection and understanding.

Ledger smiling and encouraging, thanked, Petronel. We envision this farm as a hub for gathering—where we can not only grow food but also friendships and support one another. If you have ideas for how we can work together, we want to hear them.

He gestured to a flip chart set up at the front of the room.

Feel free to share your thoughts throughout the evening. We are here to listen. We are excited about becoming part of this vibrant community, and we appreciate the chance to learn from each of you.

With that, he opened the floor for dialogue, inviting residents to share their ideas and concerns. As voices began to rise around him, Ledger felt the initial burden of skepticism start to lift, replaced by a growing sense of possibility—a sense of belonging he longed for.

The sun dipped low in the sky as Ledger approached the community center, its welcoming facade buzzing with the lively chatter of residents preparing for the weekly meeting. He took a moment to collect his thoughts, reminding himself of the importance of patience in this new chapter of his life. If he wanted to establish bonds within the community, he needed to be proactive and present.

Inside, the scent of freshly baked bread wafted through the air as people milled around. He spotted Clara, Wizen, Eliza, Louisa, and Julien setting up a small table laden with food and refreshments, a gesture meant to foster goodwill. Ledger could not help but feel grateful for their unwavering support.

He noticed a group of local farmers gathered at the far end of the room, their laughter rising above the hum of conversation. Instead of lingering on the edges of the gathering, Ledger took a deep breath and stepped forward, determined to connect.

"Hello there! I am Ledger Philogene," he began, walking up to the group with a friendly smile. "**My family and I recently purchased some land here in Colihaut—Au-Fonde and Lawi Dovant." He hoped his introduction would ease the air of uncertainty as he made eye contact with the small gathering. Ledger sensed the mix of curiosity and skepticism from the men around him, their expressions a blend of intrigue and wariness. It was clear that they were weighing his words carefully, trying to gauge exactly who he was and what his presence meant for their community.

One man in particular, David, stepped forward, crossing his arms firmly across his chest. He studied Ledger with an intensity that made him feel both seen and scrutinized. The atmosphere shifted subtly, and Ledger recognized that he was standing at a crucial juncture—the moment could shape the perception of his family and their intentions in this tight-knit community. David's body language suggested he was not easily swayed, and Ledger understood that building trust would take more than just an introduction.

"So, you've come to our little corner with plans for the land, I assume?" David asked, his tone direct but friendly. "What kind of farming do you have in mind?" Ledger could sense the underlying concerns in David's question, an invitation to explain further what they intended to do within a landscape that already had its rhythm and its pulse. This was a critical moment, and Ledger knew he needed to articulate not just his vision, but also the reverence they held for the existing ways of farming in Colihaut. As he prepared to respond, he felt Clara's presence nearby, offering quiet support, and he drew strength from it, ready to demonstrate their commitment to becoming part of the community rather than just its newest inhabitants.

"So, you're the newcomer taking over the old Marcellus places?" David's question was pointed, and Ledger felt the weight of his scrutiny, the unspoken thoughts of the group resting heavily in the air. There was an implicit challenge in David's tone, and while the skepticism was palpable, Ledger refused to let it deter him. He recognized that such an inquiry came from a place of protection for their land and traditions, and he prepared to meet it with openness and sincerity.

"Yes, that's us," Ledger replied, mustering a warm smile to soften the tension. "I am eager to get to know everyone and learn about what has made farming successful in this area. I also want to share some of my experiences if that is all right." He wanted to convey that they were not only newcomers but also potential allies who valued the community's history and knowledge. The group exchanged glances, a subtle shift occurring as they processed his words. Ledger felt a surge of determination to seize the moment, extending his hand in friendship. "I believe there's a lot we can learn from one another," he added, hoping to emphasize the spirit of collaboration he envisioned.

David hesitated for just a moment, his gaze flickering between Ledger's outstretched hand and the faces of his companions. Finally, he reached out, offering his hand firmly. "Alright," he said, his voice a touch softer now. The others watched intently, and as one by one they followed David's lead, Ledger felt the first tentative glimmers of connection forming. The handshake felt significant; it symbolized an opening, a willingness to engage. Each grip was a tiny bridge being built, and Ledger could not help but feel a swell of hope. This was the beginning of something important, a step toward mutual understanding that could grow into a lasting relationship based on respect and shared effort in their new home.

Over the next several weeks, Ledger immersed himself in the community, attending meetings at the Kai Cacao center and participating in local events. He asked questions, sought advice, and tried to share his own experiences from years of farming back home. Each interaction was a brushstroke in the larger picture he hoped to create.

One evening, during a lively community potluck, Ledger found himself beside an older farmer named Roger, who was well-known for his expertise in organic practices. The aroma of various dishes filled the air, and the atmosphere was warm with laughter and camaraderie. Ledger saw this as a perfect opportunity to deepen his understanding of local agriculture. "I'd love to hear about your methods, Roger," he said, leaning in with genuine interest. "What crops have thrived best for you here?" His tone was encouraging, reflecting his eagerness to learn from someone with a wealth of experience.

Roger brightened at Ledger's inquiry, his face lighting up with enthusiasm as he prepared to share his knowledge. As he talked about cover crops and rotation strategies, Ledger listened intently, jotting down notes in the margins of his notebook. The older farmer gestured animatedly, his passion for sustainable farming evident in the way he described the benefits of maintaining soil health. "Keep an eye on the soil. It is your best friend out there. Build it up over the years; it pays off in ways you can only imagine," Roger advised, his eyes sparkling with conviction.

These words resonated deeply with Ledger, echoing the principles of care and stewardship he believed in. He could see how Roger's respect for the land had shaped his success, and it inspired Ledger to consider how he would approach his own farming practices in Colihaut. Making a mental note to visit Roger's farm in the coming weeks, he felt a surge of gratitude for the community's willingness to share their wisdom. The prospect of learning firsthand from Roger was exciting, and Ledger envisioned how this connection could enrich both his knowledge and their mutual efforts to cultivate the land responsibly.

At a community meeting at the square, Ledger felt a mixture of excitement and apprehension as he prepared to speak about his plans for a cooperative food initiative aimed at benefiting both local families and his own. Standing in front of a gathering of residents, he took a deep breath, channeling the energy of the supportive community around him. "I envision a program that not only supports our farm but also strengthens our community," he began, scanning the faces before him. "By working together—sharing resources, celebrating our crops—we can all thrive." His voice projected both passion and determination, hoping to convey how their collective efforts could yield benefits for everyone involved.

The response from the gathered residents was mixed, with some expressions reflecting skepticism while others showed curiosity or cautious optimism. As Ledger spoke, he noticed a few nods of approval from the crowd, small gestures that fueled his confidence. Despite the varied reactions, he could tell that some members were beginning to warm to the idea, intrigued by the potential of collaboration. Ledger acknowledged the reservations he sensed and understood that trust and familiarity would take time to build.

As the conversation started to flow in the right direction, Ledger encouraged input from others. "I'd love to hear your ideas and thoughts on how we can make this work together," he continued, inviting residents to contribute their perspectives and resources. This was not just about his initiative; it was about weaving the fabric of their community tighter, ensuring that every voice was heard and valued. With each suggestion that emerged from the crowd, Ledger felt a growing sense of hope. The seeds of collaboration had been planted, and he believed that with patience and dedication, they could cultivate a thriving cooperative that would benefit everyone in Colihaut.

Emboldened by his growing relationship with the community, Ledger decided to host an open house at Au-Fonde, inviting neighbors and local farmers to explore the land and see his family's vision in action. He envisioned this gathering to showcase the potential of their farmland while fostering deeper connections within the community. To prepare, he set up hay bales for seating, arranged refreshments, and organized a small tour of the property to highlight their sustainable farming practices and future. Ledger hoped that the event would encourage dialogue and collaboration as they all worked toward a common goal.

On the day of the open house, Ledger paced anxiously, his mind racing with thoughts of whether anyone would show up. He felt a mix of excitement and apprehension as he scanned the horizon, searching for any signs of their neighbors. The familiar landscape looked beautiful under the late morning sun, but he could not shake the unease knotting in his stomach. What if no one came? Would his efforts be in vain? The fear of rejection lingered, but he also felt a glimmer of hope that the relationships he had been building would resonate with others.

Finally, as the time approached, a few familiar faces appeared on the dirt road, hesitant yet curious. Ledger's heart swelled with relief as he recognized some of the locals he had met at previous gatherings, their expressions an encouraging mix of intrigue and cautious optimism. Clara stood beside him, her presence steady and supportive. She offered him a reassuring smile as the neighbors drew closer, and he calmed slightly, drawing strength from her unwavering belief in the potential of this gathering. As they approached the entrance to Au-Fonde together, Ledger felt a renewed sense of purpose. This was not just a showcase of land; it was an invitation to collaborate and share in the journey ahead. The open house was about to begin, and with it, the opportunity to build lasting connections in their new home.

"They are here! Just stay true to yourself, Ledger," he reminded himself, feeling a surge of determination wash over him as more people gathered. As the chatter of excited voices filled the air, Ledger stood tall at the front of Au-Fonde, ready to welcome his neighbors. The sun continued to shine brightly, casting a warm glow over the land, and he gestured toward the expansive fields that stretched out behind him—a vivid tapestry of green and brown that symbolized the potential that lay ahead.

"Welcome, everyone! We are so glad you could join us today," Ledger began, his voice gaining strength with each word. "This is our new home, and we want it to feel like your home too. Our vision is to create a place where we can grow together—both in crops and in the community. He scanned the crowd, noticing a mix of expressions on their faces—some curious, others skeptical. This blend of reactions was natural, he thought, as they were all exploring what was possible together. Still, there was a palpable sense of curiosity in the air, and that alone filled him with hope.

As he continued speaking, Ledger felt the energy of the crowd shift slightly, a subtle yet promising sign that people were beginning to engage with his vision. He explained their plans for crop diversity, sustainable practices, and the ideas for their cooperative initiative, emphasizing how collaboration could lead to shared success. He encouraged questions and welcomed input, recognizing that this was not just about his family's goals but about fostering a space where everyone could contribute and feel valued. With each response and exchanged glance, Ledger felt the initial barriers slowly starting to dissolve. This gathering was the first step toward creating the nurturing community he longed for, where every neighbor's voice mattered in their collective journey.

"We're excited about what's possible here," Ledger continued, his voice steady and infused with enthusiasm. "Our goal is to implement sustainable farming practices that respect the land while producing quality crops. But more importantly, we want to engage with all of you, learn from your experiences, and understand what has worked best in this area." As he spoke, he felt a sense of warmth and determination surging within him. This was not merely about soil and seeds; it was about creating a community grounded in shared values and mutual support.

Ledger could see Clara nearby, her encouraging smile radiating pride and belief in his words, and it bolstered his confidence. Her presence reminded him of the journey they had embarked on together, and how vital their connection with the community would be for their success. Meanwhile, their youngest children, Koie and Nerisa, filled the surrounding space with their laughter, running around and collecting smiles from their new neighbors. Their carefree joy was infectious, softening the atmosphere and making the gathering feel even more welcoming.

As he watched them play, Ledger was reminded of the importance of building relationships—not just as farmers but as friends and neighbors. He envisioned Au-Fonde as more than just a piece of land; it could become a hub of friendship, learning, and collaboration. Ledger took a moment to scan the faces in the crowd again, feeling the energy shift as the earlier skepticism transformed into intrigued expressions. This was a pivotal moment for them all, and he felt hopeful about forging connections that would extend beyond the open house, fostering a spirit of togetherness in Colihaut. Each conversation, each shared smile, was a brick in the foundation of the community they all wished to cultivate.

"This land has been cared for by the Marcellus family for generations," Ledger continued, his tone respectful and earnest. "We wish to honor that legacy. We are not here to disrupt; we aim to build on what has already been established. He felt the weight of those words, understanding the significance of the connection between the land and the families that had lived and worked it for decades. Ledger knew that respect for tradition was essential if they were to forge a new path together.

He turned slightly to take in the sights around the farmers observing him with a mix of curiosity and skepticism, families exchanging whispers, and children chasing one another across the grass, their laughter ringing like a chorus through the air. It brought a smile to his face, a warm feeling blossoming within him even amid the underlying tension. Each element painted a vivid picture of community life, and Ledger felt grateful to be part of it, even if he was still a newcomer finding his place.

As he continued to speak, he drew upon the imagery of the children playing freely and the families gathered around, hoping that he could ignite a sense of shared purpose. "Together, we can cultivate not just crops but also a vibrant community that values our history and our future," he said, his gaze encompassing the crowd once more. The visible tension began to ease just a little, and he felt himself gaining traction. Ledger sensed that they were starting to consider the possibilities he was outlining, and it filled him with optimism. This was more than an open house; it was a moment of connection, a step toward blending their histories and dreams into something greater than any one of them could achieve alone.

"Tonight, we've set up some refreshments, and we'd love for you to enjoy them as we chat," Ledger said, gesturing toward the tables laden with an assortment of homemade dishes and drinks. "I would also love to hear about your farms and what you have grown over the years. Your insight would be invaluable to us as we start this journey." He meant every word; he knew that their experiences could shape his approach in ways he had yet to imagine. Community input would be vital as he and his family aimed to enrich the land and respect its heritage.

As Ledger's invitation hung in the air, he noticed some of the local farmers beginning to step forward, hands reaching for refreshments. Their expressions were more relaxed, a small but encouraging sign that they were ready to engage. However, he also noticed others who hung back, carefully observing the unfolding interactions. Their hesitance was evident, and Ledger understood that trust was not something that could be rushed. It took consistent effort and genuine connection over time to cultivate a sense of belonging.

He felt a surge of determination as he made eye contact with a few of the more reticent farmers, offering encouraging smiles to bridge the gap. Ledger was prepared to invest the time and energy needed to build those relationships, knowing that establishing a sense of community would be crucial for their initiative's success. As he encouraged conversation among those gathered, he hoped that as they shared stories of their experiences, the walls would start to come down, paving the way for a collaborative future. Each dialogue, each laugh over shared memories of farming trials and triumphs, would weave them closer together, transforming their efforts into a collective mission of support and prosperity.

"And remember, we're not just looking to take from this community," Ledger said, grinning broadly as he made eye contact with various attendees. "We want to participate, make contributions, and hopefully become valued members. Let us forge partnerships that can uplift all of us!" His enthusiasm was infectious, resonating with many in the crowd. He could see a few smiles beginning to emerge, their warmth igniting the possibility of genuine connection.

As he mingled among the guests, Ledger made it a point to engage individuals one-on-one, listening attentively to their stories and sharing snippets about his own life. He approached each conversation with an open heart, eager to understand their experiences and perspectives. The atmosphere shifted as these interactions unfolded; conversations began to bloom like the flowers emerging in spring. With every shared laugh or personal anecdote, the walls of skepticism that initially surrounded him gradually crumbled. People started to see him as more than just a newcomer seeking to establish a business; they began to view him as a potential friend and ally in their shared agricultural journey.

After some time, Ledger found himself at a table with an older farmer named Martha, who was well-known for her award-winning heirloom tomatoes. He had heard murmurs about her crops and how fiercely she cared for her garden. Sitting down across from her, he felt an immediate rapport. "I've heard so much about your tomatoes," he began, genuinely interested. "What are your secrets? What makes them so special?" As Martha leaned in, her eyes sparkling with pride, Ledger sensed that this conversation could be the beginning of a valuable friendship and mentorship. He listened intently as she shared her techniques and the care that went into her farming practices, grateful to gain first-hand knowledge from a seasoned expert. In this exchange, Ledger not only learned about tomatoes but also felt the rich history of passion and dedication that Martha brought to her work, further inspiring his vision for community collaboration.

"So, you want to grow tomatoes, do you? You will have to earn their love, you know," Martha said, leaning forward with a twinkle in her eye. Her playful challenge made Ledger chuckle, and he replied, "I am ready for the challenge! What is your secret?" This sparked a lively conversation that ignited a sense of camaraderie between them. Ledger felt invigorated by the exchange; it was more than just a discussion about gardening techniques; it was an opportunity to learn from someone who had poured her heart and soul into her craft.

As Martha spoke, her passion for her tomatoes became evident. She shared the intricacies of her cultivation methods, from the importance of crop rotation to the benefits of companion planting. "You need to listen to the plants," she advised, her tone earnest. "They'll tell you when they're thirsty or when they need nutrients." She sprinkled in community wisdom accumulated over the years, weaving personal anecdotes with lessons learned from neighbors and fellow farmers. Ledger soaked it all in, captivated by her stories of late nights spent caring for her crops and the joy that came with harvesting award-winning fruits.

With each passing moment, he felt more connected—not only to the knowledge she was imparting but also to the rich tapestry of traditions that defined farming in their community. Martha's insights illuminated the deeper relationship between a farmer and the land, revealing that success often stemmed from patience, respect, and a willingness to learn. As the sun dipped lower in the sky, casting a warm glow over the gathering, Ledger realized this conversation was not just about tomatoes; it was about cultivating mutual respect, sharing knowledge, and breathing life into the vision he had for Au-Fonde.

"Every bit of knowledge you share with me is a piece of the puzzle I need to fit into this new environment," Ledger expressed earnestly, grateful for Martha's insights. "Thank you for being so open." He could feel a genuine bond forming, one that transcended mere agriculture and hinted at the kind of community he envisioned. Martha smiled warmly, pleased to see her experiences valued.

Their shared conversation was not just passing chatter; it was a foundational moment that would help shape his understanding of local farming practices and strengthen his ties to the community.

Meanwhile, Koie and Nerisa were busy weaving their connections among the children gathered at the event, drawing them into playful activities and leading a game of tag that erupted into joyous shouts and laughter. The cheerful sounds filled the makeshift gathering area, creating an atmosphere of lightheartedness and camaraderie. As Ledger glanced over to see his children chasing after their new friends, his heart swelled with pride and hope. This spirit of play echoed a warmth he deeply longed for in their new home—a sense of belonging that transcended age.

Watching the joy on the children's faces, Ledger felt a renewed sense of purpose. It was clear that these moments of laughter were just as crucial as the farming conversations, creating an underlying foundation of connection that would support their new life. As Koie and Nerisa continued to draw in the other children, Ledger envisioned a future where community gatherings would celebrate not only the fruits of their labor but also the relationships they would cultivate along the way. It was in these shared experiences, these vibrant interactions, that he believed they would find the roots of their new life flourishing in Au-Fonde.

As the evening wore on, Ledger felt a growing sense of belonging enveloping him. Conversation flowed like the warm breeze that rustled the leaves overhead, and laughter erupted from various corners of the gathering. Despite the initial uncertainty that had marked their arrival, he could sense that seeds of friendship were beginning to sprout in the warm glow of their shared commitment to community and farming. Each dialogue, each shared smile, added richness to the fabric of the evening, transforming a simple open house into a vibrant tapestry of connection.

Underneath the stars, Ledger stood among his new neighbors, soaking in the beauty of the moment. The sky was a canvas of twinkling stars, illuminating the faces of those around him. He felt a swell of optimism in his heart just perhaps, they were on their way to building enduring relationships that would bloom alongside the crops they planned to cultivate. He could envision future gatherings filled with the same laughter and camaraderie, where the community would come together to celebrate both their challenges and triumphs in farming and life.

In that moment, Ledger realized that the journey ahead would be shaped not only by the land they tended but also by the bonds they nurtured. The potential of what they could achieve together began to form in his mind, both as individual farmers and as a unified community. With each story shared and every connection forged, he felt a deeper response from those around him, igniting the hope that Au-Fonde would not just sustain their family but also become a cherished part of a larger, thriving community. He knew that by cultivating these relationships, they were planting a foundation for future growth—one that would see their collective dreams take root and flourish.

Adapting to rural life in Colihaut required the Philogene family to immerse themselves fully in the local customs and practices that defined the vibrant community. Each day brought new lessons, as they navigated a lifestyle shaped by the rhythms of nature and the rich traditions that had been passed down through generations. The pace of life here was markedly different—slower yet infused with a depth that fostered connection and community spirit. For Ledger, Clara, and their children, this shift was not merely about adjusting to agricultural techniques; it was a profound journey of understanding the essence of the culture surrounding them.

As they learned to farm the fertile land, they discovered more than just the mechanics of planting and harvesting; they encountered the stories embedded in every crop and every technique. They listened to the wisdom of seasoned farmers, gaining insight into sustainable practices that had stood the test of time. This education extended beyond the fields, as they participated in local festivals and gatherings that celebrated the community's heritage. Clara found joy in engaging with neighboring families and sharing recipes and traditions while learning about the culinary practices that defined Colihaut's identity. Every shared meal became an opportunity to connect, reinforcing their bond with both the land and the people.

Through these experiences, the Philogene family slowly learned to navigate the intricate web of relationships that composed their new home. They were welcomed not just as newcomers but as integral parts of the community. Children from local families joined their own in the fields, creating friendships that crossed cultural boundaries. With every shared laugh, every joint effort in the garden, and every story exchanged on warm evenings, the Philogenes contributed to a larger narrative of belonging.

Additionally, the children adapted to their surroundings, embracing the slower pace of life and reveling in the simple pleasures of rural living. They discovered the joy of exploring nature, learning to appreciate the beauty of their environment while developing a respect for the land that sustained them. This cultural adaptation went beyond mere survival; it was an enriching journey that deepened their understanding of what it meant to be connected to a community, to the earth, and to each other. As they became more rooted in Colihaut, the Philogene family began to embody the spirit of resilience and cooperation that characterized their new home, further enriching their lives and anchoring them in a place they could truly call home.

The annual Colihaut St. Peter's Fishermen's Feast was in full swing, casting a vibrant spell over the town. Colorful banners fluttered in the gentle breeze, adding splashes of color that seemed to dance in the sunlight. The air was thick with the rich aromas of local delicacies—fried fish, seasoned plantains, and sweet pastries mingled, creating an enticing atmosphere that beckoned both locals and visitors alike. Families laughed and mingled, their voices weaving together to create a lively tapestry of sound that filled the streets with joy and celebration. The Philogene family arrived with excitement, their hearts full of hope as they stepped into the vibrant scene unfolding before them.

Clara took the lead, her spirit infectious as she guided their children, Nerisa, and Koie, through the festivities. They started at the church for the morning service, where the community gathered in gratitude and reverence. The atmosphere was spiritual yet uplifting, with hymns resonating through the walls and prayers uniting everyone's hearts. After the service, the real excitement began with a lively procession through the village. The streets came alive with people singing and dancing, their energy contagious as they made their way to the bayside for the blessing of the boats. Clara watched her children's faces light up, their wonder evident as they soaked in the sights, sounds, and spirit of the annual tradition.

As they navigated through La Place Dame, Clara pointed out various stalls set up by local artisans and craftspeople, each representing a unique craft or tradition associated with Colihaut. From colorful woven baskets to intricate carvings, the stalls showcased the rich cultural heritage of the area. "Look at that," she exclaimed, guiding them towards a booth where vendors demonstrated the art of fishing net making. "These," she explained, "are skills passed down through generations. It is a big part of what makes our community strong." Nerisa and Koie eagerly listened, asking questions and taking in the stories as they watched the artisan's work, their excitement growing as they learned more about the traditions that shaped their new home.

As the day wore on, the Philogene family joined in the festivities, tasting different dishes and sharing smiles with their neighbors. Clara felt a deep sense of belonging wash over her; this celebration was a brilliant representation of the community they had become a part of. With each laugh shared and every tradition embraced, the Philogenes felt their roots sinking deeper into the rich soil of Colihaut. The feast was not just a day of fun but a conduit for connection, where they could celebrate not only the bounty of the sea but also the bonds that tied them to this vibrant community.

"Look at those baskets!" Clara exclaimed, smiling brightly as she pointed to the colorful display of intricately woven baskets on a nearby stall. "They are woven by hand from palm fronds, a skill that has been passed down for generations. Let us go learn how to make one!" Her eyes gleamed with excitement, and the hustle and bustle of the festival served as the perfect backdrop for this moment of discovery. It was a chance not only to appreciate the craftsmanship but also to connect with the community's rich traditions.

Nerisa, her eyes sparkling with enthusiasm, clutched her mother's hand tightly. "Can we really make one, Mom? Please!" she asked, her voice bubbling with eagerness. Clara felt a rush of joy as she observed her daughter's excitement; Nerisa had always been drawn to creative activities, ready to embrace new experiences. Meanwhile, Koie, still shy, lingered a little behind, his gaze darting between the colorful baskets and the bustling crowd. Clara noticed his hesitation and knelt, brushing a strand of hair out of his eyes with a gentle touch.

"Hey there, buddy," she said softly, her voice reassuring. "It is just like when we learned to plant in our garden. You will be great at this! And think of all the fun we will have together." Clara understood that Koie sometimes preferred to observe before joining in, and she wanted him to feel comfortable in this vibrant setting. "We can work side by side; I'll show you the ropes," she added, smiling encouragingly. Koie looked up at her, a small smile appearing on his face, and nodded slowly, his confidence slowly growing with her support.

With a renewed sense of excitement, Clara stood up, taking her children's hands in hers. "Let's go see if we can find someone who can teach us," she said, leading them toward the basket-making stall. As they approached, Clara felt a sense of gratitude for the opportunity to share this experience with her children. It was moments like these that not only enriched their understanding of Colihaut's culture but also strengthened the bond they shared as a family. The colorful festival came alive around them, and Clara was eager to dive into a new adventure, knowing it would become a cherished memory for years to come.

"It's important for us to learn from the people here, sweetheart," Clara reminded her children, her voice warm and encouraging. "Every basket has a story; every dish has a history." She could see that her words were slowly igniting a spark of interest in Koie. With a gentle nudge of encouragement, he stepped forward, his shyness giving way to curiosity. Nervousness faded as they approached the weaving booth, and Clara felt a surge of pride watching her son take this brave step into the heart of the community.

As they gathered around the booth, they were greeted by the elderly artisan, Mrs. Arnaud, who welcomed them with open arms and a radiant smile. Her hands, skillfully weathered by years of intricate work, deftly manipulated the palm fronds as she prepared to demonstrate her craft. Clara felt a warm connection forming as Mrs. Arnaud began to share not only her skills but also her stories, weaving together the past and present of Colihaut's vibrant culture. The children listened intently, captivated by the rhythm of her voice and the passion that danced in her eyes.

"Each pattern you see here has a special meaning," Mrs. Arnaud explained, her fingers skillfully weaving the fronds together. "This design," she said, pointing to a bright yellow basket, "represents the sun, which gives us life and nourishment. And this one," she continued, indicating a deeper blue piece, "symbolizes the sea and its abundance." Clara watched as Koie's eyes widened with wonder at the thought that each creation held a connection to their community. He began to ask questions, his voice eager and free of hesitation now that they were fully engaged in the learning experience: "What do these colors mean, and how long does it take to make one?"

Mrs. Arnaud smiled and answered him patiently, encouraging his curiosity. Clara felt a sense of warmth wash over her, realizing that this moment was more than just learning a craft; it was about building bridges between cultures and fostering a sense of belonging. With each story and lesson shared, they were not only gaining practical skills but also embedding themselves deeper into the fabric of Colihaut. It was an enriching experience that Clara knew would resonate with her children long after the festival ended. As they watched and listened, Clara felt the excitement of discovery and connection enveloped them, a perfect blend of teaching and learning that would strengthen their roots in this beautiful community.

After the St. Peter's Feast, the Philogene family returned to Au-Fonde, their bags filled with local crafts and souvenirs that reflected the vibrant culture they had just experienced. Each item held a story, from the handwoven baskets to the fragrant spices they had sampled, serving as tangible reminders of the warm welcome they had received. As they settled back into their home, the atmosphere felt different, charged with a new sense of connection to the community. Ledger and Clara exchanged glances, both aware that this journey marked the beginning of a deeper relationship with their neighbors.

"I know some locals still look at us with skepticism, especially the older generation," Ledger said reflectively, as they sat together at the dining table, unpacking their treasures. "But I want to make sure our children understand the importance of respecting these traditions." His brow furrowed slightly as he considered the cautious attitudes they had encountered. Ledger felt it was vital for Nerisa and Koie to appreciate the rich history and values of Colihaut, understanding that their family's integration into the community would require patience and genuine respect for its customs.

Clara nodded in agreement, her heart full of thoughts on how they could navigate this journey as a family. "We can start by incorporating these traditions into our everyday lives," she suggested, her eyes sparkling with inspiration. "Cooking local dishes together, attending more community events, and engaging with our neighbors will help bridge that gap." She felt strongly that active participation would not only enrich their experience but also demonstrate their commitment to becoming a part of Colihaut.

Ledger smiled, feeling reassured by Clara's optimistic outlook. "You are right. It is not just about living here; it is about being a part of the fabric of this place. If we show that we respect and value their way of life, they will come to see us as neighbors, not outsiders. He felt a renewed sense of purpose, envisioning a future where their children would grow up understanding the importance of cultural respect and community. Together, they began to brainstorm ideas—attending cultural workshops, volunteering for community clean-ups, and even hosting a gathering to share their own family traditions.

As they mapped out their plans, the Philogene family felt the threads of connection begin to weave tighter. They were determined to create a home not just within the walls of their house in Au-Fonde, but also in the hearts of the people of Colihaut. The journey ahead was filled with promise, and Ledger and Clara were eager to embrace it, knowing that with each step taken, they were not only learning but also contributing to the rich tapestry of their new community.

"Absolutely. We need to show them that we are not here to change their way of life, but to join it," Clara affirmed with determination, her voice steady. She could see the potential for building meaningful connections in Colihaut. "Perhaps we can start by participating more actively in community events." It was clear to her that genuine engagement would not only help her family assimilate but also build trust and goodwill among their neighbors. The idea of rolling up their sleeves and being a part of the community invigorated her, and she quickly began brainstorming ways to get involved.

As the weeks flew by, the Philogene family committed themselves to fully immersing in their new life. They joined the congregation at the local church, where they found warmth and camaraderie among fellow worshippers. Each Sunday, they embraced the sense of community that filled the sanctuary, singing hymns and participating in prayers that connected them to the heart of Colihaut. They also took part in local cleanup days, picking up litter from the beaches and parks while chatting with residents and fostering a sense of shared responsibility for the environment. Clara and Ledger reveled in the experience, grateful for the chance to contribute positively to their new community.

In addition, the Philogenes began sharing home-cooked meals with their neighbors, inviting families over to enjoy dishes inspired by both local cuisine and their own culinary traditions. Clara made it a point to introduce her children, Nerisa, and Koie, to the joys of cooking together, explaining the ingredients and customs behind each dish. As they prepared food and laughed together, the kitchen became a hub of connection and learning. Clara encouraged the children to engage with their peers at school and during community events, highlighting the significance behind the activities and the customs they encountered. "Every tradition has a story," she would say, her eyes twinkling with enthusiasm. "And you can be part of that story."

Nerisa flourished in this environment, her confidence growing as she forged friendships and learned the local dialect. Koie, initially more reserved, found strength in his sister's enthusiasm and joined in, participating in games and community projects that drew him out of his shell. Clara watched with pride as her children adapted, their laughter ringing through their new home in Au-Fonde. The Philogene family was not merely settling into a new place; they were weaving themselves into the very fabric of Colihaut, creating bonds that would last a lifetime. Each event they attended, and each story they shared, brought them closer to understanding the rich culture surrounding them, and for Clara that sense of belonging was worth every effort they made.

During a lively community dinner, Clara gathered her children close, ready to impart another lesson about the rich traditions surrounding them. "Remember, it's not just about tasting the food; it's about understanding what it represents," she said, her voice filled with warmth and conviction. "Every dish has roots in the land and the people." Clara pointed out the colorful spreads on the tables, each plate telling a story of the island's heritage, reflecting the ingredients grown in the soil and the hands that prepared them. She encouraged Nerisa and Koie to ask questions and engage with their neighbors about the meals, instilling in them a respect for the culture that embraced them, even if it was still learning to do the same in return.

Despite their diligent efforts to integrate into the community, Clara noticed that some locals still eyed them with caution. This became glaringly apparent during a community meeting concerning the upcoming harvest festival, where the air was thick with unease. As discussions around logistics and planning began, a few voices from the crowd raised concerns about the newcomers. Clara felt a knot tighten in her stomach as she listened to murmurs about fear of change and competition for resources. The apprehension in the room was palpable, and she knew it could spark doubt about their place within this community.

"We have managed our farms for generations. How do we know you will not disrupt what has been working for us?" a local farmer challenged, skepticism etched on his face. Ledger could feel the weight of the words hanging in the air, and he sensed the tension rising among the attendees. Clara glanced at him, knowing that he would have to respond to ease their fears and reinforce their commitment to being part of Colihaut.

With resolve, Ledger stood up, addressing the crowd. "I understand your concerns; we share this land and its resources, and we deeply respect the traditions and practices that have sustained you for so long," he began, his tone earnest and steady. "Our family is here to learn, to contribute, and to support the community. We bring our skills and willingness to help, not to disrupt." He looked directly at the farmer, hoping to convey sincerity. "I want to assure you that our goal is to complement your efforts, not to compete with them. Together, we can create something beautiful for our community."

Ledger's words hung in the air, and a murmur of acknowledgment rippled through the crowd. Clara held her breath, watching as Ledger continued, detailing the ways they hoped to collaborate during the festival and beyond—whether by lending a hand in the fields or sharing innovative ideas without imposing change. Gradually, the atmosphere shifted as he engaged with the audience, taking the time to answer questions and address concerns, proving their dedication to being responsible members of the community. She could see in the eyes of the locals that he was beginning to break down the barriers of skepticism, and she felt a wave of hope that, with continued effort, they would strengthen their bonds with the people of Colihaut.

"I understand your worries," Ledger continued, looking around the room with sincerity etched on his face. "And I want to assure you that our goal isn't to disrupt but to contribute." His voice was steady, and he made eye contact with several community members, trying to bridge the gap between them. "We respect the land and the traditions that have kept this community thriving." He paused, letting his words sink in before adding, "We're eager to learn from your experiences, and we hope to collaborate on future projects." The earnestness in his tone resonated with those listening, creating an atmosphere that felt just a bit more open.

As he spoke, Ledger noticed a few locals nodding in agreement, their expressions softening. Clara held her breath, hopeful that his sincerity was making an impact. It was evident that the Philogenes' commitment to respect and understanding was beginning to shine through the skepticism that had initially confronted them. "We all want what's best for our families and our community," he continued, feeling a sense of camaraderie growing in the room. "We want to celebrate this harvest festival together and make it a showcase for our shared values and traditions."

With each word, the tension in the air began to dissipate, slowly replaced by a dialogue that felt more collaborative than confrontational. Ledger could see that by expressing their willingness to learn, the Philogenes were moving beyond being mere outsiders; they were becoming potential allies. As Clara glanced around the room, she could feel the energy shift, a budding sense of optimism building among those gathered.

After the meeting, some locals approached the Philogene family, sharing their thoughts and even inviting them to specific preparations for the festival. The warmer responses encouraged Ledger and Clara to embrace the opportunities ahead and forge deeper connections. They began to exchange ideas on how to enhance the celebration while highlighting Colihaut's rich heritage, laying the groundwork for an impactful partnership. By remaining committed to showing respect, engaging with their neighbors, and helping wherever possible, Ledger and Clara were confident that, over time, they would truly find their place within this community, alongside their newfound friends and partners in celebration.

Months passed, and the Philogene family became increasingly entwined in the rhythms of rural life in Colihaut. The landscape around them transformed into a familiar tapestry, with the sound of birdsong and the scent of earthy rain providing a comforting backdrop to their daily lives. As they immersed themselves in local customs and practices, they began to earn respect within the community. Young adults Wizen, Petronel, Julien, Eliza, Louisa, James, and Dfriel formed strong friendships with local peers, spending afternoons at lively gatherings, strumming guitars, and sharing stories under the shade of palm trees. They explored the vibrant streets together, discovering hidden cafés and participating in weekend markets, where laughter and the excitement of bustling activity filled the air. Nerisa and Koie formed friendships with their peers, laughing and playing together in the gardens and streets. They quickly learned traditional games that echoed the laughter and joy of their new friends, and even joined local sports events, showcasing their skills and eager spirits. The bonds they forged with the community members gradually grew strong, embodying the idea that they truly belonged.

Quickly adapting to the local culture, they eagerly joined in traditional games and soccer matches that echoed the joy of their youth. Their weekends were vibrant; they attended bonfires on the beach, danced to the rhythms of local music, and enjoyed friendly competitions that showcased their skills and enthusiastic spirits. As the bonds with their new friends deepened, it became clear that they were no longer just visitors; they were becoming integral members of the community, embodying the idea that they truly belonged. Each shared experience forged connections that solidified their ties to this remarkable place, blending their lives seamlessly with the rich tapestry of Colihaut's culture.

One afternoon, Clara decided to take the initiative to strengthen those connections further by organizing a small community gathering at Au-Fonde. She extended invitations to their neighbors for a potluck dinner, excited at the prospect of sharing food, laughter, and stories. As preparations began, Clara adorned their home with handmade decorations, draping colorful fabrics and weaving palm fronds into cheerful arrangements. The ambiance felt festive, and she could hardly wait to welcome everyone in. The aroma of familiar dishes filled the air as she prepared a feast that blended both their St. Barthélemy roots and the local flavors of Colihaut. Clara had carefully chosen recipes that celebrated the essence of the community's cuisine— from spicy fish dishes to comforting vegetable stews—hoping to foster a sense of connection and unity through the universal love of food.

As the sun began to set, casting a warm golden glow over the yard, Clara felt a thrill of anticipation. One by one, neighbors arrived, bringing dishes of their own. The mingling scents of spices and herbs created a rich tapestry of flavors, each dish reflecting a piece of its creator's heart and heritage. Clara moved among her guests, encouraging everyone to share the stories behind their dishes while introducing them to her own family recipes. Laughter echoed throughout the night as stories were exchanged, and cultural connections deepened.

Nerisa and Koie played with their new friends, caught up in games and laughter, and happily engaged in the spirit of the gathering. Clara watched her children, a smile spread across her face as she saw the delightful blend of cultures coming together. They were no longer outsiders, but active participants in the rhythms of Colihaut. The evening became a celebration of shared experiences, creating bridges of understanding that strengthened the community's fabric. Clara felt a true sense of achievement in bringing everyone together, realizing that these connections were what would ground their family in this beautiful new chapter of their lives. Each friendly conversation, shared meal, and collective laughter added another layer to the rich tapestry of their experience in Colihaut, further binding them to the community they now called home.

As the sun began to set, casting a warm golden glow over the landscape, the atmosphere at Au-Fonde transformed into a scene of warmth and welcome. Guests started to arrive, each bringing with them an array of dishes that filled the air with tantalizing aromas. The friendly chatter of neighbors echoed in the yard, harmonizing with the sound of laughter from children who dashed about, playing tag and enjoying the carefree freedom of the open space. Clara stood at the entrance of their home, her heart swelling with joy as she welcomed each person.

"Welcome! I am so glad you could all join us tonight!" Clara called out cheerfully, her smile reflecting her excitement. Her voice danced above the noise as she greeted familiar faces and new friends alike, her warmth inviting everyone into the festive atmosphere. She was thrilled to see how far they had come in building relationships within the community and tonight felt like a culmination of those efforts. As guests mingled, they took in the decorations Clara had hung—colorful palm fronds and handmade banners that added to the celebratory ambiance, creating a sense of togetherness that mirrored the spirit of the occasion.

Children scampered past, their laughter ringing in the air as they played hide-and-seek among the trees, free to explore the haven that the Philogene family had created. Clara made her way through the gathering, encouraging conversations, and making introductions. She pointed out the contributions of those who had brought dishes from their own kitchens, highlighting the rich tapestry of flavors that reflected the diverse backgrounds of their guests. At this moment, Clara could feel the merging of cultures and friendships, each interaction weaving them closer together.

As the kitchen filled with the enticing scents of her carefully prepared meal—a fusion of St. Barthélemy flavors blended with local delicacies—Clara took a moment to breathe it all in. Tonight was not just about sharing food; it was about celebrating connections and creating memories as a community. She felt a deep sense of gratitude for the journey that had brought them here and for the neighbors who had become friends. With a heart full of hope, Clara looked around at the gathering and knew they were not just building a home but a family among families, reinforcing the bonds that would sustain them all in the months and years to come.

She welcomed each family with heartfelt warmth, making them feel at home as they entered the beautifully decorated space. The tables were set with an array of dishes: djon-djon rice, fried plantains, callaloo, and a delicious stew made from the local catch of the day.

Ledger stepped out onto the porch, beaming with pride at the sight of their neighbors mingling while enjoying the spread. He felt a bubbling excitement as he realized that this gathering was more than just a meal; it was a bridge. A chance to further blend their lives with the community.

"Thank you all for coming!" Ledger said, raising his glass high above the table, his voice ringing with sincerity as he addressed the gathering. "Tonight is about sharing not just food but stories and laughter. We are grateful to have you here with us." His words hung in the air for a moment, accompanied by a palpable sense of warmth and camaraderie that settled over the group. He could see the smiles and nods of agreement from their neighbors, who had come together to celebrate this evening of connection.

As he lowered his glass, the neighbors responded with enthusiasm, raising their own drinks in a chorus of cheerful cheers and laughter. The sound reverberated throughout the yard, echoing the joy of collective celebration. With the initial toasts complete, everyone began to serve themselves from the beautifully arranged spread that Clara had worked so hard to prepare. Plates filled with mouthwatering dishes reflected a mosaic of tastes, from traditional local specialties to the delicious influences of their St. Barthélemy roots.

Conversations flowed freely as groups gathered around tables, sharing bites and anecdotes. Clara moved gracefully among the guests, ensuring that everyone had enough to eat and drink, her warm smile, was a constant presence that invited connection. She paused to listen to stories about the rich history of Colihaut, mingling with laughter as neighbors recounted humorous memories from their childhoods. She felt the energy of the gathering enveloped her, reinforcing the importance of these shared experiences.

Ledger watched the scene unfold, feeling a deep sense of pride in the community that was growing around his family. The atmosphere was filled with animated discussions and joyful exchanges, reflecting a sense of belonging that he had longed for since their arrival. Watching his children bonding with the local kids and his neighbors engaging in friendly banter, he realized that this gathering was not just about food but about the beautiful tapestry of lives woven together through shared moments. With every bite taken and every story exchanged, the Philogene family's place in Colihaut became even more solidified, a testament to the power of community and connection.

"Want to help me make a flower crown?" Nerisa asked her local friend, her eyes sparkling with enthusiasm. "I learned how to do it from a lady at the fair!" She knelt to gather flowers from the nearby garden, her hands deftly selecting the brightest blooms to create a crown that would reflect the colors of the evening. Her friend's eyes lit up with excitement as they began to weave the flowers together, laughter bubbling between them as they shared tips and stories about their favorite designs.

Koie, shyly tagging along with Nerisa, stood nearby, watching his sister and their new friends as they gathered materials. He observed as the other children whispered excitedly about their favorite local games, their faces animated with enthusiasm. This warmth and excitement stood in stark contrast to the initial skepticism he had felt from some of the locals when their family first arrived. Now, he felt a sense of belonging, the camaraderie among them creating an atmosphere that was truly inviting. Koie took a tentative step forward, gathering the courage to join their creative endeavor, realizing that he, too, could be a part of this joyful experience.

As the evening progressed, the gathering's vibrancy continued to grow. Ledger found himself deep in conversation with Mr. Telford, a local farmer who had been reluctant at first but now seemed to be warm to the idea of collaboration. They discussed the upcoming harvest festival and shared ideas for how the Philogene family could contribute, focusing on enhancing the festival's community spirit. Ledger listened intently, appreciating Mr. Telford's insights and recognizing how valuable this exchange of thoughts was in building trust.

The sound of laughter and conversation filled the air as Ledger and Mr. Telford struck a chord of mutual respect and understanding. With each word shared, the barriers that had initially existed began to crumble, replaced by a partnership rooted in shared goals. Ledger felt a surge of hope; moments like these signaled a bright future for the Philogene family in Colihaut and reinforced the importance of fostering relationships based on collaboration and open communication. As he glanced over at Nerisa and Koie, their laughter intertwined with the sounds of the gathering, he knew they were not just building a home but paving the way for a strong community that embraced every member, new and old.

"You've put a lot of effort into this," Mr. Telford said, taking a sip from his drink as he regarded the vibrant gathering around them. "I can see it. It takes courage to dive into community life like you have." His voice carried a note of genuine admiration, signaling the shift in his understanding of the Philogene family's intentions. Ledger appreciated the acknowledgment, recognizing that moments like these were vital for forging deeper connections.

"It's important to us," Ledger replied earnestly, his shoulders relaxing as he continued the conversation. "We want to learn and respect the traditions that make Colihaut special. We are in this together, after all." He felt the weight of their journey—leaving their home and settling into a new place—shifting into something more hopeful and collaborative. As he spoke, his passion for integrating into the community radiated from him, reinforcing his deep commitment to building relationships based on mutual respect.

Mr. Telford nodded appreciatively, his expression softening as he considered Ledger's words. The walls that had once separated them seemed to be crumbling, and Ledger could sense that their previous conversations had opened the door just a little wider. The hesitations that had once lingered in Mr. Telford's eyes were gradually being replaced by a readiness to connect.

As they continued to talk, Ledger shared stories of his family's traditions, weaving in anecdotes of their life on St. Barthélemy and how those roots intertwined with their desire to embrace Colihaut's culture. In return, Mr. Telford shared insights about farming practices handed down through generations, his voice laced with pride as he discussed the community's shared heritage. Every exchange deepened their understanding of one another, planting the seeds for a future built on collaboration. Ledger felt a renewed sense of hope, knowing that dialogues like this would help bridge the gap between newcomers and long-time residents, cultivating a spirit of unity that would strengthen their community bonds.

As the sun dipped below the horizon and twilight settled gently over Au-Fonde, the energy of the gathering shifted toward storytelling. Clara took the lead, her voice warm and inviting as she encouraged everyone to share their favorite memories centered around farming, food, or family traditions. "These stories are what connect us—our experiences and traditions shape who we are," she said, gesturing to everyone gathered. "Thank you all for sharing your part in this community." The atmosphere buzzed with excitement as neighbors eagerly took turns recounting tales filled with laughter, nostalgia, and a sense of pride in their roots.

The stories flowed freely, each one adding another layer to the tapestry of connections between the Philogene family and their neighbors. Clara felt a wave of warmth enveloping her; her vision of blending cultures and forging lasting relationships gradually manifested into a beautiful reality. The laughter and shared memories echoed in the air, creating a bond of familiarity and trust that had been slowly built over the months. Each story told was a thread weaving the lives of those present into a shared narrative, reinforcing their collective identity as a community.

As the evening ended, Ledger found himself standing back, taking a moment to absorb the vibrant scene before him. The Philogene home, once a quiet outpost, was now filled with the joyous sounds of laughter, the enticing aromas of mixed cuisines, and a rich tapestry of cultural conversations. It all blended into a harmonious celebration of life and togetherness, highlighting the connections being forged that evening. His gaze shifted to Clara, whose eyes sparkled with delight as she engaged with their guests.

At that moment, Ledger felt an overwhelming sense of gratitude wash over him. He recognized the significance of this gathering—not just as an event, but as a turning point in their journey. Surrounded by new friends and united in shared stories, the Philogene family was no longer just outsiders; they had become an integral part of this community. As they shared in the warmth of the night, Ledger knew they were laying down roots that would sustain them for years to come, nurturing a deep sense of home in Colihaut.

In the following weeks, the Philogenes continued their dedicated efforts to integrate into Colihaut, each family member contributing their unique strengths to the community. Clara, with her love for plants and gardening, initiated a small gardening club, inviting local families to join them in cultivating a community garden. This new endeavor quickly took root and thrived, flourishing under the shared hands and hearts of many eager participants. Clara watched with delight as families gathered in the garden, exchanging tips, laughter, and stories while digging in the earth together.

The collaborative effort drew in more families than Clara had anticipated, creating a vibrant blend of plant varieties and growing techniques that enriched the landscape. As colorful flowers bloomed and fresh vegetables sprouted, the garden became a symbol of unity, each plant reflecting the diverse backgrounds and traditions of those tending to it. With each meeting, the initial barriers faded further away, replaced by budding friendships rooted in mutual respect and shared dreams. Neighbors who once kept to themselves became familiar faces, their laughter and joy filling the air, transforming the garden into a lively hub of interaction.

As the seasons changed, the crops flourished, blooming in time with the relationships that had developed among the Philogenes and their neighbors. Ledger often strolled through the garden, taking in the sight of flourishing plants and gathering families, feeling a deep sense of pride. He knew that they had not just adapted to their new surroundings but had become an integral part of Colihaut. They were honoring its traditions while also contributing their own unique gifts to the community tapestry, enriching the lives of those around them.

Their journey was only beginning, yet the strength they found in each other and the support of the community reinforced their resolve. Ledger looked forward to the many seasons ahead, confident that the roots they were establishing would grow strong and deep. With every shared meal from the garden and each connection forged among the families, the Philogenes continued to cultivate not just crops, but also a beautiful sense of belonging that would endure in Colihaut for years to come.

The transition to farming at Au-Fonde proved to be a greater challenge than Ledger and his family had anticipated. What they initially envisioned as a serene life filled with the joys of planting and harvesting was quickly overshadowed by the reality of hard, labor-intensive work. As the sun crested the horizon each morning, its warm rays illuminated the fields, yet they also beckoned the Philogene family to start their days earlier than ever before.

The transition to farming at Au-Fonde proves to be a significant challenge for the Philogene family. What they initially envisioned as a serene and rewarding lifestyle quickly reveals itself to be a grueling test of endurance and dedication. Ledger, Clara, and their children soon learn that transforming their land into a productive farm demands hard, labor-intensive work that requires both physical strength and mental resilience. Each morning, the family rises before dawn, the rooster's crow echoing in the stillness as they prepare for another day of toil. The crisp morning air fills their lungs, but the weight of responsibility adds a palpable heaviness to each step as they venture into the fields.

In the early days of farming, as they set to work clearing the land, the reality of rural life became apparent. They spend long hours under the sun, tilling the soil, pulling weeds, and preparing rows for planting. The labor is relentless, and at the end of each day, they return home sore and fatigued. The physical toll of this new lifestyle strains them, testing their limits and sometimes leading to frustration and exhaustion. Yet, despite the hardships, the Philogenes remain committed to their dream of cultivating a thriving farm. They share laughter and encouragement during their labor, relying on one another for support as they battle both the elements and their own fatigue.

As days turn into weeks, the challenge of farming begins to solidify their resolve. Ledger often reminds their family of the purpose behind their hard work, the vision of a bountiful harvest, fresh vegetables, and a sustainable lifestyle. Clara, too, uplifts their spirits by creating small rituals around their work, such as celebrating the first seeds they plant and organizing picnics after long days in the fields. By transforming their labor into a family affair, they find joy in the process and learn to embrace the rhythm of rural life. The work may be challenging, but with each passing day, they become more skilled and knowledgeable, slowly transforming Au-Fonde into the flourishing farm they had always dreamed of.

The rooster's crow was the family's daily alarm clock, signaling the beginning of another laborious day. Ledger rose first, the weight of responsibility resting heavily on his shoulders. He slipped on his worn boots and stepped outside, greeted by the crisp morning air. The fields stretched out before him, inviting yet daunting, their potential masked by weeds and unturned soil.

As Clara and the children stumbled out of their rooms, still bleary-eyed, they rallied together for a quick breakfast.

Clara poured cereal for the children, her voice filled with enthusiasm as she said, "We have a big day ahead, everyone. Remember, each day we work brings us closer to making Au-Fonde a thriving farm." The breakfast was simple yet nourishing, serving as a quick refueling for the strenuous hours that lay ahead. Ledger, sensing the importance of their mission, gathered everyone around the table before heading out to demonstrate a united front.

He spoke inspiringly, laying out the plan for the day: "Today, we're going to prepare the east field for planting. We will be working hard, but we are in this together. Let us put our hands to work and our hearts into it!" As he spoke, Wizen, Petronel, Julien, Eliza, Louisa, James, and Dfriel nodded in agreement, their faces a mix of excitement and apprehension at the tasks that lay ahead. They were about to learn that farming was not just about sowing seeds; it required dedication, resilience, and the willingness to embrace the sweat and toil that came with working under the watchful sun. The family knew that this day would be challenging, but they were ready to face it together, driven by a shared vision of what their hard work could yield.

The family made their way to the east field, where the earth lay dormant, waiting for transformation. The task ahead was monumental: clearing the land of weeds, rocks, and debris. The sight of the unkempt field, overgrown and full of obstacles, was both daunting and motivating. As they set to work, Ledger grabbed a hoe, its wooden handle heavy in his hands, while Clara wielded a shovel, her determination evident in her focused stance. The children, eager to help, picked up smaller tools— Petronel with a hand trowel, James wielding a rake, Julian holding a small spade, and Dfriel managing a sturdy bucket for collecting rocks. Together, they formed a makeshift team, united in their goal of transforming their land into a vibrant farm.

With each stroke of the hoe, the physical toll of rural life became evident. The sun climbed higher, beating down on them, and Ledger's muscles began to ache, the sweat dripping from his brow as he fought against the stubborn earth. He paused every so often to catch his breath, looking around at his family, who were also wearing the marks of hard work. Wizen, panting and feeling the fatigue set in, dropped his tool, and looked up at Ledger, eyes wide with uncertainty. "Dad, how long do we have to do this?" he asked, his voice a mixture of desperation and exhaustion, reflecting the weight of the day's labor.

Ledger paused to wipe his forehead and looked at Wizen, his heart going out to his son, who was clearly showing signs of fatigue. "It's hard work, I know," he replied encouragingly. "But remember, every bit of effort we put in now will pay off later. This land can give us so much if we nurture it. We are building something together, and soon we will see the fruits of our labor." His words resonated with the rest of the family, who took a moment's respite, finding motivation in Ledger's unwavering spirit.

Eliza, her energy still high and infectious, cheered her brother on, eager to prove they could handle the task. "Come on, Wizen! We can do this together!" Her enthusiasm sparked determination in her siblings, and they resumed working side by side. A few hours passed as they dug, cleared, and toiled under the sun, the repetitive nature of the work soon transforming into an arduous rhythm. The sound of shovels striking the ground, tools scraping against stones, and the laughter interspersed with gasps of exertion created an atmosphere of relentless effort. Despite their progress, Ledger could feel the weight of exhaustion settling on the family, enveloping them like a heavy blanket, but amidst the sweat and toil, there was a sense of camaraderie as they pushed through, united in their mission to reclaim the land they called home.

The family made their way to the east field, where the earth lay dormant, waiting for transformation. The task ahead was monumental: clearing the land of weeds, rocks, and debris. As they set to work, Ledger grabbed a hoe, while Clara wielded a shovel, and the children picked up smaller tools to assist where they could.

With each stroke of the hoe, the physical toll of rural life became evident. Ledger's muscles began to ache and sweat dripped from his brow as he fought against the stubborn earth.

As evening approached, the Philogene family stood surveying their progress in the east field, their bodies bearing witness to the strain of their labors. The land, still far from finished, lay scattered with weeds and stones they had painstakingly removed throughout the day.

The once overgrown terrain was gradually showing signs of transformation, but the work was grueling, leaving their hands calloused, their muscles sore, and their clothes dust-covered from the earth they had turned.

The setting sun cast a warm glow over the scene, reflecting the family's hard work, and it ignited a sense of accomplishment within Ledger—an encouraging reminder that they were on the right path despite the lengthy journey ahead.

Clara, sensing some exhaustion etched on her family's faces, called everyone to gather for a moment of respite. Rubbing her sore hands, she offered a comforting smile as she said, "Let us take a break and drink some water. We have done a lot today!" Her voice carried warmth and authority, prompting the children to drop their tools and gather around her.

They sank down onto the soft grass, letting the weight of the day lift, even if only for a moment. The evening air began to cool, and the sound of crickets chirped around them, creating a symphony of nature that wrapped them in a tranquil embrace.

As the sky transformed into stunning hues of orange and pink, Ledger took a deep breath, feeling pride swell in his chest at what they had accomplished together, even if it was just the beginning. This moment of pause was about more than resting; it was an opportunity for the family to appreciate their shared labor.

They exchanged glances of camaraderie, each recognizing the effort that had been poured into the day. It was a reminder that they were not just transforming the land but also weaving memories and strengthening their familial bonds as they worked side by side.

"Each day will bring us closer to our goal," Ledger said, his tone encouraging as he looked at his children, their bright eyes reflecting determination. "I know it feels tough right now but look at what we have done together! This is the foundation of our future, and every bit of effort counts." His words resonated deeply with the family, instilling a sense of purpose that quelled the sting of fatigue.

They shared stories of their day—how Wizen had bravely faced the stubborn weeds and how Eliza had insisted on carrying the heaviest rocks. These tales of small victories renewed their collective spirit, highlighting that even the hardest work could be met with laughter and pride.

As they sipped water and caught their breath, Ledger glanced at his children. Despite the physical toll that the day's labor had taken, he could see the determination shining in their eyes—a spark that made all the effort worthwhile. They were learning resilience and perseverance, valuable lessons that reached far beyond the fields of Au-Fonde.

Each drop of sweat was an investment in their future, not just as farmers but as a family. In that golden hour, surrounded by the beauty of the land they were cultivating, Ledger felt a profound sense of gratitude and hope. The journey ahead would be filled with challenges, but together, they were ready to face whatever lay in store, confident that their hard work would eventually bear fruit.

Later that night, as the stars began to twinkle in the clear sky, Ledger and Clara tucked the children into bed, their muscles still aching from the day's work. Clara kissed Petronel, Eliza and Louisa, and Nerisa good night and turned to Ledger, concern etched across her tired face.

Clara sighed softly, her brow furrowed with concern as she looked at her children, who were sprawled out in the grass, visibly exhausted after just a few hours in the fields. "I worry about the physical toll this is taking on us, especially on the kids," she admitted, her voice laced with maternal instinct. It pained her to see the weariness etched on their young faces, remnants of the hard labor they had tackled together.

Ledger nodded, rubbing the back of his neck, which throbbed from the day's labor, an echo of the fatigue shared by the entire family. Although they had embraced the challenge of transforming Au-Fonde into a thriving farm, it was becoming increasingly evident just how demanding farming could be, both physically and emotionally.

They learned quickly that the dream of rejuvenating the land came at a cost, and Clara felt a stirring mix of pride and apprehension as she observed her children's resilience against the backdrop of their newfound lifestyle.

"I know, Clara," Ledger replied, his voice steady but filled with understanding. "It is not like anything we have done before. But we must remember that this is a journey. We are building something that will last—and it is worth the effort." He glanced at the window, where the sun was setting behind the hills, painting the sky in hues of orange and pink. Each day was a step toward creating a thriving farm for their family, a legacy they could all share.

Though the work was daunting, Ledger believed in the importance of enduring these challenges together, finding strength in their unity and in the knowledge that they were investing in their children's future.

Clara sat on the edge of Louisa and Eliza's bed, her fingers brushing the soft fabric of the sheets as she absorbed the calmness of the room. The familiar scent of lavender filled the air, offering a momentary comfort amidst her swirling thoughts. Her heart was a mix of pride and worry; she cherished the resilience and dedication her children displayed, but she also felt the weight of her concerns pressing down on her. She wanted her children to thrive and develop a deep connection to the land, to learn the joys and rhythms of farming, but she also did not want them to feel overwhelmed by the physical demands of this new lifestyle.

Balancing their love for the land and the realities of hard work became a delicate dance, one that Clara hoped their family could master as they navigated the journey ahead together.

"I just don't want them to burn out," Clara said gently, her concern evident in her voice. "Farming should be a source of joy, not just toil and hard work. We can adjust our approach—break things down into smaller tasks and make it more engaging for them?" She met Ledger's gaze, her eyes filled with a mixture of hope and determination.

Clara envisioned their children flourishing in an environment that inspired curiosity and excitement rather than exhaustion. By introducing playful activities and manageable responsibilities, they could help their kids develop a genuine love for the land they were cultivating, ensuring that each day spent on the farm felt rewarding, rather than burdensome.

Ledger considered her words, appreciating her sensitivity and insight. He knew she was right; it was crucial to cultivate a love for farm life in their children, rather than allowing it to become a weight they resented. After all, a thriving farm depended not only on hard work but also on the spirit and enthusiasm of those who tended to it. If the kids could learn to find joy in their tasks, whether it was planting seeds, caring for animals, or harvesting fruits, then they would grow up with a deep connection to the land and a sense of pride in their contributions.

With a newfound sense of purpose, Ledger felt motivated to reframe their approach to farming, ready to work alongside Clara to ensure their children would thrive in both their labor and their love for the farm.

"That's a great idea," Ledger said, his voice filled with enthusiasm. "We can set aside time for lighter tasks like planting seeds or watering—activities that are easier for them and still contribute to our goals."

He imagined their children joyfully sowing seeds in small, designated patches, laughter filling the air as they played in the dirt. By incorporating these manageable tasks, they could instill a sense of accomplishment and ownership in Wizen, Petronel, Julien, Eliza, Louisa, James, Dfriel and Koie, and Nerisa while ensuring the work remained enjoyable.

Ledger felt a renewed sense of optimism, envisioning their days on the farm transforming into a blend of labor and play, forging lifelong memories and a genuine passion for the land.

Clara smiled, her worries eased by Ledger's understanding. It was heartening to know they were on the same page and that they could find balance in their approach to farming, especially if they worked together to create a supportive and nurturing environment for their children. They could plan chores that not only contributed to the farm's progress but also fostered fun and learning in a way that engaged the children.

As they discussed their ideas, Clara felt a comforting warmth spread through her; the prospect of cultivating both their land and their children's spirits made the challenges of farming seem more manageable. With shared determination, she knew they could nurture a love for the earth while ensuring their family thrived amidst the toil.

"And we can incorporate some fun into our workdays," Clara suggested, her eyes sparkling with excitement. "Maybe we can listen to music while we work or take breaks for games in the field?" The idea of mixing enjoyment with their labor brought a smile to her face. Clara envisioned the family creating a lively atmosphere, where the rhythm of cheerful tunes would accompany their efforts, and laughter would punctuate their breaks. It would redefine their experience on the farm, transforming what was once solely a task into a joyful day of collaboration and camaraderie.

Ledger chuckled, picturing their children laughing and running through the vast space of Au-Fonde, their little voices echoing against the backdrop of the trees and horizon. He could see Wizen, Petronel,

Julien, Eliza, Louisa, James, and Dfriel darting after each other as they played tag between the rows of budding plants, their shared laughter creating a vibrant soundtrack to the day's work. The image filled him with warmth, reinforcing his belief that farming did not have to be just a series of hard chores. Instead, it could be a cherished family adventure, where each day held the promise of new experiences and joyful memories.

With this vision in mind, he felt invigorated by the prospect of making their time on the farm a blend of diligent work and meaningful fun, ensuring that their connections with each other and the land grew deeper every day.

"Yes! Let us plan a weekly 'family fun day' where we mix work with play," Ledger exclaimed, a spark of enthusiasm lighting up his eyes. "We could have a picnic in the field after we get some work done!" He could already envision the family spreading a blanket under the shade of a tree, enjoying sandwiches and treats while basking in the warmth of the sun and each other's company. It would not only serve as a reward for their hard work but also create cherished moments filled with laughter and bonding.

With this new tradition, Ledger felt confident they could cultivate a spirit of joy and togetherness, weaving the fabric of their family life into the work they did on the farm.

Clara beamed at the thought, feeling a renewed sense of hope about the future. As they crawled into bed that evening, fatigue washed over them, but so did a comforting warmth of shared purpose. They both knew that the challenges of farming would persist, yet it was the strength they drew from each other that made them resilient.

With Ledger by her side, Clara felt reassured that they could adapt to this demanding lifestyle while nurturing their children's love for the land. This deep connection and commitment to their family goals filled her with optimism, reminding her that together, they could turn every challenge into an opportunity for growth and joy.

The sun broke through the horizon, casting golden rays onto the fields of Au-Fonde. As the Philogene family gathered for breakfast, the chatter was lively, a stark contrast to the fatigue that had lingered the previous night. They were ready to implement their new approach.

"Alright, everyone! Today, we are going to make our work fun!" Clara announced cheerfully, her voice ringing with excitement as she gathered the family in the sunny kitchen. "Let's start by picking out some seeds to plant together!" Her enthusiasm was infectious, and as she spoke, Wizen, Petronel, Julien, Eliza, Louisa, James, Dfriel, Koie, and Nerisa's eyes lit up with curiosity and joy. The thought of selecting seeds sparked their imagination, and they rushed to the table, eager to help choose what they would plant next. Clara could see the difference in their energy; their laughter and chatter filled the room, replacing any remnants of fatigue from previous days of labor.

The promise of a lighter, enjoyable workday set the tone for the morning, infusing the air with a sense of camaraderie and purpose. Clara watched as her children sifted through the packets, discussing which vegetables or flowers they wanted to grow. Their excitement brought a smile to her face, and she felt her heart swell with pride.

This was more than just a farming task; it was a chance for them to bond as a family and instill a love for the land they were cultivating. She envisioned them planting the seeds together, sharing stories and laughter as they worked side by side. The joy of planting together with her children renewed her resolve, and Clara felt that today was just the beginning of a beautiful tradition that would integrate fun and learning into their daily lives on the farm.

"Can we plant tomatoes?" Dfriel exclaimed, his eyes sparkling with enthusiasm. "I want to make the biggest one's ever!" His excitement was palpable, and he could not wait to see how tall and juicy his tomato plants could grow. The idea of nurturing the fruits from tiny seeds into something substantial ignited his imagination, and he envisioned himself harvesting the ripest tomatoes to share with the family. The prospect of competition only fueled his determination, and he was ready to take on the challenge excitingly.

"And I want to try growing some flowers for our garden!" Louisa jumped in, her voice bright and animated. She had always been captivated by vibrant colors and fragrant blooms, and the thought of filling their garden with beauty made her heart race. Clara glanced at her daughter and smiled, knowing how much Louisa loved tending to flowers and deciding. Ledger caught Clara's gaze and smiled, feeling a wave of hope wash over him. As they engaged in their tasks, the family worked alongside each other, their laughter breaking the morning's stillness. The music Clara had set up nearby played merrily, its joyful rhythm setting a lively backdrop to their efforts. As the sounds of their shared labor blended with cheerful melodies, it became clear that this was the beginning of a delightful new routine—one that celebrated hard work while fostering their bonds as a family.

After hours of planting, the family took a much-needed break under a shade tree, grateful for the cool refuge from the sun. They spread out a picnic blanket decorated with their colorful artwork, a testament to their creativity and togetherness. Plates of sandwiches, fresh fruit, and lemonade filled the space, and as everyone settled in, Clara could not help but smile at the scene unfolding around her.

Ledger watched as Koie and Nerisa giggled while tossing a frisbee back and forth, their earlier fatigue forgotten amid the new energy that had been cultivated through their playful efforts. The laughter and excitement echoed in the tranquil air, a joyful soundtrack to their family time.

"This is what it's all about," Ledger said softly, glancing at Clara, his eyes full of warmth and pride as they observed their children reveling in the moment. He felt a deep sense of fulfillment, knowing that they were nurturing not just their land but also their children's spirits. Clara nodded, her heart full as she watched the carefree joy on her kids' faces. "I think we're finally finding our rhythm," she replied, relief evident in her voice. It felt as if they had stepped into a harmonious balance between work and play, creating meaningful memories while cultivating their farm. With Ledger by her side and their children thriving, Clara felt optimistic about their journey ahead, determined to continue building this life filled with laughter, love, and a passion for the land.

*As the sun climbed higher, the fatigue remained a part of their lives, but it no longer defined their experience. They were learning to embrace the challenge of farming while fostering a spirit of togetherness and joy. Each day brought its difficulties, but with shared laughter and bound Each day brought its difficulties, but with shared laughter and boundless determination, the Philogene family began to find their footing in the demanding life of farming.

The rhythm of their days slowly settled into a routine that balanced hard work with family bonding. They cultivated the fields early in the morning and spent afternoons nurturing their growing relationships with the Colihaut community, all while ensuring that they kept their spirits high through small moments of joy.

On some afternoons, Ledger would work alongside the children, teaching them how to tend to the young plants they had painstakingly put in the ground. He showed them how to water the saplings gently and how to recognize when weeds needed to be pulled.

"Look, Dad! That one is growing so fast!" James exclaimed in awe, his eyes wide with excitement as he pointed enthusiastically at a small tomato plant that had visibly sprouted in just a few days. Its leaves stretched eagerly towards the sun as if trying to embrace the warmth and light. James's enthusiasm was infectious, and Ledger could not help but smile at his son's pure delight. It was moments like these that reminded Ledger why he loved farming; witnessing growth in all its forms, whether in crops or in his children, filled him with an incredible sense of purpose.

Kneeling beside James, Ledger felt pride swelling in his chest as he observed the little plant. "You've done a great job taking care of it, buddy," he said, encouragingly ruffling James's hair. Seeing their hard work pay off in such a tangible way ignited a spark of joy in him. This was not about growing food; it was about growth as a family and the conversations and connections that flourished alongside the crops. As James leaned in closer, captivated by the tiny green leaves, Ledger felt a wave of gratitude wash over him. Together, they were not just nurturing the land; they were nurturing each other, cultivating bonds that would last a lifetime.

"That is right! Each plant is like a little promise," Ledger said, looking at the small tomato plant with a sense of wonder. "With care and patience, they will grow strong." He wanted his children to understand that nurturing the earth also meant nurturing hope and the future. The idea that their efforts would eventually yield food and beauty made the labor feel worthwhile. Ledger took a moment to appreciate the seedlings dotting the row, each one a testament to their hard work and dedication, waiting to bring joy and sustenance to their family.

Louisa, not wanting to be left out, chimed in with a determined spark in her eyes. "I think I'm going to name mine Sparkle!" she declared, her face beaming with excitement. Ledger chuckled as he watched his daughter's imagination take flight. This playful naming ritual was something they had always enjoyed together, and it infused their work with creativity and fun.

They often exchanged stories about the plants, giving them names and personalities as if they were cherished friends rather than mere crops. It made the work less daunting and more engaging, turning farming into a whimsical adventure. As Louisa beamed at her little "Sparkle," Ledger felt grateful for these moments of joy, which not only helped them connect with nature but also strengthened the bonds they shared as a family.

As days turned into weeks, the family adapted to the rhythms of rural life. Evenings were especially special. Clara often prepared meals using ingredients they had started to grow, allowing everyone to see the fruits of their labor come to life on the dinner table.

"Tonight's dinner is a celebration of our hard work!" Clara announced cheerfully as she served the dishes onto the table, her heart swelling with pride. "We have fresh tomato salad and roasted veggies." The vibrant colors and aromas filled the air, intertwining with the joyful chatter of her family. It felt like a fitting tribute to a day spent outdoors, working the land together and fostering a shared sense of accomplishment. She could hardly wait to see the delight on their faces as they savored their own labor, transformed into a delicious meal.

As they gathered around the table with full plates, their eyes sparkling with satisfaction, a warm sense of togetherness enveloped them. Each bite carried a taste of their efforts: the crunch of freshly harvested vegetables complemented by the rich flavors of the roasted mix created a symphony of delightful tastes. The vibrant red of the tomatoes elicited smiles and laughter, reminiscent of the joy they shared while picking them. Clara watched as her children enthusiastically recounted their favorite moments from the day, their faces animated and glowing with excitement. The sound of their laughter surrounded the table, echoing the happiness cultivated throughout the day. At that moment, Clara felt a profound sense of fulfillment. They were building not just a meal, but also cherished memories, reinforcing the bonds of family with every bite shared.

"Can we have more of those tomatoes? They are the best!" Koie exclaimed, his eyes lighting up with enthusiasm as he reached for another helping. The vibrant red of the salad seemed to tantalize him, and he savored each bite as though it were a delightful treat. His enthusiastic plea sparked a wave of laughter around the table, as everyone chimed in with their own favorite dishes, playfully arguing over who had the best palate. Clara, serving more of the fresh tomatoes, could not help but giggle at Koie's unabashed love for their hard-earned harvest, and she felt a swell of warmth knowing that their efforts were being so joyfully received.

Ledger leaned back in his chair, fully content, taking in the scene before him. It was not just the delicious vegetables that filled their bellies; it was the laughter, the playful banter, and the shared moments that made each meal special. As he watched his family enjoy their dinner, he realized that these evenings were about more than nourishment; they were about connection and gratitude. Each conversation, each chuckle, and each satisfied smile was an affirmation of the time spent together during the day, planting seeds not just in the ground but in their hearts as well. In that moment of togetherness, surrounded by love and laughter, Ledger felt truly blessed, knowing they were building lasting memories that would nourish their family for years to come.

However, not every moment was filled with joy. They faced challenges along the way—unexpected pests that threatened their crops, days of relentless rain that made the fields muddy and difficult to work, and times of uncertainty when Ledger questioned whether they were doing everything right.

"Clara," Ledger said late one evening, his voice tinged with frustration, "I keep reading about the best practices, but it feels like no matter how hard we try, there is always something that seems to go wrong. It can be so disheartening." He leaned against the kitchen counter, running a hand through his hair as he exhaled deeply. The weight of their farming challenges felt heavier in the quiet of the night, and he struggled to balance his hopes with the reality of their journey. The unpredictable nature of farming often overshadowed the small victories they celebrated, leaving him feeling defeated and questioning whether they were truly cut out for this life.

Clara, sensing Ledger's turmoil, reached out and placed a reassuring hand on his arm. Her touch was gentle and grounding, a reminder of the bond they had forged through the ups and downs of their farming adventure. "You know, every farmer faces challenges," she replied softly, her eyes meeting his with warmth and understanding. "What matters is how we respond to them.

Remember everything we have accomplished together? We have grown so much as a family, and that matters just as much as the crops." Her words wrapped around him like a comforting embrace, and Ledger felt a flicker of hope reignite within him. He knew she was right; it was not about the tomatoes or the flowers, it was about the love, resilience, and determination they cultivated alongside the land. Sitting together in the glow of the kitchen light, they shared a moment of renewed purpose, ready to face whatever challenges lay ahead with unwavering support for one another.

"Every farmer faces challenges, Ledger. It is part of the process," Clara said gently, her voice steady and reassuring. "We're learning as we go, and with each obstacle, we grow stronger—together." Her words wrapped around him like a warm blanket, reminding him of the journey they were on. She could see the weight on his shoulders and wanted him to recognize that their struggles did not define them; rather, they were integral to their growth, both as individuals and as a family. Clara understood that farming was as much about resilience and adaptability as it was about planting seeds and nurturing crops.

Her words served as a poignant reminder of the strength they had built within themselves and as a unit. The physical demands of farming were daunting, requiring hard work and dedication, but Clara believed wholeheartedly that the lessons they learned transcended the soil they tilled. Each challenge they faced—be it pests, unpredictable weather, or crop failures—taught them about patience, perseverance, and the importance of leaning on one another.

"Look at all we've accomplished," she continued, her eyes sparkling with determination. "We have created something beautiful, and we are doing it together. That is what truly matters." In that moment, Ledger felt a renewed sense of hope, inspired by Clara's unwavering support and the shared purpose that bound them. Together, they were not just farming; they were building a legacy, one rooted in love and resilience.

As the season progressed, whispers of harvest began to fill the air. Their hard work was beginning to show tangible results. The once barren fields had transformed into vibrant patches of color. Tomatoes, peppers, and herbs flourished under their care.

"Look at all the vegetables!" Nerisa exclaimed, dancing around in excitement, her energy infectious as she pointed toward the bountiful produce they had cultivated. Her eyes sparkled with joy, and she clasped her hands together as if savoring the moment. "Can we have a harvest party?" she added, her voice brimming with enthusiasm. The thought of celebrating their hard work thrilled her, and it was clear that she envisioned not just a gathering but a joyous occasion that would fill the air with laughter and community spirit.

James, nodding vigorously beside her, echoed her sentiment. "Yes! We can invite our friends from the community too!" His face lit up with the idea of sharing their achievements with others, of bringing the neighborhood together to revel in the fruits of their labor. The children's excitement was palpable, and it ignited a spark of inspiration in Ledger and Clara. They exchanged glances, each sensing the opportunity to not only celebrate their first harvest but also to deepen connections with their neighbors and friends.

Motivated by their children's enthusiasm, Ledger and Clara began planning a harvest festival, eager to create an inviting atmosphere that would honor their hard work while fostering relationships within the community. They envisioned a day filled with laughter, good food, and the warmth of shared stories. As they brainstormed activities—games for the kids, tasty meals featuring their freshly harvested vegetables, and local music, they felt a sense of purpose and excitement. Together, they crafted invitations, reaching out to local families and encouraging them to bring their loved ones. With every detail they worked on, Ledger and Clara felt the joy of the season swell around them, knowing that it was not about celebrating their harvest, but about building a more connected, vibrant community together.

On the day of the harvest festival, laughter and joy rippled through the fields as visitors arrived. Families from Colihaut brought their own dishes to share, creating a vibrant tapestry of flavors and cultures. Children played while adults exchanged stories, appreciating the fruits of the Philogene family's hard work.

"Thank you all for coming to our first harvest festival!" Ledger addressed the crowd, his voice resonating with warmth and gratitude. "It means the world to us to share this special day with our friends and neighbors." He took a moment to survey the gathering, their fields filled with smiling faces, the laughter of children playing, and the savory aromas wafting from the food stands. "When we first arrived, we knew that transforming Au-Fonde into a thriving farm would be a challenge, but we never imagined how fulfilling it would be to share this journey with all of you."

319

The crowd erupted in applause and cheers, their faces bright with smiles as they soaked in the joy of the moment. Ledger's heart swelled with emotion, knowing that this celebration was about more than just the harvest; it was about the connections formed and the community that had blossomed alongside their crops. As he spoke, he felt a palpable sense of unity in the air, a collective acknowledgment of the hard work and dedication that had woven them all together.

Standing beside him, Clara's heart brimmed with pride as she gazed at the people gathered in their fields. This gathering was not just the result of their labor, but a manifestation of the relationships they had nurtured within the community. She remembered the long hours they had spent preparing for this day, the planning, the organizing, and the sheer joy of inviting everyone to share their success. Clara glanced at Ledger, their eyes locking for a moment, and in that shared glance, they acknowledged how far they had come together. Today was a celebration of not just their first harvest, but of the spirit of community, connection, and resilience that had flourished in the heart of Au-Fonde.

"Every vegetable, every sprout we've cultivated together symbolizes something much larger than just farming," Ledger continued, his voice steady and passionate. "It represents the relationships we have built, the stories we have shared, and the resilience we have shown. Today is a celebration of not just our harvest but of community." His words resonated deeply as he looked out over the crowd, witnessing the camaraderie that had developed through their shared experiences. Each seed sown had brought them closer, knitting a tapestry of connections that extended beyond the fields.

As he continued, Ledger glanced at Louisa and James, who were happily helping distribute fresh vegetables to each guest, their faces lighting up with joy at their small acts of service. It warmed his heart to see them so engaged and proud, embodying the spirit of generosity he valued so deeply. The sight of their children actively participating in this celebration filled him with a sense of hope for the future. These were the moments that would shape their understanding of community and belonging.

Ledger paused for a moment, taking a deep breath as he embraced the moment fully. He savored the buzz of laughter, the scent of freshly harvested produce, and the smiling faces surrounding him. It was in times like these that he felt the true essence of their endeavors—the hard work, the late nights, and the struggles—had all been worthwhile. This gathering was more than just a festival; it was a testament to their journey and a promise of what was to come. With gratitude swelling in his chest, Ledger concluded, "Let's continue to grow together, celebrate one another, and nurture the bonds that make this community a thriving place for all." The crowd responded with renewed cheers, a chorus of support that echoed the sentiment of unity they had all contributed to building.

"We couldn't have done this without your support, guidance, and friendship," Ledger continued, feeling the warmth of the audience's attention. "Thank you for welcoming us into your lives. We are grateful to be a part of this community, and we look forward to many more seasons of growth—together." His heartfelt words resonated deeply with everyone present, and he sensed a shared sentiment in the air. It was a promise to nurture the relationships they had built and to continue working side by side as they faced the challenges and joys that lay ahead.

As applause erupted from the crowd, Ledger looked out and spotted Mr. Telford in the front row, nodding appreciatively with a smile that spoke volumes about the bond they had formed over the seasons. The sense of connection was palpable, a reminder that they were all in this together, facing the trials of farming in solidarity. Ledger felt an overwhelming sense of gratitude for the community that had embraced them, transforming what began as a modest farm into a vibrant gathering place.

At that moment, Clara stepped forward with a basket filled with bright red tomatoes, colorful peppers, and fragrant herbs—beautiful representations of their hard work and commitment to the land. The sight of the fresh produce glistening in the sun brought yet another wave of enthusiasm from the audience. She held the basket aloft, a symbol of abundance and shared bounty that underscored their celebration. "We want to share the rewards of our labor with all of you!" she called out, inviting the crowd to partake in the fruits of their efforts. Ledger watched proudly as she engaged with the community, her warmth and generosity shining through. Together, they had not only grown vegetables; they had cultivated a sense of belonging and togetherness that would continue to flourish in the seasons to come.

"And now, we'd love to share the bounty of our hard work with you all!" Clara announced with a bright smile, her enthusiasm infectious. "Please help yourselves to these fresh vegetables, and let's enjoy some delicious dishes made from ingredients right from our farm!" Her voice rang out with warmth and invitation, drawing the guests closer to the colorful spread before them. The vibrant array of tomatoes, peppers, zucchini, and herbs looked stunning, a testament to the hard work and dedication they had all poured into the farm.

Eagerly, the guests began to serve themselves, each exploring the flavors of the fresh produce that had been nurtured with such care. The sound of laughter and conversation mingled with the rustling of leaves and the clinking of plates, creating a joyful atmosphere that enveloped the gathering. Clara moved among the crowd, chatting with friends and neighbors, her heart swollen as she watched everyone enjoy the fruits of their labor. The connections forged during the planting and harvesting seasons were evident in the smiles shared and the stories exchanged over the meal.

As Ledger stepped back to take it all in, he felt a deep sense of belonging wash over him. This was what they had envisioned—a flourishing community built on shared labor, respect, and laughter. The sight of their friends and neighbors reveling together, savoring the food they had grown, filled him with pride and gratitude. He realized that while the journey had been filled with challenges, moments like this made every struggle worthwhile. They were no longer just farmers; they were integral parts of a vibrant community, connected through the land and each other. The festival was not just a celebration of their harvest but a celebration of the relationships that had blossomed alongside the crops, and in that light, Ledger felt hopeful for the many seasons yet to come.

As the sun began to set, casting a golden glow across the gathering, Ledger watched as neighbors danced to lively music, children chased fireflies, and families shared stories over the tables laden with food. Clara joined him, her hand slipping into his.

As the sun began to set, casting a golden glow across the gathering, Ledger took a moment to absorb the scene unfolding before him. Neighbors danced joyfully to lively music, their laughter mingling with the sounds of celebration, while children chased fireflies, their delighted squeals adding to the symphony of the evening. Families gathered around tables laden with an array of food, sharing stories and creating bonds over the delicious dishes made from the harvest. He felt a sense of warmth spread through him, knowing they had succeeded in bringing everyone together for this special occasion.

Just then, Clara joined him, her hand slipping into his as she leaned into him, her presence calm and steady. "Can you believe how far we've come?" she asked softly, her eyes sparkling with joy as she took in the vibrant atmosphere around them.

Ledger turned to her, and a smile spread across his face. "Not just us, but all of us," he replied, feeling the shared pride swell within him. "Today were about more than just vegetables; it was about creating memories together." The day had transformed into a celebration of everything they had built—a community that had flourished alongside their farm, rich in relationships and shared experiences.

As the festivities continued, neighbors began to share their own harvest stories, exchanging tips and advice that would make the following seasons even more fruitful. Ledger reveled in the camaraderie, listening intently as laughter and stories flowed between friends and new acquaintances. He realized that after the initial struggles and hard labor, the Philogene family had truly become a part of this vibrant community. They were no longer outsiders but cherished members of a larger family, bound together by shared experiences and mutual support. As the last rays of sunlight danced across the horizon, Ledger felt an overwhelming sense of gratitude and belonging, grateful for Clara by his side and the community they had all built together.

Observing the laughter around them, Clara felt a wave of optimism wash over her. "It feels like the beginning of something wonderful, doesn't it?" She scanned the vibrant scene: friends gathered, sharing stories and joy, their faces illuminated by the fading sun. It was a moment charged with possibility, a celebration of what they had achieved together. The farm, once a mere dream, had transformed into a thriving reality, and Clara's heart swelled with hope. This was not just about the crops; it was about camaraderie and shared purpose, a foundation for something greater than themselves.

Ledger nodded thoughtfully, his gaze fixed on the flourishing fields around them, the fruits of their labor. "Yes, it does. And I would not trade this for anything," he replied softly, feeling the weight of those words. Each drop of sweat and every hour spent laboring under the sun had led them to this moment of triumph. He understood that while challenges would always be a part of farm life, the rewards were profound. This farm symbolized not only physical sustenance but also emotional depth—growth in their relationships and their sense of belonging within the community that had come together around them.

As the last light of day faded and the stars began to twinkle in the night sky, Ledger felt a profound sense of gratitude wash over him. The laughter and warmth of their friends enveloped him like a comforting blanket, reminding him of the journey they had undertaken. Together, they had faced the trials of farming, learning to navigate storms—both literal and figurative. Through hard work and unity, they had emerged stronger, their roots digging deep into the rich soil of Colihaut. This land held not only crops but also the intertwined hopes and dreams of everyone present, binding them together in a shared narrative of resilience and promise.

As the weeks progressed, the initial enthusiasm surrounding the farm began to wane, met with the harsh realities of nature. Ledger's dreams of a bountiful harvest were abruptly challenged as they faced crop failures due to unpredictable weather patterns and invasive pests. What had once been a landscape of potential now bore the marks of a struggle, with wilting plants and ruined rows that mocked their efforts. The joy he had felt in teaching his children about the land began to erode as he grappled with the frustration and disappointment that came from investing so much time and energy—only to see their hopes dashed.

The day dawned ominously, the air heavy with an unsettling stillness. Ledger stood in the fields, wiping sweat from his brow while surveying the fledgling crops that were just beginning to sprout. He had poured his heart and soul into nurturing the tender plants alongside Wizen, Petronel, and Julien. With each seed they had planted, whispers of hope had flourished. But as he looked out at the rows of green, uncertainty gnawed at him. The sky darkened, churning with angry clouds that loomed like giants ready to unleash their wrath.

As the first drops of rain fell, Ledger hurried back to the house. Inside, Clara, Eliza, James, Dfriel, Koie, and Nerisa clustered together, anxiety threading through their conversations. The once-comforting sound of raindrops turned ominous as the clouds unleashed their fury. "We've done everything we can," Clara said, her voice trembling slightly, glancing toward the door as the wind began to howl. "But we can't control the weather."

"Or the pests," Petronel added bitterly, recalling the locusts that had descended upon their fields just a few weeks ago, devouring the very essence of their labor. Ledger could feel frustration bubbling within him—a heavy weight of responsibility pressing down on his chest. He had promised his family that together they would thrive here, that this new land would grant them the prosperity they sought. But with each gust of wind that rattled the windows, all those dreams seemed to hang by a fragile thread.

Outside, the storm intensified, roaring like a restless beast as the wind whipped through the trees, tearing leaves from their limbs. The sound was deafening, and Ledger felt a rising tide of panic mixed with helplessness. "We need to secure the tarps over the seedlings!" he shouted, his voice barely rising above the cacophony. "If we don't protect what we have, it could all be washed away!"

"Ledger!" Clarissa, his mother, cried out, her gaze wide with fear. "It is too dangerous! You cannot go out there!" She reached for him, her hand trembling slightly as she gripped his arm.

But he could not stand idly by. The weight of his family's survival rested heavily on his shoulders. "We can't afford to lose everything," he insisted, his determination hardening. "We've come too far." With a shared glance of reassurance, Wizen and Julien nodded, stepping up to join Ledger as they made their way outside, bracing themselves against the fury of the storm.

The wind nearly knocked them off their feet as they rushed to the fields, struggling to secure the tarps that whipped violently in the gales. Rain lashed against their skin like icy needles, and the earth beneath them turned to mud, threatening to swallow their feet. "Hurry!" Ledger shouted, pulling the tarps taut as they fought against the storm's strength. The air was charged with electricity, the sky momentarily illuminated by flashes of lightning that lit up the darkened landscape.

But just as they managed to secure the last tarp, a deafening crack echoed through the air, followed by an explosion of power as a tree was uprooted nearby. Time seemed to freeze for a moment, and Ledger's heart raced as he realized the force of nature they were up against. "Get to the house!" he yelled, adrenaline coursing through him as they sprinted against the wind, pushing through the chaos and debris.

Inside, they collapsed onto the floor, panting and drenched. Ledger's heart raced, but relief washed over him as he looked around at his family, unharmed though shaken. Yet, as the storm raged on outside, doubts crept in. He could no longer ignore the gnawing frustration in his gut. They had invested time and energy into their crops, only to have nature unleash its fury upon them, offering up a reminder of their vulnerability in this new land.

Clara, seeing the turmoil etched on Ledger's face, placed a comforting hand on his shoulder. "We've all sacrificed so much, but we can't let this define us," she said softly. "Nature can be unpredictable, but so can we. We will find a way to start over."

But Ledger could only nod, a heavy silence settling over the room as the storm continued its relentless assault. How many times would they have to rise and rebuild? How many dreams would they watch be swept away by forces they could not control? He felt the weight of his responsibilities pressing down on him again—an immense burden of expectation and hope.

In the eye of the storm, Ledger closed his eyes, taking a deep breath. When the hurricane calmed and the winds subsided, he understood they would face the aftermath together. They would rebuild what was lost, plant new seeds, and weather the next storm as a family. Still, the emotional turmoil of the moment lingered, a haunting reminder of the fragility of their aspirations.

The next morning, Ledger would walk through the fields, his heart heavy with the weight of responsibility. He felt the emotional toll of knowing that his family depended on the success of their crops for sustenance and stability. The realization that, despite their best efforts, the whims of nature could dictate their livelihood was a bitter pill to swallow. This unpredictability stirred a nagging anxiety in him, gnawing at his thoughts as he considered how to provide for Wizen, Petronel, Julien, Eliza, Louisa, James, Dfriel, Koie, and Nerisa.

His frustration often turned inward, as he questioned his choices and abilities as a farmer and a father. Was it his fault that the rain came too late, or that pests had invaded their fields? Each failure felt like a personal indictment, a stark reminder of the limits of his control. Yet, amid the despair, Ledger knew he had a choice: to allow these setbacks to defeat him or to confront them with the resilience he wished to instill in his children. He realized that these challenging moments could serve as powerful teaching opportunities, reflections of life's unpredictable nature.

Ledger contemplated how to openly share these struggles with his children, to cultivate an understanding that resilience was not merely an abstract concept but a necessity in the face of adversity. He wanted them to see that while setbacks could be painful, they also presented valuable lessons about perseverance and the importance of adapting to ever-changing circumstances. By confronting these challenges together as a family, Ledger hoped to not only navigate the current difficulties but also shape a narrative of strength and unity that would empower his children to face their own future obstacles.

As the realities of farming began to set in, Clara's worries about their financial stability intensified. The vibrant dreams of cultivating a thriving farm now clashed with the practicalities of maintaining a household with nine children. Each crop failure not only threatened their harvest but also raised the specter of economic risks that loomed large over their family. Clara felt the weight of responsibility pressing down on her, anxiety creeping in as she contemplated how to provide for their children's needs amid the unpredictability of agricultural investments. With each passing day, the pressure mounted as she grappled with her fears of inadequate resources, rising costs, and an uncertain future.

Ledger watched his wife's worries deepen, feeling the strain in their conversations as they navigated the challenges together. He knew Clara well; her nurturing instinct made her acutely sensitive to the difficulties they faced. She often voiced her concerns, fearing that their ambitions might be too grand considering their current financial situation. But in those moments, Ledger sought to reassure her, emphasizing their shared vision and the foundation of perseverance they had built as a family. He recognized the importance of acknowledging her feelings while also instilling hope in their journey.

With an empathetic heart, Ledger reminded Clara of the resilience they had already demonstrated, recalling times when hard work and determination had turned challenges into successes. "We've weathered storms before," he said softly, "and we can do it again." He believed in the potential for a turnaround, emphasizing that setbacks were, in many ways, just part of the farming journey. They had invested not just in their crops but also in the values that they wanted to pass down to their children— lessons of hard work, unity, and the importance of trusting one another through thick and thin.

While Ledger understood her concerns were valid, he remained hopeful that with their combined efforts and unwavering commitment, they could rise above current challenges and create a stable and successful future. He wanted Clara to see that their dreams, though tempered by hardships, were still within reach. Together, they could navigate the financial pressures with a clear focus on their shared goals, treating each setback as a steppingstone rather than a stumbling block. In those quiet moments of reassurance, he hoped to fortify Clara's spirit, reminding her that they were a team capable of overcoming whatever obstacles lay ahead, driven by love and an unwavering vision for their family.

Clara was not just a wife; she was an essential partner in Ledger's vision for their farm. Recognizing the challenges they faced, she stepped in eagerly to manage household responsibilities while also assisting in the fields. Her unwavering support allowed Ledger to focus on their agricultural goals, knowing that he had a steadfast ally at home. Together, they built a partnership grounded in shared dreams and mutual respect, one that combined their strengths for the benefit of their growing family.

Clara brought a wealth of knowledge to their endeavors, especially when it came to cooking and utilizing local foods. Her resourcefulness was invaluable as she creatively maximized their harvests, ensuring that nothing went to waste. She skillfully transformed their produce into nourishing meals, teaching the children the importance of savoring what they grew. Clara often involved the kids in the kitchen, showing them how to prepare family recipes and instilling a sense of pride and ownership in their food. This not only reinforced their connection to the land but also fostered an appreciation for the fruits of their labor.

Together, they created a family routine that interwove farming, cooking, and education. Mornings began with chores in the fields, where Ledger would share his insights about sustainable practices with their children, explaining the benefits of crop rotation and organic fertilizers. Clara would often join them, weaving stories about the importance of caring for the earth and respecting nature's cycles. This collaborative approach not only educated their children but also promoted a sense of community among them, where everyone played a role in their shared success.

As the days unfolded, their home became a vibrant hub of activity, where laughter and learning flourished side by side. Ledger and Clara celebrated the seasons, integrating farming lessons into family traditions. They held seasonal festivals to honor their harvests, teaching their kids about the hard work that went into bringing food to their table. These experiences solidified their shared vision, creating a legacy defined by stewardship, resilience, and teamwork.

In those moments of shared labor and learning, Clara and Ledger forged a path toward a sustainable future that thrived on cooperation and love. Their partnership became a model for their children, demonstrating that together, they could overcome challenges and realize their dreams. By working side by side, they instilled in their family the values that would carry them through difficult times, laying the groundwork for a vibrant and fulfilling life on the farm.

Despite her unwavering support for Ledger's vision and her enthusiasm for their farming venture, Clara faced the brutal reality of balancing her role as a mother with the relentless demands of farming. The long days spent toiling in the fields took a toll on her physically and emotionally. Each sunset brought with it not only the satisfaction of work accomplished but also the weight of exhaustion that settled heavily in her bones. Clara often found herself drained, struggling to muster the energy for the home front. She worried about how this fatigue might affect their children's upbringing, pondering whether they were truly meeting their needs amidst the chaos of farm life.

As the busy seasons rolled on, Clara's concerns deepened. She longed to create a nurturing environment for her children, one that was both loving and enriching. However, as the hours in the fields stretched on, she sometimes felt like she was falling short of that ideal. Her mind often raced with thoughts about missed moments—times when simply being present for her children felt overshadowed by the pressing need to keep up with their farming responsibilities. These worries gnawed at her, leading to sleepless nights where questions echoed in her head: Have we made the right decision in moving to this challenging environment? Will this lifestyle positively shape our children, or will they feel the emptiness of my absence?

Clara's introspection frequently led her to the kitchen, where she could find solace in familiar routines. Cooking offered her a chance to connect with her children, even when the world outside demanded so much of her. She would call them in to help prepare meals, using these moments as opportunities to foster bonds and teach them valuable life skills. Yet, even as she chopped vegetables or stirred pots, she could not shake the nagging doubt that lingered just beneath the surface.

While Ledger's passion for farming inspired her, the reality of their situation sometimes felt overwhelming. Clara found herself yearning for the support of a community, wishing for more time to connect with other mothers who shared similar struggles. Although Ledger would reassure her of their progress and the strength they derived from each other, Clara silently wished for a way to harmonize her parenting and farming responsibilities without feeling stretched thin.

She knew that this journey was filled with challenges, but her love for her family was a guiding light. Clara sought to find that delicate balance between nurturing her children and helping cultivate the land they all called home. Little by little, she learned to embrace the notion that it was okay to prioritize self-care, to ask for help when needed, and to recognize that navigating this path together was part of their growth as a family. In her heart, she hoped that, despite the difficulties, the lessons they were all learning—about hard work, commitment, and resilience—would become the foundations of a loving and unified family life.

To ease the transition into their new life on the farm, Clara took the proactive step of reaching out to other women in the community. Understanding the importance of connection, she sought friendships and support among those who had already navigated the challenges of rural life. These women, with their enduring smiles and stories etched with hard-earned wisdom, welcomed Clara into their circle. As they gathered over coffee or worked alongside one another in the fields, Clara found solace in their shared experiences.

Through these interactions, she discovered that many had faced similar struggles, from juggling the demands of motherhood and farming to managing the uncertainties of unpredictable weather. Each woman carried her own challenges, and hearing their tales inspired Clara to recognize the strength in the community. The resilience they exhibited became a source of motivation for her, helping her to adapt her own expectations about what life on the farm really entailed. She learned that it was okay to lean on others and acknowledge that they were all navigating the same rough terrain together.

As friendships blossomed, Clara felt encouraged and uplifted. They exchanged tips on gardening methods that thrived in their climate or shared recipes that highlighted seasonal produce, enriching not just their kitchens but also their family lives. These women became not just acquaintances, but integral parts of Clara's support network—serving as confidantes with whom she could discuss her hopes and fears. Clara realized that they could rally together during planting season or lend a hand during harvest, forming a united front against the challenges of farm life.

This deepening connection within the community also brought a sense of belonging that had been missing in her earlier reflections about their move. She began to appreciate the importance of shared resources and collective strength. Organizing weekend potlucks or seasonal festivals fostered a sense of camaraderie that made the tough days feel a little lighter. The laughter and joy during these gatherings reminded her that they were all in this together, finding joy in the simple pleasures of life, despite its unpredictability.

As Clara's confidence grew, she began to embrace her role within the community more fully, recognizing how vital these ties were to not only her well-being but also to the well-being of her family. The support she received helped her find balance in her responsibilities at home and on the farm, encouraging her to approach each day with renewed energy and optimism. By investing in these relationships, Clara fortified her own resilience, creating a ripple effect that extended to her children, who began to form their own friendships and connections as well.

In time, Clara's bond with her neighbors evolved into a cherished web of support that transformed their farming endeavors into a shared journey, rich with lessons of cooperation and community spirit. Through this experience, she came to realize that while the challenges of farm life were significant, the strength of the community made the journey not only bearable but profoundly rewarding.

❦

Chapter Ten: Community Dynamics

As the Philogene family settled into their new life at Au-Fonde in Colihaut, their journey was imbued with a deep desire to integrate into the local community. The beauty of their surroundings—the lush landscapes, the sound of waves crashing against the shore, and the warmth of the sun—was a stark contrast to the challenges they faced as newcomers. With hard work and perseverance, Ledger and Clara dedicated themselves to establishing a presence in Colihaut, eager to contribute to the community while instilling their values in their nine children. They envisioned a life rooted in collaboration and mutual respect, determined to become integral members of the social fabric that defined this small coastal town.

At first, their enthusiasm was met with a welcoming spirit from some community members. Clara quickly bonded with local women, sharing recipes and tending to gardens, while Ledger paired up with other farmers to exchange tips and labor on initiatives like community farming days. The family participated in local festivals, bringing dishes made from their own harvests, which allowed them to forge connections and demonstrate their commitment to Colihaut. They believed that by contributing actively to community events, they could build trust and acceptance, fostering genuine relationships within their new home.

However, as the Philogene family settled in, they soon encountered the rising tensions related to class and landownership that reflected the broader societal conflicts of their time. The town of Colihaut, while picturesque, was steeped in complexities rooted in socioeconomic disparities. The dynamics of wealth and landownership created rifts within the community, leaving the Philogenes to navigate a complex social landscape filled with unspoken hierarchies and underlying resentments.

Some established families viewed newcomers with skepticism, perceiving them as threats to their livelihoods and traditions. They resented the Philogene family's attempts at integration, unsure of their intentions and wary of their potential influence. This created an undercurrent of tension that began to strain the relationships Clara and Ledger had worked so hard to build. Clara could feel the weight of judgment in the eyes of some women at community meetings, where whispered conversations about land disputes and resource allocation cast shadows over their camaraderie.

Confronted with these challenges, the Philogenes had to reassess their approach and find ways to address the growing tensions. Ledger, with his background in farming and community engagement, sought to bridge the divide by focusing on mutual goals and shared interests. He organized community meetings to discuss agricultural methods, emphasizing the benefits that could arise from collaboration rather than competition. Clara continued to foster friendships, reaching out to others who felt marginalized in the community, and hoping to cultivate a support network that could unite their diverse backgrounds.

Despite their efforts, the complexities of class dynamics proved difficult to untangle. Tensions flared during town meetings, where discussions around land use and resource management highlighted divisions in priorities and perspectives. The Philogene family often found themselves caught in the middle, trying to advocate for a collaborative approach while navigating the pushback from those resistant to change. As frustrations mounted, Ledger and Clara began to realize that their journey would require not only their commitment to integration but also a deeper understanding of the historical and cultural nuances at play.

Throughout this tumult, the Philogene family remained resolute, drawing on their experiences to teach their children the importance of empathy, understanding, and resilience. They shared stories of their struggles and successes, emphasizing that true community is built on compassion and cooperation. In the face of adversity, they cultivated a sense of pride in their identity as a family committed to lifting each other up, encouraging their children to approach their interactions in Colihaut with curiosity and respect.

As they continued to navigate the evolving dynamics within the community, the Philogene family began to recognize the importance of patience and persistence. While the road to acceptance was fraught with challenges, they understood that positive change often takes time. Through their hard work and dedication, they hoped to contribute to a more unified Colihaut, one where class barriers could be broken down and connections could flourish. By remaining steadfast in their values and committed to fostering alliances across lines of division, the Philogenes aimed to weave their narrative into the broader story of their community, enriching it through their unique perspectives and unwavering spirit.

In their quest for acceptance within Colihaut, Ledger, and Clara made concerted efforts to connect with nearby families, keenly aware that building relationships was crucial to their integration into the community. They immersed themselves in local traditions, making it a priority to participate in community events like harvest festivals and church gatherings. These occasions provided perfect opportunities for them to share their experiences, showcase their values, and learn from the lives and stories of others who called Colihaut home.

At the harvest festival, Clara donned an apron and brought a selection of homemade dishes crafted from their freshest produce. She joined other local women in the bustling kitchen tent, exchanging recipes and techniques while their children played together nearby. These moments fostered bonds, allowing Clara to showcase not only her culinary skills but also her willingness to contribute to the community. The laughter and chatter among the women created an atmosphere of warmth and acceptance, demonstrating that shared experiences could bridge cultural divides.

Ledger, on the other hand, took on a more social role in honoring their desire for connection. He made it a point to introduce his family to neighbors, fostering a sense of camaraderie and shared purpose. At community events, he would approach families with a smile, engaging them in conversation about farming practices and local customs. He shared stories of their journey, their hopes for the future, and his commitment to working collaboratively with other farmers. Through these interactions, Ledger aimed to demonstrate that he saw value in the existing community and that the Philogenes wished to embrace it as they built their new life.

During church gatherings, Ledger and Clara's family sat among the congregation, observing the traditions and rituals that held significance for the local community. Ledger helped with setting up the church hall, while Clara offered her skills in the kitchen, bringing her favorite dishes to the communal potluck. They welcomed conversations with families seated nearby, often discovering shared values and common frustrations regarding the challenges of rural life. These interactions helped dismantle barriers, as small talk evolved into deeper discussions about raising children, farming challenges, and the importance of community support.

As weeks turned into months, Ledger and Clara's consistent engagement with the community began to pay off. Their genuine interest in others' lives and their willingness to contribute positively to local traditions cultivated goodwill. Families began to include them in social gatherings outside formal events, inviting them to informal barbecues and weekend get-togethers. These occasions became pivotal moments for the Philogenes, allowing them to further deepen relationships and learn about the nuances of Colihaut's social landscape.

While establishing connections took effort, Ledger and Clara remained committed to cultivating friendships rooted in mutual understanding and respect. They deliberately practiced active listening, allowing others to share their stories and experiences without interruption or judgment. This attentiveness helped forge deep-rooted relationships, and soon the Philogene name started to become associated with sincerity and hard work in the community.

The friendships that formed became more than social connections; they evolved into alliances that strengthened their sense of belonging. Neighboring families began offering advice on localized farming practices, sharing equipment, or lending a helping hand during busy seasons. The Philogenes, in turn, eagerly engaged in those reciprocal relationships, demonstrating their gratitude and reinforcing their commitment to building a resilient community.

As they embraced their roles within Colihaut, Ledger, and Clara learned that establishing connections required not only time and effort but also vulnerability and openness. Their perseverance inspired others to welcome them more fully, fostering an environment enriched by diverse perspectives and experiences. While challenges still loomed on the horizon, the Philogene family was beginning to carve their niche within the community, one heartfelt connection at a time, sowing the seeds of trust, friendship, and shared hope for the future.

As the Philogene family continued to build relationships within Colihaut, they began to experience the warmth and generosity of community support that made all the difference in their settling-in process. Neighbors, recognizing the Philogenes' dedication to becoming integral members of the community, willingly offered advice on local farming techniques, sharing insights drawn from generations of experience. These interactions became vital learning opportunities for Ledger and Clara, who were eager to adapt their practices to suit the unique rhythms of their new surroundings.

During a particularly vibrant exchange in the fields, Ledger found himself working side by side with one of the more experienced local farmers, a kind-hearted man named Samuel. As they tended to the cornfields, Samuel shared wisdom about soil management that was specific to Colihaut, explaining how to identify the best times for planting and harvesting based on the unique climatic conditions of the region. In return, Ledger shared his own knowledge of crop rotation and sustainable practices that had been effective in their previous farming ventures. This two-way exchange not only enhanced Ledger's skills but also fostered a sense of camaraderie and respect between them, building a bridge of trust that would support both families.

Similarly, Clara, while working with neighboring women during community gatherings, began to learn how to incorporate local ingredients into her cooking, which enhanced the family's meals while also honoring the traditions of her new community. The mutual support blossomed during these interactions; they shared tips and recipes, which helped Clara feel more at home and more integrated into the local culture. As she adapted their menus to incorporate regional specialties, she introduced her neighbors to dishes from their own heritage, thus fostering a rich tapestry of culinary exchange that deepened their friendships.

These exchanges cultivated a network of trust and interdependence that helped the Philogenes feel increasingly anchored in their new home. They no longer felt like outsiders navigating a complex social landscape; instead, they developed meaningful connections that created a sense of belonging. Their willingness to share knowledge, combined with the community's efforts to support them, laid the groundwork for a collaborative spirit that resonated throughout Colihaut.

For the Philogene children, witnessing this mutual support was as impactful as it was for their parents. They played alongside their neighbors' children, forming bonds that would become lifelong friendships. The adults modeled cooperation and kindness, teaching the kids that a community thrives when its members uplift one another. During harvest time, they organized communal pickings where families worked together, pooling their resources and labor for greater efficiency. The laughter and chatter that filled the air not only made the work lighter but also fortified the connections between families.

Through these shared experiences, Clara and Ledger observed that their efforts were reciprocated in ways that reinforced their ties to the community. During particularly busy seasons, neighbors would arrive unannounced to lend a hand, whether it was helping with planting, providing equipment, or simply offering a meal. This generosity reaffirmed the sentiment that in Colihaut, no one had to face challenges alone. As they watched their children grow and form bonds with others, the Philogene family began to truly feel that they were no longer just inhabitants of Colihaut but rather a vital thread in the rich fabric of the community.

The Philogenes came to realize that mutual support was not only essential for their farming success but also for their emotional well-being. The relationships they forged were fortified by the understanding that together, they could weather any storm. This interdependence created a more robust sense of identity for the Philogenes within Colihaut, lifting them as they navigated the complexities of their new life, and instilling hope for a promising future built on collaboration and shared prosperity.

In the spirit of collaboration and community-building, Ledger and Clara often opened their home to host communal meals for local families. These gatherings became a vibrant celebration of food, friendship, and cultural exchange, showcasing dishes made from their own harvest and inviting neighbors to share in the bounty of their labor. With each meal, they aimed to create a welcoming space where stories could be shared and connections could deepen, bridging the gap between newcomers like the Philogene family and the established residents of Colihaut.

Clara poured her heart into preparing these meals, using recipes passed down through her family that highlighted the flavors of their cultural heritage. She infused local ingredients, harvested fresh from their fields, with traditional spices and techniques. The aroma of her cooking wafted through their home, drawing in neighbors as they arrived for the festivities. Tables were adorned with homegrown produce, colorful salads, and hearty stews, as well as some of Clara's signature dishes that reflected their Caribbean roots. This merging of flavors not only delighted the palate but also served as a testament to the rich cultural tapestry present in Colihaut.

During these gatherings, Ledger welcomed everyone with a warm smile, encouraging stories to flow as freely as the food. He often initiated discussions about farming practices, sustainability, and the importance of preserving traditions while adapting to new challenges. This open environment invited seasoned farmers to share their experiences and insights, while also allowing the Philogenes to contribute their own knowledge. The resulting dialogues became opportunities for learning and growth, emphasizing the importance of community wisdom and shared resources in cultivating a successful life.

As they gathered around communal tables, the atmosphere was filled with laughter and heartfelt conversations. Children played together, their joyous sounds mingling with the adults' exchanges, creating a sense of unity, and belonging. Clara and Ledger listened intently as neighbors shared their family stories, traditions, and struggles. These interactions strengthened their relationships, as they recognized that every family, regardless of their history, faced challenges and celebrated victories in their own unique ways.

Through these shared meals, the Philogene family introduced Colihaut to their culinary heritage, sparking interest and curiosity among the residents. Many were eager to learn how to prepare Clara's dishes, leading to spontaneous cooking sessions in her kitchen, where women and children gathered to chop, stir, and taste together. This culinary collaboration helped meld cultures and foster friendships, as they blended ingredients and traditions to create new, unique dishes that represented the collective creativity of their community.

As the rhythm of communal meals continued, Ledger and Clara became known for their hospitality and commitment to fostering connections. They noticed that their guests, once strangers, began to form their own bonds, continuing conversations, and friendships beyond their gatherings. The meals created a network of support that extended well beyond the dinner table, fostering collaboration in other areas of community life, such as joint farming efforts or shared childcare responsibilities.

In time, the Philogene home transformed into a hub of community activity—a place where families reunited, exchanged ideas, and supported one another through both triumphs and challenges. By sharing their resources and inviting others into their lives, Clara and Ledger fostered an environment rich in collaboration, breaking down barriers between newcomers and established residents.

These communal meals served as more than just an introduction to the Philogene family's culinary heritage; they became a living embodiment of the shared values of respect, cooperation, and community. In weaving their own stories into the collective narrative of Colihaut, the Philogene family helped to strengthen the bonds that held the community together, reinforcing the idea that shared resources and shared experiences truly elevated everyone involved, fostering a deeper sense of belonging for all.

Class Divisions—Despite the Philogene family's earnest efforts to integrate into the Colihaut community, tensions began to rise as underlying class divisions surfaced. While many neighbors welcomed them with open arms, a noticeable faction harbored reservations about the newcomers and their land purchase. Some locals viewed the Philogene family's acquisition of land not as an opportunity for collaboration but as an encroachment on their territory. They feared that the changes brought by newcomers might disrupt the delicate balance that had governed their lives for generations. Whispers of discontent circulated, suggesting that the Philogenes, with their ambitious goals, posed a threat to the established way of life that many had come to cherish.

This unease was compounded by the perception that Ledger and Clara's ambitions could challenge the status quo—the norms and hierarchies that had long defined the community. For some families, the Philogene's willingness to embrace innovation in farming practices and community engagement felt like a direct challenge to traditional methods and established power dynamics. They viewed the Philogenes' success in integrating into local events and forging connections as an unwelcome intrusion, an assertion that newcomers could reshape the community without fully understanding its history and struggles. As a result, animosity and resentment began to brew among a select few families, leading to increasing unease within the once-welcoming atmosphere of Colihaut.

The tensions were subtle at first, manifesting in dismissive comments during community gatherings or the exclusion of the Philogenes from certain social circles. Clara especially felt the weight of these dynamics during her interactions with some of the local women who had previously embraced her with warmth. The cordial exchanges began to grow strained, with whispers of distrust replacing the supportive camaraderie she had once found comforting. Ledger, too, sensed the quiet chill in the air during discussions with fellow farmers. While he had initially shared insights and techniques with open hearts, he now faced skepticism and suspicion, as those who felt threatened became more guarded and less willing to collaborate.

As the divisions deepened, the Philogene family struggled to navigate the complexities of a community marked by conflicting sentiments. The ambition that had once attracted them to Colihaut now seemed to become a double-edged sword, with their vision for a thriving, collaborative future clashing with the fears and insecurities of some long-standing residents. Despite these challenges, Ledger and Clara were determined to remain committed to their original goal of fostering relationships built on trust and mutual respect. They understood that meaningful change often takes time and that the seeds of acceptance would require patience, understanding, and a willingness to confront the discomfort that comes with challenging deeply rooted social structures.

As the Philogene family continued to settle in Colihaut, the issues of land ownership and access to resources became increasingly contentious, revealing the fractures within the community. Established farmers, who had tended their land for generations, were anxious about the rising prices and the potential consequences of new, ambitious families like the Philogenes entering the fray. For them, land was not merely a commodity; it embodied a legacy, a way of life that defined their identities and anchored their place in the community. The presence of newcomers threatened to upend this delicate balance, leading to fears of displacement and loss of tradition.

Ledger found himself at the heart of these community discussions about land rights and the ethics of ownership. As he tried to advocate for collaborative farming practices and shared his vision of sustainable agricultural development, he encountered mounting resistance from established farmers who viewed his ideas with suspicion. They questioned his intentions, believing that his pursuit of agricultural prosperity could lead to the further commercialization of the land and the erosion of their long-held values. In these discussions, Ledger began to recognize that the complexities of land ownership were deeply intertwined with issues of class, power, and community identity.

The conversations surrounding land ownership often grew heated, revealing the stark divides between those who embraced change and those who resisted it. Ledger felt a growing sense of urgency to address these tensions while trying to uphold his integrity and the principles that had guided him and Clara in their farming journey. He understood that discussions about land access were not merely about property lines; they encompassed broader societal shifts, such as the impact of urbanization, environmental changes, and economic pressures on rural communities. With each meeting, Ledger sought to listen actively to the concerns of established farmers, hoping to foster understanding and create a dialogue that acknowledged their fears without dismissing his own aspirations.

In navigating these challenges, Ledger learned the importance of humility and empathy. He began seeking common ground by participating in joint community initiatives aimed at addressing local agricultural issues, such as promoting sustainable practices and enhancing resource sharing. Though tense, these engagements provided opportunities to demonstrate his commitment to the community's well-being, allowing him to articulate his vision in a way that aligned with their values. Ledger hoped this approach would help to alleviate some of the anxieties surrounding landownership and build a cooperative spirit among residents.

As discussions about local land ownership continued to unfold, the Philogene family remained steadfast in their belief that the strength of Colihaut lay in its ability to adapt and grow together. They understood that navigating these complexities would take time and effort, but they believed that through openness and mutual respect, it was possible to carve out a future where both established families and newcomers could coexist and thrive. Ledger recognized that the journey toward agricultural prosperity was not just about their family's success; it also required the ability to engage with the historical and social contexts that shaped their community, fostering a respectful dialogue that honored both tradition and progress.

As tensions rose within Colihaut, the need for open dialogue became undeniable. Local leaders convened community meetings to discuss the pressing issues surrounding landownership and the changes newcomers like the Philogene family were bringing to the area. Ledger felt compelled to attend these meetings, believing that genuine engagement could lay the groundwork for understanding and cooperation. However, as he took his seat surrounded by familiar faces, he sensed the heavy atmosphere charged with skepticism and unease.

The meetings were often held in the old community center, a space adorned with memories of past gatherings and celebrations. As residents trickled in, Ledger noticed the cautious glances exchanged among established farmers. Many had known one another for decades, their shared experiences etched in the lines on their faces. In contrast, Ledger, and Clara's family, as newcomers, represented change and uncertainty, casting a long shadow of doubt over their intentions. Taking a deep breath, Ledger prepared himself for what lay ahead, hoping to engage in constructive dialogue that could alleviate some of the community's concerns.

As the meeting commenced, local leaders outlined the agenda, addressing rising land prices and the increasing number of new arrivals who sought to stake their claim in Colihaut. Ledger listened intently as neighbors voiced their frustrations and fears. "We've worked this land for generations," one elderly farmer proclaimed, his voice cracking with emotion. "What do newcomers know about our struggles? They don't understand the complexities of rural life like we do." Ledger felt the weight of these words, realizing just how entrenched the divide was between the established residents and those who had recently arrived.

Determined to share his perspective, Ledger raised his hand when allowed to speak. "I understand your concerns," he began, trying to convey empathy and respect for their experiences. "My family is committed to becoming part of this community, and we want to learn from you. We know that farming in Colihaut is a unique challenge, and we hope to contribute positively."

But skepticism lingered in the air, and several locals folded their arms or exchanged knowing glances. One farmer interrupted, "How can we trust that you won't just come in here and change everything? You are not from here. You don't know what we've been through." Ledger's heart sank; he felt the frustration and anger behind those words, and the challenge ahead became increasingly apparent. The conversation quickly shifted toward concerns about rising land prices fueled by newcomers, with residents questioning whether their way of life could survive the changes brought on by escalating competition.

With each passing question and comment, Ledger became more acutely aware of the gulf that separated him from the very community he yearned to embrace. Each time he attempted to bridge the divide with understanding and shared experiences, he was met with resistance that felt both disheartening and overwhelming. It became clear to him that the issues of land ownership were deeply intertwined with community identity and pride. To some residents, the presence of the Philogenes was a sign of everything they feared: the potential erosion of their traditions, an unfamiliar way of life invading their agricultural heritage.

As the meeting continued, Ledger listened as stories of hardship emerged tales of droughts, crop failures, and the toll of economic pressures that had plagued family farms for years. Each story underscored the tenacity and resilience of the long-time residents and highlighted how their relationships with the land were woven into their identities. Ledger realized that merely sharing his farming knowledge was not enough; he needed to acknowledge these histories and show that he respected their struggles.

The meeting later adjourned without a resolution, leaving Ledger with a profound sense of the challenges ahead in trying to bridge this divide. As he walked home that evening, he contemplated how to continue the conversation beyond formal meetings. He considered reaching out to individuals, hoping for more personal dialogues that might foster understanding. Perhaps if he could connect one-on-one with those who held reservations, he could demonstrate the Philogene family's genuine desire to learn, collaborate, and honor the rich history of Colihaut.

The evening was steeped in uncertainty, but one thing had crystallized in Ledger's mind: building trust would be a slow process, requiring patience, humility, and a commitment to listening. He knew he had to confront the reality that, while eager for connection, the Philogene family's journey toward acceptance would demand more than just a willingness to engage. It would require deep respect for the community's values, an acknowledgment of their history, and a readiness to work alongside them to secure a shared future. As he prepared for bed that night, Ledger resolved to approach the next steps with both an open heart and a clear vision of collaboration, determined to find ways to bridge the gap that separated them from their neighbors.

In the wake of rising tensions within Colihaut, Ledger became increasingly aware of the urgent need to find common ground with local leaders and established families. He understood that simply attending community meetings and sharing his ideas was not enough; he needed to take proactive steps to foster collaboration that would benefit both the newcomers and those who had long called Colihaut home. With Clara's encouragement and support, Ledger began crafting initiatives designed to highlight the importance of unity while addressing the agricultural challenges that threatened their way of life.

One of his first initiatives aimed to establish cooperative farming projects that would bring together both local farmers and the Philogene family. Ledger envisioned community members pooling resources, sharing knowledge, and working side by side to enhance productivity. He believed that by collaborating on shared farming ventures—such as planting crops in communal fields or employing rotational grazing techniques—everyone could benefit from better yields and resource optimization. This would not only alleviate some of the burden on individual farmers but also foster shared experiences and relationships across generational lines.

To present this idea, Ledger scheduled a meeting with several established farmers, including Samuel, the kind-hearted neighbor who had previously shared invaluable insights about techniques specific to Colihaut. Ledger arrived at the meeting armed with data on the benefits of cooperative farming, but more importantly, he came with an open heart and a sincere willingness to listen. "I believe we can create something powerful together," he proposed earnestly. "By bringing our efforts together, we can increase our collective strength against the challenges we face, whatever they may be."

While the proposal was met with some skepticism, Ledger noticed a gradual shift in the atmosphere as he spoke. He highlighted examples from other regions where cooperative farming had helped communities thrive amidst adversity. "We can unite our knowledge, share resources, and rise together," he emphasized, hoping to sow seeds of collaboration in the room. Slowly, a few heads nodded in agreement, and Ledger felt encouraged by their willingness to explore the possibilities for partnership.

Beyond farming cooperatives, Ledger also proposed the idea of shared market days. "Imagine a weekly gathering where we can all come together to sell our goods, share our harvests, and celebrate the bounty of Colihaut. It would not only promote our products but strengthen our community ties," he explained. This initiative aimed to draw out the unique contributions of each family, allowing them to showcase the diversity of crops, foods, and artisan goods produced in the area.

In championing these initiatives, Ledger sought to emphasize the value of collaboration over competition. He recognized that many long-time residents feared the encroachment of newcomers on their established markets. To counter this, he proposed that local families could work together to create an inviting atmosphere at these market days, where everyone felt included and celebrated. "Let's support each other's ventures and build our economic resilience as a community," he urged, making it clear that he was not interested in overshadowing anyone's efforts but rather uplifting the entire area.

As word of the proposed initiatives spread throughout the community, Ledger began to see positive responses emerge. Some families voiced their enthusiasm, eager to discuss new ideas and come together for the benefit of all. Even those who initially harbored skepticism started to express interest, realizing that Ledger's vision encompassed not just the Philogenes, but the entire fabric of Colihaut.

Encouraged by this progress, Ledger organized a series of informal gatherings at Au-Fonde, inviting community members to brainstorm further ideas while enjoying meals together. As neighbors shared their thoughts and dreams for Colihaut's future, Ledger could feel the collective energy shift. Laughter filled their gatherings, stories flowed freely, and the walls that had once seemed insurmountable began to crumble. Conversations turned from suspicion and resistance to possibilities and hope.

In these moments of connection, Ledger became more attuned to the concerns of his neighbors, the fears tied to changes in land ownership, the economic anxieties peculiar to rural life, and the deep-seated value they placed on community support. Understanding these perspectives allowed him to approach each discussion with greater empathy and respect. He sensed that, through collaboration, they could find solutions to both long-standing challenges and newer issues while nurturing the heart and spirit of Colihaut.

Through his persistent efforts to create avenues for cooperation, Ledger held to the belief that a united community could navigate the evolving landscape together. Building on the initial groundwork of farmers' meetings, cooperative projects, and shared market days, he began to weave a collaborative narrative that resonated with the diverse voices of Colihaut. With each small victory, Ledger felt hope rekindled among the community, illuminating a path toward resolution and stronger connections for all. In the face of rising tensions, he had taken the first steps toward constructing a new, collaborative future for the Philogene family and their neighbors, rooted in shared dreams and mutual support.

Despite Ledger's earnest intentions and proactive efforts to foster collaboration in Colihaut, he soon discovered that the journey toward acceptance was fraught with challenges. The initiatives he had proposed—cooperative farming projects and shared market days—met with mixed reactions, and not all community members were willing to embrace the changes he envisioned. Resistance began to surface, creating a palpable divide that tested both his resolve and commitment to cultivating a sense of belonging in this complex community.

During a particularly tense gathering at the community center, Ledger presented his ideas, hoping to garner enthusiasm and support. While some farmers nodded in agreement, others remained visibly skeptical, arms crossed, and faces set in hard lines. One longtime resident, a wiry man named Harold, spoke up with a confrontational tone. "We have always done things a certain way here. Why should we change just because newcomers think they have a better idea? You do not know what it is like to have to fight for every crop," he challenged, his voice echoing through the halls.

Ledger felt the weight of Harold's words, understanding that they stemmed from a deep-rooted sense of pride and a fear of the unknown. Despite his attempts to address these concerns with respect and empathy, it became clear that some families felt threatened by the changes Ledger represented. For them, the Philogene family's presence was a symbol of an impending shift that might alter the way of life they had fought to preserve for generations. This resistance created an uneasy atmosphere, discouraging open dialogue and making it difficult for Ledger to connect with those who were still skeptical.

In the days that followed, Ledger became increasingly aware of the reluctance among certain community members to engage with the Philogene family. Invitations to local gatherings and events were often extended with strings attached or worded in ways that hinted they were not entirely welcome. Clara, who had initially found joy in connecting with neighbors during potluck dinners and community activities, began to share Ledger's frustrations. There were times when she would return home from the market to mention how some vendors would not acknowledge her or how conversations fell silent when she approached certain groups. The warmth they had once felt was increasingly hard to find.

These experiences weighed heavily on Ledger, who had put his heart into building bridges between himself and his neighbors. He often found himself questioning whether he had misjudged the community's openness to newcomers. Each dismissal felt like a personal rebuff, and the isolation that crept in began to test his resolve. He had envisioned creating a collaborative environment where everyone could thrive, yet it seemed that with every attempt to foster inclusivity, he encountered barriers that felt insurmountable.

During quiet evenings, Ledger would sit with Clara on their porch, reflecting on the challenges they faced. "I thought we could contribute positively, work alongside everyone," he admitted, frustration seeping into his voice. "But how do we break through this wall? How do we show them that we are here to help and not to disrupt them? Clara, gentle yet pragmatic, reminded him that change often breeds fear, and that acceptance takes time. "We just must stay true to our beliefs, Ledger. We will find our way, even if it feels slow right now," she encouraged, placing a comforting hand on his shoulder.

To better understand and address the concerns of the community, Ledger decided to reach out to individuals for one-on-one discussions rather than relying solely on public meetings. He focused on establishing personal relationships with key members of the community, hoping that building trust on a smaller scale would pave the way for broader acceptance. These smaller exchanges allowed him to share his family's story, their struggles, and their dreams while also inviting others to recount their experiences, deepening his appreciation for their histories.

Despite his best efforts, however, some families remained unmoved. Each encounter where resistance echoed through the voices of long-time farmers reminded him of the uphill battle they faced. Ledger realized he needed resilience in the face of adversity, as the path to acceptance required both patience and unwavering commitment. Although disappointment lingered with each fleeting moment of rejection, Ledger remained hopeful. He believed that even the smallest connections could lead to greater understanding if nurtured with care.

Over time, Ledger began to recognize that the challenges of acceptance were also growth opportunities, both personally and within the community. While some were unwilling to embrace change, others were beginning to see the value in his approach, responding with cautious optimism. These flickers of hope served as reminders that progress often comes through perseverance in the face of resistance. With every effort made to engage, Ledger believed that he could help foster a sense of belonging for the Philogenes in Colihaut, no matter how long it took to break down the barriers that stood in their way.

In the face of rising tensions within Colihaut, Clara recognized the urgent need to create spaces for connection and understanding between the Philogene family and their neighbors. She suggested hosting cultural exchange events—gatherings where families could come together to showcase their traditions, music, and food. Clara believed that celebrating their shared humanity through diverse cultural expressions could help foster appreciation and respect among community members. It was a hopeful initiative aimed at weaving together the fabric of Colihaut's community, one thread at a time.

With Ledger's support, Clara began planning the first cultural exchange event at their home, inviting neighbors to bring their favorite dishes, stories, and music to share. The Philogenes prepare traditional Caribbean meals, featuring dishes like jerk chicken, plantains, and rice and peas. Clara envisioned an evening filled with laughter, music, and storytelling, where each family could contribute something unique from their heritage. She promoted the idea not only as an opportunity to share but also as a chance for everyone to learn from one another, emphasizing how much richer their community could be through diversity.

As news of the event spread, Clara felt a mix of excitement and apprehension. She knew there would be those who might resist participating, but she remained hopeful that the allure of food and music could break down barriers. In the days leading up to the gathering, Clara made a point to visit their neighbors, personally inviting them and sharing her vision for the evening. She spoke enthusiastically about the opportunity to come together, enjoy good food, and celebrate the stories that shaped each family's background.

On the night of the cultural exchange, the air buzzed with anticipation as neighbors began to arrive, some with dishes wrapped in colorful cloths, while others carried musical instruments. Clara greeted each guest warmly, inviting them into their home, where the aroma of Caribbean spices mingled with the scents of familiar, local fare. The living room was adorned with decorations that celebrated both their heritage and that of their neighbors, creating an inviting atmosphere that emphasized unity in diversity.

As the evening unfolded, Clara encouraged guests to showcase their talents. Families shared stories of their cultural traditions, recounting their histories and how they had come to call Colihaut home. There were tales of harvest festivals, holiday celebrations, and childhood memories. Ledger watched as people began to open, laughter and chatter filling the air, reminding him of the power of shared experiences. Music filled the room—the Philogene family played upbeat reggae tunes while neighbors brought out homemade instruments to join in. The joyful sounds seemed to melt away the tension that had lingered in the community, if only for a while.

During a heartfelt moment, an elderly neighbor named Agnes stepped forward with a plate of freshly baked bread. She smiled warmly at Clara and Ledger, explaining how her family had always gathered to make this bread for special occasions. "It's a symbol of good fortune and welcome," she said, her eyes sparkling. Ledger could see the pride in her expression as she shared her family's tradition—a bridge between their cultures that highlighted their common humanity. Clara seized the opportunity, weaving Agnes's story into the fabric of the evening, encouraging others to share similar traditions while making everyone feel valued and respected.

As the food was shared across the table, guests eagerly sampled dishes from one another's cultures, expressing delight and curiosity about the different flavors. Someone was particularly enamored with Clara's jerk chicken, while others found themselves surprised by the sweetness of the plantains. Conversations flowed more freely as they enjoyed the diverse array of cuisines, revealing an eagerness to learn about one another's backgrounds. Clara felt a sense of joy watching the barriers between families begin to erode, replaced by a newfound kinship.

With each shared story, song, and plate passed around, the cultural exchange event transformed into a communal celebration of identity, history, and the vibrant threads that wove them all together. Even those who had initially been skeptical began to join in, appreciating the richness of the experience. Clara saw heads nodding in agreement as neighbors connected over similarities rather than differences, fostering a growing sense of belonging and understanding.

As the evening ended, Clara reflected on the success of the gathering. The walls that once seemed solid and unyielding had begun to crack, allowing warmth and light to seep through. She felt encouraged by how the community had embraced this opportunity for cultural exchange, recognizing that unity could flourish from mutual respect and shared experiences. Ledger, too, felt reinvigorated by the event, hopeful that the connections nurtured that night could pave the way for further collaboration and acceptance in Colihaut.

As guests left, promising to return for future gatherings, Clara knew that the journey to integration and acceptance would be ongoing. Yet, she was confident that the shared experiences of the cultural exchange had planted seeds of understanding that could grow deep roots in the heart of Colihaut. By celebrating their differences while honoring their shared humanity, the Philogene family and their neighbors could navigate the path toward a more inclusive and vibrant community together.

As the social dynamics of Colihaut shifted around him, Ledger found himself grappling with a profound sense of isolation and frustration. The cultural exchange event, while a success in many ways, had not completely erased the barriers between the Philogene family and some long-time residents. Despite the laughter and shared stories that had filled their home, he could still sense the lingering skepticism in the air. It felt as though acceptance was a distant shore, just out of reach. Ledger often found himself lost in thought, contemplating the sacrifices his family had made to pursue their dream of building a life in this community.

In quieter moments, he would sit on the porch of their home, watching the sun dip below the horizon, casting warm hues across the landscape. He remembered the long journey they had taken to get here, the late nights filled with plans and hopes, the risks they had embraced investing in land that held the growth potential, both for crops and for their family. Yet now, every step forward was met with resistance—a reminder of the complexities in moving not just into a new physical space, but also into the hearts and minds of a community steeped in history and tradition. As he gazed out over the fields, Ledger questioned whether the sacrifices they had made were worth the fight for acceptance.

These thoughts triggered a whirlwind of emotion within him: frustration at the closed doors he encountered, anger toward those who refused to acknowledge their efforts, and overwhelming sadness that he was not yet part of the fabric of Colihaut. Ledger felt the weight of this isolation pressing down on him, questioning if he truly belonged in a place that seemed so unwilling to welcome change. With every dismissive glance or cold shoulder, he found himself wrestling with a deeper question: What did it mean to be truly accepted and respected within a community so bound to its traditions and past?

He often replayed interactions in his mind, dissecting each conversation for signs of progress or retreat. He recalled conversations with Harold and the other skeptics, their words echoing in his thoughts: "You don't know what it's like to have to fight for every crop." Those words stung with an honesty that he could not ignore. Ledger acknowledged that he could never fully grasp the depth of their experiences, but he was determined to understand. He sought not to replace their way of life or overshadow their history, but to pave a path for shared futures. Yet, as he stewed over these reflections, doubt crept in.

The internal struggle weighed heavily on Ledger, blurring the lines between hope and despair. There were days when he felt empowered, ready to take on any challenges that lay ahead, convinced that their collective experiences would lead to meaningful relationships. But there were also moments when he felt utterly defeated, questioning whether he had the strength to endure the long, slow process of building trust. The duality of his feelings reflected the complexity of the community, with history yet resistant to change.

He pondered the stories he wanted to write in Colihaut—the legacy he wanted to leave for his children. Ledger wanted his family's narrative to be linked with their neighbors, not divided by it. But with each setback, he felt himself retreating into protective silence, unsure of how to push through the walls that continued to rise around him. He had envisioned a future built on collaboration, yet the words of some community members haunted him. How could he convince them of his intentions when they saw only the threat of change?

In his heart, Ledger knew he had to persist despite these challenges. His family had come to Colihaut seeking a better life, inspired by a dream that was worth fighting for, but the battle was proving to be more daunting than he had anticipated. He realized that true acceptance would not come simply through initiatives or shared meals; it would take time, patience, and resilience.

Determined to break through the isolation creeping in, Ledger resolved to keep pressing forward. He reflected on what being part of a community meant—sharing joys, facing struggles together, and fostering an environment where every voice mattered. He understood that if he wanted to create a sense of belonging for himself and his family, he would need to embody the values of empathy, humility, and perseverance, even when faced with adversity.

With renewed clarity, Ledger committed to taking each day as it came, ready to confront the challenges that lay ahead. He resolved to continue reaching out to his neighbors, building connections one conversation at a time. He would extend the hand of friendship, even when it felt heavy, and strive to illustrate the value of unity over division. As the stars began to twinkle in the darkening sky, Ledger felt a flicker of hope ignite within him—he may not yet be fully accepted, but he would never stop working toward a place where his family could belong. In his heart, he knew that every effort, no matter how small, counted in the journey toward building their life in Colihaut.

As Clara settled onto the porch beside Ledger, she watched the sun melt into the horizon, casting long shadows across their fields. The beauty of the landscape often brought her solace, but tonight, even the vibrant colors felt muted under the weight of societal expectations that loomed over them. She could see in the way Ledger furrowed his brow during meetings, how his shoulders sagged a little more each time they were met with resistance. She felt it creeping into her own heart, as the external tensions within the community began to seep into their family life.

Clara worried deeply about the impact of these growing tensions on their children. She could sense the unease among the community and the whispers that carried through the wind the subtle exclusion her little ones sometimes faced at school or during playdates. Each furrowed brow on the faces of neighbors, when she greeted them, felt heavy with implications that her children might notice—lessons about belonging and acceptance that were more about how others viewed them rather than who they truly were. Their innocence was precious, and she wanted to shield them from any hurt that might stem from being seen as outsiders in a community so steeped in its own traditions.

Clara determined to cultivate a sense of pride and resilience in her children, an inner strength that would enable them to confront challenges head-on. She began weaving stories of their heritage into their daily lives, celebrating their roots and traditions. At dinner, she shared tales of her childhood,

340

dances at family gatherings, and the joy of harvesting fresh vegetables from their garden. She taught her children about the Caribbean culture they came from, emphasizing the beauty in diversity and the value of embracing one's identity. "You have so much to be proud of," she would tell them, her voice infused with warmth. "Your roots run deep, and your story is a part of this land now, too."

Clara believed that by instilling this sense of pride, her children could navigate the complexities of being part of a community that was not always welcoming. She watched with joy as they began to embrace who they were, sharing their own stories and traditions with newfound enthusiasm. In those moments, Clara felt a flicker of hope, believing that her children could build bridges where the adults were faltering.

However, Clara's unwavering support for Ledger remained her anchor in the storm. She admired his tenacity and commitment to their shared dream, and his determination fueled her own resolve. On nights when he came home disheartened from community gatherings, Clara would listen as he vented his frustrations, her empathetic eyes reflecting his struggles. She would remind him of the courage he displayed in reaching out, of the lives they were touching, one conversation at a time. "We are building something beautiful together," she would reassure him. "It will take time, but it's worth every effort."

Even as they navigated the difficulties they faced, Clara found herself increasingly aware of the need for community cohesion. Inspired by Ledger's initiatives, she began brainstorming ways to strengthen ties among neighbors—a garden project that involved all families, where they could plant crops together, or community art days where they could collaborate on a mural celebrating their diverse heritages. She envisioned these gatherings as platforms for connection, where laughter could drown out the whispers of doubt.

Yet, amidst her optimism, Clara, too, felt the weight of reality pressing down on her. Some days, the harshness of rejection felt so palpable that it seeped into her bones. There were moments when she questioned whether their efforts could truly shift the dynamics of the community or whether acceptance was simply an unreachable dream. She often found herself wondering how they could continue to strive for belonging in a place where the past held such strong influence over the present.

But then, she would look at her children, filled with hope and resilience, and remind herself that their journey was part of a larger story—one that could inspire change within Colihaut. Clara believed that if she and Ledger could model the values of compassion and collaboration, their children would carry that legacy forward, creating a ripple effect that might just break down the barriers in their community.

In these moments of uncertainty, Clara drew strength from her commitment to her family and to Ledger. They were in this together—deeply intertwined in their aspirations and struggles, their love acting as a counterbalance to external pressures. She held onto the belief that, despite the challenges they faced, they were paving the way for a future steeped in understanding rather than division. And as they built their lives on the foundations of love and support, Clara knew deep down that they could weather any storm if they stood steadfast together.

Amidst the challenges and setbacks, they faced in Colihaut, the Philogene family's commitment to their goals remained unwavering. Each day brought new obstacles—whether it be the lingering skepticism from some long-time residents or the uncertainty of the agricultural seasons—but Ledger, Clara, and their children met these hurdles with steadfast determination. Together, they cultivated not only their land but also their hopes of becoming integral members of the community.

The early mornings were quiet and peaceful, a stark contrast to the whirlpool of thoughts that occupied Ledger's mind. With the dawn's first light breaking over the hills, he and Clara would rise to tend to the farm, their daily routine a testament to the work they had committed to together. They worked side by side, tilling the soil, planting seeds, and nurturing the crops that promised both sustenance and prosperity.

Despite the whispers of doubt and the emotional weight of seeking acceptance, Ledger found solace in the rhythm of their labor. The earth beneath his hands felt familiar and reassuring. It reminded him of the dreams that had driven them here, the aspirations of a sustainable life built from hard work and collaboration. As he sank his hands into the warm, rich soil, he often spoke to Clara about their vision for the farm, weaving in hopes of community connection as he planted each seed.

"One day, I want to see our fields filled with plants shared with everyone," he would say, his eyes lighting up with the possibilities. "Imagine a harvest festival with everyone contributing their crops. A day where we celebrate the land and each other." Clara would smile at his enthusiasm, inspired by his resilience even on days when frustrations lingered in the air like a summer haze.

Clara, too, poured her heart into the farm, balancing her responsibilities with the need to instill pride and resilience in their children. She often pulled Koie and Nerisa into the fields, teaching them the importance of hard work and the lessons that come with patience and care. "Every plant has its time to grow," she would explain, her voice gentle yet encouraging, "and so do we." As they worked together, Clara emphasized the significance of nurturing not only the land but also the familial bonds that lay at the heart of their resilience.

One afternoon, Clara organized a small family project—a patch of land dedicated to growing vegetables they would offer to local families in need. "Let's give back to the community," she proposed, hoping to connect with neighbors through generosity. "If we share the fruits of our labor, we can show that we're invested in this community, too." Ledger nodded, appreciating her perspective. This initiative could be a powerful statement—an expression of their determination to be seen not just as newcomers, but as active participants in the life of Colihaut.

As they cultivated this new patch of land, Nerisa and Koie reveled in the experience. They planted seeds, watered the ground, and shared laughter as they picked weeds. Through these simple tasks, Clara imparted lessons of resilience, reminding them that every setback was part of a larger journey. Whenever a plant struggled or a storm threatened to disrupt their efforts, they would discuss how perseverance could lead to growth even in adversity.

"Just like us," Nerisa would say, her eyes bright with understanding. "We have our rough days, but we keep trying." Clara beamed with pride at her daughter's insight, recognizing the strength of their family unit. With each lesson, Nerisa and Koie were learning more than just how to farm; they were absorbing the very essence of resilience, the capacity to rise above challenges and take root even in difficult conditions.

The family's resilience was tested further when an unexpected storm swept through the region, threatening to damage the crops they had worked so hard to cultivate. As the wind howled and rain lashed against their windows, Ledger gathered his family together in the living room. They huddled close, sharing stories of strength and determination while the storm raged outside. Clara shared tales from her childhood—of storms that had come and gone, of how the crops always bounced back with time and care.

"Every storm has its end," she reminded them all, her voice steady. "And when it does, our farm will still be here, waiting for us to nurture it back to life." Ledger joined in, emphasizing the importance of their collective strength. "Together, we have already faced so much, and together we will rebuild. That is the truth of our family," he affirmed, reinforcing their bond during this tumultuous time.

When the storm finally passed, they ventured outside to assess the damage. Although some plants had been battered, their most treasured crops remained resilient, having taken root deep enough to weather the tempest. With determination glittering in their eyes, Ledger, and Clara, joined by Wizen, Petronel, Julien, Eliza, Louisa, James, Dfriel, Koie, and Nerisa, got to work immediately, repairing what the storm had damaged. The sense of community in their efforts served as a powerful reminder that they were not alone in their commitment to the land or each other.

The morning sun broke through the clouds, illuminating the scene in a glow that reflected their resolve. Neighbors who had attended the cultural exchange event arrived with tools and encouragement, ready to lend a hand. The Philogene family's initiative to grow food for the community had ignited a spark, drawing people together, and now, in the wake of the storm, it was clear that this bond could withstand even the toughest tests.

"Let's gather the fallen branches first," Ledger directed, pointing to the remnants scattered across their field. Wizen and Petronel grabbed rakes, while Julien and Eliza started clearing debris from the pathways, their laughter rising above the wind as they worked side by side. Clara nodded, impressed by how quickly the community mobilized to help.

"Look at that!" Clara exclaimed as James and Dfriel teamed up to inspect the damaged rows of vegetables. "They are checking which plants can be saved. That is the spirit!"

Nerisa, inspired by Clara's enthusiasm, added, "We can replant any of the seedlings that can still thrive! It is just like life; we will flourish as long as we keep nurturing each other.

The group moved with purpose, reinforcing not just the crops but their connections. The work, though physically demanding, carried an energy that lifted their spirits. As they repaired what they needed mending, Clara seized the moment to remind everyone why they were coming together and how far they had come since the family moved to Colihaut.

"Let's take a break!" she called out after a while, wiping her brow. "How about we gather around for some refreshments? We can share what we love about our farms and our families."

Everyone took a moment to catch their breath, gathering beneath a large mango tree that provided shade. A meal was quickly laid out — fresh coconuts, breadfruit chips, and some leftover jerk chicken from the cultural exchange. As they enjoyed the food, laughter flowed more freely than ever before.

Julien, full of energy, stood up. "Let us each share a story about our farms! I want to hear how each of us started." The suggestion ignited a wave of excitement and one by one, they shared their personal tales, revealing the challenges and triumphs that had shaped their relationships with the land.

Nerisa spoke of the goats her family had raised, recounting the day they had all escaped and led her on a wild chase down the hillside. The group roared with laughter, and even the most skeptical community members found themselves smiling. Louisa chimed in next, sharing how she had learned to weave baskets from the palm leaves growing on her property. "My grandmother taught me that nothing goes to waste; it all has a purpose. Just like our community—everyone has something to contribute."

As each story unfolded, the barriers between newcomers and established families began to dissolve even further. Clara's heart swelled with pride at how her children soaked in the wisdom being shared, their faces alight with the realization that they were becoming part of a larger tapestry of life in Colihaut.

With renewed energy, they returned to work, motivated not just by the need to restore their land but by the sense of unity that surrounded them. Together, they planted new seedlings, reinforced damaged rows, and shared tips on sustainable farming techniques. The children played nearby, learning from their parents by example, their laughter mingling with the sounds of hard work.

As the sun began to set, casting a golden hue across the fields, Ledger took a moment to look around at the scene before him. He felt a wave of gratitude wash over him. In the face of adversity, they had found a connection. The community was starting to bloom into something beautiful, and he realized how essential these relationships were to build a shared future.

"Thank you all for being here today," he said, his voice filled with emotion as he addressed everyone. "You have not only helped reinforce these crops but have reinforced the bonds that tie us together as a community. Together, we are stronger, and I believe we can overcome any storm that comes our way."

The day's hard work had forged new friendships, deepened existing ones, and illuminated the resilience of the Philogene family. As they looked toward the horizon, Ledger, Clara, and their children felt the warmth of belonging wrapping around them, a reminder that even in the face of uncertainty, they were not alone in their journey. The shared laughter, stories, and hard work had forged an invisible thread of connection that tied them to their neighbors.

Together, they had weathered the storm, both literally and metaphorically, and emerged stronger on the other side. Ledger glanced at Clara, her smile radiant in the fading light, and felt a surge of hope. Their dreams of building a life intertwined with the community were no longer distant wishes but tangible realities fueled by collaboration and support. With each passing day, they were creating a future where acceptance thrived, rooted in the rich soil of mutual respect and shared experiences. The horizon before them gleamed with the promise of new beginnings—an affirmation that through resilience, love, and unity, they could cultivate not just their farm, but a flourishing community.

CB

Part Four: Intersecting Lives

Chapter Eleven: Henri Sebastien

As the vibrant tapestry of Colihaut continued to evolve, a pivotal figure emerged Henri Sebastien. A middle-class Venezuelan with deep cultural roots, Henri embodied a different set of ambitions and values that intertwined with those of the Philogene family in surprising ways. He stood as a bridge between worlds, captured by the dynamic energy of his adopted community, yet anchored in the traditions of his homeland.

Henri was born in Caracas, where he grew up surrounded by rich culture, art, and music. His early life was marked by a wealth of experiences that molded his worldview, instilling in him a deep appreciation for education and the arts. Raised in a family that valued intellectual pursuits, Henri excelled in his studies, earning a scholarship to study literature and anthropology at the University of Simón Bolívar. His passion for learning would later evolve into a commitment to education as a means of empowering others, a legacy he carried into his marriage with Isabelle.

Isabelle, a passionate artist, and educator with a knack for connecting with children, complemented Henri's dedication beautifully. Their shared values created a strong bond, grounded in mutual respect and the belief that education and creativity could transform lives. Together, they envisioned a future where art and knowledge flourished, inspiring those around them to embrace their potential. This shared dream fueled their journey, leading them to Colihaut, where they hoped to foster a sense of community and provide young minds with the tools to dream beyond their immediate circumstances.

As they settled into their new home at Lagon, Henri's vision took form; he and Isabelle began to explore ways to engage with the local community. They dreamed of establishing an arts and education center, a space where both children and adults could come together to learn and create. With each passing day, Henri poured his energy into building connections, meeting with local leaders, and organizing workshops that showcased the importance of culture and creativity in everyday life.

However, as Henri navigated the complexities of his relationship with Ledger and the wider community, he found himself grappling with the differences in their perspectives. Ledger, deeply rooted in the practical world of agriculture and survival, was focused on the immediate challenges facing the Philogene family. His pragmatic approach often clashed with Henri's idealism, leading to a tension that was palpable at community gatherings. While Ledger saw the land to provide for his family and build a legacy, Henri viewed his aspirations through the lens of cultural expression and community-building.

Henri often felt that Ledger's practicality overshadowed the importance of nurturing creativity and imagination in the community. He believed that while crops and sustenance were essential for survival, the cultivation of minds through art and education was equally vital for a thriving society. This dichotomy between their worlds created friction, leading Henri to question whether Ledger understood the potential for transformation that education and creativity could bring to Colihaut.

Despite their differences, there was a mutual respect that underpinned their interactions. Ledger admired Henri's passion and dedication, even if he did not always agree with his methods. He recognized that Henri's pursuits held value; indeed, they could enrich the community in ways that agriculture alone could not. For Henri, Ledger's resilience and hard work were commendable, yet he felt a sense of urgency about expanding the community's focus beyond mere survival to embrace a more holistic approach to development.

Their relationship, marked by both collaboration and contention, reflected the complexities of a community in transition. As Colihaut evolved, so too did the dynamics among its residents. Henri, with his Venezuelan roots, brought a new layer of cultural richness to the village, challenging traditional notions of identity and belonging. His presence encouraged others to think beyond the constraints of their circumstances, igniting aspirations that had long been dormant.

Through the lens of Henri Sebastien, readers are invited to explore not only the individual journey of a man striving to uplift his community but also the broader narrative of a village grappling with the intersection of tradition and innovation. His story serves as a testament to the resilience of the human spirit, reminding us that progress often comes from the convergence of diverse perspectives and the willingness to bridge the gaps that separate us.

As Henri continued to forge connections in Colihaut, his impact began to ripple through the community, creating an environment where collaboration, understanding, and creativity could flourish. Within this evolving landscape, the interplay between Henri and Ledger would come to shape the future of Colihaut in unexpected and profound ways, illustrating that the path to belonging and acceptance is often navigated through the complexities of shared dreams and differing values.

Henri Sebastien hailed from a middle-class family in Venezuela, where his childhood was steeped in the vibrant cultural heritage that defined his homeland. Growing up in the bustling streets of Caracas, he was enveloped by an atmosphere rich with literature, music, and artistic expression. His parents, both dedicated educators, played a pivotal role in shaping his appreciation for the world around him, fostering a sense of curiosity and a love for learning that would follow him throughout his life.

From an early age, Henri was surrounded by books. His father, a literature teacher, often shared his passion through evenings filled with poetry and prose, reading aloud the works of Gabriel García Márquez and Mario Vargas Llosa. His mother Elena, a history teacher, introduced him to the tales of Venezuela's past—stories of resilience, revolution, and the country's dazzling cultural tapestry. These narratives ignited a fire within Henri, instilling in him a profound respect for the power of words and the stories they carried. He learned that literature was not just a form of entertainment but a tool for understanding the complexities of human experience.

Music was another foundational pillar of his upbringing. Henri's home was often alive with the soulful rhythms of salsa, merengue, and traditional Venezuelan folk music. His parents regularly took him to cultural events and local festivals, where traditional dancers filled the streets with vibrant colors and contagious energy. Henri delighted in the sounds of the cuatro and the maracas, each note weaving a story of his cultural identity. These moments taught him that art was a communal experience, a way to connect with others while celebrating the richness of their shared heritage.

As he navigated the complexities of growing up, Henri developed a strong sense of identity rooted in this cultural background. He became aware of the political and social realities surrounding him—the struggles faced by his community and the value of education in fostering change. In a country marked by both beauty and turmoil, Henri recognized that an empowered society was reliant on access to knowledge and artistic expression. He envisioned a future where education served as a beacon of hope, allowing individuals to transcend their circumstances and aspire to something greater.

Driven by this vision, Henri excelled academically, earning a scholarship to attend the University of Simón Bolívar, where he pursued a degree in literature and anthropology. His time at university further deepened his appreciation for the arts as a means of cultural expression. He engaged with a diverse community of thinkers, artists, and activists, participating in discussions that challenged norms and explored the intersection of culture, identity, and social justice. Henri's passion for education crystallized into a commitment to uplift those around him, believing firmly that art and knowledge were essential catalysts for empowerment.

As Henri looked ahead to his future, he envisioned a life dedicated to nurturing creativity and education within the framework of community. He dreamed of establishing a space where individuals could come together to explore their artistic talents, share their stories, and learn from one another. This dream became even more profound after marrying Isabelle, a talented artist and educator who shared his vision of cultivating minds and hearts through creative expression.

When Henri and Isabelle decided to relocate to Colihaut, they brought with them a wealth of cultural richness and an unwavering commitment to education and the arts. Their shared passion for community engagement and empowerment fueled their aspirations, motivating them to create an arts and education center that would serve as a beacon of possibility for the residents of their new home. They envisioned workshops in painting, music, and creative writing, envisioning a space that fostered collaboration and inspiration.

However, the transition to Colihaut was not without challenges. Henri quickly realized that while the community was rooted in its deep traditions, there were hurdles to overcome in reconciling his cultural ambitions with the more pragmatic perspectives of some of the local families, including Ledger Philogene's. Henri's aspirations often felt at odds with Ledger's singular focus on agriculture and survival, as they navigated the complexities of building relationships within the community that was both welcoming and resistant to change.

For Henri, the richness of his cultural heritage became both a source of strength and a lens through which he viewed the world. It motivated him to connect with those around him, to share his passion for education and the arts, and to contribute to the burgeoning identity of Colihaut. Henri's journey would prove to be more than just an exploration of his own dreams; it would also entail weaving his narrative into the larger story of the community, celebrating both the differences and the shared aspirations that united them all.

As he stepped into this new chapter of his life, Henri Sebastien was determined to leave his mark on Colihaut—a mark defined by the vibrancy of his culture, the power of education, and the transformative potential of art. Through his journey, he would discover that amidst the contrasting ambitions and values, the bonds of humanity could create an intricate tapestry richer than any single thread.

Seeking opportunities for a better life, Henri Sebastien relocated to Dominica several years prior, hoping to establish a new beginning for his family. The decision to migrate stemmed from both economic pressures and a strong desire to provide his children with a stable environment where they could flourish. In Venezuela, Henri had witnessed the struggles of his fellow citizens as political unrest and economic instability threatened the livelihoods of many families, including his own. The rising cost of living and uncertainty about the future gnawed at him and weighed heavily on his heart.

Henri had always held a deep commitment to education, believing it to be a powerful vehicle for change. As a teacher, he understood that knowledge could uplift individuals and communities alike, equipping them with the tools needed to navigate the challenges of life. Yet, in a country fraught with turmoil, the educational opportunities he prized were becoming increasingly scarce. The realization that his children might grow up without the support and resources they needed to thrive ignited a spark of urgency within him.

The idea of moving to Dominica began to take shape as he learned about its reputation as a haven of stability and opportunity. Henri envisioned a place where his family could not only escape the uncertainties of their homeland but also immerse themselves in a community that valued education and cultural exchange. Dominica's diverse population and rich cultural landscape promised a fresh start—one where his children could grow in a nurturing environment that celebrated creativity and learning.

Fueled by this hope, Henri made the difficult decision to uproot his family and set off for a new life on the island. Alongside his parents and siblings, his wife Isabelle, her parents, and siblings, and their five young children, Alton, Aldie, Algar, Nun, and Theresa, he prepared for the journey with a mixture of excitement and trepidation. They sold what little belongings they could, gathering only the essentials for their new life. As they boarded the Steamship, Curacao, that would carry them away from everything they had ever known, Henri clutched his children's hands tightly, reassuring them that a brighter future awaited.

The voyage to Dominica was long and filled with uncertainty, the ocean stretching endlessly before them. As they sailed, Henri reflected on the hope and possibilities that lay ahead. He envisioned a life where he could contribute his skills as an educator, infusing the local community with his passion for knowledge and the arts. He dreamed of establishing a connection with families seeking to enrich their children's lives through creativity and education. The journey was as much about seeking refuge as it was about laying the groundwork for a legacy of learning.

Upon arriving in Portsmouth, Dominica, Henri was captivated by the island's beauty. Lush green mountains rose steeply from the coastline, and the vibrant sounds of nature surrounded them. Yet, even in this paradise, there were challenges to face. Henri quickly realized that establishing a place for his family and carving out a role in the community would require perseverance and resilience.

He set to work immediately, seeking out opportunities to teach and share his knowledge. He visited local schools, introducing himself to educators and community leaders, eager to learn how he could contribute to the educational landscape. His enthusiasm was infectious; Henri's passion for reading and the arts resonated with many, and he soon found himself welcomed into the local community.

In his interactions with fellow educators and parents, Henri recognized a shared desire for growth and improvement. Dominica's children were hungry for knowledge, and he was determined to provide them with the tools to explore their creativity. He began organizing workshops in art, storytelling, and music, creating platforms for children to express themselves and develop their talents. Each session was infused with energy and excitement, as Henri encouraged young minds to embrace their potential.

As he nurtured his role within the community, Henri remained focused on his goal: providing a stable and fulfilling life for his family. He understood the struggles they faced as newcomers but took comfort in the support he received from the individuals and families he was beginning to know. The sense of belonging began to take root, bolstered by the shared values of education, creativity, and community spirit.

Through hard work and determination, Henri sowed the seeds of a promising future not just for himself and his family, but also for the children of Dominica. His efforts brought together diverse voices and perspectives, blending cultural influences to create a vibrant atmosphere of learning. In this new land, Henri found not just refuge but a community that embraced his vision, one that resonated deeply with the core of who he was.

As he reflected on their journey from Venezuela to Dominica, Henri felt a profound sense of purpose. They had survived the uncertainties of migration, and now, with the love and support of their new community, they were beginning to thrive. Henri's dream of contributing his talents to a place that valued education, and creativity was coming to fruition, fostering hope and resilience in both his family and the community around them. Dominica was not just a new home; it was a canvas for Henri's aspirations, painted with the colors of hope, love, and the promise of a brighter tomorrow.

Upon arriving in Dominica, Henri became actively involved in local cultural initiatives, focusing on promoting the arts and education. Eager to immerse himself in the community and share his passion for creativity, he wasted no time in organizing workshops and events that celebrated Caribbean culture. By bringing together diverse cultural expressions, Henri aimed not only to enrich the lives of the residents but also to foster a profound sense of pride in their heritage.

His first initiative was a series of storytelling workshops at local schools, where he invited children and parents to share their own tales and legends. Henri understood the power of stories in shaping identities, and he believed that recounting local folklore would instill a strong sense of belonging among the younger generation. He also introduced them to the works of Caribbean authors, encouraging discussions around literature's role in reflecting and nurturing cultural identity.

The response was overwhelmingly positive. Families returned week after week, excited to participate in discussions and share their narratives. Children laughed and cheered as they embraced their cultural roots, and Henri watched proudly as they discovered the magic of storytelling and the joy of creativity. Over time, these workshops grew, attracting not only families but also members of the wider community who were eager to engage in conversations about identity, history, and art.

Henri's commitment did not stop there. He organized cultural fairs that showcased local talent, from musicians and dancers to visual artists. He worked alongside musicians to create a platform for local bands, where they could perform and share the rhythms of Caribbean music. The sounds of calypso, reggae, and traditional folk melodies filled the air, uniting residents in celebration of their rich musical heritage. Each event included art displays, allowing painters and sculptors to exhibit their work in a space that felt welcoming and inclusive.

Through these endeavors, Henri quickly gained respect within the community, becoming a bridge between different cultural expressions. He understood that Dominica was a melting pot of influences—an interplay of Indigenous, African, European, and Caribbean heritage—and he sought to honor each thread in the cultural tapestry. He forged connections with artists from various backgrounds, creating collaborative projects that intertwined different art forms and demonstrated the beauty of diversity.

One memorable project involved creating a mural on the side of a community center, where artists from different backgrounds came together to depict scenes of island life, historical events, and the shared dreams of the residents. The mural's colorful imagery served as a reminder of their collective identity and aspirations, drawing attention from both locals and visitors. It became a focal point in the neighborhood, where individuals gathered to share ideas, laughter, and stories.

As Henri continued to immerse himself in the cultural landscape of Dominica, he began to see and address the needs of marginalized groups within the community, offering workshops tailored to those who had limited access to artistic resources. By providing art supplies and mentoring aspiring artists, he cultivated an inclusive environment where everyone had the opportunity to express themselves creatively. Through his efforts, he empowered individuals who felt overlooked, helping them find their voices and share their perspectives.

The respect he garnered extended beyond the realm of arts and education; it became a testament to his character and commitment to building community. Henri's ability to connect diverse individuals through shared passions made him a valued figure in the community. Elders spoke highly of him, appreciating his dedication to preserving local traditions while encouraging innovation. Parents felt grateful for the opportunities he created for their children, and soon, even those who were initially skeptical began to acknowledge his positive influence.

Through his work, Henri transformed into a community leader, someone who embodied the very values he advocated: inclusivity, creativity, and resilience. He stood at the helm of a cultural renaissance in Dominica, advocating for an arts education that honored the past while envisioning a vibrant future. His initiatives not only celebrated the richness of Caribbean culture but also inspired a sense of ownership and pride among residents, breathing new life into the collective identity of Dominica.

As he reflected on his journey from Venezuela to this vibrant community, Henri felt a deep sense of fulfillment. What had begun as a quest for a better life had blossomed into a mission to enhance the lives of others, proving that immigration could be a path not just to survival but to thrive—for himself, his family, and the community he now called home. Through the arts and education, Henri Sebastien had indeed become a catalyst for change, demonstrating that the richness of culture lies in the connections we forge and the stories we share.

Henri's marriage to Isabelle, a local artist and educator, reflects their mutual dedication to nurturing minds and fostering creativity in the next generation. Together, they embody the belief that education and artistic expression are essential for personal and social development. Their home is a vibrant sanctuary filled with books, art supplies, and music, providing an inspiring environment for their five children—Alton, Aldie, Algar, Nun, and Theresa—to explore their talents and grow.

Books line the shelves of every room, creating a warm atmosphere of knowledge and imagination. From classic tales of adventure to thought-provoking works of philosophy, Henri and Isabelle curated a library that encouraged their children to dive into stories and ideas from all corners of the world. Each evening, the family would gather in the cozy living room, where Henri would read aloud to them. Alton, the eldest, often sat beside him, captivated by the tales of distant lands and brave heroes, while Aldie and Algar scribbled notes and colorful illustrations inspired by the stories. Nun, with her inquisitive nature, asked questions that sparked conversations, and little Theresa, with her boundless energy, would occasionally chime in with her thoughts, adding her unique perspective to the discussion.

Art supplies overflowed from a dedicated corner in their home, creating an inviting space for creativity to flourish. Isabelle encouraged her children to express themselves freely, providing them with everything from paints and brushes to markers and canvas. She often led art sessions where they would explore different techniques, learning about famous artists and the cultural significance of their work. The walls of their home were adorned with the children's masterpieces, showcasing their growth as budding artists. From Alton's bold abstracts to Theresa's whimsical landscapes, each piece reflected their individuality and creativity.

Music echoed throughout the house, weaving itself into the daily routines of the family. Isabelle played the piano, filling the rooms with harmonies that inspired everyone to join in. Alton and Aldie took up the guitar, frequently practicing their chords and harmonizing with one another. Algar could not resist the rhythm of the drums, giving free rein to his energy during family jam sessions. Nun and Theresa danced around the living room, creating their own routines that infused joy into the atmosphere. These impromptu performances became cherished family rituals, where laughter and creativity intertwined, and the deep bonds among them grew stronger.

Henri and Isabelle's commitment to education extended beyond their family to the broader community, where they worked tirelessly to promote artistic engagement and learning. Together, they organized workshops that welcomed families from all backgrounds, creating a space where children could discover their artistic abilities and share their stories. During these events, Henri facilitated creative writing sessions while Isabelle led art projects, encouraging collaboration among participants. They believed that fostering creativity was a communal effort, one that strengthened the fabric of their society.

Through these initiatives, Henri and Isabelle instilled in their children the importance of empathy, understanding, and open-mindedness. They encouraged Alton, Aldie, Algar, Nun, and Theresa to embrace their unique identities while appreciating the richness that diversity brings. The children often interacted with peers from various backgrounds, sharing ideas and experiences that deepened their connection to the community and broadened their horizons.

Henri and Isabelle also emphasized the value of resilience and hard work. They taught their children that learning is a lifelong journey filled with challenges and opportunities for growth. Whether it was through tackling difficult math problems or experimenting with new artistic techniques, the Sebastien children learned to persevere, finding joy in the process of discovery. They understood that creativity flourishes in the face of challenges and that every setback could be transformed into a valuable lesson.

As Henri reflected on their life together, he felt immense pride in the nurturing environment he and Isabelle had created for their children. Their home was not just a place of residence; it was a hub of creativity, learning, and love. Each child was flourishing in their own way, developing not only their talents but also a strong sense of purpose and community.

Although the Sebastien family lived in Bioche, they attended church in Colihaut, and the children—Alton, Aldie, Algar, Nun, and Theresa—initially went to school there as well. Henri and Isabelle's shared dedication to education became a powerful foundation for positive change in their community. Their unwavering commitment to learning and growth inspired their children to embrace values like creativity, empathy, and resilience, shaping their perspectives and ambitions.

As they matured, Alton, Aldie, Algar, Nun, and Theresa were destined to become champions of education and the arts, carrying forward the legacy of nurturing young minds and fostering creative expression. This legacy, rooted in their upbringing and their parents' teachings, would continue to ripple through generations, inspiring future communities to value knowledge, compassion, and artistic exploration. In doing so, they ensured that the seeds of hope planted in their home would blossom into a lasting movement of empowerment and cultural richness.

The differing ambitions and priorities of Ledger Philogene and Henri Sebastien create an intriguing contrast within the Colihaut community. While Ledger is dedicated to establishing a strong agricultural foundation for his family, Henri's aspirations lean more toward fostering cultural development and education. This juxtaposition of paths not only underscores their pursuits but also highlights the broader spectrum of dreams and goals that exist within their close-knit community.

Ledger embodies the hardworking farmer, channeling his energy and resources into cultivating the fertile land of Dominica. He believes that agriculture is the backbone of the community, providing sustenance, economic stability, and a sense of pride. With each season, Ledger meticulously plans his crops, ensuring that his family and neighbors have access to fresh produce. His deep connection to the land reflects his commitment to sustainability and the preservation of traditional farming practices that have sustained generations before him. Ledger envisions a thriving agricultural enterprise, where his children can carry on the legacy of farming, cultivating both the earth and their family's heritage.

In contrast, Henri's ambitions reach beyond the practicalities of agriculture. He is driven by a desire to cultivate the minds and spirits of the children in Colihaut through education and the arts. Henri views creativity as a vital component of the community's growth and development, believing that nurturing artistic expression can lead to profound societal change. He envisions a future where children are equipped not only with academic knowledge but also with the tools to explore their identities, communicate effectively, and appreciate the richness of their shared culture. His commitment to cultural development positions him as a champion of the arts, seeking to create an environment where creativity blooms alongside traditional values, much like Ledger's crops in the fields.

These contrasting ambitions often place Ledger and Henri at different ends of community discussions. During town meetings, Ledger advocates for agricultural initiatives, urging fellow farmers to collaborate on sustainable practices and to invest in better equipment that can increase yields. He passionately speaks about the importance of providing stable livelihoods through farming, emphasizing that a strong agricultural foundation is essential for the well-being of families in Colihaut. His resolve reflects his deep-seated belief that feeding the community physically is paramount to its survival and prosperity.

On the other hand, Henri champions the need for cultural enrichment, advocating for programs that inspire creativity and critical thinking among the youth. He passionately argues that education should encompass the arts, enriching children's lives and allowing them to engage with the world around them in meaningful ways. Henri believes that nurturing a generation of creative thinkers will benefit the community, encouraging innovation and adaptability in the face of challenges. He often points out that, while traditional farming practices are important, fostering a mindset that values creativity can lead to new ideas and solutions for community issues.

This contrast in perspectives occasionally leads to tension between the two men, as they grapple with their differing definitions of progress. Ledger sometimes views Henri's focus on the arts as a distraction from the immediate needs of the community—namely, the necessity of food security and agricultural sustainability. He worries that an emphasis on cultural development might dilute the practical ambitions that keep families grounded and fed. Conversely, Henri sees Ledger's singular focus on agriculture as potentially limiting. He fears that neglecting the arts and education could stifle creativity and self-expression, leaving the community at risk of becoming overly reliant on traditional practices without room for growth and transformation.

However, rather than allowing these differences to create a permanent rift between them, both Ledger and Henri recognize the value of their distinct contributions to the community. Through respectful dialogue, they explore ways to bridge their visions, finding common ground. They begin to understand that both agriculture and cultural development are integral to the community's identity and prosperity. This evolving recognition fosters a sense of partnership as they collaborate on community projects that integrate both of their ideals.

One such initiative emerges when they decide to host a local festival celebrating both the agricultural bounty and the rich cultural tapestry of Colihaut. Ledger provides fresh produce for the festival while Henri curates a series of artistic performances that showcase local talent, including music, dance, and storytelling. Together, they create an event that honors their shared values, attracting families and neighbors eager to celebrate the interplay of food and culture. The festival becomes a resounding success, demonstrating how the union of agriculture and the arts can elevate the community's spirit while enriching the lives of its members.

Through their collaboration, Ledger and Henri exemplify the dynamic spectrum of dreams and goals present in Colihaut. Their contrasting paths, rooted in deep convictions, serve to strengthen the community. As they navigate their respective ambitions, they forge an understanding that encompasses both the immediate needs of the land and the aspirations of the mind and heart. In doing so, they ensure that Colihaut remains a vibrant and nurturing environment—one where the seeds of creativity and agriculture can thrive together, shaping a brighter future for all.

As tensions regarding land ownership and class dynamics rise in Colihaut, Henri's perspective as an immigrant from a middle-class background profoundly shapes his understanding of these changes. Coming from Venezuela, where socioeconomic disparities have often been stark, Henri has witnessed firsthand how class tensions can fracture communities. This background informs not only his empathy for Ledger's struggles as a farmer but also his vision for fostering collaboration that promotes cultural understanding and strengthens the community.

Henri is acutely aware of the challenges faced by landowners like Ledger. He sees how the increasing pressures of urbanization, tourism, and external economic interests can threaten the livelihoods of farmers who have nurtured the land for generations. Ledger's dedication to sustaining his family's agricultural legacy is an embodiment of resilience, yet Henri recognizes that this commitment is often tested by the encroaching demands of change. As a newcomer, Henri has developed an appreciation for the deep-rooted traditions that define Colihaut, making him more inclined to empathize with local landholders who face uncertainty about their future.

However, Henri's immigrant experience also exposes him to different ways of viewing community dynamics. Having navigated the complexities of adapting to a new cultural landscape, he understands the transformative potential of embracing diversity. He believes that rather than allowing tensions over land ownership to create rifts, there are opportunities for collaboration that can enrich the community. Henri is driven by the notion that cultural exchange can bridge divides, fostering mutual respect and understanding among residents from various backgrounds.

In conversations with Ledger and other community members, Henri often advocates for initiatives that promote collective engagement—initiatives that honor both agricultural practices and cultural expressions. He sees the potential for community projects that combine farming and the arts, inviting local artists to showcase their work during harvest festivals or markets. Such events would not merely celebrate the fruits of farmers' labor but also elevate the voices and stories of those who cultivate the land, weaving together agricultural pride with cultural identity.

By facilitating dialogues that explore the intersections of land and art, Henri seeks to foster relationships rooted in shared experiences. He believes that when the community comes together to celebrate its heritage, whether through music, storytelling, or visual arts—residents can find common ground, reducing the tensions that often come with differing perspectives on land ownership and class dynamics. These gatherings serve as opportunities for residents to share their challenges and aspirations, allowing them to recognize that they are, in fact, allies in their collective journey.

Moreover, Henri promotes educational programs that emphasize the importance of understanding both the agricultural and cultural dimensions of Colihaut. By partnering with Ledger and other local farmers, he encourages initiatives that teach children about the significance of farming while also incorporating the artistic narratives that accompany the land. Through workshops that intertwine gardening with visual arts, storytelling, and performance, Henri hopes to cultivate a generation that appreciates the rich tapestry of experiences and talents present in their community.

As tensions heighten in Colihaut, Henri remains steadfast in his belief that empathy and collaboration can lead to sustainable solutions. He understands that acknowledging the struggles of landowners like Ledger must be accompanied by a broader vision that includes everyone in the community, newcomers, and long-time residents alike. By creating spaces for dialogue and collaborative projects,

Henri envisions a future where cultural understanding enhances social cohesion, allowing residents to navigate challenges together.

Henri's perspective as an immigrant allows him to see the potential for unity amidst diversity. While he empathizes deeply with Ledger's fears and aspirations, he also recognizes that their common goal— building a thriving community—can be enriched by integrating cultural perspectives and artistic expression. By championing collaboration and understanding, Henri seeks to contribute to a Colihaut that not only honors its agricultural roots but also embraces the creative possibilities that arise from its rich tapestry of cultures.

Despite their differences, Henri recognizes that Ledger's extensive agricultural experience could complement his own community initiatives, creating valuable opportunities for collaboration. By involving local farmers like Ledger in cultural projects and educational programs, Henri believes they can enhance both agricultural sustainability and artistic appreciation within Colihaut. This vision for collaboration offers a pathway for mutual growth, allowing both families to learn from one another and cultivate a synergy that benefits the entire community.

Henri envisions a series of collaborative projects that showcase the intersection of agriculture and the arts. He knows that Ledger's deep understanding of farming practices could lend authenticity and credibility to initiatives aimed at teaching children and community members about sustainable agriculture. For instance, they could host workshops where Ledger shares his knowledge of crop rotation, organic farming, and the importance of biodiversity. In these sessions, local children could learn how to plant their own gardens while simultaneously exploring the artistry involved in nature, such as drawing plants, creating sculptures from found materials, or composing songs inspired by the rhythms of farming life.

Incorporating artistic elements into agricultural education would not only enrich the learning experience but also highlight the beauty and complexity of nature. Henri believes that by intertwining farming with creative expression, they can foster a deeper connection to the land. He imagines community events where children and families come together to celebrate the harvest through art and performance—painting murals that depict scenes from local farms, writing poems about the agricultural cycle, or creating theatrical pieces that tell the stories of farmers. These activities would allow the community to express its collective identity while honoring the hard work of the land.

Furthermore, Henri believes that incorporating cultural elements into agricultural projects can help bridge the gap between different generations within the community. They could organize seasonal festivals, where Ledger's produce takes center stage, accompanied by artistic displays and performances from local talents. These festivals could encourage intergenerational storytelling, where older farmers share their experiences with younger community members, fostering respect and understanding across age groups. Henri imagines vibrant market days filled with local produce, food stalls featuring Caribbean flavors, and spaces for musicians and artists to perform, creating a lively atmosphere that celebrates both agriculture and the arts.

By working together, Henri and Ledger could also develop educational programs that emphasize the importance of environmental stewardship and cultural heritage. Through field trips to local farms, community members can gain firsthand insights into sustainable practices, learning not just the how is but also the whys of agriculture. Educators can incorporate art projects that reflect the themes of these experiences, enabling students to express their newfound knowledge visually or through performance. Such programs could instill values of sustainability and creativity, ensuring that the next generation understands the significance of both the land and cultural expression.

Additionally, Henri envisions opportunities for collaborative grants that could fund initiatives benefiting both farmers and artists. By coming together as a unified front, they could apply for funding aimed at promoting rural development and cultural preservation, thus strengthening their combined voices within the community. This collaborative approach could serve as a model for other towns and neighborhoods grappling with similar challenges, showcasing the potential that arises when diverse talents and backgrounds unite.

Henri's vision for potential collaborations with Ledger creates a hopeful narrative for Colihaut. By acknowledging their differences and understanding the strengths each brings to the table, they can cultivate a vibrant partnership that enhances community cohesion. Their combined efforts could breathe new life into both the agricultural sector and the arts, allowing Colihaut to flourish as a place where creativity and sustainability coexist harmoniously.

Through these collaborations, Henri and Ledger not only stand to benefit personally but also contribute to a legacy that enriches the entire community, ensuring that future generations appreciate and nurture the artistic and agricultural treasures of their home. In doing so, they foster a spirit of unity and resilience that embodies the essence of Colihaut—a community that values both its roots and its creative aspirations.

As the story unfolds, Henri and Ledger's paths cross during a community event aimed at fostering dialogue among residents. The event, organized by local leaders to encourage collaboration and understanding among Colihaut's diverse community members, serves as a perfect backdrop for the men to engage in meaningful discussions about their respective ambitions.

As Henri enters the vibrant Kai Cacao, he is struck by the energy in the room. Tables are adorned with colorful banners showcasing local art, and murals created by children line the walls, celebrating Colihaut cultural heritage. The air is filled with the sounds of laughter and chatter, as old and young residents gather to discuss their hopes, dreams, and challenges. Henri is excited about the opportunity to create connections that could pave the way for his vision of integrating the arts into community life.

In another corner of the room, Ledger stands with a group of farmers, discussing the latest agricultural techniques and the challenges posed by new land ownership regulations. He radiates commitment to the agricultural legacy of Colihaut, aware that the survival of his family's farm and those of his neighbors depends on their ability to adapt and thrive amidst change. Ledger is initially cautious about engaging in conversations beyond agriculture, viewing Henri's artistic pursuits as a distraction from the more pressing issues facing farmers like him.

However, as the event progresses, Henri and Ledger find themselves seated at adjacent tables during a breakout session focused on community development. It begins with a simple exchange of pleasantries, but as discussions unfold, both men quickly realize their shared commitment to improving life in Colihaut. Henri passionately speaks about the importance of fostering creativity and community engagement through the arts, emphasizing how cultural expression can serve as a vehicle for healing and connection. Ledger, intrigued, listens intently and begins to appreciate the insights Henri provides about how art can enrich daily life.

"What you're saying makes sense," Ledger responds thoughtfully, reflecting on his own experiences. "Farming is important, but maybe our community needs more than just food—it needs a sense of belonging and understanding." His words resonate with Henri, who realizes that they are both striving for the same goal: a thriving and connected Colihaut.

As the conversation deepens, Henri shares stories from his own background, recounting how art and education played a pivotal role in shaping his values. He speaks of the community-driven projects he envisioned, ones that could merge agriculture with artistic expression, and how they might benefit everyone in Colihaut. Ledger begins to see beyond their initial differences, recognizing opportunities for collaboration that could address both their passions.

"I've always thought of farming as an isolated endeavor," Ledger admits, tapping his fingers on the table. "You've got me thinking about how I could share more of what I do with the community—not just through crops but through storytelling about the land and its history."

Henri nods enthusiastically. "Exactly! Imagine hosting workshops where children can learn about planting seeds while painting the landscapes they see around them. We could host a community festival to celebrate harvests alongside local art and performances. It could strengthen our community's identity and show everyone the beauty in what we do!"

As the event continues, Ledger finds himself more engaged in the possibilities Henri presents. He begins to see that Henri's perspective is not a departure from his own interests but rather an extension of them. By integrating arts and agriculture, they could foster a deeper connection among residents— an understanding of each other's passions and struggles.

Throughout the event, they begin to brainstorm ideas, excitedly outlining potential collaborations that could come to life. They discuss the prospect of a community garden project that includes educational components for local children, with decorated plots for art, stories, and performances intermingled with vegetables and herbs. Ledger's knowledge of farming complements Henri's vision for creativity, and they realize they can leverage each other's strengths for the greater good.

As they wrap up their discussions, Ledger extends a hand. "I would like to explore this further, Henri. We can meet next week to plan something specific?"

A smile spread across Henri's face as he shook Ledger's hand. "I would love that. Let us create something meaningful together for Colihaut."

This pivotal moment marks the beginning of a friendship anchored in respect, understanding, and a shared commitment to the community. Through their discussions, Henri and Ledger not only forge a bond but also sow the seeds for future collaborations that hold the potential to unite their passions for agriculture and the arts. As they leave the community event invigorated by their newfound connection, both men are filled with hope for the possibilities ahead, ready to embrace the rich tapestry of experiences that will emerge from their partnership for the benefit of all in Colihaut.

As their friendship begins to blossom, both families face distinct challenges—Ledger's family grapples with the difficulties of farming, while Henri's family sustains the pressures of managing arts initiatives. Despite these differences, their interactions offer a comforting space for shared experiences and understanding that transcends their ambitions. As they lean on one another for support, both Ledger and Henri find a source of growth, inspiration, and renewal as they confront the evolving dynamics of Colihaut.

For Ledger, the daily rigors of farming are often overwhelming. The pressure to maintain productivity amidst changing land use policies, unpredictable weather, and economic fluctuations weighs heavily on him. He worries about the future of his farm—not just for his own family but for the entire community, many of whom depend on agriculture for their livelihoods. With each crop cycle, there is an underlying fear of drought, pests, or market instability that could threaten what he has worked so hard to build.

Ledger often feels isolated in his struggles, believing that the concerns of farmers are perceived as secondary to the more creative pursuits that Henri passionately promotes. However, as he spends more time with Henri, he begins to realize that they face similar pressures, albeit from different angles. Henri's commitment to nurturing artistic expression and education comes with its own challenges, such as securing funding for initiatives and engaging the community in ways that truly resonate with them.

On the other hand, Henri feels the weight of responsibility when managing arts initiatives in Colihaut. While he is enthusiastic about the potential for cultural enrichment and community building through creative projects, he often grapples with the difficult task of garnering support from residents who may not readily embrace the arts. The struggle to balance his family's needs while advocating for educational programs can be taxing. Each setback in securing resources feels like an uphill battle, often leading to moments of doubt about whether his efforts can contribute meaningfully to the community.

Through their conversations, Ledger witnesses Henri's unwavering passion for the arts and education, which ignites a spark of inspiration within him. He sees how Henri pours his heart into projects, organizing workshops and festivals that aim to uplift and strengthen the community. This dedication resonates with Ledger and prompts him to consider the broader impact of his own work on the farm.

As their friendship deepens, Ledger and Henri frequently sit together, reflecting on their challenges and sharing ideas about how to navigate the evolving dynamics of Colihaut. Henri encourages Ledger to view farming not merely as an end but as a canvas for cultural expression and connection. Ledger begins to see potential in intertwining these aspects, realizing that the farm can be a place not just for growing crops but also for fostering creativity, dialogue, and community engagement.

Inspired by Henri, Ledger contemplates integrating cultural initiatives into his own vision for the farm. He imagines hosting farm-to-table events where local artists and musicians perform amid the fields, creating an atmosphere that celebrates both agriculture and the arts. These gatherings could become events that bring families together, cultivating a sense of ownership and pride in the harvest while allowing community members to experience the beauty of artistic expression firsthand. By bridging the gap between farming and culture, Ledger envisions a vibrant space where people can gather, celebrate, and learn about the land and its significance.

Their conversations naturally shift toward implementing collaborative projects that engage both their passions. Ledger shares his ideas about creating educational programs on sustainable farming practices, while Henri suggests incorporating elements of art and storytelling into the curriculum. The two men begin brainstorming how to combine their strengths to create a series of workshops—one that teaches the community about the importance of sustainable agriculture while simultaneously encouraging artistic expression through the lens of nature.

As they work through these ideas, Ledger finds himself increasingly energized by Henri's vision. He begins to understand that art can serve as a powerful tool for conveying the rich narratives of agriculture and the importance of community sustainability. Conversely, Henri feels buoyed by Ledger's practical knowledge, recognizing that incorporating local farming traditions into artistic endeavors will give their projects authenticity and depth.

Through their friendship, Ledger and Henri have developed a mutual respect and admiration that transcends their initial differences. As they support one another through the unique challenges they face, both men grow in ways they never anticipated. Ledger's desire to integrate cultural initiatives into his farming vision reflects a willingness to evolve, while Henri gains a fresh perspective on the importance of connecting creativity with the realities of the land.

This burgeoning friendship blossoms into a collaborative partnership that promises to strengthen both families and the wider Colihaut community. Together, they begin to lay the groundwork for a series of projects that marry the practicalities of farming with the transformative power of the arts, paving the way for a richer, more interconnected community experience.

As Ledger and Henri stand on the cusp of this new path forward, they do so with a shared sense of purpose, inspired by each other's dedication and resilience. Their combined efforts symbolize the very essence of Colihaut—a place where diverse ambitions can intertwine, fostering a spirit of unity, creativity, and growth that will benefit all who call the community home.

Henri and Ledger's friendship deepens, each man learns from the other in profound ways. Conversely, Henri finds inspiration in Ledger's resilience and practicality when faced with the uncertainties of agriculture. Ledger's steadfast commitment to his farm in the face of challenges serves as a reminder to Henri of the importance of grounding his creative endeavors. He begins to recognize that while artistic expression is vital, the success of his initiatives relies on practical considerations and community needs. This newfound perspective urges Henri to adopt a more pragmatic approach to his projects, ensuring they resonate meaningfully with Colihaut's farmers and their families.

As both families grow closer, their children also begin to form friendships that mirror the development of the bond between their fathers. Henri's children, introduced to Ledger's family, revel in the excitement of shared experiences, spending afternoons together in the fields, exploring nature, and learning about the art of farming from Ledger's children. They engage in playful activities that blend the best of both worlds—planting seeds while also envisioning stories and art related to what they will harvest. These interactions enrich their lives, fostering mutual respect and understanding rooted in shared experiences.

Building on their friendship, both families also make a point to share meals together. These gatherings become not just opportunities to break bread but symbolic occasions where their worlds converge. Ledger's family prepares dishes made from their freshest produce, while Henri's family brings along dishes infused with local spices and flavors, celebrating the cultural diversity of Colihaut. As they sit around the table, they share laughter and stories, weaving together their different backgrounds. These meals foster a sense of community, allowing both families to appreciate each other's traditions and life experiences.

Motivated by their growing camaraderie, Ledger and Henri begin to organize collaborative events that further entwine agriculture with artistic expression. They imagine hosting seasonal festivals that not only celebrate the harvest but also showcase local artists, musicians, and performers. These events provide a platform for the community to come together, engage with local talent, and appreciate the beauty of their land. Both Ledger and Henri work tirelessly to plan these gatherings, involving their families and encouraging participation from other community members.

One memorable festival features a "Harvest and Art" theme, where local farmers display their produce alongside art installations created by community members. Children's artwork, inspired by the natural beauty surrounding them, adorns the festival grounds, while Ledger and Henri's combined efforts create workshops where families can learn about sustainable farming practices while also expressing themselves artistically. There are painting stations, storytelling corners, and cooking demonstrations, all set against the backdrop of the lush agricultural landscape.

Through these shared meals, collaborative events, and community projects, the two families exemplify the potential for unity amidst diversity in Colihaut. They demonstrate how intersecting lives can lead to greater understanding and collective progress. Ledger's practicality and Henri's creativity become complementary forces, inspiring others to explore their own unique contributions to the community.

As both men encourage their families to participate in the planning and execution of these initiatives, they witness the resulting bonds forming among community members. Neighbors who have long lived alongside one another become more connected, sharing ideas and aspirations that might have once felt out of reach. The children, having grown up in a community marked by a rich tapestry of cultures and traditions, foster friendships that reflect this interconnectedness.

As the festival approaches, excitement ripples through Colihaut, drawing residents together in anticipation. Families come together to decorate the market space, with Ledger's children helping to organize displays while Henri's children create art that captures the essence of the farm's stories. The festival becomes a vibrant tapestry, combining the colors of bountiful harvests with the vivid expressions of artistic creativity.

Together, Ledger and Henri begin to pave the way for a more inclusive and harmonious Colihaut. They champion the idea that by blending their passions—agriculture and the arts—they can create a community that embraces diversity while harnessing it as a strength. This approach transforms the way residents relate to one another, fostering an atmosphere of collaboration that invites open dialogues about the challenges they face.

In their shared commitment to fostering unity, Henri and Ledger evolve from acquaintances to allies, forging a partnership that not only enriches their own families' lives but also leaves a lasting impact on the entire community. Their friendship reveals the transformative power of collaboration, demonstrating that when individuals come together to celebrate their differences, they can cultivate an environment of understanding and support.

As the festival day dawns, the spirit of Colihaut shines brighter than ever, signaling the dawn of a renewed sense of purpose among its residents. Amidst the laughter, artistic showcases, and the aromas of local cuisine, Henri and Ledger stand side by side, grateful for the journey that has brought them together. In the vibrant atmosphere filled with the sounds of music, children's laughter, and the joyful chatter of families, they reflect on how far they have come since their initial encounters. The festival, once just a dream, has blossomed into a heartfelt celebration of community, showcasing the unique blend of agriculture and creativity that Colihaut has to offer.

As they take in the scene, Ledger glances at a group of children painting murals on repurposed wooden panels, their expressions radiant with joy and excitement. "Look at them," he says to Henri, his voice filled with pride. "This is what it's all about bringing everyone together, sharing our stories."

Henri nods in agreement, his eyes sparkling. "These moments remind me of the real power of community. When we come together to celebrate our roots and our creativity, we create something beautiful and lasting."

The two men share a knowing smile, understanding that their collaboration is reshaping the narrative of Colihaut. No longer are they simply farmers and artists in separate spheres; they have fused their efforts to create a shared vision that encompasses both agricultural legacy and cultural expression.

As the festival progresses, Ledger and Henri take time to interact with the festivalgoers, hearing their stories and witnessing the joy this new tradition has ignited within the community. Families mingle at the produce stalls, sampling freshly harvested fruits and vegetables while enjoying performances from local musicians. The arts and crafts area buzzes with activity as people quickly visit to create their own artwork, inspired by the natural beauty that surrounds them.

As dusk begins to settle, Henri steps away momentarily to check on the final preparations for a performance set to take place as the sun sets behind the hills. He feels a wave of gratitude wash over him, knowing how much this event means to Colihaut. He catches Ledger's eye and gestures to the stage area, where community members are gathering for a storytelling session that highlights the history and traditions of the land.

"Do you think we've made a difference?" Henri asks, turning to Ledger with sincerity in his voice.

Ledger thinks for a moment, eyes scanning the joyful faces that surround them. "Absolutely. Look at the way people are engaging with each other. We have created a space where they can learn from one another, share their stories, and find common ground. This festival is not about celebrating what we grow or what we create, it is about building relationships."

With that realization, the two men feel a deep sense of fulfillment. Their friendship has not only blossomed, but it has also sparked a ripple effect of connection throughout Colihaut. In their commitment to blending their passions, they have fostered a new chapter for their community—one that cherishes both its agricultural roots and its burgeoning artistic identity.

As the sun sets, casting a warm golden hue over the festival grounds, Ledger and Henri stand side by side once more, watching as community members gather for a final dance performance, the energy of celebration flowing through the air. It is a beautiful tapestry of music, laughter, and camaraderie, and in this moment, they know they have laid the groundwork for a future rich with potential.

Together, they have sown the seeds of unity, demonstrating how intersecting lives can lead to greater understanding, collective progress, and a flourishing Colihaut that embraces its diversity. The journey they embarked on may have started with their individual ambitions, but it has grown into a shared mission that strengthens their families and their community, leaving a legacy of collaboration and cultural appreciation that will resonate for generations to come.

ぐる

Chapter Twelve: The Venezuelan War of Independence

Amidst the backdrop of the Venezuelan War of Independence, Henri and Isabelle Sebastien find themselves engulfed in turmoil that compels them to reevaluate their future. The chaos surrounding them escalates daily, with the sounds of conflict echoing in the streets of Caracas and the growing sense of instability threatening the very foundation of their family life. As fierce battles rage between those seeking freedom and those clinging to power, the couple is faced with the harsh reality that their cherished values of education and cultural expression may no longer be safe in their homeland.

Henri, a dedicated teacher and ardent supporter of the ideals of liberty and enlightenment, has always believed in the transformative power of knowledge. Isabelle, a passionate artist, views her work as a reflection of the beauty and complexity of life—an expression of the culture and traditions that have defined their Venezuelan heritage. Together, they have fostered a loving home that nurtures their children's growth and encourages exploration through education and creativity. Yet now, as violence draws closer, the very essence of their lives hangs in the balance.

Driven by an overwhelming desire for stability and security, they grapple with the heart-wrenching decision to leave everything they know behind. The thought of abandoning their homeland, their family, and their dreams fills them with sorrow, but the looming threat of danger makes it a choice they cannot ignore. Convinced that the future of their family depends on finding a place where they can live freely and safely, Henri and Isabelle begin the arduous task of planning their escape.

The journey ahead is fraught with uncertainty. As they navigate the turmoil of conflict, they encounter numerous challenges, anxieties about leaving loved ones behind, concerns over how they will provide for their children in an unfamiliar land, and fears about the cultural dislocation that awaits them. Despite the chaos, they cling to the hope that a new life awaits, one where they can rebuild their dreams in peace.

Their path leads them to the island of Dominica, a place known for its natural beauty and rich cultural tapestry. As they disembark from the ship that carries them away from the ravaged landscapes of Venezuela, they are filled with trepidation and optimism. The warm, vibrant essence of the island initially captivates them, yet the reality of starting anew looms large.

Settling in Bioche, they discover the estate of Lagon, a once-grand property that stands as a reminder of a different time. The lush surroundings and the gentle lapping of the waves against the shore offer a sense of solace, inspiring Henri, and Isabelle to envision a life rebuilt on the values they hold dear. At Lagon, they begin to forge connections within their new community, immersing themselves in the local culture while striving to maintain their own traditions.

Through their journey from conflict and chaos to finding a new home, Henri and Isabelle embark on a daunting yet transformative adventure. They are determined to create a haven for their children, a place where education and artistic expression can flourish once more. Their resilience in the face of adversity teaches them valuable lessons about adaptability and the importance of community, leading them to discover that even amidst change, hope and renewal can thrive.

Through their journey from the chaos of conflict to the promise of a new home, Henri and Isabelle demonstrate remarkable resilience and determination. Each day presents fresh challenges as they navigate their new environment, yet they hold steadfast to their dreams of nurturing their children's education and fostering a creative spirit.

In the estate of Lagon, amidst the whispering palms and the sound of the waves, the Sebastien family embarks on a transformative adventure—one that will not only lead to personal growth and adaptation but also deepen their understanding of the strength found within the community, culture, and the unyielding human spirit.

As the Venezuelan War of Independence intensifies, Henri and Isabelle Sebastien become increasingly aware of the escalating violence and uncertainty that envelops their community. The once vibrant streets of Caracas, filled with laughter and life, now reverberate with the sounds of cannon fire and distant cries. What was once a bustling center of culture and education is gradually transforming into a landscape marked by fear and unease, creating a chilling contrast to the lively town they once cherished.

Factions clash openly in the streets, their ideologies spilling into public spaces where families used to gather. As the war progresses, it becomes evident that no one is immune to its destructive force. Neighbors who once shared meals and laughter now find themselves divided, caught up in a conflict that rips at the very fabric of their society. Long-standing friendships dissolve into distrust, while the threat of violence looms larger with each passing day.

For Henri and Isabelle, the impact of the war is especially profound as they observe its disruptive effects on their children's education. Henri's classroom, once a sanctuary for learning and exploration, is abandoned as schools shutter their doors in response to the unrest. The children, eager to absorb knowledge and creativity, now find themselves isolated from resources and opportunities crucial to their growth. Henri grapples with the loss of his students, mourning the relationships he has built and the critical lessons that will go untaught while the war rages on.

The arts, which have always served as a source of joy and inspiration for Isabelle, seem to wither under the weight of conflict. Galleries that once showcased beautiful works and celebrated artistic expression are closed, their walls now silent. The vibrant cultural life that flourished in Caracas, filled with music, theater, and literature, begins to fade, stifled by the harsh realities of war. Isabelle fears that the very essence of their society, the creativity, and spirit that define their identity—will be lost amidst the chaos.

Witnessing families torn apart by the conflict adds a deeper layer of anguish to their plight. Neighbors flee their homes in search of safety, while others are forced to pledge allegiance to factions at odds with their principles. Henri and Isabelle are acutely aware of how their own family may soon be swept up in the turmoil and are haunted by the reality that the safety of their children hangs precariously in the balance.

Dining tables that used to be filled with laughter and lively discussions now bear witness to tense conversations steeped in worry and uncertainty. As they gather with friends, the threat of violence looms over them, and hushed whispers replace the joyous banter. Henri and Isabelle find themselves contemplating a future clouded by doubt, grappling with the implications of a protracted conflict.

Night after night, they hear the distant rumblings of artillery, a somber reminder of the fragility of the life they hold dear. The air becomes thick with an omnipresent sense of dread, and visions of the idyllic family life they once envision morph into stark realities of fear and survival.

Amidst the turmoil, Henri's commitment to education and Isabelle's passion for the arts became even more vital to them, serving as anchors in a world turned upside down. They begin to discuss what they can do for their children. As there is no way to guarantee their safety in a simmering conflict, they start to contemplate the unimaginable finding a way to escape the violence that threatens to engulf them.

Each day brings new challenges, and as the war continues to escalate, Henri and Isabelle make an urgent and poignant realization: it may be time to seek refuge away from the uncertainty that haunts their homeland. The rising tensions not only threaten their safety but also risk obliterating the very values of family, education, and culture that define who they are. The couple stands at a crossroads, forced to confront difficult decisions that will forever alter the course of their lives and those of their children.

With five young children along with their parents and siblings to protect, Henri and Isabelle Sebastien confront a heavy burden that weighs on their hearts and minds. The chaos surrounding them, the echoes of gunfire, the cries of desperation in the streets, and the ever-growing uncertainty, instill an overwhelming sense of urgency. Each day feels like a precarious tightrope walk, and the reality of their situation deepens their concerns for what lies ahead.

Amidst the clamor of conflict, the couple often gathers in the dim light of their home to share their fears and hopes for their children's futures. The intimate setting rings with a palpable tension as their discussions turn grave. "Can we truly keep them safe here?" Henri asks, his voice barely above a whisper, as the sound of distant rumbling casts shadows over every word. Isabelle looks to their children—playing innocently in the corner, oblivious to the turmoil outside—and feels a pang of anguish in her heart.

The prospect of a stable upbringing for their children, filled with laughter, education, and creativity, seems increasingly bleak as the war wages are on. Henri fears that the ideals they hold dear, the dreams of a nurturing environment where their children can learn and grow without fear, are slipping through their fingers like sand. "Every day that passes, I worry that this chaos will steal their childhood from them," he confesses, the weight of uncertainty evident in his weary eyes.

Isabelle nods, tears brimming in her eyes as she reflects on the life they had envisioned for their family. "I want them to know the beauty of art, the power of knowledge," she replies, her voice trembling. "But how can we provide that in a world that feels so hostile? The creativity we have cherished is relegated to memory; it is as if we are living in a nightmare that refuses to end."

Their fears are compounded by the knowledge that the ongoing conflict disrupts the education of their children. Schools have closed, teachers have fled, and daily life has devolved into survival mode. The family has resorted to creative measures to nurture their children's minds, finding bits of paper to draw on or sharing stories by candlelight when the electricity fails. But they both know these makeshift solutions cannot replace the enriching environment they once took for granted.

The couple finds themselves questioning not only their ability to provide a nurturing space but also their decision to remain in Venezuela. With every clash reported in the news, with each frightened whisper from neighbors, their resolve wavers. They wonder how long they can endure the escalating violence without it tearing their family apart. The fear that grips their hearts at night often transforms into sleepless hours filled with anxious contemplation.

"Henri, what if the unrest lasts for years?" Isabelle asks one evening, her voice thick with worry. "Will our children grow up knowing only fear, understanding only conflict as they connect with the world? I cannot bear the idea of them losing their childhood or their innocence."

Henri takes a deep breath, his mind racing. "We must do what is best for them, even if it means making the hardest decision of our lives." He gazes at their children, who now tumble into a gentle heap of giggles and warmth, unaware of the turmoil that looms outside. "We cannot risk their futures for the sake of our pride. If this war continues, they will never know the life we dreamed for them."

With each conversation, Henri and Isabelle delve deeper into the possibility of leaving their homeland. It is an excruciating prospect filled with loss—loss of their roots, their community, and the familiarity of the life they have built together. Yet, the thought of abandoning their children to a future of instability and fear becomes unbearable, leading them to turn their hearts and minds toward the possibility of a new beginning.

During their concern for the future, they begin to explore options that could lead them to safety. Henri reaches out to family and friends living abroad, seeking guidance on what steps to take next. They envision a life in Dominica, one where their children can roam free, where education flourishes and creativity is encouraged. But with each potential avenue explored, the weight of their decision looms larger, stirring both hope and fear in equal measure.

As tensions continue to rise in Venezuela, Henri and Isabelle feel an increasing urgency to act. Each day spent in a chaotic reality heightens their resolve to secure a safer future for their children, even if it means making the heart-wrenching choice to leave behind their birthplace. They embrace the uncertainty of what lies ahead with cautious optimism, determined to protect their family and nurture the aspirations they hold so dearly for their children. The dream of a stable upbringing—one filled with love, education, and artistic expression—burns bright in their hearts, guiding them through the darkness of chaos toward the promise of a new beginning.

After much deliberation, Henri and Isabelle Sebastien arrive at a heart-wrenching conclusion: they must leave Venezuela for the sake of their family's safety. The discussions that had transpired in the dim light of their home, filled with uncertainty and fear, finally crystallized into an unwavering resolve. Yet this decision is fraught with emotion, representing not only a profound loss of the life they have built but also a courageous leap into the unknown, one that will alter the course of their family's future forever.

Each conversation about their children's well-being has painted a stark picture of the reality they face, one that becomes increasingly intolerable. Henri and Isabelle recognize that their current circumstances threaten the very essence of their family—education, creativity, and security—making it clear that remaining in Venezuela is no longer an option. This realization weighs heavily on their hearts, as they mourn the life they had envisioned, filled with cultural richness and familial bonds that may now feel out of reach.

As they begin to prepare for their departure, a mix of anxiety and determination marks their every action. They gather their belongings, carefully choosing what to take with them—children's books, cherished family photos, Isabelle's sketchpad, and paints—items that serve as connections to their past and reminders of who they are. It is a task filled with bittersweet emotions; each piece they pack represents both a farewell to their homeland and a hope for a new beginning.

They also reach out to friends and family for assistance, in navigating the complex web of logistics required for their escape. Henri contacts distant relatives who have settled in Dominica, seeking advice on the best routes and potential resources available to newcomers. Every message feels fraught with urgency as they share their plans, hoping their loved ones can provide guidance that might ease their transition.

Isabelle takes special care in explaining their situation to supportive friends, who express heartbreak yet understanding. Many help—helping them to secure transportation and even sharing supplies. The couple feels a swell of gratitude for the connections they have forged, and in these moments, they are reminded that while the decision to leave brings loss, it also reveals the depth of their relationships with those who share their struggles.

As they prepare for the logistical challenges ahead, fear of the unknown begins to mingle with flickers of hope. They discuss what their new life might look like— the possibility of a quieter, safer existence in Dominica where their children can play freely and attend school. Henri imagines the day he will share lessons with eager young minds again, while Isabelle envisions an open canvas where creativity can flourish, unhindered by the specter of conflict.

The reality of their imminent departure begins to settle in, evoking emotions that ebb and flow like the tides. There are moments filled with tears as they contemplate leaving behind the only home they have ever known, the friends they have grown up with, the memories etched into every corner of their neighborhood and the cultural richness that has shaped their identities. Yet amidst the sorrow, there is a steadfast commitment to their children and a shared understanding that courage lies not in the absence of fear, but in the determination to act in the face of it.

On the eve of their departure, Henri and Isabelle gather the children for a family meeting. Holding their hands tightly, they explain their decision, sensing the gravity of the moment. With tenderness in their voices, they reassure the children that this journey is a step toward safety and a new beginning. The children's eyes reflect a mixture of confusion and apprehension, but also a glimmer of excitement at the prospect of adventure.

As they prepare to leave, a comforting warmth fills the air—a recognition that though they are stepping into the unknown, they are doing so together as a family. Their bonds of love and courage become their guiding light, illuminating a path through the uncertainty and fear that lies ahead.

In choosing to leave Venezuela, Henri and Isabelle are not merely abandoning their home; they are crafting a new possibility for their family. It is a decision born of love, resilience, and hope, one that reaffirms their commitment to nurturing their children's future during chaos. As they embark on this journey, they carry both the weight of their past and the promise of a brighter tomorrow, ready to face whatever challenges may come in their pursuit of safety and stability.

With their bags packed and hope in their hearts, the Sebastien family stands at the docks, ready to embark on a journey across the sea to Dominica. As they look out at the steamship waiting to take them away from Venezuela, a mixture of excitement and apprehension ripples through their bodies. Each member of the family clings to their small belongings, which serve as a tangible connection to their past, but within them also stirs an eagerness to discover what the future holds.

As they board the ship, the salty sea breeze fills their lungs, offering a taste of freedom yet to come. The sight of the vast ocean, shimmering under the sun, evokes a sense of both wonder and trepidation. Henri holds Isabelle's hand tightly, sensing her unease as they navigate the vessel, surrounded by fellow travelers on their own journeys. The atmosphere is charged with mixed emotions, and the air is filled with whispers of hope and uncertainty.

The ride begins, and the ship steadily cuts through the waves, creating a rhythm that reflects the tumultuous feelings within the Sebastien family. Each wave beckons them closer to the promise of a new beginning, but the chorus of apprehension lingers in their hearts. As the shoreline of Venezuela fades into the distance, the reality of their departure sinks in—what they have left behind and what lies ahead.

Seated together on the deck, the children gaze wide-eyed at the endless expanse of water, their innocence contrasting with their parents' burdened hearts. They ask questions, curious about their destination and the adventures that await them. As a means of distraction, Isabelle begins to tell them stories of the lush landscapes and vibrant culture they will soon encounter, painting vivid images in their minds.

Yet beneath the surface, both Henri and Isabelle wrestle with their fears. "Will we be safe there? Will we find a place we can truly call home?" they each wonder silently. The sense of loss hangs heavily; leaving family, friends, and the familiar world they grew up in weighs on their hearts.

Sensing her unease, Henri leans closer to Isabelle, enclosing her hand in both of his. "We are heading toward a place where we can rebuild our dreams," he assures her, his voice steady despite the tide of apprehension that washes over him. He gazes out toward the horizon, where the sky meets the sea, tinged with the colors of a new dawn. "This journey is not just an escape; it is a new beginning for us—a chance to create a life for our children that they deserve."

Isabelle turns to him, searching for reassurance in his gaze. "I believe in us," she replies quietly, a flicker of determination igniting within her. "But I cannot help but feel the weight of what we've left behind."

Henri nods, understanding her turmoil. "I know it is hard, Isabelle. It is normal to feel this way." He takes a deep breath, focusing on the steady rhythm of the ship as it navigates the waves. "But we will find our footing again. Our love and commitment to each other and our children will be our guiding light. Dominica offers us a chance to embrace a new life full of possibilities—one where they can grow up free and unafraid."

As the sun begins to set, casting a golden hue across the water, the Sebastien family gathers at the ship's railing. The children's laughter fills the air, and Henri marvels at their resilience. This moment, amidst the sea of uncertainty, highlights their unity and spirit.

They share a collective bond, fortified by hope and love, knowing they are journeying toward a future that allows them to nurture their dreams. With each wave crashing against the hull, the past drifts further away, giving rise to a new chapter.

As night descends and the stars begin to twinkle in the vast sky above, the Sebastien family stands together, looking out over the water. The unknown stretches before them, filled with both challenges and opportunities, but in that moment, they feel a spark of excitement ignite within their hearts. With hope as their compass, they sail onward into the future—ready to embrace whatever awaits them in Dominica.

Upon their arrival in Portsmouth, Dominica, the Sebastien family is met with a breathtaking sight: the island's lush green landscape unfolds before them, its vibrant foliage glistening in the warm tropical sun. The air is thick with the scent of salt and blooming flowers, an intoxicating mixture that fills their lungs and awakens their senses. As the ship docks, the children press their faces against the railings, wide-eyed with wonder, absorbing the beauty surrounding them.

As they step onto the dock, the friendly faces of the local community greet them with warm smiles and inviting waves. Henri and Isabelle exchange glances, their hearts swelling with a newfound sense of hope. At this moment, the initial anxiety of their journey begins to ebb, replaced by the excitement of what lies ahead. The vibrant culture of Dominica is palpable, woven into the very fabric of island life, and they feel an immediate pull towards the possibilities that await them.

The couple watches as their children dart ahead, captivated by the sights and sounds of their new home. The lively chatter of the locals, the laughter of children playing nearby, and the rhythm of island music create a symphony of life that envelops them. In the distance, bold waves crash against the shore, a reminder of nature's power and beauty that resonates deep within their spirits.

As they explore the town, Henri and Isabelle are inspired by the resilience of the Caribbean people they encounter. Stories of hardship lived alongside tales of triumph and community reinforce their belief that they can forge a new life here. The warm hospitality they receive confirms that they are no longer just strangers; they are part of a larger tapestry of people determined to thrive amidst their challenges.

Having secured a temporary home on the outskirts of Portsmouth, the family begins to settle into their new life. The vibrant colors of the wooden houses, the sounds of the market bustling with energy, and the rich aromas of local cuisine invigorate their spirits. They eagerly embrace the culture, eager to learn and connect with their neighbors. Isabelle feels inspired to rediscover her artistic expression, while Henri lunges into teaching opportunities, ready to share his passion for knowledge with the local youth.

The Sebastien family's initial fears gradually transform into a renewed sense of purpose. Each day unfolds as a new adventure, filled with the lessons of resilience and hope that Dominica embodies. They attend community gatherings, where dances and music ignite a sense of belonging and joy. Henri and Isabelle both contribute to discussions about education and the arts, eager to share their perspectives and learn from the diverse experiences of those around them.

They find solace in the local customs—the blending of cultures creates a rich tapestry that speaks to not just survival but thriving together as a community. The lessons of acceptance and unity resonate deeply with the couple, reaffirming the importance of cultivating connections in their new environment.

With every passing day, the lush surroundings and warm climate foster their dreams of flourishing in this new land. The island's natural beauty becomes a backdrop for their family's transformation, a place where they can nurture their children's education, embrace creativity, and rebuild the values that once seemed lost.

As they settle into their new rhythm, the Sebastien family realizes they have found more than just a new home; they have discovered a sanctuary that offers the promise of growth and renewal. This vibrant island, rich with cultural history and the spirit of its people, fuels their aspirations, whispering to them that they are exactly where they are meant to be.

In the heart of Dominica, the Sebastien family begins to plant their roots, embracing the challenges and joys this new chapter brings. With hopeful hearts and open minds, they embark on the journey of reclaiming their dreams amidst the beauty and resilience of their new home.

After exploring the region and immersing themselves in the vibrant life of Dominica, Henri's eyes widen with excitement upon discovering the estate of Lagon in Bioche. Nestled in the lush mountains with a stunning view of the crystalline sea, the property captivates him. The sprawling gardens are alive with vibrant flora—bright flowers bursting with color, tall palms swaying gently in the breeze, and a multitude of plants that seem to sing with life. The serene sounds of birds chirping harmonize with the soft rustling of leaves as the wind dances through the trees, creating a delightful symphony of nature that invites Henri deeper into the estate.

As he walks through the expansive grounds, Henri envisions the possibilities. Vegetable gardens that will provide fresh produce for their family, shaded areas perfect for storytelling and lessons, and open spaces where the children can run and play freely create a vivid picture of the life they dream of building for their family. Lagon feels alive, whispering promises of inspiration and opportunity, coaxing Henri to turn dreams into reality.

Eager to bring Isabelle to see the estate, Henri rushes back to share the news. When they walk through the gates together, Isabelle's eyes light up with wonder. She strolls through the gardens, taking in the colorful blooms and the inviting nature of the land. "This place feels like it has a spirit of its own," she declares, observing how the gentle breeze rustles through the leaves. "It's magical."

Together they explore the dilapidated yet charming buildings, each room echoing stories of the past and alluding to the future they could create. They discuss how they could transform the house into a warm, inviting home, one that reflects their values and passions. "Imagine having an art studio here," Isabelle suggests, her excitement palpable as she points out a sunlit room with large windows that frame views of the mountains. "This could be a space for the children to explore their creativity freely!"

As they tour the estate, Henri begins to envision an area dedicated to education, a small library, or a classroom space where he can host local children eager to learn. "This property can be so much more than just a home; it could be a place where knowledge and creativity intersect," he reflects, his heart swelling with hope. The thought of nurturing the local community through education invigorates him, and he feels a calling to make this vision a reality.

However, the couple is acutely aware of their financial constraints. Despite their limited savings, the lure of Lagon is strong. They gather their thoughts and prepare to negotiate the purchase, understanding that this opportunity is a rare one. Henri recalls the struggles they faced while escaping Venezuela, and he knows that taking this leap of faith could shape not only their family's future but also the lives of others in their community.

Together, they meet with the current owner, a kind elderly gentleman who recognizes the passion in Henri and Isabelle's eyes. They express their heartfelt intentions to restore the estate and to create a nurturing environment for their family and the community. The negotiations feel tense yet hopeful, as the couple explains how they envision transforming Lagon into a haven for creativity and learning.

Their resolve and enthusiasm resonate with the owner, who sees their potential and the genuine love they have for the land. After several discussions and heartfelt proposals, a deal is struck. The purchase will test their financial limits, but the joy that radiates from finally owning Lagon fills Henri and Isabelle with a renewed sense of purpose. It is a profound moment that solidifies their commitment to rebuilding their lives in this new land.

With the paperwork signed and their dreams beginning to take shape, the couple stand together on the sprawling grounds, taking in the beauty that surrounds them. As the sun sets behind the mountains, casting a golden sheen over the estate, Henri and Isabelle clasp hands, their hearts brimming with anticipation.

"This is just the beginning," Henri whispers, looking toward the horizon. "We will cultivate our passions here, nurture our children, and build a legacy that contributes to this community."

Isabelle nods, eyes shining with conviction. "Lagon will be our sanctuary—a place where our family can grow and where we can share our love of education and the arts with others."

As they take their first steps toward making that dream a reality, the Sebastien family feels a profound sense of belonging wash over them. The decision to purchase Lagon in Bioche marks the dawn of a new chapter, one filled with hope, creativity, and the promise of a bright future. Here, amid the gardens and the sea, they will cultivate not just their dreams but also the lives of those they touch—a testament to their resilience and unwavering spirit.

As the Sebastien family begins to unpack their belongings in Lagon, excitement fills the air. The scent of fresh paint and the sounds of chirping birds mix, creating an invigorating atmosphere that feels alive with possibility. The children rush in and out of rooms, eyes wide with wonder as they explore their new surroundings. They are captivated by the beauty of the estate—each corner bursting with vibrant tropical plants, towering trees, and expansive gardens that promise countless adventures.

With a sense of delight, the children discover a small stream winding through the property, its crystal-clear water glinting in the sun. They squeal with joy as they dip their toes in it, making splashes and laughing, their carefree spirits resonating through the air. Henri and Isabelle watch fondly, knowing this idyllic setting is the perfect backdrop for their children to grow, learn, and create lasting memories.

While the children explore, Henri and Isabelle roll up their sleeves, diving into the task of transforming Lagon into a nurturing space filled with laughter, creativity, and learning. They work together, unpacking boxes filled with cherished belongings—family photos, books, art supplies, and even their Venezuelan mementos. Each item they remove from the boxes sparks conversations about their past and their hopes for the future.

As they settle into their new roles as both owners of Lagon and educators for their children and the community, they prioritize establishing a rhythm that honors both their Venezuelan roots and the culture of their new home. Mornings begin with the aroma of fresh coffee brewed from beans they sourced locally, mixed with the sound of children's laughter in the background as they play in the gardens. Henri and Isabelle agree to incorporate both Venezuelan dishes and local Caribbean flavors into their meals, creating a delightful fusion of tastes that reflects their journey.

Isabelle is especially excited to set up a dedicated art space, where sunlight floods in through large windows and brushes await her touch. She plans to invite the local children to join her for art lessons, hoping to inspire creativity and provide a space where they can express their ideas freely. Alongside this vision, Henri sketches out a plan for small outdoor classrooms where he dreams of holding workshops for local youth. His passion for educating young minds fuels his determination to make Lagon a center for learning, community engagement, and artistic expression.

As days turn into weeks, the rhythm of their new life begins to take shape. The family joins local events, mingling with neighbors and forging connections that integrate them into the community. Festivals filled with music, dance, and delicious food invite them to celebrate the vibrant culture of Dominica. They learn the island's history, its inhabitants' resilience, and the unique customs that enrich their new home, grounding them as they adapt to their surroundings.

Evenings at Lagon are filled with laughter and storytelling. Henri shares tales from their lives in Venezuela, weaving in lessons of resilience and hope, while Isabelle encourages the children to share their newfound experiences. These gatherings become a cherished tradition, reinforcing their bonds as a family and embracing the beauty of their journey.

Through it all, the Sebastien family finds that Lagon is more than just a house; it is a sanctuary where they can cultivate their passions and create a nurturing environment for their children. With each corner of their home filled with warmth and creativity, they begin to solidify their new identity as a family rooted in love, resilience, and the shared vision of a brighter future.

As they look out across the lush gardens and the blue expanse of the sea, Henri and Isabelle exchange knowing smiles, their hearts filled with gratitude for the journey that has brought them here. Their home at Lagon becomes a place of transformation, where dreams are nurtured, cultures blend beautifully, and the laughter of their children echoes through the air—a testament to their new beginning in Dominica.

Eager to integrate into the vibrant local culture, the Sebastien family actively engages with their neighbors and local schools in Colihaut. Understanding that fostering connections is essential for their new life in Dominica, Henri and Isabelle set out to contribute their unique gifts and experiences to the community around them.

Henri steps up first, tapping into his passion for education and the arts. He approaches the local school, where he introduces himself to the principal and expresses his desire to offer workshops in visual arts. With an enthusiastic smile, he shares his vision of inspiring creativity in the students, encouraging them to explore their artistic potential. The principal, impressed by Henri's background and dedication, eagerly agrees to collaborate, and soon, Henri finds himself leading classes filled with eager young minds.

In these workshops, Henri introduces various art forms, from painting and drawing to sculpture and mixed media. Much to his delight, the students respond with enthusiasm, their eyes shining with curiosity as they experiment with different techniques. Henri encourages them to express their identities and stories through art, fostering a sense of pride and ownership in their work. The classroom buzzes with energy, laughter, and creativity, forming an enriching environment that strengthens the bond between Henri and the local children.

Meanwhile, Isabelle focuses on sharing her love for storytelling and cultural traditions. Recognizing the importance of nurturing connections among families, she organizes storytelling sessions in Kai Cacao, inviting local children and parents to gather. With her captivating presence and expressive storytelling, she brings tales from their Venezuelan heritage to life, weaving in lessons about resilience, love, and adventure.

Isabelle combines these stories with local folklore, creating a rich tapestry of narratives that resonate with everyone. As she shares stories under the shade of a large tamarind tree, the children sit wide-eyed, fully engrossed, bridging the gap between cultures. Parents gather too, appreciating the unique perspectives and insights that emerge during these sessions. The sense of camaraderie grows as families share their own stories, traditions, and laughter, fostering an atmosphere of connection and mutual respect.

Through their efforts, the Sebastien family gradually becomes embraced by the community. Neighbors invite them over for casual gatherings, sharing local delicacies and introducing them to the intricacies of island life. They bond over meals, laughter, and conversations about their respective cultures, allowing friendships to blossom that transcend differences.

As Henri and Isabelle connect with their new neighbors, they also become aware of the community's challenges—the economic struggles, the importance of education, and the resilience of the people who face these realities with unwavering spirit. The Sebastien family finds that their contributions extend beyond arts education and storytelling; they become part of a larger movement to uplift and empower the community itself.

The Sebastien children's friendships with local kids deepen, grounded in shared experiences and adventures in the gardens of Lagon and around the vibrant village of Colihaut. They play together, learn from one another, and explore the island's breathtaking landscapes, developing lasting bonds that further entwine the Sebastien family within the community.

As the months pass, their efforts to connect solidify valuable relationships that support their aspirations and foster a sense of belonging. Henri and Isabelle's commitment to enriching the lives of others while sharing their own journey becomes a central theme in their lives at Lagon. They realize that community is built on trust, shared experiences, and a genuine desire to uplift one another.

In embracing community, the Sebastien family finds their place in Dominica—a place where they can continue to grow, learn, and contribute. Together with their neighbors, they lay the groundwork for collaborative endeavors, creative projects, and a nurturing environment that weaves both their Venezuelan roots and Caribbean traditions into a beautiful tapestry of shared life. As they invest in the communities of Bioche and Colihaut, the Sebastians find that they, too, are enriched by the love and support that surrounds them, creating a network of connection and hope that they will anchor them in their new home.

Yet, despite their determination and hope, the Sebastien family still faces challenges in adapting to life in Dominica. The realities of their new environment come with a set of hurdles that test their resilience and commitment to creating a stable life.

One of the most pressing difficulties is finding consistent work. While Henri has been able to offer his arts education workshops at the local school, the position is part-time and does not provide the financial stability the family needs. He begins to explore other job opportunities, reaching out to local organizations and businesses. However, many positions require fluency in Creole, and although Henri has a basic understanding of the language, he struggles to communicate effectively. Frustration mounts as he navigates job applications and interviews, feeling the weight of responsibility to provide for his family.

Meanwhile, Isabelle faces her own challenges. Although she has successfully established storytelling sessions in the community, she soon realizes that limited access to resources hampers her ability to enhance these programs. Art supplies, books, and educational materials are often scarce or expensive. Determined to create a nurturing environment for the children, she seeks out local resources and community support, yet each step often feels like an uphill battle.

Additionally, language barriers significantly complicate their interactions. While Isabelle's storytelling sessions bring together families from various backgrounds, she often lacks the conversational fluency in Creole necessary to fully connect with everyone. Understanding local customs and communication styles is crucial for building deeper relationships, and she finds herself exhausted from continuous efforts to bridge the gap. As she practices her language skills, she remains eager to improve, but the learning curve feels steep and sometimes discouraging.

Amidst these challenges, Henri and Isabelle are also determined to keep their children grounded. They recognize that their transition to a new life can be overwhelming for the kids, who may struggle with feelings of uncertainty and homesickness. To address this, they create a routine that provides structure and stability—a balance of work, play, and family time.

Each evening, Henri and Isabelle gather the family to share stories about their day, reflecting on their experiences with humor and gratitude. They emphasize the importance of resilience, reminding their children that challenges are part of the journey. They encourage their kids to voice their feelings and concerns, fostering an environment where open communication thrives. This approach not only strengthens their family bond but also helps to ease their children's anxiety about adapting to their new environment.

On weekends, they explore Dominica together, immersing themselves in the island's vibrant culture and breathtaking landscapes. They hike through lush forests, visit local markets, and participate in community events, allowing the children to embrace their new home while creating cherished memories. These outings serve as a reminder that, despite the struggles they face, there is joy and beauty to be found in each day.

During this whirlwind, Henri and Isabelle find solace in each other's support. Together, they brainstorm creative solutions to the obstacles they encounter. They reach out to other expatriates and residents for advice and resources, building a network of support that helps ease their path.

They forge connections with people who have faced similar challenges and can empathize with their situation. These conversations lead to collaborative initiatives, like resource-sharing programs with other families, and engagement with local artists who can provide insights on how to navigate opportunities in the arts.

Though challenges persist, the Sebastien family remains dedicated to their vision of a hopeful future in Dominica. They learn to adapt, focusing on small victories and moments of joy that punctuate their busy lives. Through it all, they find that the strength of their family unit is an unwavering foundation, allowing them to take strides forward, one day at a time.

As they face these new challenges together, Henri and Isabelle reaffirm their belief that resilience, love, and community will guide them through the complexities of their new life. Even when the path seems daunting, they embrace the journey, knowing that every challenge is an opportunity for growth and discovery.

The experience of fleeing their homeland weighs heavily on Henri and Isabelle, lingering in their hearts like a distant echo of a life left behind. Memories of their previous struggles and the uncertainty of their journey to Dominica often surface, reminding them of the hardship that has shaped their identity. Despite their emotional weight, they remain resolute in their mission to build a future that honors their values and aspirations for their family.

Every evening, as they gather around the dinner table, Henri, and Isabelle share reflections on their past. They discuss the lessons learned from their harrowing journey—lessons about resilience, community, and the profound importance of education for their children's growth. These conversations serve as a source of strength, reinforcing their commitment to one another and their shared vision for a brighter future.

Isabelle often speaks of the stories they have encountered along the way, weaving in tales of adversity turned into triumph. These narratives remind their children that challenges can lead to personal growth and greater resilience. She emphasizes the power of storytelling to process their experiences, encouraging their children to embrace vulnerability and find strength in their voices. Through storytelling, they keep the memory of their homeland alive while simultaneously weaving themselves into the fabric of their new community.

Henri, too, draws from the wisdom of their past. His insights about the value of education create a guiding principle for their family. He is deeply committed to ensuring that his children not only receive a good education but also understand that learning extends beyond the confines of a classroom. He often engages them in discussions about the world, encouraging curiosity and exploration of ideas. He reminds them that knowledge is a powerful tool that can open doors and create opportunities, regardless of their current circumstances.

This commitment drives Henri and Isabelle to overcome obstacles and find innovative ways to support their family and engage with their new home. They seek local partnerships that can help enhance the educational opportunities available to their children, scouting for resources, workshops, and mentors who can amplify their learning experiences. They tap into the local community, utilizing libraries and community centers, and even searching for online resources to supplement their children's education.

In every interaction, they strive to model resilience for their children, showing them how to adapt to challenges with grace and determination. Whether it is navigating language barriers, forging new friendships, or embracing the diverse cultural landscape of Dominica, Henri and Isabelle demonstrate the importance of remaining optimistic and proactive.

During moments of frustration or despair, they remind each other of the strength they have shown as a family throughout their journey. They draw on the support of their growing network of friends and neighbors—people who uplift them, offer encouragement, and share their own stories of resilience. This sense of community bolsters their spirits, reminding them that they are not alone in their struggles.

Through their daily routines, the Sebastien family cultivates resilience as a cherished family value, understanding that it is not merely the absence of difficulties but rather the ability to rise above them. They celebrate small victories together, whether it is a successful art class led by Henri or a storytelling session that ignites laughter and connection among local children.

As challenges arise, the family becomes more adept at finding creative solutions. They brainstorm ideas for collaborative projects that engage the local youth in the arts and education, seeking to create spaces where both Spanish and Creole can be spoken and celebrated. They make the most of their experiences, learning from the community and sharing their own unique contributions.

The weight of their past is heavy, but it drives Henri and Isabelle to continue forging ahead, building a future where their children feel secure, valued, and empowered. Each obstacle they encounter becomes an opportunity to demonstrate the power of resilience, honoring their journey while steadfastly focusing on the bright potential that lies ahead.

Together, the Sebastien family continues to navigate their new life in Dominica with the unwavering belief that their dedication to resilience, community, and education will pave the way for a flourishing future—one where their values shine brightly, and where their children can thrive amidst the beauty and vibrancy of their new home.

As Henri and Isabelle continue to settle into life in Bioche and Colihaut, they draw immense strength from their growing network of friends and neighbors. The warmth and kindness they experience from the local community becomes a vital lifeline, offering both encouragement and understanding as they navigate the complexities of their new life.

From their first days on the island, Henri and Isabelle have been embraced by their neighbors, who share their own stories of struggle and resilience. These connections create a sense of solidarity that reinforces the idea that they are not alone in their journey. Each conversation with a neighbor reveals a tapestry of experienced people who have faced adversity, overcome challenges, and emerge stronger. This shared understanding fosters deep bonds, allowing the Sebastien family to feel more at home in their new environment.

The couple eagerly participates in community initiatives, finding opportunities to connect with others while also giving back. They join local clean-up days at the beach, plant trees in neighborhood parks, and participate in cultural festivals that celebrate the rich heritage of Dominica. These activities not only provide a sense of purpose but also allow them to engage with their community in meaningful ways.

As they work side by side with other families, they create lasting friendships based on mutual respect and shared values. Henri teams up with local artists, organizing collaborative workshops that highlight both Venezuelan and Caribbean artistic traditions. These programs draw participants from all walks of life, fostering creative exchanges that enrich their collective experiences.

Isabelle also finds a sense of purpose in these community efforts. She collaborates with other parents to organize storytelling sessions in local schools and community centers, combining traditional Caribbean tales with her Venezuelan heritage. This initiative creates a vibrant platform for children and families to come together, sharing stories that reflect their diverse backgrounds while celebrating their shared humanity.

Through these interactions, Henri and Isabelle discover that they are part of a broader community that thrives on empathy and support. They witness the strength of resilience manifested in their neighbors' lives, whether in the form of resilience against the elements or in the face of personal hardships. This environment not only inspires them but also reassures them that they can overcome their challenges together.

The support they receive fuels their determination to establish a stable and fulfilling life for their children. With their neighbors' encouragement, Henri seeks additional teaching opportunities and begins to establish creative partnerships with local schools. Isabelle, inspired by the friendships she is nurtured, expands her storytelling sessions, inviting islanders to share their own stories, further deepening the connections within the community.

As they nurture these relationships, Henri and Isabelle find themselves becoming advocates for educational and artistic initiatives that empower local youth. They collaborate on programs aimed at providing resources, mentorship, and artistic expression opportunities, instilling hope, and inspiration among the younger generation. In doing so, they not only enrich their own lives but also create pathways for others to follow, reinforcing the sense of interconnectedness that defines their community.

Months pass, and the Sebastien family becomes a cherished part of the fabric of Bioche and Colihaut. Their children forge friendships with local kids, learning about the island's culture while sharing glimpses of their Venezuelan heritage. Henri and Isabelle's home fills with laughter, creativity, and the echoes of stories exchanged with friends—each moment a testament to the power of community.

Through their involvement, they cultivate a sense of belonging that transcends the challenges they once faced. They find purpose in their shared efforts to uplift one another, recognizing that they are part of a collective narrative woven together by the threads of perseverance, hope, and solidarity.

Henri and Isabelle realize that finding strength in the community is not merely about receiving support but also about giving back. In forging deep connections and actively participating in the life of their new home, they create a nurturing environment for their children, a place where they can thrive amidst the love and encouragement of their newfound family. Together, they embrace the journey, knowing that through community, they will continue to build a future filled with hope and possibility.

Faced with resource limitations in their new surroundings, the Sebastien family becomes adept at finding creative solutions that allow them to thrive in Bioche and Colihaut. The realities of life in Dominica push Henri and Isabelle to innovate, drawing on their resourcefulness and the cultural wealth around them.

As Henri develops his educational programs, he begins to incorporate local materials into his projects. Understanding the importance of connecting his students to their environment, he gathers natural resources—fallen leaves, branches, and stones—to create art supplies and extend learning beyond traditional methods.

He organizes outdoor workshops where children make sculptures from twigs and leaves, encouraging them to see beauty in their surroundings while fostering creativity. By integrating these local elements into his teaching, Henri minimizes costs while enriching the educational experience. The children are excited to explore these hands-on projects, igniting their imaginations and deepening their connection to the land.

Henri also takes great care to draw from the cultural traditions of Dominica in his classes, introducing students to local artists and techniques that inspire creativity. He invites community members to share their skills, whether in pottery, music, or dance. This collaborative approach not only enhances the curriculum but also builds a strong sense of community, allowing students to learn from one another and celebrate their diverse talents.

Isabelle similarly finds innovative ways to incorporate local artistry into her storytelling sessions. She immerses herself in the rich folklore and legends of Dominica, learning tales of the island's history and culture. As she weaves these stories into her narrative sessions, she highlights important cultural symbols and themes that resonate with the children.

To enhance her storytelling, Isabelle collaborates with local artisans who create traditional costumes, puppets, and props that enrich the stories she tells. This collaboration not only brings the tales to life but also supports local artists by providing them with a platform to showcase their work. By engaging with the community in this way, Isabelle fosters pride in local culture while deepening the children's understanding of their heritage.

This adaptability transforms the challenges the Sebastien family faces into opportunities for growth and connection. Rather than seeing resource limitations as obstacles, they recognize them as a chance to innovate and engage more deeply with their new home. Their resourcefulness cultivates a mindset of perseverance, teaching their children the value of creativity and collaboration in overcoming difficulties.

As they implement these creative solutions, the Sebastien family feels a growing sense of fulfillment in their efforts to contribute to the community. Their commitment to integrating local elements into education and storytelling resonates with neighbors, reinforcing the sense of belonging they have cultivated.

Through workshops, storytelling sessions, and community collaborations, Henri and Isabelle build a supportive network that thrives on shared creativity and resourcefulness. They discover that by embracing their surroundings and drawing from the strengths of their community, they not only support each other but also enrich the lives of those around them.

In doing so, they create a landscape where learning, artistry, and cultural pride flourish, allowing the Sebastien family to turn challenges into the building blocks of their new life. Each initiative they undertake reinforces their connection to Dominica and highlights the beauty of blending their Venezuelan heritage with the vibrant traditions of their new home. Together, they show their children—and the community—what can be achieved through creativity, adaptability, and a shared commitment to growth.

Throughout their struggles in adapting to life in Dominica, Henri and Isabelle remain steadfast in their commitment to family values. Recognizing that the foundation of their strength lies in their unity, they prioritize quality time spent together as a source of comfort and motivation throughout their challenges.

In their efforts to cultivate a strong family identity, Henri and Isabelle create rituals that blend both Venezuelan and Caribbean customs. They understand the importance of instilling a sense of belonging in their children while celebrating their cultural heritage. This intentional blending of traditions allows the kids to appreciate their roots in Venezuela while also embracing the vibrant culture of Dominica.

Every Sunday, the family gathers for a "cultural day," where they dive into different aspects of their heritages. They might cook traditional Venezuelan dishes like arepas or pabellón, while also preparing local favorites like callaloo or fish in coconut sauce. The aromas of spices and fresh ingredients fill their home, wrapping them in warmth and nostalgia.

These family dinners, filled with laughter and storytelling, become a cornerstone of their household. Throughout the meal, Isabelle encourages everyone to share stories about their day, recount their adventures, and reflect on lessons learned. Henri, with his passion for storytelling, often interjects with tales from their homeland, infusing the evenings with captivating narratives that transport them all to different times and places.

As they gather around the table, the tablecloth adorned with bright Caribbean patterns, the conversations flow freely, nourishing their spirits. They share not just meals but also life lessons, values, and laughter—each moment reinforcing the importance of unity and connection within the family.

In these rituals, Henri and Isabelle purposefully incorporate elements that help their children maintain a strong sense of identity. They teach them about the significance of their Venezuelan heritage, sharing stories of their ancestors and the culture they come from. At the same time, they encourage their children to embrace the new experiences and traditions of their Caribbean home.

To further enrich this cultural exchange, Henri introduces local folklore into their evenings, weaving his own artistic flair into the stories. The children learn about the legends of Dim Dim, the local "forest man," and the spirit of the sea, helping them forge their identities within the rich tapestry of their new culture.

The family also celebrates both Venezuelan and Caribbean holidays, ensuring that their children feel connected to their roots. Whether it is Christmas with lively Venezuelan music and traditional dances, or Carnival festivities filled with vibrant colors and excitement, these celebrations create a rich interplay of customs that tie their past to their present.

By participating in local events, the Sebastien family becomes an active part of the community while sharing their own traditions and fostering understanding and appreciation with their neighbors. This dual commitment to both cultures serves as a reminder of the beauty of diversity and the importance of honoring one's roots.

As challenges arise, whether related to language barriers or financial struggles, Henri and Isabelle lean on their family values, using their rituals to guide them through tough times. They remind each other of their collective goals and dreams, fostering resilience and motivating one another to face adversity together.

In moments of uncertainty, they draw strength from their shared experiences, recognizing that their unity will carry them through even the most daunting challenges. They often sit down to discuss their aspirations, such as Henri's dreams of expanding his art programs or Isabelle's desire to unlock more storytelling opportunities for local kids, weaving in encouragement and optimism into each conversation.

Through their unwavering commitment to family values, Henri and Isabelle create a nurturing environment where their children can flourish—one grounded in love, creativity, and the beautiful tapestry of their combined heritage.

By prioritizing family time, building rituals that celebrate their identities, and reinforcing the importance of unity, the Sebastien family transforms their struggles into opportunities for growth and connection, fostering a rich sense of belonging in their new home while honoring the legacy of their past.

Looking ahead, Henri and Isabelle cultivate a vision for their family that transcends mere survival. They embrace the belief that education and creativity can pave the way for a brighter future, envisioning a life where their children not only thrive but also become contributing members of society who honor their rich heritage.

For Henri, the cornerstone of this vision lies in expanding his arts education programs. Drawing on his passion for creativity and teaching, he imagines a future where local schools collaborate with him to enhance their curriculums. He dreams of creating a dynamic arts education initiative that introduces students to a wide array of artistic disciplines, including visual arts, music, and theater.

Henri envisions workshops where children can explore their talents, express their emotions creatively, and learn from local artists. By weaving cultural appreciation into his programs, he aims to instill a sense of pride in both their Venezuelan roots and the vibrant Caribbean culture that surrounds them. His goal is to cultivate an environment where children feel free to explore their artistic potential, fostering a community of confident and inspired young creators.

Simultaneously, Isabelle nurtures her dream of empowering young girls in the community through storytelling and artistic expression. She believes that instilling confidence and creativity in these girls is vital for their personal development and future success. Isabelle envisions starting workshops specifically designed for young girls, where they can learn the art of storytelling, engage in creative writing, and explore various forms of artistic expression.

Her workshops would encourage girls to share their experiences and perspectives through narratives, fostering a sense of belonging and self-worth. By incorporating elements of both Venezuelan folklore and Caribbean storytelling traditions, Isabelle aims to create a rich cultural tapestry that helps participants honor their heritage. Through these initiatives, she hopes to build a supportive community that inspires young girls to express themselves fearlessly and cultivate their unique voices.

At the heart of Henri and Isabelle's vision is the desire for their children to embrace their dual identities while positively contributing to their new community. They aim to instill a sense of responsibility in their children, guiding them to not only pursue their dreams but also to uplift others along the way.

Henri and Isabelle encourage their kids to participate in community activities, fostering connections with neighbors and peers who share similar values. They want their children to understand the importance of collaboration, empathy, and respect for diverse cultures. By engaging in local projects, their children will develop a sense of belonging and a commitment to making a difference in the lives of others.

As they share their dreams for the future, Henri and Isabelle realize that their vision extends far beyond their immediate family. They aspire to build a legacy rooted in creativity, education, and community involvement—one that paves the way for future generations to thrive. They dream of creating a cultural nexus in their town, where families can come together to celebrate art, storytelling, and shared experiences.

Through collaborations with local organizations, schools, and artists, they hope to create lasting partnerships that enrich the community. By fostering an environment that values education and artistic expression, Henri and Isabelle aspire to contribute to a culture of creativity that empowers everyone to share their stories and talents.

In this vision for the future, Henri and Isabelle are driven by love, determination, and a deep commitment to raising compassionate and capable children. They are excited about the journey ahead and ready to embrace challenges as opportunities for growth and connection. With a clear vision in their hearts and minds, they step forward into the future, eager to bring their aspirations to life and inspire their children to dream big.

At the heart of Henri and Isabelle's determination to build a new life in Dominica is a profound desire to empower their children. They recognize that nurturing their kids' sense of identity is crucial for their confidence and resilience in a foreign environment. Henri and Isabelle strive to instill in their children a strong sense of pride in their Venezuelan roots while encouraging an openness to the diverse cultures that surround them.

From early on, Henri and Isabelle make a concerted effort to cultivate an appreciation for their heritage. They share stories of their family's history, traditions, and the vibrant Venezuelan culture. Through music, food, and festivities, they bring a piece of their homeland to life in their home. Venezuelan dishes become a staple at family dinners, where they gather to enjoy arepas, pabellón, and hallacas, often sharing stories about family gatherings back in Venezuela.

Henri tells tales of his childhood, highlighting family traditions that celebrate unity and resilience, such as the joyous gatherings during El Carnaval. He emphasizes the importance of music and dance, introducing their children to traditional Venezuelan songs and rhythms. These moments not only nurture their children's connection to their roots but also serve as a reminder of the rich cultural tapestry from which they come.

While honoring their Venezuelan identity, Henri and Isabelle equally emphasize the importance of embracing the diverse cultures they encounter in Dominica. From the outset, they encourage their children to engage with peers from various backgrounds, fostering friendships that help broaden their horizons. Through interactions with local families and imported cultural events, the children learn about the island's rich traditions, folklore, and unique history.

As they participate in community gatherings and festivals, Henri and Isabelle accompany their children to immerse themselves in the local culture, encouraging them to ask questions and seek understanding. They visit local markets, celebrate Carnival, and participate in traditional dances, allowing their kids to appreciate the beauty of cultural diversity while reinforcing the significance of their own identity.

Understanding that dialogue is essential for nurturing cultural awareness, Henri and Isabelle prioritize open conversations about culture, history, and global citizenship. They create a family environment where discussing ideas, experiences, and values is encouraged. This open channel of communication allows their children to express their thoughts and feelings about their experiences in a new country.

During family dinners, they often engage in discussions about different cultures' contributions to society. Henri and Isabelle prompt their children to think critically about the world and its complexities, asking questions such as, "What have you learned from your friends?" or "How do you think our experiences shape your understanding of others?"

These discussions help the children develop empathy for people from different backgrounds and foster a global perspective. The family reflects on current events, historical narratives, and social issues, emphasizing the importance of understanding differing viewpoints and fighting against stereotypes. They instill in their children the idea that being a global citizen means not just recognizing one's own identity, but also appreciating and respecting others.

Encouraging critical thinking becomes a central aspect of Henri and Isabelle's parenting philosophy. They teach their children to ask questions and seek knowledge, empowering them to frame their thoughts independently. When their children express confusion or concern about cultural differences, Henri and Isabelle guide them through thoughtful discussions, helping them constructively navigate their emotions while building understanding.

In practical terms, this can be as simple as encouraging their children to share their opinions based on what they have learned, whether it is about a recent cultural event they attended or a story they have heard at school. By guiding their children to express themselves clearly and respectfully, Henri and Isabelle prepare them to navigate complex social interactions with confidence and grace.

They also instill empathy by creating opportunities for their children to participate in community service projects, such as helping at local schools or participating in environmental cleanup initiatives. These experiences not only strengthen their sense of responsibility but also help the children develop compassion for others and a deeper appreciation for their community.

As their children engage with diverse peers and navigate the complexities of their multicultural environment, Henri and Isabelle stand firmly beside them, ready to provide guidance and support. They understand that these formative experiences will equip their children with the skills needed to navigate an increasingly interconnected world.

They instill the belief that adaptability is a strength and that embracing diversity enriches life. Their family culture becomes one of inclusivity, open-mindedness, and love—principles that will serve as a compass as their children embark on their unique paths.

Through these dedicated efforts, Henri and Isabelle empower their children to embrace their identities with confidence while also cultivating curiosity and respect for the beautiful mosaic of cultures that surround them. In doing so, they prepare their children not only to face the complexities of a multicultural world but also to thrive within it as compassionate, thoughtful, and informed individuals.

In overcoming adversity and nurturing their family's values, Henri and Isabelle lay the groundwork for a legacy of resilience that will echo through generations. They recognize that the struggles they face are not isolated incidents but part of a broader narrative that encompasses immigration, adaptation, and the quest for belonging. Each challenge becomes an integral chapter in their family's story, teaching their children valuable lessons about perseverance and strength in the face of hardship. By openly discussing their experiences, they help their children understand that struggles can be transformative and that embracing adversity is a crucial aspect of growth.

Henri and Isabelle's unwavering commitment to education serves as a cornerstone of this legacy. They believe that knowledge is power, and they instill in their children the importance of lifelong learning. By prioritizing education, they create an environment where curiosity is celebrated, and critical thinking is cultivated. Henri's desire to expand his arts education programs and Isabelle's aspiration to empower young girls through storytelling reflect their dedication to fostering a community that values intellectual and artistic endeavors. They encourage their children to view learning as a tool not only for personal growth but also for contributing positively to society.

Through their active participation in community initiatives, Henri and Isabelle demonstrate the significance of building connections and supporting one another. They aim to show their children that resilience is not just an individual trait but a collective strength that can be cultivated within a community. By engaging with their neighbors and sharing their experiences, they foster a sense of camaraderie that reinforces the idea that no one is alone in their struggles. Their involvement in local projects underscores the importance of empathy and solidarity, essential values they hope their children will carry forward as they navigate their own paths.

Henri and Isabelle understand that the challenges they endured must not be seen merely as burdens to bear, but rather as steppingstones to a future filled with hope and possibility. They teach their children that setbacks are not failures but opportunities for growth and learning. By sharing stories of perseverance and triumph, they inspire their family to approach life's challenges with optimism and resilience. They encourage their children to see themselves as architects of their own futures, capable of overcoming obstacles with creativity and grit.

As they lay the foundation for their family's legacy, Henri and Isabelle envision a future where their children carry forward the values of resilience, adaptability, and compassion. They aspire to empower them to become proactive individuals who embrace diverse cultures and perspectives, standing firm in their identities while remaining open to the world around them. In doing so, they ensure that the lessons learned from their journey remain alive, guiding the next generation toward a future filled with promise and potential—a legacy marked not by the struggles faced, but by the strength cultivated in overcoming them.

As the Sebastien family continues to settle into life in Bioche, they embody the spirit of resilience and determination that defines their journey. Each day unfolds as a new opportunity to embrace their surroundings, marked by trials, triumphs, and the unwavering bonds of family. Their experiences serve as a testament to the incredible capacity of the human spirit to adapt and thrive even in unfamiliar territory. With every challenge they overcome, they not only reinforce their commitment to one another but also strengthen their identity as a family anchored in hope and perseverance.

Together, Henri and Isabelle look to the future with optimism, ready to embrace the myriad opportunities that lie ahead. They understand that while the path may still hold uncertainties, their collective efforts will guide them toward fulfilling their dreams. They are committed to weaving their unique backgrounds and cultural identities into the vibrant fabric of Bioche, ensuring that their children grow with a strong sense of belonging and purpose. The lessons learned from their journey will be instilled in their children, fostering a legacy that champions resilience, creativity, and compassion.

In honoring their past and the values that have shaped them, the Sebastien family acknowledges the importance of their roots while remaining open to the diverse experiences around them. They actively contribute to their community, participating in local initiatives that reinforce connections and foster a sense of belonging. Their willingness to share their story and engage with others transforms their individual experiences into a collective narrative that enriches the lives of those around them. By doing so, they not only carve out a new chapter for themselves but also play a vital role in the evolving story of Bioche, helping to weave their unique experiences into the rich tapestry of life in this vibrant community.

As they embark on this new journey, the Sebastien family stands united, ready to face the future with courage and hope. They remain dedicated to empowering one another and actively shaping their destinies. Through their journey, they illustrate that resilience is not merely the ability to withstand challenges, but a powerful force that propels individuals and families forward, creating pathways to growth, connection, and a brighter tomorrow. With their hearts set on the future, the Sebastien family is poised to embrace all that life in Bioche has to offer, reflecting the enduring strength and beauty of the human spirit.

ॐ

Chapter Thirteen: Settling in Bioche

As the Sebastien family settles into their new life in Bioche, Dominica, they are met with a landscape rich in natural beauty and cultural diversity, teeming with both promise and challenge. This idyllic Caribbean setting offers stunning vistas of lush mountains and shimmering coastlines, yet the family's journey is marked by the complexities of acclimatizing to a new environment. Henri and Isabelle are acutely aware that this transition will require resilience and adaptability, and they approach it with open hearts and minds. They feel a deep commitment to creating a nurturing atmosphere where their children can thrive academically, socially, and emotionally.

Central to Henri and Isabelle's vision for their family is the importance of education, which they see as the cornerstone of their children's future. They understand that to flourish in their new surroundings, their children must not only excel in their studies but also develop a strong understanding of and appreciation for both their Venezuelan roots and the local culture. With this goal in mind, Henri and Isabelle are making a conscious effort to blend their cultural roots with their current surroundings. Their goal is to honor and preserve their heritage by incorporating meaningful traditions, language, cuisine, and practices into their everyday routines. Simultaneously, they actively participate in the local customs of Bioche and Colihaut, two communities that have become an integral part of their lives.

Although they lived in Bioche, they spent most of their time in Colihaut, which influenced their social and cultural experiences. Their frequent visits to the church, attendance at local schools, and trips to the Laplace Dame Market highlight their deep integration into the community life of Colihaut. These activities are not just routine; they serve as ways for Henri and Isabelle to forge connections, understand local ways of life, and feel a sense of belonging in both settings.

By doing so, they aim to create a rich, harmonious identity rooted in their heritage while embracing the unique customs of each place they inhabit. This dual approach not only strengthens their personal sense of identity but also fosters cultural continuity across generations.

They foster an environment where curiosity and respect for diversity are paramount, encouraging their children to explore the beautiful tapestry of culture around them.

However, their journey is not without obstacles. The Sebastien family grapples with the challenges of navigating a new education system, overcoming language barriers, and building connections within an unfamiliar community. Henri and Isabelle often find themselves reflecting on how to bridge the gap between their past experiences in Venezuela and the new realities of life in Dominica. Additionally, they face the practical challenges of establishing a comfortable home, securing employment, and embracing the local way of life. Yet, amid these trials, they remain steadfast in their commitment to each other and to the values they hold dear.

Through their commitment to family traditions and cultural values, the Sebastien family aims to foster a strong sense of identity in their children. They weave stories of their Venezuelan heritage into their daily rituals, whether it be through cooking traditional meals, sharing folk tales, or celebrating holidays that resonate with their roots. By doing so, they not only reinforce their children's connection to their heritage but also cultivate pride in who they are. At the same time, Henri and Isabelle encourage their children to embrace the vibrant culture of Dominica, engaging in local traditions and celebrations to create a sense of belonging in their new community.

In this rich and dynamic context, the family embarks on a profound journey of growth, learning, and adaptation. Their experiences in Bioche and Colihaut represent more than just a physical relocation; they symbolize a larger metamorphosis that encompasses their identities as immigrants, parents, and members of a newly adopted community. As they navigate the intricate balance between honoring their Venezuelan roots and embracing their new life in Dominica, the Sebastien family becomes a testament to the power of resilience, love, and the human spirit's capacity to adapt and flourish even in the face of uncertainty.

Instilled with a belief in the transformative power of education, Henri and Isabelle prioritize their children's learning from the moment they arrive in Bioche. Understanding that a supportive learning environment can significantly impact their children's academic growth and personal development, they set up a cozy study area in their home. This inviting space is filled with books, art supplies, and educational materials carefully curated to reflect both their Venezuelan roots and the vibrant Caribbean culture that surrounds them. The couple understands that integrating aspects of their heritage into their children's education will nurture a sense of identity while also inspiring a curiosity about the world outside their door.

With Henri's background as a teacher, he actively takes on the role of an educator, infusing his lessons with creativity and enthusiasm. He crafts engaging learning experiences that are tailored to each child's interests and academic needs, promoting critical thinking and curiosity. Using storytelling techniques, Henri introduces his children to the rich history and traditions of Venezuela, encouraging them to think deeply about their cultural identity. He also includes lessons on local Caribbean history and customs, helping them understand their new community and appreciate its unique contributions to the broader narrative of the region. By blending the two cultures, he fosters an appreciation for diversity and encourages a global perspective.

In this nurturing atmosphere, creativity flows freely. Henri and Isabelle encourage their children to express themselves through various artistic mediums, whether it is drawing, painting, or writing. The study area becomes a hub of creativity, where the children are invited to explore their thoughts and emotions through art projects that celebrate both their Venezuelan roots and the local culture. This blend of cultural expression not only enhances their artistic skills but also helps them process their experiences as new immigrants, allowing them to articulate their feelings and perspectives in meaningful ways.

Furthermore, Henri and Isabelle emphasize critical thinking in their educational approach. They encourage their children to ask questions and seek answers beyond the textbook, fostering a sense of inquiry that will serve them well in their academic journey. Henri introduces thought-provoking topics during their study sessions, prompting discussions that challenge their children to evaluate information critically and think independently. By engaging in collaborative discussions and problem-solving activities, the children learn invaluable skills that transcend the classroom.

To complement the formal learning experience, Henri and Isabelle seek opportunities for their children to engage with the community. They participate in local events, workshops, and cultural festivals that enrich their educational experience and deepen their understanding of the world around them. By encouraging their children to interact with peers from various backgrounds, they promote social learning and help them build essential relationships that contribute to their sense of belonging in Bioche.

In cultivating this enriching learning environment, Henri and Isabelle not only support their children's academic growth but also lay the foundation for lifelong learning. They instill the belief that education is a continuous journey, one that extends beyond formal schooling to encompass every experience and interaction. As their children adapt to their new surroundings, they embrace the transformative power of education, ready to explore the diverse world around them with open minds and eager hearts. In doing so, the Sebastien family reinforces an unshakeable bond built on love, curiosity, and the joy of learning together.

Motivated to become part of the local community, the Sebastien family enrolls Alton, Aldie, Algar, Nun, and Theresa in Colihaut School, seeing it as a crucial step for building meaningful relationships and enriching their children's education. They want their kids not just to learn academically but to immerse themselves fully in the vibrant local culture. By choosing a school that reflects the community's values, Henri, and Isabelle hope to facilitate their children's adjustment to life in Dominica while also establishing a sense of belonging in their new environment.

Recognizing the importance of active involvement in their children's education, Henri and Isabelle participate in parent-teacher meetings and school events. They prioritize communication with teachers, advocating for collaborative learning experiences that celebrate both local history and cultural diversity. During these meetings, they share their perspectives as newcomers to the community while also listening to the insights of seasoned parents and educators about the school's curriculum and initiatives. This engagement not only allows them to advocate for educational innovations but also helps them better understand the unique challenges and opportunities that the school community faces.

Through these interactions, the couple forms meaningful connections with other parents and teachers, fostering a network of support that enhances their family's integration into Colihaut. Henri and Isabelle share their children's backgrounds and interests, discovering common ground with other families who also value education and cultural enrichment. They initiate conversations about potential opportunities for collaboration, aiming to create programs that expose children to the rich histories and traditions of both the local community and their own Venezuelan culture. By bridging these two worlds, they hope to enrich their children's learning experiences and promote mutual understanding among families from different backgrounds.

In addition to advocating for collaborative educational efforts, Henri and Isabelle actively explore opportunities for their children to participate in extracurricular activities, arts, and community service projects. They encourage their children to join clubs that align with their interests, whether in sports, music, or the arts, viewing these activities as essential avenues for social integration and personal development. By engaging in local events and initiatives, the Sebastien children can connect with their peers outside the classroom, fostering friendships and a deeper appreciation for the diverse tapestry of cultures that make up Colihaut.

These extracurricular involvements also serve a dual purpose by reinforcing the couple's commitment to community service. Henri and Isabelle believe in the value of giving back and encourage their children to participate in projects that benefit their new community. Whether it is helping clean up local parks or volunteering for community events, these experiences not only instill a sense of responsibility but also enhance their children's understanding of teamwork and the importance of contributing to the greater good.

Through their active engagement in the local school and community, the Sebastien family lays a solid foundation for a meaningful and fulfilling life in Bioche. By immersing themselves completely in their new surroundings, they cultivate a sense of belonging while instilling core values of cultural appreciation, empathy, and community involvement in their children. Together, they navigate the joys and challenges of this new chapter, committed to making the most of their experiences in Dominica.

In addition to their children's formal education, Henri and Isabelle are committed to encouraging a love for learning through everyday experiences. They understand that education extends far beyond the classroom and that some of the most significant lessons can be found in the world around them. Whether it is cooking traditional Venezuelan dishes together or visiting local markets, the Sebastien family actively involves their children in a variety of enriching activities that teach valuable skills while deepening their appreciation for both their heritage and their new home. In the kitchen, for example, cooking becomes an opportunity to discuss cultural traditions, the history of different ingredients, and the significance of family recipes, allowing the children to engage with their Venezuelan roots in a tangible and meaningful way.

Moreover, Henri and Isabelle frequently take their children to the local market at La Place Dame, in Colihaut, where they explore the vibrant offerings of the community. This experience serves multiple purposes: it exposes them to local produce, crafts, and culinary delights while also providing an avenue to practice language skills, negotiate prices, and learn about the importance of supporting local businesses. Through these outings, the Sebastien children not only gain practical knowledge about commerce and nutrition but also learn to appreciate community engagement and the diverse cultural influences that shape their new environment.

Henri and Isabelle also place a strong emphasis on engaging their children in discussions about current events. They believe that instilling a sense of awareness about the world promotes responsible citizenship and helps their children develop a well-rounded worldview. During family dinners, they often mention news stories relevant to their community and the world at large, encouraging open dialogues about these topics. By discussing different perspectives and the implications of various events, they nurture critical thinking skills and ensure their children understand the importance of being informed citizens who can engage thoughtfully with the world around them.

By fostering a love for learning through these daily interactions, Henri and Isabelle instill in their children a sense of responsibility toward both their cultural heritage and the broader world. They teach them that education is not a finite pursuit confined to books and classrooms; rather, it is a lifelong journey that involves curiosity, exploration, and a willingness to learn from every experience. This mindset becomes a guiding principle for the Sebastien family, shaping their approach to life in Bioche and the lessons they carry with them.

The Sebastien family's commitment to fostering a love for learning not only enriches their children's education but also fosters a deeper connection to their cultural roots and their new community. As they navigate their journey together, they promote a nurturing environment that values inquiry, creativity, and adaptability, empowering their children to approach the world with an open mind and a passionate spirit. This devotion to continuous learning becomes a cornerstone of their family's identity, creating a legacy of curiosity, resilience, and cultural appreciation that will influence the generations to come.

The Sebastien family actively seeks to engage with their new communities in Bioche and Colihaut, viewing these interactions as vital opportunities to foster relationships and integrate into their surroundings. They understand that building connections extends beyond mere social interactions; it symbolizes their commitment to becoming an integral part of the community. To this end, they eagerly attend local events, festivals, and gatherings, immersing themselves in the vibrant cultural fabric of their new home. Each event serves as an opportunity not only to learn about the local customs but also to share their own Venezuelan heritage with their neighbors.

The Sebastien family introduced themselves to the community through their rich and diverse cuisine. At local gatherings, they eagerly bring traditional Venezuelan dishes such as arepas, empanadas, and pabellón. These culinary offerings often become talking points, inviting neighbors to engage in conversations about the ingredients, preparation techniques, and the stories behind each dish. Sharing food is a universal language, and through these exchanges, the Sebastians create an atmosphere of warmth and hospitality. They find that each bite serves as a bridge to mutual understanding, sparking dialogues that foster connections based on curiosity and appreciation for one another's backgrounds.

In addition to sharing cuisine, the Sebastien family also embraces the practice of storytelling—an integral part of both Venezuelan and Caribbean cultures. During gatherings, Henri and Isabelle take turns sharing tales from their homeland, weaving together history, folklore, and personal anecdotes that highlight the resilience and beauty of their culture. These storytelling sessions not only provide entertainment but also offer valuable insights into the values that shape the Sebastians' identity. As they recount their experiences, they invite their neighbors to share their own stories, creating a space where diverse narratives intersection. Through this exchange, they find common ground, emphasizing shared values that transcend cultural boundaries and foster a sense of belonging.

The Sebastians' willingness to engage actively with their new communities cultivates an atmosphere of mutual respect and appreciation. Their efforts to build bridges between their past and present help diminish the barriers often found between immigrants and established residents. By participating wholeheartedly in local festivals and events, the Sebastians make their presence felt while simultaneously showing their commitment to honoring both their Venezuelan roots and their new Caribbean surroundings. These shared experiences deepen their connections, enriching the community with their unique perspectives and experiences.

As the Sebastien family continues to forge these important relationships, they create a network of support that enhances their own sense of belonging in Bioche and Colihaut. They grow to feel at home within the community, where friendships bloom and cultural exchanges thrive. Through their engagement and willingness to learn, they lay the groundwork for a vibrant, interconnected life that honors their heritage while celebrating the diverse cultural mosaic that surrounds them. These connections become a source of strength for the family, reinforcing their sense of identity and belonging in this new chapter of their lives.

As Henri works to incorporate arts education into the local community, he takes the initiative to collaborate with local artists and educators, recognizing that creativity plays a crucial role in both personal development and community engagement. Understanding that art fosters a sense of belonging and encourages self-expression, Henri sets out to organize workshops and cultural programs in Bioche and Colihaut. By bringing together talented artists from various disciplines, he can create a platform where children can explore their artistic abilities while also learning about the richness of their cultural heritage.

These workshops invite children from the community to participate in a diverse range of activities, including painting, music, and dance. Through hands-on experiences, participants not only develop new skills but also gain exposure to different forms of artistic expression. For instance, during painting sessions, participants might explore themes related to local history and the natural world surrounding them, allowing them to connect their artistic endeavors with the community they inhabit. By fostering this environment of creativity, Henri and his collaborators create opportunities for the children to express themselves freely, nurturing their confidence and igniting their imaginations.

The cultural programs that Henri organizes often culminate in community showcases, where children display their artistic creations and perform music and dance routines for their families and neighbors. These events not only provide a platform for young artists to shine but also strengthen the bonds within the community as families come together to celebrate their children's talents. The Sebastien family's involvement in these initiatives reinforces their commitment to nurturing a vibrant arts culture in Bioche, and Colihaut, making them integral members of the community while advocating for the importance of creative education.

Moreover, through collaboration with local artists, Henri blended his Venezuelan heritage with the distinct Caribbean influences that define the region. This fusion not only enriched the workshops but also promoted cultural exchange, as local artists and participants shared their unique stories and techniques. By highlighting the interconnectedness of various artistic traditions, Henri fosters an appreciation for diversity among all participants, demonstrating how art can serve as a unifying force in a multicultural community.

As these initiatives flourish, they not only enrich the lives of local children but also solidify the Sebastians' place within the fabric of Bioche and Colihaut. By championing arts education and collaborative creativity, the family cultivates a sense of community that reflects their values of connection, growth, and cultural appreciation. Their efforts leave a lasting impact, inspiring the next generation of artists to embrace their creativity and become active contributors to the vibrant cultural landscape of their new home. Through this journey of collaboration and creativity, the Sebastien family continues to weave their story into the larger narrative of Bioche, illustrating the profound ways in which art can connect, heal, and uplift communities.

The Sebastien home evolves into a welcoming haven for families in the area, a sanctuary where the spirit of cultural diversity is celebrated and embraced. In this warm and inviting atmosphere, Henri and Isabelle host gatherings that encourage community members to come together, share experiences, and learn from one another. They understand that such gatherings are essential not only for strengthening local bonds but also for fostering an environment where individuals feel safe and supported in expressing their unique identities. This commitment to inclusivity transforms their home into a cultural hub that reflects the vibrant blend of identities that characterize the communities of Bioche, and Colihaut.

At these gatherings, the Sebastians prioritize creating safe spaces for dialogue and exchange, where participants can engage in meaningful discussions about the importance of preserving one's heritage while also embracing new customs. Families share stories of their cultural practices, traditions, and personal experiences, fostering mutual respect and understanding among attendees. By facilitating these conversations, Henri and Isabelle create a platform that highlights the beauty of individuality and encourages each person to find pride in their roots while exploring the richness of diverse backgrounds.

The Sebastien family's home is adorned with artifacts and decorations that celebrate their Venezuelan heritage alongside elements inspired by the local Caribbean culture. This careful curation serves as a visual representation of their belief in the beauty of cultural integration. When guests walk into their homes, they are greeted with an atmosphere that conveys a profound respect for all cultures, inviting them to share their own stories and experiences. The Sebastians encourage children to participate in activities that celebrate cultural traditions, such as storytelling sessions, music performances, and traditional dance, further enriching the experience for all who attend.

Through these gatherings, the Sebastien family fosters community resilience and solidarity. They create not just a space for socializing but also a forum for discussing challenges and solutions that families face in their daily lives. The safe space they have cultivated allows for the exploration of complex topics, such as identity, belonging, and the integration of immigrant experiences within the fabric of the local community. By openly addressing these themes, they promote healing and understanding, encouraging their guests to reflect on their journeys while supporting one another through shared experiences.

As the Sebastians continue to host these gatherings, their home becomes a symbol of unity and collaboration within the communities of Bioche, and Colihaut. They contribute significantly to the narrative of cultural exchange, showing that the blending of diverse heritages enriches the local landscape rather than dilutes it. Through their efforts, Henri and Isabelle establish their home as a sanctuary where cultural identities are celebrated, stories are shared, and friendships are forged. In doing so, they exemplify the power of community in nurturing a sense of belonging, demonstrating that creating safe spaces for dialogue is fundamental to building a harmonious and inclusive future for all.

Despite their unwavering commitment to community engagement, the Sebastien family encounters significant challenges as they strive to adapt to certain aspects of life in Dominica. Henri and Isabelle, while passionate about integrating their Venezuelan heritage with the local culture, find themselves grappling with the intricacies of a new educational system and differences in societal expectations for their children. The family must navigate the delicate balance between honoring their customs and embracing the norms of Caribbean society.

One of the most prominent challenges they face involves varying educational philosophies. In Venezuela, Henri and Isabelle were accustomed to a more traditional approach to education, which emphasizes structure and a particular hierarchy in the classroom. In contrast, the schools in Dominica may prioritize different teaching methods that stress creativity, collaborative learning, and a more relaxed classroom dynamic. As their children transition into this new system, Henri and Isabelle find themselves needing to reevaluate their expectations regarding academic achievement and engagement. They recognize that supporting their children in this adjustment will not just require practical changes but also an open-minded approach to how learning and education can be perceived and valued in this new context.

Additionally, the Sebastien family confronts different societal expectations when it comes to parenting and community involvement. In Venezuela, family life often revolves around close-knit familial structures and a strong emphasis on respect for elders. However, in Dominica, Henri and Isabelle observe a more community-oriented approach where families often partake in collective activities that fuse social engagement with child-rearing. They realize that blending these differing expectations calls for adaptability; Henri and Isabelle must be willing to adjust their parenting styles, balancing their desire to instill their Venezuelan values in their children with the locals' more communal way of fostering relationships and support networks.

As they reflect on these adjustments, the Sebastians understand that this cultural shift is a process that requires time and patience. They engage in open discussions with each other about their experiences and feelings, allowing space for vulnerability and honesty as they navigate these challenges together as a family. Henri and Isabelle also rely on their connections within the community to gain insights into best practices for integrating their family dynamics within the local expectations. By building relationships with local parents, teachers, and community leaders, they can access valuable perspectives that can help them navigate this transition more effectively.

The Sebastien family's journey of cultural adjustment is a balancing act that requires flexibility and understanding. They learn to appreciate that adaptation does not mean compromising their identity or heritage; instead, it is an opportunity to enrich their family's narrative by blending Venezuelan customs with the local Caribbean lifestyle. This dynamic process not only shapes their children's upbringing but also deepens their family's connections within the community. As they continue to navigate the complexities of life in Dominica, the Sebastien family embodies resilience and adaptability, evolving through their experiences to create a harmonious blend of traditions that honors both their past and their present.

As the Sebastien family immerses themselves in life in Dominica, they encounter practical challenges, particularly related to resource limitations in accessing educational materials and supplies. Despite their enthusiasm for integrating into the community and fostering a rich educational environment for their children, Henri often finds himself grappling with financial constraints that necessitate careful budgeting. Determined to provide for his family while pursuing his vision for educational initiatives, he navigates the fine line between meeting basic needs and promoting a culture of learning at home.

To manage these limitations, Henri is required to be inventive and resourceful, often seeking alternative ways to procure necessary materials for educational activities. He explores local markets, looking for affordable supplies that can be transformed into learning tools or art projects. From repurposed everyday items to creating DIY educational resources, Henri embraces a hands-on approach that encourages creativity not only in himself but also in his children. This process not only helps alleviate financial strain but also teaches his children valuable lessons about resourcefulness, sustainability, and the importance of thinking outside the box.

Furthermore, with their focus on building a sustainable life, the Sebastien family actively draws on the support of their local community. Henri and Isabelle recognize that collaboration can help bridge the gaps created by resource limitations. They connect with other families and educators to share resources, knowledge, and ideas. For example, Henri organizes community workshops where families can come together to exchange materials and collaborate on projects, creating a sense of shared purpose and mutual support. This collaborative spirit reinforces the notion that education thrives not just in isolation but through communal effort.

The family also seeks out local organizations and businesses that support educational initiatives, exploring partnerships that might provide additional resources or opportunities. By advocating for the importance of arts education and community involvement, Henri positions the Sebastien family as active contributors to the broader educational landscape in Bioche and Colihaut. Together, they work to foster an environment where learning is accessible to all, demonstrating that challenges related to resources can be transformed into opportunities for growth and connection.

Through these experiences, the Sebastien family learns that while resource limitations pose real challenges, they can also serve as catalysts for innovation and collaboration. Embracing a mindset of creativity in problem-solving, they navigate the complexities of their situation by fostering resilience within themselves and their children. As they continue to adapt and grow, Henri and Isabelle become role models for their children, illustrating that overcoming obstacles often leads to deeper connections and meaningful experiences. In doing so, the family reinforces the idea that even in the face of difficulties, the power of community and ingenuity can provide pathways to success and fulfillment.

During adjustments and struggles, Henri and Isabelle remain steadfast in upholding their cultural traditions, ensuring that their Venezuelan heritage continues to thrive in their new environment. They celebrate Venezuelan holidays with enthusiasm, transforming their home into a vibrant space filled with love and nostalgia. The sights, sounds, and smells of traditional festivities bring back cherished memories, allowing them to share stories of family gatherings, spirited music, and the joy of festive meals with their children. This dedication to their roots not only enriches their family life but also provides a comforting anchor as they navigate the challenges of cultural adjustment in Dominica.

During celebrations like Arepas Day or Christmas, the Sebastien household is bustling with activity. They prepare traditional dishes—fluffy arepas, savory hallacas, and sweet natilla—attending to each recipe's intricate details while involving the children in the cooking process. These moments become invaluable opportunities for bonding, where the family shares laughter, stories, and the rich history behind each dish. As they gather around the table to feast, they reinforce the importance of togetherness and the value of their heritage, reminding everyone of the love and warmth embedded in their customs.

Henri and Isabelle also take joy in teaching their children about the significance of these celebrations, highlighting the values they represent. Whether it is the spirit of generosity during the Christmas season, or the sense of community found in festival gatherings, they emphasize lessons about family, gratitude, and resilience. By sharing these values, they foster a sense of identity in their children, helping them understand that their heritage is a source of strength and pride. Through storytelling and cultural practices, the Sebastians create a bridge between their old life in Venezuela and their new life in Dominica, ensuring that their children appreciate both their roots and their current experiences.

These traditions serve as a foundation for their family values, creating a strong sense of unity and belonging amidst the inevitable adjustments that come with relocation. In difficult times, especially when facing the challenges of resource limitations and cultural differences, Henri and Isabelle find comfort and reassurance in their traditions. They remind their children that no matter where they are, the essence of their family and the love they share remain unchanged. It is this steadfast commitment to their cultural values that not only provides solace but also empowers the family to face obstacles with resilience and courage.

The Sebastien family's dedication to celebrating their Venezuelan traditions nurtures a deep connection among family members and cultivates a rich cultural tapestry in their home. By intertwining their heritage with their daily lives, they create a supportive environment that fosters emotional well-being and resilience. As they move forward in their journey, Henri and Isabelle ensure that their customs remain a source of joy, inspiration, and strength, helping their family navigate the complexities of adapting to a new culture while honoring the legacy of their past.

As the Sebastien family integrates into life within the Bioche, and Colihaut communities, Henri and Isabelle make it a priority to instill their cultural heritage in their children's upbringing. Understanding that a strong sense of identity is essential for navigating a new environment, they actively introduce their children to Venezuelan customs that celebrate their roots. Traditional dances, lively music, and captivating storytelling become essential components of their family life, allowing their children to experience the richness of their heritage firsthand. This dedication not only helps the children connect with their cultural background but also serves as a foundation for resilience and a deeper understanding of their place in the world.

Henri and Isabelle often organize family nights dedicated to immersing their children in Venezuelan culture. These evenings are filled with the upbeat rhythms of folk music, prompting everyone to join in traditional dances and learn the steps that have been passed down through generations. As they twirl and sway to the music, the children feel a sense of connection to their ancestors and the larger history of Venezuela. Furthermore, Henri shares stories of family gatherings in their homeland—tales filled with humor, lessons, and the heartwarming spirit of togetherness—that resonate deeply with their children and spark curiosity about their heritage. This blend of movement and narrative helps to create an emotional bond between the children and their cultural lineage.

In their efforts to transmit these traditions, Henri and Isabelle also embrace the local customs of Dominica, recognizing the value of weaving together both cultures to create a rich tapestry of experiences. They encourage their children to participate in local festivals and community events, learning about Caribbean traditions and forging friendships with their peers. This blending of cultures fosters an appreciation for diversity and promotes a sense of belonging in their new community. By allowing their children to explore both their Venezuelan and Dominican identities, Henri and Isabelle cultivate an open-minded perspective that enriches their children's lives and broadens their understanding of the world.

As a result of this commitment, the Sebastien children develop a profound appreciation for their heritage, gaining a sense of pride in their identity that will carry with them throughout their lives. They learn that their cultural background is not just a part of their past but also an integral aspect of who they are becoming in this new setting. This understanding empowers them to embrace their unique blend of traditions as strengths, enabling them to navigate the complexities of their environment with confidence and adaptability.

The Sebastien family's efforts in transmitting their traditions create a vibrant and nurturing home environment where cultural heritage is celebrated and interwoven with the experiences of their new life in Dominica. By passing down the values and customs dear to them, Henri and Isabelle ensure that their children not only remember their roots but also carry them forward into the future. Through this journey of cultural integration, the family thrives, enriching their lives and the lives of those around them, while demonstrating the beauty and strength that come from embracing both heritage and community.

The Sebastien family's efforts to blend their Venezuelan customs with local traditions have a remarkable impact on the communities of Bioche, and Colihaut, fostering a sense of reflection among their neighbors. Through their dedication to cultural sharing, Henri and Isabelle create an inviting atmosphere that inspires others to delve deeper into their own heritage. As the Sebastians host gatherings and participate in local events, the vibrant display of their traditions catalyzes broader community engagement, encouraging residents to explore and celebrate the richness of their cultural backgrounds.

Neighbors begin to take notice of the Sebastians' commitment to weaving their Venezuelan customs into the fabric of everyday life in Dominica. They see firsthand how traditional music, dance, and storytelling can bring people together, regardless of their origins. This inspiration spurs individuals and families within the community to reflect on their own cultural narratives, prompting conversations about their histories, traditions, and the importance of cultural preservation. The result is a growing appreciation for the diversity that exists within the communities, where different backgrounds and customs are highlighted and cherished.

As local families engage in discussions about their own heritage, they find opportunities to share unique elements of their cultures with one another. Potluck-style gatherings arise, where people bring traditional dishes from their own cultures, creating a culinary feast that celebrates the flavors of various backgrounds. Community events expand to include dance performances, artistic showcases, and storytelling circles, showcasing the rich tapestry of traditions that define the area. The Sebastien family's initiative turns into a collective endeavor, as more and more residents embrace the idea of sharing and learning from one another.

Henri and Isabelle's willingness to embrace and share their traditions not only enriches the lives of their own family but also encourages local families to actively engage with their cultural stories. This collective reflection cultivates a deeper sense of belonging within the community, as residents celebrate their diverse identities while forging new connections. By creating spaces for dialogue and cultural exchange, the Sebastians help foster a communal identity that is inclusive and vibrant, reflecting the unique contributions of each member of the community.

The Sebastien family's influence encourages a cultural renaissance in the villages of Bioche, and Colihaut, transforming the area's into a place where diversity is not only recognized but actively celebrated. This evolution fosters a spirit of unity and resilience, as neighbors support one another in their journey of cultural exploration. Through their shared experiences and newfound connections, the community grows stronger, demonstrating that the blending of different traditions can lead to a richer, more harmonious existence for all. In this way, the Sebastians leave an indelible mark on their new home, illustrating the profound impact that cultural sharing and appreciation can have on building a cohesive community.

To further foster appreciation for diversity and cultural sharing, Henri takes the initiative to organize cultural exchange events that draw community members together, celebrating the rich tapestry of traditions present in Bioche, and Colihaut. These gatherings serve as a platform for families to come together and share their unique customs, creating an atmosphere of unity and understanding. Each event is designed to highlight the vibrant cultures within the community, promoting connection and collaboration among attendees.

One of the central features of these cultural exchange events is the potluck, where families contribute dishes that reflect their culinary heritage. The table becomes a feast of flavors, showcasing everything from savory Venezuelan arepas and sweet natilla to traditional Caribbean dishes like callaloo and roti. This culinary diversity not only satisfies the palate but also sparks conversations about recipes, cooking techniques, and the stories behind each dish. As community members sample and savor one another's creations, they engage in lively discussions that deepen their understanding of different cultures and foster a sense of appreciation for culinary art.

In addition to food, Henri incorporates storytelling sessions into these events. Families can share folklore, legends, and personal narratives that reflect their cultural backgrounds. These stories, rich in history and meaning, captivate listeners and inspire a sense of wonder and reflection. By listening to one another's tales, community members gain insights into diverse experiences and perspectives, fostering empathy and mutual respect.

Art showcases also play a significant role in these gatherings, where local artists, including children, can display their work. From paintings that depict Caribbean landscapes to crafts that use traditional techniques, these exhibitions highlight the creativity and talent within the community. Participants are encouraged to discuss their artistic processes and the cultural significance behind their creations, further enriching the exchange of ideas and traditions.

The Sebastians' home becomes a focal point for these celebrations, transforming into a vibrant hub of activity and connection. As laughter and conversation flow freely, the gatherings create lasting bonds among diverse community members. Henri and Isabelle's warm hospitality and inclusive spirit invite everyone to participate, ensuring that people from all backgrounds feel welcomed and valued. These events not only strengthen existing friendships but also cultivate new relationships, enabling community members to connect meaningfully across cultural lines.

Through these cultural exchange events, Henri and Isabelle successfully promote a greater understanding of identity and heritage within their community. As neighbors celebrate their differences, they also uncover commonalities that unite them, creating a shared sense of belonging in Bioche, Dublanc, and Colihaut. This ongoing dialogue and exchange lay the groundwork for a more cohesive community, where diversity is not merely acknowledged but cherished, enriching the lives of everyone involved.

Henri and Isabelle's children embrace the opportunity to be ambassadors of their family's cultural legacy, actively participating in the cultural exchange events organized by their parents. With enthusiasm and pride, they showcase traditional Venezuelan dances, performing graceful movements that captivate their audience and bring a piece of their heritage to life. Their cheerful performances, filled with vibrant energy and joyful expression, spark curiosity among their peers, inviting questions about their culture and encouraging others to share their own traditions in return.

During these events, the Sebastien children also take the time to share stories from their heritage, recounting tales of beloved family gatherings and significant cultural rituals. They weave narratives that highlight the values of community, resilience, and love, effectively drawing listeners into the heart of their Venezuelan customs. As they speak, they notice their friends leaning in, captivated by the imagery and lessons woven into each tale. This sharing of stories not only showcases the beauty of their culture but also fosters a sense of connection and understanding between children of varying backgrounds.

Through their active engagement, the Sebastien children help to break down cultural barriers, fostering friendships across lines that may have previously felt insurmountable. They create a welcoming space for their peers to learn about and appreciate different customs, contributing to an environment that emphasizes inclusivity and collaboration. As they dance, tell stories, and make new friends, the children model a form of cultural diplomacy that enhances community spirit and encourages an appreciation for diversity.

The interactions and friendships formed during these events are testimonies to the positive impact of the Sebastien family's commitment to bridging cultures. Through laughter, shared experiences, and collective learning, the children embody a collective vision of harmony that resonates throughout the community. They demonstrate that cultural exchange is not merely about sharing food or traditions but also about building relationships that transcend differences, promoting unity and mutual respect.

In this way, Henri and Isabelle's children become vital players in the cultural narrative of Bioche, and Colihaut. Their role as ambassadors fosters a sense of belonging among their peers and reinforces the idea that embracing diversity enriches the lives of everyone involved. By encouraging their children to take pride in their heritage and share it openly, Henri and Isabelle help cultivate a new generation that values connection, celebrates differences, and actively contributes to a harmonious communal identity. This commitment to cultural exchange paves the way for a brighter, more inclusive future, where children learn to appreciate the beauty of diversity from a young age.

As time progresses, the Sebastien family takes a moment to reflect on their journey and the significant transformations within their community of Bioche. Looking back on their arrival, they remember the initial challenges of adapting to a new culture, navigating resource limitations, and finding their place in a diverse environment. However, through determination and resilience, they have turned those struggles into opportunities for growth and connection, both for themselves and for their neighbors.

Henri and Isabelle acknowledge that their dedication to education, engagement, and cultural exchange has played a pivotal role in influencing their surroundings. By organizing events that celebrate both Venezuelan traditions and local customs, they have created a platform for dialogue and mutual respect among community members. They recognize how these gatherings have become spaces where people can share their stories, celebrate their backgrounds, and learn from one another, thereby fostering deeper relationships that transcend cultural boundaries.

Their commitment to their heritage, combined with their willingness to embrace new experiences within Caribbean culture, has sown the seeds of understanding and acceptance throughout the community. The Sebastians have modeled the importance of openness and curiosity, encouraging others to explore their own cultural narratives while appreciating the rich diversity of their neighbors. They have seen firsthand how this spirit of collaboration not only enriches community life but also nurtures a true sense of belonging among residents.

As they reflect on the evolution of Bioche, and Colihaut, the Sebastians feel a profound sense of gratitude for the friendships they have forged and the connections that have blossomed. They see their children not merely as ambassadors of their Venezuelan traditions but as inspiring leaders within their community, fostering camaraderie and cultural exchange. The once-quiet gatherings in their home have now transformed into vibrant celebrations of diversity that draw attendees from various cultural backgrounds, highlighting the beauty of their shared humanity.

This journey of cultural integration has not only strengthened the Sebastien family but also enriched the entire community, creating a collective identity marked by appreciation, inclusion, and harmony. The transformations they witness serve as a testament to the power of cultural exchange and the profound impact that dedicated individuals can have in shaping their environment.

In reflecting on their experiences, Henri and Isabelle continually reaffirm their commitment to community engagement, recognizing that their journey is ongoing. They express hope for the future, envisioning a Bioche where cultural diversity is celebrated and where every individual feels a sense of connection and belonging. Through their efforts, they have indeed paved the way for a deeper understanding and acceptance within the community, leaving a legacy of unity and resilience that they hope will flourish for generations to come.

With the bonds of friendship and community strengthened the Sebastien family begins to envision a brighter future in Bioche. Embracing the growth, they have experienced, Henri and Isabelle remain committed to their mission of creating a nurturing environment for their children that honors their Venezuelan roots while also celebrating the beauty of Caribbean culture. They recognize the importance of instilling values of resilience, creativity, and cultural appreciation in their children, empowering them to navigate the complexities of a diverse world.

In their vision for the future, education plays a crucial role. The Sebastien family seeks to establish a home where learning extends beyond academic subjects to include cultural literacy and the arts. Henri and Isabelle encourage their children to explore their Venezuelan heritage through music, dance, and storytelling, while also immersing them in local Caribbean traditions. By fostering a love for both cultures, they aim to equip their children with a rich understanding of their identity and the ability to appreciate the diverse tapestry of human experiences.

The arts will remain a central focus in their family life, as Henri and Isabelle understand that creative expression is a powerful tool for bridging cultural divides. They hope to inspire their children to engage in artistic endeavors that reflect their heritage while also integrating local influences, promoting a unique blend of cultural expression. Whether through dance performances, art exhibitions, or music, the Sebastians envision their home becoming a hub of creativity that invites others to join in and share their talents.

Additionally, Henri and Isabelle are determined to build a legacy of cross-cultural understanding within the community. They aspire to continue organizing cultural exchange events that highlight the diverse backgrounds of their neighbors while fostering an atmosphere of collaboration and respect. By actively involving their children in these initiatives, they ensure that the spirit of cultural sharing is passed down to the next generation, reinforcing the idea that unity can thrive amid diversity.

As they look toward the future, the Sebastien family feels an overwhelming sense of hope and optimism. They envision a Bioche and Colihaut where mutual respect and appreciation are the norms, rather than the exceptions. They dream of a community where children grow up recognizing the value of their unique identities while appreciating the rich traditions of others. In this collective vision, cultural narratives intertwine, creating a dynamic environment that nurtures growth, understanding, and harmony.

With their unwavering dedication to family and community, Henri and Isabelle are inspired to continue their journey of cultural integration and engagement. They know that the path ahead may not always be easy, but their commitment to creating a legacy of resilience, creativity, and cross-cultural understanding will undoubtedly resonate for generations to come. As they forge ahead, the Sebastien family takes pride in knowing that their efforts are contributing to a brighter, more inclusive future, not only for themselves but for the entire community of Bioche, and Colihaut.

As the Sebastien family settles into their new life in Bioche, their journey becomes one of adaptation, connection, and shared growth. Each challenge they face is met with determination, and through their unwavering commitment to their cultural heritage and family traditions, they not only shape their identity but also leave a lasting impact on the community around them.

In embracing their new home, Henri, Isabelle, and their children embody the essence of resilience. They demonstrate that by fostering understanding, prioritizing education, and actively engaging in collaboration, distinct cultures can intersect to create a rich and harmonious tapestry of life in Bioche. Through cultural exchange events, shared stories, and artistic expressions, the Sebastians weave their Venezuelan roots into the fabric of Caribbean life, illustrating the beauty of cultural integration.

Their journey inspires others in the community to reflect on their own traditions, nurturing an environment where diversity is celebrated and cherished. The bonds of friendship forged through shared experiences redefine the meaning of community, bringing together neighbors from various backgrounds in a spirit of unity and respect.

In this new chapter, the Sebastien family not only lays a foundation for their children's future but also contributes to a legacy of cross-cultural understanding that resonates beyond their immediate family. As they continue to navigate the complexities of their new life, they exemplify how embracing both heritage and innovation can lead to a vibrant and inclusive community.

With every shared meal, dance, and story, the Sebastians plant seeds of connection that will flourish for generations to come. Their commitment to cultural pride and openness ensures that the story of their journey in Bioche will be one that echoes in the hearts and minds of those around them, creating a lasting impact that enriches the entire community. As a new chapter unfolds for the Sebastien family, it serves as a testament to the power of love, respect, and the enduring strength of community.

ⓒℬ

Part Five: Seeds of Change

Chapter Fourteen: Community Contributions

As Ledger and the Philogene family, along with Henri and the Sebastien family, begin to establish themselves in Dominica, their individual contributions to the community start to take shape, creating a tapestry of impact that enhances the local landscape. Each family brings unique experiences and perspectives, shaping their roles within the community and fostering connections that transcend cultural boundaries.

Ledger channels his efforts into agriculture and trade, recognizing the importance of sustainable food systems and economic empowerment. With a deep understanding of the land and its potential, he works diligently to implement innovative agricultural practices that not only benefit his family but also contribute to local food security and economic resilience. Through collaboration with other farmers, Ledger cultivates relationships that strengthen the agricultural community, promoting a spirit of cooperation and mutual support.

Meanwhile, Henri focuses on education and cultural enrichment, believing that knowledge is a powerful tool for empowerment and change. He is dedicated to creating educational programs that celebrate cultural heritage while equipping the next generation with the skills needed to navigate the complexities of modern society. Henri's initiatives foster an appreciation for diversity and encourage critical thinking, enabling children and families to thrive in an ever-changing world.

As these two families work towards their individual goals, their contributions inevitably intersect, revealing the interconnectedness of their efforts. Ledger's focus on agriculture complements Henri's educational pursuits, providing students with hands-on learning opportunities about sustainable farming, nutrition, and the significance of local produce. In turn, Henri's educational initiatives raise awareness about the importance of food security, encouraging a culture of sustainability that resonates throughout the community.

Together, the Sebastien and Philogene families navigate the complexities of colonial legacies, community dynamics, and aspirations for a brighter future. Their shared experiences enhance their understanding of the historical context within which they operate, prompting them to consider how past injustices can inform their present actions. By fostering dialogues about heritage and mutual respect, they encourage a more nuanced understanding of identity and belonging in Dominica, paving the way for healing and collaboration.

Their collective efforts serve as a model for community engagement, demonstrating that through collaboration, respect, and a shared vision for the future, diverse cultures can coalesce into a cohesive community. As Ledger and Henri continue to work together, they embody the spirit of resilience and innovation necessary to overcome challenges and foster a thriving environment for all. The impact of their contributions will not only benefit their families but also resonate throughout the community, inspiring others to join in the pursuit of a brighter, more inclusive future for Dominica.

Driven by his dedication to farming, Ledger works tirelessly to optimize his land in Au-Fonde, believing that sustainable agriculture is essential not only for his success but for the health of the entire community. Understanding the delicate balance between farming and environmental stewardship, he experiments with innovative techniques that honor both the local ecosystem and his commitment to building a robust agricultural community.

One of Ledger's primary initiatives involves implementing crop rotation, a practice that enhances soil health and minimizes pest issues. By rotating different crops in sequential seasons, he prevents nutrient depletion and reduces the likelihood of diseases that can affect specific plants. This method not only boosts its yields but also improves the overall quality of the soil, making it more fertile for future harvests.

In addition to crop rotation, Ledger adopts intercropping techniques, planting complementary crops in proximity to one another. This strategy allows different plants to benefit from one another, promoting biodiversity and maximizing land use efficiency. For instance, pairing legumes with nutrient-demanding crops helps naturally enrich the soil with nitrogen, reducing the need for chemical fertilizers. By diversifying his planting strategy, he creates a more resilient agricultural system that can better withstand pests, diseases, and climate fluctuations.

As Ledger's practice flourishes, he becomes a living example for his neighbors, demonstrating the tangible benefits of environmentally mindful agriculture. His success encourages fellow farmers in the Au-Fonde area to reconsider their own methods, sparking conversations about sustainable practices and the importance of preserving the local ecosystem. Ledger welcomes these dialogues, often inviting his neighbors to visit his farm and share their insights and experiences. He believes that through collaboration and shared knowledge, the community can collectively improve their agricultural practices.

Furthermore, Ledger actively participates in local farmer's markets and agricultural fairs, where he showcases the fruits of his labor and shares his innovations. By openly discussing the benefits of sustainable farming, he inspires others to adopt similar practices, fostering a culture of environmental responsibility that resonates throughout the community.

Through his unwavering commitment and visionary approach to farming, Ledger plays a crucial role in reviving local agriculture in Au-Fonde. His initiatives not only yield greater food production but also cultivate a sense of camaraderie among farmers who recognize the importance of working together for the common good. As the community embraces more sustainable practices, they move closer to achieving food security and environmental stewardship, highlighting the transformative power of dedicated individuals like Ledger in shaping a brighter future for Dominica.

Recognizing the importance of trade in fostering community relationships, Ledger takes a proactive step by establishing a local market where farmers can gather to sell their produce. This initiative transforms a simple open space into a vibrant hub of activity, where the richness of local agriculture and the diversity of culinary traditions can flourish.

The market becomes a lively venue for community engagement, where farmers not only sell their fresh fruits, vegetables, and other products but also exchange ideas and experiences with one another. Ledger's leadership in organizing the market is pivotal in creating a welcoming atmosphere that encourages collaboration, knowledge-sharing, and mutual support among local producers.

In curating the market, Ledger ensures that it reflects the unique offerings of the community, highlighting seasonal crops and artisanal products. He invites farmers from surrounding areas to participate, fostering a spirit of inclusiveness and diversity that enriches the market. The stalls come alive with colorful displays of produce, homemade goods, and culinary delights, showcasing the bounty of Dominica and allowing farmers to take full ownership of their products and livelihoods.

Beyond mere commerce, the market serves as a platform for cultural exchange. Community members gather not only to shop but also to share recipes and cooking tips, engaging in conversations about their culinary traditions. This sharing of knowledge helps preserve and celebrate the rich heritage of the region while introducing new flavors and techniques to local cuisine. Ledger facilitates these interactions, reminding attendees of the importance of food education and the stories behind each product.

By establishing this local market, Ledger promotes food security within the community. He encourages local consumption of produce and goods, reducing dependence on imported products while supporting the local economy. The market empowers farmers to set fair prices for their goods, providing them with opportunities to earn a sustainable income. This economic empowerment fosters greater resilience within the community and enhances the overall well-being of its members.

As the market thrives, it becomes a symbol of unity, drawing people from various backgrounds together around a shared appreciation for local agriculture and culinary traditions. Ledger's vision of fostering community relationships through trade proves successful, creating trust and collaboration among local producers while ensuring that everyone has access to fresh, nutritious food.

In this dynamic space, friendships blossom, and community ties strengthen, reinforcing the idea that when individuals come together for a common purpose, they can effectively create a supportive and thriving environment. Ledger's commitment to market engagement not only enhances the economic landscape of Au-Fonde but also enriches the social fabric of the community, paving the way for a brighter, more interconnected future for all.

Understanding that knowledge is a vital component of sustainable farming, Ledger takes the initiative to hold workshops aimed at educating local farmers about modern agricultural techniques and organic practices. Recognizing that many farmers may feel intimidated by new methods, Ledger creates an inclusive environment where knowledge is shared openly, fostering community collaboration and empowerment.

In these workshops, Ledger invites experts in various fields such as soil health, pest management, and sustainable agriculture to share their insights and experiences. These guest speakers bring a wealth of knowledge and practical advice, equipping local farmers with the tools they need to improve their farming practices. By providing valuable resources, Ledger ensures that his neighbors have access to the latest information, making it easier for them to implement effective strategies on their own farms.

During these sessions, Ledger emphasizes the importance of soil health, teaching farmers about composting, cover cropping, and natural fertilizers. He illustrates how these practices not only enhance soil fertility but also contribute to higher yields and reduced environmental impact. By demystifying these concepts and demonstrating their practicality, Ledger encourages farmers to adopt organic methods that lead to long-term sustainability.

Additionally, Ledger addresses pest management, introducing integrated pest management (IPM) techniques that focus on ecological balance rather than chemical reliance. Farmers learn about beneficial insects, natural repellents, and crop rotation methods that help control pests while nurturing the health of their crops. The workshops create a platform for discussing common challenges and brainstorming solutions collectively, reinforcing a sense of camaraderie among participants.

As Ledger shares his insights and experiences, he builds trust within the community. Farmers often express their gratitude for the opportunity to learn and collaborate, and this goodwill fosters stronger relationships among neighbors. Through open dialogue and shared learning, Ledger emphasizes the notion that together they can overcome challenges and thrive.

These educational workshops not only enhance individual farming practices but also contribute to the overall resilience of the agricultural community in Au-Fonde. As farmers adopt new techniques and share their successes, they inspire one another to continuously improve and innovate. This shared commitment to education and collaboration strengthens the bonds within the community, ensuring that everyone is equipped to navigate the complexities of modern agriculture.

Ledger's efforts in educating local farmers cultivate a culture of continuous learning and support. By prioritizing knowledge sharing and sustainable practices, he is nurturing a thriving agricultural community that can withstand challenges and adapt to future needs. The workshops represent a significant step toward empowering local farmers, enhancing food security, and fostering a resilient agricultural landscape in Dominica.

In contrast to Ledger's focus on agricultural practices, Henri channels his passion for the arts and education into crafting innovative programs at local schools in Dominica. Understanding that education extends beyond traditional subjects, he designs curriculum modules that incorporate cultural history and the arts, ensuring that children receive a well-rounded education that encompasses the rich legacies of both Venezuelan and Caribbean cultures.

Henri's curriculum is thoughtfully crafted, blending academic learning with artistic expression. He introduces lessons that explore the history, music, dance, and visual arts of both cultures, allowing students to understand their heritage while appreciating the diversity of their community. By integrating cultural content into subjects like history and language arts, Henri creates a holistic learning experience that fosters critical thinking and cultural pride among students.

One of Henri's notable initiatives is the introduction of cultural exchange days, where students engage in hands-on activities such as traditional music workshops, dance classes, and art projects that celebrate the contributions of both Venezuelan and Caribbean traditions. These interactive sessions not only enhance students' artistic skills but also build a sense of community, as they learn to respect and appreciate each other's backgrounds.

Henri's innovative approach inspires local teachers to adopt similar methodologies, encouraging them to create lessons that reflect the multicultural makeup of the classroom. As teachers witness the positive impact of Henri's programs, they begin to incorporate more inclusive practices into their own teaching, fostering diverse educational environments where all students feel valued and represented. This collaborative spirit enhances the overall educational landscape, promoting a rich tapestry of learning experiences that celebrate cultural heritage.

Moreover, Henri emphasizes the importance of parental and community involvement in the educational process. He encourages families to participate in school events, share their own cultural stories, and contribute to the curriculum. This engagement strengthens the bond between the school and the community, creating a supportive network that enriches the learning environment for all students.

Through these innovative educational programs, Henri not only enhances the curriculum but also cultivates a spirit of creativity and cultural awareness among the children of Dominica. His efforts contribute to a deeper understanding of identity and heritage, helping students develop a sense of belonging that transcends societal divisions.

Henri's commitment to integrating cultural history and the arts into education is transformative. By equipping students with a diverse and inclusive academic experience, he empowers them to become culturally aware and engaged citizens. As his programs receive recognition and support from the community, they lay the groundwork for a more expansive and dynamic educational approach that enriches the lives of students and fosters a renewed appreciation for the beauty of cultural diversity in Dominica.

To further enrich the communities, Henri organizes cultural workshops where families can come together to share their stories, music, and dances. These events serve as vibrant gatherings that foster a sense of belonging and community pride, allowing individuals of all ages to connect through the arts. By creating a safe and inclusive space, Henri invites artists, educators, and community members to collaborate and share their unique experiences, enhancing the cultural fabric of Dominica.

Each workshop is thoughtfully designed to encourage participation and engagement. Henri incorporates various activities, including storytelling sessions, traditional music performances, and dance workshops, where community members can showcase their talents and learn from one another. These interactive events allow children and adults alike to explore their cultural heritage, fostering a deeper appreciation for the diverse backgrounds that comprise their community.

During storytelling sessions, participants gather in a circle, sharing folktales, personal anecdotes, and historical narratives that reflect their cultural identities. This exchange of stories not only strengthens interpersonal connections but also ignites curiosity among younger participants, encouraging them to ask questions and engage with their own traditions. The stories exchanged serve as bridges between generations, preserving cultural legacies while instilling pride and respect for one another's histories.

In addition to storytelling, the workshops feature live music and dance performances that celebrate the rhythmic and expressive aspects of both Venezuelan and Caribbean cultures. Participants are invited to join in, whether by playing instruments, dancing, or singing along, creating a lively atmosphere filled with joy and enthusiasm. These shared artistic expressions allow attendees to experience the richness of their multicultural heritage firsthand and promote a sense of unity that transcends individual differences.

By emphasizing collaboration and interaction among participants, Henri helps to break down barriers and build a strong sense of community. The cultural workshops empower attendees to embrace their unique identities while recognizing the strengths and beauty that arise from multicultural interactions. As families come together to celebrate and learn, they foster friendships and camaraderie that extend beyond the workshops, enriching everyday life in Dominica.

The impact of these workshops extends far beyond the events themselves. They create a ripple effect throughout the community, inspiring participants to engage in cultural exchange initiatives and encourage artistic endeavors within their own homes and neighborhoods. By prioritizing cultural education and collaboration, Henri is laying the groundwork for a more inclusive, vibrant, and resilient community that values the contributions of all its members.

Henri's commitment to organizing cultural workshops catalyzes healing and understanding. By bringing families together to share their stories and celebrate their cultural identities, he cultivates an environment where diversity is cherished, and collective strength is recognized. Through these enriching experiences, participants not only gain a deeper understanding of one another but also unite in their shared aspirations for a harmonious and interconnected community in Dominica.

Henri is dedicated to empowering and uplifting young voices within the community, recognizing that the next generation holds the potential to shape the future. To nurture the artistic talents of children, he develops targeted programs designed to encourage self-expression through various art forms. By establishing after-school art clubs and writing workshops, Henri provides a platform for children to explore their creativity, fostering an environment where their unique perspectives can thrive.

The after-school art clubs serve as a creative haven for young artists. Henri introduces them to different mediums—such as painting, sculpture, and digital art, allowing them to experiment and discover their preferred forms of expression. Each session is tailored to explore themes relevant to their lives and cultures, encouraging participants to reflect on their experiences and articulate their thoughts through art. This hands-on approach not only develops their artistic skills but also instills a sense of pride and ownership over their creative work.

In parallel, Henri organizes writing workshops that invite children to express their stories, thoughts, and dreams through the written word. By introducing them to various literary styles—such as poetry, fiction, and creative non-fiction, Henri encourages them to articulate their emotions and experiences. Through writing exercises and group discussions, the children learn the power of storytelling and the impact it can have on their communities. This process not only builds their writing skills but also enhances their confidence as they recognize the value of their voices.

Central to Henri's mission is his belief that every child has the potential to become a leader and changemaker. By providing them with the tools and support to cultivate their artistic talents, he empowers them to advocate for their ideas and beliefs. The skills they acquire in the art clubs and writing workshops serve as a foundation for their growth, equipping them with the confidence needed to engage in broader community issues as they mature.

The impact of these programs extends beyond individual expression. As children develop their talents and gain confidence, they begin to engage more actively in their communities. Henri encourages them to showcase their work at local events, enabling them to share their stories and art with family and neighbors. These showcases not only validate their efforts but also inspire others in the community to recognize the rich diversity of voices present in Bioche, Dublanc, and Colihaut.

Henri also emphasizes the importance of mentorship within these programs, inviting local artists and writers to guide the children. This connection fosters a sense of community and continuity, as established artists share their experiences and insights, creating a supportive network that empowers young talents. Through these mentorship experiences, children learn the significance of collaboration, resilience, and passion for the arts.

Henri's commitment to empowering local voices lays the groundwork for future leaders and changemakers. By fostering creativity and confidence in young artists and writers, he nurtures a generation that values self-expression and cultural heritage. As these children grow, they carry with them the lessons learned through Henri's programs, ready to contribute positively to their communities and advocate for the change they wish to see. Through his dedication, Henri is not just cultivating artistic talents; he is shaping the future of Bioche, Dublanc, and Colihaut, ensuring a vibrant, expressive, and engaged society for years to come.

Both Ledger and Henri grapple with the remnants of colonial legacies that continue to shape community dynamics in Dominica. Recognizing that history profoundly influences current social structures, they are acutely aware of the complexities surrounding land ownership, social hierarchies, and access to resources. By acknowledging these legacies, Ledger and Henri inform people of their approaches to community building, prompting them to foster inclusivity and equity in their interactions and initiatives.

Ledger, as he invests in sustainable agriculture and trade, understands that land ownership in Dominica is often laden with historical injustices. The legacy of colonialism has resulted in complex land disputes and a lack of equitable access to agricultural resources for many families. As he optimizes his land in Au-Fonde, he works not only to improve his own farming practices but also to advocate for a fairer distribution of resources among local farmers. He encourages dialogue about land rights, inviting community members to participate in discussions that address historical grievances and explore collaborative solutions. By fostering a sense of shared ownership and responsibility, Ledger strives to create a more equitable agricultural landscape for all.

Similarly, Henri's commitment to education and the arts is profoundly shaped by his awareness of social hierarchies and the historical context of access to education in Dominica. He is mindful that certain communities have been marginalized, often lacking the resources and opportunities available to others. By developing inclusive programs that celebrate cultural diversity and artistic expression, Henri directly addresses these disparities. His workshops and after-school clubs provide a platform for children from all backgrounds to engage with their heritage, empowering them to reclaim their narratives and assert their identities.

Henri encourages conversations around the historical context of education itself, emphasizing the importance of teaching students about their histories and the legacies of their ancestors. This approach not only fosters pride in their cultural identities but also arms them with the knowledge necessary to navigate the complexities of contemporary society. By helping young people understand the historical forces that have shaped their lives, Henri equips them with the tools to challenge existing inequalities and advocate for a more just community.

Together, Ledger and Henri exemplify a thoughtful engagement with the past as they navigate the complexities of their present. They recognize that understanding the historical context is essential for fostering meaningful community connections and for building a future that is inclusive and equitable. Their commitment to addressing the remnants of colonialism in their initiatives reflects a broader understanding that true community building requires introspection and a conscious effort to dismantle oppressive structures.

In their respective roles, Ledger and Henri are not only addressing immediate community needs but are also working to reshape the narrative around colonial legacies. By fostering inclusivity and equity in their interactions and initiatives, they embody a vision for a community where all voices are heard and valued, allowing for the healing of historical wounds and the forging of a brighter, more unified future for Dominica.

Despite their different focuses, Ledger and Henri share a common aspiration: to empower their community. Both men recognize that agricultural sustainability and educational enrichment are not isolated endeavors; rather, they are interconnected facets that contribute to the broader goal of building a resilient and self-sufficient community in Dominica. By leveraging their unique strengths, Ledger and Henri aim to create a transformative environment where all members can thrive.

Ledger's commitment to sustainable farming practices not only enhances food security but also promotes environmental stewardship and economic independence. He understands that a vibrant agricultural sector is essential for community wellbeing, providing local families with fresh produce while cultivating an appreciation for the land and its resources. Ledger believes that when farmers are empowered to practice sustainable agriculture, they contribute to preserving the local ecosystem, ensuring that future generations can continue to benefit from their resources.

In turn, Henri's focus on educational enrichment complements Ledger's agricultural initiatives. By nurturing the artistic talents of young people and incorporating cultural history into the curriculum, he fosters creative thinking and critical awareness among the next generation. Henri's belief in the power of education as a tool for social change aligns seamlessly with Ledger's vision for a self-sufficient community. When children are educated and empowered, they grow into informed adults who can advocate for their needs and contribute positively to society.

Their collaboration on community events serves as a testament to their commitment to creating a brighter future for their children, unmarred by the inequalities of the past. By organizing festivals, workshops, and market gatherings together, they exemplify how agriculture and education can intersect to strengthen community bonds. These events not only celebrate local talent and tradition but also provide platforms for families to come together and share their stories, experiences, and aspirations.

Moreover, Ledger and Henri recognize that addressing the remnants of colonial legacies requires collective action. Through their partnership, they create a holistic approach to community building, ensuring that both agricultural sustainability and educational opportunities are accessible to all. Their combined efforts embody a vision of equity and inclusivity, where everyone has the chance to voice their concerns and play a role in shaping the community's future.

As they work side by side, Ledger and Henri inspire others to join their cause, fostering a sense of unity and shared purpose within the community. Together, they empower individuals to dream big and strive for change, laying the groundwork for a resilient, self-sufficient community that honors its heritage while looking forward to a hopeful future. With shared aspirations and collaborative spirit, they are paving the way for a Dominica where both agriculture and education thrive hand in hand, creating lasting impact for generations to come.

As Ledger and Henri navigate the complexities of colonial influences within their community, they inevitably encounter resistance from some members who are skeptical of change. This skepticism often stems from historical grievances and a distrust of new initiatives, making it challenging to rally widespread support for their vision of empowerment and sustainability. However, Ledger and Henri are undeterred. Their determination to create opportunities for collaboration and growth paves the way for meaningful dialogue and understanding.

Recognizing that change can be intimidating, Ledger and Henri proactively engage with community leaders and residents, seeking to foster open conversations about their initiatives. They listen carefully to the concerns expressed by skeptics, acknowledging the complexities of the past while highlighting the potential for a renewed and equitable future. By ensuring that all voices are heard, they cultivate trust and demonstrate that their intentions are rooted in respect and inclusivity.

Through their discussions, Ledger shares the tangible benefits of sustainable agricultural practices, illustrating how these methods not only enhance food security but also bolster local economies. He provides examples of successful farms that have adopted these practices and the positive impact that such changes can have on the community. By presenting data and real-life success stories, he addresses fears head-on and illustrates how innovation can coexist with tradition.

Similarly, Henri emphasizes the importance of education in breaking the cycle of inequality and fostering a more culturally informed generation. He invites parents and community members to participate in workshops that showcase the positive outcomes of his programs, such as improved creativity and academic performance among children. Through demonstrations and interactive sessions, Henri makes it clear how investing in education enriches not just individual futures but the collective well-being of the community.

In their advocacy, both Ledger and Henri embody a spirit of patience and perseverance. They understand that changing deeply rooted beliefs takes time and sustains effort. By remaining committed to their vision, they serve as role models for resilience, demonstrating that progress can be achieved through respectful engagement and collaboration.

To further bridge divides, Ledger and Henri also organize community forums that encourage participation from all demographics. These forums provide a platform for open dialogue where community members can express their doubts, ask questions, and share their own experiences related to both agriculture and education. Leveraging these interactions, Ledger and Henri adapt their initiatives based on the feedback received, ensuring that the community feels invested in the changes being proposed.

The challenges they face strengthen their resolve to create a collective vision that honors the past while working toward a more equitable future. By building trust and cultivating understanding, Ledger and Henri transform skepticism into a catalyst for change. Through their commitment to dialogue and collaboration, they inspire others to reimagine the possibilities for their community, fostering a sense of shared purpose and unity that transcends historical divisions.

As they continue this journey, Ledger and Henri remain hopeful that, with persistence and patience, they can empower their community to embrace change and cultivate a brighter, more inclusive future for all.

The contributions of Ledger and Henri significantly lead to the emergence of strong ties within the community, fostering a dynamic environment where relationships are built across cultural lines. Ledger's market has evolved into a vibrant hub, not just for trade but also for cultural exchange. By creating a space where local farmers can sell their produce, Ledger facilitates not only economic growth but also the sharing of stories, traditions, and practices that enrich the community's cultural landscape.

Recognizing the market's potential as a focal point for cultural interactions, Henri actively encourages artistic demonstrations and performances that celebrate the diverse backgrounds of local farmers and their families. He organizes events such as music festivals, dance performances, and craft fairs, inviting artisans, musicians, and dancers from various cultural traditions to showcase their talents. These events not only draw crowds but also create opportunities for the community to engage with different art forms and narratives, allowing residents to learn about and appreciate each other's heritages.

Through these cultural exchanges, residents begin to break down the barriers that often separate them, fostering a spirit of collaboration and unity. As they share meals featuring local dishes, participate in dance workshops, or listen to storytelling sessions that highlight their unique histories, community members celebrate their differences while recognizing their shared humanity. Henri's emphasis on inclusivity and cultural appreciation reinforces the idea that diversity is a strength, and these interactions ensure that no voice goes unheard.

These events also serve as a platform for dialogue, where residents can discuss not only their cultural practices but also the challenges they face as a community. By creating an atmosphere of understanding, Ledger and Henri facilitate conversations that bridge gaps and encourage cooperation. For example, farmers may share sustainability practices rooted in their cultural traditions, while artists discuss how their work can contribute to community initiatives. This exchange of ideas fosters mutual respect and inspires collective problem-solving.

As families come together to support each other's creative endeavors and agricultural pursuits, new friendships blossom. Children play together, learning from each other while engaging in cultural exchanges, such as cooking traditional dishes or participating in local festivals. These interactions nurture a sense of belonging and solidarity, empowering the younger generation to embrace diversity as a natural part of their community fabric.

Moreover, Ledger's market becomes an example for other communities on the importance of building relationships across cultures. By demonstrating how cultural exchange and collaboration can enhance community welfare, Ledger and Henri inspire neighboring towns to adopt similar approaches, enriching the entire region.

The collaborative efforts of Ledger and Henri not only strengthen individual relationships but also contribute to the collective identity of the community. By celebrating diversity and encouraging cultural exchange, they lay the groundwork for a resilient, interconnected society, where residents appreciate their differences and work together toward common goals. This shared commitment to building relationships across cultures fosters a sense of pride and unity, ensuring that the legacy of their collaborative spirit continues to thrive in Dominica for generations to come.

As community ties strengthen, Ledger and Henri bring their visions together to collaboratively organize festivals that spotlight both agricultural and artistic achievements. These events become highly anticipated occasions, attracting families from all corners of the community who come together to celebrate not only the fruits of the harvest but also the creativity and talents that flourish within their midst.

During these vibrant festivals, Ledger showcases the season's bountiful produce, inviting local farmers to display their fresh fruits, vegetables, and artisanal goods. At the same time, Henri curates artistic exhibitions featuring local artists' work, ranging from paintings and sculptures to performances by musicians and dancers. This fusion of agriculture and the arts creates a festive atmosphere, highlighting the diverse offerings of the community and reinforcing the idea that both sectors are vital to their collective identity.

As families gather at the festivals, the excitement is palpable. Children run between stalls, eager to taste freshly made dishes and engage in hands-on activities like vegetable painting or crafting cultural masks. Live music fills the air, and dance performances captivate audiences, creating shared moments of joy and celebration. The festivals serve as a reminder that everyone's contributions, whether through farming, artistry, or hospitality, are integral to the community's success.

Moreover, these celebrations foster a deep sense of pride among residents, as they showcase their unique cultural heritages while acknowledging the interconnectedness of their efforts. Residents take turns sharing stories about their families' agricultural practices and artistic traditions, enriching the celebration with personal narratives that weave together the community's history. By spotlighting these stories, Ledger and Henri cultivate a climate of appreciation for the diverse backgrounds that shape their collective identity.

The festivals also serve as a platform for community engagement, inviting local leaders and organizations to participate and collaborate. Workshops, discussions, and information booths provide opportunities for residents to learn about sustainable practices, cultural preservation, and community health initiatives. These elements ensure the festivals are not simply moments of celebration but also vehicles for education and empowerment.

Through their collaborative efforts, Ledger and Henri reinforce the idea that the health of the community relies on the strength of its relationships. The festivals symbolize a collective commitment to unity, resilience, and growth. As families come together to share their harvests and talents, they further solidify the understanding that their aspirations for a better future are intertwined.

The positive impact of these shared celebrations extends beyond the event itself, inspiring community members to engage in collaborative efforts year-round. The enthusiasm generated during the festivals motivates individuals to participate in local projects, whether it is supporting sustainable farming practices or encouraging artistic expression in schools and community centers.

The shared festivals and celebrations orchestrated by Ledger and Henri capture the spirit of community unity and resilience. They remind everyone of the value of collaboration and the strength that comes from celebrating both agricultural bounty and artistic achievement together. Through these cherished events, the community not only honors its past but also embraces a hopeful future, where the rich tapestry of cultures and shared dreams continues to thrive in Dominica.

The seeds of change planted by Ledger and Henri have blossomed into a powerful collective commitment to shaping an inclusive community where the aspirations of all families are recognized and nurtured. Through their collaborative efforts, they foster an environment that values every individual's contributions, emphasizing that the strength of the community lies in its unity and shared goals.

As Ledger and Henri engage with their neighbors, they discover that true progress is achieved not through isolated efforts, but through the collaboration and support of the community. They witness firsthand how their initiatives—whether in agriculture or the arts—thrive when connected with others who share the same vision for a brighter future. This realization serves as a guiding principle for their work, motivating them to encourage a spirit of partnership among residents.

Their commitment to inclusivity becomes a hallmark of their legacy. By ensuring that all voices are heard, Ledger and Henri create opportunities for families to participate in decision-making processes that affect their lives. Community meetings and open forums allow residents to express their ideas, concerns, and dreams, fostering a sense of ownership in the direction of their community. This participatory approach cultivates deep-rooted relationships, enhancing trust and solidarity among families.

Furthermore, Ledger and Henri celebrate the shared achievements of the community, regularly highlighting the stories of those who contribute to its richness. By showcasing the diverse talents and backgrounds of their neighbors, whether through cultural events, markets, or public recognition, they instill a sense of pride in collective identity. Families are reminded that their individual successes are part of a larger narrative that reflects the resilience and creativity of the entire community.

The legacy of collaboration not only propels Ledger and Henri forward but also inspires others to take an active role in shaping their environment. As the community witnesses the positive changes resulting from their efforts, more residents are motivated to join in, contributing their skills and resources to various initiatives. This ripple effect strengthens the foundations of community life, creating a culture where mutual support and collaboration become second nature.

With a clear vision for the future, Ledger and Henri remain determined to cultivate pride, resilience, and hope for generations to come. They understand that the culture of collaboration they have nurtured will empower future leaders and changemakers, ensuring that the community continues to flourish.

As they move forward, they acknowledge the importance of passing on this legacy to the younger generation. They actively engage youth through educational programs and mentorship, fostering a new wave of community stewardship. By teaching them the value of collaboration and the significance of their contributions, Ledger and Henri plant the seeds for a more connected and dynamic future.

The legacy of collaboration forged by Ledger and Henri extends far beyond their individual efforts. It embodies a vision for a cohesive community that prioritizes inclusivity and collective success. As these seeds of change take root, they promise a flourishing future where every family feels valued and empowered, forging a path of shared aspirations and a vibrant, united Dominica.

As Ledger and Henri contribute to the community in their unique ways, their efforts intertwine to create a solid foundation for a better future in Bioche and Colihaut. Together, they navigate the complexities of colonial legacies and shared aspirations, fostering a spirit of collaboration and resilience that uplifts the entire community.

Through Ledger's dedication to sustainable agriculture and Henri's commitment to education and cultural enrichment, they address the pressing needs of their neighbors while simultaneously celebrating the diverse strengths present within their community. Their individual initiatives complement each other, creating a holistic approach to community empowerment that not only addresses immediate challenges but also lays the groundwork for lasting change.

As they work side by side, Ledger and Henri sow the seeds of change that will empower their children and future generations. They instill a sense of pride in their heritage, encouraging the younger members of the community to appreciate their roots while also dreaming of a bright future. The festivals, markets, and educational programs they create are not just events; they are milestones in the community's journey toward growth and inclusivity.

In this spirit of collaboration, Ledger and Henri illuminate a path forward that emphasizes unity and shared purpose. Their efforts remind everyone that progress is achievable through mutual support and understanding, as well as through recognizing the interconnectedness of agriculture, education, and culture.

The story of Bioche and Colihaut is one of hope and possibility. The foundation built by Ledger and Henri reflects a commitment to nurturing a resilient community that honors its past while actively working toward a more equitable and flourishing future. As the seeds they have planted continue to grow, they inspire all members of the community to participate in shaping a world filled with opportunity and promise, ensuring that the legacy of collaboration lives on for generations to come.

೫

Chapter Fifteen: Challenges Arising

As the Sebastien and Philogene families continue to make strides in contributing to their community, they inevitably encounter unforeseen challenges that threaten their progress. Ledger's agricultural efforts, while aimed at fostering sustainability and food security, are met with economic hardships that test his resilience and determination. Rising costs, market fluctuations, and issues related to land access complicate his mission to enhance agricultural practices and support local farmers. These obstacles create tension not only for Ledger but also for the entire community, as the success of local agriculture is intricately linked to the wellbeing of families in Bioche, and Colihaut.

Simultaneously, Henri's advocacy for education presents its own set of conflicts, particularly as it intersects with traditional views on societal roles. His efforts to promote educational equity and cultural enrichment challenge long-standing norms about education and its purpose within the community. Resistance from those who hold on to conventional beliefs about education often creates friction, with some community members questioning the value of incorporating creativity and cultural history into the curriculum. This tension highlights the broader struggle between progressive ideals and entrenched traditions, prompting important discussions about the direction in which the community should move.

As local events unfold and political tensions rise, both families find themselves navigating a complex landscape of community dynamics and socio-political issues affecting Dominica. Political instability, economic pressures, and social inequalities create a backdrop where conflicts can easily escalate. Ledger and Henri must contend not only with their respective challenges but also with the reactions and interactions of their neighbors, who are often grappling with their own struggles and differing perspectives.

Despite these challenges, the interactions between the Sebastien and Philogene families, and within their communities, also pave the way for mutual respect and collaborative action. As they confront conflicts related to agricultural sustainability and educational reform, they recognize the importance of solidarity and dialogue in addressing broader socio-political issues. Their shared experiences of resilience in the face of adversity inspire them to work together, promoting a vision of a united community that can overcome challenges collectively.

Through these shared conflicts and the pursuit of common goals, Ledger and Henri demonstrate how embracing differences and fostering understanding can lead to constructive change. Their journey encapsulates the complexities of community life, highlighting how conflict can catalyze collaboration, and enrich the social fabric of Dominica. As they navigate this intricate terrain, the Sebastien and Philogene families embody hope for a future where respectful dialogue and teamwork help to mitigate tensions and drive positive transformation within their communities.

Ledger's commitment to sustainable agriculture is increasingly strained as market prices fluctuate unpredictably. These fluctuations create a precarious environment for farmers, making it challenging for Ledger to forecast his profits and plan effectively for the future. As prices for his crops drop or fail to meet expectations, the pressure mounts, leaving Ledger to grapple with the harsh realities of maintaining a profitable agricultural business.

Additionally, the rising costs of supplies and labor complicate his efforts to sustain profitability. Essential inputs such as seeds, fertilizers, and equipment have seen significant price increases, forcing Ledger to reevaluate his farming practices. He strives to use organic methods and sustainable resources, but the cost of these eco-friendly options is often higher than conventional alternatives.

This dilemma puts him at a crossroads, as he must balance his commitment to sustainable practices with the immediate need to keep his operation financially viable.

With expenses mounting, Ledger finds it increasingly difficult to keep up with the financial demands of running his estate. This struggle has far-reaching implications—not just for his business but also for the local farmers depending on him for leadership and support. Many of these farmers look to Ledger for guidance on sustainable practices and rely on his success as a benchmark for their own. If his estate falters, it could jeopardize the livelihoods of those who have invested their hopes and resources in sustainable agriculture within the community.

As Ledger navigates this challenging landscape, he faces a profound sense of responsibility. The pressure to sustain his family and uphold his vision for agricultural resilience weighs heavily on his shoulders. Balancing his ideals with the pressing realities of the market leads to sleepless nights and difficult decisions. He often contemplates whether to pivot to more conventional farming methods that might offer immediate financial relief but at the expense of long-term sustainability.

In this context, Ledger's determination is tested as he seeks innovative solutions to combat the financial strain. He begins exploring potential partnerships with local cooperatives to share resources and minimize costs, hoping to create a more supportive network for farmers facing similar challenges. Ledger also contemplates diversifying his crops, potentially focusing on high-demand products that can cushion the impact of market volatility.

Despite the mounting challenges, Ledger remains steadfast in his belief that sustainable agriculture is the path forward for not just his estate but the entire community. He continues to advocate for greater awareness around the importance of buying local, hoping to cultivate a sense of solidarity among consumers. By educating the community about the benefits of supporting local farmers, he aims to stabilize market demand for his products, a crucial step in ensuring that both his ambitions and those of his fellow farmers do not fade away.

Ledger's journey through the turmoil of market fluctuations highlights the fragility of sustainable agriculture in a volatile economic landscape. His experience serves as a reminder of the interconnectedness of local farming systems and the profound impact that external economic factors can have on the resilience of communities. As he grapples with these challenges, Ledger remains committed to finding a way forward, deeply aware that his efforts are not just about maintaining an estate; they are about nurturing a community and preserving the future of sustainable agriculture in Dominica.

The agricultural landscape in Dominica is becoming increasingly competitive, as larger farms and agricultural businesses emerge, reshaping the market dynamics that small-scale farmers like Ledger rely on. As these larger entities expand, they bring with them increased resources and infrastructure that allow them to produce at scale, often at a lower cost. This shift creates a formidable challenge for Ledger, who is committed to sustainable practices and the support of local farming initiatives.

One of the most significant pressures Ledger faces is the influx of imported goods. These products, often subsidized in their home countries, can undercut local prices significantly, making it difficult for Ledger and his fellow small-scale farmers to compete. Consumers, drawn to lower prices, increasingly turn to these imports, further threatening the viability of local agriculture and destabilizing the community's economic foundation. Ledger watches as shelves filled with cheaper foreign produce outshine the hard-earned fruits of local labor, deepening his frustration and sense of urgency.

Confronting these external pressures forces Ledger to grapple with feelings of frustration and helplessness. His dedication to farming is driven by a desire to cultivate healthy, sustainable practices that benefit both his family and the community. However, as he sees his sales dwindle and hears of neighbors struggling to keep their farms afloat, he starts to question whether his principles can stand up against the harsh realities of economic disparity. The emotional toll of these struggles weighs heavily on him, igniting doubts about the viability of his farming enterprise in an increasingly hostile environment.

Codec's struggles with competing against larger, more industrialized operations lead Ledger to consider drastic changes. He begins to contemplate whether he should pivot his focus toward alternative crops that may capture niche markets or invest in marketing strategies to better communicate the value of locally sourced produce. Nonetheless, the uncertainty surrounding these decisions only adds to his anxiety. He fears that any misstep could further jeopardize the future of his estate and the welfare of the local farmers who depend on him for guidance.

Moreover, the competitive landscape raises questions about access—not just to markets but to resources essential for farming. Larger farms have the financial backing to invest in advanced technology and efficient supply chains, enabling them to optimize production and reduce waste. In contrast, Ledger struggles to access the same level of investment or resources, which puts him at a disadvantage. The disparities in access to funding, infrastructure, and information create a barrier that is difficult to overcome, leaving Ledger feeling isolated in his pursuit of a sustainable farming model.

Despite the challenges, Ledger refuses to abandon his vision. He actively seeks alliances with other local farmers, understanding that collaboration is vital in navigating this competitive landscape. By forming co-operatives, they can pool resources, share knowledge, and collectively negotiate better terms with suppliers and distributors. This collaborative approach empowers small-scale farmers to regain some control over their circumstances and enhances their ability to respond to market pressures.

Ledger's experience in dealing with competition and access challenges highlights the broader implications for small-scale agriculture in Dominica. As he grapples with his frustrations and the viability of his enterprise, he recognizes that the fight for local agriculture is also a fight for the community's identity and future. Through perseverance and a commitment to collaboration, he strives to carve out a space for sustainable farming amidst an evolving agricultural landscape, reaffirming his belief in the importance of local food systems and community resilience.

The economic challenges that Ledger experiences reverberate throughout the community, creating a ripple effect that underscores the interconnectedness of local agriculture. As he struggles to maintain his business amidst fluctuating market prices and increasing competition, his persistence becomes a source of both inspiration and concern for his neighbors. Local farmers, who have long looked to Ledger for guidance and support, begin to express doubts about the sustainability of their own practices in the face of mounting pressures.

Witnessing Ledger's difficulties, many farmers start questioning whether they can continue to rely on traditional methods and local markets as their primary sources of income. The anxiety within the community builds as they discuss their own vulnerabilities, contemplating the future of agriculture in their region. Conversations shift from potential growth and resilience to worries about survival, creating a palpable sense of unease.

Determined to provide support and foster a sense of unity, Ledger takes on the role of a community leader, rallying his neighbors to share resources, ideas, and techniques for overcoming common obstacles. He organizes meetings where farmers can voice their concerns and collaboratively brainstorm solutions. Ledger emphasizes the importance of adapting to the changing landscape—not just to survive, but to thrive collectively. He encourages discussions about diversifying crops, exploring alternative markets, and implementing sustainable practices that respect both the land and their shared values.

Despite his proactive approach, the weight of financial stress takes a toll on Ledger's mental resilience. As he invests time and energy into bolstering the community while grappling with his own fears about the future, feelings of isolation and doubt begin to creep in. He starts questioning whether their collective efforts can truly make a difference in the face of overwhelming economic disparities and competition from larger agricultural entities.

Ledger's internal struggle becomes a reflection of the broader emotional landscape of the community. As economic pressures mount, the sense of hope that once characterized their endeavors begins to wane. Farmers share their frustrations and fears, expressing doubts about their ability to navigate the increasingly hostile environment. Although Ledger tries to inspire and cultivate positivity, he cannot ignore the discouragement that hangs in the air.

In these moments of vulnerability, Ledger recognizes the need for self-care and support—not just for himself, but for the entire community. He advocates for mental health awareness within agricultural circles, urging farmers to seek assistance and cultivate resilience together. By fostering an environment where individuals feel safe to share their struggles and seek help, Ledger hopes to strengthen both individual mental health and communal solidarity.

The impact of Ledger's challenges on the community becomes a powerful catalyst for action. As they confront their fears and uncertainties, local farmers begin to realize that they are not alone in their struggles. Together, they harness their collective strength to face the economic realities of the agricultural landscape, transforming their doubts into a renewed sense of purpose.

Through collaboration, resource-sharing, and open dialogue, the community starts to cultivate a spirit of resilience that inspires hope for the future. While Ledger may wrestle with his own doubts, his commitment to supporting his neighbors reinforces the notion that they can navigate these challenges together. As they build a support network grounded in empathy and shared goals, the farmers of Bioche and Colihaut foster not only their own futures but also the enduring strength of their community.

Henri's commitment to education and the arts often clashes with the traditional views held by some community members in Bioche and Colihaut. While Henri envisions a future where children have access to a well-rounded education that includes both academics and cultural enrichment, many local families prioritize practical trade skills and labor as the most viable paths to success. For these families, immediate income-generating skills take precedence over broader educational pursuits, creating a significant cultural divide within the community.

Many community members dismiss Henri's emphasis on cultural enrichment as unnecessary. In their view, focusing on practical skills—such as farming, craftsmanship, and trades—is far more beneficial, as these skills directly translate into financial stability. Families often encourage their children to follow in their footsteps, linking education closely to job readiness and economic survival. This practical approach stems from years of navigating economic challenges, where immediate returns on investment are critical for the well-being of the household.

This pervasive cultural attitude poses a considerable challenge for Henri, who feels passionately that a well-rounded education is essential for breaking cycles of poverty and fostering future leaders. He understands that while practical skills are vital, a comprehensive education that includes arts and humanities can empower children to think critically, innovate, and contribute to their community in meaningful ways. Henri believes that exposure to the arts can cultivate creativity, compassion, and cultural awareness—qualities that are crucial for personal and social development.

Feeling the weight of this cultural clash, Henri works diligently to bridge the gap between his vision and the traditional perspectives of the community. He organizes educational workshops and community events that highlight the value of both practical skills and cultural enrichment. By bringing local artisans and craftsmen together with artists and educators, Henri aims to demonstrate that the arts and trades can coexist and enhance one another.

Despite his efforts, Henri often faces resistance from parents who remain skeptical of the benefits of the arts. Some express concerns that prioritizing education in music, literature, or visual arts could distract their children from learning essential trade skills that guarantee immediate employment. Henri listens to their apprehensions but gently counters by sharing stories of how a holistic education can lead to innovative thinking and better problem-solving skills—qualities that can benefit any job, whether in agriculture, trade, or the arts.

The ongoing dialogue about education highlights a deeper issue: the community's struggle to envision a future that accommodates both pragmatism and creativity. For many families, the desire for stability and security creates a narrow focus on immediate skills, making it difficult to see the long-term advantages of a diversified education. Henri's challenge lies in shifting this mindset, encouraging families to invest in futures that include not only economic viability but also cultural depth and critical thinking.

Through persistent advocacy and community engagement, Henri aims to create a cultural shift that recognizes the importance of a multifaceted education. He seeks to inspire families to view education not merely as an end but as a holistic tool for empowerment and societal development. Henri's journey underscores the complexities of navigating cultural traditions while striving for a brighter, more inclusive future for the children of Dominica, illustrating the need for collaboration between different viewpoints to nurture a generation of well-rounded leaders.

As Henri advocates progressive educational practices, he encounters significant resistance from those in the community who believe that education should strictly adhere to existing societal roles. Many parents voice concerns that emphasizing arts and humanities may clutter their children's schedules with what they deem "frivolous" subjects, fearing these pursuits could detract from vital, practical hard skills necessary for securing stable employment. This skepticism presents a formidable obstacle for Henri in his mission to expand the educational framework in Bioche, and Colihaut.

The entrenched belief among some community members is that education should serve immediate economic needs, prioritizing skills that directly translate into job opportunities. This perspective emphasizes the traditional routes of farming, craftsmanship, and trade, viewing arts and critical thinking as secondary, if not irrelevant. As a result, many parents strongly advocate for a curriculum focused on practical skills, arguing that the future success of their children hinges on mastering these competencies.

This resistance frustrates Henri deeply, as he recognizes the potential of a well-rounded education to transform lives and break the cycles of poverty. He believes that creativity and critical thinking are essential skills that foster innovation and adaptability—qualities increasingly necessary in a rapidly changing world. Despite the pushback, Henri remains committed to his vision, seeing the resistance as an opportunity to engage skeptics in meaningful dialogue about the broader implications of education.

Fueled by his determination, Henri approaches community meetings and discussions with empathy and openness. He invites parents to share their concerns while also presenting the benefits of incorporating arts and humanities into the education system. Through storytelling, he illustrates how creativity can lead to unexpected solutions in various fields, from agriculture to entrepreneurship. By showcasing successful individuals who have found value in both practical skills and creative pursuits, he aims to inspire families to reconsider their notions of what constitutes a valuable education.

Henri also frames the conversation around the idea of preparing children for a future that is uncertain and multifaceted. He argues that cultivating critical thinking skills not only enhances problem-solving abilities but also equips children to navigate challenges that may not yet exist. In his discussions, Henri emphasizes the importance of adaptability, highlighting how a diverse educational background can help young people thrive in an evolving job market where creativity and innovation are prized.

While Henri's efforts to engage the community in dialogue about educational reform are met with varying degrees of openness, the resistance remains a tough hurdle to overcome. Despite the frustration he feels, Henri channels that energy into finding common ground with parents. He seeks to build trust by organizing community workshops that blend practical skills with creative exploration, allowing families to experience firsthand how these pursuits can complement one another.

Through patience and perseverance, Henri aspires to shift the narrative surrounding education in his community. He understands that change takes time and that fostering a culture that values both creativity and practicality requires consistent effort. By demonstrating the tangible benefits of a well-rounded education and actively involving the community in the process, Henri hopes to gradually dismantle the resistance to change and inspire a new generation to embrace a broader vision of learning.

Henri's experiences with resistance remind him that progress is often met with challenges, but he remains dedicated to advocating for a future where children are equipped not only with skills for immediate employment but also with the creativity and critical thinking needed to become influential leaders and change-makers in their community.

To address the tensions surrounding educational practices in Bioche, and Colihaut, Henri takes the initiative to organize community education workshops. These workshops aim to highlight the benefits of education in various forms, showcasing how a comprehensive approach can enrich the lives of children and the community. Understanding that open dialogue is crucial in overcoming resistance, Henri carefully curates these events to foster engagement and promote understanding among community members.

Henri invites local leaders and respected figures—farmers, artisans, educators, and business owners—to share their experiences and successes, illustrating the diverse paths that education can open. By featuring individuals who have benefited from both practical skills and creative endeavors, Henri seeks to reinforce the idea that a holistic education is not just about academic achievements but also about personal growth, cultural appreciation, and social responsibility.

At these workshops, discussions are framed around the theme of empowerment. Henri emphasizes how education can enhance children's economic prospects while also nurturing their social and cultural identities. He invites participants to consider stories of individuals who have integrated their trade skills with creative pursuits, demonstrating how this combination can lead to innovative solutions and opportunities. By showcasing successful local entrepreneurs who have utilized their education in diverse ways, Henri hopes to inspire families to broaden their definitions of success.

The workshops also provide a platform for parents and community members to express their concerns about education. Henri encourages open dialogue, creating a safe space for participants to voice their opinions and fears. By listening to their perspectives, he builds rapport and trust, allowing for more constructive conversations about the value of integrating arts and humanities into the curriculum. Through these interactions, he aims to unpack the misconceptions surrounding creative education and illustrate its potential to enhance practical skills rather than detract from them.

Henri incorporates hands-on activities into the workshops, allowing participants to engage with both practical skills and creative expression. This experiential learning approach enables attendees to witness firsthand how skills from different domains can complement each other. For instance, a workshop might involve a local artist working alongside farmers to create art from organic materials, illustrating the beauty of merging creativity with agricultural practices. This not only highlights the potential for cross-disciplinary collaboration but also fosters a sense of community and shared purpose.

As families begin to see the possibilities that a more holistic educational approach can offer, Henri gains momentum in shifting perspectives. The workshops spark lively discussions and inspire parents to envision a future where their children can thrive socially, culturally, and economically. Over time, the dialogue around education starts to change, with more community members expressing interest in exploring creative opportunities alongside traditional skills.

Henri's community education workshops serve as a vital bridge between traditional views and forward-thinking ideologies. Through these gatherings, he not only advocates educational reform but also reinforces the notion that learning is a lifelong journey influenced by various experiences and perspectives. By cultivating a spirit of collaboration and respect for diverse educational paths, Henri aims to empower the next generation to embrace their identities fully and pursue multifaceted opportunities, ensuring a brighter and more inclusive future for all in Dominica.

As the Sebastien and Philogene families navigate their respective challenges within the communities of Bioche, and Colihaut, they are increasingly drawn into local political meetings and community events designed to address the pressing economic and social issues affecting their neighborhoods. Ledger and Henri initially focused on their separate endeavors—Ledger with sustainable agriculture and Henri with progressive education—and began to recognize the profound value of dialogue and collaboration in fostering community resilience.

At these gatherings, community members come together to discuss a broad range of issues, including market fluctuations, educational barriers, and the impact of imported goods on local agriculture. Ledger and Henri discover that their individual challenges are not isolated; rather, they are deeply intertwined with the collective well-being of their community. As they listen to the concerns of their neighbors, they gain insights into how economic sustainability and educational reform can work hand in hand to create a more robust and resilient society.

For Ledger, hearing from other farmers who share similar struggles instills a renewed sense of purpose and camaraderie. He realizes that the sustainability of his agricultural practices is not only vital for his own family but also essential for maintaining the cultural and economic fabric of the community. This understanding reinforces the importance of advocating policies that support local agriculture. He begins to see how educational initiatives that encourage youth to appreciate sustainable farming practices can help ensure a new generation of informed and engaged farmers.

Simultaneously, Henri finds that his push for a more holistic educational approach resonates with the community's broader goals. The discussions about economic empowerment and workforce readiness reveal the importance of equipping children with both practical skills and critical thinking abilities. As he shares his vision for integrating creative education within the local curriculum, he sees community members become more receptive to innovative ideas. Henri begins to envision partnerships where local farmers can collaborate with schools to teach students about sustainable practices, blending education with hands-on experiences in agricultural settings.

As Ledger and Henri engage in these dialogues, they come to appreciate their shared purpose. Private conversations between the two reveal their mutual respect and eagerness to collaborate for the greater good. They outline potential projects that could align with their goals, such as creating community gardens where educational workshops on agriculture and arts can occur simultaneously. By intertwining their efforts, they aim to cultivate not only the land but also a deeper understanding of the interconnectedness of their struggles and aspirations.

Over time, the community meetings foster an atmosphere of collaboration, creating a supportive network of individuals dedicated to tackling the issues facing Bioche, and Colihaut. Ledger and Henri find inspiration in the shared stories of resilience and innovation, encouraging them to push past the barriers they once faced as isolated entities. This collective spirit drives them to advocate for policies that support both sustainable agriculture and educational advancement, illustrating the strength that lies in community unity.

Through fostering dialogue and collaboration, Ledger and Henri's efforts transcend their individual struggles, weaving together a narrative of hope and collective action. Their commitment to working together not only strengthens their families but also contributes to the community's ongoing efforts to navigate socioeconomic challenges. As they bridge the gaps between agricultural sustainability and education, they create a legacy of resilience and empowerment that inspires future generations to engage with their communities, ensuring a brighter and more sustainable future for all.

As Ledger and Henri navigate their individual challenges in Bioche and Colihaut, they begin to create meaningful opportunities for mutual support. Through their interactions at local political meetings and community workshops, they come to a profound realization: a strong agricultural foundation is essential not only for their own families' livelihoods but also for uplifting the entire community. Meanwhile, Henri recognizes that education plays a pivotal role in equipping the next generation with the essential tools needed to thrive in an increasingly competitive world.

This acknowledgment of shared interests becomes the catalyst for their collaboration. They engage in thoughtful conversations with other community members, exploring how sustainable agricultural practices and progressive education can work in tandem to create a more resilient and empowering environment. In these discussions, Ledger emphasizes the value of supporting local agriculture as a means of bolstering the economy, while Henri advocates for educational initiatives that integrate practical skills with creativity and critical thinking.

Together, they encourage community members to see the interconnectedness of their struggles. Ledger explains how investing in sustainable farming not only enhances food security but also creates job opportunities for local youth, while Henri highlights how fostering creativity in education can inspire innovative solutions to agricultural challenges. This shared advocacy emphasizes a collective responsibility to address the community's pressing issues and empowers people to actively participate in shaping their future.

Recognizing that traditional barriers often hinder progress, Ledger and Henri focus on crafting collective solutions that promote both education and sustainable practices. They propose the establishment of collaborative programs that bring together farmers and educators, where knowledge flows freely between generations. This could take the form of workshops that teach students about sustainable farming practices or community service projects that allow young people to gain hands-on experience in local agriculture. Through these initiatives, they aim to break down the divides that have historically separated the realms of education and practical labor.

As they advocate for change, Ledger and Henri also address the concerns of families entrenched in traditional views about education. They invite parents into discussions to explore the tangible benefits of integrating arts and critical thinking into the curriculum. By showcasing local success stories—individuals who have succeeded through a blend of practical skills and creative education—they inspire others to see the possibilities that lie in a more holistic approach.

Their collaborative efforts gain traction, and soon other community members begin to rally behind their vision. As more families become engaged in discussions about the future of education and agriculture, the sense of unity strengthens. Individuals start to view themselves not just as isolated workers and caretakers but as part of a larger community that thrives on shared knowledge and interdependence.

Through continuous dialogue and advocacy, Ledger and Henri cultivate an atmosphere of empowerment where community members can find common ground despite their differing backgrounds and perspectives. They inspire each other and those around them to envision a community where education and sustainability go hand in hand, leading to a future that embraces innovation while honoring tradition.

This common ground in advocacy not only enhances the individual endeavors of Ledger and Henri but also lays the groundwork for a more collaborative and resilient community. By focusing on collective solutions and mutual empowerment, they forge a path forward that encourages everyone in Bioche, and Colihaut to contribute to the well-being of their families and enhance the social fabric of their neighborhoods, paving the way for a brighter future for all.

As Ledger and Henri deepen their commitment to fostering a more resilient community in Bioche and Colihaut, they step confidently into leadership roles within local forums. Embracing the responsibility that comes with these positions, they advocate tirelessly for policies that not only support local farmers but also enhance access to education for all children in the community. Understanding that transformation begins with strong leadership, they aim to be catalysts for change.

In these community forums, Ledger and Henri lead by example, encouraging open discussions that highlight the diverse experiences and needs of their fellow residents. They create spaces where individuals feel safe to voice their concerns, share their stories, and propose solutions. By actively listening to the community members, they reinforce the idea that leadership is not about dictating change but about fostering a collaborative environment where everyone's input and experiences are valued.

Ledger's advocacy focuses on sustainable agricultural practices and the need for policies that protect and empower local farmers. He uses his platform to educate community members about the impact of globalization and the importance of supporting local produce. Through workshops and discussions, Ledger engages residents in conversations about how local agriculture can be revitalized not just for economic benefit, but also for environmental sustainability and community health. He emphasizes that strong support for farmers benefits the entire community.

Meanwhile, Henri underscores the significance of education as a vehicle for change. He champions initiatives aimed at equitable access to quality education, believing that all children deserve an opportunity to thrive. Henri invites educators, parents, and young people to participate in discussions about curriculum development, inclusivity, and innovative teaching methods. By gathering insights from diverse community members, he aims to create an educational framework that reflects the unique needs and aspirations of the entire community.

Through their combined efforts, Ledger and Henri inspire others to join the movement toward change and cooperation. Their presence in community forums transforms passive audiences into active participants, fostering a sense of ownership among residents. People begin to recognize that they have a role to play in shaping their community's future, whether through advocating for policies, supporting local initiatives, or volunteering for educational programs.

As more individuals engage in these conversations, a collective momentum builds. The shared commitment to improving agricultural practices and educational access begins to dissolve previous barriers and divisions. Community members actively collaborate to identify challenges, brainstorm solutions, and implement actionable plans that reflect their shared vision for a vibrant and sustainable community.

The influence of Ledger and Henri extends beyond their immediate circles. Their leadership inspires neighboring communities to also consider how local collaboration can address socio-political issues effectively. They model a new approach to leadership that prioritizes inclusivity, respect, and mutual support, encouraging other aspiring leaders to emerge and contribute their voices to the ongoing dialogue.

Through their leadership roles, Ledger and Henri pave the way for a more inclusive approach to tackling socio-political issues. Their efforts not only uplift the immediate communities of Bioche and Colihaut but also create a ripple effect that encourages systemic change at larger scales. By fostering open dialogue and community cooperation, they lay the foundation for a brighter, more sustainable future—where everyone's voice is heard, and each person's contribution is valued.

Over time, Ledger and Henri cultivate a mutual respect for contributions and the unique perspectives they bring to their community. Through their shared experiences in local forums and community events, they come to recognize that their individual struggles, whether related to sustainable agriculture or educational challenges, mirror broader societal issues affecting Bioche, and Colihaut. This realization becomes the foundation for a strong partnership grounded in collaboration rather than competition.

As they engage in deeper conversations, Ledger and Henri explore the potential for their combined efforts to effect meaningful change in their community. Ledger's expertise in sustainable agricultural practices complements Henri's understanding of educational frameworks, allowing them to devise innovative strategies that leverage their unique strengths. They begin brainstorming programs that integrate agriculture and education, aiming to create initiatives that not only benefit their families but also uplift the entire community.

One of the first collaborative projects they envision is a community agricultural education program. This initiative would involve workshops where local farmers, led by Ledger, teach students about sustainable farming techniques, crop rotation, and environmental stewardship. In parallel, Henri would facilitate discussions on the importance of these practices in the context of food security and health. The combination of hands-on agricultural knowledge with classroom learning aims to foster a generation of informed, engaged citizens who appreciate the significance of both farming and education.

Moreover, they discuss the possibility of creating seasonal farm-to-school programs that provide fresh produce to local schools while offering students the chance to learn about nutrition, cooking, and the value of supporting local agriculture. By connecting the dots between education, health, and sustainability, Ledger, and Henri hope to create a comprehensive approach that benefits all stakeholders in the community.

As this partnership evolves, they actively include other community members in their planning. They seek input from parents, teachers, and local leaders to ensure that the programs they develop are inclusive and address the diverse needs of the community. Through these collaborative efforts, they foster a sense of ownership among residents, motivating them to contribute their ideas and skills to the initiatives.

Ledger and Henri also work together to advocate for policy changes that support the integration of agricultural education in schools. They unite their voices to lobby for funding and resources that can enhance educational programs, ensuring that agriculture and the arts are respected and valued within the local curriculum. Their collective efforts draw attention to the importance of these subjects, emphasizing their role in fostering community resilience and sustainability.

Throughout this journey of building bridges, Ledger and Henri not only impact their families and immediate neighborhoods but also create a framework for future collaboration among community members. Their partnership serves as a model for how individuals can come together despite differing backgrounds and perspectives to work toward common goals.

In successfully combining their efforts, Ledger and Henri demonstrate the power of collaboration and mutual respect in addressing complex societal issues. They inspire others to recognize the potential in working together, creating a more unified community that is capable of tackling challenges with innovative solutions. As they establish programs that support both agricultural sustainability and educational enrichment, they lay the groundwork for a thriving, interconnected community—a place where all members have the resources and knowledge they need to succeed.

Fueled by their mutual respect and shared vision for a thriving community, Ledger and Henri take proactive steps to initiate comprehensive programs that integrate agriculture and education. Understanding that a strong foundation in both areas can lead to significant improvements in the quality of life in Bioche, and Colihaut, they design initiatives aimed at fostering collaboration and knowledge exchange among community members. Their commitment to creating a cohesive framework for addressing local challenges inspires them to explore innovative solutions that resonate with a diverse audience.

One of their primary strategies involves hosting community events that underscore the importance of sustainable farming practices in conjunction with educational workshops. These events draw in families, local farmers, educators, and community leaders, providing a platform for dialogue and shared learning. Ledger takes the lead in showcasing practical agricultural techniques, demonstrating methods such as organic farming, crop rotation, and composting. At the same time, Henri facilitates discussions around nutrition and healthy eating, engaging parents and children in conversations about the benefits of consuming locally grown produce. By pairing these workshops, they create a holistic understanding of how agriculture intersects with everyday life and well-being.

As families participate in these interactive events, they begin to recognize the profound interconnectedness of food security, education, and cultural enrichment. Ledger and Henri incorporate storytelling into their presentations, sharing their personal journeys and the agricultural and educational traditions that shape their lives. This narrative approach fosters empathy and connection, helping community members see that their individual struggles are part of a larger tapestry of experiences. Through hands-on activities such as planting and cooking demonstrations, families actively engage with the concepts being taught, further reinforcing the bond between sustainable practices and educational growth.

The impact of these initiatives extends beyond individual events, as they cultivate a growing sense of unity and purpose within the community. As awareness of the benefits of sustainable agriculture and education increases, participation in their programs rises significantly. Families not only gain valuable knowledge but also develop a collective identity rooted in shared goals. Community members become more invested in local initiatives, recognizing that their contributions, whether through volunteering, advocating for policy changes, or simply engaging in educational activities, are vital to the community's success.

The programs led by Ledger and Henri epitomize the power of collaboration and collective action in tackling pressing social issues. By intertwining agriculture and education, they create a vibrant network of support and engagement that empowers families to take control of their futures. This comprehensive approach not only enriches the lives of individuals but also lays the groundwork for a sustainable and resilient community where food security and educational opportunities are accessible to all. As families continue to come together to learn, share, and grow, they forge a brighter path forward that promises cultural enrichment and lasting positive change for generations to come.

As the families in Bioche, and Colihaut collaborate to tackle pressing socio-political issues, they begin to forge a powerful legacy of positive change that resonates throughout their communities. Ledger and Henri's combined efforts act as a beacon of hope, illustrating how collaboration and shared purpose can generate meaningful progress. Their partnership not only addresses immediate challenges but also inspires a fundamental shift in the mindset of community members, encouraging them to unite around common goals and envision a brighter future.

The transformative journey of Ledger and Henri reflects the strength that emerges when individuals come together to confront shared challenges. They demonstrate that through open dialogue and mutual respect, it is possible to break down the barriers imposed by traditional norms and explore innovative solutions. As families witness the tangible benefits of integrating sustainable agricultural practices with educational initiatives, the community's collective confidence grows. This newfound confidence empowers them to embrace a more proactive approach to socio-political issues, advocating for changes that enhance both their livelihoods and their educational opportunities.

Inspired by Ledger and Henri's commitment to positive change, the community begins to reevaluate traditional roles and norms that have long shaped their interactions. The dialogue sparked by their initiatives encourages families to reconsider what it means to be a contributor to society, fostering an environment where collaboration replaces competition. This shift is particularly significant for the younger generation, who are encouraged to engage with both their cultural heritage and modern practices. As they embrace this shared vision, community members start to see themselves not just as isolated individuals but as integral parts of a dynamic and interconnected community.

The legacy of change cultivated by Ledger and Henri resonates beyond their immediate efforts, spreading throughout Bioche, and Colihaut. Their initiatives lay the groundwork for future generations to continue the work of building a more sustainable and inclusive future. Families begin to take ownership of their roles within the community, participating in ongoing dialogues and initiatives that advocate educational equity and agricultural sustainability. This collective momentum instills a sense of pride and responsibility, encouraging community members to uphold the values of cooperation and mutual support.

The legacy of change sparked by Ledger and Henri's collaboration serves as a powerful reminder of what can be achieved when individuals come together for a common cause. Their journey inspires others to think critically about their societal roles and to engage actively in shaping their community's future. As this legacy unfolds, it establishes a resilient foundation for Bioche, and Colihaut, where collective strength, shared vision, and the pursuit of knowledge empower the community to flourish for generations to come.

In the face of economic hardships and cultural clashes, Ledger and Henri's paths converge, showcasing the transformative power of collaboration and mutual respect. As they navigate their individual challenges, they realize that their journeys are intricately linked by the shared goal of fostering a prosperous future for their families and communities. By recognizing the value of their unique strengths and perspectives, they exemplify how unity can be harnessed to tackle broader socio-political issues impacting Dominica.

Together, Ledger and Henri embark on a mission to address the pressing challenges faced by their communities, cultivating a spirit of cooperation that transcends their differences. Their initiatives spark important conversations about sustainable agriculture, educational access, and cultural enrichment, drawing in diverse community members who contribute to a shared vision. By fostering an inclusive environment where ideas can flourish, they inspire others to join their efforts, creating a ripple effect of positive change throughout Bioche, and Colihaut.

Through their commitment to nurturing their families' aspirations, Ledger and Henri not only work toward a better future for themselves but also lay the foundation for generations to come. Their collaborative approach serves as a testament to the strength that can emerge when individuals come together with a common purpose. As they continue to navigate challenges hand in hand, they illuminate a path forward that embodies resilience, mutual support, and hope.

In this journey toward a brighter future, Ledger and Henri remind us that fostering dialogue, advocating for positive change, and building bridges between diverse perspectives are essential components of progress. As the community rallies around its vision, they collectively navigate the complexities of its socio-political landscape, paving the way for a sustainable and inclusive future that reflects the aspirations of all its members. Together, they demonstrate that through collaboration and respect, it is possible to overcome obstacles and create a thriving, united community in Dominica.

☙

Chapter Sixteen: Building Alliances

As Ledger and Henri navigate the complexities of their individual challenges amid the broader socio-political landscape in Dominica, they stumble upon a transformative opportunity for collaboration. Both men are acutely aware of the historical and systemic issues that shape their communities, particularly the enduring impact of colonial legacies on local livelihoods and rights. Motivated by a shared commitment to advocating community rights and enhancing the well-being of their families, Ledger and Henri forge a partnership that catalyzes change.

In this chapter, we explore how their alliance not only empowers them to confront their own struggles but also inspires a wider network of support for families facing similar challenges in Bioche, and Colihaut. Leveraging their unique strengths, Ledger's agricultural expertise, and Henri's educational insights, they develop initiatives that address the pressing needs of their communities. Through their collaboration, they create a platform for dialogue and collective action that resonates throughout the region.

As their partnership grows, it becomes a symbol of resilience and hope, encouraging others in their communities to reevaluate their roles and actively participate in the movement for social justice and empowerment. The impact of Ledger and Henri's alliance extends beyond their immediate efforts, fostering a robust network of families who unite to share resources, knowledge, and support. This is the highlight of not only the transformative power of their collaboration but also the broader implications it holds for the community as they work together to build a more equitable and sustainable future for all.

As Ledger and Henri deepen their conversations, they begin to bond over their shared experiences, particularly the common challenges imposed by lingering colonial legacies that continue to affect the lives of their community members. These discussions delve into the historical injustices that have shaped agricultural practices and educational opportunities in Bioche, and Colihaut. Both men acknowledge how the weight of history has created barriers that limit access to essential resources, leaving many families struggling to achieve their full potential. Their dialogue becomes a safe space to express frustrations and hopes, fostering a connection grounded in understanding and empathy.

Reflecting on their respective journeys, Ledger and Henri recognize that their personal struggles are intricately tied to the broader socio-political context. Ledger shares his insights on how colonial exploitation has led to unsustainable agricultural practices, undermining local farmers' ability to thrive. He recounts the stories of his ancestors and their deep-rooted connection to the land, emphasizing the importance of embracing sustainable techniques to honor that legacy. Meanwhile, Henri discusses the impact of colonial education systems, which often prioritize outdated curricula that do not reflect the diverse cultural backgrounds and realities of their students. His commitment to promoting educational equity and relevance resonates deeply with Ledger, reinforcing their shared vision.

These conversations illuminate a mutual desire to honor their heritage while advocating for a better future. Ledger and Henri begin to articulate a collective aspiration to empower their communities by reclaiming their narratives and promoting practices that celebrate their cultural identity. They envision a future where families have equitable access to resources, including educational opportunities that prioritize local knowledge and traditions. This shared understanding acts as a catalyst for their alliance, solidifying their resolve to work together in advocating for systemic change. As they discuss tangible initiatives, they become increasingly aware of the collective strength found in unity, motivating them to forge ahead in their mission to uplift their communities and dismantle the barriers imposed by history.

As Ledger and Henri continue their discussions, they discover a shared vision that crystallizes into common goals: enhancing food security through sustainable agricultural practices and ensuring equitable access to education for all children in their communities. This alignment of purpose serves as a strong foundation for their partnership, allowing them to combine their strengths in agriculture and education to tackle the systemic issues plaguing Bioche, and Colihaut. They understand that by addressing these interconnected areas, they can make a significant impact on the overall well-being of their families and neighbors.

Recognizing the urgency of these issues, Ledger emphasizes the need for sustainable practices that will not only improve food security but also restore ecological balance to their agricultural systems. He shares innovative techniques he has learned that can help local farmers increase their yields while preserving the environment. Henri, in turn, articulates the importance of providing children with educational options that are culturally relevant and accessible. He aspires to create a curriculum that integrates local history and practices, empowering students to appreciate their heritage while preparing them for future challenges. Together, they formulate a plan to advocate for policies that support these initiatives, ensuring that food security and education are prioritized within the community.

Moreover, they recognize that their combined knowledge and networks can be powerful tools in elevating the voices of their community members, particularly those who have long felt marginalized and overlooked. By uniting their efforts, Ledger, and Henri plan to organize community forums that encourage widespread participation and dialogue. These gatherings will serve as platforms for residents to express their needs, share their experiences, and collaborate on solutions. They believe that by amplifying these voices, they can advocate for rights and resources that are crucial for the development of their community.

Through their dedication to these collective goals, Ledger and Henri not only strengthen their alliance but also foster a sense of solidarity among community members. Their partnership symbolizes hope and empowerment, illustrating that by working together, they can challenge the status quo and effect meaningful change. As they align their efforts toward enhancing food security and educational access, they lay the groundwork for a future where all families can thrive, rooted in dignity and the recognition of their inherent rights. This collective aspiration drives them forward, inspiring others to join the movement and work toward a more sustainable and equitable future for Dominica.

Motivated by the insights gained from their discussions, Ledger and Henri commit to setting aside time each week to strategize and plan their next steps. They recognize that meaningful change requires careful preparation and a clear roadmap. During their meetings, they create a dynamic space for brainstorming initiatives aimed at raising awareness about the critical importance of agricultural sustainability and educational equity. With a shared vision, they explore a variety of ideas that can engage their community members and foster a sense of collective purpose.

One of their focal points is the organization of workshops designed to educate local farmers about sustainable agricultural practices. They discuss topics such as crop rotation, organic farming methods, and soil conservation techniques to not only enhance food security but also improve environmental health. Ledger shares his experiences with successful practices, while Henri emphasizes the importance of incorporating these ideas into a community-centric approach, ensuring that all voices are heard. They agree that inviting experts to facilitate these workshops will further enrich the learning experience, making it more impactful for attendees.

In addition to workshops, Ledger and Henri envision hosting community forums where residents can discuss their challenges and share their insights on the socio-political issues affecting them. These forums will serve as vital platforms for open dialogue, allowing families to articulate their needs and aspirations while also fostering a sense of unity. They brainstorm ways to promote these events, leveraging social media and local networks to maximize participation. By creating an inviting atmosphere that encourages participation from all community members, they hope to amplify the collective voice advocating for change.

Moreover, they explore the idea of joint events that celebrate local culture while promoting their initiatives. For instance, a community harvest festival could not only showcase sustainable farming practices but also highlight the importance of education through interactive displays and performances by local students. These events would serve to strengthen community bonds, making the concepts of sustainability and educational equity more relatable and engaging for families.

As they lay the groundwork for a unified front against existing inequalities, Ledger and Henri feel a renewed sense of purpose. Their collaborative efforts not only solidify their partnership but also signal to the community that collective action is both possible and necessary. By dedicating their time and energy to strategizing together, they are building a robust framework that empowers families to confront the challenges they face, fostering resilience and hope for a more equitable future. Through their shared commitment, Ledger and Henri are paving the way for transformative initiatives that can inspire lasting change across their communities.

With the strength of their newfound alliance, Ledger and Henri take a proactive step by organizing a series of community workshops that emphasize the critical relationship between agriculture and education. Recognizing that both sectors are essential for the overall development of their communities, they design these workshops to serve as platforms for education, collaboration, and empowerment. By bringing together families, educators, and local experts, they aim to cultivate a deeper understanding of how farming practices and education systems can work in harmony to support sustainable community growth.

To enrich the workshops, Ledger and Henri invite local experts in sustainable farming, educational theory, and community development. These knowledgeable individuals share their insights on innovative agricultural techniques that not only enhance food production but also promote environmental stewardship. They cover topics such as organic farming, water conservation, and crop diversity, demonstrating how such practices can lead to more resilient food systems. Alongside these discussions, experts also highlight the importance of integrating agricultural studies into local curriculums, helping students connect theoretical knowledge with practical applications in their own communities.

The workshops are designed with a focus on hands-on learning, engaging families in interactive activities that illustrate the concepts being discussed. Participants can explore techniques such as planting and maintaining a sustainable garden, which can directly improve their food security at home. Additionally, Ledger and Henri facilitate discussions that encourage families to reflect on how agricultural knowledge can be incorporated into everyday learning for their children. Through group activities, parents and children are prompted to discuss their aspirations, sharing ideas on what agricultural education could look like in their schools.

By promoting the interconnectedness of food security and educational development, these workshops aim to foster a holistic approach to community growth. They encourage families to see the value in supporting one another by sharing knowledge and resources, creating an environment where collective progress becomes possible. As community members engage with the material and participate in lively discussions, they begin to realize that improving their agricultural practices is not just about enhancing crop yields; it also involves preparing future generations to continue the work of sustainable farming and advocating for their educational rights.

Through these workshops, Ledger and Henri successfully cultivate a sense of community pride and responsibility, inspiring participants to take an active role in shaping both their agricultural practices and their children's education. As families leave each session with new skills, ideas, and a greater sense of agency, they embark on a path toward fostering a resilient community that is well-equipped to face the challenges of the future. In this way, Ledger and Henri's efforts not only empower individuals but also create a ripple effect of positive change that extends throughout Bioche, and Colihaut.

Ledger and Henri's collaborative efforts go beyond the confines of workshops as they dive into grassroots advocacy to further their mission. Recognizing the importance of fostering a dialogue around community rights, they actively participate in local events to raise awareness of the socio-political issues facing their neighborhoods. One of their most effective tools is storytelling, which allows them to connect emotionally with community members and make the complex topics of justice and equity more relatable and accessible.

At these gatherings, Ledger and Henri share their personal narratives, weaving in their experiences with the ongoing impact of colonial legacies on their lives and the lives of their neighbors. They discuss how these historical injustices have shaped access to resources, education, and opportunities in Bioche, and Colihaut. By drawing on their stories, they vividly illustrate the tangible consequences of systemic inequality, making it clear that the struggles they face are not isolated incidents but part of a larger narrative that many in their community can resonate with.

As they speak, families begin to see the importance of uniting in their pursuit of justice and equity. Ledger and Henri encourage these groups to recognize their collective strength and the power of their voices. They emphasize that by standing together and sharing their stories, they can challenge the status quo and advocate for meaningful change. Their authenticity and vulnerability create a safe space for others to open, leading to shared experiences and feelings of validation among attendees.

The conversations sparked by Ledger and Henri's storytelling do not stop at the events; they ripple through the community, inspiring discussions around systemic change in homes, schools, and local gatherings. People begin to reflect on their own experiences and consider how they can contribute to the movement for justice too. As awareness spreads, community members become more engaged and willing to participate in initiatives aimed at addressing these long-standing issues.

By raising awareness through grounded, heartfelt advocacy, Ledger and Henri play a pivotal role in transforming the community's outlook on its rights and responsibilities. Their grassroots efforts foster a sense of solidarity, empowering families to reclaim their narratives and demand the equitable treatment they deserve. As conversations turn into action, they set the stage for a collective journey toward justice, healing, and empowerment, paving the way for a brighter future forged through unity and resilience.

As Ledger and Henri's influence within their communities continues to grow, they recognize the importance of reaching out to other families in Bioche, and Colihaut who are facing similar struggles. Determined to create a sense of belonging and shared purpose, they begin to build a support network that encompasses not only agricultural workers but also educators, parents, and families from diverse backgrounds. This diverse coalition is essential for addressing the complexities of the challenges they all face in their respective sectors.

To lay the groundwork for this network, Ledger and Henri facilitate open forums and discussions where community members can come together to share their experiences, challenges, and aspirations. These gatherings become safe spaces where individuals can speak freely about the issues that affect their lives, whether it is overcoming barriers in agriculture, advocating for better educational opportunities, or navigating the legacies of colonialism. By promoting open dialogue, they encourage community members to articulate their needs and desires, creating a rich tapestry of voices that represent the community's collective strength.

The support network quickly evolves into a powerful platform for solidarity and empowerment. As families hear each other's stories, they begin to realize they are not alone in their struggles. This realization fosters a sense of camaraderie and trust, as individuals come to see their shared experiences as a source of strength rather than isolation. Together, they explore solutions to common problems, leveraging their diverse perspectives and expertise to advocate for their rights more effectively.

Ledger and Henri emphasize the value of collaboration, encouraging members of the network to support one another in their advocacy efforts. They facilitate joint initiatives aimed at raising awareness about educational inequalities, food security issues, and the importance of sustainable practices. By pooling their resources and knowledge, families within the network find that they can have a greater impact than they might individually.

Moreover, the formation of this alliance sends a powerful message to the wider community: collective action can drive substantive change. As families unite to advocate for their rights, they become more visible and formidable allies in the fight for justice and equitable treatment. Ledger and Henri's efforts to create these community alliances not only empower families to take a stand for their needs but also strengthen the very fabric of their communities. Together, they cultivate an environment where everyone feels valued and heard, laying the groundwork for a brighter future forged through mutual support and shared ambitions.

Recognizing the profound impact that policy change can have on their community, Ledger and Henri take a proactive approach to advocate for local educational reforms that confront the enduring realities of colonial legacies. They understand that equitable access to education is essential not only for individual growth but also for the overall progress of Bioche, Dublanc, and Colihaut. They set out to engage local leaders and policymakers, striving to create a more inclusive and relevant educational landscape.

Their advocacy efforts focus on addressing the barriers to educational access that many families face. They highlight issues such as inadequate resources, outdated curricula, and the lack of representation of local cultures and practices in schools. Ledger and Henri work tirelessly to gather data and personal stories from community members, illustrating how these barriers impact children's ability to learn and thrive. By presenting a compelling case for reform grounded in the lived experiences of their neighbors, they aim to create a sense of urgency among decision-makers.

A key aspect of their advocacy is the push for the inclusion of agricultural education in local school curriculums. They argue that such programs not only provide practical skills that are directly applicable to the community's agricultural economy but also foster a deeper understanding of sustainability and environmental stewardship among students. Recognizing agriculture's cultural significance, Ledger and Henri believe that integrating agricultural education can empower the next generation to contribute to their family's livelihoods and the community's well-being.

Through persistent dialogue with local leaders and policymakers, Ledger and Henri strive to influence educational policies that truly reflect the community's needs and values. They attend school board meetings, participate in public forums, and collaborate with like-minded advocates to ensure that their voices and the voices of their community members are heard. By building coalitions with other stakeholders—such as educators, parents, and agricultural organizations—they amplify their impact and demonstrate the broad support for reform.

As they navigate the complexities of the legislative process, Ledger and Henri remain committed to their mission, recognizing that advocacy is often a long and challenging journey. However, their determination and passion for creating a more just and inclusive educational system shine through in their efforts. By championing these critical reforms, they not only work toward enhancing educational access but also seek to dismantle the remnants of colonial legacies that have hindered progress in their communities for too long.

Through their advocacy for educational legislation, Ledger and Henri are laying the groundwork for a future where every child has the opportunity to learn, grow, and thrive in an environment that honors their heritage and prepares them for a sustainable future. In doing so, they inspire hope and foster a sense of possibility that can transform the educational landscape for generations to come.

In response to the economic hardships faced by local farmers, Ledger and Henri actively advocate for government support of sustainable agricultural initiatives. They understand that small-scale farmers are crucial to the community's economy and cultural identity, yet they are often overwhelmed by external competition and the impacts of climate change. By promoting sustainable practices, Ledger and Henri aim to bolster the resilience of these farmers while ensuring the long-term viability of agriculture in Bioche, and Colihaut.

Their advocacy efforts focus on pushing for grants and programs that provide financial assistance to small-scale farmers looking to adopt eco-friendly practices. Ledger and Henri emphasize the importance of transitioning from conventional farming methods to sustainable alternatives, such as organic farming, crop rotation, and permaculture. They argue that these practices not only enhance soil health and biodiversity but also reduce input costs and increase yields over time, leading to greater economic stability for local farmers.

To amplify their message, Ledger and Henri organize workshops and community meetings where they educate farmers about the benefits of sustainable practices and the resources available to them. They invite expert speakers to share insights on new agricultural techniques, funding opportunities, and success stories from other communities that have embraced sustainability. By creating a supportive environment for knowledge sharing, they empower farmers to embrace change and view it as an opportunity rather than a burden.

As their advocacy gains traction, it becomes a rallying point for the community. Families begin to see the connection between sustainable agriculture and their rights to a healthy environment and fair economic opportunities. Ledger and Henri encourage everyone to unite in the fight for their livelihoods, emphasizing that collectively advocating for government support is essential for creating lasting change. This sense of solidarity strengthens the community, fostering a culture of mutual support and joint action.

With their grassroots efforts, Ledger and Henri engage local leaders and policymakers in discussions about the importance of prioritizing sustainable agricultural initiatives in government agendas. They present compelling data and narratives that showcase how supporting small-scale farmers benefits the entire community—creating jobs, preserving cultural heritage, and ensuring food security. Their strategic advocacy becomes a beacon of hope for families struggling to navigate the challenges of a rapidly changing agricultural landscape.

Through their commitment to promoting sustainable practices, Ledger and Henri are not only seeking to alleviate economic pressures faced by local farmers but also nurturing a broader movement toward environmental stewardship and community resilience. Their work fosters a sense of pride in local agricultural traditions while laying the foundation for a sustainable future where farmers can thrive alongside their communities. Together, they inspire a collective vision of hope, encouraging families to stand firm in their rights and cultivate a vibrant, sustainable local economy.

Ledger and Henri deeply understand that reclaiming cultural practices is essential for healing the wounds left by colonial history. They recognize that cultural identity plays a crucial role in community resilience and individual well-being, and they are determined to champion programs that honor and celebrate their local traditions and heritage. By fostering a sense of pride in cultural roots, they inspire community members to embrace their identity while also striving for equitable futures.

To facilitate this cultural revitalization, Ledger and Henri initiate a series of community programs designed to highlight and celebrate local customs, stories, and traditions. Through art, music, and storytelling festivals, they create vibrant, engaging spaces where community members can come together to share their heritage. These events allow individuals of all ages to participate, encouraging the younger generation to learn from their elders and experience the richness of their cultural legacy firsthand.

At these festivals, local artists and musicians showcase their talents, bringing traditional rhythms and styles to life. Workshops are held to teach community members various art forms, such as pottery, weaving, and dance, ensuring that these skills are passed down through generations. Storytelling sessions, featuring tales of historical significance and cultural wisdom, become a focal point, allowing participants to connect emotionally with their shared history. Through these activities, Ledger and Henri aim to foster a deeper understanding and respect for their cultural narrative, reinforcing the importance of cultural preservation.

In promoting these initiatives, Ledger and Henri also emphasize the role of collaboration. They encourage partnerships with local schools, cultural organizations, and government entities to secure support and resources for their programs. By involving a diverse array of stakeholders, they enhance the visibility of cultural revitalization efforts and create a collective momentum that amplifies their reach and impact.

As the community engages with these vibrant celebrations of cultural identity, a renewed sense of pride and belonging emerges. Families begin to view their cultural practices not only as artifacts of the past but as living traditions that can inform their present and future. This transformation fosters an environment where individuals feel empowered to advocate for their rights while also honoring the legacy of their ancestors.

Through their commitment to cultural revitalization, Ledger and Henri not only aim to heal the divisions created by colonialism but also strive to build a more cohesive community grounded in shared values and experiences. By reconnecting with their cultural roots, community members become more resilient and united, forging a path toward an equitable future that honors their heritage. Their efforts to revitalize cultural connections serve as a powerful catalyst for understanding, celebration, and collective action, enriching the community's tapestry and ensuring that its story continues to thrive for generations to come.

As Ledger and Henri actively work to empower local leaders within the community, they see the potential in their children and other young individuals. They nurture their interests, knowing that the future lies in the hands of the next generation. One such young leader is Theresa, who has developed a keen awareness of the socio-economic challenges facing their community. Inspired by her parents' dedication to sustainable agricultural practices, she approaches her studies at Convent High School with a focus on Economics and Trade.

Driven by a desire to create positive change, Theresa has taken it upon herself to advocate for local farmers and promote fair trade initiatives. Her passion ignites a flame of hope among her peers as she organizes events and projects that not only educate others about the importance of supporting local businesses but also encourage them to actively participate in community advocacy. Through her determination and creativity, Theresa embodies the spirit of empowerment that Ledger and Henri have instilled in their family and the broader community, making her a beacon of inspiration for those around her.

The bustling halls of Convent High School, where students move between classrooms, chatting excitedly about their day. In a bright, airy classroom with large windows that overlook the school's garden, students are preparing for a special presentation day focused on Economics and Trade.

Theresa sat at her desk, a mix of excitement and nerves swirling in her stomach. Today was a significant day—she would be presenting her project on the importance of sustainable trade practices in their community to a panel of local business owners, teachers, and her classmates. Her father, Henri, had heavily influenced her interest in economics with his passionate discussions about the challenges faced by local farmers and the need for equitable trade practices.

As she glanced at her project materials, she noticed Alton, her older brother, sliding into the seat next to her. "You ready for this?" he whispered, giving her an encouraging smile.

"Yeah," she replied, adjusting her notes. "I just hope they see how important this is for us—not just for business, but for the environment too."

Alton leaned back, crossing his arms. "You've got this. Just remember how passionate Dad is about these issues. You're speaking from the heart."

The bell rang, signaling the start of the presentation session. Theresa felt her heart race as she stood and walked to the front of the room, the colorful visuals of her poster board depicting local agricultural products and sustainable practices catching everyone's attention. She took a deep breath and began.

"Good morning, everyone. My name is Theresa, and today I want to talk to you about sustainable trade practices and how they can benefit our community—especially in Bioche, Dublanc, and Colihaut."

She scanned the audience, locking eyes with her teacher and a few familiar faces from the community who had come to support the students. "As we know, our traditional agriculture practices have faced challenges due to external competition and changing global markets. But we have opportunities to reclaim our local economy by prioritizing sustainable methods."

Her voice grew stronger as she detailed her research on how eco-friendly practices not only help the environment but also lead to better long-term profits for farmers. She talked about the importance of supporting small-scale farmers, many of whom are struggling to keep their businesses afloat.

"By advocating for fair trade and sustainability," she continued, animatedly pointing to the graphs and statistics on her poster, "we can create a better system for our community. Imagine our local products—the fruits, vegetables, and crafts—reaching larger markets while respecting our traditions and protecting our land."

As she spoke, she saw nods of agreement from both her peers and the panel. Theresa's passion shone through, echoing the conversations she often had with Ledger and Henri about community rights and economic justice. She included stories of families impacted by economic changes, noting that her own father had shared stories of their struggles, and how important it was to ensure their voices were heard in the market.

After her presentation, the room buzzed with questions and discussions. Her classmates engaged with the topic, suggesting ideas for further initiatives, while the panelists offered insightful feedback, impressed by her knowledge and clarity.

"Great job, Theresa," her teacher said, beaming as she wrapped up the session. The students clapped, and Alton gave her a thumbs-up from the back of the room, pride evident on his face.

As the session concluded, Theresa stepped down, feeling a sense of accomplishment wash over her. She had not only shared her knowledge but had also sparked conversations that could lead to real change. She knew that her education was not just about learning theories but also about applying those lessons to make a difference in her community.

"As she walked out of the classroom, bursting with pride, she bumped into Ledger, who had come to support the students, he smiled at her. 'You did fantastic, Theresa!' he remarked, Your passion for sustainable practices really shone through," he praised. Recognizing that the voices of the youth would play a pivotal role in the community's future. Henri, watching from the back, felt a swell of pride. His children were becoming the advocates they desperately needed, showing not just knowledge but also a deep connection to their heritage and the issues facing their community.

He recalled the countless conversations they had shared at the dinner table, discussing sustainable practices and the importance of preserving their cultural identity. It inspired him to see how those discussions had translated into action. The way Theresa spoke so passionately about sustainable trade not only reflected her education but also the values he and Ledger had instilled in her. As she posed for photos with classmates, her laughter ringing out through the hallway, Henri felt a renewed sense of hope.

This was not just about one presentation; it was a glimpse into a future where this generation could lead with empathy and resilience. He felt grateful that, even amid the economic challenges they faced, they were cultivating a generation equipped to uplift their community. As students gathered around to share their thoughts and continue the discussion sparked by Theresa's project, Henri knew that change was not only possible but already unfolding in front of him, one inspired voice at a time."

"Thanks, Ledger! It meant a lot to share what we have been talking about at home," she replied, a sense of purpose filling her heart. She realized that through her studies and community involvement, she was, in her own way, following the footsteps of her father, Henri—building a foundation for a brighter, more equitable future for their community.

They believe that true transformation comes from within and are committed to nurturing the potential of passionate individuals who are eager to take initiative. By providing mentorship and resources, Ledger and Henri create pathways for these emerging leaders to organize local events and advocate effectively for the changes their community needs.

To facilitate this empowerment, Ledger and Henri host leadership workshops that focus on essential skills such as effective communication, event planning, and advocacy strategies. These workshops serve as platforms for aspiring leaders to learn from one another, share experiences, and develop their unique voices. By fostering a sense of collaboration, they create an environment where participants feel supported and encouraged to step into leadership roles.

Additionally, Ledger and Henri connect these emerging leaders with valuable resources, including access to funding opportunities, training materials, and best practices from successful community initiatives. They emphasize the importance of cultural relevance and grassroots engagement in all advocacy efforts, ensuring that leaders understand how to communicate the community's needs and aspirations to decision-makers.

As these local leaders begin to act, they organize their own community events, ranging from educational workshops to cultural festivals, that reflect the unique interests and concerns of their neighborhoods. This bottom-up approach ensures that the needs and voices of community members are not only acknowledged but actively prioritized. Ledger and Henri remain available for guidance and support, celebrating the successes of these leaders while helping as they navigate challenges.

The empowerment of local leaders becomes a transformative force within the community. As they take ownership of initiatives, the sense of agency among residents grows, leading to increased participation and engagement in community affairs. People start to realize that they have the power to influence decisions that affect their lives, which cultivates a lasting culture of grassroots leadership.

Through their dedicated efforts to empower community leaders, Ledger and Henri are not only amplifying the voices of their community but also fostering a sustainable framework for future advocacy. By encouraging individuals to step up and take charge, they create a ripple effect of leadership that inspires others to follow suit. As these leaders champion causes that resonate with the community, they build a more inclusive and responsive network that reflects the true essence of collective action.

In the end, Ledger and Henri's approach to empowering local leaders paves the way for a stronger, more resilient community. Together, they cultivate a culture of collaboration and empowerment, ensuring that the voices and visions of the people remain at the forefront, leading to meaningful change and a brighter future for all.

By organizing collaborative community events that blend agricultural showcases with educational exhibitions, Ledger and Henri create vibrant opportunities for families to come together in celebration of their collective identity. These events serve as dynamic platforms for local farmers to display their produce, artisans to showcase their crafts, and educators to share knowledge on sustainable practices and economic development. From colorful farmer's markets to interactive workshops, each gathering is designed to resonate with the community's values and strengths.

As families arrive, the atmosphere hums with excitement and camaraderie. Parents chat about their crops and share gardening tips, while children participate in hands-on activities like planting seeds or crafting with local materials. Ledger and Henri encourage local chefs to prepare dishes using the produce, highlighting the connection between agriculture and nutrition, and allowing families to taste the fruits of their labor together.

These events foster relationships among community members, reinforcing the power of unity in addressing common challenges. With each gathering, people learn from one another, exchanging ideas about sustainable practices and support networks. Workshops led by local experts become a focal point for meaningful discussions, empowering families to take ownership of their roles within the community and advocate for their needs.

As the network strengthens, families begin to feel a renewed sense of purpose and belonging. They realize that their individual efforts contribute to a larger tapestry of resilience and collective support. Parents who once felt isolated now find themselves surrounded by fellow community members with shared values and aspirations. The joy of reconnecting with their roots and the commitment to a brighter future infuse the gatherings with a palpable energy.

Through these collaborative events, Ledger and Henri effectively lay the groundwork for a thriving community spirit. By celebrating their shared identity and the diverse talents within their neighborhood, they cultivate an environment where everyone feels valued and empowered. This sense of togetherness not only enhances local pride but also strengthens their resolve to work together in facing future challenges, ensuring that their collective identity remains vibrant and impactful for generations to come.

In the vibrant communities of Bioche, and Colihaut, Ledger and Henri's tireless efforts have sparked a transformative movement that transcends generations. Recognizing that the children are the essential catalysts for change, they have focused their initiatives on breaking the cycle of disadvantage perpetuated by colonial legacies. Through innovative mentorship programs, Ledger and Henri empower young leaders to embrace their potential, instilling in them the values of social responsibility, environmental stewardship, and cultural pride. This approach not only addresses the immediate challenges faced by their communities but also ensures that future generations are equipped with the knowledge and confidence to advocate for a more equitable and sustainable world.

At a vibrant outdoor community fair held at La Place Dame, in Colihaut, the communities of Bioche, and Dublanc, were present. The colorful stalls showcased local crafts, food, and initiatives resulting from Ledger and Henri's efforts. The atmosphere is alive with laughter, music, and chatter, creating an infectious sense of community pride.

Under the bright Caribbean sun, families gathered in the heart of Colihaut for a celebration of community spirit, the culmination of Ledger and Henri's collective efforts to instigate meaningful change. Colorful banners fluttered in the warm breeze, each one emblazoned with powerful words: Unity, Empowerment, Heritage. The fair was not just a showcase of local culture, but a testament to the strength of the communities of Bioche, and Colihaut.

"Look at this turn-out, Henri!" Ledger exclaimed, gesturing to the sea of smiling faces—children running freely, elders sharing stories, and local artisans displaying their crafts. "We did this together!"

Henri beamed, taking in the scene with a mixture of pride and gratitude. "It is incredible to see everyone coming together like this. All those hours of planning and meetings were worth it."

As they meandered through the fair, Ledger stopped watching a group of children at the Environmental Stewardship Station, where kids were learning about recycling and sustainable practices. Young leaders were springing up right before their eyes; a teenage girl named Amina led a demonstration on creating compost bins from household waste.

"Let's tidy up our community and be responsible for the environment!" Amina encouraged, her passion evident as she enthusiastically explained the benefits of composting. Ledger and Henri exchanged a proud glance. This was exactly the kind of empowerment they had envisioned.

"Look at her," Ledger remarked, nodding toward Amina. "She is exactly what we were hoping for—someone who understands the importance of responsibility and sustainability. Imagine how far this influence will reach."

"Absolutely," Henri replied, his voice warm with enthusiasm. "By mentoring these young leaders, we are not just changing lives today. We are breaking the cycle of disadvantage for future generations. They will carry these lessons forward, instilling pride in their community."

As they continued through the festive atmosphere, they came across a performance stage where local youth showcased traditional dances and songs. The audience erupted with applause as Amina and her friends performed a vibrant cultural dance that celebrated their heritage. Ledger felt a swell of pride, recognizing the deep-rooted connections to their history being honored in such a lively way.

"Remember when we first started this journey?" Ledger asked with a reflective tone in his voice. "Back then, it felt like such a monumental challenge. But now, look what we have accomplished."

Henri nodded, his expression thoughtful. "It is more than just projects; it is about fostering a sense of belonging and responsibility. We are building a foundation where our culture can thrive, and our youth can become stewards of this legacy."

As the fair progressed, Henri and Ledger took a moment to connect with young attendees who had participated in their mentorship program. They offered workshops on leadership, community engagement, and self-expression.

"Hi, Ledger! Hi, Henri!" called out James, his face lighting up with excitement as he approached. "Thanks to your program, I just organized a cleanup event in Dublanc! We had over thirty kids show up!"

"That's fantastic, James!" Henri replied, clapping him on the shoulder. "You are making a real impact. This is just the start of what you can achieve."

"I have plans for more events, too," James continued, his eyes gleaming with ambition. "I want to inspire others to join us and take care of our community, just like you both have."

"Keep that spirit alive," Ledger encouraged. "You and your friends are the future. Your leadership can spark even more change and inspire others to step up.

As day turned to dusk, the fair transformed under a canopy of twinkling lights, casting a warm glow that filled the atmosphere with a sense of hope and camaraderie. Families gathered around, sharing food and stories, while laughter and music floated through the air.

As Ledger and Henri watched the scene unfold, they felt a profound sense of fulfillment. They had not only influenced their immediate community but also inspired a movement that resonated with future generations—a movement that embraced social responsibility, environmental stewardship, and deep cultural pride.

"Tonight, we've celebrated our past, but more importantly, we're paving the way for the future," Ledger said, his voice steady with conviction. "With every child committing to this community, we ensure that the legacies of colonial disadvantage can be rewritten."

Henri nodded in agreement, his heart full. "It is all about connecting the past with the future. These kids have the tools to redefine their narratives, to truly own their stories. And I believe they will."

As they joined in the festivities, Ledger and Henri knew that this was just the beginning. Together, they had ignited a fire within their community that would burn brightly for generations to come, ensuring a legacy of empowerment, resilience, and hope.

Ledger and Henri recognized the untapped potential within the youth of Bioche, and Colihaut, prompting them to introduce comprehensive youth engagement programs focused on leadership development, agriculture, and the arts. These initiatives operate on the principle that when young people are given the tools to explore their interests, they not only grow as individuals but also contribute meaningfully to their communities. By creating a safe and supportive environment, Ledger and Henri encourage participants to pursue their passions while instilling in them the core values of social responsibility and community involvement. This holistic approach aims to cultivate a new generation of leaders who are aware of their surroundings and committed to making a difference.

The programs offer a diverse range of workshops designed to equip young individuals with essential life skills. Topics such as public speaking and advocacy skills are integrated into the curriculum, empowering participants to voice their opinions and champion the causes they care about. Additionally, practical sessions on sustainable farming practices not only provide valuable knowledge about agriculture but also demonstrate the importance of environmental stewardship. Through interactive learning experiences, youth discover how to implement sustainable methods within their own communities, turning knowledge into action. This blend of education and hands-on experience helps to create informed citizens who understand the intricacies of their local environment and the global implications of their actions.

As the programs gain momentum, a vibrant community of passionate individuals emerges, dedicated to tackling the challenges that lie ahead. Young participants develop confidence, creativity, and critical thinking skills, preparing them not just to face their futures, but to reshape them. The arts component of the program encourages self-expression and cultural pride, providing a platform for youth to showcase their talents and connect with their heritage. By participating in cultural events, performances, and artistic collaborations, these young leaders create a sense of unity and shared purpose, reinforcing the idea that they are a vital part of their community's ongoing transformation.

The youth engagement programs spearheaded by Ledger and Henri catalyzes change. By cultivating emerging leaders who are well-versed in advocacy, sustainability, and the arts, they are fostering a future where community involvement is second nature. The impact of these initiatives extends far beyond the immediate environment, creating a ripple effect that inspires other young people to engage, contribute, and strive for a brighter, more equitable future. As these leaders continue to grow and evolve, they carry with them the lessons learned and the values instilled through the program, ensuring that the spirit of community empowerment thrives in Bioche, and Colihaut for generations to come.

Recognizing the profound value of cultural interchange, Ledger and Henri embark on an initiative to organize cultural exchanges with schools in neighboring communities. This program aims to broaden the horizons of young individuals by exposing them to diverse perspectives and practices, cultivating a deeper understanding and appreciation for different cultures. Through heartfelt collaboration, students from Bioche, and Colihaut engage with their peers in nearby areas, participating in joint activities that delve into agriculture, art, and local customs. These exchanges create a unique opportunity for children to learn from one another, fostering a sense of unity while celebrating the rich tapestry of traditions that exist within their region.

The cultural exchanges are thoughtfully designed to connect agriculture with local customs, allowing students to explore how these elements intertwine. For example, during visits to farms or community gardens, children are encouraged to share their agricultural practices, recipes, and stories that reflect their respective heritages. This immersive experience not only enhances their understanding of sustainable farming but also highlights the significance of food traditions and their role in cultural identity. By participating in hands-on activities such as cooking workshops or traditional craft sessions, students draw meaningful connections between their own practices and those of their peers, inspiring a deeper appreciation for both their heritage and the diversity that surrounds them.

As interactions unfold, the emphasis on inclusivity and collaboration becomes a cornerstone of the exchanges. Students learn the art of communication and teamwork while engaging in dialogue about their experiences, challenges, and aspirations. Through storytelling sessions and collaborative projects, they discover common ground, breaking down barriers and nurturing friendships that extend beyond their immediate communities. This newfound awareness fosters a generation that embraces diversity, understanding that their differences are assets that enrich their lives and strengthen their communities. Ledger and Henri witness the transformative power of these exchanges as the children celebrate their newfound friendships through laughter, shared meals, and creative expressions, solidifying the idea that collaboration is vital for collective growth.

The cultural exchanges initiated by Ledger and Henri not only enhance the educational experience of young people but also instill critical values that transcend mere tolerance. As participants embrace their own heritage alongside the traditions of others, they develop a strong sense of identity rooted in respect and empathy. This proactive approach to cultural interchange not only prepares the youth for a diverse world but also cultivates a community of future leaders who are committed to inclusivity and collaboration. The bonds forged during these exchanges lay the groundwork for a united and resilient generation, equipped to advocate for understanding and cooperation in an increasingly interconnected world.

As the community of Bioche, and Colihaut begins to witness tangible changes stemming from their collective efforts, Ledger and Henri take time to reflect on the growth of their alliance and the progress made since their journey began. What once seemed like distant dreams evolved into concrete achievements, showcasing the remarkable resilience and determination of the people they serve. To commemorate these milestones, Ledger and Henri host annual events that celebrate the accomplishments of the community, turning moments of reflection into vibrant celebrations of unity. These gatherings are not merely ceremonies; they are vibrant expressions of community spirit, encapsulating the heart and soul of their shared journey.

During these annual celebrations, families are honored for their excellence in sustainable farming practices and educational advancements, recognizing those who have gone above and beyond to implement eco-friendly techniques and foster academic success among the youth. As community members come together, the positive energy is palpable; proud parents and children alike share stories of their achievements, radiant with the joy of their hard work paying off. Food stalls overflow with locally grown produce, while cultural performances fill the air with music and dance, creating an atmosphere of festivity and pride. These events become a platform for individuals to showcase their talents and innovations, highlighting the diverse fabric of the community.

In addition to acknowledging individual achievements, these celebrations serve a deeper purpose—fostering a profound sense of pride and belonging among all participants. As families gather to share their journeys, the collective narrative of struggle and triumph unites them, reinforcing the bonds that hold the community together. Ledger and Henri watch with satisfaction as connections deepen, friendships are formed, and a shared vision for the future crystallizes in the hearts of attendees. The events serve as a poignant reminder of where they started and how far they have come, helping to instill a sense of accountability and purpose within the community.

These annual celebrations also act as a beacon of motivation for continued growth and engagement. They inspire attendees to set new goals for the coming year, reminding them that their efforts contribute to a larger movement of empowerment and sustainability. Ledger and Henri use these occasions to evaluate progress, discussing both successes and areas for improvement, fostering an environment where community feedback is valued and encouraged. As the community reflects on its achievements, it reinforces its commitment to collaboration and nurtures the hope that their shared journey will continue to thrive, paving the way for future generations to lead informed and empowered lives. Through these celebrations, Ledger and Henri not only honor the strides already made but also illuminate the path forward, invigorating the community to embrace the challenges and opportunities that lie ahead.

During the vibrant annual events organized by Ledger and Henri, a key focus is placed on gathering success stories from families who have directly benefitted from their support network. As community members share their experiences, whether it is a young farmer who has mastered sustainable practices or a family that has successfully integrated educational advancements into their daily lives, these narratives unfold like a rich tapestry, showcasing the resilience and determination of the community. Ledger and Henri take careful notes, understanding that each story is a testament to the collective effort that has transformed their community. By documenting these successes, they aim to illuminate the positive impact of their initiatives, capturing the spirit of hope and perseverance that has emerged from working together.

This collection of stories serves not only to celebrate individual achievements but also as a powerful advocacy tool for future efforts. Ledger and Henri recognize that these narratives have the potential to resonate beyond their community, influencing policymakers and stakeholders who hold the keys to broader support and investment. By articulating the tangible benefits gleaned from community-driven initiatives—like increased agricultural productivity, educational attainment, and improved social cohesion, they can effectively communicate the need for continued resources and attention to their cause. Each documented story becomes a compelling argument, illustrating how investment in local programs yields significant returns for the community, therefore advocating for policies that prioritize grassroots efforts.

Moreover, these success stories foster a strong sense of pride among community members, reinforcing the idea that their hard work and collaboration are making a real difference. Families feel empowered to contribute their narratives, knowing that their experiences are valuable pieces of a larger movement. Ledger and Henri ensure that these stories are shared widely, utilizing social media, community newsletters, and local events to amplify their reach. This not only builds awareness within their own community but also connects them to similar movements and initiatives in other regions, fostering a network of shared learning and support.

As they compile these success stories into a comprehensive report, Ledger and Henri see it as more than just documentation; it becomes a narrative of triumph that speaks to the core values of resilience, unity, and empowerment. This living document serves as a blueprint for future initiatives, illustrating the efficacy of community engagement and the importance of sustained support. By sharing these successes, Ledger and Henri not only celebrate the achievements of the families within Bioche, and Colihaut but also pave the way for continued advocacy, ensuring that their collective journey toward empowerment remains in the spotlight, inspiring others to invest in community-led change.

While the progress made within the communities of Bioche, and Colihaut is commendable, Ledger and Henri recognize that significant challenges still lie ahead. Climate change, with its increasingly erratic weather patterns and rising sea levels, poses a pressing threat to local agriculture and food security. Additionally, economic shifts—which can lead to job loss and reduced investment in rural areas—exacerbate existing vulnerabilities. Compounding these issues are the lingering effects of colonial policies that continue to shape socio-economic disparities. Despite these obstacles, Ledger and Henri remain committed to their mission, drawing on the strength of their alliance to foster a spirit of resilience within the community.

Their collaborative approach enables community members to confront these challenges with unity and determination. Ledger and Henri emphasize the importance of open dialogue, encouraging people to express their concerns and ideas for navigating the evolving landscape. By facilitating workshops and town hall meetings, they provide a platform for sharing knowledge and experiences, enabling families to collectively brainstorm solutions to the issues they face. This process not only enhances individual agency but also solidifies the bonds of trust and cooperation among community members, reinforcing their commitment to work together for a common purpose.

Through their ongoing efforts, Ledger and Henri introduce innovative strategies aimed at building resilience in the face of these pressing challenges. For example, they collaborate with local scientists and agricultural experts to implement climate-smart farming techniques that minimize environmental impact while maximizing yields. Education initiatives are also expanded to equip young people with the skills needed to navigate economic changes and capitalize on new opportunities. By focusing on adaptability and sustainability, they are preparing the community to withstand and thrive amid uncertainties.

Despite the gravity of these challenges, the alliance between Ledger, Henri, and community members remains a powerful source of hope and strength. They understand that tackling these issues will not happen overnight, but the collective resolve to face adversity enables them to envision a brighter future. As they confront climate change, economic shifts, and historical inequities, Ledger and Henri are steadfast in their belief that with collaboration, creativity, and unwavering support, the community can not only survive but thrive. Together, they transform challenges into opportunities for growth, forging a path forward that is defined by resilience, unity, and shared purpose.

As part of their unwavering commitment to building resilience, Ledger and Henri continuously assess the evolving needs of their community. They understand that in a rapidly changing world, flexibility and responsiveness are essential. By maintaining an open line of communication with community members, they create an environment where feedback is not only welcomed but actively sought. This proactive engagement allows them to stay attuned to the pressing challenges faced by families in Bioche and Colihaut, enabling them to adapt their strategies accordingly. Whether it is addressing a sudden economic downturn or implementing new agricultural practices to combat climate change, their ability to pivot ensures that the alliance remains effective and relevant.

Collaboration is at the heart of Ledger and Henri's adaptive strategy. They routinely engage with local experts—such as agricultural scientists, educators, and sustainability advocates—to co-create innovative solutions tailored to the community's specific context. By leveraging local knowledge and expertise, they can develop initiatives that are not only grounded in practical realities but also resonate with the cultural fabric of the community. For instance, when faced with the challenges of soil degradation due to climate change, they partner with agronomists to design workshops on regenerative farming techniques that empower local farmers to restore their land while increasing productivity. This collaborative approach maximizes the impact of their efforts while fostering a sense of ownership among community members.

Furthermore, Ledger and Henri recognize that adaptability goes beyond just responding to immediate challenges; it is about fostering a culture of innovation and learning. They encourage experimentation within the community, where new ideas can be tested and evaluated, leading to continuous improvement. By celebrating both successes and failures as learning opportunities, they create an atmosphere that empowers individuals to take initiative and contribute to problem-solving efforts. This culture of innovation not only enhances the community's capacity to adapt to change but also builds confidence among its members, reinforcing their belief in collective agency.

The adaptive strategies employed by Ledger and Henri become a hallmark of their approach, distinguishing their alliance in a landscape marked by uncertainty. By remaining open to change and collaborating closely with both local experts and community voices, they ensure that their initiatives are responsive and effective. This resilience is not only crucial for addressing current challenges but also for preparing the community for future uncertainties. As they weave adaptability into the very fabric of their work, Ledger and Henri empower the community to thrive amid change, fostering a sense of hope and possibility that inspires all.

Looking ahead, Ledger and Henri are filled with a deep sense of optimism for the future of Bioche, and Colihaut. Their alliance, built on the foundations of collaboration and resilience, not only strengthens community ties but also ignites a shared sense of hope for what can be achieved when families come together for a common purpose. They envision a vibrant future where sustainable practices not only thrive but become the norm, fostering a balanced relationship between the community and its natural resources. This vision includes agricultural innovation that prioritizes environmental stewardship, ensuring that the land remains fertile and productive for generations to come.

In addition to sustainable farming, Ledger, and Henri advocate for a future where education is accessible to all members of the community. They dream of a Bioche and Colihaut where every child, regardless of their background, can pursue their studies and develop their talents. By continuing to expand educational initiatives—such as after-school programs, mentorship opportunities, and vocational training—they aim to equip young people with the skills necessary to navigate a rapidly changing world. This commitment to education not only empowers individuals but also uplifts the entire community, creating a ripple effect of knowledge and opportunity that fosters economic stability and social cohesion.

Cultural heritage also plays a pivotal role in Ledger and Henri's vision for the future. They see a community that celebrates its diverse history and traditions while embracing new ideas and influences. By integrating cultural education into their programs and organizing events that spotlight local art, music, and storytelling, they foster an environment where pride in one's heritage flourishes. This celebration of culture not only strengthens individual identities but also builds bridges between different groups within the community, reinforcing the values of inclusivity and respect.

Ledger and Henri's vision for the future is one marked by unity, sustainability, and empowerment. They believe that as families continue to work together and support one another, they can create a strong foundation for generations to come. Their optimism is rooted in the belief that change is not just possible, but already underway, fueled by the dedication and resilience of the community. With each step taken together, they are paving the way for a brighter future, one that reflects the aspirations and dreams of the people of Bioche, and Colihaut, where hope flourishes, and possibilities abound.

By laying the groundwork for collaboration, advocating for community rights, and empowering future generations, Ledger and Henri create a lasting impact that transcends their own families and ripples throughout the wider region. Their commitment to fostering unity and resilience serves as a beacon of hope and a practical model for communities striving to overcome the vestiges of colonialism and address contemporary challenges. As they actively engage in discussions around land rights, social equity, and environmental sustainability, Ledger, and Henri not only remedy local issues but also empower community members to recognize their value and advocate for their needs. This groundwork cultivates a collective consciousness that inspires individuals to take ownership of their future and assert their rights within the larger socio-political landscape.

The success of Ledger and Henri's initiatives resonates beyond Bioche, and Colihaut, inspiring similar movements in neighboring communities grappling with the legacies of colonialism. Their story of transformation becomes a powerful narrative that demonstrates the efficacy of grassroots organizing and collaborative problem-solving. As community networks flourish and advocacy efforts gain momentum, other regions begin to implement their own versions of the alliance's strategies—sharing knowledge, resources, and support to uplift one another. This interconnectedness fosters a regional movement rooted in shared values of sustainability, education, and cultural pride, reinforcing the idea that together, communities can tackle systemic challenges and create meaningful change.

Moreover, the focus on empowering future generations ensures that the impact of Ledger and Henri's work is both profound and enduring. By mentoring young leaders and integrating community-defined educational pathways, they foster a new cohort of advocates equipped to champion their causes. These youth, emboldened by the examples set before them, carry the lessons of resilience, collaboration, and social justice into the next chapter of their community's narrative. The legacy of Ledger and Henri is not merely one of localized change but one that plants seeds for broader activism around equity and rights, inspiring young people to become agents of change.

In summary, the long-term impact of Ledger and Henri's work is characterized by their ability to galvanize community spirit, promote sustainable practices, and empower individuals to claim their rights. Their alliance symbolizes a shift toward collective agency, encouraging communities across the region to unite in the pursuit of justice and equity. As their influence spreads, they help to weave a resilient fabric of interconnected communities that honor their past while courageously shaping their future together, ensuring that the legacy of their efforts continues to inspire and uplift countless others for generations to come.

Through their alliance, Ledger and Henri have profoundly transformed the socio-political landscape of Bioche, and Colihaut, creating an environment where community rights are not only recognized but revered. By promoting a culture of inclusivity and collaboration, they have ensured that the lessons of history guide current practices and inform a more equitable future. Their work champions the voices of marginalized individuals, empowering them to engage actively in the local governance of their communities. This emphasis on honoring rights and history fosters a sense of belonging and purpose, essential for building a cohesive and forward-thinking society.

By uniting their efforts, Ledger and Henri not only drive meaningful change within their own community but also plant seeds of resilience that promise to flourish for generations to come. Their initiatives have laid a foundation that will endure, cultivating an engaged citizenry capable of navigating the complexities of the challenges they face. As families learn to work together creatively and collaboratively, they develop a strong sense of agency that will empower future leaders to carry forth the mantle of advocacy and innovation. This continuity of purpose ensures that the ethos of resilience and community empowerment remains vibrant and active long after their initial efforts.

Their journey serves as a powerful testament to the efficacy of collaboration, highlighting the strength that emerges when individuals collectively advocate for justice, equality, and shared aspirations. In confronting both historical and contemporary challenges, Ledger and Henri illustrate that transformation is possible when communities come together with a common vision and a commitment to support one another. The lessons learned from their work resonate well beyond the borders of Bioche, and Colihaut, inspiring other communities grappling with similar issues to adopt inclusive and collaborative approaches.

As they reflect on their accomplishments, Ledger and Henri recognize that their legacy is not just about the tangible changes they have made but also about the enduring spirit of solidarity that has been cultivated among the people. They have shown that genuine transformation is built on relationships, trust, and shared hope for a brighter future. Through their alliance, they have forged a path defined by resilience, demonstrating that when individuals unite under a common banner, they can indeed effect lasting change. Their story will continue to inspire new movements, proving that the road to justice and equality is illuminated by the collective strength of those who dare to dream and act together.

ᘓ

Part Six: Legacy of Hope

Chapter Seventeen: Tensions and Resolutions

As the sun began to set over the lush hills of Dominica, casting a warm golden hue across the landscape, members of the Sebastien and Philogene families gathered at Coco's Tavern, it had become a hub for dialogue and activism. The air was thick with anticipation and trepidation, amplified by the palpable tension that had been building within their villages. The complexities of landownership issues, exacerbated by the historical injustices of colonial policies, had resurfaced, igniting long-simmering grievances among community members. The Philogene family, known for their agricultural expertise but struggling against bureaucratic obstacles, found themselves increasingly frustrated alongside the Sebastians, who had long fought for labor rights and access to quality education for their children.

As the families took their seats in the dimly lit room, Ledger, an articulate and passionate member of the Philogene family, stood at the front, flanked by Henri from the Sebastien family. Both men felt the weight of the moment as they prepared to address their gathered friends and neighbors, their expressions reflecting the urgency of the times. "We are here today not just as families, but as a community that has been pushed to its limits," Ledger began, his voice steady yet filled with emotion. "For too long, we have lived under the shadow of inequity—inequity in land ownership, inequity in our labor rights, and inequity in education for our children. Today, we must confront these issues together."

The audience murmured in agreement, their expressions a mix of concern and determination. Henri stepped forward, ready to amplify Ledger's message. "Every time we should be celebrating our harvests, we are instead fighting for the right to plant. Every time our children should be learning in proper schools, they face overcrowded classrooms and outdated materials," he said, his voice rising with fervor. "This is unacceptable, and we cannot wait any longer for change to happen on its own. We need action!"

As emotions swirled, the tension in the room transformed into a collective energy, igniting a spark of motivation among the families present. Hands shot up, voices raised in agreement, each person sharing their experiences of struggle—stories of land disputes with large landowners, accounts of unfair treatment in the fields, and the heartbreak of watching children drop out of school due to financial pressures. A sense of community began to swell, each spoken word weaving a stronger bond among them, uniting their voices in a shared purpose.

The Sebastien and Philogene families recognized that they would need to rally their communities to seek resolutions and lasting change. They proposed forming a coalition to advocate for land reform, push for fair labor practices, and ensure equitable access to education. "We need to organize a community meeting and invite local leaders," Ledger suggested, "to present our concerns and demand accountability. If we stand together, they will have to listen!"

As the discussion intensified, plans were made for a town hall meeting that would bring together not just the families but the entire community. They would map out a strategy, collect stories, and prepare a presentation that reflected the collective grievances of all those impacted by the systemic inequalities that had plagued their lives. With every nod of agreement, the group felt empowered, their resolve solidifying amidst the rising tensions.

In the weeks to come, the towns of Bioche, Dublanc, and Colihaut would see a transformation as more families joined the coalition. The Sebastien and Philogene families understood that this was just the beginning, but together, they were ready to confront the challenges ahead. With clarity of purpose and the power of their community behind them, they set out on a journey to foster lasting change—

one that would resonate well beyond their struggles and inspire others grappling with similar injustices across Dominica. The rising tension had ignited a movement, and there would be no turning back.

The atmosphere of Dominica felt electric as summer clouds loomed ominously over the village square in Colihaut. Word had spread like wildfire about a recent government announcement—a series of new policies aimed at addressing land tenure and economic disparity while being governed under the lingering shadows of British Rule. Yet, instead of hope, these proposals have sparked outrage and fear among the populace. Ledger and Henri stood at the edge of the crowded square, their expressions mirrored in the frustration and concern that rippled through the crowd. The gathered community, a tapestry of faces representing families from Bioche, and Colihaut, buzzed with anxious voices debating the meaning and potential consequences of the government's latest initiative.

Ledger leaned closer to Henri, his brow furrowed. "These policies sound good on paper, but we know our people. They will not just alleviate the issues we have been facing. They are talking about consultation, but what does that really mean for us if we have no representation?" Henri nodded, his gaze scanning the crowd as individuals and families tossed worried glances at one another. The elders, once the respected voices of their communities, now looked uneasy, their concerns overshadowed by the imposing presence of the governing authorities.

As the crowd swelled, a local leader stepped onto a makeshift platform—it was Marlene, a fierce advocate known for her eloquence and unwavering commitment to community rights. She raised her hand to silence the crowd, her fiery spirit igniting a spark of unity. "We have gathered today to listen, to learn, and to speak!" she proclaimed. "These new policies may seem like a step forward but let us not forget the centuries of neglect and disenfranchisement we have endured. We must not be lulled into complacency when our needs have always been ignored!" The crowd erupted in a chorus of agreement, voices rising in a powerful symphony of dissent.

Ledger felt the tension in the air shift as the folks around him rallied to Marlene's call. "We need to come together, to advocate for real change. We demand a seat at the table where our fates are being decided!" she continued, her voice resonating through the square. "If we do not band together now, we risk further marginalization!" The words struck a chord, igniting the urgency of their shared struggle in the hearts of everyone present.

Henri exchanged glances with Ledger, their unspoken agreement solidifying their resolve. "We need a plan," Ledger urged, his voice firm amid the rising fervor. "It is not just about voicing our concerns. We need to organize, to present our demands clearly and powerfully, or we will just be shouting into the void.

With Marlene's guidance, they quickly formed committees, electing representatives to ensure all voices were heard—from farmers grappling with land disputes to families struggling with access to education. They even designated a group to draft a petition that would outline their collective grievances and proposed solutions, emphasizing the urgency for meaningful consultation with the governing bodies.

As the meeting ended, the atmosphere transformed from anxiety to hope, a shared vision taking root. "We must remember that we are stronger together," Marlene said, her eyes shining with conviction. "If we can unite our communities, our voices will be amplified beyond this square. We have a chance to shape our future!" The crowd erupted in cheers, their commitment solidified, moments of doubt replaced by determination.

Walking home later that evening, Ledger, and Henri felt a renewed sense of purpose. They understood that the road ahead would be challenging, but the spark of solidarity ignited that day signaled a shift in the political climate of Dominica—a shift towards empowerment, resistance, and the promise of change. The community had banded together; now, armed with resolve and unity, they were prepared to confront the injustices that had long plagued their lives, ready to shape their destiny rather than allow it to be dictated by forces beyond their control.

The sun hung low in the sky, casting long shadows across the fields of Au Fonde, where the fading light only highlighted the stark contrasts between the overgrown plots of struggling farmers and the meticulously cultivated lands of affluent landowners. Ledger stood at the edge of his family's Estate, a somber expression on his face as he surveyed the worn-out soil that used to yield vibrant crops. He turned to Clara, who had joined him, their shared frustration palpable amidst the clamor of a nearby meeting of struggling farmers contemplating their next steps.

"It's worse than ever, my dear," Ledger said, running his fingers through his unkempt hair. "The new government policies are only widening the gap. Look at what is happening around us. Families are losing their land to big agribusinesses because they can pay the taxes we cannot. It feels like we are being pushed off our own soil." Clara nodded, her face etched with concern as she looked over the fields once rich with life, now barren and struggling.

The meeting had drawn a crowd of concerned community members to the community center, each face reflecting the mounting pressure and despair. Shouts rang out as farmers voiced their grievances—stories of loss, anxiety, and the ever-present threat of eviction that loomed over those who could not keep pace with the wealthier business interests. "We've worked this land for generations!" one older farmer shouted, anger tinged with sorrow. "And now they want to take it away from us?"

As the voices filled the room, Ledger and Henri exchanged glances, understanding that this was more than a meeting; it was a turning point. They stepped forward to address the crowd, Ledger's heart racing with the burden of leadership. "We need to stand united against these inequalities!" he began, his voice steady despite the tumult around him. "We cannot let our families be sacrificed for the sake of profit. Access to land is our right, and we must advocate for equitable land rights that support small-scale farmers like us!"

His words settled over the crowd, the intensity of the moment igniting a fire within the gathered families. Henri took his turn, bolstered by Ledger's passion. "It is not just about surviving for today; it is about the legacy we leave for our children. Without land, our future is uncertain. We must lobby for policies that protect small farmers and ensure we get the resources we need to thrive.

The room erupted in applause and shouts of agreement, voices intertwining in a chorus of determination. Ledger felt the energy swell as he stepped closer and laid out a plan—one that involved organizing a coalition of farmers to advocate for their rights. "We must demand fair treatment, not just from our government but also from the powerful landowners who have been exploiting us for too long. It is time we asserted our needs as the backbone of this community."

As they discussed strategies that evening, Ledger felt a shift in the atmosphere. Families began to share stories of resilience and collaboration—ideas for cooperatives, resource sharing, and community gardens that could unite them in their struggle. Henri added, "If we can create a network that supports each other, we can amplify our voices. We need to go beyond just fighting for our rights; we must cultivate a movement that insists on equity and access!"

The excitement in the room was palpable, a testament to the strength of their collective resolve. But beneath the surface buzz of hope lay an undeniable current of urgency. The threat posed by government policies that favored large agribusiness was real and pressing. Families felt the need for immediate action, yet Ledger and Henri knew it was also a long-term battle that required meticulous planning and unwavering solidarity.

As the meeting ended, Ledger felt an overwhelming sense of purpose flooding through him. This collective moment was not merely about addressing today's challenges—it was about redefining the very foundation of how their communities would stand against societal inequalities. Together, they would advocate for a future where equitable land rights were not just a dream but a fundamental principle of their existence. The time for action was now, and with the support of their neighbors, Ledger and Henri were ready to fight for the resilience and dignity of their community.

The warm afternoon sun streamed through the open windows of the small schoolhouse in Colihaut, where Henri sat at an old wooden desk, the sound of children's laughter floating in from the playground. For a moment, he felt a sense of peace watching the eager faces of the students chasing one another under the shade of the mango trees. But that tranquility was shattered by the grim news he had heard earlier that day—proposed budget cuts aimed at educational reforms that could drastically affect the resources allocated to rural schools like theirs.

Henri's fingers drummed nervously against the desk as he mentally replayed the heated discussions in the bustling town hall meeting. The government's plan, which was framed as a necessary adjustment to streamline education funding, threatened to scale back crucial programs that supported not just schools but also after-school tutoring initiatives and nutritional programs for children from low-income families. "How can they even think about cutting funds?" he pondered, his heart heavy with concern for the children he had devoted himself to supporting. "These kids already face enough hurdles; they don't need their education under threat."

As the bell rang, signaling the end of recess, the children streamed back into the classroom, their energy infectious. Henri greeted them with a warm smile, but beneath his façade of cheerfulness lay a growing sense of urgency. "Alright, everyone! Today, we will continue our project about community heroes!" he said, trying to uplift their spirits. However, the weight of the impending threat loomed in his mind. He glanced across the classroom, imagining the bright futures of these young minds, potentially overshadowed by decisions made far from their reach.

After class, Henri gathered a few of the older students who often stayed behind to help arrange books and clean up the classroom. They were bright and motivated, and he loved to hear their ideas about the future. "Listen, I need your help with something important," he began, lowering his voice so only they could hear. "Talks are going on that could severely cut back on our school resources. We may lose programs that help us learn and grow."

The students exchanged worried glances, the realization of the threat settling over them. "But we need those programs!" a girl named Amina exclaimed, her brow furrowing with concern. "I rely on the tutoring classes after school to keep up with my studies!"

"I know, and that's why we have to act," Henri replied, urgency lacing his words. "I want us to organize a meeting—invite your parents, your friends, and other families in the community. We need to raise awareness about what is at stake. Education should never be a privilege; it is a right for all of us!"

The resilience in their young faces ignited hope in Henri's heart. They nodded in agreement, ready to rally their families to advocate for their rights. "We can make posters!" suggested Marlon, his eyes bright with determination. "And we can share our stories with everyone in Bioche and Colihaut!"

"Yes! We need everyone to understand how education affects our lives," Henri encouraged, feeling the strength of their resolve. "We will write letters, gather signatures, and even present at the upcoming community meeting. It is time for our voices as students, parents, and educators to be heard!"

As the children brainstormed ideas for their campaign, Henri felt a surge of motivation. Instilling a sense of agency in these young minds was part of the solution. He envisioned a future where every child in Bioche, Dublanc, and Colihaut had access not just to basic education, but to enriching experiences that would equip them for the challenges ahead. Education was not merely a luxury; it was an essential foundation that could reshape their entire community.

That evening, as he walked home under the fading light, Henri held onto the hope that had blossomed among his students. They were not just children; they were future leaders, capable of effecting change. If he could rally their families and the broader community, they could collectively challenge the narrative being pushed by those in power. Together, they would strive to protect the right to quality education—not just for themselves, but for every child in their villages, ensuring that knowledge and opportunity would remain a fundamental part of their lives. The fight for education access was more than a challenge; it was a mission, and Henri felt invigorated knowing he was not alone in this endeavor.

The Kai Cocoa in Colihaut buzzed with energy as families began to filter in for the first of a series of community forums organized by Ledger and Henri. Brightly colored banners proclaimed, "Voices of Change," while chairs were arranged in a large circle to foster openness and conversation. The scent of fresh bread and local fruits wafted through the air, adding to the warmth of the setting. As attendees filled the seats, a sense of anticipation crackled among them, a collective acknowledgment of the challenges ahead and the hope that this gathering could spark change.

Ledger stood at the front of the room, his heart pounding with excitement and a hint of anxiety. He shared a determined look with Henri, who was welcoming families and encouraging them to settle in. "Thank you all for coming," Ledger began, raising his voice to capture the attention of the growing crowd. "Today marks a step forward in our journey to seek justice for our communities. This space is yours—an opportunity to share your experiences with land ownership, education, and the issues we face together."

Henri nodded vigorously, stepping beside Ledger to add his words of encouragement. "We are here to listen, to learn, and to discuss how we can work together towards solutions. Your stories are powerful, and they matter! Let us create a space where everyone's voice is heard."

After the introductions, families began to share their stories. An older woman named Madam Elise spoke first, her voice trembling yet resolute as she recounted the painful experience of losing her family's land to a corporate agribusiness. "My parents worked this land for over fifty years," she said, her eyes glistening with tears. "Now, they want to take it away for a few dollars. I feel like I am losing my heritage."

A murmur of empathy spread through the room, and another attendee, a young father named Antoine, spoke up next. "I've faced the same thing," he said, his tone fierce but filled with despair. "We are given scraps while they benefit. My children deserve better; they deserve to grow up with a future on this land!"

As each person took their turn to speak, their shared narratives built a tapestry of frustration and resilience. A woman named Kiara, who struggled to keep her children in school despite the rising costs of supplies and fees, opened about her fears. "I want them to succeed, but how can I support their education when I can barely keep food on the table?" she asked, her voice cracking. "It feels like our dreams are slipping away. Education— it is supposed to be our right, and yet we feel it is a privilege we cannot afford."

Through the heartfelt exchanges, the atmosphere shifted from isolation to solidarity. Families began to see themselves in each other's stories, recognizing that their struggles, whether with land, education, or economic pressure, were interconnected. Ledger felt this bond deepening, and he sensed a movement taking shape amidst the pain.

Encouraged by the stories and buoyed by a sense of shared purpose, Henri stood up to propose actionable ideas. "What if we form committees focused on our issues? One for land rights, and another for education access. Together, we can advocate for policy changes and ensure our voices are heard where it matters most!"

The audience erupted with enthusiasm, excitement stirring the air. People began to clap and shout affirmations—this was precisely what they needed: a platform to collectively push for change. As families discussed how to organize, Ledger scanned the room filled with vibrant faces bonded by a common goal, realizing how powerful unity could be.

By the end of the forum, plans were made for additional meetings, and lists began to form for those wanting to participate in committees. The sense of agency blossoming in the room was palpable, transforming frustration into action. Ledger and Henri exchanged proud smiles, knowing this was just the beginning.

As families departed, a warmth lingered in the space—something they had all been searching for. The forums had provided more than just a venue for grievances; they had united diverse voices into a harmonious chorus demanding change, igniting a fire of resilience that would extend beyond the walls of the community center.

That night, as Ledger and Henri reflected on the day's events, they felt an invigorating hope. They understood that real change required not just voices but collaboration, relationships, and a commitment to walking the path together. The seed of solidarity had been planted, and now, it was up to them to nurture it into a movement that would stand firm against the inequalities faced by their families and communities.

The vibrant colors of the sunset poured into the community center as Ledger stepped up to the front of the room, the soft hum of conversation fading into an expectant silence. The gathering was larger than he had anticipated; families from Bioche, and Colihaut had come together, united by a rising discontent over land access issues that had become increasingly desperate. Ledger felt a surge of determination coursing through him as he looked out at the sea of faces, each reflecting a shared struggle and fierce longing for change.

"Thank you all for being here tonight," Ledger began, his voice steady yet passionate. "We are here not just to discuss our concerns—we are here to mobilize for action. The land we work on is not just soil; it is our heritage, our livelihood, and the foundation of our future. And right now, it is under threat."

He paused, allowing his words to sink in, sensing the tense atmosphere charged with anticipation. "For too long, we have been voiceless in the face of policies that prioritize large agribusinesses over smallholder farmers like us. The government needs to hear our demands! We need equitable land rights that recognize the importance of small-scale agriculture and the role it plays in sustaining our communities."

Hands began to rise in agreement, nods of affirmation spreading through the crowd. Encouraged by their reactions, Ledger continued, "We cannot let our livelihoods be dictated by people who see land as just another commodity. It is time we held our local authorities accountable! To do that, we need to present a united front. Each story shared tonight, each voice raised, adds to the power of our collective narrative."

Henri, standing beside Ledger with a notepad ready, was poised to take notes, but he also caught the eye of a woman across the room, Madam Elise, who had previously shared her painful experiences of losing her family land. She stood, her voice strong, echoing Ledger's urgency. "We need a plan. We cannot just complain; we must act! Not just for ourselves but for our children and future generations. If we do not stand up now, what will the next generation inherit?"

"Exactly!" Ledger exclaimed, driven by the shared conviction resonating through the room. "Let us start by drafting an open letter to our local government representatives. We will detail our grievances, share stories of how these land policies have impacted our lives, and demand a meeting to discuss equitable reforms."

The idea sparked excitement. "What if we also create a petition?" suggested a young farmer, eager to contribute. "We can gather signatures from families across our villages, showing just how many of us are affected!"

"Great idea!" Henri chimed in, eager to build on the momentum. "We can have stations at each community's market where people can sign. If we reach out to our network and neighboring communities, we can amplify our voices!"

With each suggestion, the voices in the room grew louder, the energy surging as people began discussing strategies and crafting language for their proposals. Ledger felt the transformative power of unity encapsulated in that moment. People were not just expressing their frustrations; they were taking the reins of their futures, ready to advocate for their rights as a collective force.

As the discussion continued, Ledger facilitated dialogues around the importance of sustainable agriculture. "We must emphasize that our farming practices promote biodiversity and protect our environment," he explained. "Policies should not only support equitable land distribution but also encourage sustainable practices that can benefit everyone in our community."

A ripple of agreement passed through the crowd, each person becoming increasingly animated as they envisioned a future where their children would inherit not only land but also rich traditions of sustainable farming.

After hours of brainstorming and solidifying their action plan, Ledger stepped back, taking a moment to observe the group. He felt a profound sense of pride swelling in his chest. Together, they had converted their fears into action, transforming frustration into a rallying point for change.

As the meeting wound down and families lingered to chat, the atmosphere was alive with hope and determination. Ledger and Henri exchanged satisfied nods, their hearts buoyed by the collective resolve they had kindled that night. It was a pivotal moment, a commitment to advocacy grounded in shared experiences, ensuring that their call for equitable land rights would not just echo in the walls of the community center but resonate through every corner of their villages and beyond. Together, they were ready to confront the injustices of the past and carve out a future defined by fairness, sustainability, and respect for their land.

Under a canopy of bright blue skies, Henri stood in the village square of Colihaut, flanked by a colorful array of handmade banners and posters created by local students. Today was the launch of his education equity campaign, an initiative he had been tirelessly coordinating over the past few months. Families from various backgrounds—teachers, parents, and students—had come together, their presence underscoring the urgency of the cause.

"Thank you all for joining us today!" Henri called out, a broad smile breaking across his face as he surveyed the crowd. "We are here to shine a light on the importance of equitable access to education for every child in our community. As you all know, the proposed budget cuts threaten to strip vital resources from our rural schools, leaving our children without the opportunities they deserve.

He paused to let his words resonate, the murmurs of agreement from the crowd encouraging him to continue. "Education is a fundamental right, not a privilege. Without the proper resources, how can we expect our children to thrive?" His voice carried strength, fueled by the determination forged in the countless conversations he had had with families who shared heart-wrenching stories of their struggles to keep their children in school.

The atmosphere buzzed with energy as Henri introduced the key elements of the campaign. "Today, we will be gathering signatures for our petition, urging policymakers to allocate more funding to our rural schools. We want to ensure that every child has access to quality education—comfortable classrooms, qualified teachers, and the supplies necessary for them to succeed!"

At the front of the crowd, a group of teachers stood in solidarity, nodding in agreement. One of them, Ms. Martin, stepped forward, her eyes fierce with passion. "We see firsthand the effects of underfunding on our students. Many of them lack basic resources like textbooks and technology, which puts them at a disadvantage compared to children in more affluent areas. Together, we can amplify our voices and demand the support we need!"

Encouraged by Henri's fervor and Ms. Martin's words, a wave of energy swept through the gathered families. Parents began to discuss their own experiences, the difficulty of affording transportation to schools, the lack of after-school programs, and the heartbreak of watching their children struggle to learn in overcrowded classrooms.

As Henri moved through the crowd, he actively engaged individuals and families, listening to their stories and inviting them to share. "What would your child's education look like if they had the resources they need?" he asked, drawing in parents and students alike. Slowly, they began to envision a brighter future filled with hope.

"I would like to see my daughter have access to computers and science labs," said one father, his voice earnest. "She dreams of becoming a doctor, but without the right resources, it seems impossible."

Henri nodded empathetically. "These are exactly the kind of stories we need to share in our petition! It is not just about funding, it is about dreams, futures, and the potential of our children.

As the sun dipped lower, casting a golden light across the square, Henri organized small groups to begin circulating the petitions among the crowd. Students teamed up with their parents, teachers paired with families, and together they moved from person to person, collecting signatures and sharing stories. The atmosphere transformed into a vibrant tapestry of community spirit, each signature representing a demand for change.

"Now, here's the next important step!" Henri announced as the initial wave of signatures began to accumulate. "We will present this petition to our local elected officials during a community meeting next month. We want them to understand how critical it is to invest in our future."

The crowd erupted in applause, their collective resolve solidifying as they envisioned the impact of their advocacy. Henri felt a surge of hope as he engaged further, reminding them of the power they possessed as a united community. "Together, we will show them that our children matter and that education equity is not just a dream—it's a necessity!"

As dusk fell, the event ended, but the atmosphere remained charged with purpose. Satisfaction washed over Henri as laughter and chatter filled the square, families exchanging contact information, forming bonds that would carry their campaign forward. He looked around to see the commitment in each face, the determination to fight for what is right, ignited by the shared understanding that advocacy was an essential tool.

That night, as Henri returned home, he could not shake the sense of accomplishment. The success of their campaign launch was just the beginning, but it had already shown families the strength of unity and the potency of their voices. By prioritizing educational access, they were not just advocating for policy reform; they were investing in the future of their community, forcing change, one petition at a time.

The air in the town hall was thick with tension as Ledger and Henri sat at a long, polished table, flanked by local officials who regarded them with expressions that danced between skepticism and irritation. The faint hum of conversation died down as the room filled with community members, eager to witness the meeting between their grassroots leaders and the local authorities. Ledger could feel the weight of expectation on his shoulders, not just for himself but for the families who had come to rely on their advocacy for change.

"Thank you for taking the time to meet with us today," Ledger began, trying to exude confidence despite the heavyweight in his stomach. "We're here to discuss the urgent need for policies that support equitable land rights and educational access for our community."

The room was silent for a moment before Councilman Harris leaned forward, fingers steepled. "While we appreciate your passion, Ledger, I must remind you that these discussions are delicate. The changes you are advocating for might disturb the social balance we have maintained in this community." His tone was smooth, but there was a clear warning in his words as if he were daring them to challenge the status quo.

Henri exchanged a quick glance with Ledger, each recognizing the precariousness of their position. "With all due respect, Councilman, our community is already experiencing disruption," Henri replied, his voice steady but steely. "Families are losing their land, children are lacking basic educational resources, and we cannot simply remain silent because it might disrupt things further. We need to advocate for a future where everyone can thrive."

Councilman Harris's brows furrowed as he shot a glance at the other officials seated beside him. "And what you propose would require a significant shift in funding and policy. We need to consider the implications on the agribusiness sector and the local economy. These entities provide jobs, and sweeping changes could endanger that stability."

"Stability?" Ledger echoed, leaning forward, his heart racing. "With the current model, many families are being pushed into poverty while the wealthy landowners profit. Your definition of stability is leaving our community behind. We want to create a system where small farmers and children have a fighting chance, too."

A murmur of agreement rippled through the audience, the tension in the room escalating. Ledger could see community members leaning forward in their seats, clearly invested in the exchange. The stakes were high; they could not afford the authorities to dismiss their concerns.

An older woman from the audience, Madam Elise, raised her hand, her voice carrying a gravitas that commanded attention. "We have lived through these oppressive situations for too long. We are not here to disrupt; we are here to build something sustainable for all of us. Ignoring our voices is what disturbs the harmony in our society!"

Councilman Harris sighed, his irritation visible. "While I understand your passion, advocating for these changes in such a confrontational manner could lead to unrest. I urge you to reconsider your approach. There are ways to work within the system."

Henri took a deep breath, grounding himself against the rising frustration. "We understand that change can be uncomfortable, but genuine dialogue is vital for progress," he said. "We are here not just as individuals, but as representatives of families who are desperate for help. If we do not speak up now, we fear for the future. We believe that constructive solutions can be found through collaboration rather than silence."

Another council member, a younger woman named Clary, frowned thoughtfully. "What if we scheduled a follow-up meeting to discuss potential compromises? There are pilot programs we could explore that would provide funding for local education without jeopardizing agribusiness."

Ledger seized the opportunity, nodding vigorously. "Absolutely! We are open to exploring collaborative solutions, but we need assurances that the concerns of our community are taken seriously. We want to be part of the solution, but we also need transparency and commitment from you all."

The atmosphere in the room shifted slightly, tension mingling with cautious optimism. Ledger and Henri exchanged hopeful glances, sensing a fragile opening among the authorities, yet fully aware of the remaining hurdles ahead.

Councilman Harris looked back at Ledger and Henri, his expression less hostile but still guarded. "Alright. Let us talk about a follow-up meeting. But I must stress that changes take time, and I cannot promise immediate action."

"We understand that" Henri replied, settling back in his chair, feeling the heaviness of the moment. "But every day we wait is another day our community suffers. We need to move beyond dialogue that leads nowhere. Action is what will build trust and heal our community."

As the meeting concluded, Ledger felt a flicker of hope amidst the lingering uncertainty. It was clear that the authorities were wary, and they would need to tread carefully to get their demands heard. However, the experience reinforced what they knew deep down: the experience reinforced what they knew deep down: the community's struggles were too great to be ignored, and the fight for equitable land rights and educational access was far from over. They understood that real change would require perseverance, unity, and a willingness to challenge the status quo despite the resistance they faced from those in power.

As families began to filter out of the town hall, Ledger felt energized by the support and determination shared in the room, even in the face of opposition. The conversations they had initiated today were just the beginning—every voice that had been raised, every story that had been shared, added weight to their cause.

Henri joined Ledger, both men feeling the gravity of their responsibility but also the excitement of harnessing this collective momentum. "We may not have won over the council today," Henri said, his brow still furrowed with focus, "but we planted seeds of change. They listened. We can build on that."

Ledger nodded, running his hand through his hair as they stepped outside into the cool evening air. "We need to harness this energy right away. Let us organize a follow-up meeting with the community, share what happened, and plan our next steps. We cannot let their pushback deter us—we need to keep advocating and keep pushing."

Back in the square, the community buzzed with discussion. Families gathered in small clusters, sharing their thoughts on the meeting and proclaiming their commitment to the cause. Ledger and Henri stood at the center, listening to the renewed optimism around them.

"We have to keep pushing the narrative of what education can mean for our children," Ledger said to the group, his voice rising above the crowd. "We must show the impact of equitable land access not just for today, but for generations to come. We cannot back down now!"

The crowd erupted in applause, and a sense of solidarity hung in the air, the embodiment of a community ready to face the challenges ahead.

"Together, we can demand change," Henri continued, emboldened. "Together, we can raise our voices until they cannot ignore us! Let us formulate our next steps. We have petitions to gather, stories to share, and a future to reclaim.

Motivated by their leaders, families felt invigorated and empowered to act. The barriers erected by authority were daunting, but they no longer felt insurmountable. Ledger and Henri exchanged glances, a quiet acknowledgment passing between them: they were at the forefront of something monumental.

Tonight, they would regroup, strategize, and rally their community to reassure every family that they mattered. No longer would their voices be drowned out by the status quo. The struggle ahead would be challenging, but they were committed to fighting for equitable land rights and access to education, thriving off the very resistance that sought to stifle them.

As the stars began to twinkle overhead, the community buzzed with laughter and dialogue, igniting visions of a future where every child would have the chance to dream and flourish. Together, Ledger and Henri, along with their community, were ready to face the trials ahead, undeterred, and resolute in the pursuit of justice for a

Kai Caco's atmosphere was charged with unease as Ledger prepared to address a gathering that had been called to address growing internal tensions among families regarding their activism. Henri sat nearby, his expression reflecting concern for the unity they had worked so hard to build. The room was filled, but a palpable divide lingered among the attendees, some families sitting together, whispering among themselves, while others exchanged wary glances.

"Thank you all for coming tonight," Ledger began, projecting warmth and familiarity into his voice despite the tension that crackled in the air. "I know we have all been feeling the pressure of our cause and the challenges we face as a community. We must open a dialogue about our differences so we can move forward together."

He could see a few faces tense at his words, particularly those of families who were feeling overwhelmed by their daily struggles. A father named Michel, his brow furrowed, stood to speak. "Look, I understand that education and land rights are important, but what good is that if I cannot put food on the table today? We need to think about our survival first. I cannot risk my livelihood for the sake of change!"

Nods of agreement surfaced in the crowd, voices murmuring support for Michel's sentiment. Ledger's heart sank for a moment as he recognized the urgent need for daily survival, overshadowing the broader goals they had been championing.

"Michel, your concerns are valid, and they echo the fears of many in this room," Ledger replied calmly. "But we must remember that the challenges we face are intertwined. Investing in quality education and advocating for our land rights will not just benefit us in the long run; it will create an environment where we can sustain ourselves better as a community."

But another voice broke through the murmurings—It was Amina, a young woman whose family had been actively involved in the campaigns. "But what if those changes take too long?" she asked, her voice firm but tinged with anxiety. "What if we advocate for something that will not help us now? I have seen families suffer while we are waiting for something that may never happen."

Henri jumped in, sensing the need for clarity. "We're facing a critical crossroads," he said, leaning slightly towards Amina. "Yes, personal survival is essential, and it is absolutely a priority. But this fight is about more than just the here and now—it is about ensuring that the next generation also has what they need to thrive. If we do not advocate for these systemic changes, we risk perpetuating a cycle that will make survival increasingly difficult for all of us in the future."

Ledger nodded in agreement, encouraging the community to engage in further discussion. "We need to recognize that both perspectives matter. Survival and long-term change are not mutually exclusive, they are two sides of the same coin. We cannot afford to lose the momentum of this movement while pursuing immediate needs."

After a few moments, an older woman in the back of the room, Madame Elise, slowly stood, her voice steady and full of wisdom. "When we advocate for our rights, we are not only securing our own single futures but also the future of every family here. I have children and grandchildren who deserve a better life than I had. If we unite our voices, we can demand resources that not only address today's challenges but also head off future crises."

The room fell silent as her words sank in, and Ledger seized the moment. "Madame Elise is right," he said earnestly. "We must channel our energy collaboratively. Let us focus on immediate solutions—we can create a food co-op to help families in need, while simultaneously working on initiatives that advocate for long-term resource allocation and educational funding."

A wave of murmurs swept through the crowd, and Ledger saw faces shifting from skepticism to contemplation. "Let us not create an 'us versus them' mentality within our community. We are all here because we want a better life for ourselves and our children. What are some immediate steps we can take together that will fortify our community while we also fight for systemic change?"

As the discussion continued, families exchanged thoughts about forming a combined effort—a task force that would address immediate resource needs while keeping the larger goals of education access and land rights in sight. Voices that had previously expressed concern about the risks of activism now began suggesting practical ideas for short-term relief and long-term advocacy.

By the time the meeting concluded, Ledger felt a renewed sense of hope. Although the path forward was not without its challenges, the community had begun to mend the rifts that could have threatened their collective effort. They understood that their struggles were deep-rooted and interconnected, and through open conversations and transparent communication, they had reaffirmed the importance of solidarity in the face of adversity.

As they all left the center that evening, Henri could sense the energy shift. The somber expressions that had filled the room at the start of the meeting had been replaced with a hint of optimism. Families lingered outside in clusters, talking animatedly about the ideas discussed, sharing hopes and concerns, and forging connections that had previously felt tenuous.

Henri and Ledger stood together on the steps of the community center, watching as people filtered out, and engaged in conversations about both immediate action and long-term goals. Ledger turned to Henri, his expression was a mixture of relief and determination.

"I think we managed to turn a corner tonight," Ledger said, a slight smile creeping onto his face. "Even if it was just a small step, we showed them that they can voice their fears and still advocate for change. That is what we need—dialogue."

Henri nodded, still feeling the buzz of the positive atmosphere. "I was concerned about losing their trust with the pushback we faced. But tonight, they showed they wanted to be part of the discussion. They do not want to just survive; they want to thrive together."

In the distance, they could hear the laughter of children playing as their parents exchanged ideas about starting a community garden and food co-op that would help relieve immediate stresses while also fostering cooperation. The thought of families growing their own food and sharing resources felt revolutionary, a tangible way to address survival without losing sight of the larger goals.

Ledger glanced at Henri, his brow thoughtful. "What do you think we should focus on next? We have so many ideas coming from that meeting—the food co-op, immediate educational resources, continuing our petitions… It is hopeful but overwhelming."

Henri crossed his arms, joy mingling with pragmatism as he contemplated their next steps. "Let us begin with the food co-op. It makes sense as a first move. It addresses the immediate needs of families while simultaneously reinforcing community ties. We can also form subcommittees to handle different initiatives, managing them without overwhelming ourselves or losing momentum."

Ledger nodded enthusiastically. "Let us get a planning meeting set up for that next week. We can distribute flyers to spread awareness and invite everyone to contribute. If we show them that tangible change is possible, it might also reinforce their commitment to the broader activism goals we are pursuing."

"Absolutely. But we need to remind them that while we are tackling these immediate issues, we cannot lose sight of our advocacy for land rights and educational funding," Henri emphasized, his eyes reflecting their shared vision. "It is all interconnected. We must keep reinforcing that importance."

As they stepped off the steps of the community center, they were joined by a small group of parents who had overheard their conversation. "We were just talking about starting the food co-op," one of them exclaimed—a mother named Lila, her eyes shining with excitement. "What do we need to do to help get that going? I can help organize meetings with neighbors!"

Henri smiled widely. "That is exactly the kind of enthusiasm we need! If we can gather others who are interested, let us outline some tasks and set a date for our first planning session. You would be surprised how quickly we can get this off the ground."

The discussions spread among the exiting families like wildfire, excitement bubbling over as the parents began to exchange contact information and brainstorm ideas. Ledger and Henri exchanged glances of satisfaction, both knowing they had sparked a renewed sense of purpose in their community.

As darkness fell, the town square was filled not with the weight of struggle but with the promise of change. The conversations continued to flow, laughter mixed with serious discussions about solutions and gathering support. There was a sense of solidarity building—a shared understanding that even with their differences, they were bound together by the desire for a more equitable future.

"Tonight was a success," Ledger said quietly, watching the scene unfold around them. "This is what community looks like."

Henri nodded, warmth filling his chest as they watched the laughter of children mingling with the fervor of the adults. "And this is just the beginning," he replied, a glint of hope shining in his eyes. "With every step we take together, we're paving the way for the changes we want to see."

With renewed energy and collective resolve, Ledger and Henri turned to join the gathering crowd, ready to lead their community into the brighter future they all believed was possible.

The community center buzzed with excitement as attendees filed in for the workshop hosted by Ledger, Henri, and their friends. Colorful banners hung from the ceiling, adorned with slogans advocating for land rights and educational access, setting a hopeful tone for the day. The scent of freshly tilled earth and vibrant flowers wafted in from the pots and planters set up around the room, ready for hands-on demonstrations of sustainable farming methods.

Ledger stood at the front, nervously adjusting his notes. He was flanked by Wizen and Petronel, who were busily preparing tools and materials for the first part of the workshop. Alton and Aldie, two enthusiastic members of the community known for their educational outreach, approached Henri to discuss his segment on educational resources.

"Are you ready for this?" Alton asked, grinning widely. "It's all about showing them how education ties into everything we're trying to achieve."

Henri nodded, feeling the weight of responsibility but also a thrill of anticipation. "Absolutely. If we can make that connection clear, we will help everyone understand that advocating for educational access is essential for our long-term success."

As the attendees settled down, Ledger stepped forward, his voice steadying as he smiled at the community members eager to participate. "Welcome everyone! We are so glad you could join us today. Our goal is to show how securing land rights and improving our farming practices can positively impact our livelihoods. Let us showcase the role that education plays in this journey."

Wizen stepped in next, his demeanor shifting from playful to serious. "Let's get started by diving into some sustainable farming practices," he said, holding up a handful of seeds. "Today, I want to share with you how choosing the right crops can not only increase our yields but also improve our financial situation. When we grow what our land can support best, we can enjoy better profits, which allows us to invest in our families and futures."

Petronel joined in, gesturing to the various tools laid before them. "We are going to demonstrate techniques that are easy and effective. The first thing we will discuss is crop rotation and its importance. These methods can lead to healthier soil and increased productivity over time."

As Wizen and Petronel led their demonstration, Henri moved to the side with Alton and Aldie, who carried materials related to educational resources. Henri began to outline the importance of marrying agricultural practices with educational initiatives.

"Education is key to understanding sustainable practices and expanding our options," Aldie emphasized, holding a handout that highlighted available educational programs and resources. "Both for adults and children. These resources can include workshops, tutoring, and even online courses that help us adapt to new agricultural technologies.

Alton added, his voice passionate, "By focusing on education, we are not just helping ourselves now; we are ensuring that the next generation is equipped to take on these challenges. Imagine our children learning how to farm better and more sustainably, continuing the fight for land rights with knowledge behind them!"

As the workshop continued, Ledger veered the group into a hands-on activity where participants paired up to plant seeds according to the techniques discussed. Wizen roamed the room, stopping to encourage discussions about specific crops and their benefits.

"Remember," he said enthusiastically, "the crops you choose can signal to others that we are capable of more than just survival; we are cultivating a future full of opportunities. This is as much about economic independence as it is about land rights."

Ledger watched as the community engaged, laughter and conversations filling the air. He felt optimistic; this collaboration was fostering a sense of shared investment among everyone present.

After the hands-on activity, Ledger and Henri gathered the group back together for a discussion. "Let's talk about how we can continue this momentum," Ledger began. "What we have learned today is just a starting point. How can we ensure that the knowledge we share here translates into action?"

"The first step is to look for ways to connect with our local schools," Henri suggested. "We can propose incorporating agricultural education into their curriculum—teaching children from a young age about sustainable practices and the significance of land rights."

Wizen raised his hand, his enthusiasm clear. "And we could establish a mentorship program where experienced farmers can guide newcomers, sharing knowledge on what crops work best in our area and how to navigate the land ownership process."

Petronel chimed in, "We can also create a community forum to discuss challenges we face in both farming and education. Allies from other villages may have useful insights to share."

People began to buzz with ideas, forming small groups to brainstorm potential initiatives. Ledger felt a sense of joy as he observed the collaborative spirit enveloping the room. Every suggestion contributed to a growing tapestry of hope and resilience.

As the workshop concluded, Henri smiled at Ledger, Alton, Aldie, and their friends. "Today was more than just a workshop Henri said, beaming at the group as they gathered their materials. "It was a turning point. Everyone here is beginning to see how our individual efforts connect to our collective future.

Ledger nodded in agreement, the weight of their shared accomplishment lifting his spirits. "Absolutely. We have shown that when we work together—sharing knowledge and strategies—we can empower each other. This is how we build a movement."

The atmosphere in the community center was charged with excitement as families chatted animatedly about the techniques they had learned and the ideas that had surfaced. Parents discussed the possibility of forming study groups for their children and sharing resources related to sustainable farming.

Alton spread out a list of local educational programs across a table, eager to engage more families. "Let us go over this together. I believe we can get everyone on board to help teach these methods in schools. The younger people learn about their rights and agriculture, the stronger our community will become.

Aldie was already jotting down additional ideas that had emerged during the discussions. "We should also consider setting up regular workshops if there is enough interest. The more we share, the more we grow—not just our crops but our knowledge," she said, her eyes shining with enthusiasm.

Wizen approached Ledger and Henri, his hands on his hips, a broad grin on his face. "You both did well, bringing everyone together like this. Even though some families are still worried about immediate survival, they are seeing that the fight for land rights involves real, usable skills we can implement right now."

Henri felt a swell of gratitude for his friends. "This wouldn't have been possible without you all," he said, his eyes scanning the room filled with hopeful faces and animated discussions. "It's about showing that by learning from one another, we can address both our urgent needs and our broader aspirations."

As participants began to exit, Ledger called out, "Do not forget to take your seed packets and handouts! And let us keep this conversation going. We will schedule our next meeting soon to discuss these initiatives in more detail.

Families nodded, clutching their materials tightly, some already asking each other for help as they headed toward the exit.

Once the last few people had left, Henri turned to the group standing around him, gratitude bubbling within him. "That was amazing. We are on the right path."

Petronel grinned widely. "And what is even better is that we are not just advocating for land and education—we are finally becoming the change we want to see. Our families are investing in this community and in each other."

"Next time, we might even bring in experts—agricultural educators who can teach us more advanced techniques," Alton suggested, his mind already racing with possibilities.

"That would be incredible," Ledger replied. "Imagine the potential for collaboration and how it could strengthen our advocacy even more."

As they cleaned up the tables, Wizen stopped and suggested. "You know, if we combine our efforts with the youth in the community, we could reach even more people. The kids bring in new ideas, and their energy is contagious. We could create a youth outreach program that incorporates farming and educational advocacy.

Henri smiled at the thought. "That is perfect. Engaging the younger generations will not only empower them but also help us build a legacy of advocacy that lasts."

With plans beginning to take shape, Ledger felt a renewed sense of purpose wash over him. They were no longer just a group of individuals with concerns; they were a united community ready to fight for their rights together.

"This is just the start," Ledger said, looking around at his friends and feeling the collective excitement for what lay ahead. "Let us keep building on this momentum and continue collaborating. Together, we will create a future where our community thrives."

The group nodded in agreement, laughter echoing as they left the community center, their hearts full of hope and determination for the journey ahead.

The sun hung high in the sky, casting a warm glow over the town hall as Ledger and Henri gathered their notes and materials for the upcoming meeting with local leaders and policymakers. They had spent weeks preparing, driven by the urgency of their community's need for change regarding land rights and access to education. The sense of anticipation crackled in the air as they approached the building, their hearts pounding with determination.

Inside the polished conference room, local council members and officials were already seated at the long, mahogany table. Ledger and Henri exchanged a glance, both aware that this meeting could set the course for their community's future.

"Remember," Henri said quietly, brushing off his sleeves nervously. "Stay focused on the facts and share the stories of our families. We need to highlight the urgency."

The Ledger replied, taking a steady breath. "We are here to bridge gaps, not create divides. Mutual respect is key." He nodded to a few allies from the community who had also arrived, ready to share their experiences.

As they entered the room, the council members greeted them with polite nods. Councilman Harrison, who had been a vocal opponent of their grassroots efforts, sat at the head of the table, his expression unreadable. "Thank you for coming, Ledger and Henri. I trust you have something important to discuss?"

"Yes, we appreciate the opportunity to speak with you," Ledger began, his voice steady. "We're here representing our community—a coalition of families who are deeply concerned about the injustices surrounding land rights and educational access."

Henri added, "We believe that constructive dialogue can lead to meaningful solutions. This is not just about policies; it is about the real lives of our community members—people who rely on stable land ownership and quality education to secure their futures.

Councilman Harrison leaned back in his chair, his brow furrowed as he listened. "I understand there are challenges, but the current systems are designed to maintain balance and order. Disrupting them can lead to unintended consequences. What specific changes are you advocating for?"

"We come with solutions," Henri said, pulling out a detailed outline of their proposals. "Firstly, we are requesting a review of land distribution policies. We propose that equitable land access be prioritized to ensure that small farmers can thrive alongside larger agricultural enterprises. This change could invigorate the local economy, allowing everyone to prosper."

An older woman from the community, Madame Elise, spoke up, her voice echoing with years of experience. "I have lived in this town for over fifty years and have seen it evolve. I have watched families struggle because they do not have the security of ownership. We want to nurture the land, not deplete it, and we can do that if we have a stake in it.

The council members exchanged glances, and Councilwoman Sandra, who had remained silent, finally interjected. "What do you envision regarding education access?"

Henri smiled, thankful for the opening. "We believe education reforms are essential for cultivating future leaders within our community. We propose introducing agricultural education programs into local schools, ensuring children learn about sustainable farming practices and the importance of land rights."

Ledger added, "By providing resources for community tutoring and workshops, we can empower families to understand their rights and responsibilities. This investment will not only benefit our children but can also transform the entire community, making it resilient and self-sufficient."

Councilman Harrison considered their words, his demeanor less rigid. "These changes would require significant investment and commitment from our office and the local government. What assurances do you have that our community can sustain these initiatives?"

A young father from the audience, Bony, stood up, his voice confident and clear. "The community is ready to contribute. We have already demonstrated this through grassroots efforts like workshops and co-ops. With the right support, we can implement these proposals, and we are begging for your partnership in making this happen.

The council members appeared more engaged now, acknowledging the power behind Bony's words. Ledger took a deep breath, hopeful. "We are asking for your trust as we navigate this process together. If we establish a clear partnership, we can work towards resolving these issues collaboratively."

An engaged discussion erupted among the council members, their earlier wariness shifting into a more open dialogue. Councilwoman Sandra mentioned concerns about potential pushback from larger agribusinesses, and Ledger used this moment to reinforce the notion of compromise.

"If we can incentivize sustainable practices among big agricultural players while supporting small farmers, it can become a win-win situation. We believe in solutions that benefit the entire community, not just a select few."

Finally, Councilman Harrison leaned forward, regarding Ledger and Henri with newfound respect. "You have presented compelling arguments, and I appreciate the passion behind your words. While I have my reservations, it is worth holding further discussions with community representatives to explore these proposals in more depth," Councilman Harrison concluded, his tone more conciliatory than before. "If we can draft a plan that addresses both the community's needs and the concerns of various stakeholders, we may be able to find common ground."

A wave of relief washed over Ledger and Henri, and they exchanged hopeful glances. "Thank you, Councilman," Ledger said, his voice full of gratitude. "We are not asking for a complete overhaul overnight, but rather a commitment to start the conversation. Together, we can outline a realistic approach that benefits everyone involved."

Councilwoman Sandra nodded, leaning in with interest. "I would suggest forming a task force that includes community members, agricultural experts, and policymakers. This way, we can create actionable steps based on the input from all sides. It will be crucial to ensure that the voices of those most affected are part of the decision-making process.

"That's a fantastic idea," Henri replied, excitement bubbling in his chest. "Engaging community members directly in the formulation of these policies will foster ownership and increase the likelihood of successful implementation."

Another community member, Sion, standing toward the back of the room, chimed in. "And we can host workshops to gather more data and feedback from families. We want to make sure this task force is representative of our community's diversity."

Councilman Harrison glanced at his colleagues, who were whispering to one another before returning his attention to the community representatives. "Very well, consider this meeting the first of many. Let us schedule follow-up discussions and work sessions to flesh out the specifics of what a policy change would entail.

Ledger felt the surge of hope transformed into actionable energy within the room. "Thank you! We are committed to ensuring this process is transparent and inclusive. Together, we will gather stories and data to illustrate the impact of these changes on our community.

The conversation continued, now saturated with ideas on how to structure the task force and collaborate on drafting a proposal. Henri took the lead, suggesting that they hold a community meeting to inform everyone of the progress and to encourage more voices to join in.

As the meeting wrapped up, Ledger felt a tremendous sense of gratitude toward his friends and allies who had supported them throughout this journey. He turned to the gathered community members, their expressions reflecting hope and determination.

"We're making real progress," he said, his heart full. "This is the start of a new chapter for our community. By standing together, we are showing that our voices can create positive change, not just for today, but for generations to come.

With firm handshakes exchanged and a sense of shared purpose uniting them, they began to leave the conference room. Outside, the sun shone brightly over the town square, illuminating the path ahead. Ledger and Henri walked side by side, buoyed by the energy of their recent success.

"I can't believe it," Henri said, still buzzing from the momentous meeting. "We have taken a significant step forward, but we need to maintain momentum. The community is counting on us."

Ledger nodded, determination setting in. "We will keep the lines of communication open and ensure everyone feels heard. This is not about us anymore; it is about every family that stands behind us."

As they exited the town hall, passing families who were beginning to gather in anticipation of their next discussion, Ledger felt a profound sense of pride. They were building something meaningful—a movement rooted in connection, empathy, and shared purpose.

"Let's get to work," he said to Henri, clapping him on the back. "There's a lot more to do, and with the community united, I know we can make their vision a reality."

The journey ahead would undoubtedly be challenging, but Ledger felt a renewed strength in their collective voice and the solidarity of their community. Together, they could navigate the complexities of negotiation and advocacy, forging a path toward a just and equitable future.

The late afternoon sunbathed the community square in warm light as families began to trickle in, their laughter and chatter filling the air with a palpable sense of excitement. Ledger and Henri stood at the edge of the square, surveying the space they had transformed into a vibrant hub of community solidarity. Colorful banners fluttered above, painted by children as part of a local art initiative, adorned with slogans like "Together We Thrive" and "Our Voices, Our Strength."

"Look at this turnout," Henri said, beaming with pride as he watched neighbors setting up booths with homemade goods, fresh produce, and crafts. "I can't believe how many people showed up to support our first solidarity event."

Ledger nodded, feeling the energy of their shared purpose glowing in the atmosphere. "This is exactly what we need—to showcase our strength as a community and remind everyone that we're in this together, not just for ourselves but for our future."

As they approached the main stage, Wizen and Petronel were busy arranging chairs and organizing sound equipment. "You two look like proud parents," Wizen teased, his broad grin making Ledger laugh. "Just wait until you see how many people step up to share their stories. That is what will make this day memorable."

Petronel chimed in, holding up a clipboard with their schedule for the day. "We have the baking competition starting soon, followed by community testimonials. Plus, the kids have prepared some performances to celebrate our heritage. Everyone is excited!"

Henri gestured toward the growing crowd. "I love seeing families come together like this. It reminds us all why we are fighting for our rights. Each booth they set up tells a story of resilience and creativity."

Just then, Ledger's younger sister, Margot, came running up, her cheeks flushed with enthusiasm. "The kids are ready for their performance! They have been practicing their dance all week," she said, practically bouncing on her toes.

"Let's get everyone's attention then," Ledger replied, stepping onto the stage with a wave to the audience that had gathered. He raised his hands to calm the excited chatter. "Thank you all for being here today! This event is a celebration of our community's strength and the unity we are building. Today, we honor our shared challenges and achievements."

Applause erupted from the crowd, and Ledger felt energized as he continued. "We have a special performance to kick things off from our talented youth. Their dance celebrates our culture and resilience, reminding us that together, we can overcome any obstacle."

With that, the audience's attention shifted to the stage where a group of children dressed in bright traditional clothing lined up, giggling nervously but fueled by the supportive smiles from their families. As the music started, they performed a lively dance, their movements full of joy and energy. The crowd clapped along, the camaraderie making their hearts swell.

As the performance concluded, Ledger stepped back to the microphone. "Wasn't that fantastic? A huge round of applause for our amazing kids!" The cheers echoed through the square, instilling a sense of pride.

Afterward, the baking competition was underway, with families showcasing their culinary skills. The aroma of fresh bread and sweet pastries filled the air, and participants eagerly sampled each other's creations. "This is a great way to get everyone talking," Henri noted, savoring a slice of cherry pie. "Food has a way of bringing people together."

As the competition unfolded, Ledger and Henri moved between booths, engaging families about their farming practices and sharing the latest developments regarding their fight for land rights. "By participating in events like these," Ledger explained to a group, "we can amplify our message and show that our community is united in purpose. We must keep sharing our stories and advocating for our needs."

Midway through the event, Ledger spotted Madame Elise standing next to a booth filled with hand-painted pots and local herbs. Encouraged by the presence of so many families, she stood ready to speak. "I want to share how our fight for land rights means securing our future. As a community, we can empower one another," she said, inspiring those around her to voice their own experiences.

Henri nodded appreciatively at her message. "This is what it is all about. We are not just sharing our successes but also our struggles. Each story builds our solidarity, showing how our individual challenges are part of a much larger picture. Together, we can advocate for change."

The sun began to set, casting a magical glow over the square as people mingled, laughter and conversation weaving through the crowd. Ledger looked around, feeling a swell of pride as he saw familiar faces animatedly discussing ideas for future initiatives.

As the event ended, Ledger gathered everyone around. "Thank you all for showing up today. This is just the beginning. We will keep building on this momentum, continuing to come together as a community to advocate for our rights and support one another," Ledger announced, his voice ringing with enthusiasm. The sun dipped lower, casting a golden hue over the crowd gathered around him.

Henri stepped beside him, a look of determination in his eyes. "What we have shown today is that we are stronger together. Each of you plays a crucial role in this journey. Whether it is sharing your stories, participating in events, or educating our children, every action counts.

The crowd murmured in agreement, and Ledger could see the spark of passion igniting in the eyes of those around him. He pointed toward Alton and Aldie, who were busy cleaning up the last of the baking contest entries. "We are organizing regular meetings to discuss policy changes with local leaders, and we want all of you to be involved. Your voices matter, and we will ensure they are heard."

A father from the crowd raised his hand, a hopeful smile on his face. "What can we do in the meantime? How can we keep the energy up and support each other?"

"We can keep the conversation going," Henri replied, beaming at his fellow community member. "Attend community forums, reach out to your neighbors, and invite them to join us at our next meeting. Share what you have learned today. Build those connections."

"Absolutely!" Ledger added with enthusiasm. "And let us brainstorm some new ideas for outreach. If anyone has thoughts on workshops, educational programs, or even social events, we want to hear them. Your ideas can make a significant impact on how we move forward as a united front."

As people began to discuss amongst themselves, Ledger noticed a few parents pulling their children into conversations, emphasizing the importance of every voice, young and old. He felt a swell of pride in his chest, knowing that they were forging a path forward together.

The evening air was filled with laughter and chatter as families began to exchange contact information, forming small groups to discuss ways to stay connected. Henri turned to Ledger and grinned. "Look at this. We have created not just a community event, but a launchpad for deeper collaboration.

"Exactly," Ledger replied, watching as small groups formed around their tables, enthusiasm written on everyone's faces. "And it is moments like these that remind us why we are fighting. We are not just advocating for our rights; we are celebrating who we are as a community.

As the sun set and twinkling string lights began to illuminate the square, Ledger reminded the crowd one last time, "Let us continue to stand strong together, lifting each other. Together, we will make our voices echo until they reach those who can make a difference. This is only the beginning, and I cannot wait to see where this journey takes us next!"

The audience erupted in applause, their spirits high as they felt the shared determination in the air. They began to gather their things, but the atmosphere remained electric with ideas and connections formed throughout the day.

As Ledger and Henri exchanged proud smiles, they knew they had ignited something special within their community—a powerful movement rooted in solidarity, shared purpose, and a commitment to fight for their rights. With each step they took forward, they felt the weight of their collective aspirations, lifting them higher, toward a future where their hopes could finally take root.

The early morning sun gleamed over the community farm, casting a golden glow on the vibrant fields as Ledger stood at the entrance of the sprawling gathering space. Banners adorned with colorful drawings of fruits and vegetables flapped gently in the breeze, welcoming families, and friends to the highly anticipated harvest festival. With his wife Clara by his side and their nine children bustling around him, Ledger felt a wave of excitement and gratitude wash over him.

"Dad, can we help with the activities?" asked Julien, one of the eldest of their children, his eyes sparkling with enthusiasm as he adjusted his apron. Eliza, his younger sister, nodded excitedly. "Yeah! I want to show everyone how to make pumpkin pie!"

"Everyone's going to love your pie, Eliza," Ledger said, beaming with pride as he tousled her hair. "And yes, you all can help. There is plenty to do before we kick off the festival!"

Their younger siblings, Koie and Nerisa, ran up holding handmade signs they had painted together. "Look, Dad! We made these to direct people to the workshops and booths!" Koie exclaimed, her voice bubbling with enthusiasm.

"Fantastic work!" Ledger responded, his heart was swelling with pride. "Take them to the front entrance and make sure everyone sees where they're going."

As they dashed off, Clara smiled, leaning against Ledger's shoulder. "You have really outdone yourself with this festival, love. It is amazing to see how far we have come as a community. All our hard work is finally paying off."

"Yes, and it shows what we can achieve when we come together," Ledger replied, his eyes scanning the vibrant setup of stalls filled with local produce, each table showcasing the fruits of their neighbors' labor. Wizen and Petronel, the young adults, were finishing the last touches on their booth, arranging baskets brimming with fresh vegetables and herbs.

"Hey, Dad!" Wizen called out with a grin, wiping his hands on his apron. "Are you ready to kick off the festival? Our heirloom tomatoes and fresh herbs are all set to impress the crowd!"

"Absolutely! And I cannot wait to see the folks come together for the workshops later. They will learn so much about sustainable farming!" Ledger replied, a sense of purpose filling his chest.

As the festival approached its start time, Henri joined Ledger and Clara, holding a clipboard with the day's schedule. "We are all set! The first workshop on crop rotation is about to begin, and I know Dfriel has brought some great new ideas he has been working on."

Just then, Dfriel, Ledger's determined teenage son, approaching, holding a handful of local flyers. "I'm excited to lead the workshop today," he said. "I want to highlight the connection between food security and land rights, so I'll be discussing how better practices can strengthen our communities."

"Perfect, Dfriel," Ledger responded with encouragement. "Your insights will help everyone understand the bigger picture."

As the sun climbed higher, the first families arrived, greeted by the laughter and shouts of children running between stalls. The smell of freshly baked goods wafted through the air, drawing people toward Eliza's pie booth, where she was enthusiastically serving slices with a smile.

"Welcome! Come try our famous pumpkin pie!" she called out, beaming with pride as she served a piece to an intrigued mother and her child.

Nearby, Wizen demonstrated how to plant seedlings while Petronel engaged attendees in discussions about organic pest control. The crowds began to gather, their faces alight with curiosity.

"Look at them!" Clara exclaimed, her eyes shining with joy as she observed families gathered around their booths. "It's incredible to witness this community spirit."

Ledger nodded, feeling a profound sense of accomplishment. "This is exactly what I had hoped for—an environment where we can learn from one another while celebrating our harvests. It is about creating a sustainable future together."

As the sun reached its peak, Ledger made his way to the center of the festival and gathered everyone's attention. "Thank you all for coming! Today is about celebrating not just our harvests but also our unity as a community. The workshops will show how our efforts in sustainable farming impact our ability to secure our land rights and provide for our families."

After Ledger's heartfelt introduction, cheers erupted from the crowd, enthusiasm palpable in the air. He gestured to Dfriel, who stepped up by the makeshift stage, ready to lead the first workshop.

"Thank you, everyone! Today we will discuss crop rotations and why they are essential for maintaining soil health and increasing our yields. This practice connects directly to our mission of advocating for sustainable and equitable land rights," Dfriel began, his voice steady as he engaged the audience.

Throughout the day, laughter mingled with shouts of encouragement as children participated in games and families explored the various booths, sampling fresh produce and culinary delights. The community square was alive with activity, each corner brimming with the fruits of their labor and the spirit of collaboration.

At one station, Koie and Nerisa set up a fun challenge for the younger kids, a "mini market" where they could pretend to buy and sell vegetables. "You have to haggle, or you might not get the best deal!" Koie instructed, handing out play money to giggling toddlers. Their laughter echoed, bringing smiles to everyone nearby. Parents stood to the side, happy to let their children immerse themselves in this local flavor of the community, basking in the sense of camaraderie filling the square.

Meanwhile, Ledger roamed between booths, encouraging conversations and sharing ideas. He paused at Wizen's stall, where a line formed for herb bundles and seedlings. "What's the trick to your herbs?" an eager customer inquired.

"Patience and a little love," Wizen answered with a wink. "And don't forget, organic methods keep the flavor intact and the soil healthy." The customer nodded appreciatively, excited to get started in her own garden.

As lunchtime approached, the delicious aroma of various dishes wafted through the air, drawing families closer to the shared picnic area. Eliza laid out her pumpkin pie along with other baked goods crafted by community members, including pies, breads, and cookies—creating a small but inviting dessert table. "Let's see who comes back for seconds!" she exclaimed, her eyes bright with enthusiasm.

A friendly competition began, with families enjoying food from one another's stalls. Clara had baked a large batch of her famous apple cider donuts, which drew a crowd of children and parents alike. "These are the best!" one excited boy shouted while licking cinnamon sugar off his fingers, prompting giggles from his friends.

After lunch, Henri took to the stage again, calling everyone's attention to the next workshop—this time on organic farming. "Join us and learn how you can improve your yield without compromising the health of our land. Our actions can lead to sustainable futures for all our families," he encouraged, gesturing to the crowd, which now included everyone in the festival.

As families settled in for the workshop, Ledger moved to a nearby booth where Julien was showcasing local honey and discussing the importance of bees in the farming ecosystem. "Did you know that bees pollinate about one-third of the food we eat?" Julien explained, demonstrating with a small play hive he had built. His passion was infectious, drawing even more curious attendees to his display.

"Remember to be kind to your bee friends!" he said, handing out small leaflets with tips on creating bee-friendly gardens. The children listened with rapt attention, fascinated by the idea of helping the bees thrive.

With the sun beginning its descent toward the horizon, the festival atmosphere felt almost magical. The sound of clinking glasses and cheerful chatter filled the area as families gathered for a final toast to their hard work. Ledger stepped up to the microphone once more, sensing it was time to bring the day to a close.

"Thank you all for joining us today at our harvest festival! This event is not about celebrating our crops; it is about nurturing our community spirit and advocating for sustainable agriculture," he said, his voice resonating with emotion. "Together, we are stronger, and together, we can ensure that every family has the opportunity to thrive."

As Ledger concluded his remarks, thunderous applause erupted from the crowd. The warmth of unity and shared purpose was palpable, making the day truly unforgettable.

Families began to gather their things, but instead of rushing to leave, many lingered to chat and exchange ideas about future events and collaborations. Clara leaned against Ledger, both soaking in the energy of the moment. "We did it," she whispered, her eyes gleaming with pride. "Look at all these smiles and connections. This is what it means to be a community."

"Yes," Ledger agreed, his heart swelling with joy and gratitude. "This is just the beginning. If we can harness this unity, we can pave the way for a better future for all of us."

With that shared dream resonating among them, Ledger and Clara watched as their children played with newfound friends, their laughter echoing through the square, a perfect centerpiece for the thriving community they had all worked so hard to build.

The sun rose brightly over the community center, casting a warm glow on the colorful banners fluttering in the gentle breeze. Today was the day of the much-anticipated Educational Arts Fair, a celebration of creativity and knowledge that Henri had poured his heart into organizing. As families arrived, the vibrant atmosphere buzzed with excitement and anticipation.

Henri stood near the entrance, greeting attendees with a broad smile. Clad in a comfortable shirt and jeans, he looked every bit the proud father and community leader every bit. His wife, Isabelle, was setting up a table adorned with art supplies and crafting materials, ready to welcome children for hands-on activities. "This is going to be so much fun!" she said, her eyes sparkling with enthusiasm.

"Absolutely," Henri replied, glancing around the bustling area. "Look at all the creativity already on display! We are really embracing the collective spirit of our community."

Their five children—Alton, Aldie, Algar, Nun, and Theresa—were eagerly assisting throughout the fair. Alton was helping to coordinate the storytelling sessions, ensuring that each child had a chance to share their cultural heritage. Aldie, ever the artistic spirit, was busy organizing a community mural project where attendees could contribute their own artistic touch.

"Dad, can I help with the storytelling?" Alton asked, his excitement palpable as he adjusted his glasses. "I think hearing everyone's stories will bring us all closer together."

"Of course, Alton. Your passion for storytelling makes you the perfect guide," Henri replied, his pride evident. "You'll do great!"

Nearby, Nun and Theresa were arranging the artwork created by local children, ranging from paintings to intricate crafts. "Look at this one!" Nun exclaimed, holding up a colorful painting of a family garden. "The colors are so bright! It really captures what we are trying to celebrate today."

"It's beautiful!" Theresa agreed. "We should display it front and center."

Algar was overseeing the preparation for the performance stage, where local children would share songs and dances inspired by their cultural backgrounds. "Everyone's going to love seeing all this talent come together," he remarked, adjusting the microphone and checking the sound system.

As families entered the fairgrounds, a wave of laughter and joyous chatter enveloped the space. Children, excited to show off their projects, ran from booth to booth. Henri took a moment to appreciate the joy on their faces. "Isabelle, look at this! They are all so eager to share what they have learned. This is exactly why we organized this event," he said, glancing at the bustling activity around them.

Soon, it was time for the opening remarks. Henri stepped up to the microphone, gathering the attention of the crowd that had gathered. "Welcome, everyone, to our Educational Arts Fair! Today, we celebrate the creativity, heritage, and knowledge of our community," he began, his voice resonant with passion. "This is a chance for our children to showcase their projects on cultural heritage, environmental stewardship, and the importance of education."

The crowd erupted in applause, their enthusiasm palpable as Henri continued. "Through storytelling, performances, and art exhibitions, we will remind ourselves of the vibrant history we share and the bright future we can create together. Let us embrace the creativity that unites us!"

With that, Alton took over the storytelling session, inviting the first child to the stage. As their young friends began to share their stories, the audience listened attentively, immersed in tales of family traditions, environmental awareness, and personal dreams. Laughter and cheers filled the air as children performed dances and songs that celebrated their cultures.

Isabelle watched with pride as Aldie guided younger children in a crafting workshop, her energy contagious as they collaborated on a group mural. "This is going to be the best mural ever!" Aldie cheered, helping them splash bright colors on the canvas.

As the day progressed, more performances took place, ranging from traditional dances to modern interpretations, illustrating the rich tapestry of the community's heritage. The infectious joy spread throughout the fair, with families celebrating not only their backgrounds but their connections to one another.

As the sun began to set, casting a warm golden light over the fair, Henri gathered his family together. "Today was a remarkable celebration of who we are," he said, wrapping his arms around Isabelle and their children. "We created an environment where everyone could express themselves and learn from each other. It is a reminder of the power of creativity and knowledge."

Isabelle smiled, her heart swelling with pride as she looked at her children and the bustling festivities around them. "I am so proud of all of you. This fair showed just how vibrant our community is. I cannot wait to do this again next year!"

The family stood together, soaking in the atmosphere—the laughter, the music, and the sense of collective achievement. This day was not about showcasing talents; it was about nurturing their community's spirit, fostering a love for learning, and reinforcing the ties that would bind them together for years to come.

The afternoon sun streamed through the large windows of the Cocoa house, (Kai Cacao), illuminating the space where families had gathered for the panels and discussions portion of the day's events. Rows of folding chairs filled the room, each occupied by eager listeners—parents, children, and community members ready to engage in meaningful conversations about advocacy and their rights.

At the front of the room, Henri took a deep breath, feeling a mix of excitement and responsibility. He stood beside a panel of local advocates, educators, and farmers, each ready to share their insights on overcoming systemic barriers. The atmosphere buzzed with anticipation as attendees exchanged quiet conversations, setting the stage for an impactful dialogue.

"Thank you all for being here today," Henri began, addressing the crowd. "We are excited to host this panel discussion focused on empowerment, advocacy, and finding solutions together. Our community is rich with talent and resilience, and today, we will explore how we can channel that strength into meaningful action.

He gestured to the panelists seated beside him. "Joining us are experts in agriculture, education, and community organizing. They will share their experiences and insights on the challenges we face and how we can work together to overcome them.

As Henri introduced each panelist, the audience leaned forward in their seats, eager to absorb every word. First to speak was Lady, a local educator who had dedicated her life to ensuring that every child had access to quality education. "We need to understand that education is not just about school—it's about community engagement and support," she said, her voice resonating with passion. "When families advocate for educational resources and policies, they become powerful agents of change in their children's lives."

A ripple of agreement passed through the crowd, with parents nodding appreciatively. Henri could sense the momentum building, feeling proud of the way their community was coming together to champion back-to-school initiatives.

Next up was Phillip, a local farmer whose family had faced numerous challenges in securing land. "We've all encountered barriers, from unjust policies to lack of access to resources," he said, his voice steady. "But it is our collective action that can change the landscape. When we stand together, we can demand the rights we deserve—whether it is for our land, our crops, or our livelihoods."

The audience erupted in applause, encouraged by Philip's words. He continued, "Start by knowing your rights. Understand what resources are available to you and do not hesitate to reach out to each other for support. The power lies in unity."

A young woman in the front row raised her hand. "How can we engage with policymakers effectively?" she asked, her tone earnest and deliberate.

Henri smiled at the engagement from the audience. "Great question. Let us explore that further," he replied, opening the floor to the panelists.

Educational advocate Lisa spoke up, leaning into the dialogue. "One crucial step is to build relationships with your local representatives. Attend town hall meetings, share your stories, and let them know how policies directly affect your lives. When they hear from you, they will understand the importance of your voice."

As the conversation flowed, families shared their personal experiences and frustrations with local policies. A father spoke about difficulties accessing educational funds for his children, while a mother recounted her journey in advocating for more sustainable farming practices. Each story resonated, connecting attendees through shared struggles and collective hopes.

"This is what it's all about," Henri said, his voice rising above the chatter as people engaged with one another. "The stories we share give weight to our cause and enable families to advocate more effectively. Our journeys might be different, but the goal remains the same: to empower ourselves and our children."

The audience grew more animated, and soon, a lively discussion led to ideas on forming a community advocacy group. "If we pool our resources and knowledge, we can have a greater impact," a woman suggested, her voice full of conviction. "Let's hold regular meetings to discuss policies and practices that affect us all."

Henri nodded in agreement, feeling the energy of the room shift as a shared vision began to take shape. "Absolutely! This is the empowerment for which we are striving. Through regular dialogue and collaboration, we can make our collective voice stronger."

As the panels wrapped up, Henri encouraged the audience to take the insights they had gained and translate them into action. "Remember, advocacy is not just about the loudest voices; it is also about grassroots movements and building networks. When we stand together, we are unstoppable."

As the event concluded, families chatted animatedly with one another, exchanging contact information and discussing how they could support each other in the future. Henri watched with pride, knowing that this day had sparked a new chapter for his community, one filled with renewed hope, agency, and determination.

As attendees began to disperse, Henri posed for a quick photo with the panelists, their faces radiating the shared commitment to inspire their community. The day's discussions had laid the groundwork for a brighter future, and he could not wait to see where this newfound energy would lead.

The sun hung low in the sky as Ledger and Henri gathered at the community center, surrounded by a dynamic group of leaders and advocates. The excitement in the room was palpable, a collective anticipation for the new opportunities that lay ahead. Inspired by the success of the recent solidarity events, they were ready to mobilize their community for meaningful change.

"Alright, everyone, let's get started!" Ledger said, stepping up to a makeshift podium crafted from repurposed wood. The room was filled with eager faces, each one reflecting their determination to improve their lives and the community they loved. "As we have witnessed in our recent gatherings, there's incredible strength in our unity. Today, we are here to talk about how we can harness that energy into powerful collective action campaigns.

Henri nodded, glancing around the room. "We've connected with several organizations across Dominica that share our vision for sustainable development, education, and social justice," he said. "By building these coalitions, we can amplify our efforts and broaden our impact."

A young woman from the back of the room raised her hand. "What specific campaigns are we initiating, and how can we get involved?" she asked, her voice filled with curiosity.

"Great question," Ledger replied with a smile. "Our first campaign will focus on advocating for environmental sustainability. We want to raise awareness about the importance of protecting our local resources while pushing for policies that promote conservation and responsible land use."

Henri chimed in, his enthusiasm infectious. "We are already in talks with local agricultural organizations to develop workshops and community clean-up projects. This way, we can engage families directly while also educating them about their environmental rights."

"Can we also include a component on climate resilience?" an older man interjected. "With the shifts we're witnessing in weather patterns, we need to ensure our farmers are prepared for whatever comes their way."

"Absolutely! That is a critical aspect," Henri responded emphatically. "We will include resources on climate adaptation and resilience techniques in our outreach materials. Together, we will organize training sessions and distribute informational pamphlets to ensure every family knows what they need to do to protect their livelihoods.

With the ideas rolling in, Ledger moved to the whiteboard and began jotting down key points. "Next, we are launching a campaign focused on educational advocacy. We want to ensure every child has access to quality education, regardless of their circumstances. This includes working with schools to secure more funding and resources. We will reach out to parents, teachers, and local leaders to rally support."

Another participant, a teacher named Clara, expressed her excitement. "I would love to coordinate parent-teacher meetings to discuss our strategy! Getting families involved is crucial to building momentum."

"Excellent idea, Clara!" Ledger replied, smiling broadly. "The more voices we have advocating for change, the stronger our campaign will be. Let us also consider using social media to spread the word and engage the community in dialogue."

As the meeting continued, participants shared their expertise, forming committees and delegating tasks. Henri kept the energy high, encouraging everyone to contribute their unique skills and perspectives. The room was filled with buzzing discussions, quick brainstorming sessions, and laughter—each person inspired by the possibilities that lay ahead.

After hours of planning, Ledger stepped to the front once more. "Before we wrap up, let us talk about how we will keep ourselves accountable. We need to establish regular meetings and set clear goals for our campaigns. Working together means staying connected and supporting one another along the way."

"No more meetings in isolation," Henri added, nodding in agreement. "This is a collective effort, and we need to maintain a strong communication network to share successes, challenges, and any new opportunities that arise."

As the group began to close out the meeting, Henri could sense a palpable shift in the dynamic. People were not just participants; they were becoming empowered leaders committed to driving change within their community.

"Let's make sure to stay connected after today," Ledger encouraged. "We will create a mailing list and a social media group so we can share updates and stay engaged. Remember, this is just the beginning. Together, we have the strength to advocate for our rights and empower our community."

As participants began to gather their belongings, the room buzzed with excitement and determination. Small groups began to form, with individuals exchanging contact information and discussing their next steps. Ledger and Henri shared a proud glance, knowing they had successfully ignited a passion for collective action.

Once the chairs were all stacked and the tables cleared, Ledger turned to Henri. "I cannot believe how much enthusiasm we generated today. This is exactly what I envisioned when we started these solidarity events."

"Absolutely," Henri responded, beaming. "We just harnessed the spirit of our community. Now it is time to turn that spirit into action. I cannot wait to see how far we can go when we work together."

With the sun setting outside, casting a beautiful orange hue over the town, Ledger and Henri felt a renewed sense of purpose as they stepped outside. Together, they were ready to lead their community toward a brighter future, one marked by unity and shared determination for lasting change.

In the weeks following the vibrant planning sessions and discussions sparked by Ledger and Henri's community events, the momentum for change continued to build. Fueled by a collective sense of purpose, community members began mobilizing petition drives aimed at advocating for crucial land reform and increased educational funding. Flyers and announcements filled the local bulletin boards, and word of mouth traveled quickly, rallying families from neighboring communities to join the cause.

On a bright Saturday morning, Ledger stood outside Kai Cacao, flanked by a colorful banner that read "Land Reform and Educational Funding Now!" He felt invigorated as he welcomed families, friends, and new supporters who had come together under a shared vision. Children ran around, clutching handmade signs that called for justice in education and land rights.

"Thank you all for being here today!" Ledger called out, raising his voice to reach the growing crowd. "Today, we are not just gathering signatures; we are standing together to demand the changes that our community deserves. Our voices matter!"

Clara, his wife, stood nearby with their younger children, helping them craft signs adorned with drawings and slogans. "Let your voices be heard!" she encouraged them, guiding their small hands as they painted vibrant colors on poster boards. "Every signature counts, and our kids' futures depend on it!"

The excitement was palpable as Henri joined Ledger, holding a stack of petitions and a clipboard. "We've already received significant support from several neighboring communities," he announced, grinning. "People are recognizing how these issues affect us all. Let us make sure our message reaches the ears of those in power!"

Families began to form lines at different tables, where volunteers had set up to collect signatures and personal testimonies. A long table bore a bold sign that read "Share Your Story." Here, community members could express their experiences with land access issues and inadequate educational resources. A touching series of testimonies began to unfold.

A young mother stepped up, her voice steady despite her nerves. "My children have had to change schools multiple times because of funding cuts. I want them to have stability and the education they deserve," she said as she penned her name on the petition. Her honesty resonated with many, prompting others to share similar stories of challenges and aspirations.

Nearby, an elderly farmer spoke of the struggles he faced in retaining land he had cultivated for decades. "Without reform, my children will not have the same opportunities I had. We need to protect our land for future generations," he urged, his weathered hands gripping the clipboard tightly as he signed his name.

As the day progressed, the atmosphere buzzed with conversations, laughter, and renewed hope. People moved from table to table, their eagerness to make a difference evident in their animated discussions. Ledger watched as neighbors exchanged stories and offered support to one another, recognizing the shared struggles within their community.

At the end of the day, several hundred signatures had been collected, each one representing a commitment to change. Ledger stood before the crowd once more, a sense of pride swelling within him. "Today, we have shown that when we come together, our voices become a powerful force," he said, addressing the gathered community members. "This petition is only the beginning. Our next step is to present these signatures to local authorities and demand that they take our concerns seriously."

Henri added, "We will compile these testimonies and statistics to strengthen our case. We must demonstrate just how widespread these issues are. Together, we can put pressure on our leaders to act."

As people began to disperse, Ledger felt an overwhelming sense of hope. He tucked the complete petitions under his arm, ready to be shared and amplified. The energy of the day was not about gathering signatures; it was about building relationships and reaffirming their collective agency.

That evening, as Ledger and Henri met at the community center to discuss their next steps, an excited group of families filtered in, eager to help. "We want to keep this going! What can we do next?" a father asked, his determination evident.

Henri looked around at the enthusiastic faces. "The next step is organizing a community meeting with local officials," he suggested. "We need to ensure they understand the urgency of these petitions—that they hear your stories and see the impact these issues have on our lives."

With renewed resolve, they began to plan the logistics of the meeting, leveraging the petitions as a centerpiece. The gatherings took on a life of their own, evolving into a mobilization of voices eager for reform—a unity that demonstrated the strength of their community.

As the sun set that evening, casting a warm glow across the town, Ledger and Henri felt a sense of triumph. They were transforming their hope into action, and together, they were igniting a movement that had the potential to reshape their collective future. The campaign for change was just beginning, and together, they were determined to see it through.

With the momentum from their petition drives growing each day, Ledger and Henri recognized the crucial role that media could play in amplifying their message. Understanding that stories of struggle and resilience resonate deeply, they set out to engage local journalists to help share the narratives of families affected by land ownership issues and educational disparities.

One crisp morning, Ledger arranged a meeting with a local journalist named Sophia, known for her commitment to social justice reporting. He and Henri sat at a small café, reviewing their talking points and discussing the families whose stories could highlight the urgent need for change.

"Thanks for meeting us, Sophia," Ledger said, leaning forward with sincerity. "We believe that sharing these personal stories can help the community understand just how wide-reaching these issues are."

Sophia nodded, her notebook open and ready. "Absolutely. Stories bring statistics to life," she replied. "Can you tell me more about the families you've worked with?"

Henri spoke passionately about a young mother named Lucilla, whose children faced uncertainty due to school funding cuts. "Lucilla has been fighting tirelessly for equitable educational resources. If we share her story, it will resonate with so many people who are facing the same struggles.

"I can see the potential here," Sophia said, jotting down notes. "We need detailed accounts—a couple of interviews and photographs to really capture their challenges and aspirations. When readers connect with these stories, it could ignite broader support."

With that, Ledger and Henri began organizing interviews with families, each one a powerful testament to the difficulties faced in their community. They set up sessions in homes, parks, and community centers, capturing photos of children studying, parents working in gardens, and the everyday realities of life in their vibrant but challenged environment.

In the days that followed, Ledger and Henri took to media, sharing snippets of their work and encouraging community members to participate. They generated a buzz about the upcoming articles, calling on supporters to stay tuned for the stories that would soon hit the press.

As Sophia published the first article, titled *Voices of Change: A Community's Fight for Fair Land and Education*, the response was immediate. The piece included heartfelt narratives, stunning visuals, and compelling statistics that illustrated the depth of the issues. It detailed Lucilla's struggles to secure adequate facilities for her children and highlighted Phillip, a local farmer, whose land ownership had been threatened by bureaucratic obstacles.

"Reading about Lucilla felt personal. This could be my neighbor or friend," a reader commented on the post shared on social media. "These issues affect us all."

Encouraged by the article's impact, Ledger and Henri organized a small press conference to further engage with media outlets. They invited Sophia and additional journalists to the community center, where families could share their stories directly and answer questions about their experiences.

On the day of the press conference, a flurry of cameras and notebooks filled the room. Ledger opened the session, welcoming attendees and emphasizing the importance of media in telling their community's story. "This is not about us; it is about everyone facing these challenges. We need to ensure that our voices are heard in broader circles."

One by one, families stepped forward to share their experiences. Lucilla spoke passionately about her children's needs, her words punctuated by the fervor of a mother advocating for her family. "This fight for education is a fight for our future," she declared, her voice steady but emotional. "We deserve schools that prepare our kids for a better life."

Reinforced by the press attention, the coverage quickly gained traction. Other journalists from regional and national outlets began to take interest, approaching Ledger and Henri for more information. Within days, the story had reached advocacy groups beyond their immediate community, drawing in new allies committed to supporting their cause.

"We've received requests for potential partnerships and support from organizations like the Land Rights Advocates and Educational Equity Coalition," Henri informed Ledger excitedly after one particularly successful day of outreach. "This is exactly what we aimed for—spreading the word and garnering support!"

Thanks to the journalists' efforts, letters of solidarity began pouring in, along with resources and offers to aid their campaigns. Advocacy groups reached out with potential funding opportunities for educational programs, while other communities sought to learn from their model of organizing.

As the sun set at Kai Cacao community center, Ledger and Henri shared a moment of reflection. "We really did this," Ledger said, a smile breaking across his face. "By sharing our stories, we have opened new doors. People are starting to listen."

"Absolutely," Henri replied, a sense of gratitude washing over him. "This is only the start. With the support of our community and allies, we can ignite real change. Let us keep pushing forward."

With renewed determination, Ledger and Henri turned to each other, ready to strategize their next steps. They understood the path ahead might be long, but with the power of media behind them, they were more confident than ever in their ability to advocate for a brighter future, a future where every child could thrive, and every family had a place to call home.

Weeks turned into months, and the vibrant energy created by Ledger and Henri's campaigns began to ripple throughout the region. Families from Bioche, and Colihaut, once hesitant to engage in advocacy, now found themselves stepping out of the shadows, empowered by the sense of purpose that the collective efforts had awakened within them. They began to realize that their voices indeed mattered in the ongoing fight for social justice.

The community center buzzed with activity as people gathered for a series of workshops designed to educate and empower residents. Led by local advocates and educators, these sessions focused not only on environmental sustainability and educational funding but also on the importance of civic engagement and advocacy. The once-intimidating barriers to participation began to dissolve as community members shared knowledge and strategies for enacting change.

One evening, as families settled into folding chairs for a workshop on land rights led by Phillip, the enthusiasm in the air was palpable. "We've all faced challenges regarding access and ownership, but together, we can change the narrative," Phillip declared, his passionate demeanor electrifying the crowd. "Our stories, our voices—they hold power."

Seated among the audience was Lucilla, who had become a cornerstone of advocacy in her neighborhood. She had organized a group of mothers to discuss school funding, and her confidence had grown tremendously. "I used to think my voice didn't matter," she shared during a breakout session. "But when I saw how sharing my story resonated with others, I realized that we are not alone. We are a community, and we need to stand together."

The participants listened intently, inspired by Lucilla's transformation. It was moments like these that fed the movement, encouraging more families to speak up and share their experiences. Progress was visible—those who once feared coming forward were now leading discussions, brainstorming solutions, and forming committees.

The atmosphere of solidarity reached new heights as families from neighboring communities interacted, sharing their challenges and strategies. Ledger observed this blossoming camaraderie during a community potluck organized to celebrate their victories and acknowledge their ongoing struggles. The long table was laid with an array of traditional dishes, each family contributing a unique recipe, symbolizing the diverse heritage of their community.

As they gathered, Ledger stood to share his thoughts. "Look around you! We are not just three separate communities; we are growing into one. When we unite our strengths, we create a powerful force for change. Our shared identity is rooted in resilience and activism.

Henri added, "Just as our food represents our cultures, so too does our fight for justice represent our shared hopes for a better future. The stories we have shared have united us in ways we never imagined."

As laughter and conversations swirled, families began to share their aspirations openly, brainstorming ideas for future initiatives. "What if we organized a community-wide event to showcase our cultures while also highlighting our advocacy?" a young father suggested. "We could invite local leaders and the media to bring attention to our causes."

"That's a fantastic idea!" Lucilla said enthusiastically. "We can include performances, art, and storytelling to engage everyone while raising awareness for land reform and educational funding."

The excitement in the air was palpable. The event planning took on a life of its own, with teams formed around various aspects: logistics, outreach, cultural showcases, and educational materials. As they shared ideas and coordinated their efforts, the previously hesitant families were now interwoven in a fabric of solidarity that knit together their diverse backgrounds and shared struggles.

Social media played an essential role in this growing engagement as well. Families began to use platforms to share their stories and updates about upcoming events. They created a community page to promote their initiatives, highlighting personal testimonials and success stories to inspire others to join the fight. The digital space became a hub of motivation and support, reaching even those who might not have been able to participate in person.

As the weeks went on, the momentum was unmistakable. The community had shifted from viewing their struggles in isolation to recognizing their shared identities as advocates. They began organizing regular community meetings not just around concerns but also around celebration and recognition of their achievements.

As the sun began to set on a particularly successful workshop, Henri and Ledger stood together outside the Kai Cacao community center, reflecting on the transformation they had witnessed. "Look at how far we've come," Henri said, pride evident in his voice. "These families are no longer hesitant; they're empowered—leading with purpose and passion."

Ledger nodded, a sense of fulfillment washing over him. "Exactly. We have built a foundation of engagement that will carry forward. We have created a culture of activism where voices matter, and that is something we can sustain.

As families walked by, animated conversations spilling into the evening air, Ledger and Henri knew that they had catalyzed a movement—a collective identity rooted in resilience and activism that would shape the future of Bioche, Dublanc, and Colihaut. Together, they were not just fighting for social justice; they were forging a legacy of empowerment that would echo through the generations to come.

With the swell of community engagement at their backs, Ledger and Henri set out to turn their vision for local educational programs into reality. They recognized the importance of tailoring these initiatives to the specific needs and challenges faced by families in Bioche, and Colihaut. With renewed determination, they began forming partnerships with local schools and community centers to create a series of workshops designed to empower the next generation.

On a sunny Saturday morning, Ledger and Henri convened a meeting with school administrators and community leaders at the local community center. The room was buzzing with energy like-minded individuals gathered around a large table, eager to brainstorm educational opportunities. Henri opened the meeting with an inspiring message.

"We've seen tremendous momentum in our community," he began, his voice steady and passionate. "Now, let us leverage that energy into creating lasting educational programs that address our needs and aspirations. We want to equip our young people with the skills they need to thrive and lead."

As they discussed potential areas of focus, Ledger outlined their key goals. "We envision workshops centered around entrepreneurship, agricultural management, and critical thinking skills. Our youth need relevant knowledge that reflects our local context, encouraging them to think creatively about their futures."

One of the school administrators, Ms. Davis, leaned in, her enthusiasm evident. "I love this idea! Our students have incredible potential, but we need to provide them with opportunities to explore that potential. Entrepreneurship training could be especially beneficial, helping them understand how to create businesses that contribute to our local economy.

Henri nodded, encouraged by her support. "Absolutely! We could incorporate mentorship from local business owners, allowing students to learn from those who have successfully navigated challenges in our community."

The group buzzed with ideas. They talked about organizing sessions on agricultural management where young people could learn about sustainable practices and modern farming techniques. Mr. Perez, a local farmer, offered to lead the workshops and share his expertise. "I'd be honored to show the next generation how to manage their plots responsibly," he said. "It's crucial that they learn not just to farm, but to think about how farming impacts our environment."

By the end of the meeting, everyone had signed on to collaborate, committing resources and support to bring the programs to fruition. They agreed to host a series of workshops every month, starting with a kickoff event that would generate excitement around their initiatives and showcase community talent.

As the team worked to promote the upcoming kickoff event, the energy was contagious. Flyers were distributed throughout the communities, local businesses helped sponsor snacks and materials, and word spread quickly. Ledger and Henri watched with pride as community members rallied behind the cause, excited about the potential impact these programs could have on young lives.

The day of the kickoff event dawned bright and beautiful, with decorations adorning the community center. Families gathered, and children buzzed with anticipation as Ledger and Henri welcomed them to a celebration of learning and opportunity.

"Thank you all for coming!" Ledger announced that his heart was swelling with gratitude and purpose. "Today marks the beginning of a journey towards a brighter future for our children. Together, we are creating spaces where they can explore their passions, develop skills, and envision themselves as leaders."

Throughout the day, a variety of workshops were introduced. In one corner of the community center, volunteers facilitated hands-on activities focused on entrepreneurship, encouraging young people to brainstorm business ideas and draw up plans. In another area, Mr. Perez and a team of local farmers led discussions on innovative practices that promote sustainability in farming.

An area dedicated to critical thinking featured interactive games and problem-solving activities, designed to challenge students and ignite their creativity. "Let's train our minds to think outside the box!" a volunteer shouted as the children eagerly engaged in the challenges.

The response was overwhelming. Parents watched with pride as their children participated eagerly, their faces alight with enthusiasm. Many expressed gratitude for the opportunity and vowed to support the initiative however they could.

As the event ended, Ledger gathered everyone for one last announcement. "We are just getting started! Based on today's enthusiasm, we will be rolling out a full schedule of workshops in the coming months. Together, we will continue to empower our youth and set them up for success."

With laughter and chatter filling the air, families began to leave, each one carrying with them the excitement of a new beginning. Henri and Ledger stood at the entrance, sharing smiles as they watched the community come together for a collective purpose.

"We did it," Henri said, filled with satisfaction. "This is only the first of many steps we'll take towards creating a sustainable future for our youth."

Ledger nodded, turning his gaze toward the children laughing and playing with their newfound friends. "And just look at the impact we are already having. It is about fostering leadership and inspiring aspirations in our young ones. They are our future."

As the sun began to set, casting a golden hue over Kai Cacao, Ledger and Henri felt a profound sense of accomplishment wash over them. The joyous chatter of children intermingled with the laughter of parents, creating a warm atmosphere that underscored the day's success. The excitement that permeated the space was not just about the workshops; it was the realization of a collective dream to foster growth, resilience, and leadership in the next generation.

"Look at them," Henri said, gesturing toward a group of children animatedly discussing their business ideas. "They're full of ambition and creativity—this is exactly what we hoped for."

Ledger nodded, his gaze shifting to a nearby group of parents who were deep in conversation about how they could support the ongoing programs. "It's amazing to see how engaged everyone has become," he replied. "This is more than just education; it's about building a community that feels empowered to take action."

As the sun dipped lower on the horizon, casting long shadows across the event, Ledger stepped back to take it all in. The decorations flapped lightly in the evening breeze, and the smell of fresh food lingered in the air, remnants of the potluck contributions that had brought everyone together.

"Shall we hold a debrief meeting in a few days?" Ledger suggested, turning back to Henri. "We can gather feedback from the families and plan the next set of workshops based on what we've learned today."

"Great idea," Henri replied, his enthusiasm evident. "We should also reach out to the local high school to involve older students as mentors. They can help facilitate workshops and inspire younger children. It will foster a sense of leadership and responsibility."

As they discussed the next steps, Anya approached them, her face alight with excitement. "I wanted to thank you both for this incredible opportunity. My son was so inspired today; he came home bursting with ideas! He wants to start a small gardening business," she said, beaming with pride.

"That's fantastic!" Ledger responded, genuinely pleased. "Encouraging entrepreneurship will not only empower him but will also strengthen our community."

Anya's eyes glimmered with tears. "I did not realize how much support there was for us. I have struggled for so long, thinking my voice did not matter. Today changed that."

As more families echoed similar sentiments, Ledger and Henri recognized that the seeds of change had taken root. The initial focus on workshops expanded into a movement, where voices were amplified, and futures were being envisioned anew.

With the last remnants of sunlight spilling across the sky, the event began to wind down. Children reluctantly packed away art supplies and business plans, their minds buzzing with newfound knowledge and excitement. Parents swept them up, exchanging smiles and gratitude with each other, their connections strengthening through a shared purpose.

As the community members began to depart, Ledger and Henri stood at the entrance, watching families walk away with their children's laughter ringing in the air. They shared a moment of silence filled with pride and hope; they knew they had ignited something special.

"Together, we're building a legacy," Henri said softly, still gazing at the thriving families. "This is just the beginning."

"Exactly," Ledger replied with a determined smile. "This community has the potential to thrive; it is all about continuing to nurture that spirit of resilience. Let us keep pushing forward."

As the last rays of sunlight faded and twilight descended, the community center stood as a beacon of hope, marked by the promise of growth and a united future. And in the hearts of those who participated, the movement for change was alive and well, ready to pave the way for generations to come.

After months of tireless advocacy and community engagement, the efforts led by Ledger, Henri, and the passionate families of Bioche, and Colihaut began to bear fruit. The seeds of change that they had planted through petition drives, community workshops, and a unified push for justice began to blossom into tangible legislative impacts.

The culmination of their hard work came in the form of a much-anticipated meeting with local lawmakers, a gathering that brought together key community leaders and government officials. The room was buzzing with anticipation as advocates shuffled in, clutching folders filled with testimonials, data, and success stories from their educational programs. Among the attendees were Anya, Marco, and several members of the community who had been instrumental in the movement. Their presence was a powerful reminder of the real lives affected by the policies at stake.

Ledger stood at the front of the room, addressing both the community leaders and the officials with a palpable sense of urgency. "We are here today not just to advocate for change, but to present the voices of those who have been directly impacted by existing policies. Our small-scale farmers, educators, and children deserve equitable opportunities that ensure their futures.

As he spoke, Henri circulated the room, ensuring that each attendee felt supported and confident in voicing their concerns. "Today marks a turning point for our communities," he echoed, rallying the passion that had brought them all together. "It is time for our local authorities to listen and act. We have come together for our future, and we need your commitment to make it happen."

After an intense round of discussions, local policymakers began to engage with the community. One official, a longtime advocate for land reform named Councilman Rivers, shared his thoughts. "I have seen firsthand the struggles of small-scale farmers and the barriers you face. It is time to re-evaluate our landownership policies to create pathways for equitable distribution. We must find a way to empower local farmers who are the backbone of our economy."

Applause erupted in the room as community members exchanged glances of hope. They had fought hard for this moment, and it felt as though their voices were finally being heard. Negotiations unfolded passionately over the next few weeks, with Ledger, Henri, and Councilman Rivers collaborating on proposals that could bring about the change they so desperately sought.

As a result of sustained pressure and community advocacy, local authorities eventually agreed to a set of reforms. They announced plans to establish a framework that prioritized equitable access to land for small-scale farmers. The new policies included measures for providing grants and resources to help those farmers improve their agricultural practices, prioritizing sustainability, and community involvement.

The victories did not stop there. The renewed focus on education was equally monumental. Following discussions about the funding disparities faced by rural schools, the government pledged increased financial support for educational initiatives across the region. This meant improved infrastructure, access to digital resources, and hiring additional teachers, which were vital to enhancing the quality of education.

When the announcement was made public, the community erupted in celebration. A local news outlet featured the triumph on its front page with the headline: "Communities Unite: Landmark Policy Changes for Land and Education." The article detailed the community's journey, highlighting personal stories of hardship and perseverance that had led to this momentous occasion.

At a celebratory gathering held at the community center, Ledger and Henri stood before a crowd overflowing with gratitude. "Today, we celebrate not just the policy changes, but the power of our collective voices," Henri declared, his voice filled with emotion. "This is proof that when we work together, we can create lasting impact. We have shown what can happen when a community unites for a common cause.

Anya took to the floor, beaming as she expressed her gratitude on behalf of the families in attendance. "This journey has been about our children and their futures. I never imagined we would see this level of support, but here we are—beginning a new chapter where our voices matter and our struggles are acknowledged."

The atmosphere was electric, filled with laughter and tears of joy. Families, educators, and farmers embraced one another, their shared victories reinforcing the bonds of solidarity that had grown over the months.

As the celebrations unfolded, Ledger and Henri reflected on the road they had traveled—the challenges, the setbacks, and the triumphs. "This moment is just the start," Ledger said to Henri. "Now we must continue to hold our leaders accountable and ensure these changes are implemented effectively. Our fight for justice is not over; it is evolving."

Henri nodded, determined. "Absolutely. We must remain engaged, to encourage others to participate in the process. We have ignited a spirit of activism in our community, and there is no turning back now."

As the sun set on that momentous day, casting a warm glow across the jubilant faces of the community, it was clear that their collective efforts had transformed not only policies but also the very fabric of their community. The air was thick with a sense of hope and renewed purpose, a feeling that they were on the brink of a brighter future. Families laughed and shared stories, children played freely, and the spirit of triumph lingered over the gathering like a comforting embrace.

The celebration was punctuated by music and dance, with local bands providing lively rhythms that brought everyone to their feet. Ledger and Henri moved through the crowd, exchanging hugs and high-fives with neighbors who had become dear friends throughout their journey. They marveled at how far they had come—from initial hesitance and skepticism to an inspired movement driven by shared goals and determination.

As the night deepened, Ledger and Henri found a moment to step aside from the festivities. They leaned against a nearby wall, watching the scene unfold before them. "Look at everyone," Henri said with a soft smile. "It is incredible to see this level of engagement. They are no longer passive; they are active participants in their future."

"Absolutely," Ledger replied, his heart swelling with pride. "But we must remember that this is just the beginning. We must ensure these new policies are effectively implemented and that our community remains engaged. Education does not stop here; it is an ongoing process."

Henri nodded, considering the path ahead. "We will need to establish a community advisory board to keep the conversation going and to ensure that our voices remain at the forefront as these changes occur. We must make sure local authorities follow through on their commitments."

"That's a great idea," Ledger agreed, his mind racing with possibilities. "We can build on this success by training community leaders to facilitate continued discussions on land reform and education. We need to empower others to take the mantle and maintain the momentum we have built."

As they contemplated the future, Anya approached them, her face still glowing from the celebrations. "Thank you both for believing in us," she said, her voice full of emotion. "You have shown us that when we unite, we can create real change. I am committed to helping other parents understand our rights and engage more actively in our children's education.

"We're all in this together," Ledger replied, touched by her commitment. "Your voice matters, and we're excited to see you take on that leadership role."

With the night sky now dotted with stars, the community's energy remained high, filled with laughter and the promise of new opportunities. Ledger and Henri knew that the victories they had achieved were not just about the policies themselves but about the empowerment of individuals to advocate for their own rights and the rights of their neighbors.

As the festivities began to wind down, families started to gather their belongings, still buzzing from the excitement of the day. Ledger and Henri applauded the community for their resilience, knowing that they had forged a strong foundation for future collaborations. The path ahead would involve hard work and vigilance, but with the solidarity of their community, they felt invincible.

In the quiet moments as families prepared to leave, but before parting ways, Ledger addressed the crowd one last time. "Let us take this energy into our everyday lives. Our collective power does not end here; we must carry it forward into our conversations, our schools, and our farms. Together, we will build a legacy of empowerment for generations to come."

The cheers and applause echoed through the night, a powerful reminder that they were a community united in purpose. As they dispersed, the bonds they had formed were stronger than before, woven together by shared experiences and the collective fight for justice.

With the sun setting behind them and the stars twinkling overhead, Ledger and Henri could not help but feel a deep sense of gratitude for the journey they were on. They were not just advocates but catalysts for change, and as they watched their community rise together, they knew they were part of something much larger than themselves, a movement rooted in hope, resilience, and the promise of a brighter future.

As Ledger and Henri continued to navigate the complexities and tensions arising from systemic inequities, their collaborative efforts became a beacon of hope for the communities of Bioche, and Colihaut. What began as a grassroots movement for land reform and educational equity evolved into a broader spirit of activism that resonated deeply within the hearts of their neighbors. The struggles against injustices related to land ownership, labor rights, and access to education forged a powerful alliance among the community members, bringing them together in ways they never thought possible.

Through their unwavering commitment to social justice, Ledger and Henri showcased that collective action was not only possible but profoundly transformative. They inspired families to raise their voices, share their narratives, and stand firm against injustices that had long been overlooked. Workshops, community meetings, and advocacy events became platforms for empowerment, helping individuals develop the confidence to advocate for their rights and the rights of their children.

As the spirit of activism intertwined with the daily lives of the residents, parents began to understand the power of their influence. They shared stories of resilience, illustrating to their children the importance of standing up for what is right. In classrooms and community spaces, dialogues flourished about justice, equality, and the significance of civic engagement. Ledger and Henri's efforts empowered not just the adults but also the youth, who were eager to learn and participate in shaping their futures.

Together, the communities embodied a formidable belief that lasting change could emerge from the seeds of solidarity that they had cultivated together. They organized community-wide events to celebrate their diversity and strength, reinforcing the notion that everyone had a role in driving progress forward. The intergenerational bonds that formed during this movement were woven through shared goals and collective dreams, ensuring that knowledge and passion were passed down to future generations.

As the months turned into years, Ledger and Henri witnessed firsthand the transformation of their communities. Young leaders emerged, inspired by the legacy of hope that had been established. These new advocates carried the torch, promoting social justice and continuing the fight for equality, proving that the groundwork laid by their predecessors had truly taken root.

Ledger and Henri's story became a cornerstone of resilience and empowerment, reminding everyone that in the face of adversity, hope and determination could cultivate a future overflowing with possibilities. Their narrative showcased that even when confronted with daunting challenges, unity, and perseverance could yield profound change.

As they stood together, watching the next generation learn and grow, Ledger turned to Henri and said, "We have created something beautiful here, something that will outlast us. This legacy of hope will inspire future champions of justice."

Henri nodded with a proud smile. "Yes, and it is just the beginning. Our communities will continue to thrive if we remind each other that our voices are powerful, and together, we can shape the future we want to see."

The story of Bioche and Colihaut became a testament to the enduring spirit of community—a vivid reminder that collective action, fueled by hope, can transform not just individual lives but entire societies. As they stepped forward into an unexplored future, the resilience and solidarity that had been nurtured would continue to resonate, guiding generations to come toward a brighter, more equitable world.

ভ

Chapter Eighteen: Passing Down Traditions

As Ledger and Henri's advocacy efforts to address socio-political issues in Dominica began to gain traction, both families recognized that their mission extended beyond immediate civil rights and community empowerment. They understood that a vital aspect of their fight for equity included the preservation of their cultural legacies. Amidst their activism, they felt a strong responsibility to maintain and celebrate their unique identities within their adopted homeland, ensuring that future generations would inherit a rich tapestry of traditions, values, and heritage.

For Ledger's family, this meant reconnecting with their Caribbean roots by fostering an appreciation for local customs, music, and culinary traditions. They initiated family gatherings that revolved around traditional cooking, where recipes and cooking techniques were shared with younger members. Grandparents and parents came together with children to prepare dishes like *mountain chicken* and *breadfruit salad*, turning mealtime into a spirited affair filled with storytelling and laughter. Through these experiences, they hoped to instill a sense of pride in their heritage and promote the importance of cultural continuity.

Similarly, Henri's family placed great emphasis on the oral traditions that had been passed down through generations. Recognizing that storytelling is a powerful vehicle for cultural expression, they organized storytelling nights at Kai Caco, inviting elders to share folk tales, legends, and historical accounts that reflected their roots and experiences. These gatherings became a beloved ritual within the community, where children and adults alike gathered to listen and learn, forging connections to their history and fostering a sense of collective identity.

Both families also understood the importance of incorporating local languages and dialects into their cultural preservation efforts. They worked to create workshops focused on the use of Creole and other linguistic practices, ensuring that younger generations felt comfortable embracing their linguistic heritage. By doing so, they nurtured not only their unique identities but also a deeper appreciation for the diversity of language within the broader Dominican context.

In their quest to instill values in the younger generation, Ledger and Henri emphasized the importance of activism alongside cultural preservation. They believed that a strong cultural identity empowers individuals to advocate for their rights effectively. Therefore, they engaged with schools and community organizations to develop educational programs that highlighted both cultural traditions and social justice themes. These programs encouraged young people to explore their identities, understand their rights, and actively participate in their communities' struggles for equality.

By introducing youth to the history of their ancestors' struggles and triumphs, the families fostered a sense of responsibility and agency. Children learned about iconic figures in their culture who had fought for justice and equality, inspiring them to see themselves as potential leaders and advocates. Ledger and Henri emphasized the critical role that culture plays in shaping one's identity, which, in turn, fuels the desire to work towards a better future.

Through festivals, art exhibits, and cultural showcases, both families sought to highlight the value of their traditions while promoting constructive dialogues around social change. They created spaces where traditional music, dance, and crafts coexisted with contemporary forms of advocacy, weaving cultural pride into the very fabric of their activism.

As Ledger and Henri worked tirelessly to address socio-political issues, they understood that the heart of their struggle lay in preserving the rich legacies of their families while forging ahead to create a more equitable society. This holistic approach to advocacy underscored the belief that cultural preservation and social justice are intricately connected. By simultaneously advocating for their rights and nurturing their cultural identities, both families were laying a strong foundation for future generations—one where pride in heritage and a commitment to activism coexist harmoniously, ensuring that their unique identities flourish in a rapidly changing world.

In the spirit of collaboration and community, Ledger and Henri embarked on a mission to host a cultural festival that would celebrate the rich heritages of both the Venezuelan and Caribbean communities. With enthusiasm and determination, they began planning the event, envisioning a vibrant celebration that showcased the diversity and unity of their neighborhoods in Bioche, and Colihaut.

The festival was set to take place on a sunny Saturday at the community park, with the goal of bringing together families from various backgrounds to share their traditions through food, music, dance, and storytelling. As preparations commenced, the excitement was palpable. Posters decorated with bright colors and illustrations of traditional instruments and dishes adorned every corner of the park, building anticipation among residents.

On the day of the festival, the park erupted into a kaleidoscope of sights and sounds. Booths lined the main pathway, each representing different cultural backgrounds. The air was filled with the enticing aromas of grilled meats, spiced stews, and sweet tropical desserts. Ledger's booth featured local Caribbean favorites like *jerk chicken* and *coconut rice*, while Henri and his family proudly displayed their Venezuelan specialties, including *arepas* and *patacones*.

Families flowed from booth to booth, their faces illuminated with joy as they sampled diverse dishes. Children laughed and played, their mouths full of sweet tropical fruits, while parents engaged in conversations, swapping recipes and stories of their cultural heritage. Ledger took a moment to step back and take in the scene, his heart swelling with pride as he witnessed the beautiful melding of cultures.

"Look at this, Henri! It is exactly what we envisioned," he said, gesturing to the throngs of people enjoying the festivities. "Everyone is celebrating not just their own heritage but each other's as well."

"I know! It is incredible to see how food brings us all together. This is a community in its truest form," Henri replied, beaming as he handed out samples of *pabellón criollo* to eager festivalgoers.

As the sun began to set, casting a warm golden glow over the park, live performances kicked off on the main stage. Dancers clad in colorful traditional costumes showcased the lively movements of both Venezuelan folk dances and Caribbean rhythms. The pulsating beats of *salsa, merengue,* and *calypso* resonated through the crowd, encouraging everyone to join in the celebration.

Families gathered around the stage, clapping along to the infectious rhythms. Ledger and Henri took the opportunity to share the significance of the dances, explaining how each movement told a story of their ancestors' struggles and triumphs. Young children jumped up and down with excitement, while elders stood proudly, reminiscing about their own experiences with the dances of their youth.

"Let's get everyone involved!" Ledger shouted, encouraging festivalgoers to join the dancers. "Come on, everyone! Let us show them how we celebrate!"

With a burst of enthusiasm, families joined in the dance, laughter, and joy echoing throughout the park. The interplay of Venezuelan and Caribbean dance styles created a breathtaking spectacle that illustrated the beauty of cultural exchange.

As the evening progressed, the festival featured a storytelling segment, allowing families to share tales from their cultures. Henri's grandmother sat beneath a large, colorful tent, her voice strong and captivating as she recounted folktales rich with lessons and morals. Families gathered around, enthralled by the rhythms of her speech, as she wove stories of clever tricksters and brave heroes.

Not to be outdone, Matilda Sebastien shared tales from Venezuela, illustrating the importance of family, community, and resilience. The children listened wide-eyed, enraptured by the vivid imagery of her storytelling, while adults were reminded of the rich tapestry of history that shaped their identities.

As the stars twinkled above the park, Ledger and Henri smiled at one another. They had succeeded in creating an event that not only showcased their unique heritages but also fostered a sense of belonging and unity among all participants. The festival had blossomed into a vibrant celebration, revealing the beauty of their intertwined cultures.

As the night ended, festivalgoers released colorful lanterns into the sky, each representing a wish for the future, a future filled with understanding, acceptance, and the preservation of their diverse heritages. The festival had not only strengthened communal bonds but had also planted seeds of appreciation for cultural exchange.

"Let's make this an annual event," Ledger suggested, his excitement evident. "We've seen the power of unity, and this festival can be a cornerstone for future generations."

Henri nodded in agreement. "Absolutely. It is a celebration of who we are and a reminder that our cultural legacies belong not just to us but to our children and our community as

The sun hung low in the sky, casting a golden glow over the bustling community center in Colihaut, where families from every corner of the neighborhood had gathered for the highly anticipated culinary showcase. The air was filled with enticing aromas as the Sebastien and Philogene families worked alongside neighbors, all eager to share their culinary heritage.

In one corner of the spacious main hall, the Sebastien family had set up their vibrant booth, adorned with colorful decorations that reflected their Venezuelan roots. Lucia Sebastien, Henri's sister, wearing a bright apron, skillfully shaped cornmeal dough into *arepas*. Her children, Karen, and Diego, stood by her side, giggling as they stuffed the flattened disks with a mix of cheese, shredded beef, and avocado.

"Don't forget to seal the edges, mojo!" Lucia gently reminded her son, who was focusing intently on his task. "You want to make sure nothing spills out while they're cooking!"

"I am ready! Watch how I do it, Mom!" Diego replied proudly, his small hands working diligently as he pressed the dough together.

Nearby, the Philogene family was effortlessly capturing the essence of St. Barts. Leon Philogene Ledger's younger brother, expertly sautéed onions and peppers in a large skillet, their fragrant aroma wafting through the air. He turned to his daughter, Amélie, who was organizing the ingredients for their famous *conch fritters*.

"Amélie, can you help me chop up those herbs?" Leon asked, gesturing to the fresh parsley and thyme on the table. "We need them for the seasoning."

"Of course, Papa!" Amélie said, her face lighting up with enthusiasm as she grabbed a small knife. "I can't wait for everyone to taste these!"

As the cooking intensified, Ledger walked around the room, harmonizing the flavors and energy emanating from each booth. He had organized the event to unite the families of Bioche, and Colihaut, and now it was morphing into a beautiful tribute to the diverse culinary traditions that thrived in their community.

"Don't forget to try the *callaloo* over at Maria's booth!" he called out to a group of families passing by, pointing to a vibrant display of dishes. "She's using fresh local greens, and you won't want to miss it!"

Attendees enthusiastically moved from booth to booth, reveling in the culinary offerings. Laughter and joy filled the air as they sampled and shared stories about the dishes being prepared. Children raced between tables, nibbling on *plantain chips* and sipping freshly squeezed juices, their faces beaming with excitement.

A mother approached the Sebastien booth with her young daughter, who was shyly clutching a plate. "What's your favorite dish?" she asked Lucia, her curiosity evident.

"I love making *hallacas* for special occasions," Lucia replied, her eyes sparkling with nostalgia. "They are like Venezuelan tamales, filled with meats and vegetables, wrapped in banana leaves. It takes a bit of time, but it is worth every moment when we gather as a family to make them!

"Can we make that next time?" the little girl asked, her face lighting up at the idea.

"Absolutely! Next family gathering, we will teach you how to make it," Lucia promised, smiling broadly.

As the showcase continued, the sounds of sizzling food and chatter filled the room. Ledger observed families working together in the spirit of collaboration, teaching their children not only how to cook but also the importance of their heritage. The atmosphere buzzed with energy, and he felt a deep sense of fulfillment watching the communal bonds strengthen.

A group of teenagers gathered in front of the Philogene booth, watching Leon as he flipped *conch fritters* in the hot oil. "Can we help?" one asked, stepping forward with an eager grin.

"Absolutely! Here, come over here and I will show you how," Leon welcomed them. "Cooking together is half the fun, after all!"

Amélie laughed as the teenagers clumsily attempted to mix the batter. "Just wait until you taste these— you'll be begging for the recipe!"

With the sun beginning to set outside, casting warm hues through the windows, families gathered around long tables set up in the center of the hall. Dishes from each family created a colorful mosaic— a perfect representation of their diverse heritages. Each bite told a story, a homage to culture, history, and the love that connected them all.

"Everyone, gather around!" Ledger called, raising a glass of local juice to the crowd. "Let us toast to the flavors that unite us, to our rich cultural heritage, and to the memories we create today! Here is to family, food, and community!"

Cheers erupted as glasses met in joyful clinking, laughter mingling with the clamor of clattering utensils. This culinary showcase had transcended mere cooking; it had fostered an appreciation for their intertwined cultures and strengthened the bonds that held their community together.

As the evening wore on, children continued to run around, adults shared stories, and the kitchen buzzed with excitement, creating a tapestry of flavors and laughter that would resonate for years to come. With every dish shared and every tradition passed down, the families of Bioche and Colihaut knew they were crafting a legacy of hope and unity, one delicious bite at a time.

The vibrant hum of excited voices and lively music filled the air as the community gathered in the heart of the park, ready for the festival's highlight — the performances of traditional dance, music, and storytelling. Children and young teens from Bioche, and Colihaut lined up on the stage, eager to showcase their talents and deepen their understanding of their cultural roots.

Ledger's younger children Louisa, James, Dfriel, Koie, Nerisa, and Henri's younger children, Algar, Nun, and Theresa—stood side by side, their faces lit with anticipation. Each of them had spent weeks practicing traditional Caribbean dance steps and music routines, eager to perform in front of their families and neighbors.

Henri, standing nearby, clapped his hands encouragingly. "Remember, this is more than just a performance," he told the children. "It's a chance to honor our ancestors, celebrate our heritage, and pass our stories—and our spirit—on to the next generation."

The music kicked off with a lively Belle beat, and Louisa and James led a traditional dance, their movements sharp and filled with joy. The rhythm spread across the crowd, inviting others to join in. Nearby, James and Dfriel played handmade drums, their steady beats setting the tone for the next act.

As the dance reached its energetic peak, the stage was quieted by Henri's voice, inviting a series of elders to take the stage for storytelling. An older man, his face etched with lines of experience, stepped forward—a community elder known for his wisdom. His deep voice wove tales of colonial legacies, resilience, and hope, storytelling rooted in the struggles and victories of their ancestors.

"Long ago, our ancestors faced hardships, but they never lost their spirit," the elder began. "They fought to preserve their traditions, their land, and their dignity. Today, we must remember that their resilience is the foundation of our strength."

A hush fell over the crowd as he spoke, children leaning forward, wide-eyed, absorbing the stories of their heritage. Henri's children—Algar and Theresa—listened intently, clutching their small hands, feeling a newfound pride swelling inside them.

Following the elder's tale, Nerisa and Louisa took turns sharing short, lively stories about legendary heroes and clever tricksters, illustrating lessons of resilience, community, and hope. A sense of pride and identity blossomed among the young audience, who clapped and cheered, eager to learn more.

Next, the young performers returned to the stage for a song led by Julien and Eliza, blending traditional melodies with rhythms that made everyone want to dance. Wizen and Petronel led the crowd in singing familiar Caribbean folk songs, their voices strong and clear, echoing into the evening sky.

As the performances continued, Henri stepped onto the stage, addressing the crowd. "These stories, dances, and songs connect us to our past," he said warmly. "And they remind us that our culture is alive — vibrant, resilient, and full of hope. Today, we pass that legacy to our children, ensuring it lives on."

The sunset cast a golden glow over the gathering as the children's performances culminated in a group dance, symbolizing unity, and shared heritage. Music, laughter, and stories wove through the crowd, a powerful reminder of how art and tradition serve as vessels for identity and resilience.

With applause ringing out, the children bowed shyly, their faces shining with pride. They had not only performed but had also learned that their stories and traditions are the heart of their community—an enduring legacy of hope, strength, and cultural pride that would carry them forward.

As the evening skies painted a soft hue of orange and pink, the Kai Cacao in Colihaut buzzed with activity. Ledger and Henri had transformed the space into a lively hub of learning, hosting a series of workshops designed to preserve and pass on cherished traditional crafts and practices.

Families gathered around tables filled with bright-colored threads, clay, and homemade instruments, eager to learn from the skilled artisans they had invited from both communities. The air was rich with anticipation and a sense of purpose — this was more than a festival; it was about keeping alive the heart of their cultural heritage.

Ledger stood beside the weaving loom set up at the front, warmly introducing Maria, a respected artisan from Dublanc. "Maria has mastered the art of traditional weaving passed down through generations," he explained to a small group of children and adults. "Today, she's going to teach us how to weave using locally sourced fibers — a skill that connects us to our ancestors and the land."

Maria smiled, her hands demonstrating intricate weaving techniques. "It's a labor of love," she said softly, encouraging everyone to try. "When you weave, you are holding onto your roots. Each thread is a story."

Next to her, Jean-Baptiste, a potter from Colihaut, shaped a piece of clay with slow, deliberate movements. "Pottery is an ancient craft that tells a story of resilience," he said, his voice gentle yet proud. "Creating with your hands connects you to your history and your community." He patiently guided a young boy's fingers as they formed a simple bowl, sharing tips and stories from his childhood.

Meanwhile, in a corner of the room, a group of teenagers clustered around Eliza, who strummed her homemade folk guitar. She showed them traditional Caribbean songs, teaching them melodies that had been passed down for generations. As they practiced, her voice blended harmoniously with the strumming, creating a soothing, timeless rhythm.

Henri moved among the groups, fostering conversations and encouraging participation. "Every craft has a story," he said to an older woman showing younger girls how to braid palm leaves into traditional baskets. "By sharing these skills, we're passing on more than just techniques — we're passing on our history, our resilience, and our pride."

Children eagerly took turns trying their hand at pottery, weaving, and singing, their faces lit with accomplishment and joy. Parents watched with grateful smiles, knowing that these moments of hands-on learning were vital for their cultural continuity.

As the evening deepened, lanterns were lit, casting a warm glow over the gathering. The sounds of laughter, teaching, and shared stories echoed through the community center, emblematically, of a collective effort to keep their traditions alive.

Ledger and Henri exchanged a satisfied glance, knowing that these workshops would plant seeds that grew far beyond the festival. They had created a space where skills and stories intertwined — reinforcing their communities' strength, pride, and resilience. The act of sharing knowledge was a profound step toward ensuring that their vibrant cultural legacy would endure for generations to come.

At the heart of the workshops and cultural preservation efforts, ledgers and Henri prioritized encouraging youth participation, believing that involving young people was essential to keeping their legacies alive. As children and teens engaged in hands-on activities like weaving baskets or crafting traditional instruments, they embraced a sense of responsibility to protect and Continue their cultural heritage.

Youngsters quickly found themselves captivated as they carefully wove fibers into intricate baskets, supervised by skilled artisans. They learned that each twist and turn reflected generations of tradition, patience, and community effort. Their small hands, sometimes hesitant at first, grew more confident with each completed piece, fostering pride in their growing skills.

In another corner, children pasting and tuning homemade drums and maracas discovered the significance of their music—learning the rhythms and melodies that had carried stories of resilience through the ages. Some even crafted their own simple instruments, feeling a profound connection to their ancestors whose melodies had once echoed through history.

"Your hands are creating more than just crafts," Henri told a group of teens as they carefully wrapped palm leaves into baskets. "You're helping to keep alive the stories and skills that define us."

Wizen and Petronel looked at their finished basket, eyes shining with accomplishment. "We want to show others how to do this," Petronel said excitedly. "Maybe one day, we'll teach more kids in our community."

By actively participating, the youth learned to appreciate the cultural significance of each craft and song, understanding that these traditions were not just old customs—they were vital parts of their identity and resilience. The experience cultivated a deeper respect for their heritage while empowering them with practical skills that could benefit their community.

Ledger and Henri watched as the young participants enthusiastically shared what they learned, eager to pass it on. They knew that nurturing youth involvement was key to the sustainability of their cultural legacy. By engaging the next generation in active learning, they were planting seeds of pride, responsibility, and continuity—ensuring that these artistic and cultural expressions would endure far into the future.

Both the Sebastien and Philogene, families place great value on mentorship as a vital component of cultural preservation. They believe that connecting the younger generation with elder community members is essential for transmitting not only traditions and skills but also the wisdom gained from navigating adversity throughout history.

Elders like Henri's grandmother Emilien, the veteran storyteller, and seasoned artisans like Maria and Jean-Baptiste have become revered mentors. They sit with young children and teenagers, sharing stories of resilience, struggles, and triumphs from their lives, highlighting the importance of cultural roots in overcoming challenges. These personal accounts make history tangible, inspiring confidence, pride, and a deep understanding of their community's journey.

In one ongoing mentorship circle, Henri's children—Alton, Aldie, and Algar—sit beside elders like uncle Jacques, and Uncle Georges, during storytelling sessions. The elders recount tales of colonial legacies, cultural resilience, and hopes for the future. As they speak, they demonstrate traditional crafts or techniques, allowing the youth to observe and learn firsthand. These direct exchanges foster a sense of continuity, where cultural knowledge is passed seamlessly from experienced elders to eager younger listeners.

Witnessing these relationships, Ledger often reminds the community, "Our history lives through these stories and skills. When our elders share their experiences, they pass down more than knowledge, they pass down the spirit of resilience and hope that keeps our culture alive.

These mentorship bonds do more than preserve culture—they cultivate a sense of responsibility within the youth to carry the torch forward. Young people begin to see themselves as custodians of their heritage, grounded in the lessons of those who came before them. As they learn directly from elders, their identities deepen, fueling pride and a sense of purpose.

This ongoing connection ensures that the community's cultural narrative continues to thrive, with each generation learning from and honoring the previous. It is a living chain—strengthened through stories, shared wisdom, and active mentorship—guaranteeing that their legacy endures over time.

Elders in the community serve as living repositories of both cultural traditions and invaluable life lessons. During mentorship sessions and storytelling gatherings, they go beyond sharing recipes, dances, and songs—they also impart their experiences of resilience, activism, and community strength. These conversations become powerful lessons in advocating for rights, standing united, and preserving identity in the face of adversity.

One elder, Henri's grandmother, often speaks passionately about overcoming obstacles: how she and others fought to protect their land, maintain their customs, and seek justice during difficult times. Her words remind the young generation that resilience is rooted in unity and a deep respect for their heritage. She emphasizes that their cultural traditions are more than symbols; they are acts of resistance and pride.

"Never forget where you come from," she tells her grandchildren. "Our ancestors faced hardships, but they stood tall fighting for their dignity and their land. We carry that strength in everything we do. We must honor them by continuing that fight for justice and respect."

Others share stories of activism, illustrating how their community members fought to protect their rights and community spaces, inspiring a spirit of advocacy among the youth. These lessons reinforce that celebrating culture is also about defending it—standing up for their community's well-being and future.

The conversations often include advice on standing together during challenging times, emphasizing that collective action and shared values are the keys to overcoming adversity. These insights help the younger generation see themselves as active participants in shaping their community's future, not just passive inheritors of tradition.

Through these shared stories and life lessons, elders nurture a sense of responsibility and purpose in young people. They teach that cultural pride and resilience are intertwined—each generation carrying forward the fight for dignity, rights, and cultural continuity. These exchanges forge more than cultural understanding; they instill enduring values of activism, solidarity, and respect that will guide the community for generations to come.

As the evening sun dipped lower, casting a warm amber glow over the community gathering, a circle had formed in the community park—elders seated comfortably on benches and in folding chairs, children and teenagers gathered around, eager to listen. The air was thick with anticipation; tonight's focus was on stories that carried lessons of resilience, justice, and hope.

Henri's grandmother Emilien, her voice steady and warm, sat at the center, surrounded by attentive young faces. She began recounting tales of her youth—of fighting to preserve their land and their culture amidst colonial pressures, of standing shoulder to shoulder with neighbors in times of hardship.

"You see, my children," she said, "our ancestors faced many storms, but they never let fear break their spirit. They knew that our strength as a community came from standing together, fighting for what is right, and holding onto our roots."

Wizen and Petronel listened intently, eyes wide with wonder as she described how their community fought to protect their land rights, how they organized protests, and how they maintained traditions despite oppression. She then looked at them with a gentle smile.

"Now it's your turn," she continued. "Your voice matters. Use what you have learned, stand up for your rights, speak out against injustice, and always remember who you are. Our culture is our strength, and you must keep it alive—not just for yourselves, but for everyone who comes after you."

Next, Henri's son Alton shared a story of activism from his own childhood: participating in peaceful protests, advocating for better schools, and standing firm when faced with discrimination. His words stirred a quiet determination in the young listeners.

A ripple of inspired whispers spread through the crowd. Louisa and James whispered to each other about ways they could help their community. Eliza nodded, her gaze full of pride and resolve.

Henri, observing the scene, spoke softly but confidently, "Stories are not just old tales—they are maps guiding us to a future where we can honor our past and create change. Every one of you has the power to make a difference. When you speak up, you are carrying forward the legacy of your ancestors— build on that strength."

The young people felt a renewed sense of purpose—an understanding that honoring their roots meant actively shaping a better future. They exchanged looks of determination, inspired by the stories they had just heard.

As the night deepened, the circle remained the stories echoing in the hearts of those present. This intergenerational exchange had done more than share wisdom—it had ignited a spark of empowerment, promising a future where their cultural pride and pursuit of justice would walk hand in hand.

The community center hummed with energy as Ledger and Henri gathered a group of motivated young people in a sunlit room. Several teens, including Wizen, Petronel, Louisa, Alton, and Theresa, sat attentively, their faces eager and curious. These were youth already demonstrating a passion for activism and community service.

Ledger stood at the front, holding a small, handmade plaque. "You all have shown through your actions and words that you care deeply about our community's future," he began, his voice firm yet encouraging. "That is exactly what a leader does—stands up and fights for what is right. And today, we want to help you become those leaders."

Henri nodded in agreement. "Leadership is not about being in charge—it is about taking responsibility, inspiring others, and working together to create change. You are the future—the voices that will advocate for your peers and protect our land and education."

He looked around at the young faces, eyes shining with purpose. "We are launching a youth leadership initiative. You will have opportunities to lead campaigns, organize community meetings, and serve as representatives advocating for land rights and access to quality education. We believe in your power to make a difference."

Wizen raised his hand, voice tinged with excitement. "I want to help organize workshops about land preservation. We need to make our voices heard about protecting our community's future."

Petronel nodded vigorously. "And I want to make sure other kids can go to school without fear of discrimination. We can start a campaign to get better resources for our schools!"

Ledger clapped his hands once, smiling proudly. "That is what we are talking about! Acting where it counts. We will support you every step of the way—helping you learn the skills, connect with allies, and build confidence."

Alton and Louisa exchanged determined looks. "We'll be the voice for those who can't speak for themselves," Louisa said quietly, but with conviction.

The room filled with a sense of possibility—a shared understanding that these young leaders were not just future hope; they were active catalysts for today's change. Henri and Ledger knew that empowering these youth would magnify their efforts, inspiring a ripple effect through the community.

As the meeting wrapped up, teenagers stepped forward, ready to take on their roles. They shook hands, exchanged ideas, and committed to making their community better—standing tall as the next generation of advocates, champions of land rights, and guardians of their cultural legacy.

Empowered by leadership training and community support, the young advocates from Colihaut launched dynamic campaigns that spoke directly to their generation. Using media, local radio, and community events, they harnessed the power of platforms familiar to their peers to raise awareness about critical issues like land rights, educational access, and cultural preservation.

Wizen and Petronel led a vibrant media initiative, creating an eye-catching order to spotlight their causes. They used stories of resilience, intertwining modern activism with cultural pride, highlighting the importance of defending their land while honoring their heritage. Their content drew widespread attention, sparking conversations among youth beyond Colihaut as posts were shared across islands and even across borders.

Louisa and Alton organized community rallies, creatively combining traditional music and dance with empowering messages. They engaged peers by turning advocacy into celebrations of their culture, transforming protests into cultural festivals that drew more young people into active participation.

They also collaborated with local radio stations, hosting youth-led talk shows and interviews where they discussed their struggles and aspirations. Their messages blended humor, storytelling, and call-to-action, making complex issues relatable and inspiring for their generation.

The campaigns were marked by remarkable creativity—using art, music, humor, and media to articulate their demands while celebrating their roots. They succeeded in making their voices heard in ways that resonated deeply, fostering a sense of pride and agency among their peers.

Beyond their immediate community, these youth-led initiatives forged connections with other young advocates across the islands, creating a network of young leaders committed to social change. Their innovative approach proved that when the younger generation leads with authenticity, creativity, and cultural pride, they can spark widespread awareness and inspire collective action—building momentum toward a future shaped by their voices and visions.

The young advocates from Colihaut recognized the importance of integrating their fight for justice and cultural preservation into education. They formed partnerships with local schools, working together with teachers and administrators to develop programs that celebrated community history, land rights, and cultural identity.

Together, they designed engaging lessons, storytelling sessions, and extracurricular activities that brought the community's struggles and heritage directly into the classroom. Students learned about their ancestors' resilience, the importance of land sovereignty, and the ongoing fight for equity in Dominica—creating a sense of pride and responsibility among the youth.

The advocates often visited classrooms, sharing their personal experiences and organizing interactive discussions about rights, activism, and cultural traditions. They also coordinated school projects—such as heritage exhibitions, folk music performances, and land rights campaigns—that involved both students and community elders.

Working with local educators, they ensured that these topics became a regular part of the curriculum, empowering their peers with knowledge and inspiring them to participate actively in community initiatives. The collaboration helped foster a shared sense of purpose, encouraging students to see themselves as agents of change and custodians of their cultural legacy.

By embedding community history and activism into education, the young leaders helped create an informed generation—aware of their rights, proud of their roots, and motivated to pursue justice and equality. This partnership strengthened the bond between schools and the community, ensuring that the fight for land, culture, and fairness would continue to be nurtured through generations.

The younger generation begins to see themselves as true custodians of their cultural identity and advocates for their community's future. Inspired by the legacies of pioneers like Ledger and Henri, they learn that activism is not about protest—it is a powerful expression of pride, responsibility, and ongoing change.

Through involvement in campaigns, community projects, and educational initiatives, they take ownership of their roles as cultural ambassadors. They understand that standing up for their land, rights, and heritage is a continuation of the courageous efforts of those who came before them. Each rally, social media post, and classroom discussion becomes a way to honor their predecessors' sacrifices while forging their own path forward.

As they see the real consequences of their efforts, whether it is raising awareness about land rights, inspiring peers to participate, or strengthening community bonds, they deepen their sense of empowerment. Their voices become tools of change, and their actions echo the resilience embedded in their history.

This realization fuels a new confidence: they are not just followers of their ancestors' footsteps but active architects of their community's future. Their activism becomes a source of pride, constantly reminding them that their advocacy is part of a broader legacy—one that demands courage, resilience, and unwavering commitment. In this way, they fully embrace their identity as both protectors of their culture and champions for justice.

Motivated by their families' long-standing advocacy and their own commitment to justice, many young activists from Colihaut step into the arena of local governance. They attend town hall meetings, community forums, and discussions with local leaders, eager to make their voices heard.

These young leaders speak passionately about issues that matter most to their peers—land ownership, access to quality education, and fair policies that promote equity. They listen carefully to community concerns, then articulate their ideas and demands with clarity and conviction, advocating for tangible changes that can improve everyday life.

By actively engaging in local governance, these youth become more than just beneficiaries of their community—they become essential participants in shaping their future. Their involvement helps bridge the gap between generations and encourages a more inclusive decision-making process, where the voices of young people are valued and respected.

Their participation also inspires other youth to take an active role, creating a ripple effect that strengthens community ties and promotes collective responsibility. In becoming part of ongoing conversations about land principles and educational reform, they help ensure that their community's narrative continues to evolve—guided by fresh ideas, youthful energy, and a shared vision for a just and equitable future.

Fueled by deep cultural pride and confidence in their ability to make a difference, the younger generation in Colihaut begins to articulate a clear and compelling vision for change. This vision reflects their collective aspirations, aspirations rooted in community empowerment, cultural preservation, and social justice.

They imagine a future where land rights are protected and respected, where every child has access to quality education, and where their heritage is celebrated and passed down with pride. Their voices emphasize the importance of unity, respect for tradition, and ongoing activism to ensure the community's voice remains strong.

This shared vision becomes more than just words; it serves as a moral compass and a rallying point for their actions. Every campaign, community project, and advocacy effort are guided by this long-term goal—to create a society where justice, equality, and cultural dignity thrive.

In articulating this future, the youth inspire others to see beyond immediate struggles and work toward sustainable change. Their collective hopes and values form a beacon of hope and resilience, lighting the way for their community's ongoing journey toward equity and cultural vitality. This vision, carried forward by their energies and ideals, becomes the heartbeat of their activism and community leadership.

To strengthen their collective voice, Ledger, and Henri champion the organization of youth summits and conferences that bring together young advocates from across Dominica. These gatherings provide a vital space for children and teenagers—like Wizen, Petronel, Louisa, Alton, and Theresa—to share their experiences, exchange ideas, and discuss common challenges related to land rights, education, and cultural preservation.

At these events, young people participate in lively discussions about their community's future, forging connections beyond their local areas. They collaborate on strategies for promoting equity and inclusion, inspiring one another with stories of resilience and activism.

Workshops are a key component of these summits. Led by experienced facilitators, they focus on developing practical skills—such as effective advocacy, public speaking, and community organizing. Children learn how to craft compelling messages, lead campaigns, and engage their peers and leaders confidently.

These conferences empower the youth with tools to become impactful leaders, giving them the confidence and competence to champion change both within their communities and on larger platforms. By fostering collaboration among young advocates from different parts of the country, Ledger and Henri help nurture a generation of leaders who are informed, connected, and committed to building a more just and inclusive Dominica.

During these youth summits, participants come together to craft a clear, strategic action plan that transforms their ideas into practical steps for change. Guided by Ledger and Henri, the young advocates collaboratively identify their primary goals—such as securing land ownership rights, improving access to quality education, and integrating cultural education into school curricula.

They analyze their target issues, prioritize actions, and decide on effective methods of engagement, including community outreach, advocacy campaigns, and direct dialogues with policymakers. Components like setting timelines, assigning roles, and choosing communication channels ensure their efforts are organized and focused.

This structured approach empowers the youth to move beyond mere discussion. It gives them a roadmap to initiate concrete steps—organizing awareness events, lobbying local leaders, and initiating school programs—that actively advance their causes. By developing a strategic plan, these young advocates become intentional agents of change, equipped to turn their collective energy into meaningful, lasting progress in their communities.

In their passionate pursuit of justice, these young advocates harness the power of the burgeoning communication methods of their time—broadsheets, pamphlets, and postal services—to spread their message far beyond their immediate surroundings. With skillful writing and heartfelt speeches, they seek to raise awareness of the injustices they face and inspire others to join their cause. Each carefully composed article or handwritten letter acts as a beacon, rallying those who share their hopes for change and urging collective action across villages, towns, and even distant regions.

These printed materials and communal gatherings serve as vital tools in building a broader movement. The dissemination of information fuels a sense of solidarity among disparate groups, uniting them in their shared desire for reform. As ideas circulate and support grows, a network of like-minded individuals begins to form—a strong, interconnected community driven by a common vision. Through these means, the advocates aim not only to challenge the status quo but also to ignite an enduring spirit of resistance and hope in the hearts of many.

As their vision for change takes shape, the younger generation understands that broad community backing is essential to turning their aspirations into reality. Building on their advocacy, cultural pride, and strategic plans, they actively reach out to parents, elders, local organizations, and community leaders to share their goals and ideas.

They organize gatherings, cultural events, and discussions to inform and motivate others about the importance of land rights, education reform, and cultural preservation. By sharing stories, hosting workshops, and demonstrating their commitment, they foster a sense of unity and shared purpose.

This collective support amplifies their voice, making their efforts more impactful and sustainable. When the community stands together—rooted in shared values and mutual respect—the young advocates gain strength and legitimacy for their initiatives. Engaging the broader community transforms their movement into a collective effort, ensuring that the seeds of change are deeply rooted and widely supported, paving the way for lasting progress.

Recognizing the strength in collective wisdom, the young advocates actively seek to collaborate with Ledger, Henri, and other seasoned community leaders. They understand that meaningful change is rooted in the shared knowledge and experiences of all generations.

The youth invite elders to join discussions about their vision for the community's future, listening to stories of past struggles, successes, and cultural traditions. These intergenerational dialogues help weave the valuable insights and lessons of previous generations into their plans and strategies.

By fostering respectful partnerships, the young advocates ensure that their initiatives honor the community's history while building on the foundations laid by their elders. This collaboration cultivates mutual respect, deepens understanding, and enriches their collective efforts. It also guarantees that the community's cultural legacy remains central as they work toward a more just and equitable future, blending past wisdom with youthful energy and innovation.

The young advocates recognize that active participation in local governance is vital for meaningful change. To this end, they organize civic engagement initiatives designed to foster community involvement and empower families to have a say in their future.

They host informational sessions on topics like voter registration, how local elections work, and the importance of civic participation. These sessions demystify political processes, answering questions and providing practical guidance for community members who may be unfamiliar with how they can influence decision-making.

The advocates also encourage families to attend town hall meetings, dialogue with elected officials, and participate in community debates. By increasing awareness and confidence, they inspire more people to engage in civic activities, strengthening the community's voice in governance.

Through these efforts, the youth aim to build a more active, informed citizenry that can advocate for policies aligned with their needs and values. Their civic initiatives help create a culture of participation, ensuring that every community member understands their power and responsibility to shape their community's future.

To maintain momentum and foster a sense of collective ownership, the youth organize regular community forums where neighbors gather to discuss their shared vision for the future. These forums create an open, welcoming space for people to voice concerns, share ideas, and collaborate on actionable steps toward change.

Facilitated by the young advocates, these discussions promote honest dialogue, ensuring that everyone, whether young or old, is heard and valued. They provide an opportunity to revisit goals, address challenges, and celebrate progress, keeping the community engaged and motivated.

By involving diverse voices, these forums strengthen the collective commitment to their shared aspirations. They also reinforce the idea that creating lasting change is a communal effort, with each person's input vital to shaping a future that reflects everyone's hopes, needs, and values. This ongoing dialogue helps sustain energy, unity, and purpose within the community.

As the young advocates put their action plan into motion, they start to see tangible results—whether it is a successful land rights workshop, increased voter participation, or new cultural programs in schools. These small victories serve as powerful reminders that their efforts are making a difference.

Celebrating these achievements reinforces their sense of purpose and fuels their passion to keep working toward their goals. Community members join in these celebrations, sharing pride and hope for a brighter future.

Each success, no matter how modest, builds momentum and confidence, inspiring continued commitment, and engagement. Together, they foster a spirit of optimism, demonstrating that collective effort and perseverance can lead to meaningful change, transforming their dreams into reality and nurturing hope for generations to come.

As the young advocates' efforts gain momentum, their dedication begins to attract recognition from local authorities and community leaders. Acknowledging the impact of their advocacy, officials start to see the value of youth participation in shaping the community's future.

This recognition often results in tangible changes, such as policy adjustments that better reflect the needs and voices of young people—whether through new land rights initiatives, educational reforms, or community development projects. Their contributions help shift decision-making processes toward greater inclusivity, ensuring that diverse perspectives are considered.

This acknowledgment not only validates the efforts of these young leaders but also encourages a continued culture of engagement and partnership. It signals a meaningful step toward a community where every generation's voice is valued, fostering a more equitable and participatory society for all.

As the community witnesses the tangible results of their collective advocacy, inspiring stories of success begin to unfold. Families gain access to land they once struggled to secure, opening new possibilities for livelihood and security. Educational opportunities expand, enrich students' lives, and strengthen community knowledge. Cultural programs thrive within schools, revitalizing traditions and fostering pride.

These victories serve as powerful reminders that meaningful change is achievable through perseverance and collaboration. Sharing these stories inspires hope and sparks motivation among community members, encouraging them to stay engaged and continue working toward their shared goals. Each success deepens their confidence that, together, they can shape a brighter, more inclusive future.

The perseverance and dedication of the young advocates begin to establish a legacy that transcends their immediate struggles. Their efforts not only bring tangible improvements—such as land rights, educational access, and cultural revitalization—but also lay the foundation for ongoing community resilience.

Emerging as strong, confident advocates, they are deeply rooted in their cultural traditions while skillfully navigating contemporary challenges. This balance ensures that their advocacy is rooted in heritage but adaptable to the evolving needs of their community.

Their legacy inspires future generations to continue leading with pride, purpose, and a sense of responsibility, ensuring that the spirit of activism and cultural preservation endures long after their immediate goals are achieved. It is a testament to their transformative impact and the enduring strength of their community.

Inspired by their earlier successes and active engagement, the young advocates come together to establish dedicated youth organizations. These groups aim to sustain the momentum of their initiatives, providing a structured platform for continued leadership and collective action.

These organizations serve as spaces for ongoing dialogue, where youth can share ideas, voice concerns, and collaborate on new projects. They also foster mentorship, empowering emerging leaders to develop skills and confidence to carry the movement forward. Additionally, strategic planning within these groups helps anticipate and address future challenges, ensuring the community's advocacy remains resilient and adaptive.

Through these youth organizations, the younger generation strengthens their role as stewards of change, securing a vibrant, empowered future for their community and preserving the spirit of activism for generations to come.

They dedicate themselves to training and mentoring the next generation of young leaders, understanding that true change is built on ongoing efforts. By sharing their knowledge, experiences, and lessons learned, they inspire a sense of responsibility in their younger peers, encouraging them to carry the torch of advocacy forward. This act of nurturing ensures that the cycle of empowerment remains unbroken, passing resilience and hope from one generation to the next.

In doing so, they reinforce the idea that their heritage is deeply intertwined with their fight for justice and equality. Each young leader mentored becomes a vital link in an enduring chain—one that links past struggles with future hope. Through continuous mentorship, they foster a community rooted in collective responsibility, ensuring that the pursuit of a fairer world remains alive and thriving through the efforts of those who come after.

A group of young advocates, now seasoned leaders, gather under a shade tree, surrounded by younger children and teens sitting attentively on blankets and benches. The air hums with anticipation and hope.

Louisa's voice is warm and steady as she speaks, her words resonating with a quiet but powerful conviction. "Today," she begins, "we are not only here to share what we have learned but to help you recognize your own incredible potential. Each of you has the strength to become a leader in your community, to carry forward the work that needs doing." She gestures encouragingly toward Miguel, a bright-eyed teen who looks eager yet uncertain, caught between doubt and hope.

Turning to Miguel, Louisa gently adds, "You already show a deep passion for our culture and for land rights. When I started, I felt just like you—uncertain but driven to make a difference." Her words soften as she emphasizes the importance of their shared journey, "That's why we're here— to support one another and ensure that this cycle of empowerment continues." Miguel nods, a spark of confidence igniting in his eyes, ready to embrace his role. Nearby, Nun steps forward, prepared to share her voice, embodying the spirit of future leadership and community resilience.

Nun's voice is steady yet heartfelt as she speaks, "Mentoring is about passing on your experiences— the wins, the setbacks, the lessons learned along the way. We are not just shaping individuals; we are building something that will endure beyond us, for the generations to come. It is our responsibility— our duty—to ensure that knowledge and hope are passed down, like a sacred flame that will never fade." Her words resonate with the young listeners, inspiring a sense of purpose and duty within their hearts.

A few of the younger children whisper excitedly among themselves, eyes wide with curiosity and admiration. Listening to the stories of challenges faced and victories achieved, they begin to understand the true power of unity and perseverance. The elders' shared experiences serve as a bridge connecting the past with the future, reinforcing the idea that their collective strength can overcome obstacles. As the stories unfold, the group's bond deepens, rooted in a common commitment to continue the work of justice and community empowerment.

Louisa steps forward again, her voice calm and encouraging. "Remember, empowerment is a cycle," she reminds them gently. "When we teach you, it is not just about today—it is about preparing you to become the leaders who will inspire others tomorrow. This is a journey we share, woven together by trust, hope, and a shared vision for a brighter future. Let us continue this journey hand in hand, supporting each other along the way."

As the sun begins to dip lower in the sky, casting a warm, golden glow over the gathering, the younger peers stand up with renewed confidence. Their faces reflect a blend of excitement and determination, ready to step into their own paths of leadership. Feeling empowered and motivated, they carry the torch of hope and resilience in their hearts, eager to ignite change in their community and beyond. Together, they pledge to keep the cycle of advocacy alive, ensuring that the legacy of their ancestors continues to shine brightly into the future.

Seeing their children and the younger generation actively preserving cultural traditions and advocating for their rights fills Ledger and Henri with deep hope. The passing down of stories, values, and the spirit of activism solidifies a legacy rooted in resilience. They understand that their heritage is not just a connection to the past but a powerful foundation for social change.

Together, the families embrace the idea that their cultural heritage is a source of strength and a catalyst for transformation. By drawing wisdom from their ancestors and celebrating their traditions, they inspire pride and purpose within the community. This shared identity fosters resilience amid adversity and underscores the importance of unity and collaboration in the fight for justice.

The intertwining of cultural preservation with activism ensures their lessons endure, guiding future generations to remain true to their roots while striving for equity and opportunity. In this way, they build a legacy that honors their history, celebrates their resilience, and paves the way for a future where hope, strength, and community thrive—empowering all to continue the journey toward a brighter, more equitable tomorrow.

ം

Chapter Nineteen: Seeds of Bravery

As Ledger and Henri stand amidst the vibrant celebration of their cultural festival, they feel a deep sense of pride and gratitude. The air is alive with the echo of laughter, the rhythmic pulse of drums, and the joyful chatter of their community in Colihaut. In this moment, they reflect on the extraordinary journey they have traveled—one filled with challenges, sacrifices, and unwavering hope.

Surrounded by their families and neighbors, they see the fruits of their efforts—young faces brimming with pride, traditions kept alive, and a community united in resilience. The music and festivities remind them of the enduring bonds they have cultivated and the strength they have nurtured through perseverance.

Ledger and Henri recognize that every struggle and obstacle has planted the seeds of bravery within their community, seeds that will flourish in the lives of their children and future generations. Their sacrifices have not been in vain; instead, they have built a legacy rooted in courage, hope, and cultural pride. With hearts full, they look forward—knowing that their work has laid a foundation for a brighter, more resilient future for all.

Ledger and Henri sit quietly together, watching the lively festivities unfold around them. As they reflect on their journey, both men are reminded of the personal sacrifices they have made—sleepless nights pondering strategies, tough conversations that challenge their patience, and the emotional toll of constantly fighting for their community's future. These moments of struggle were often painful, demanding resilience and unwavering commitment.

Yet, amidst these hardships, they recognize how much they have grown. Ledger recalls feeling lost and uncertain during his early days of activism, questioning whether change was truly possible. Henri, too, reflects on his moments of doubt, wondering if their efforts were enough. In their shared struggles, they found strength in their friendship, supporting each other through the darkest times. Their bond became a source of solace and renewed purpose, deepening their understanding that true leadership often requires sacrifice but also leads to profound personal growth.

Together, they see that these challenges have shaped them, transforming their doubts into determination and their sacrifices into symbols of hope. Their journey has not only reinforced their dedication to justice but also helped them become stronger, more compassionate leaders for their community.

Ledger looks out proudly at the younger generation, confident advocates, and proud custodians of their cultural heritage. A swell of pride fills his chest as he observes their growth and resilience. He realizes that the lessons ingrained in their journey—perseverance, collaboration, courage—are the true legacies they are passing on. These values will guide their children long after the challenges have passed, embedding a sense of strength and identity that no obstacle can erase.

For Henri, the importance of legacy extends beyond tangible gains like land rights or educational opportunities. It is about cultivating a deep understanding of their cultural roots—the traditions, stories, and values that form the core of their community. He sees that by instilling this sense of identity, they have planted seeds of resilience and pride that will empower future generations to thrive.

Together, Ledger and Henri have built more than just progress; they have laid a solid foundation— one of cultural pride, hope, and unwavering purpose. Their legacy ensures that their children will carry forward not only the fruits of their labor but also the enduring strength of their heritage, inspiring them to face whatever the future may hold with confidence and grace.

As Ledger and Henri stand amidst the lively festival, a sense of profound realization settles over them: the true strength of their story is rooted in the unity of their community. They have seen how solidarity can turn despair into hope, transforming individual struggles into collective victories. Every hand, every voice—no matter how small—has contributed to their journey toward justice and resilience.

The celebration embodies the spirit of collaboration, where each person's contribution amplifies the collective voice, making their progress possible. This sense of unity not only fuels their current efforts but also shapes the future their children will inherit—a world where everyone's voice is valued and heard, where community bonds are the foundation of strength.

In that moment, they understand that their story is not about personal or family achievement; it is about building a legacy rooted in cooperation, shared purpose, and hope. The power of unity, they realize, is what will continue to propel their community forward and ensure that justice, respect, and cultural pride endure for generations to come.

The festival is more than a vibrant celebration; it is a powerful act of cultural revival that weaves together the diverse stories of both families. Children proudly display traditional crafts and culinary skills they have learned, their faces shining with pride and curiosity. Meanwhile, elders share stories rich with history and wisdom, echoing the collective spirit of resilience that has carried their community through hardships.

Ledger and Henri watch with gentle smiles, moved by the unwavering pride radiating from their children's faces. They understand that this renewal of traditions—is vital for nurturing a strong sense of identity. It is a bridge connecting the past to the future, fiercely honoring their heritage while embracing new possibilities.

In this celebration, they see their community's enduring spirit alive—a testament to the resilience, creativity, and unity that continue to shape their collective story. They know that by passing down culture and pride, they are laying a foundation that will empower their children to grow with confidence and purpose, rooted in the strength of their shared heritage.

Amidst the festive atmosphere, the families' conversations spark a forward-looking vision—one rooted in resilience and hope. Despite ongoing challenges, they remain unwavering in their commitment to building a more equitable future. The discussions during the celebration inspire community members to stay engaged in the fight for justice, ensuring that the spirit of activism is passed on and continues to grow.

They recognize that while vestiges of colonial legacy may cast shadows over their journey, the collective light of community spirit and cultural pride serves as a powerful beacon. This illumination guides them toward pathways of opportunity and equality, reaffirming their belief that persistent effort, unity, and unwavering hope can transform obstacles into new beginnings.

With eyes set on the future, they carry the legacy of resilience forward, inspiring their children and neighbors to imagine a world where justice prevails—where every voice is valued, and every person has the chance to thrive. Their shared vision fuels the ongoing journey toward a brighter, more inclusive tomorrow.

Ledger and Henri, in their quiet moments of reflection, recognize that the bravery displayed by their community is the foundation of a legacy. The efforts and sacrifices they have made are like seeds that, with care and perseverance, will grow into a vast forest of resilience and hope. Their journey stands as a testament to the unwavering spirit of those who fought before those who dreamed of a land free from colonial constraints, where their children can truly thrive and flourish.

This quest for justice goes beyond individual struggles; it becomes a shared legacy that unites them. It is a collective story of courage, hope, and perseverance that binds generations together. As they look ahead, they know that the sacrifices of the past pave the way for a brighter, freer future—one where their children's potential is limitless, and the spirit of resistance continues to inspire new chapters of resilience and progress.

Ledger and Henri stand side by side, their eyes fixed on the horizon where the future awaits. The golden light of dusk casts a warm glow over them, symbolizing both the closing of one chapter and the dawn of another. They feel the deep satisfaction of knowing that the seeds of bravery and hope they have planted—through efforts in cultural preservation, community advocacy, and unwavering resolve—have begun to take root. Their work has laid a strong foundation, and as they look to their children, they see the living embodiment of possibility: young hearts and minds eager to carry the torch of change, blending the strength of their heritage with the promise of new paths.

This moment encapsulates the essence of their journey—one rooted in hope, resilience, and the collective power of community. The story of their struggle is a rallying call for others who seek to reclaim their identities, stand for justice, and build a future where every voice matters. Surrounded by the warmth of their cultural traditions and united by a shared purpose, Ledger, Henri, and their families embrace the journey ahead. They understand that their legacy is more than a past; it is a living, breathing force that continues to shape the present and inspires future generations to thrive in a world of equity and dignity.

In the end, their story echoes as a testament to the enduring strength of hope and community—that through collective effort, resilience, and cultural pride, a brighter future is crafted. As the first light of dawn emerges, casting new possibilities on the horizon, they hold onto the knowledge that their shared journey is building a legacy that will transcend time. Together, they stand ready to face whatever comes next, knowing that their unwavering commitment will guide their descendants toward continued growth, freedom, and the realization of their dreams.

☙

Epilogue: Seeds of Friendship

The future unfolds in a scene of promise and unity, where Wizen Philogene, Ledger and Clara's lively son, and Theresa Sebastien, Henri and Isabelle's imaginative daughter, forge a deep friendship. As they navigate the ups and downs of adolescence in the lively heart of Colihaut, their connection becomes a symbol of the enduring legacy of both families.

Their bond reflects the shared struggles and triumphs that Ledger and Henri endured reminders of resilience, hope, and love that have helped shape their community. It embodies not just friendship, but the unbreakable promise of a future built on unity, understanding, and mutual respect. Together, these young souls carry forward the legacy of courage and perseverance, weaving a new chapter of possibility where their children's dreams can flourish beyond the shadows of the past.

Wizen and Theresa often meet at the Kai Cacao, a hub of activity where locals gather to discuss initiatives and celebrate their shared culture. It is here, amidst the colorful murals depicting their rich heritage, that both young leaders recognize the importance of continuing their families' legacies. As they share stories of their parents' sacrifices and their community's ongoing struggles for land rights and educational access, a deep understanding forms between them.

Together, they brainstorm solutions to issues facing their community, such as reestablishing community gardens and launching educational outreach programs in local schools. Wizens' keen interest in sustainable farming complements Theresa's passion for Sewing and trading, allowing them to collaborate effectively. Their complementary strengths create a dynamic partnership, enabling them to rally their peers and engage the community in projects that reflect their shared vision for a sustainable and equitable future.

As their friendship deepens, Wizen and Theresa often share their dreams for the future. Wizen envisions a world where young farmers can leverage technology to enhance traditional farming methods, ensuring food security for all families. Theresa dreams of becoming an educator, empowering children with knowledge and instilling in them the values of their heritage. These aspirations fuel their determination to contribute positively to Colihaut, reminding them of the sacrifices made by their parents.

During late afternoon meetings under the shade of a giant mango tree, they sketch out plans for initiatives that promote community cohesion and cultural pride. Their discussions often lead to laughter, sparking innovative ideas as they find creative ways to intertwine their passions with the community's needs. This shared vision becomes a binding force, strengthening their friendship and uniting their families in purpose and commitment.

As Wizen and Theresa's endeavors gain traction, the Philogene and Sebastien families see their bond grow stronger. Both families come together at community events, celebrating successes and sharing stories of hope. Ledger and Henri take pride in watching their children carry on the legacy they fought so hard to build. They often reminisce about their own childhood friendships and the resilience required to overcome adversity, knowing that Wizen and Theresa's partnership is rooted in the same courage.

The collaborative projects led by the two young leaders foster deeper ties between the families, turning them into allies in advocating for positive change in their community. Through shared experiences filled with laughter, resilience, and vision, the alliances formed to become a testament to the power of unity in the face of challenges.

Wizen and Theresa continue to work together, their friendship embodies the resilience of the human spirit and the seeds of bravery sown across generations. They inspire others within the community, cultivating a new generation of activists who understand the importance of cultural heritage and social justice. Their youthful energy and dedication become contagious, encouraging their peers to join in the efforts aimed at improving Colihaut.

Together, they create an atmosphere of activism infused with hope, demonstrating that the sacrifices of their parents were not merely about overcoming adversity but also about building a foundation for a brighter future. As they plan events and initiatives that honor their cultural identities, they perpetuate the legacy of courage and determination rooted in both the Philogene and Sebastien families.

In the heart of Colihaut, the blossoming friendship of Wizen and Theresa stands as a testament to the ongoing journey towards justice, equality, and community empowerment. Their collaboration not only strengthens the ties between their families but also serves as a beacon of hope for the entire community. As they dream, create, and advocate together, they uphold the spirit of their parents' sacrifices, ensuring that the legacy of resilience and bravery continues to flourish for generations to come.

In this promise of tomorrow, the seeds of friendship sown today will grow into a flourishing future, nurturing a community that embodies the ideals of unity and shared prosperity. And so, with hearts full of dreams and minds set to action, Wizen and Theresa embark on the path toward creating a better world—not only for themselves but for every member of Colihaut, honoring the enduring legacy of love, strength, and hope.

℃

The End